SCOUT IS NOT A BAND KID

JADE ARMSTRONG

This book is dedicated to Annabel Scott.

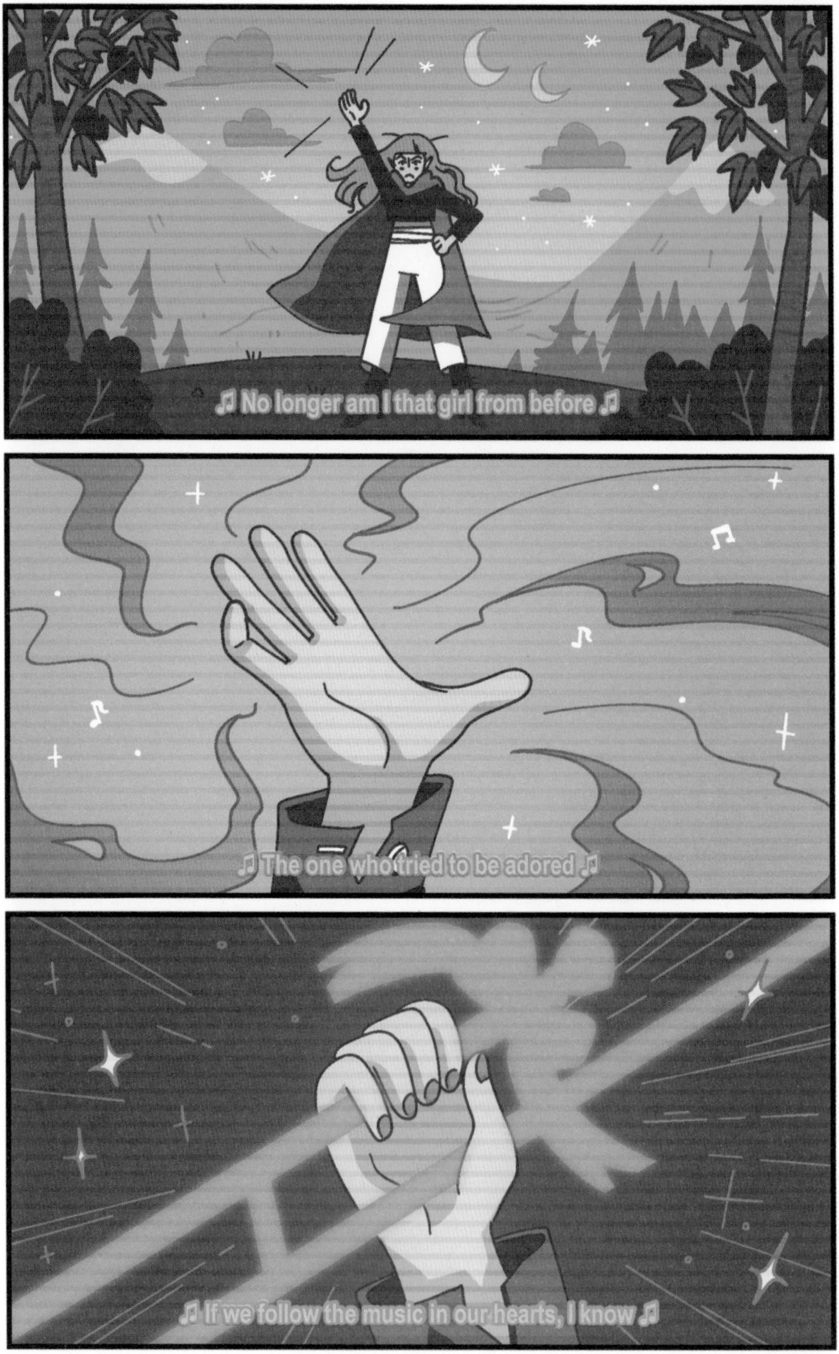
♫ No longer am I that girl from before ♫
♫ The one who tried to be adored ♫
♫ If we follow the music in our hearts, I know ♫

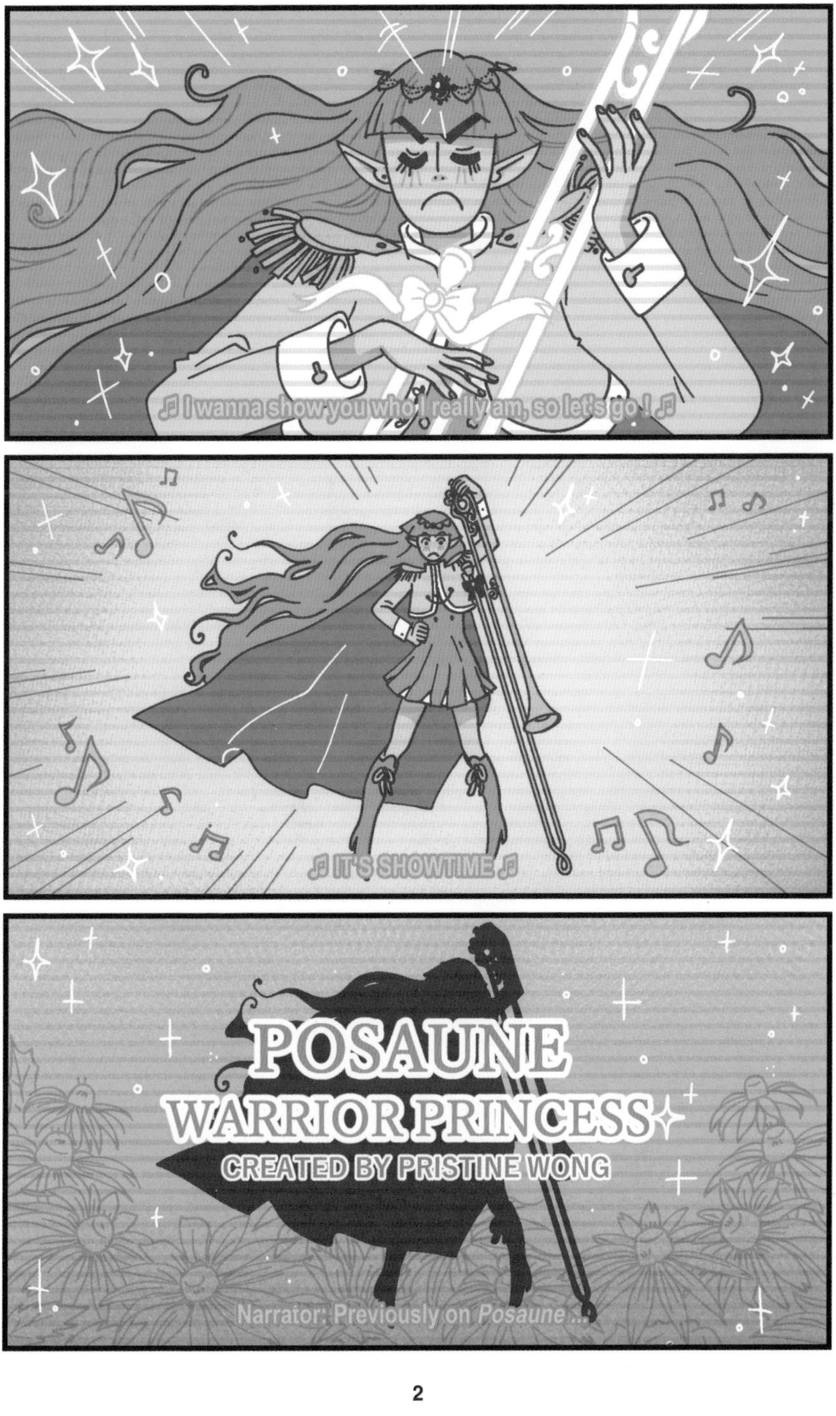
♬ I wanna show you who I really am, so let's go ! ♬
♬ IT'S SHOWTIME ♬
POSAUNE
WARRIOR PRINCESS
CREATED BY PRISTINE WONG
Narrator: Previously on *Posaune* ...

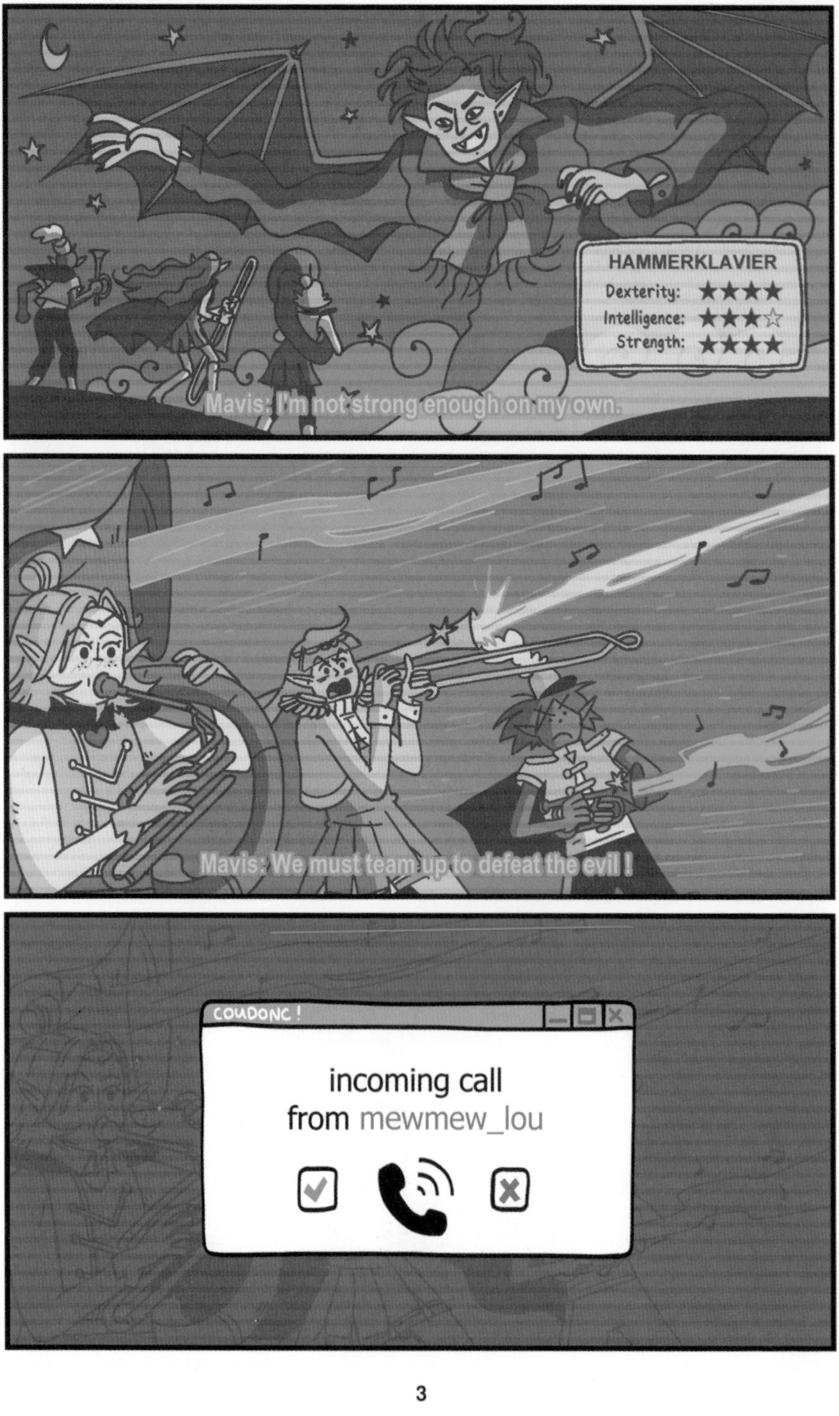
HAMMERKLAVIER
Dexterity:
Intelligence:
Strength:
Mavis: I'm not strong enough on my own.
Mavis: We must team up to defeat the evil !
COUDONC !
incoming call
from mewmew_lou

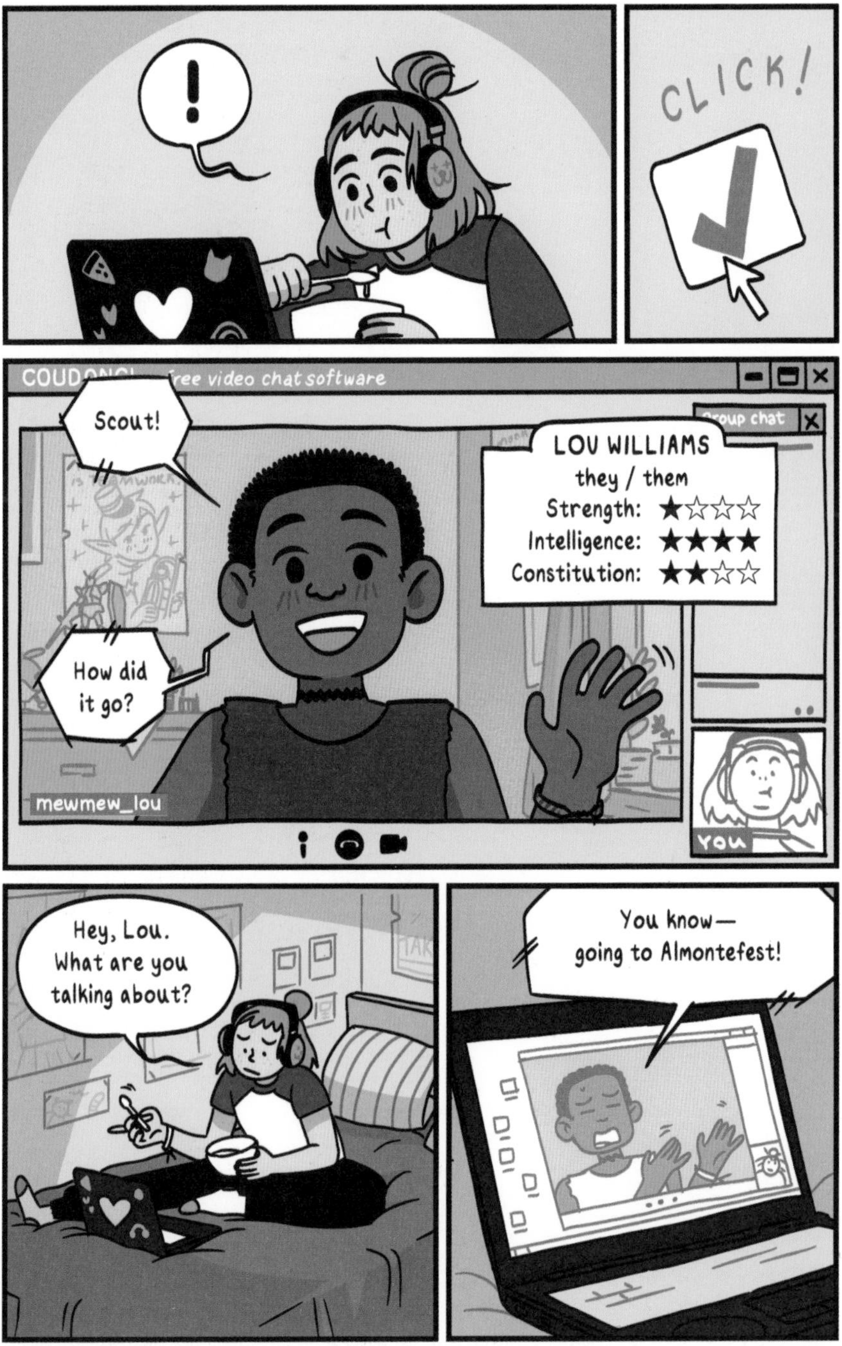
!
CLICK!
video chat software
Scout!
How did it go?
LOU WILLIAMS
they / them
Strength: ★☆☆☆
Intelligence: ★★★★
Constitution: ★★☆☆
mewmew_lou
YOU
Hey, Lou. What are you talking about?
You know— going to Almontefest!

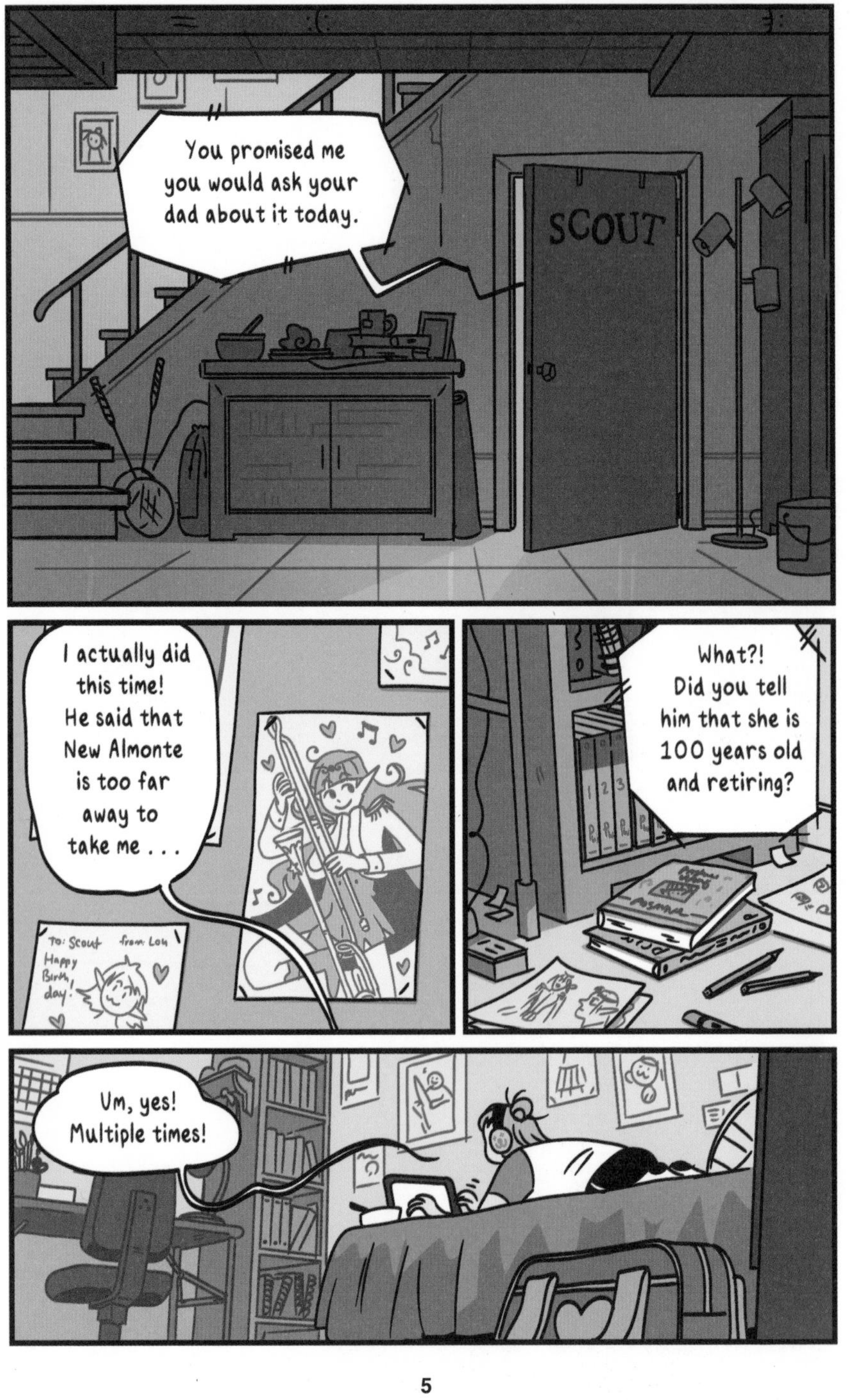
You promised me you would ask your dad about it today.
SCOUT
I actually did this time! He said that New Almonte is too far away to take me . . .
To: Scout from: Lou
Happy Birth, day!
What?! Did you tell him that she is 100 years old and retiring?
Um, yes! Multiple times!

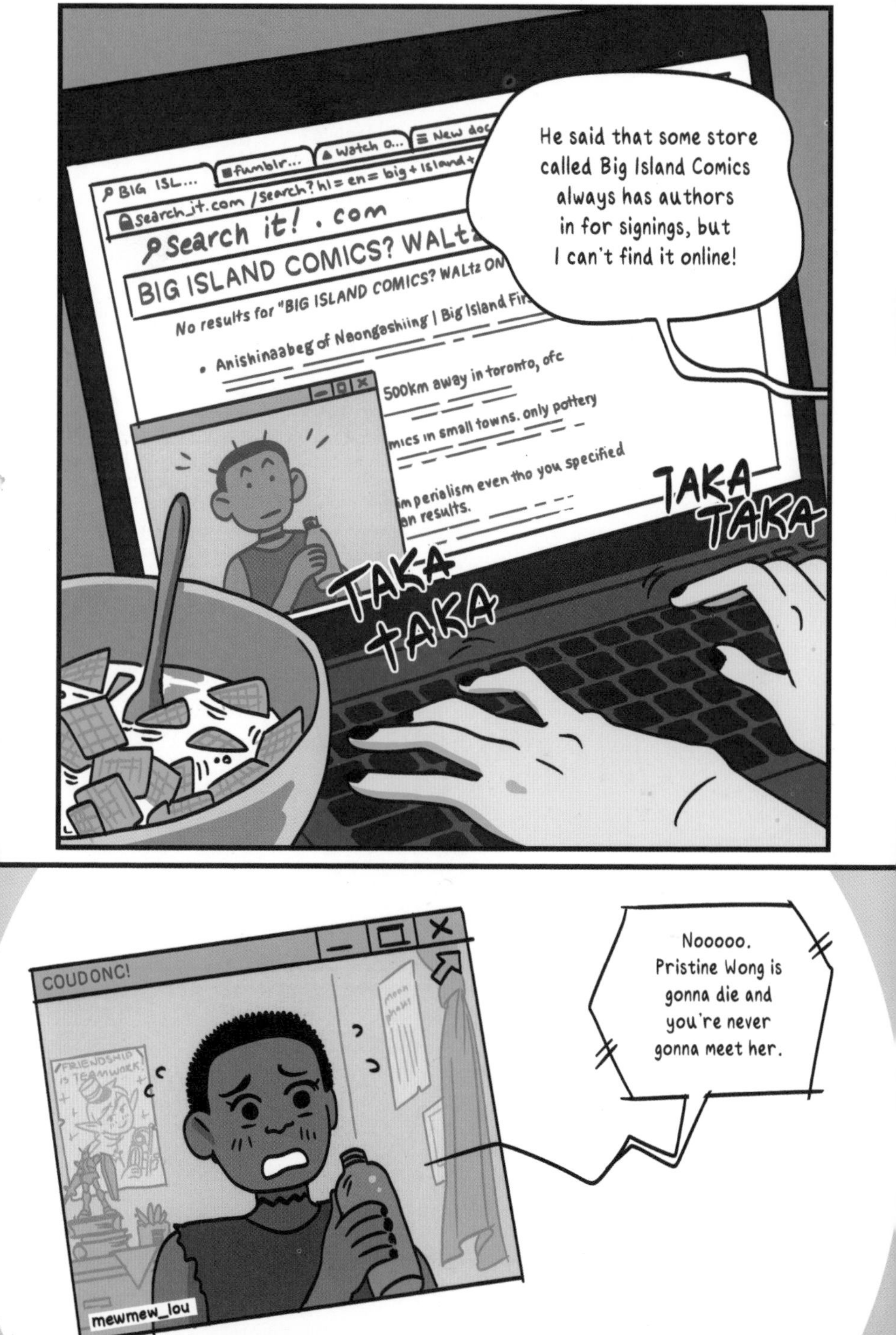
BIG ISL...
fumblr...
Watch o...
New doc
search_it.com /search?hl=en=big+island+
Search it! .com
BIG ISLAND COMICS? WALtz ON
No results for "BIG ISLAND COMICS? WALtz ON
Anishinaabeg of Neongashiing | Big Island First
500km away in toronto, ofc
mics in small towns. only pottery
imperialism even tho you specified
He said that some store called Big Island Comics always has authors in for signings, but I can't find it online!
TAKA TAKA
TAKA TAKA
COUDONC!
FRIENDSHIP IS TEAMWORK!
mewmew_lou
Nooooo. Pristine Wong is gonna die and you're never gonna meet her.

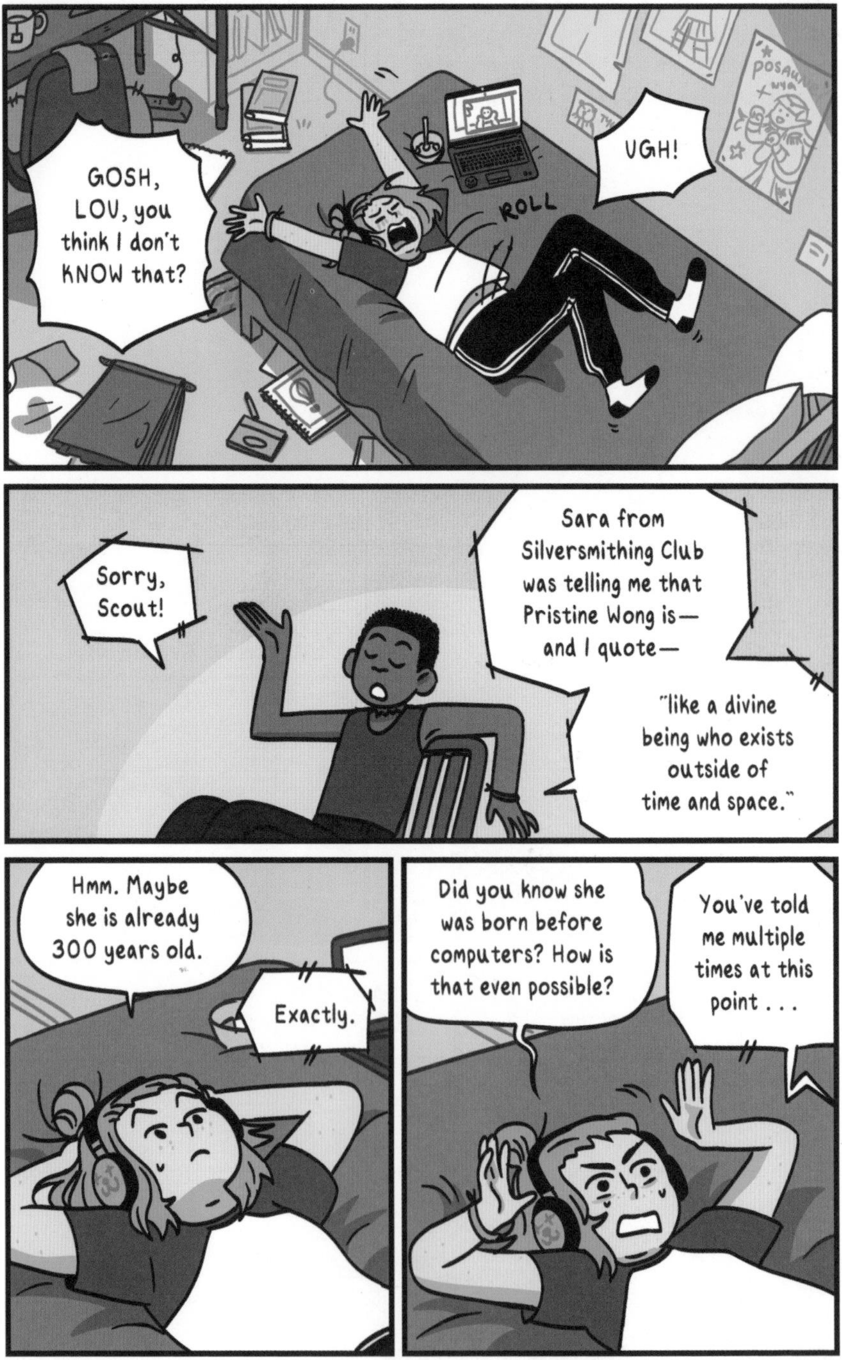
GOSH, LOU, you think I don't KNOW that?
UGH!
ROLL
Sorry, Scout!
Sara from Silversmithing Club was telling me that Pristine Wong is— and I quote—
"like a divine being who exists outside of time and space."
Hmm. Maybe she is already 300 years old.
Exactly.
Did you know she was born before computers? How is that even possible?
You've told me multiple times at this point . . .

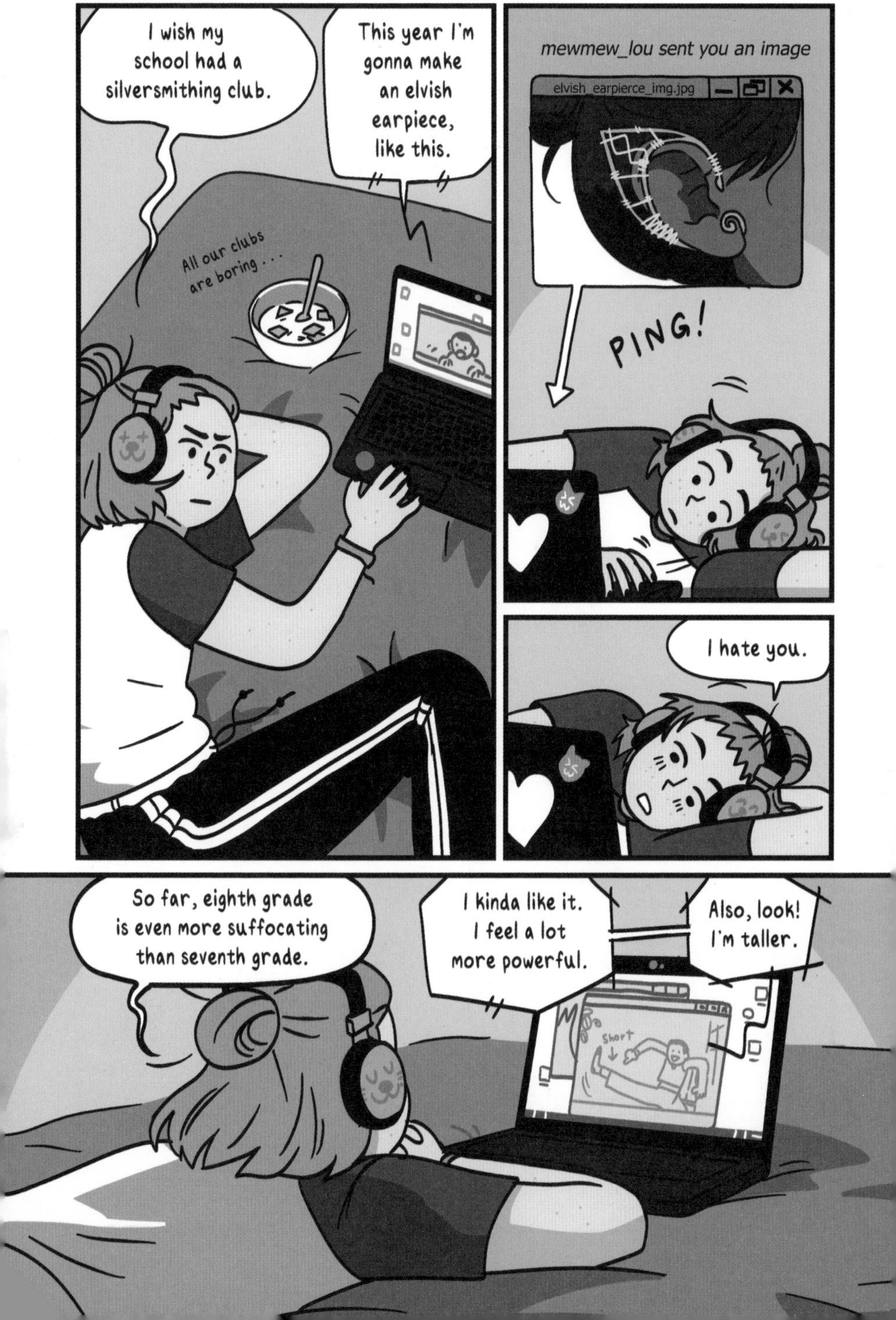
I wish my school had a silversmithing club.
All our clubs are boring . . .
This year I'm gonna make an elvish earpiece, like this.
mewmew_lou sent you an image
elvish_earpierce_img.jpg
PING!
I hate you.
So far, eighth grade is even more suffocating than seventh grade.
I kinda like it. I feel a lot more powerful.
Also, look! I'm taller.
Short

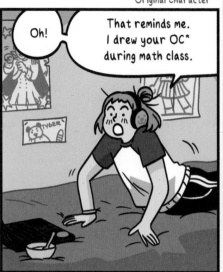

Oh!

That reminds me. I drew your OC* during math class.

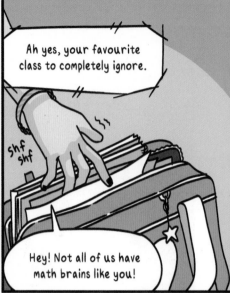

Ah yes, your favourite class to completely ignore.

shf shf

Hey! Not all of us have math brains like you!

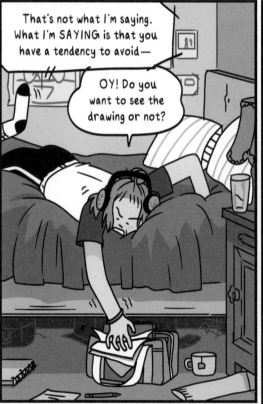

That's not what I'm saying. What I'm SAYING is that you have a tendency to avoid—

OY! Do you want to see the drawing or not?

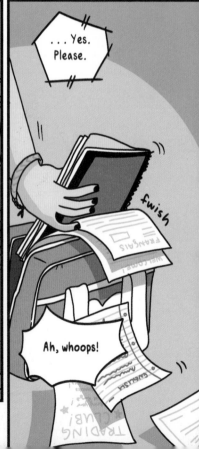

. . . Yes. Please.

fwish

FRANÇAIS

Ah, whoops!

ENGLISH

TRADING CLUB!

9

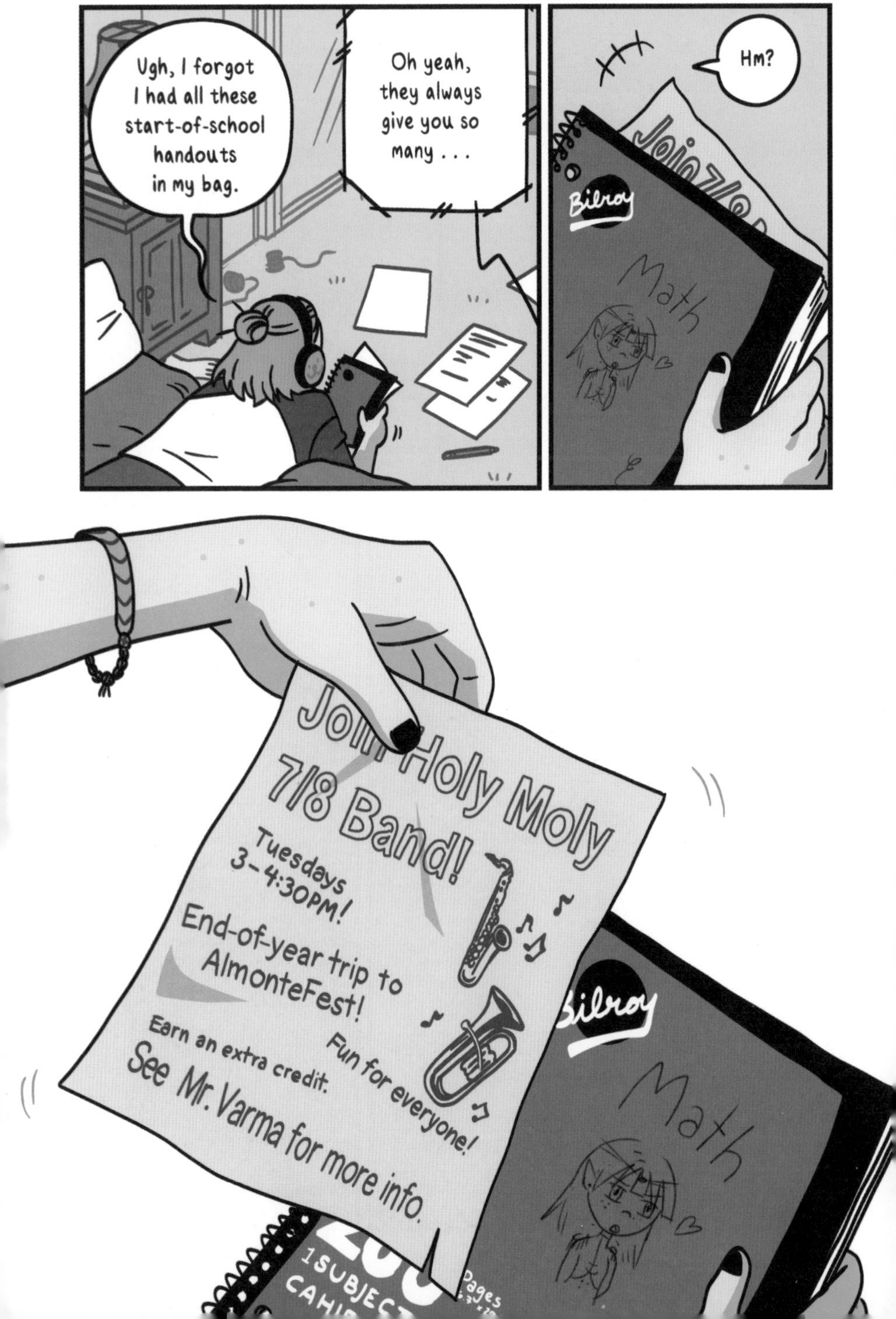
Ugh, I forgot I had all these start-of-school handouts in my bag.
Oh yeah, they always give you so many . . .
Hm?
Bilroy
Math
Join Holy Moly 7/8 Band!
Tuesdays 3–4:30PM!
End-of-year trip to AlmonteFest!
Fun for everyone!
Earn an extra credit.
See Mr. Varma for more info.
Bilroy
Math
1 SUBJECT
Pages

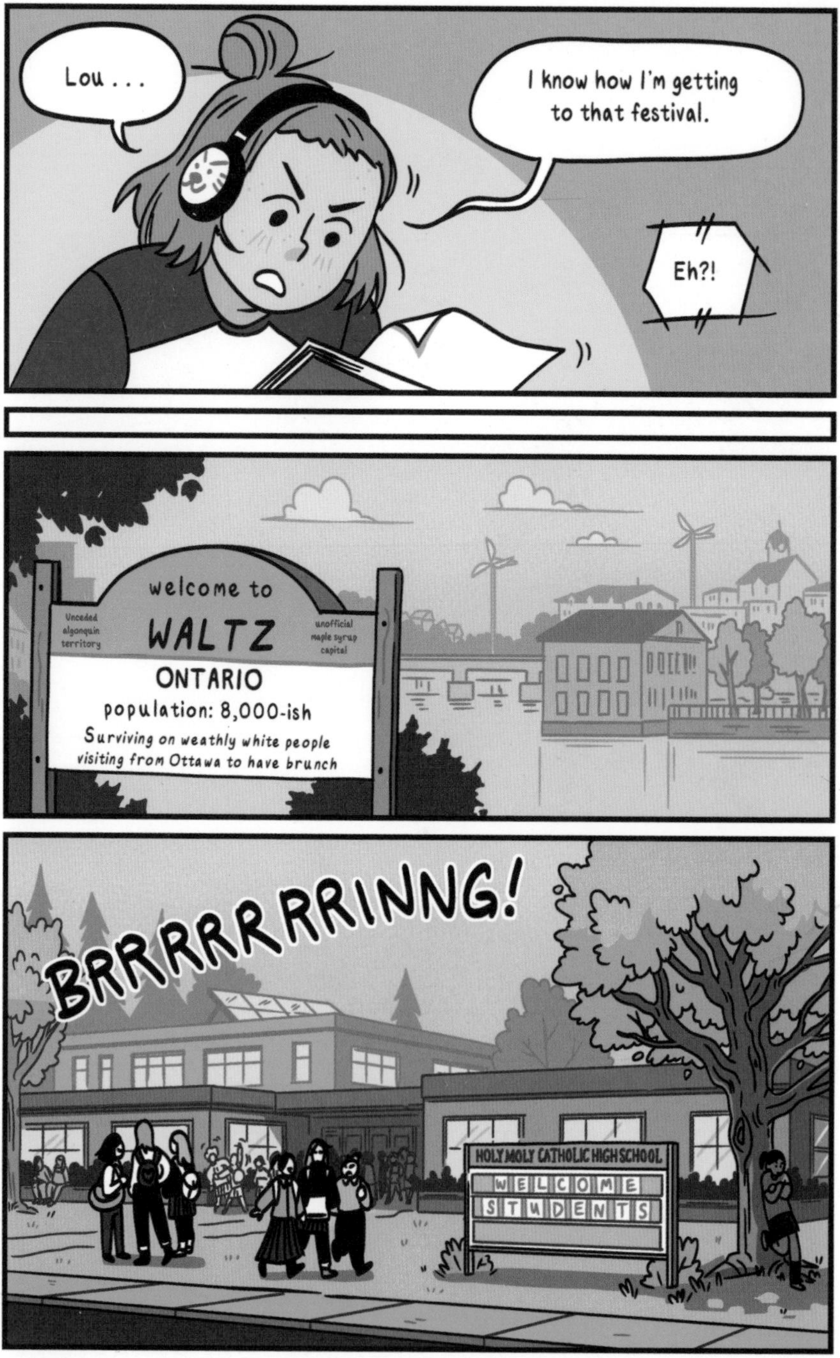
Lou . . .
I know how I'm getting to that festival.
Eh?!
welcome to
Unceded algonquin territory
WALTZ
unofficial maple syrup capital
ONTARIO
population: 8,000-ish
Surviving on weathly white people visiting from Ottawa to have brunch
BRRRRRRRINNG!
HOLY MOLY CATHOLIC HIGH SCHOOL
WELCOME
STUDENTS

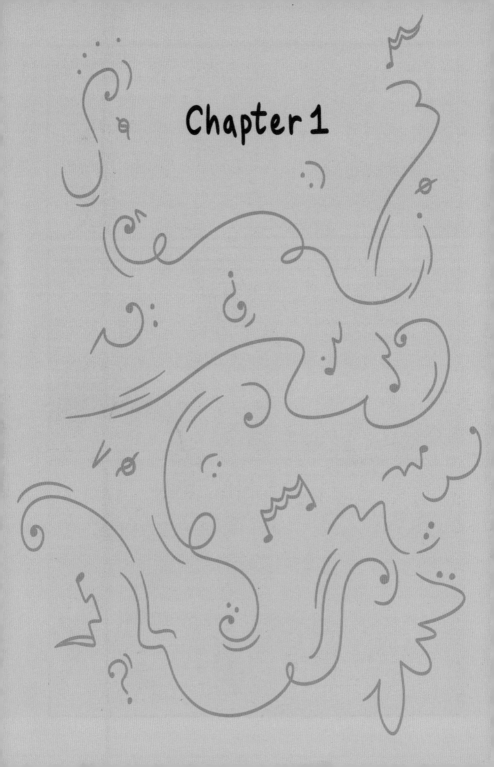

Chapter 1

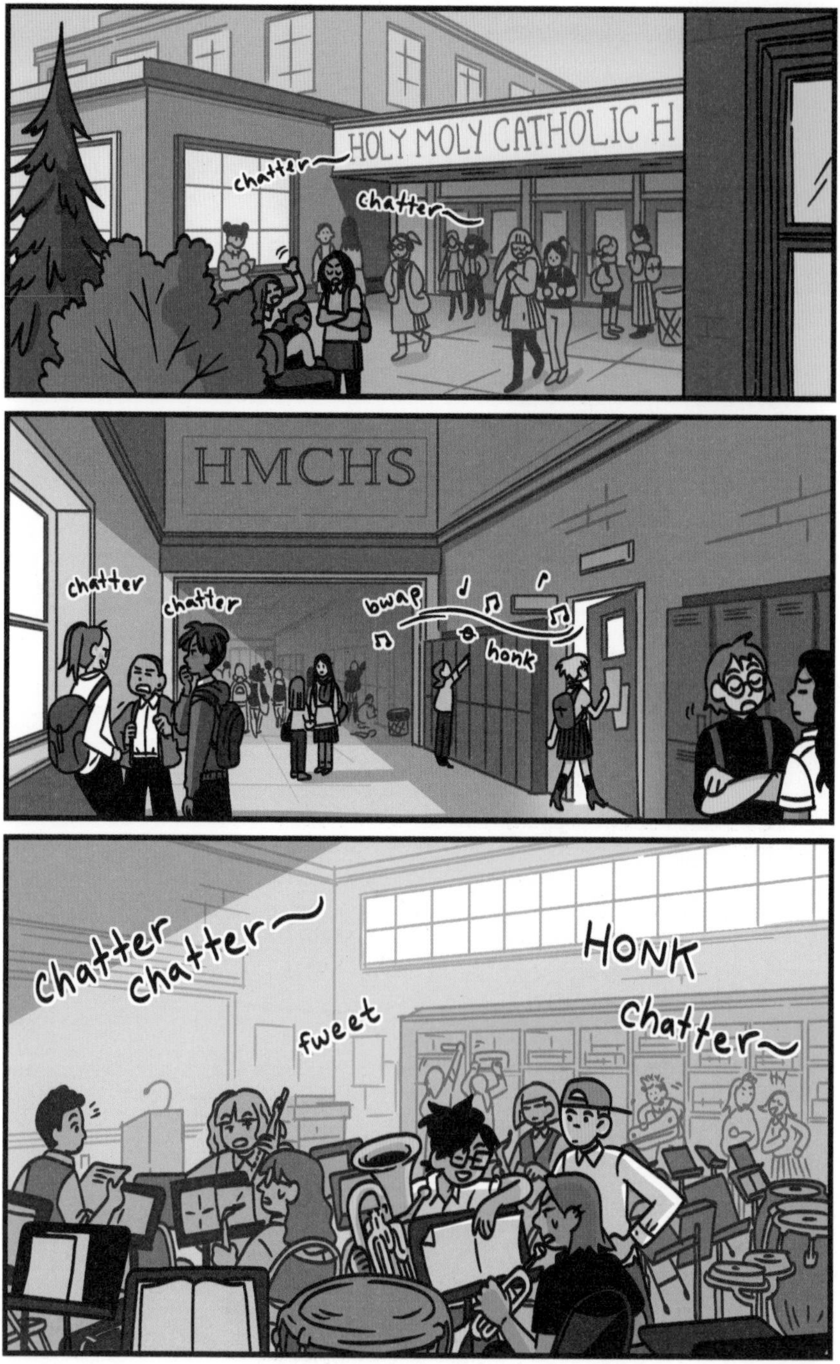
HOLY MOLY CATHOLIC H
chatter~
chatter~
HMCHS
chatter
chatter
bwap
honk
chatter chatter~
HONK
fweet
chatter~

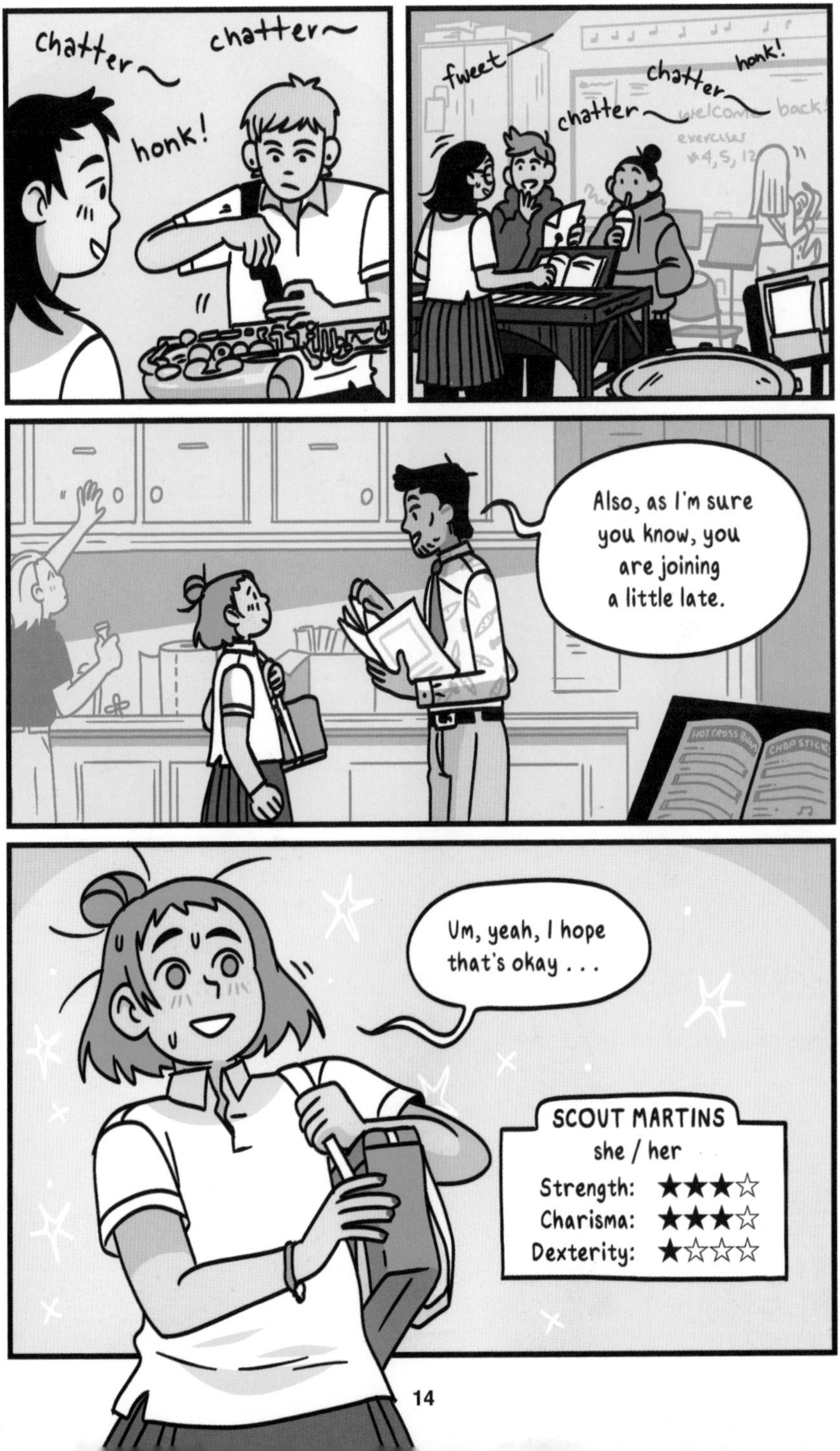
chatter~
chatter~
honk!
fweet
chatter~
honk!
chatter~
welcome back!
exercises #4, 5, 12
Also, as I'm sure you know, you are joining a little late.
Um, yeah, I hope that's okay . . .
SCOUT MARTINS
she / her
Strength: ★★★☆
Charisma: ★★★☆
Dexterity: ★☆☆☆

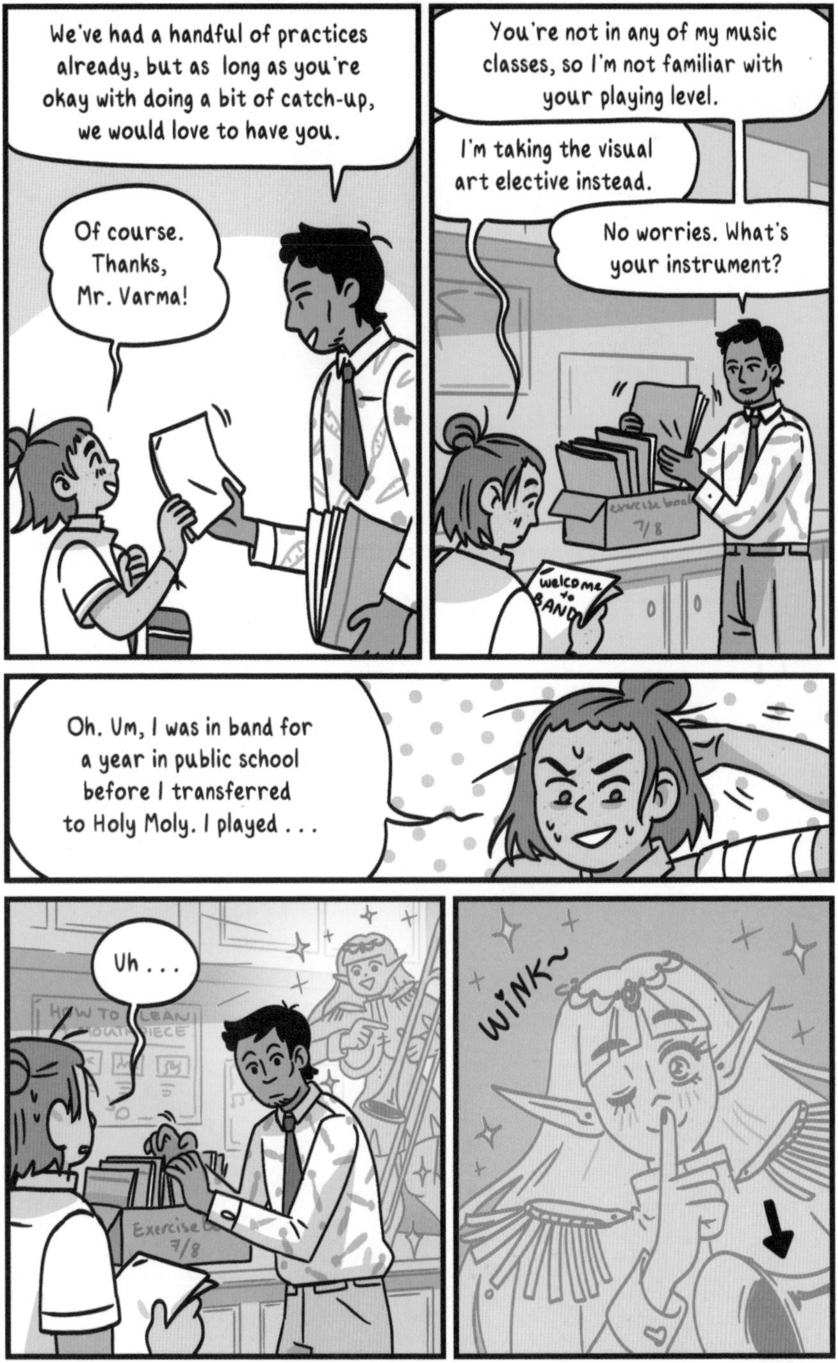
We've had a handful of practices already, but as long as you're okay with doing a bit of catch-up, we would love to have you.
Of course. Thanks, Mr. Varma!
You're not in any of my music classes, so I'm not familiar with your playing level.
I'm taking the visual art elective instead.
No worries. What's your instrument?
exercise book 7/8
welcome to BAND
Oh. Um, I was in band for a year in public school before I transferred to Holy Moly. I played . . .
Uh . . .
Exercise 7/8
WINK~

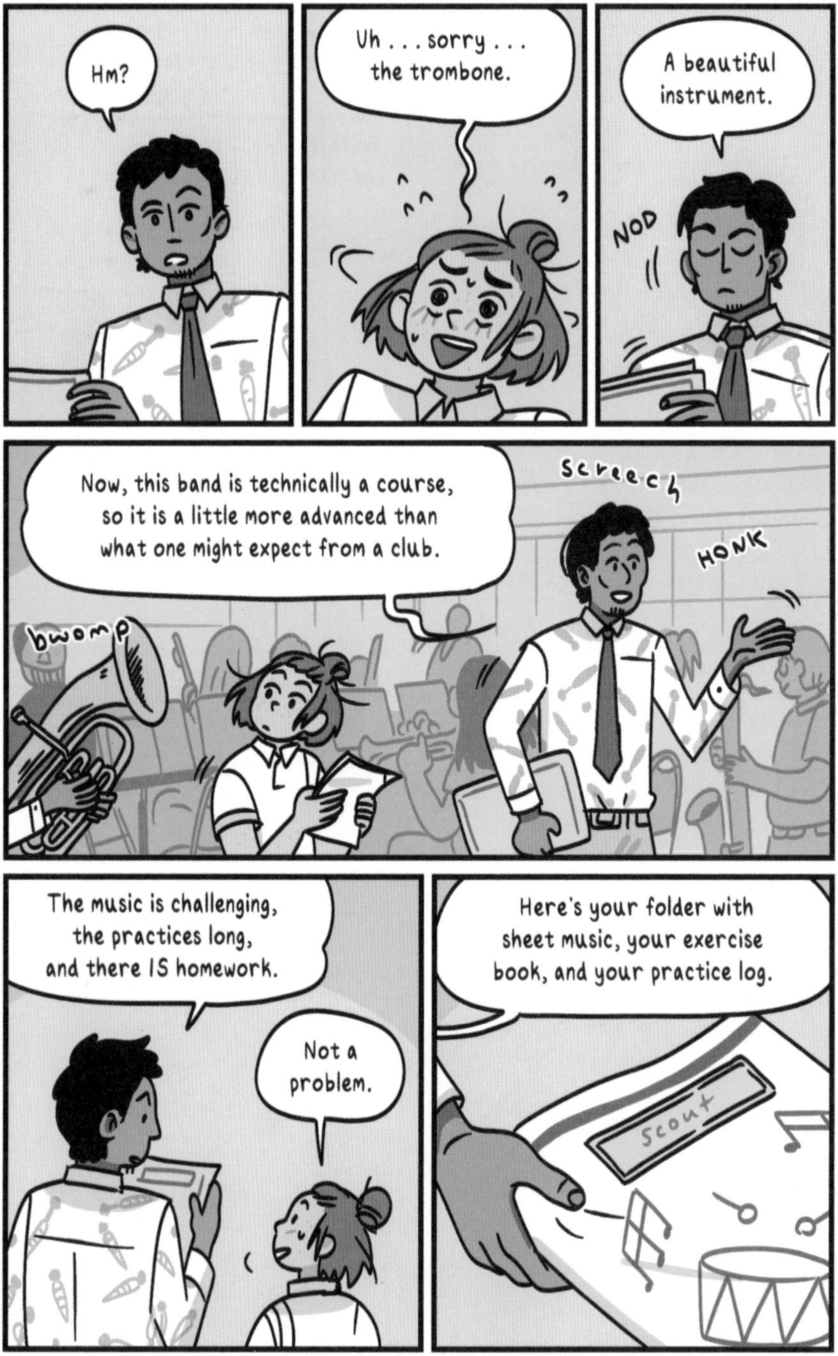
Hm?
Uh . . . sorry . . . the trombone.
A beautiful instrument.
NOD
Now, this band is technically a course, so it is a little more advanced than what one might expect from a club.
screech
HONK
bwomp
The music is challenging, the practices long, and there IS homework.
Not a problem.
Here's your folder with sheet music, your exercise book, and your practice log.
Scout

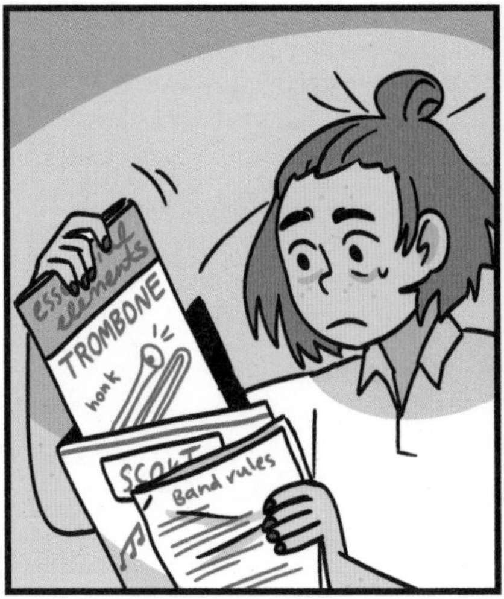
TROMBONE
honk
Band rules

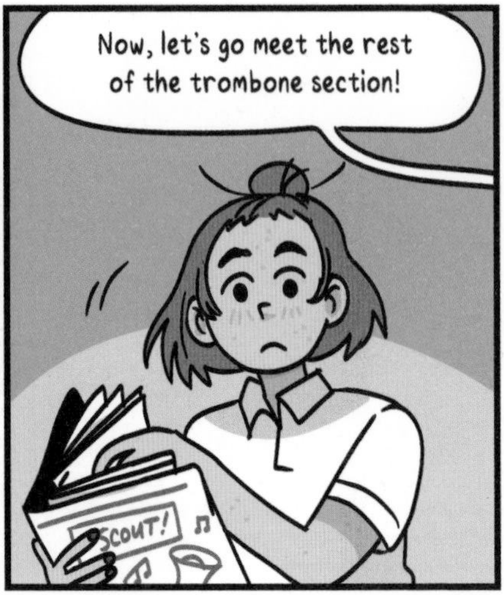
Now, let's go meet the rest of the trombone section!
SCOUT!

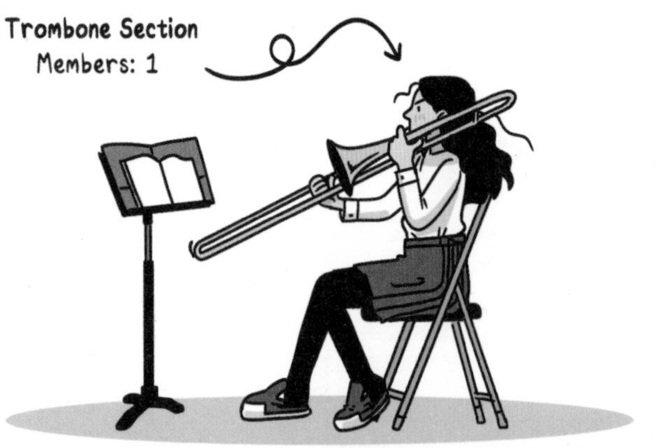
Trombone Section
Members: 1

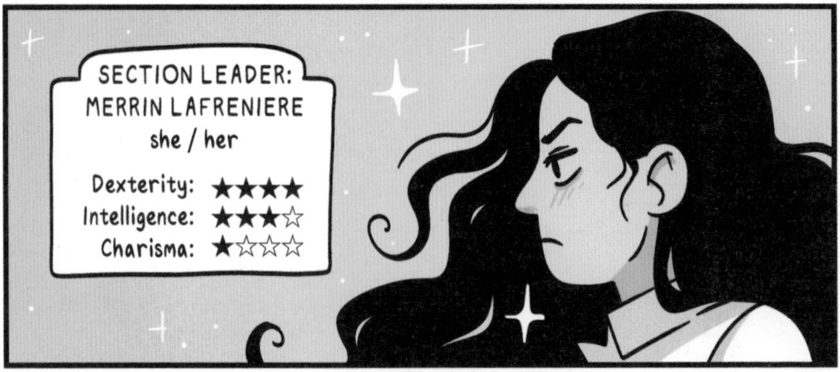
SECTION LEADER:
MERRIN LAFRENIERE
she / her
Dexterity: ★★★★
Intelligence: ★★★☆
Charisma: ★☆☆☆

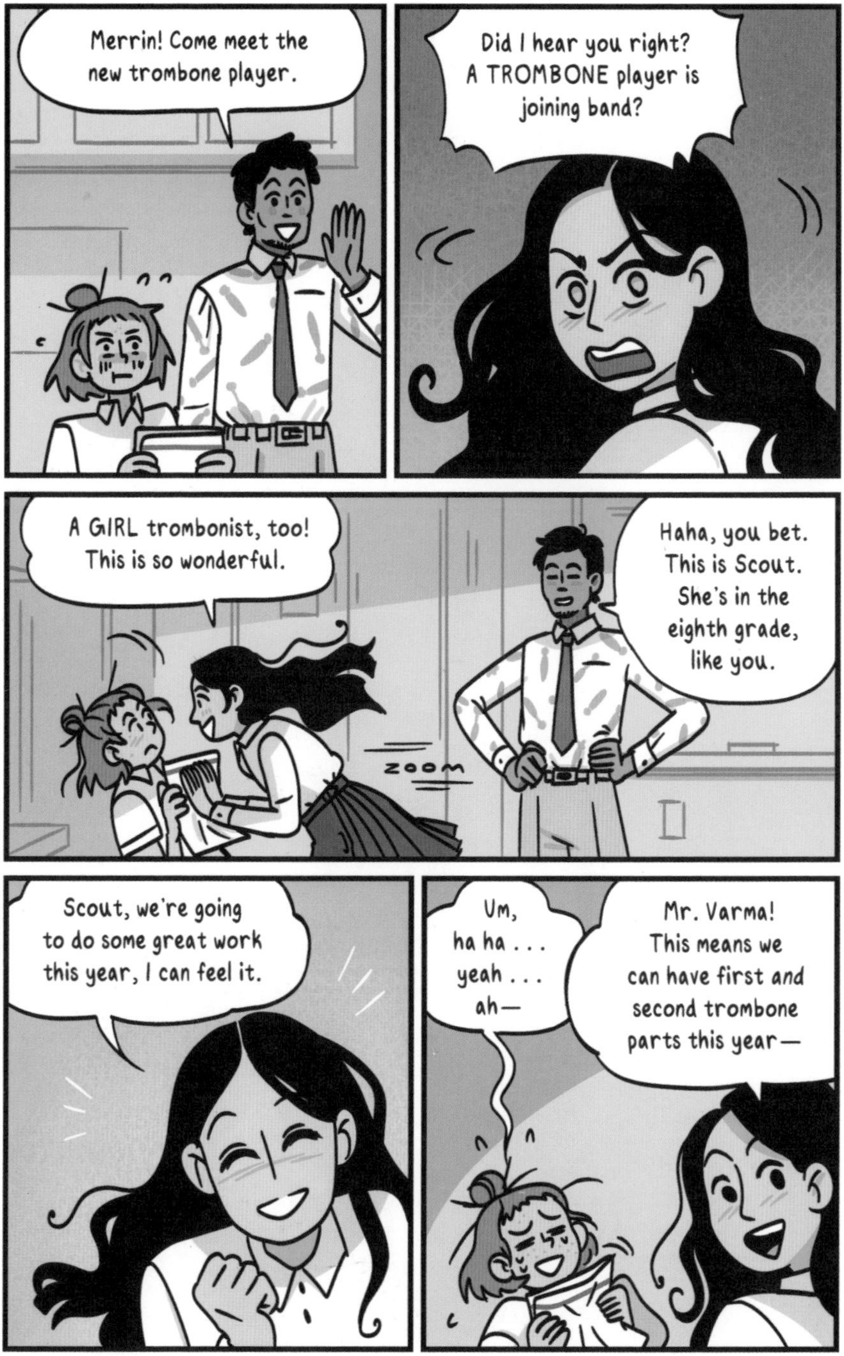
Merrin! Come meet the new trombone player.
Did I hear you right? A TROMBONE player is joining band?
A GIRL trombonist, too! This is so wonderful.
Haha, you bet. This is Scout. She's in the eighth grade, like you.
ZOOM
Scout, we're going to do some great work this year, I can feel it.
Um, ha ha . . . yeah . . . ah—
Mr. Varma! This means we can have first and second trombone parts this year—

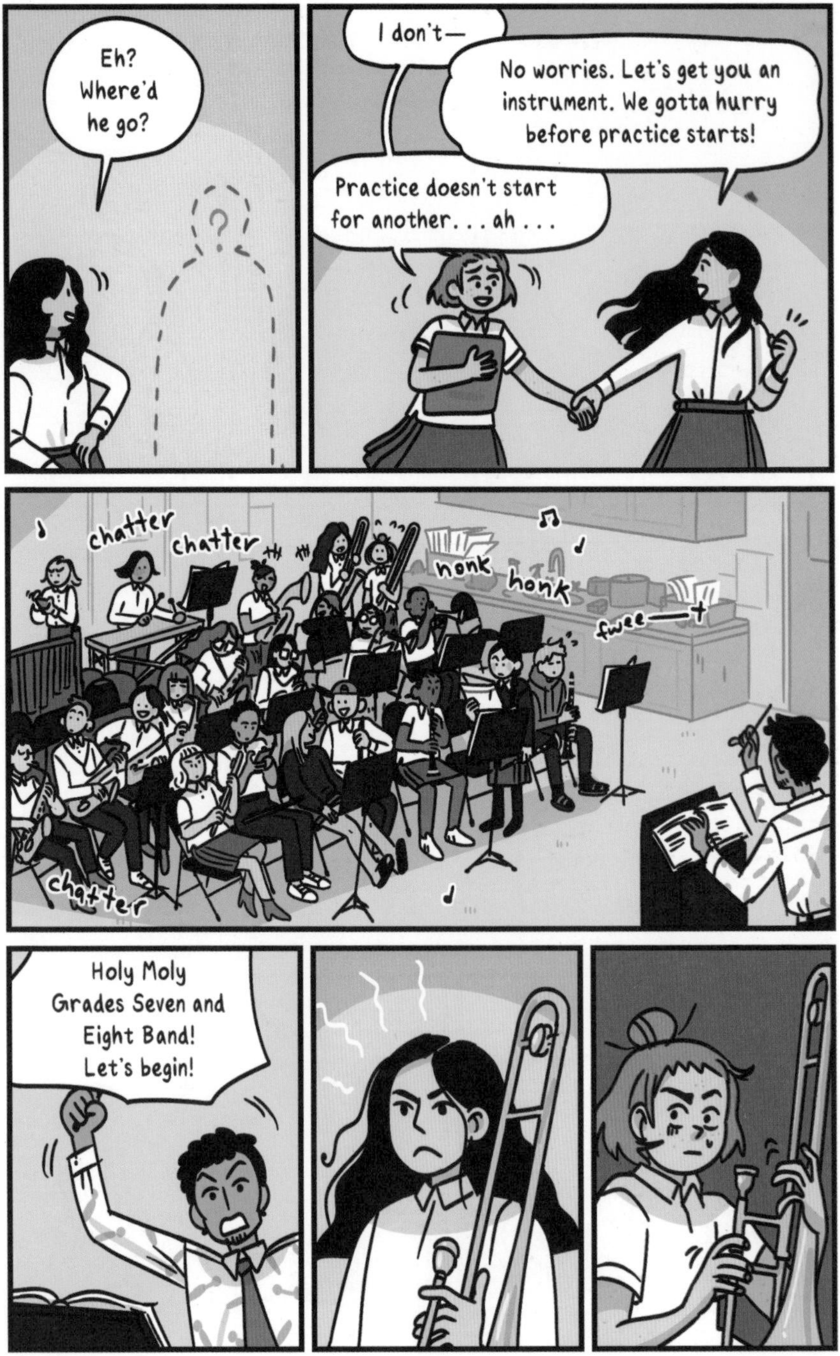

Eh? Where'd he go?
?
I don't—
No worries. Let's get you an instrument. We gotta hurry before practice starts!
Practice doesn't start for another. . . ah . . .
chatter
chatter
honk
honk
fwee—t
chatter
Holy Moly Grades Seven and Eight Band! Let's begin!

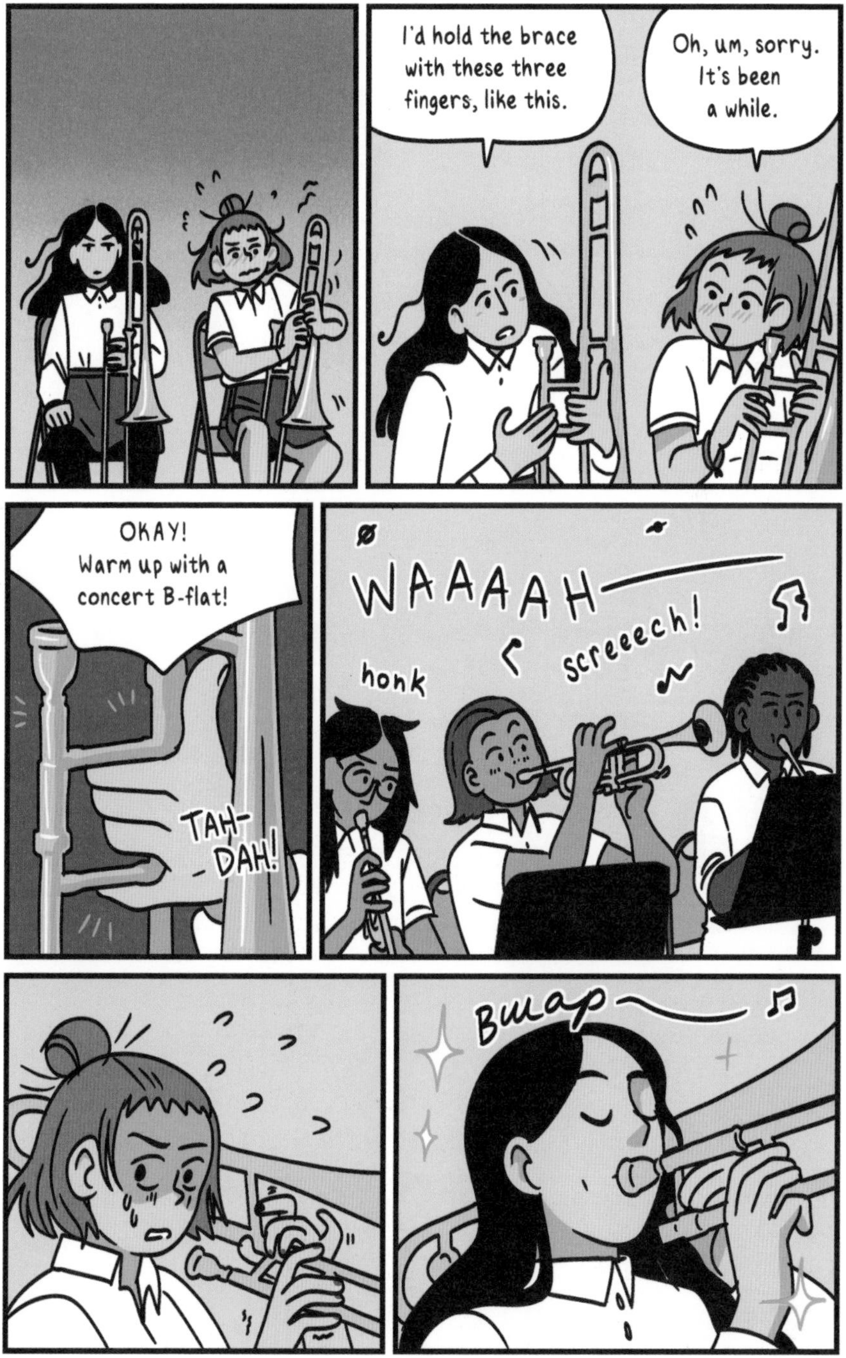
I'd hold the brace with these three fingers, like this.
Oh, um, sorry. It's been a while.
OKAY! Warm up with a concert B-flat!
TAH-DAH!
WAAAAH
honk
screeech!
Bwap

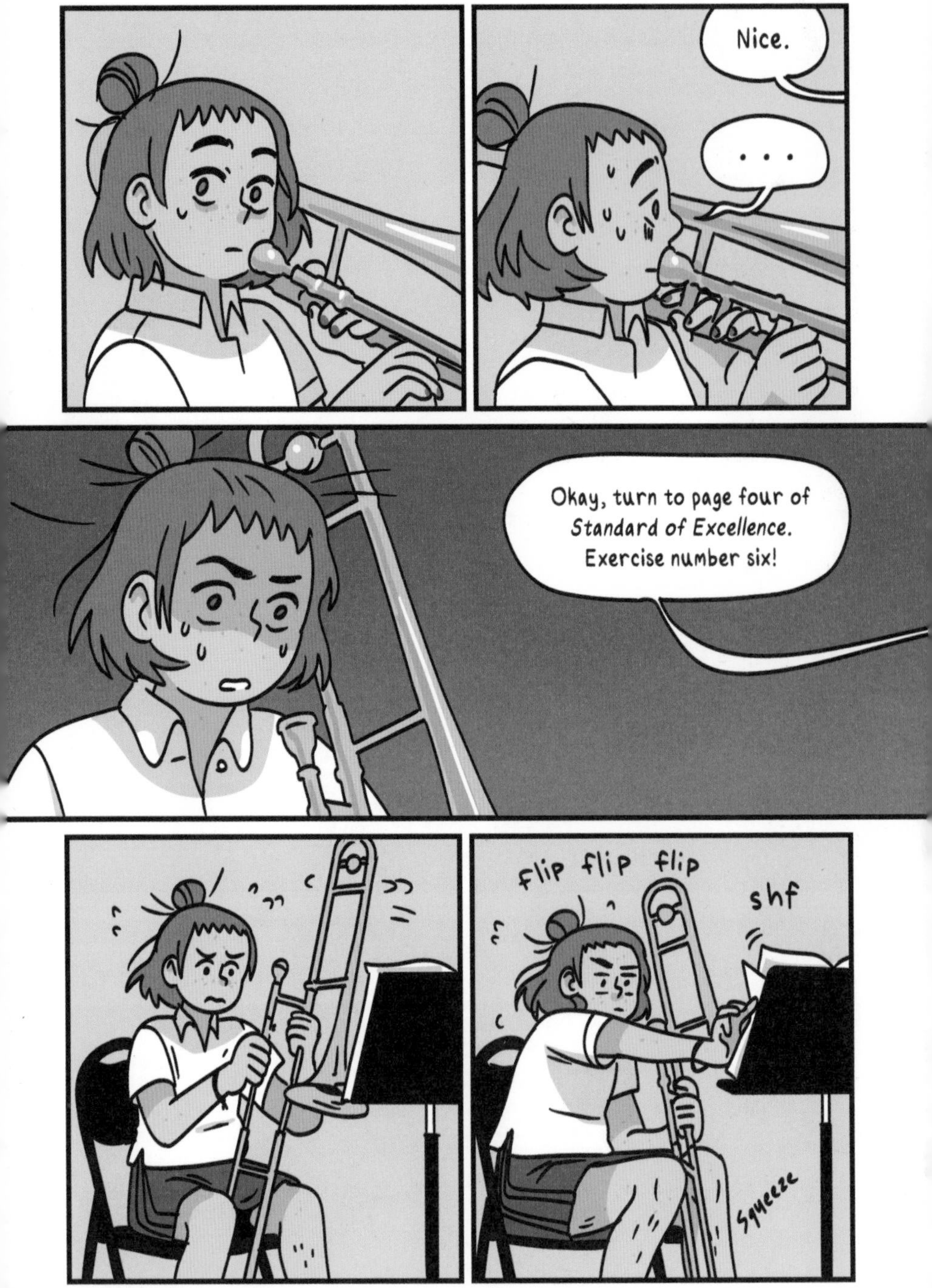
Nice.
. . .
Okay, turn to page four of *Standard of Excellence.* Exercise number six!
flip flip flip
shf
squeeze

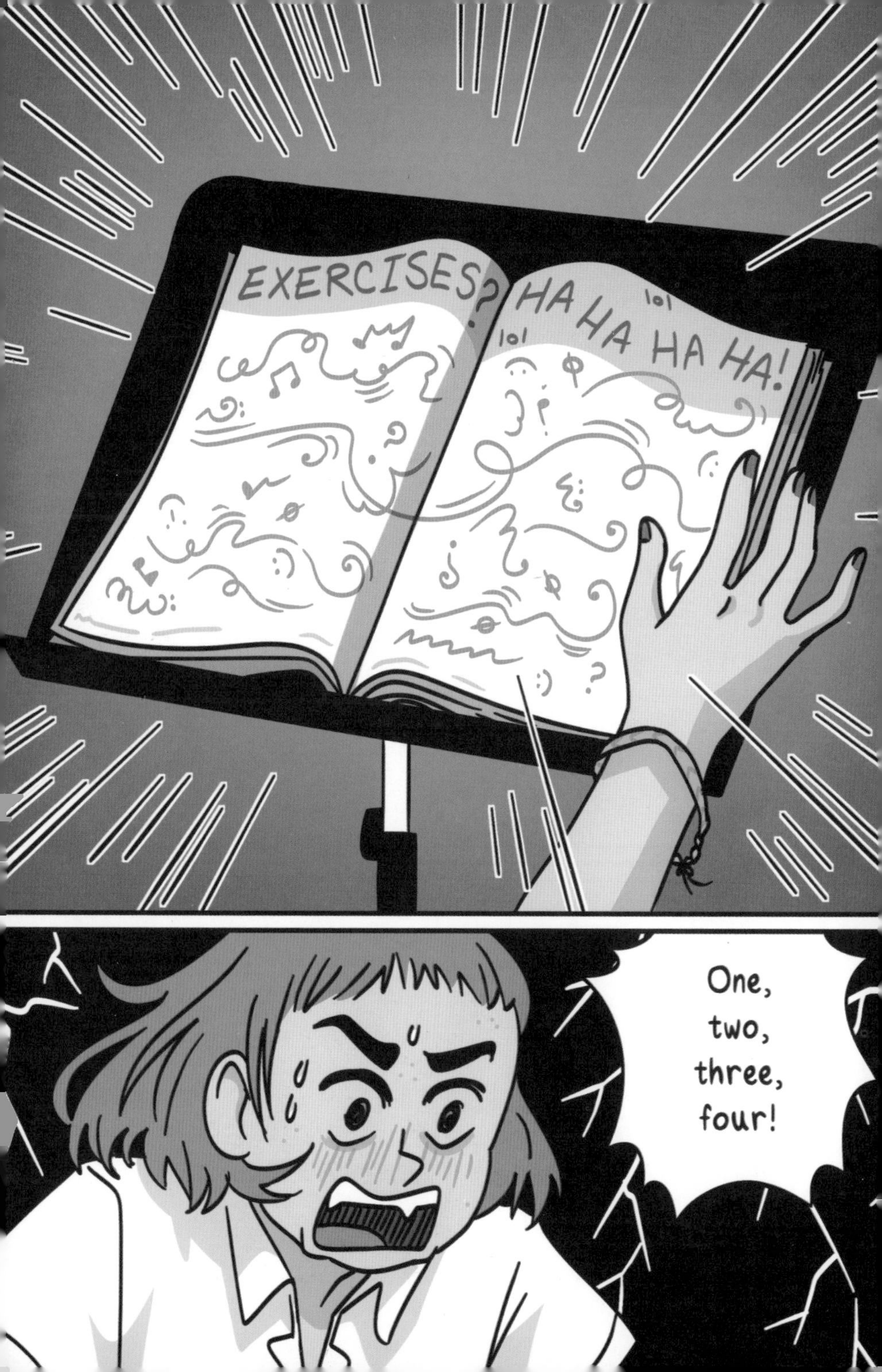
EXERCISES? HA HA HA HA!
One, two, three, four!

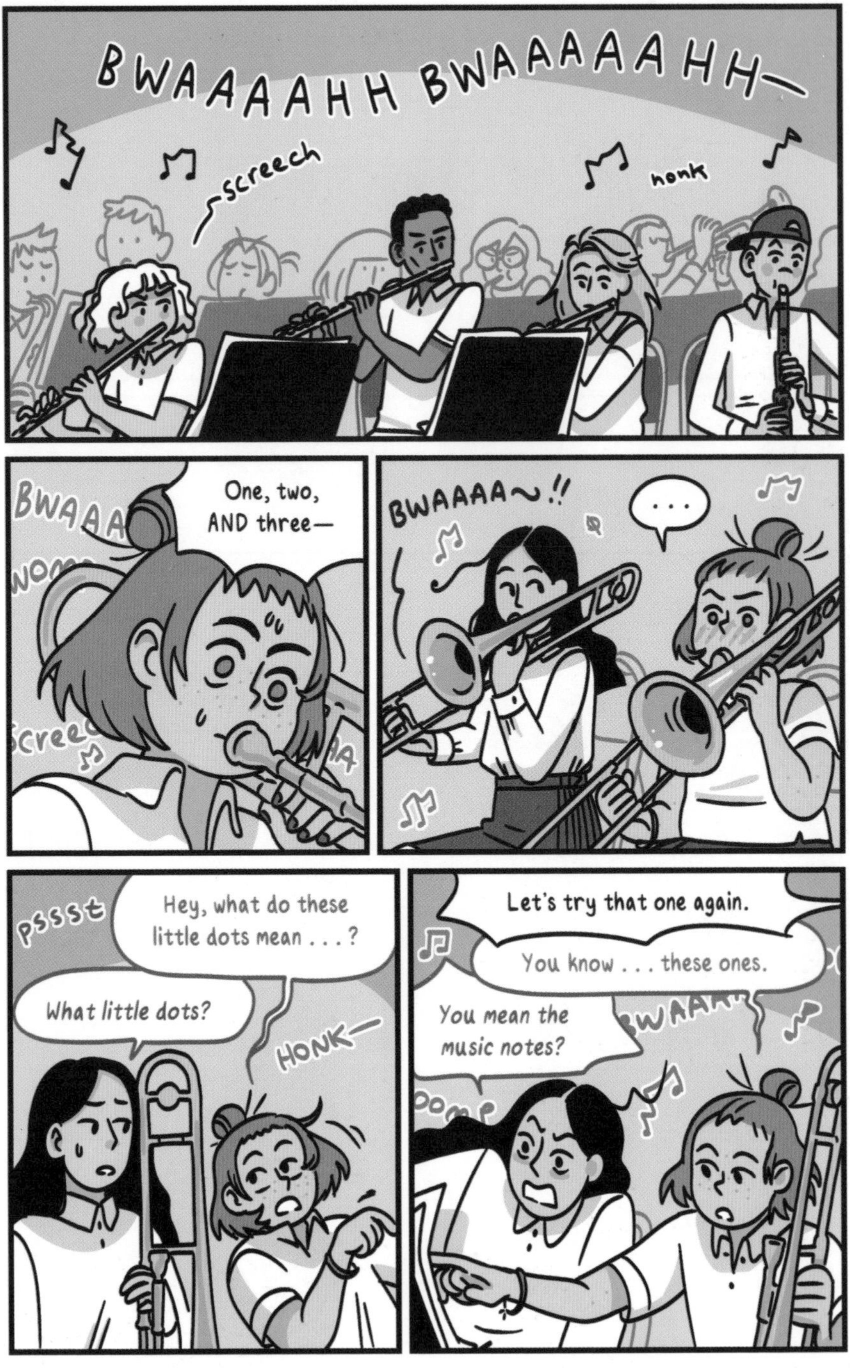
BWAAAAAHH BWAAAAAAHH—
screech
honk
BWAAA
One, two, AND three—
BWAAAA~!!
. . .
pssst
Hey, what do these little dots mean . . . ?
What little dots?
HONK—
Let's try that one again.
You know . . . these ones.
You mean the music notes?

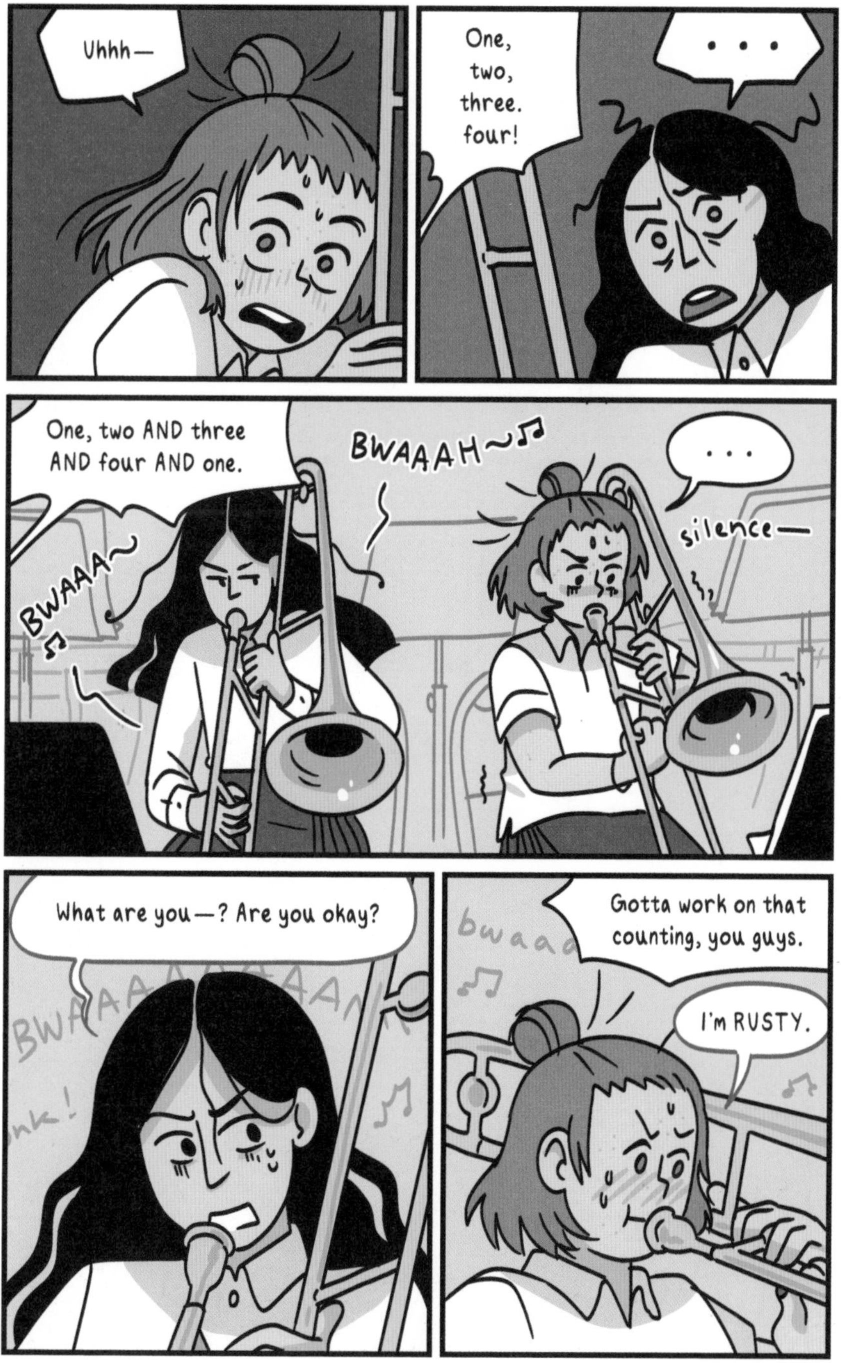
Uhhh—
One, two, three. four!
. . .
One, two AND three AND four AND one.
BWAAA~♫
BWAAAH~♫
. . .
silence—
What are you—? Are you okay?
Gotta work on that counting, you guys.
I'm RUSTY.

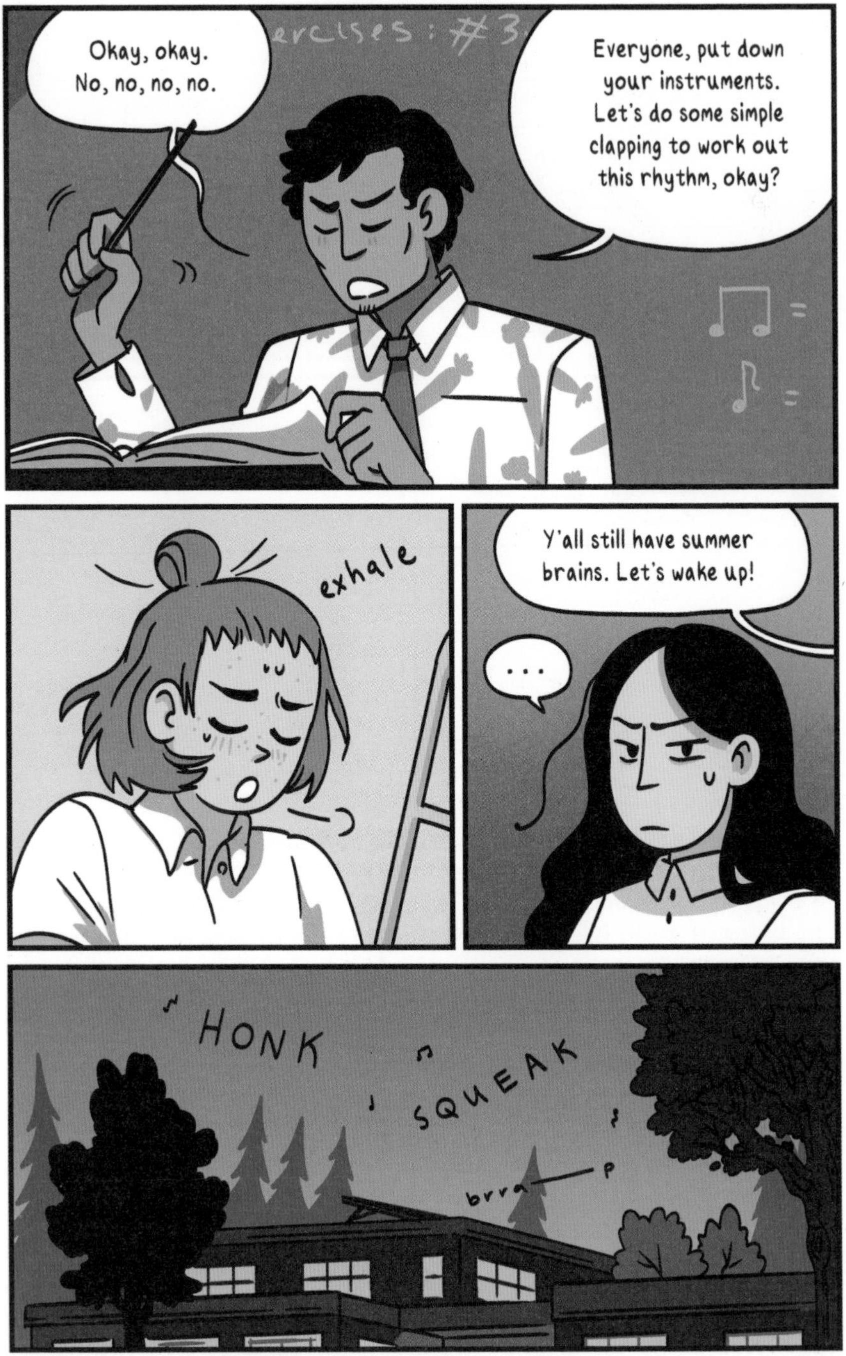
Okay, okay. No, no, no, no.
Everyone, put down your instruments. Let's do some simple clapping to work out this rhythm, okay?
exhale
Y'all still have summer brains. Let's wake up!
...
HONK
SQUEAK
brra—p

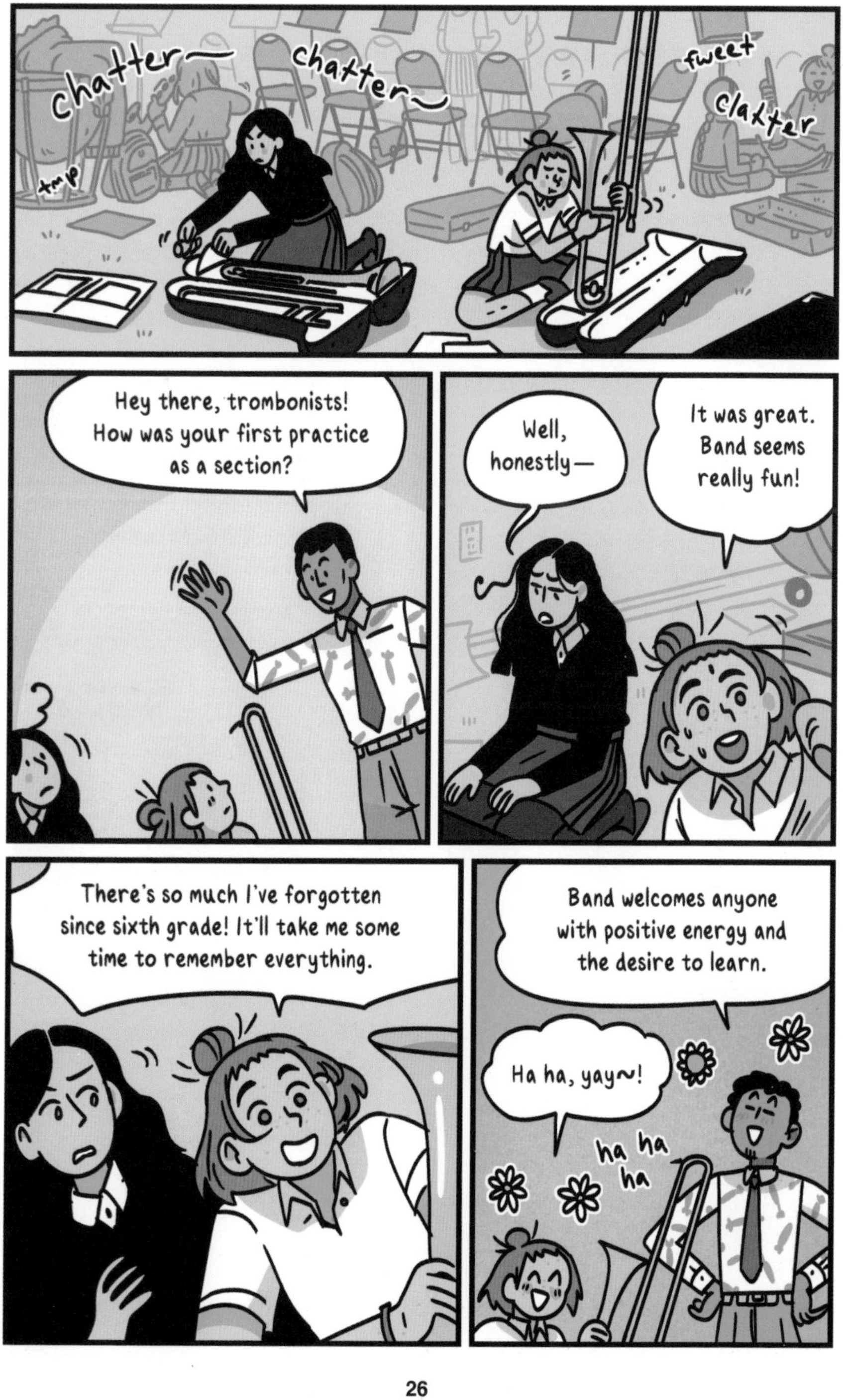
chatter—
chatter~
tmp
fweet
clatter
Hey there, trombonists! How was your first practice as a section?
Well, honestly—
It was great. Band seems really fun!
There's so much I've forgotten since sixth grade! It'll take me some time to remember everything.
Band welcomes anyone with positive energy and the desire to learn.
Ha ha, yay~!
ha ha ha

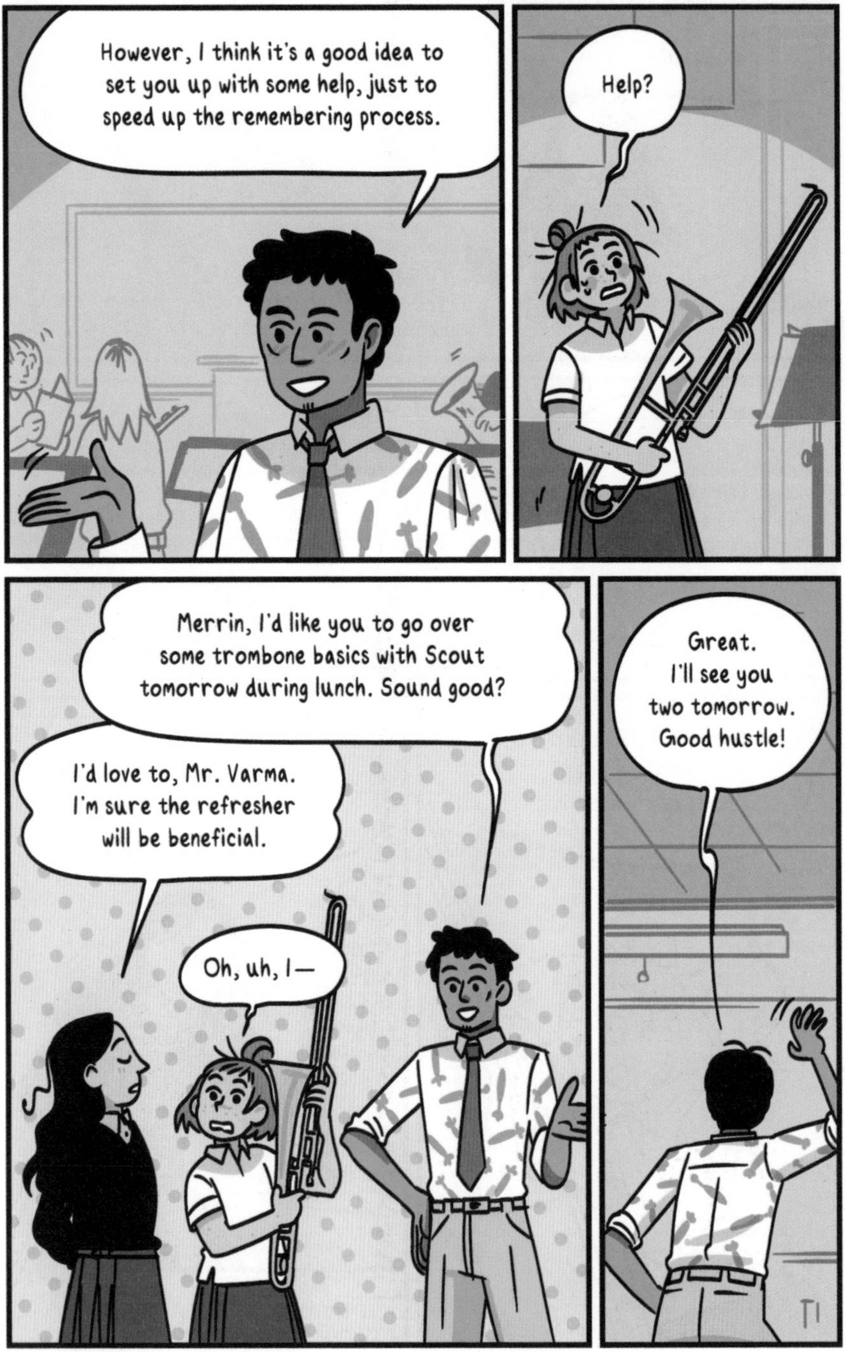
However, I think it's a good idea to set you up with some help, just to speed up the remembering process.
Help?
Merrin, I'd like you to go over some trombone basics with Scout tomorrow during lunch. Sound good?
I'd love to, Mr. Varma. I'm sure the refresher will be beneficial.
Oh, uh, I—
Great. I'll see you two tomorrow. Good hustle!

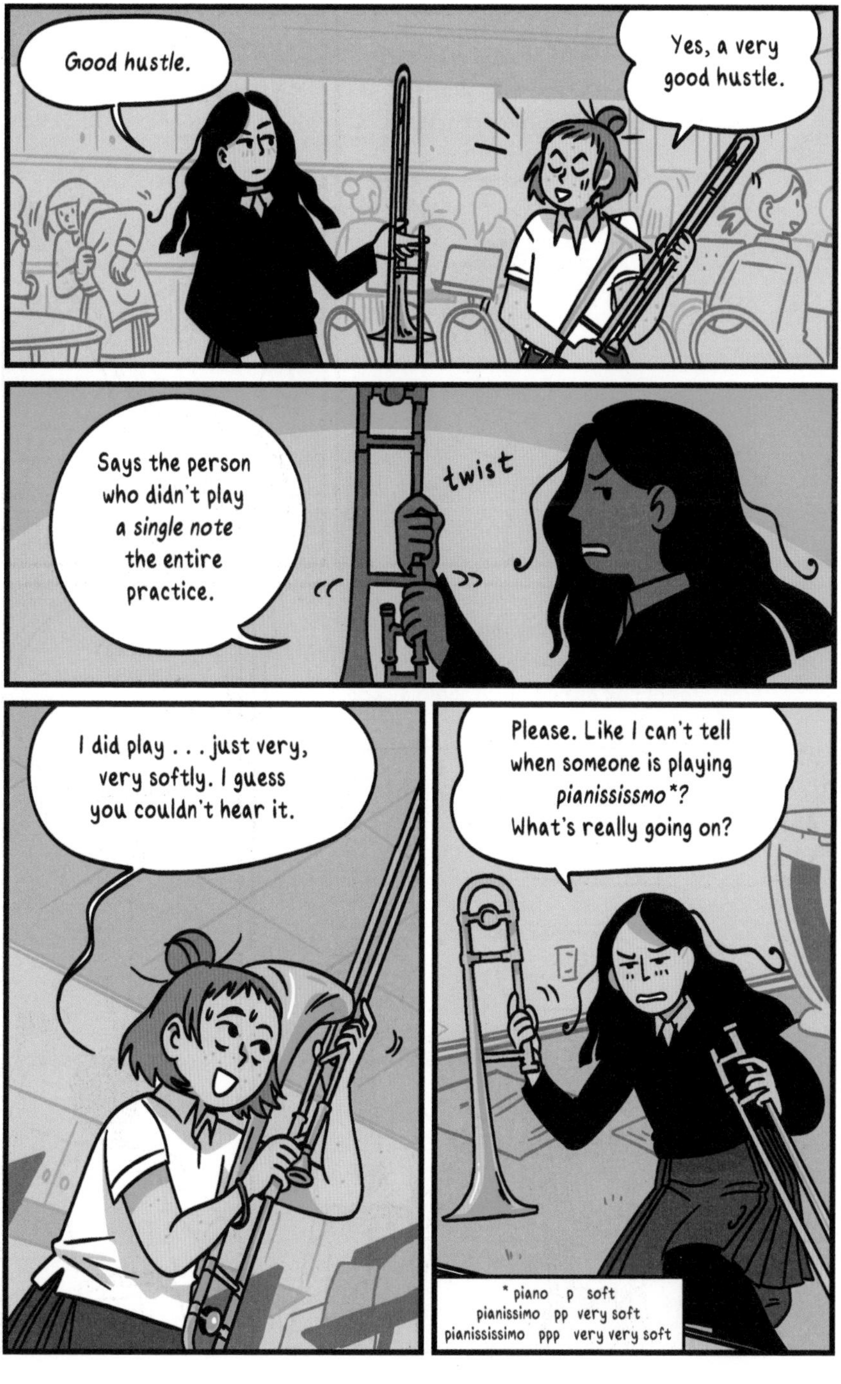
Good hustle.
Yes, a very good hustle.
Says the person who didn't play a *single note* the entire practice.
twist
I did play . . . just very, very softly. I guess you couldn't hear it.
Please. Like I can't tell when someone is playing *pianississmo**? What's really going on?
* piano p soft
pianissimo pp very soft
pianississimo ppp very very soft

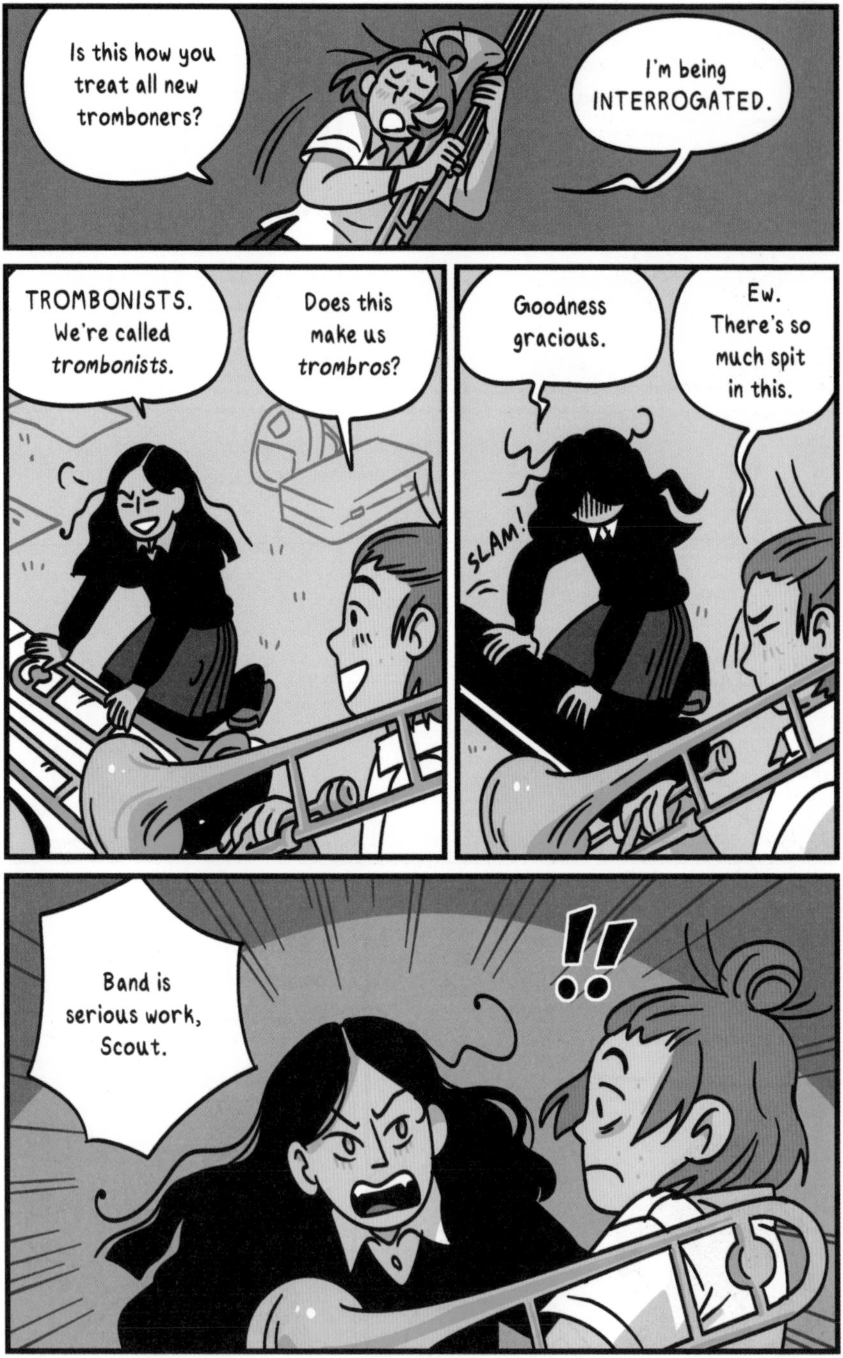
Is this how you treat all new tromboners?
I'm being INTERROGATED.
TROMBONISTS. We're called *trombonists.*
Does this make us *trombros?*
Goodness gracious.
Ew. There's so much spit in this.
SLAM!
!!
Band is serious work, Scout.

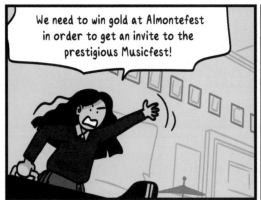

We need to win gold at Almontefest in order to get an invite to the prestigious Musicfest!

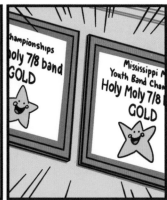

hampionships
oly 7/8 band
GOLD

Mississippi
Youth Band Chan
Holy Moly 7/8
GOLD

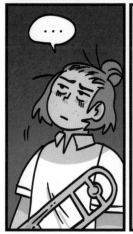

...

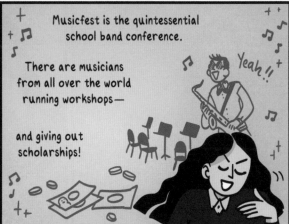

Musicfest is the quintessential school band conference.

There are musicians from all over the world running workshops—

and giving out scholarships!

Yeah!!

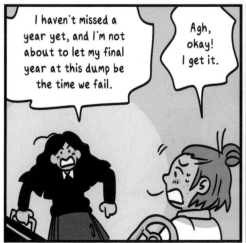

I haven't missed a year yet, and I'm not about to let my final year at this dump be the time we fail.

Agh, okay! I get it.

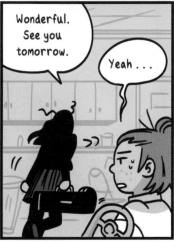

Wonderful. See you tomorrow.

Yeah . . .

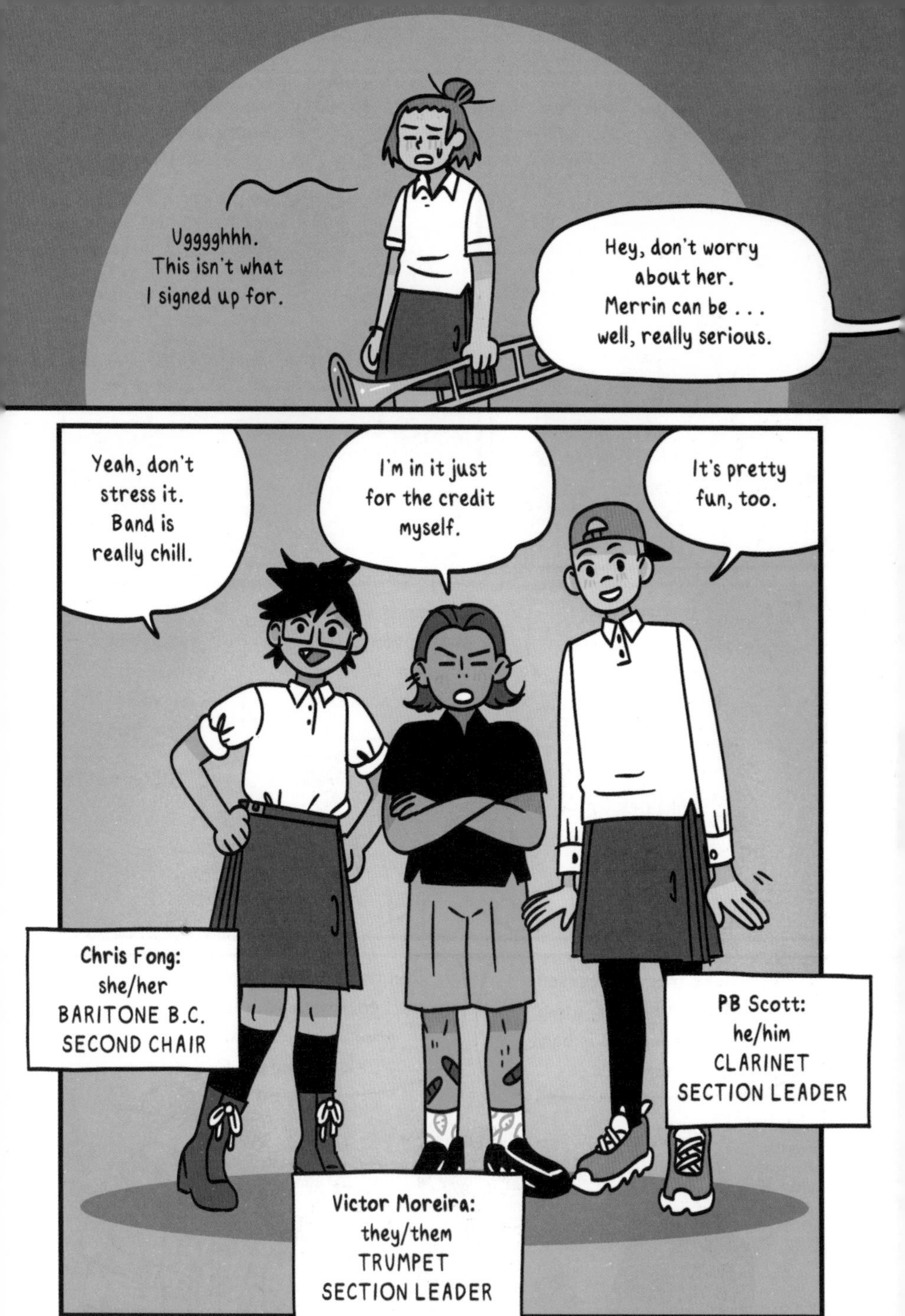
Ugggghhh. This isn't what I signed up for.
Hey, don't worry about her. Merrin can be . . . well, really serious.
Yeah, don't stress it. Band is really chill.
I'm in it just for the credit myself.
It's pretty fun, too.
Chris Fong: she/her BARITONE B.C. SECOND CHAIR
Victor Moreira: they/them TRUMPET SECTION LEADER
PB Scott: he/him CLARINET SECTION LEADER

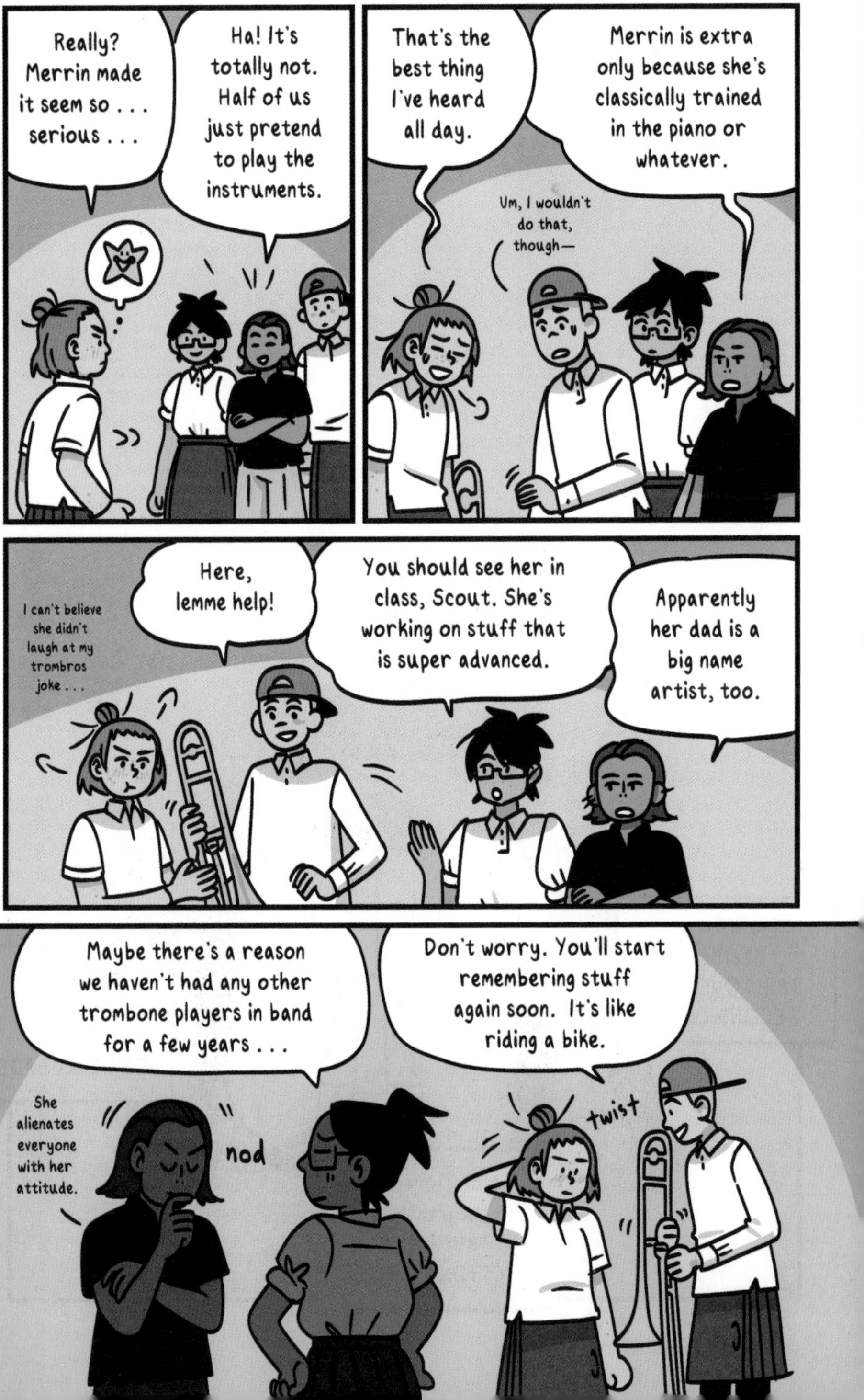
Really? Merrin made it seem so . . . serious . . .
Ha! It's totally not. Half of us just pretend to play the instruments.
That's the best thing I've heard all day.
Merrin is extra only because she's classically trained in the piano or whatever.
Um, I wouldn't do that, though—
I can't believe she didn't laugh at my trombros joke . . .
Here, lemme help!
You should see her in class, Scout. She's working on stuff that is super advanced.
Apparently her dad is a big name artist, too.
Maybe there's a reason we haven't had any other trombone players in band for a few years . . .
She alienates everyone with her attitude.
nod
Don't worry. You'll start remembering stuff again soon. It's like riding a bike.
twist

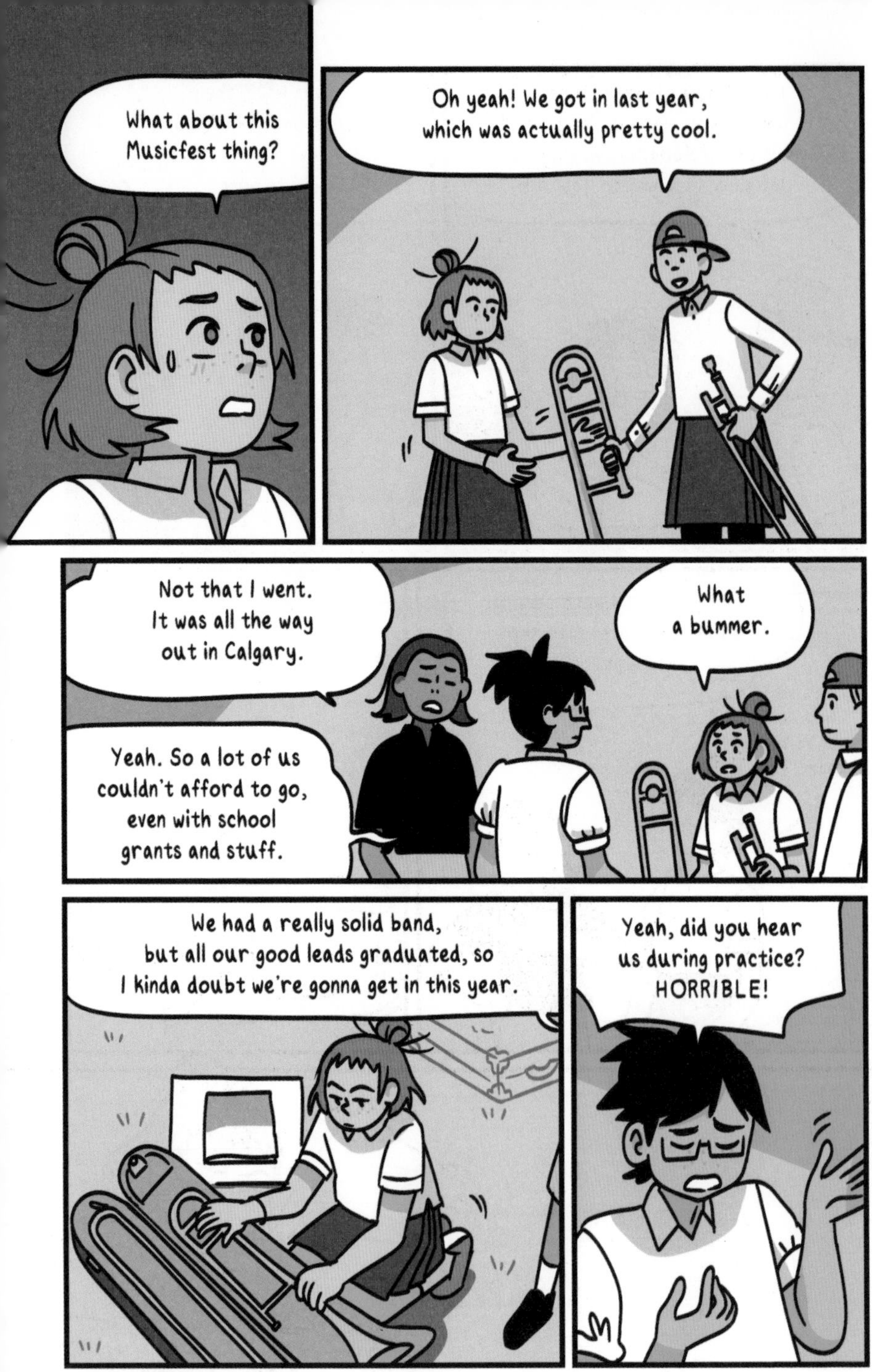
What about this Musicfest thing?
Oh yeah! We got in last year, which was actually pretty cool.
Not that I went. It was all the way out in Calgary.
What a bummer.
Yeah. So a lot of us couldn't afford to go, even with school grants and stuff.
We had a really solid band, but all our good leads graduated, so I kinda doubt we're gonna get in this year.
Yeah, did you hear us during practice? HORRIBLE!

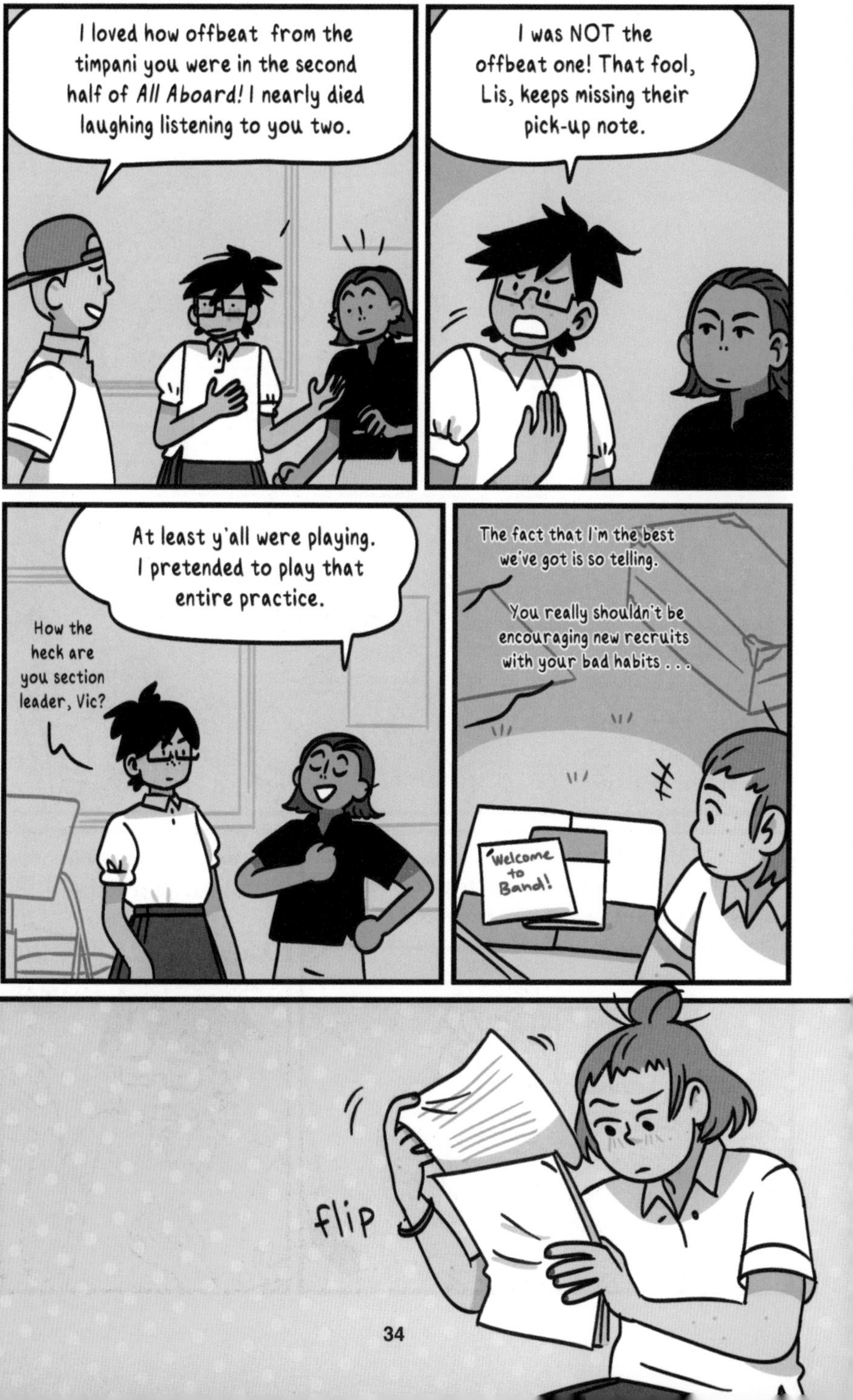
I loved how offbeat from the timpani you were in the second half of *All Aboard!* I nearly died laughing listening to you two.
I was NOT the offbeat one! That fool, Lis, keeps missing their pick-up note.
At least y'all were playing. I pretended to play that entire practice.
How the heck are you section leader, Vic?
The fact that I'm the best we've got is so telling.
You really shouldn't be encouraging new recruits with your bad habits . . .
Welcome to Band!
flip

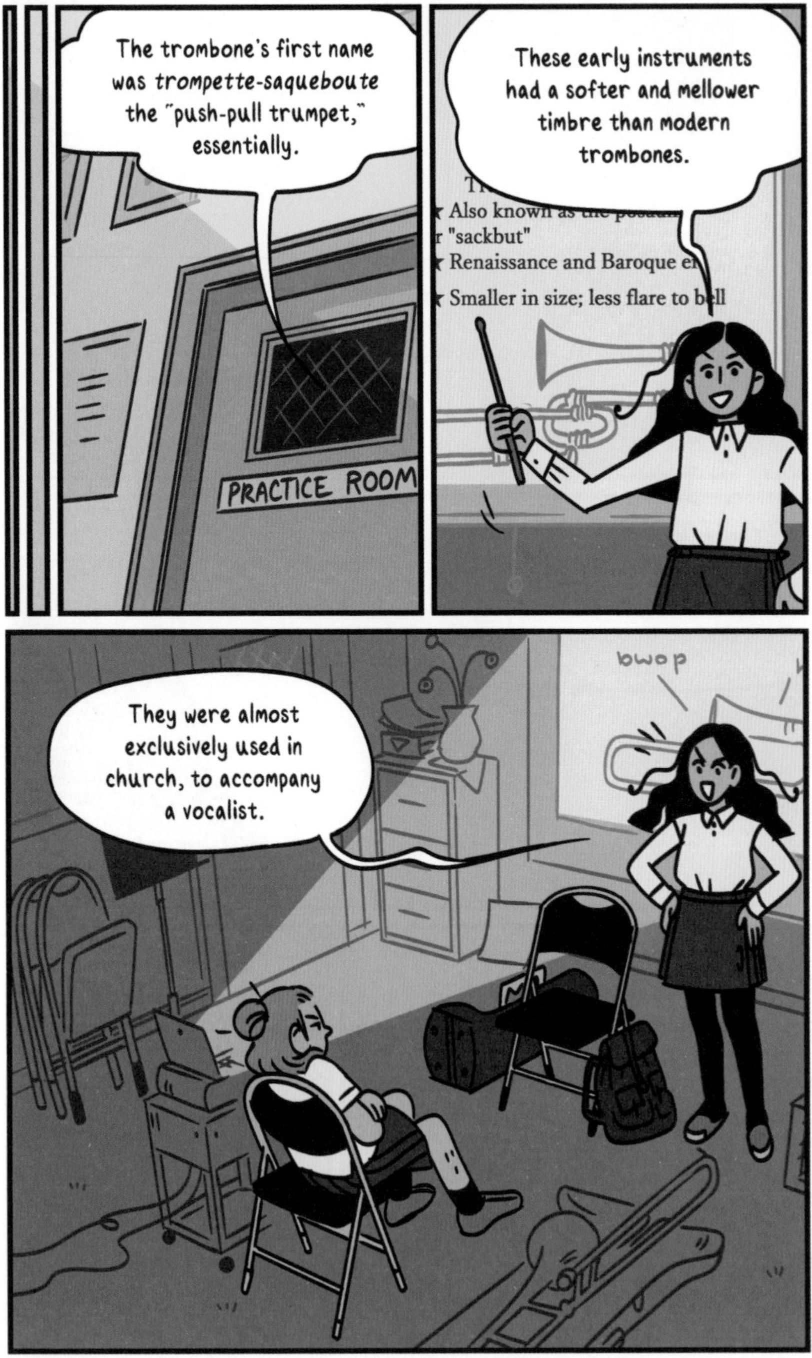
The trombone's first name was *trompette-saqueboute* the "push-pull trumpet," essentially.
PRACTICE ROOM
These early instruments had a softer and mellower timbre than modern trombones.
"sackbut"
Renaissance and Baroque
Smaller in size; less flare to bell
They were almost exclusively used in church, to accompany a vocalist.
bwop

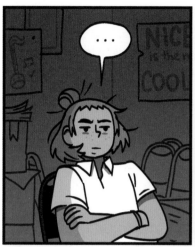

...

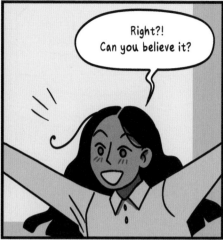

Right?! Can you believe it?

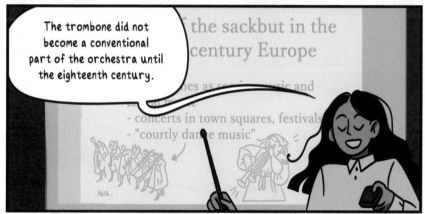

The trombone did not become a conventional part of the orchestra until the eighteenth century.

...f the sackbut in the ...century Europe

...es as se... ...sic and ...
- concerts in town squares, festivals...
- "courtly dance music"

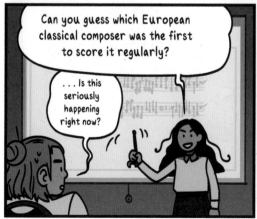

Can you guess which European classical composer was the first to score it regularly?

...Is this seriously happening right now?

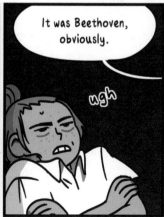

It was Beethoven, obviously.

ugh

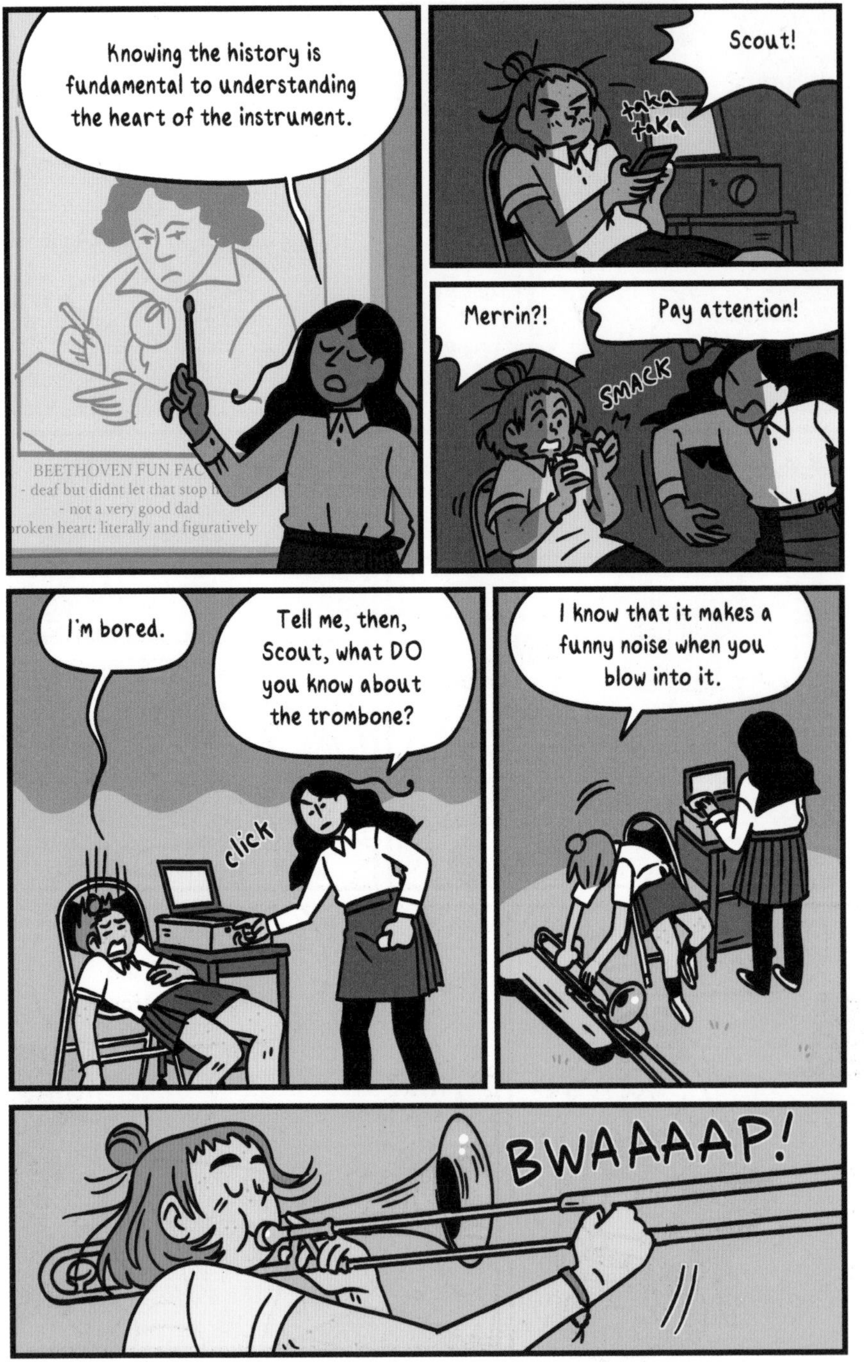

Knowing the history is fundamental to understanding the heart of the instrument.
BEETHOVEN FUN FAC
- deaf but didnt let that stop h
- not a very good dad
roken heart: literally and figuratively
Scout!
taka taka
Merrin?!
Pay attention!
SMACK
I'm bored.
Tell me, then, Scout, what DO you know about the trombone?
click
I know that it makes a funny noise when you blow into it.
BWAAAAP!

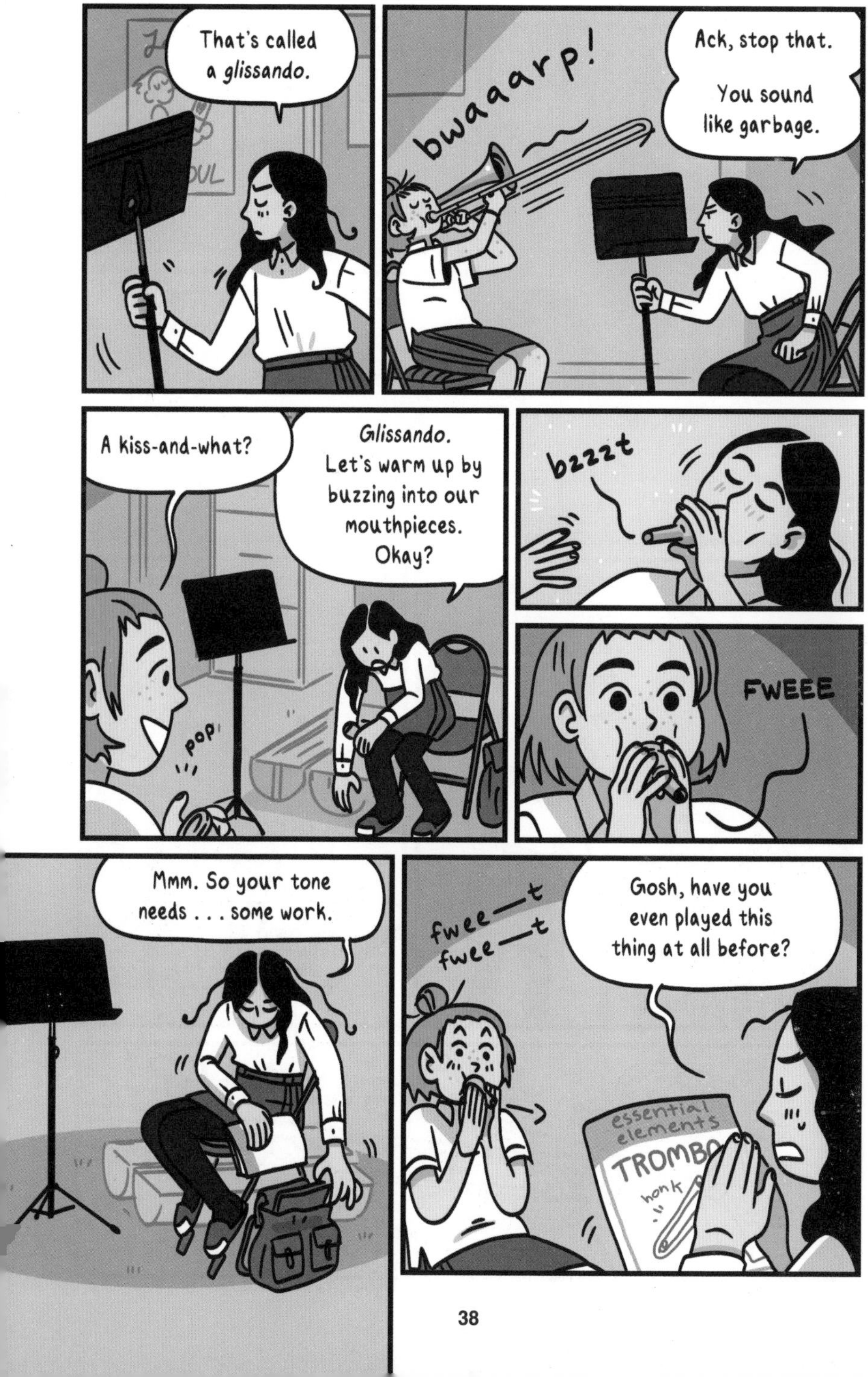

That's called a *glissando.*
bwaaarp!
Ack, stop that.
You sound like garbage.
A kiss-and-what?
Glissando. Let's warm up by buzzing into our mouthpieces. Okay?
pop
bzzzt
FWEEE
Mmm. So your tone needs . . . some work.
fwee—t
fwee—t
Gosh, have you even played this thing at all before?
essential elements
TROMBO
honk

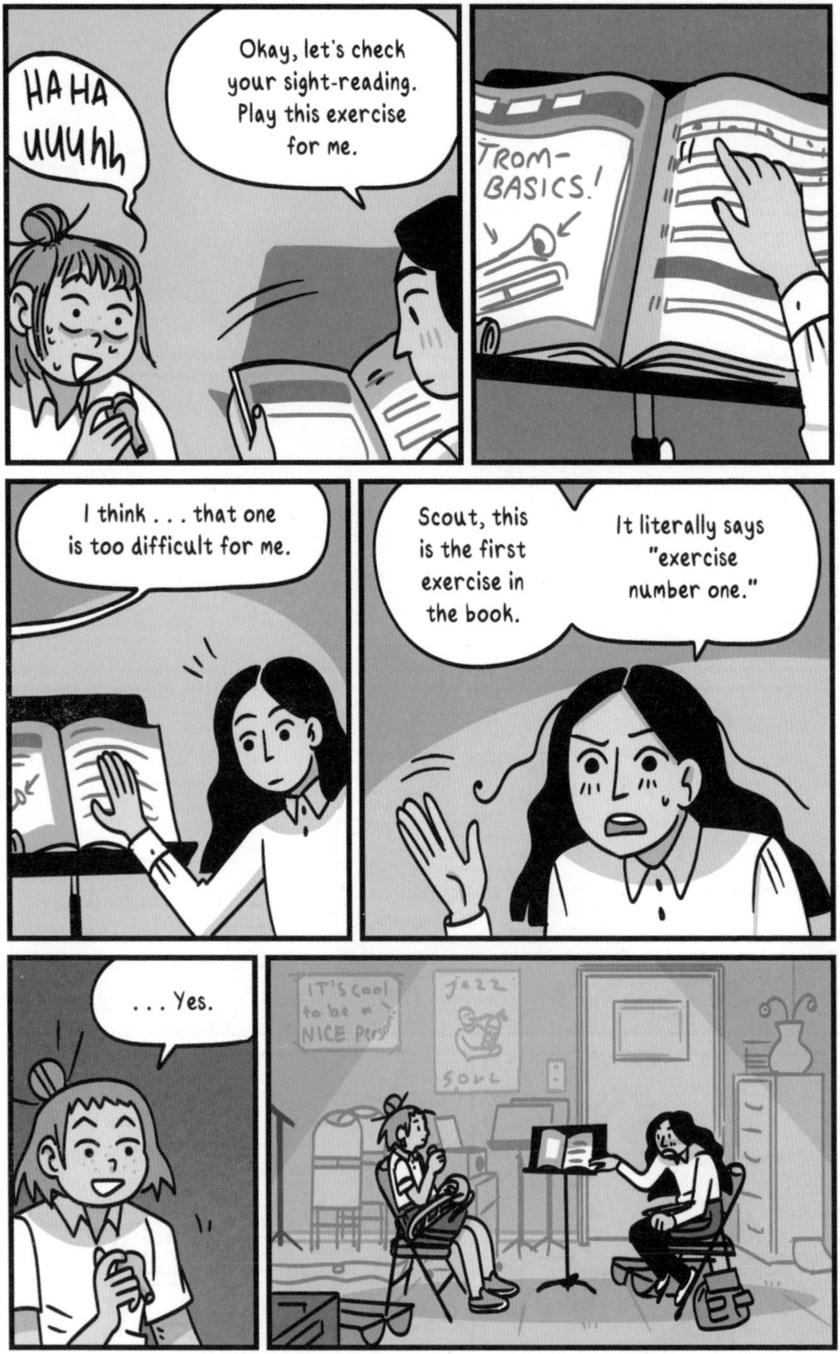
HA HA uuuhh
Okay, let's check your sight-reading. Play this exercise for me.
TROM-BASICS!
I think . . . that one is too difficult for me.
Scout, this is the first exercise in the book.
It literally says "exercise number one."
. . . Yes.
IT'S cool to be a NICE Pers
JAZZ
SOUL

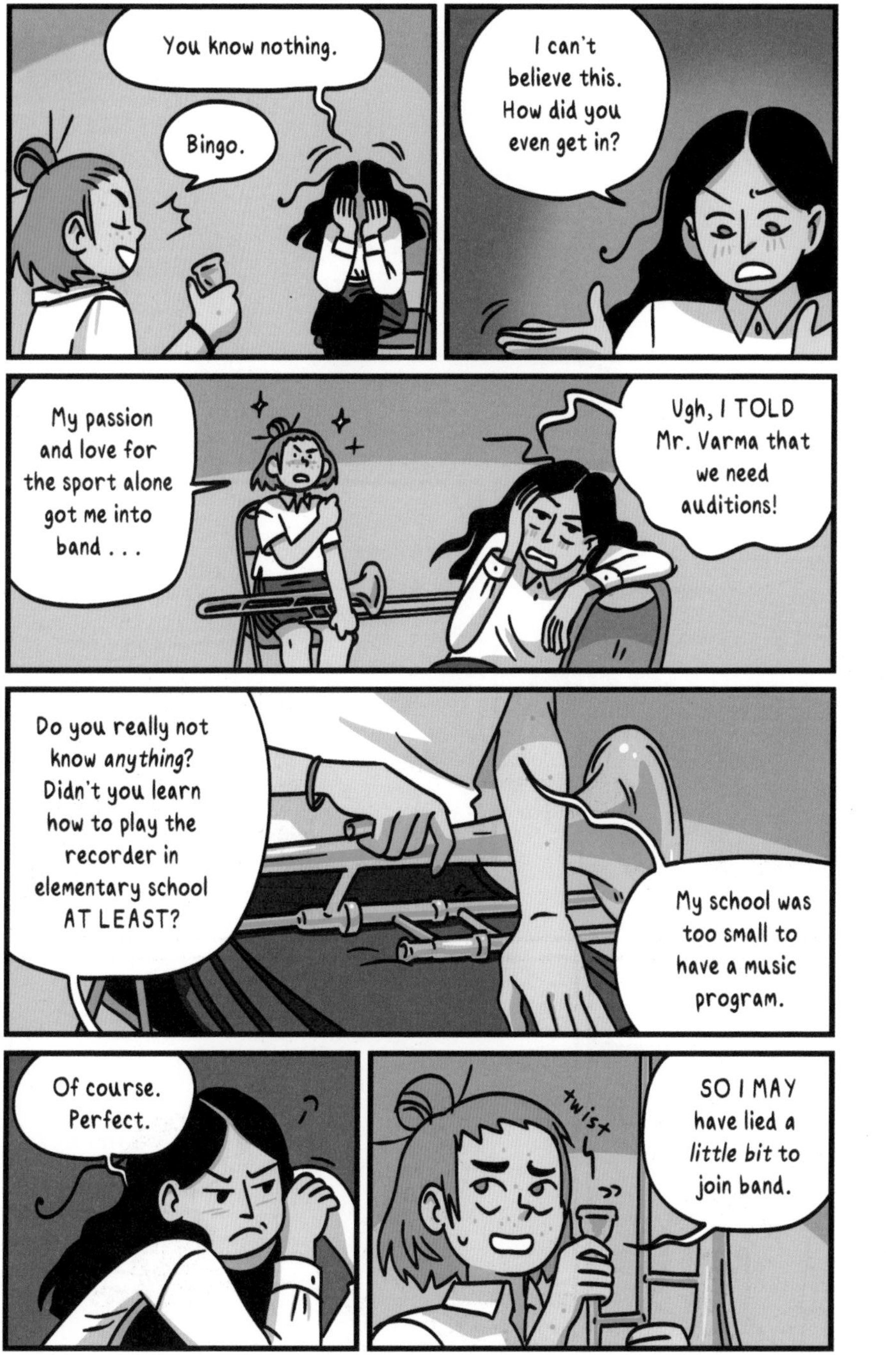
You know nothing.
Bingo.
I can't believe this. How did you even get in?
My passion and love for the sport alone got me into band . . .
Ugh, I TOLD Mr. Varma that we need auditions!
Do you really not know *anything*? Didn't you learn how to play the recorder in elementary school AT LEAST?
My school was too small to have a music program.
Of course. Perfect.
twist
SO I MAY have lied a *little bit* to join band.

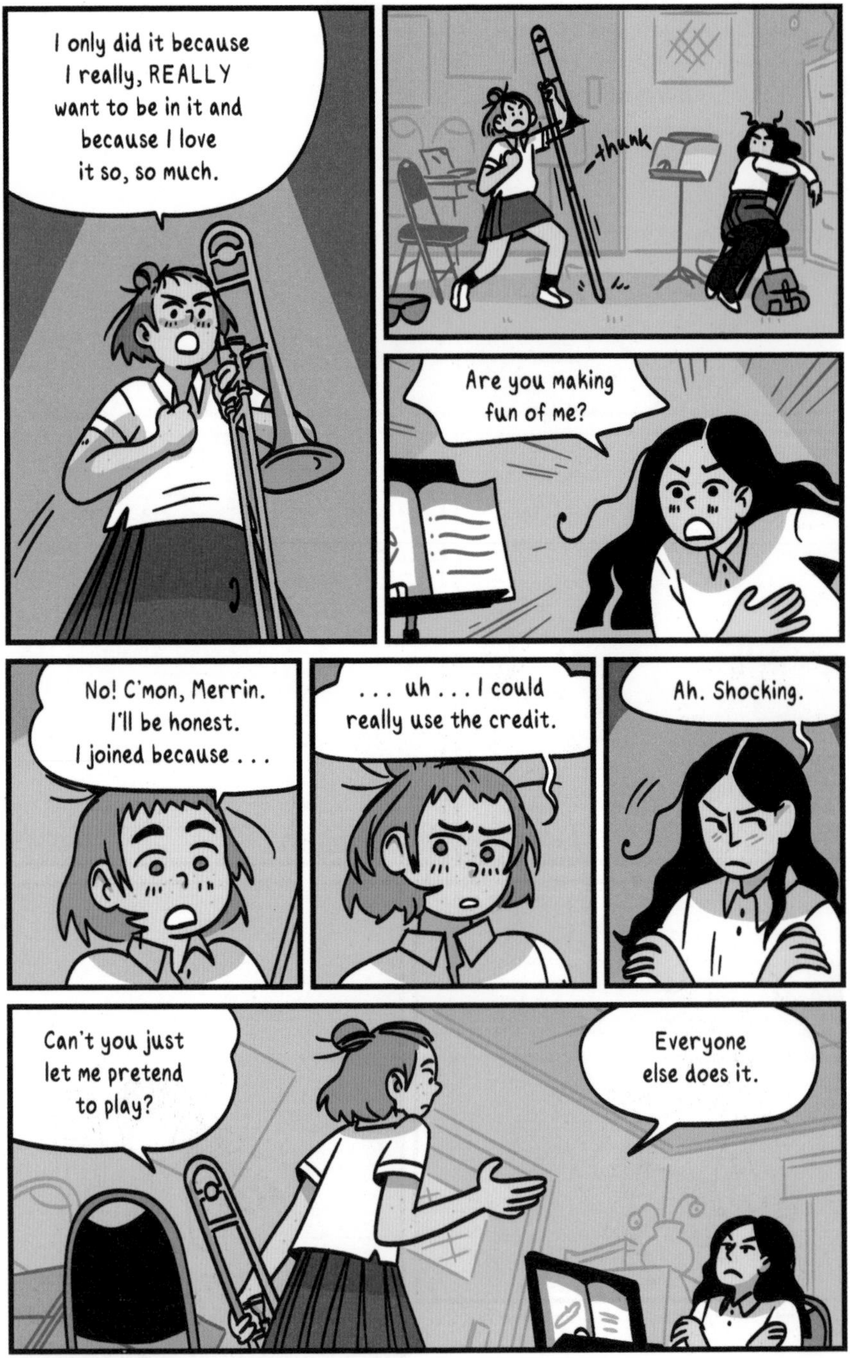
I only did it because I really, REALLY want to be in it and because I love it so, so much.
-thunk
Are you making fun of me?
No! C'mon, Merrin. I'll be honest. I joined because . . .
. . . uh . . . I could really use the credit.
Ah. Shocking.
Can't you just let me pretend to play?
Everyone else does it.

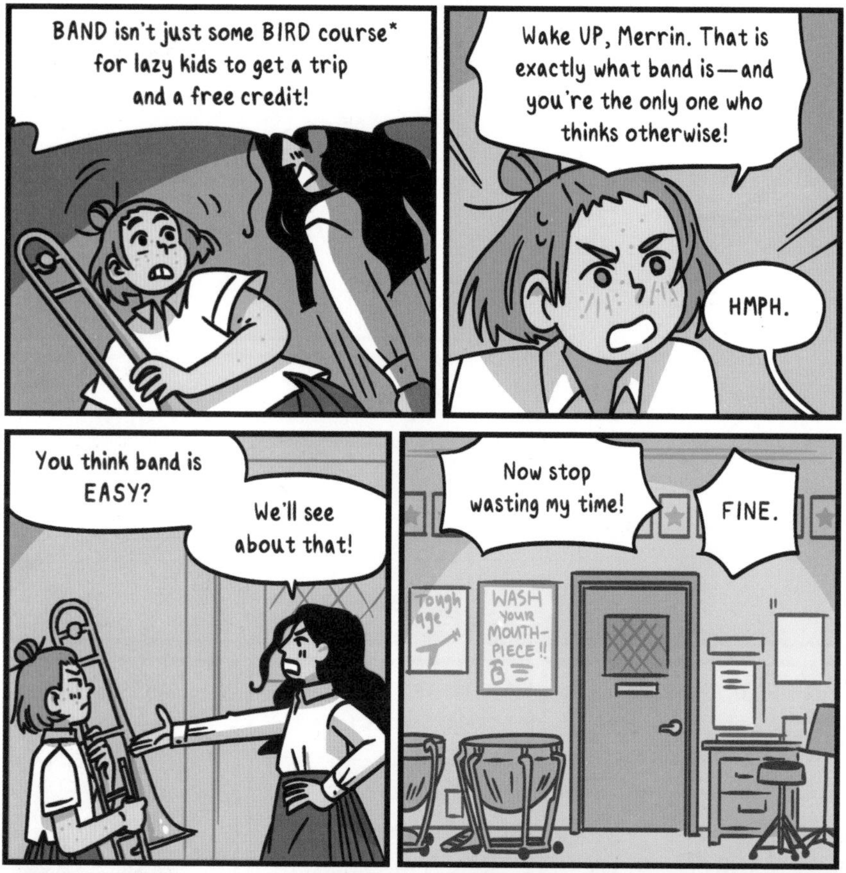
BAND isn't just some BIRD course* for lazy kids to get a trip and a free credit!
Wake UP, Merrin. That is exactly what band is—and you're the only one who thinks otherwise!
HMPH.
You think band is EASY?
We'll see about that!
Now stop wasting my time!
FINE.
WASH YOUR MOUTH-PIECE!!

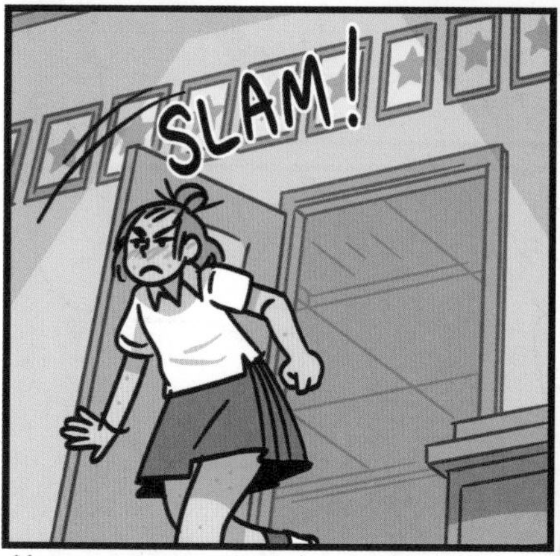
SLAM!

*A term used to describe a class that requires little work. An easy pass!

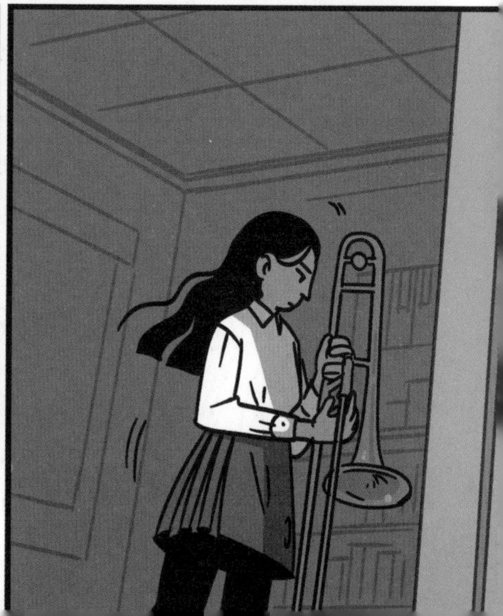

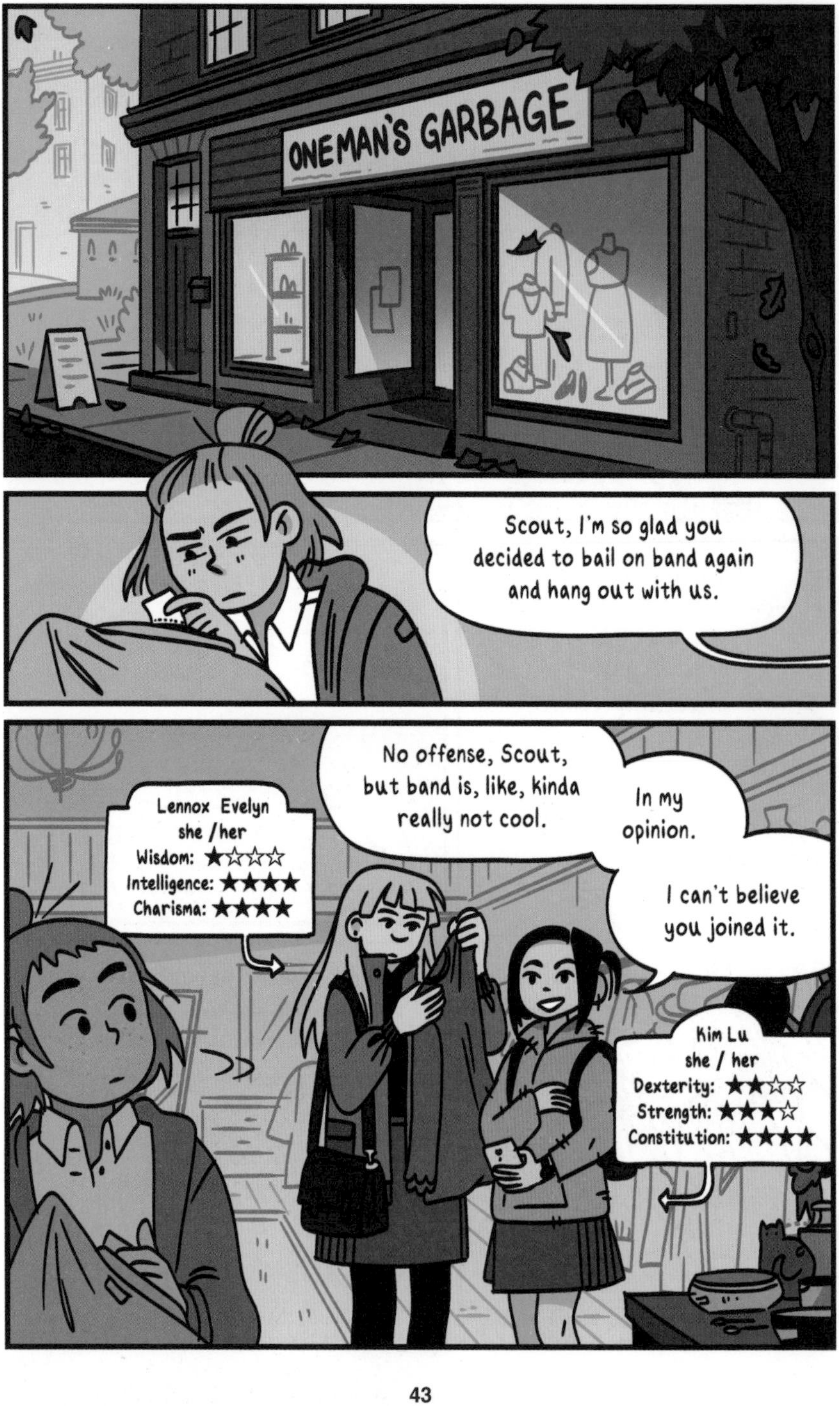
ONE MAN'S GARBAGE
Scout, I'm so glad you decided to bail on band again and hang out with us.
Lennox Evelyn she /her Wisdom: ★☆☆☆ Intelligence: ★★★★ Charisma: ★★★★
No offense, Scout, but band is, like, kinda really not cool.
In my opinion.
I can't believe you joined it.
Kim Lu she / her Dexterity: ★★☆☆ Strength: ★★★☆ Constitution: ★★★★

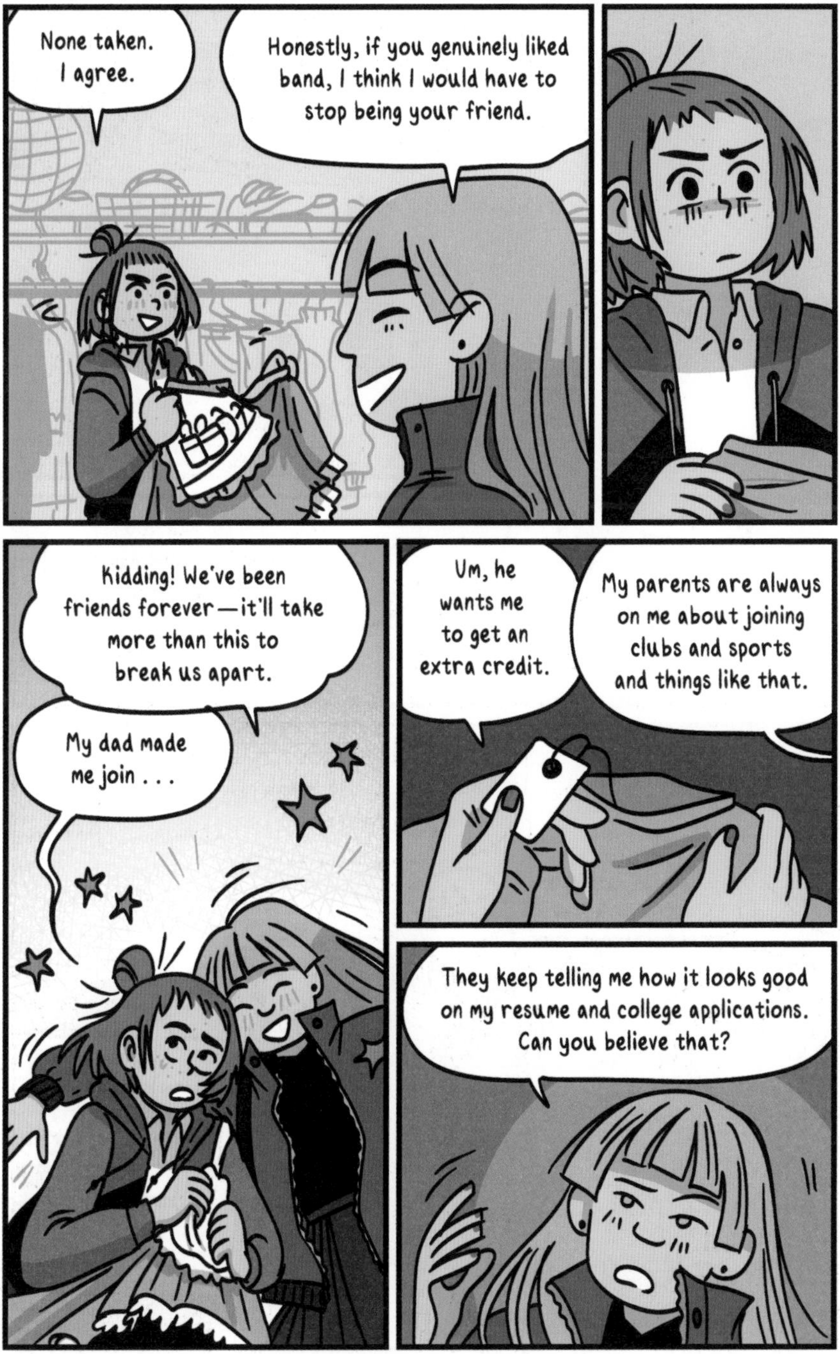
None taken. I agree.
Honestly, if you genuinely liked band, I think I would have to stop being your friend.
Kidding! We've been friends forever—it'll take more than this to break us apart.
My dad made me join . . .
Um, he wants me to get an extra credit.
My parents are always on me about joining clubs and sports and things like that.
They keep telling me how it looks good on my resume and college applications. Can you believe that?

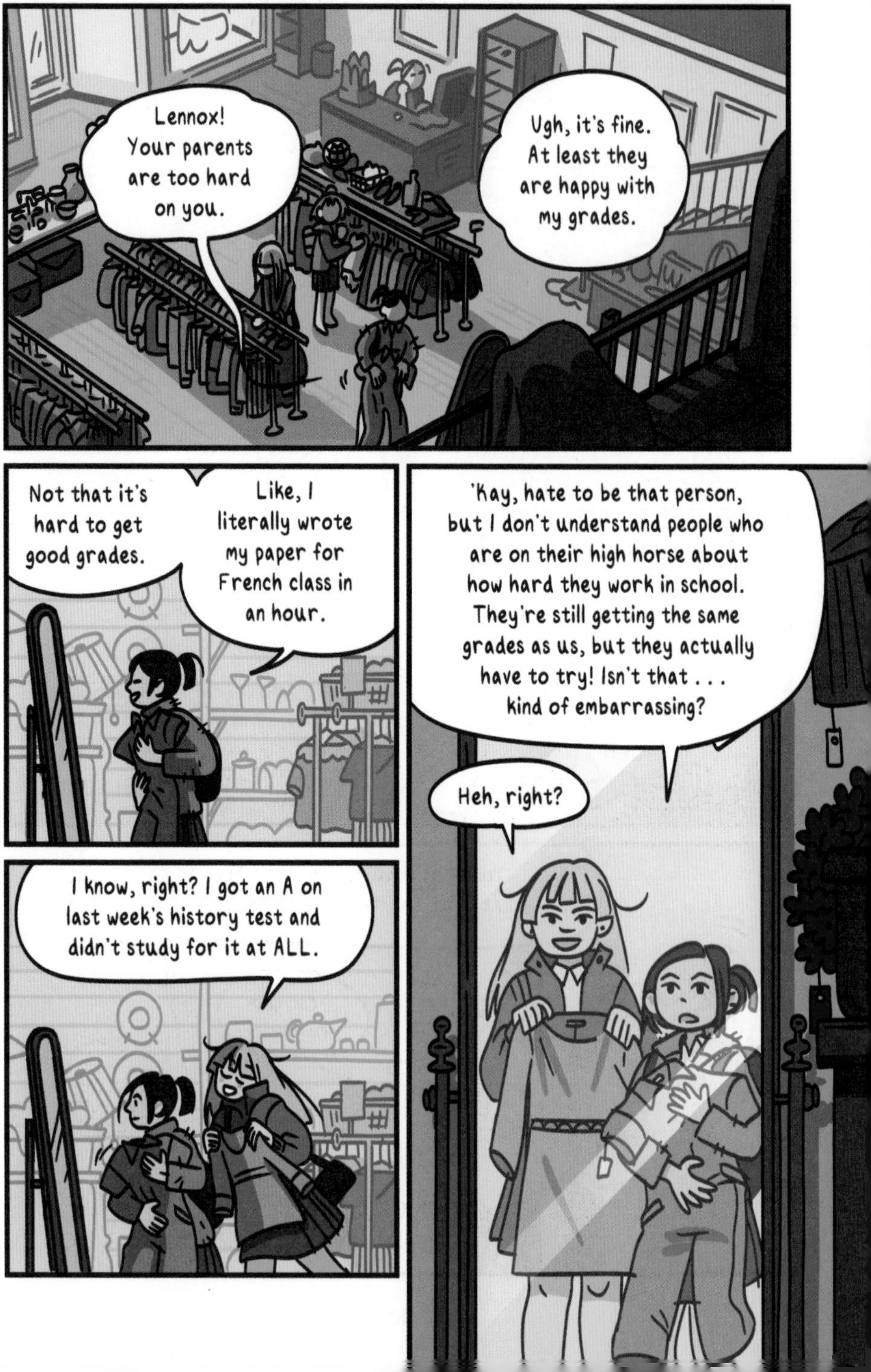
Lennox! Your parents are too hard on you.
Ugh, it's fine. At least they are happy with my grades.
Not that it's hard to get good grades.
Like, I literally wrote my paper for French class in an hour.
I know, right? I got an A on last week's history test and didn't study for it at ALL.
'Kay, hate to be that person, but I don't understand people who are on their high horse about how hard they work in school. They're still getting the same grades as us, but they actually have to try! Isn't that . . . kind of embarrassing?
Heh, right?

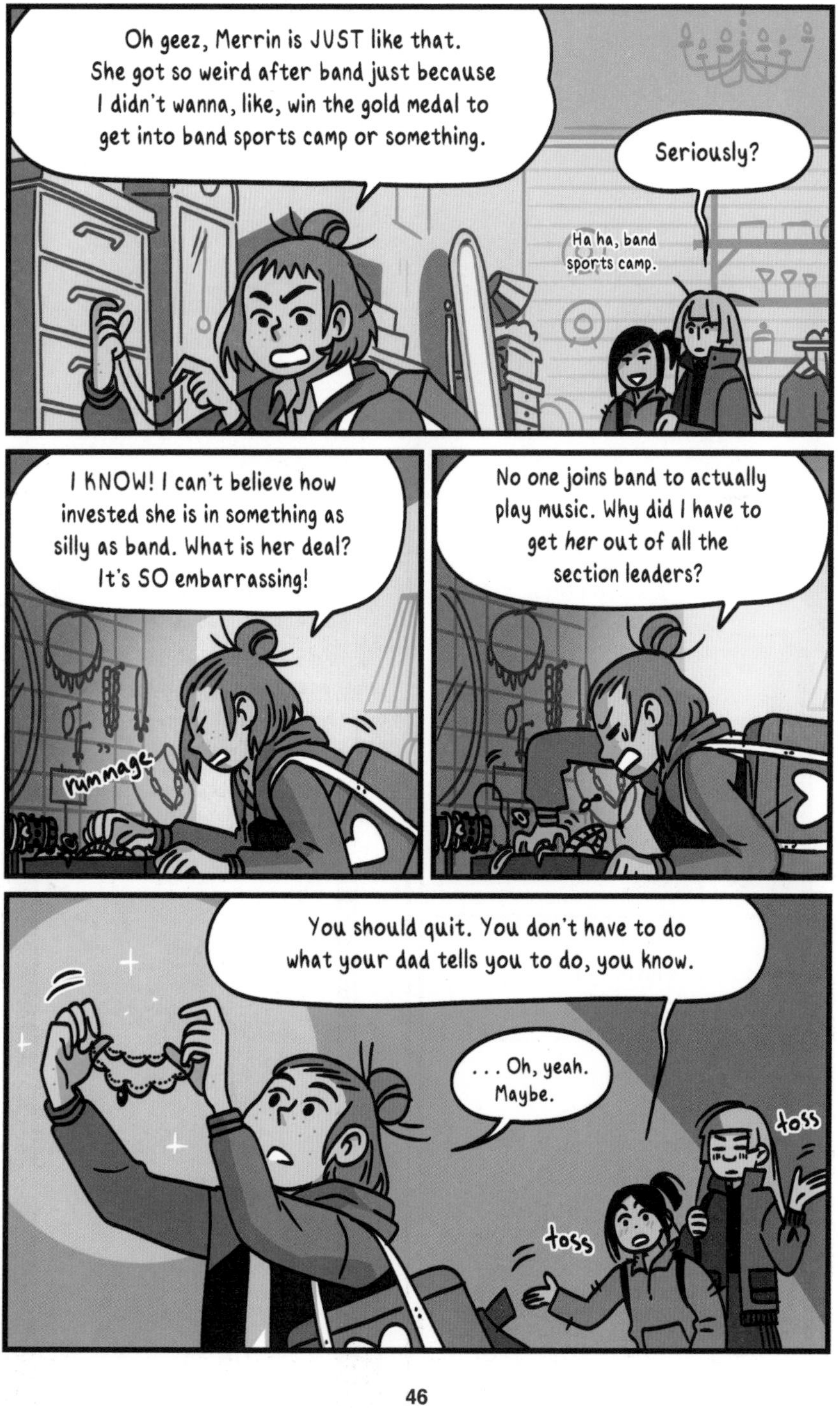
Oh geez, Merrin is JUST like that. She got so weird after band just because I didn't wanna, like, win the gold medal to get into band sports camp or something.
Seriously?
Ha ha, band sports camp.
I KNOW! I can't believe how invested she is in something as silly as band. What is her deal? It's SO embarrassing!
rummage
No one joins band to actually play music. Why did I have to get her out of all the section leaders?
You should quit. You don't have to do what your dad tells you to do, you know.
. . . Oh, yeah. Maybe.
toss
toss

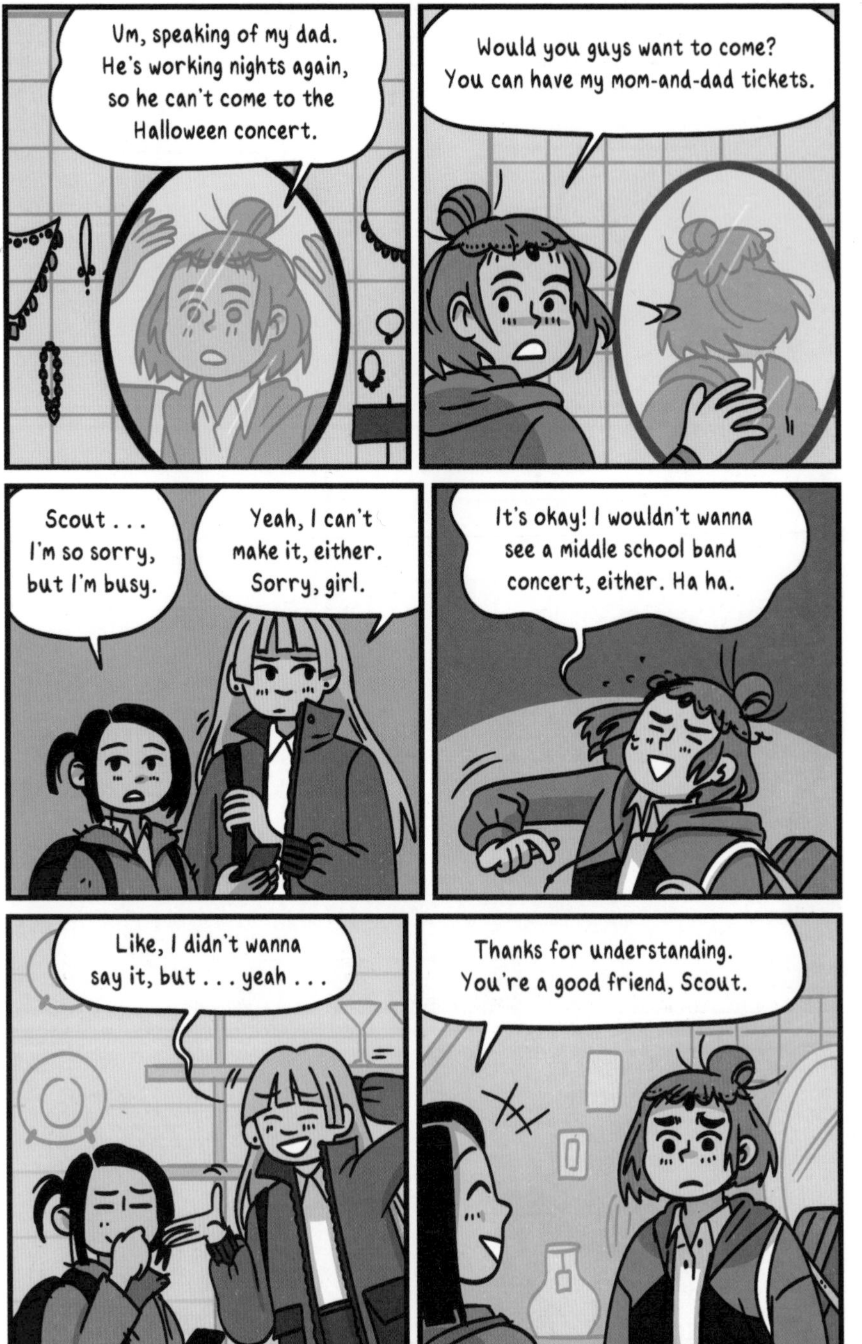
Um, speaking of my dad. He's working nights again, so he can't come to the Halloween concert.
Would you guys want to come? You can have my mom-and-dad tickets.
Scout . . . I'm so sorry, but I'm busy.
Yeah, I can't make it, either. Sorry, girl.
It's okay! I wouldn't wanna see a middle school band concert, either. Ha ha.
Like, I didn't wanna say it, but . . . yeah . . .
Thanks for understanding. You're a good friend, Scout.

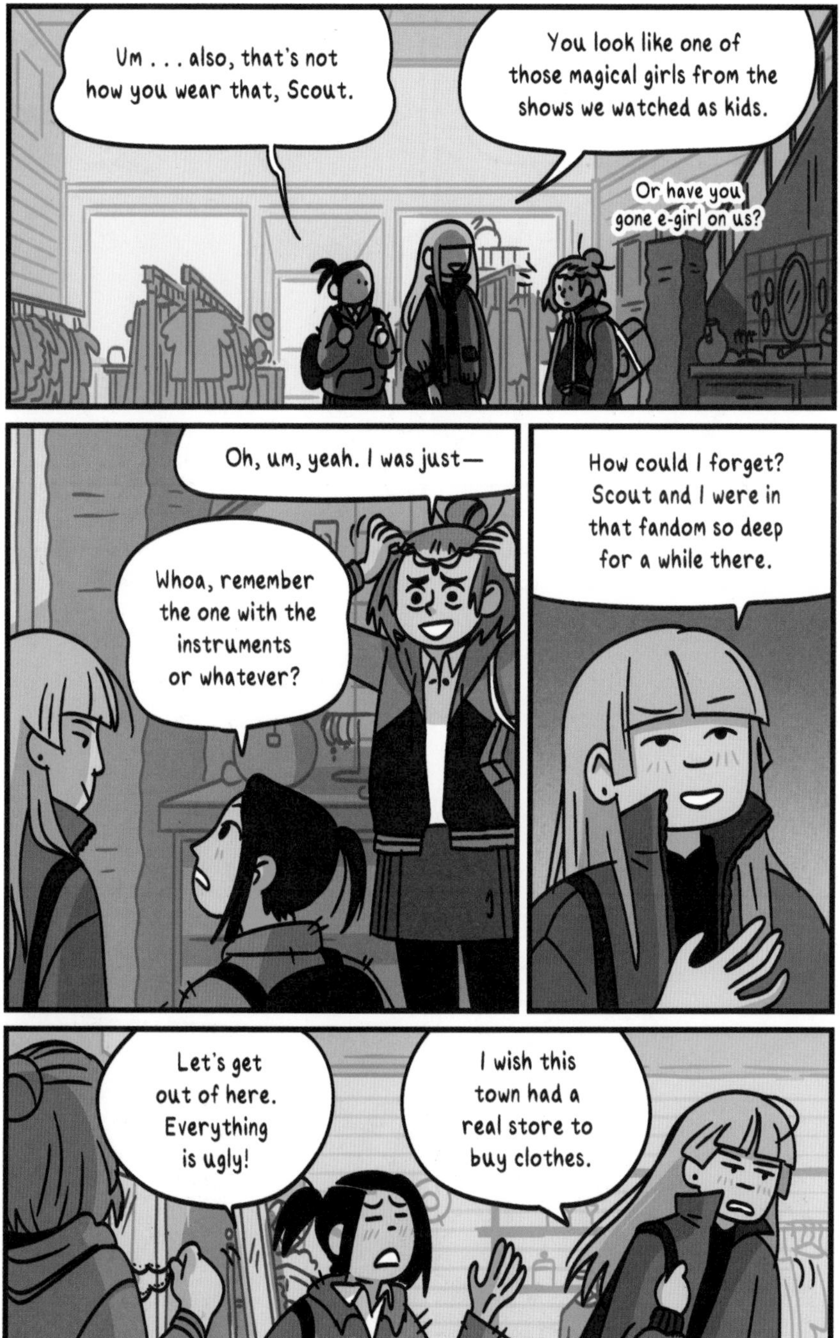
Um . . . also, that's not how you wear that, Scout.
You look like one of those magical girls from the shows we watched as kids.
Or have you gone e-girl on us?
Oh, um, yeah. I was just—
Whoa, remember the one with the instruments or whatever?
How could I forget? Scout and I were in that fandom so deep for a while there.
Let's get out of here. Everything is ugly!
I wish this town had a real store to buy clothes.

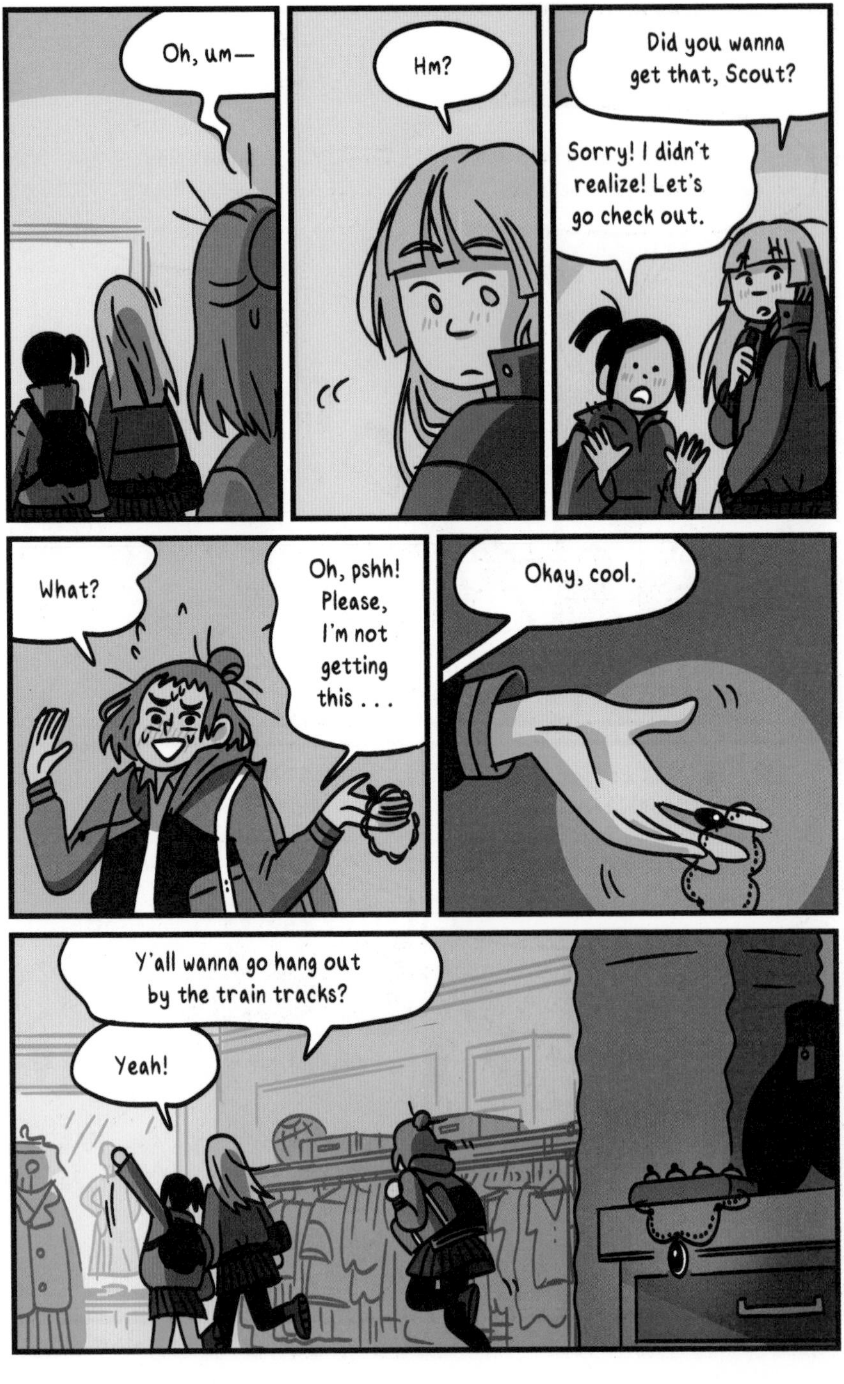
Oh, um—
Hm?
Did you wanna get that, Scout?
Sorry! I didn't realize! Let's go check out.
What?
Oh, pshh! Please, I'm not getting this . . .
Okay, cool.
Y'all wanna go hang out by the train tracks?
Yeah!

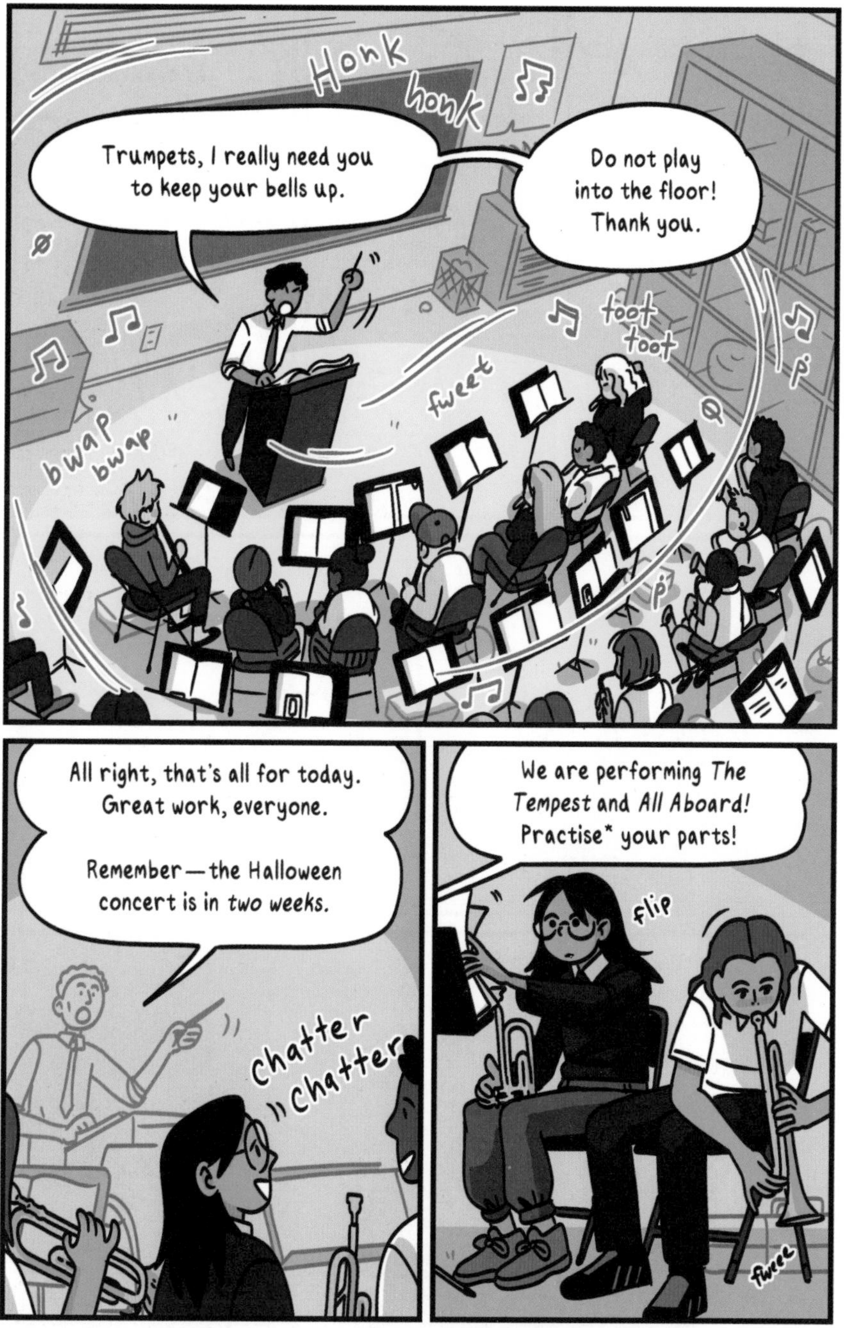
Honk
honk
Trumpets, I really need you to keep your bells up.
Do not play into the floor! Thank you.
toot
toot
fweet
bwap
bwap
All right, that's all for today. Great work, everyone.
Remember—the Halloween concert is in *two weeks.*
chatter
chatter
We are performing *The Tempest* and *All Aboard!* Practise* your parts!
flip
fweee

*In Canadian English, *practise* is a verb and *practice* is a noun.

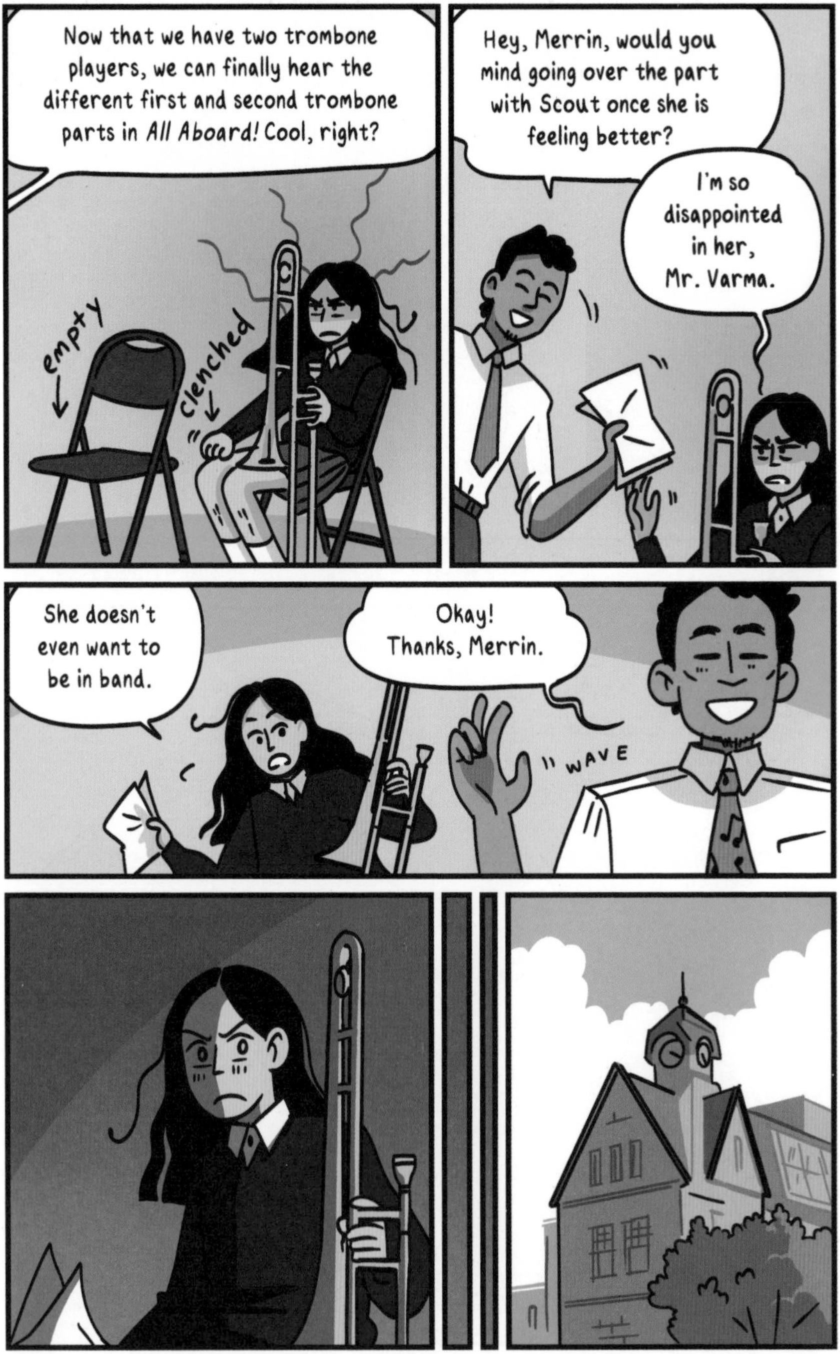
Now that we have two trombone players, we can finally hear the different first and second trombone parts in *All Aboard!* Cool, right?
empty
clenched
Hey, Merrin, would you mind going over the part with Scout once she is feeling better?
I'm so disappointed in her, Mr. Varma.
She doesn't even want to be in band.
Okay! Thanks, Merrin.
WAVE

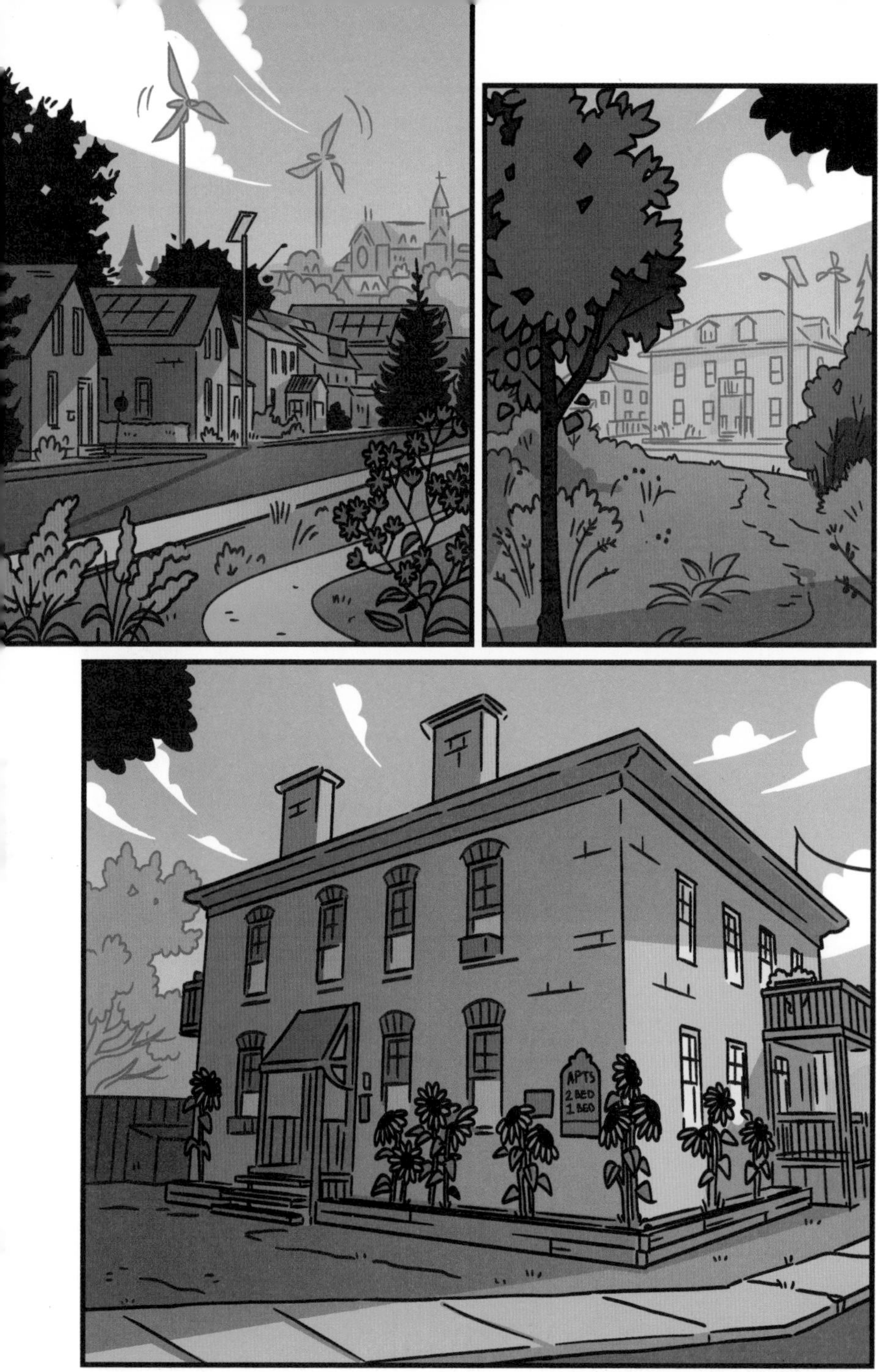
APTS
2 BED
1 BED

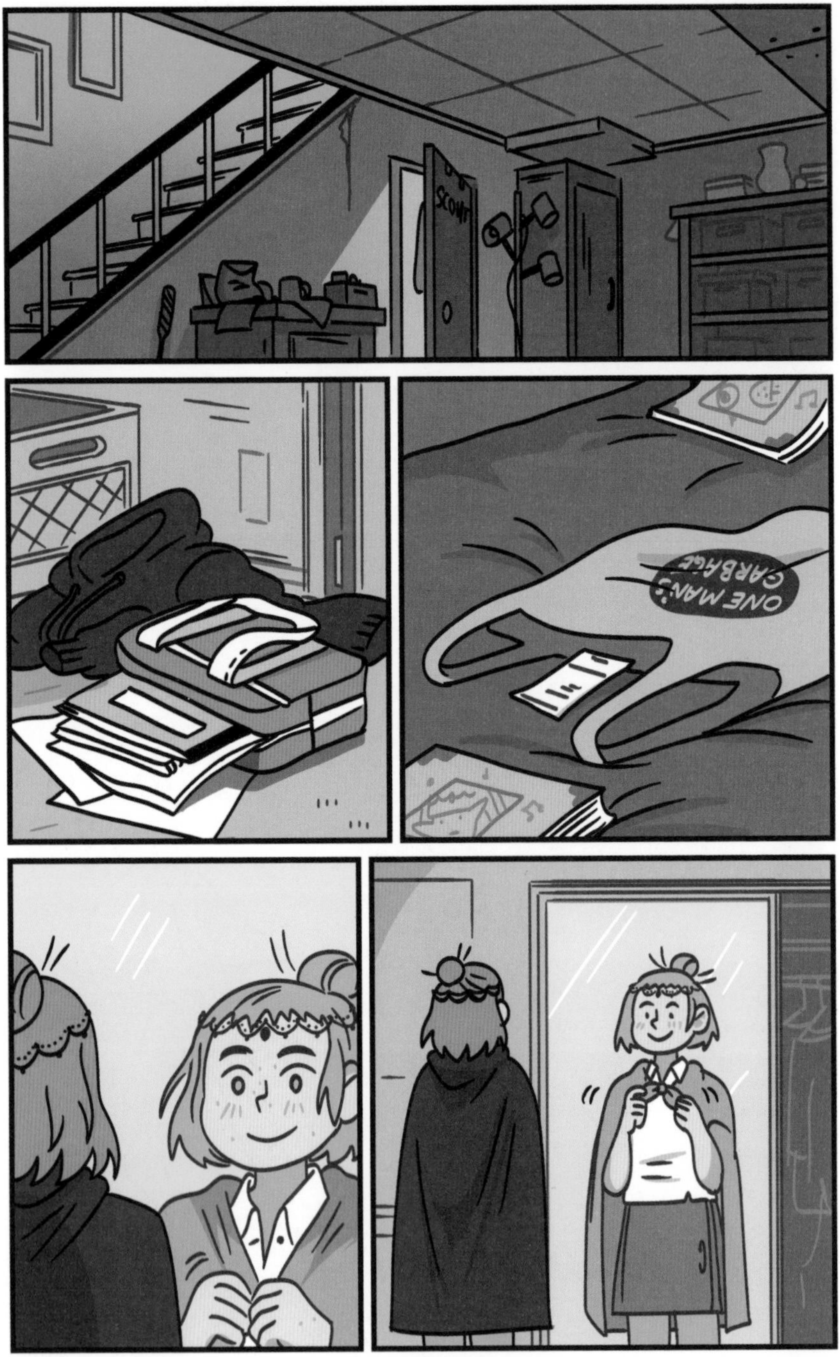
SCOUT
ONE MAN'S GARBAGE

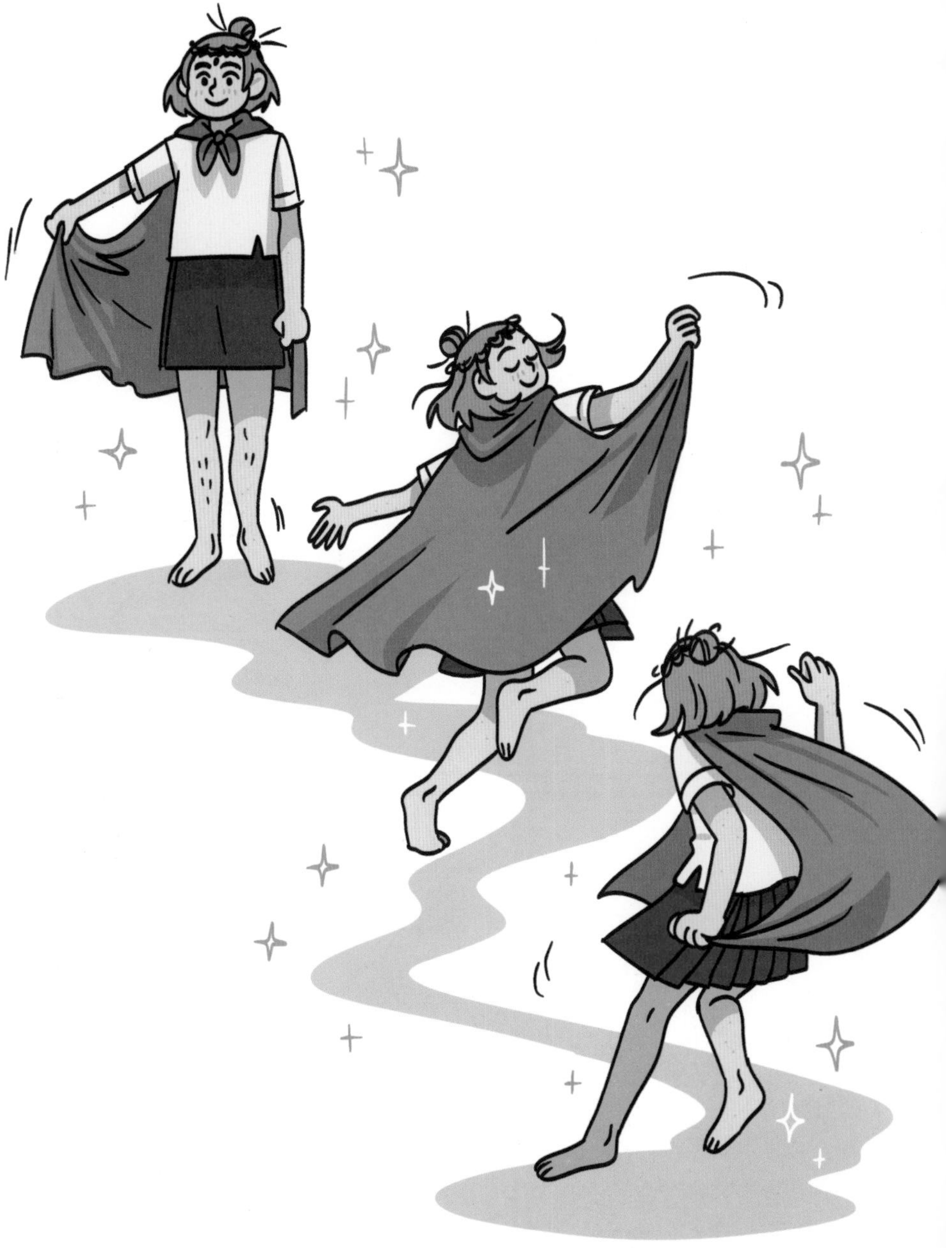

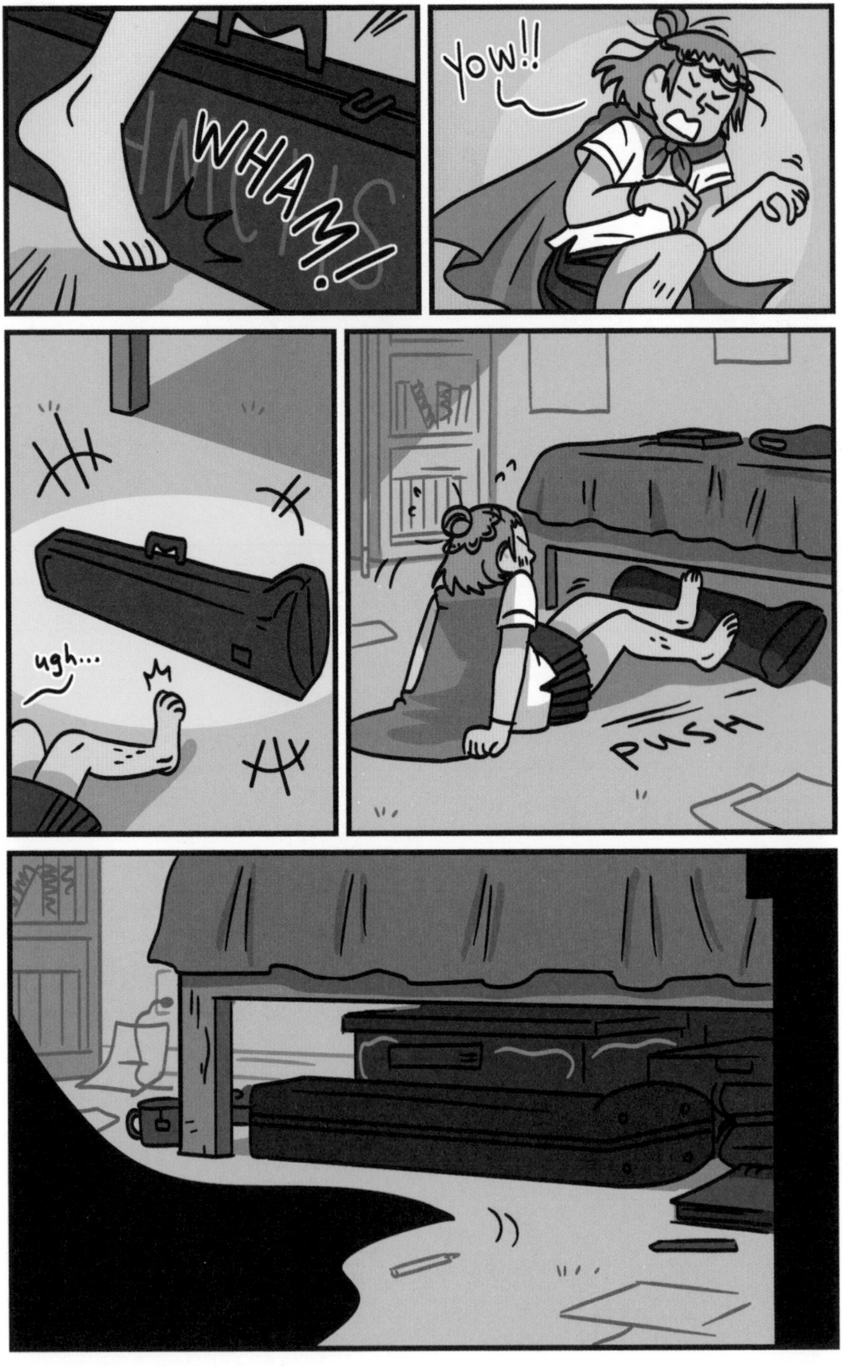
WHAM!
YOW!!
ugh...
PUSH

Chapter 2

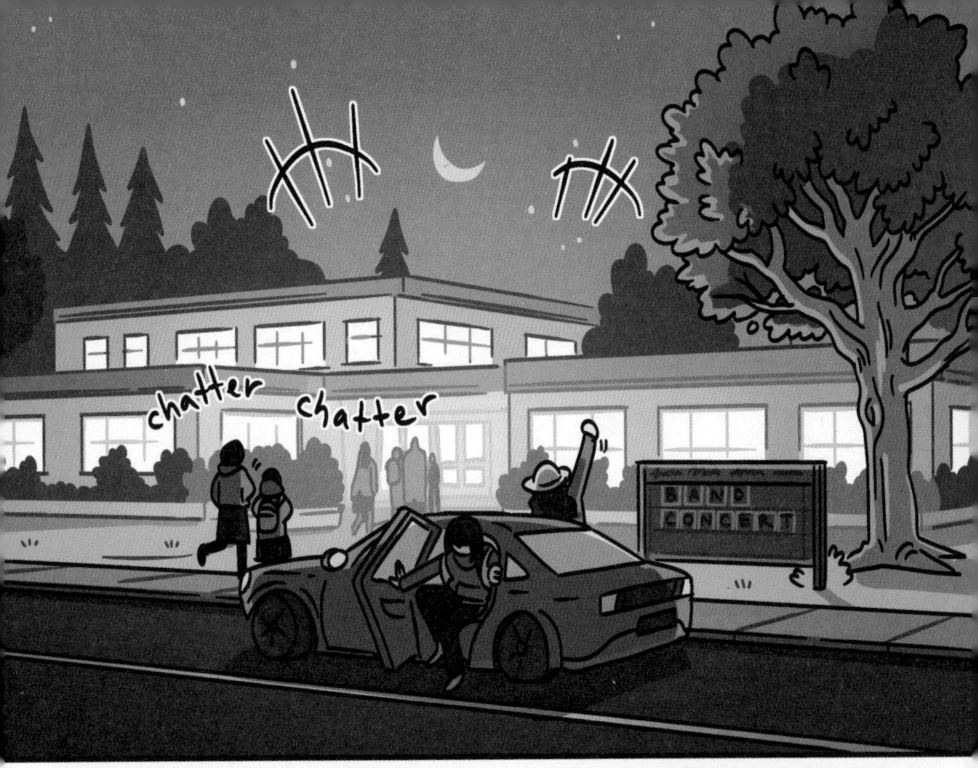
chatter
chatter
BAND
CONCERT

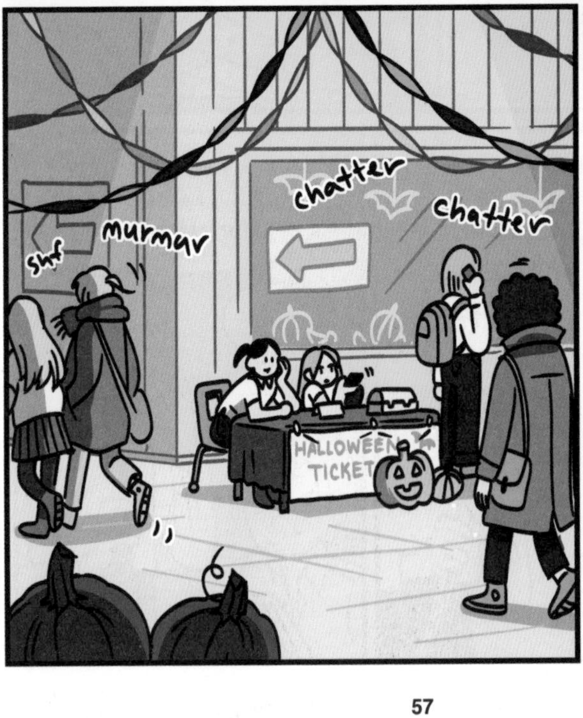
murmur
shf
chatter
chatter
HALLOWEEN
TICKET

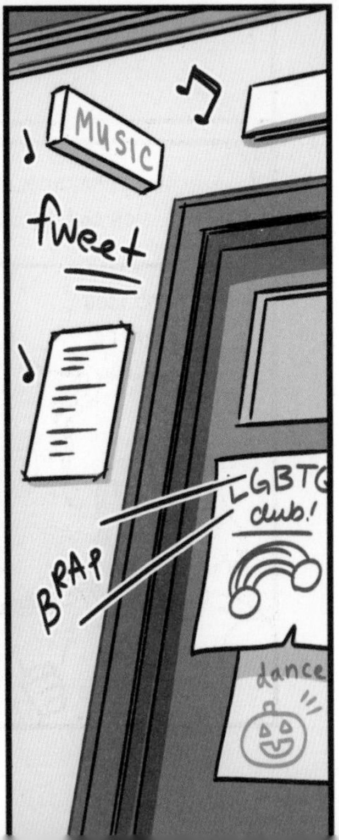
MUSIC
fweet
BRAP
LGBTQ
club!
dance

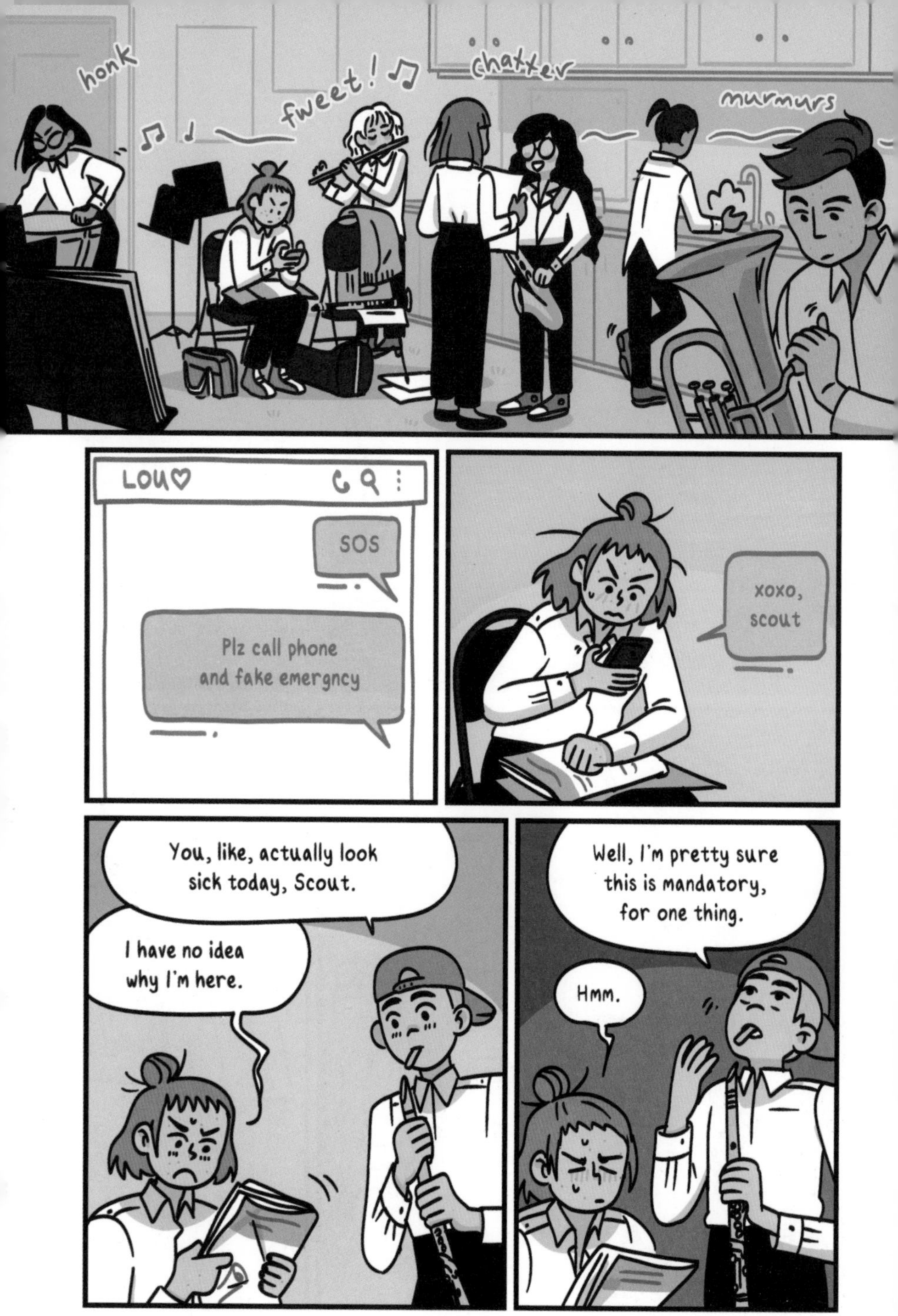
honk
fweet!
chatter
murmurs
LOU♡
SOS
Plz call phone and fake emergncy
xoxo, scout
You, like, actually look sick today, Scout.
I have no idea why I'm here.
Well, I'm pretty sure this is mandatory, for one thing.
Hmm.

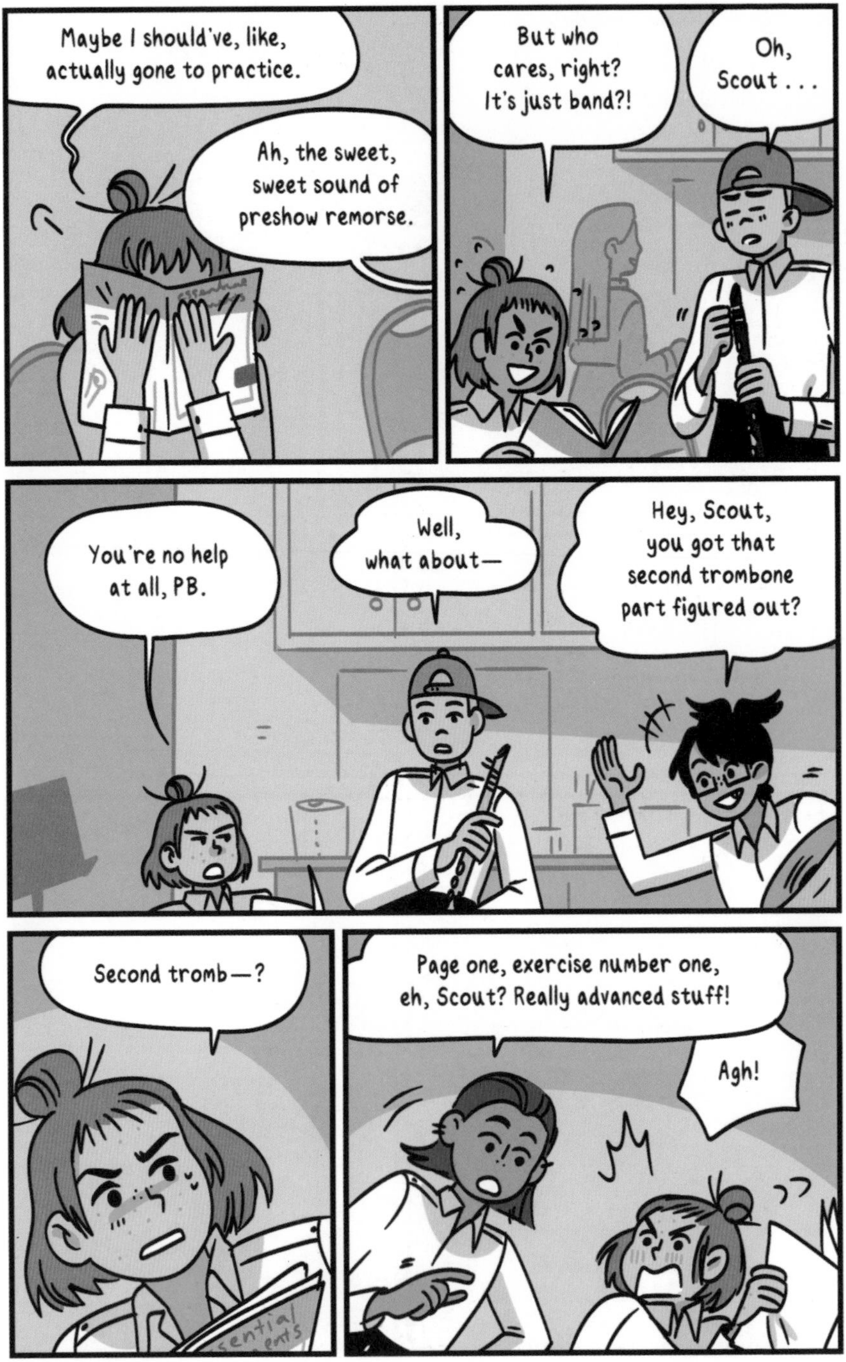

Maybe I should've, like, actually gone to practice.
Ah, the sweet, sweet sound of preshow remorse.
But who cares, right? It's just band?!
Oh, Scout . . .
You're no help at all, PB.
Well, what about—
Hey, Scout, you got that second trombone part figured out?
Second tromb—?
Page one, exercise number one, eh, Scout? Really advanced stuff!
Agh!

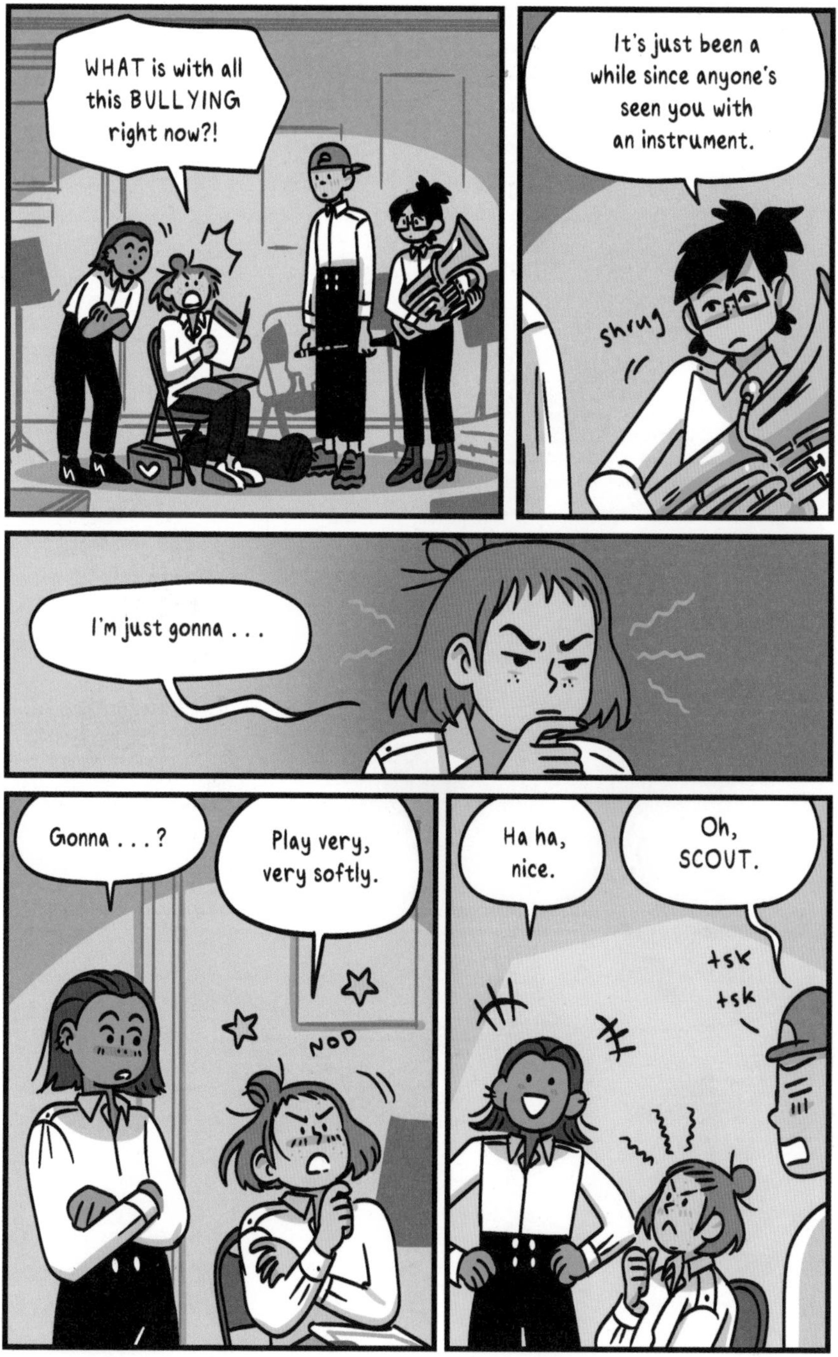
WHAT is with all this BULLYING right now?!
It's just been a while since anyone's seen you with an instrument.
shrug
I'm just gonna . . .
Gonna . . . ?
Play very, very softly.
NOD
Ha ha, nice.
Oh, SCOUT.
tsk
tsk

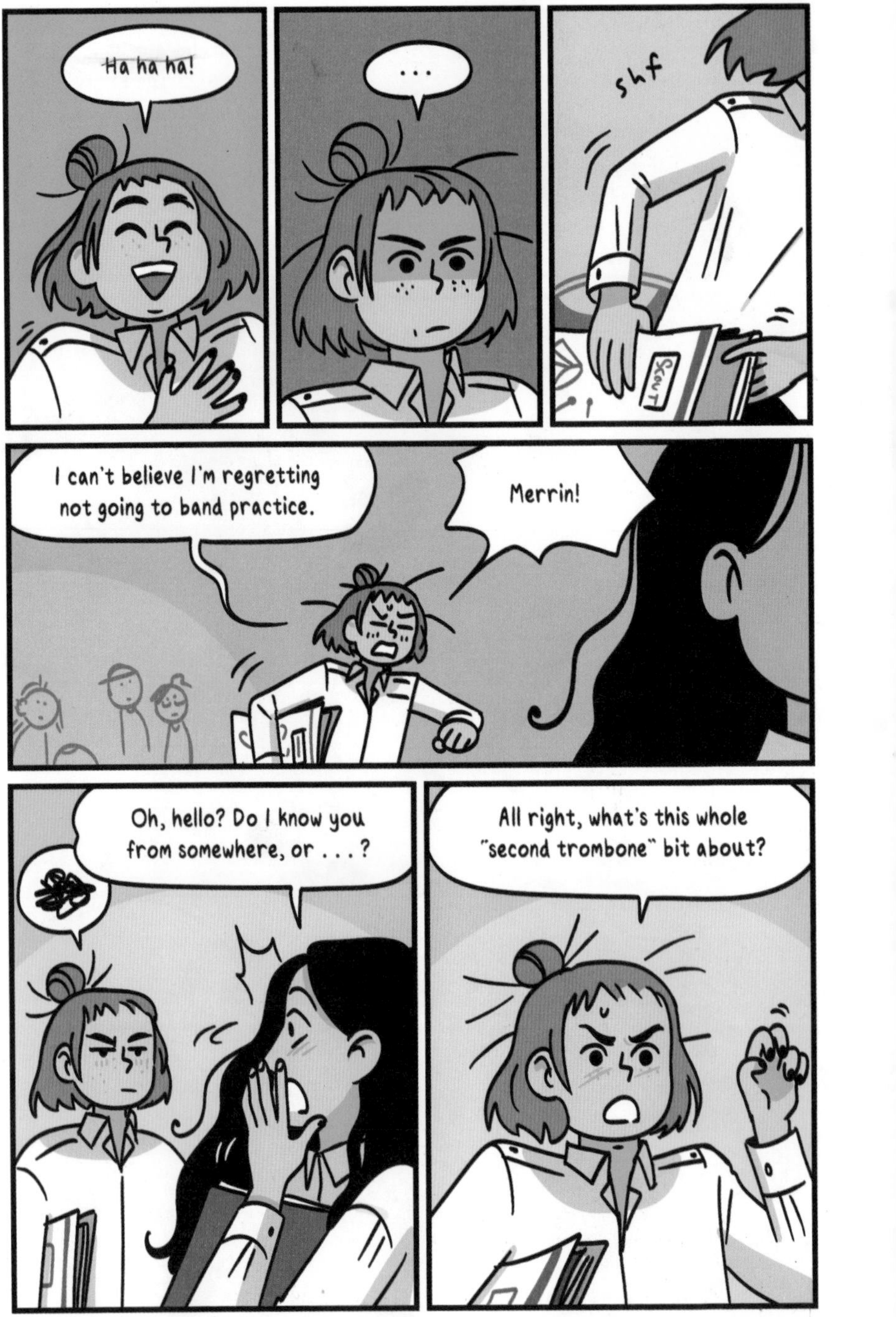
Ha ha ha!
. . .
shf
SCOUT
I can't believe I'm regretting not going to band practice.
Merrin!
Oh, hello? Do I know you from somewhere, or . . . ?
All right, what's this whole "second trombone" bit about?

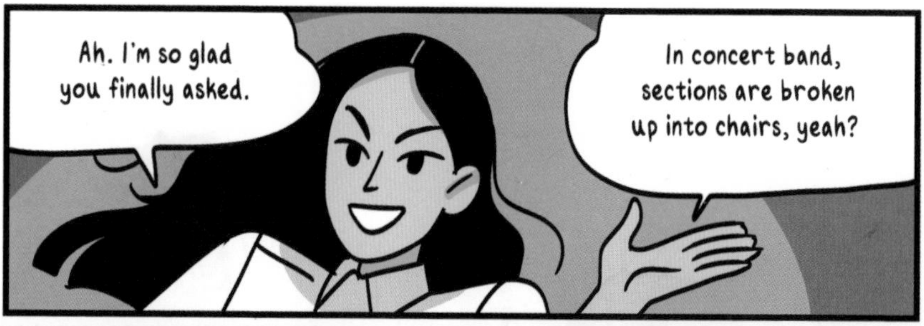
Ah. I'm so glad you finally asked.
In concert band, sections are broken up into chairs, yeah?

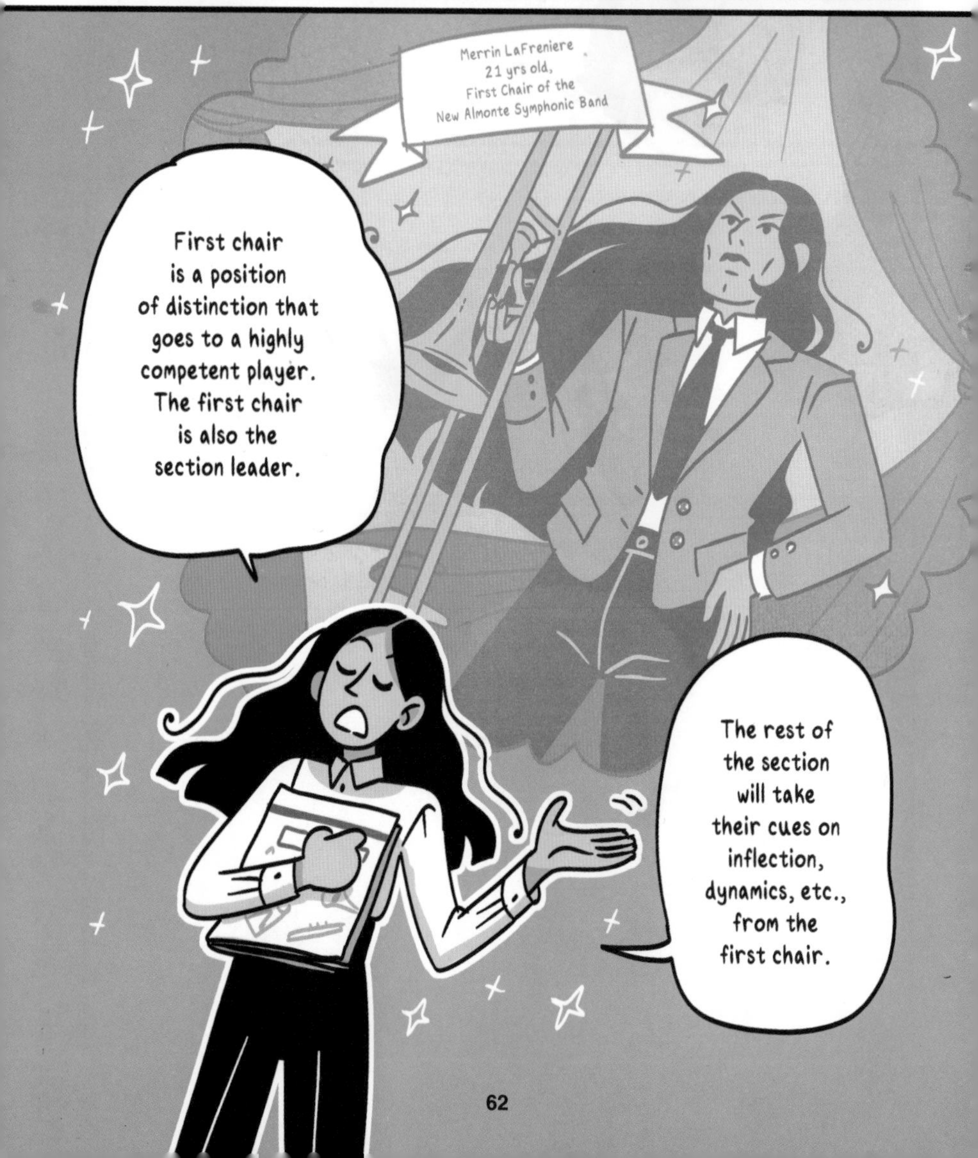
Merrin LaFreniere 21 yrs old, First Chair of the New Almonte Symphonic Band
First chair is a position of distinction that goes to a highly competent player. The first chair is also the section leader.
The rest of the section will take their cues on inflection, dynamics, etc., from the first chair.

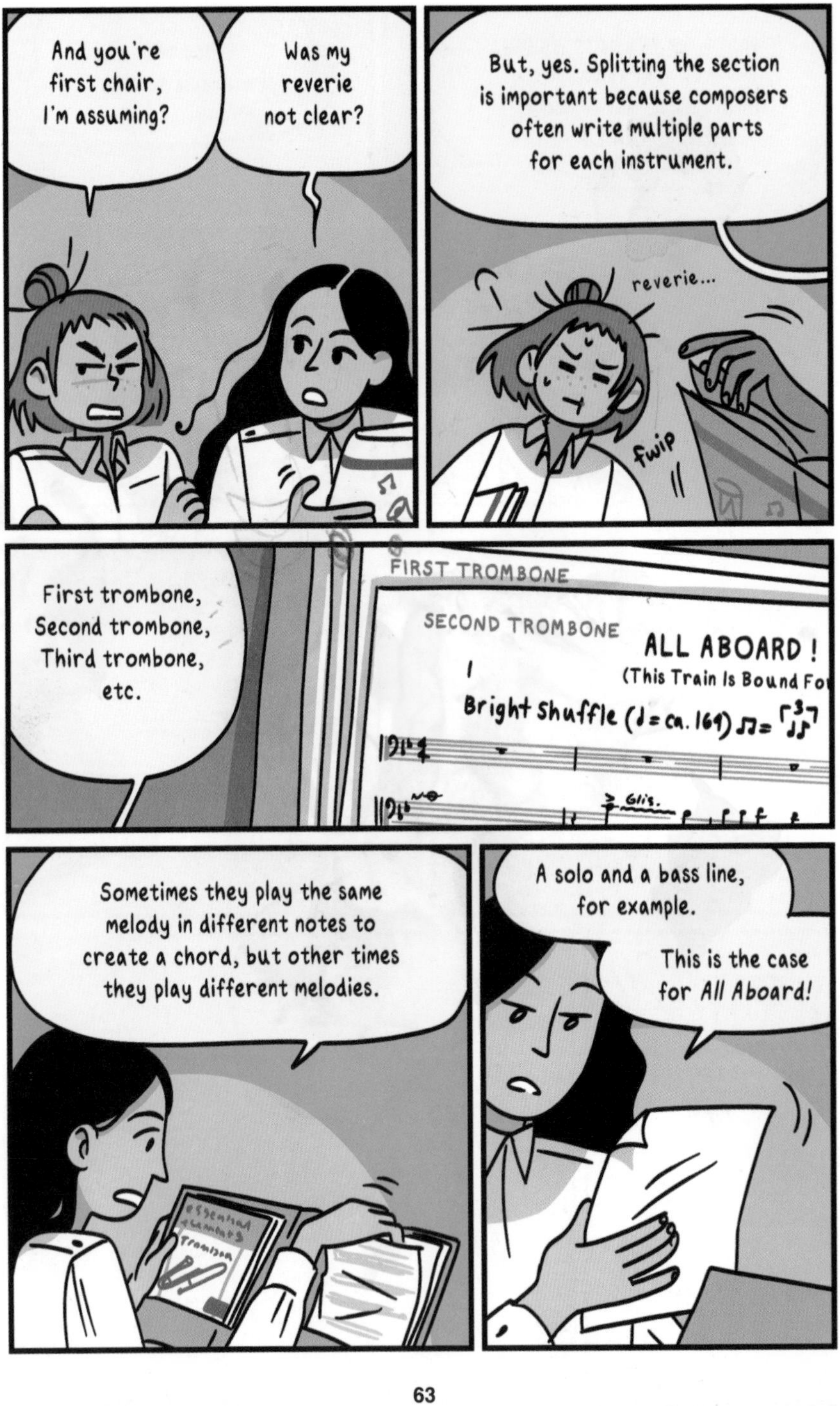
And you're first chair, I'm assuming?
Was my reverie not clear?
But, yes. Splitting the section is important because composers often write multiple parts for each instrument.
reverie...
fwip
First trombone, Second trombone, Third trombone, etc.
FIRST TROMBONE
SECOND TROMBONE
ALL ABOARD!
(This Train Is Bound Fo
Bright Shuffle
Glis.
Sometimes they play the same melody in different notes to create a chord, but other times they play different melodies.
A solo and a bass line, for example.
This is the case for *All Aboard!*

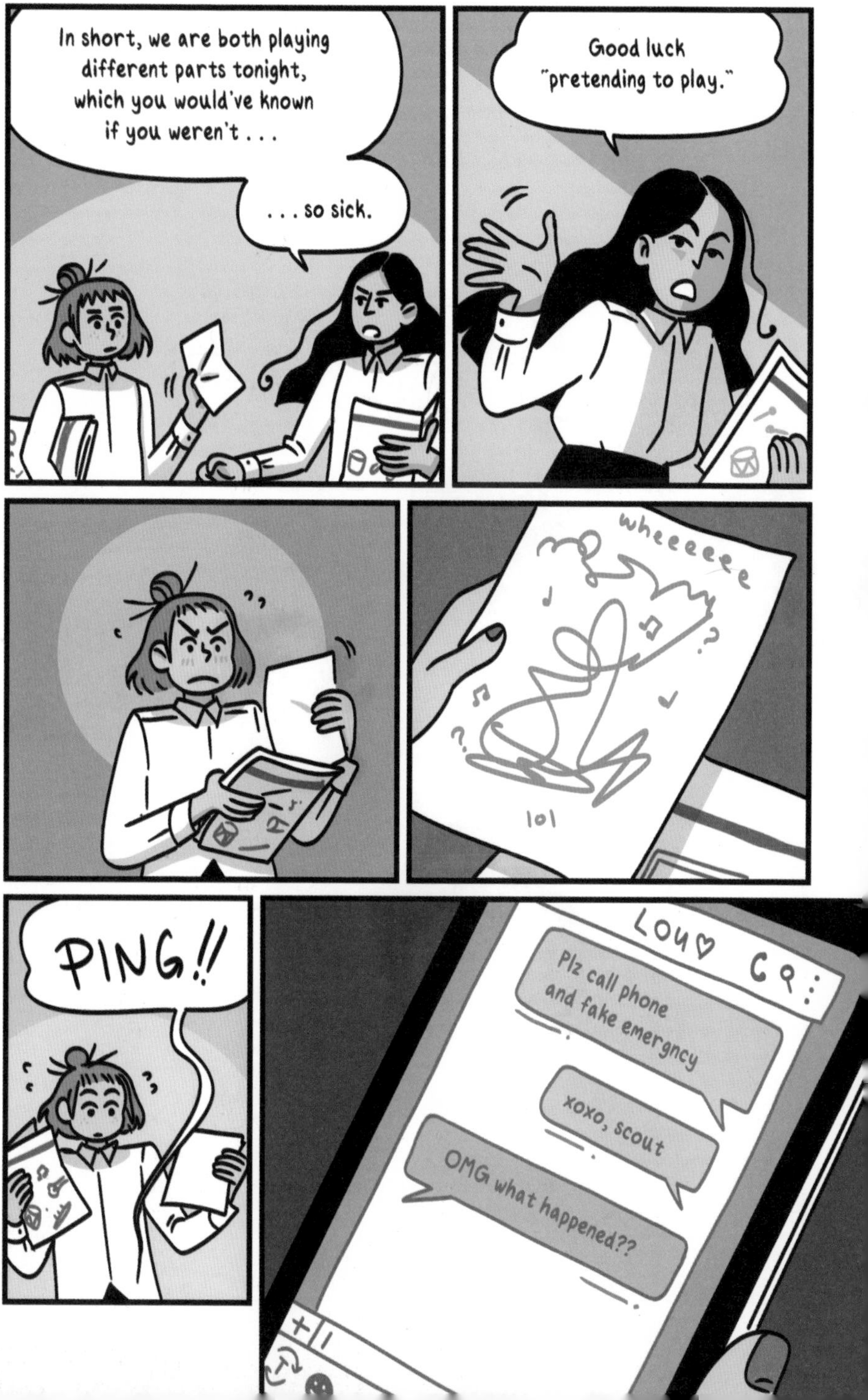
In short, we are both playing different parts tonight, which you would've known if you weren't . . .
. . . so sick.
Good luck "pretending to play."
wheeeeee
lol
PING!!
LOU♡
Plz call phone and fake emergncy
xoxo, scout
OMG what happened??

*In Canadian English, *gray* is spelt *grey*.

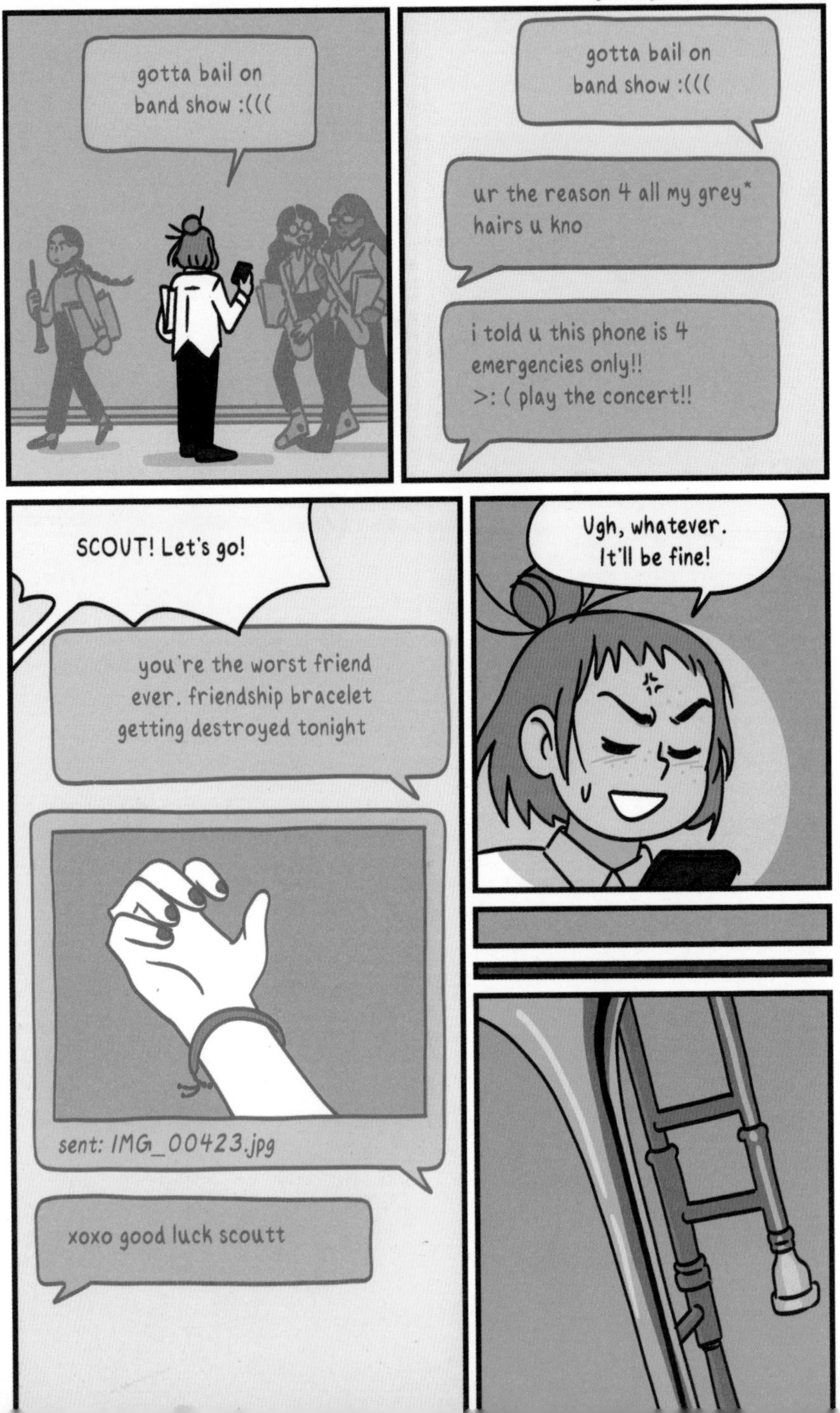
gotta bail on band show :(((
gotta bail on band show :(((
ur the reason 4 all my grey* hairs u kno
i told u this phone is 4 emergencies only!! >: (play the concert!!
SCOUT! Let's go!
you're the worst friend ever. friendship bracelet getting destroyed tonight
sent: IMG_00423.jpg
xoxo good luck scoutt
Ugh, whatever. It'll be fine!

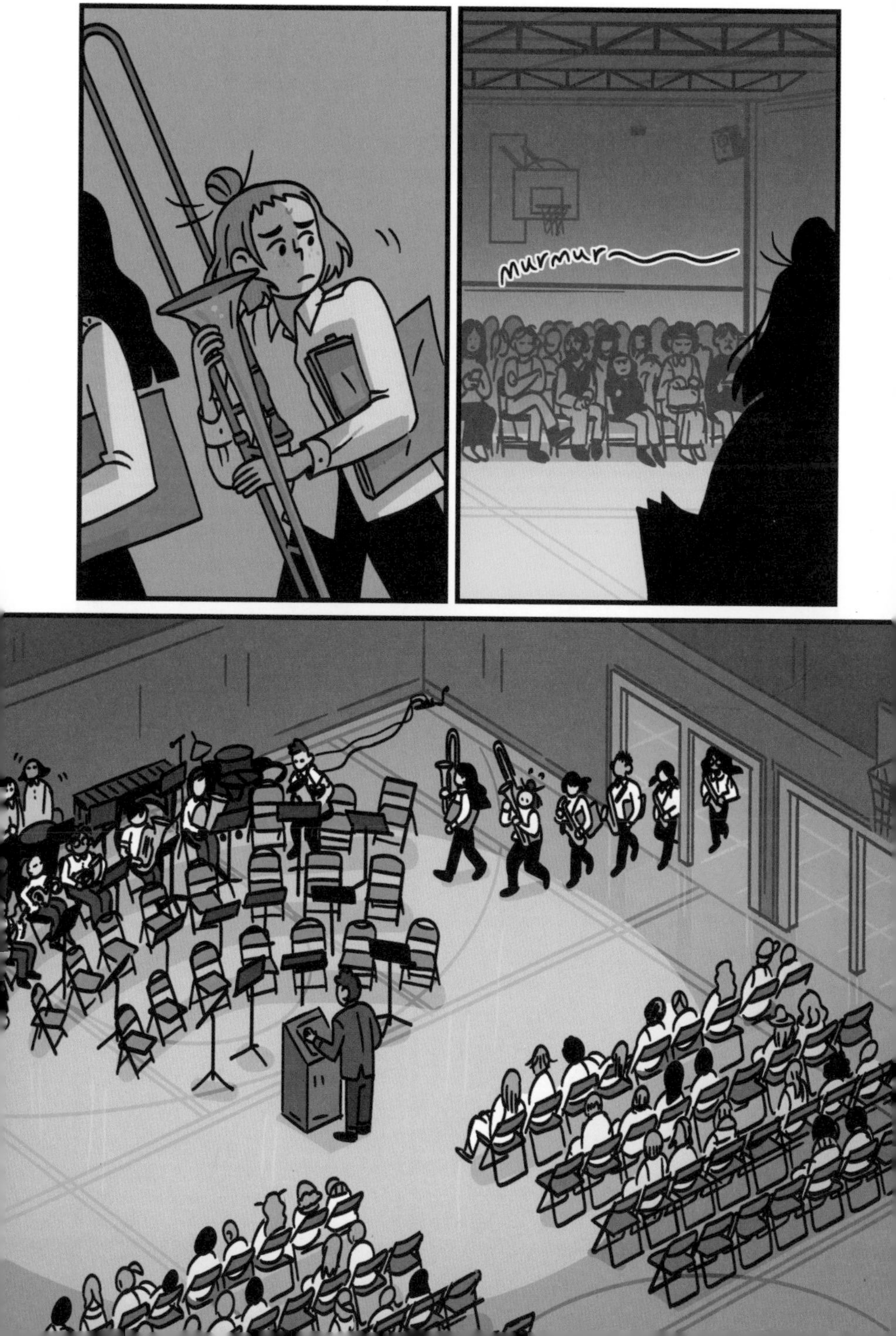
murmur

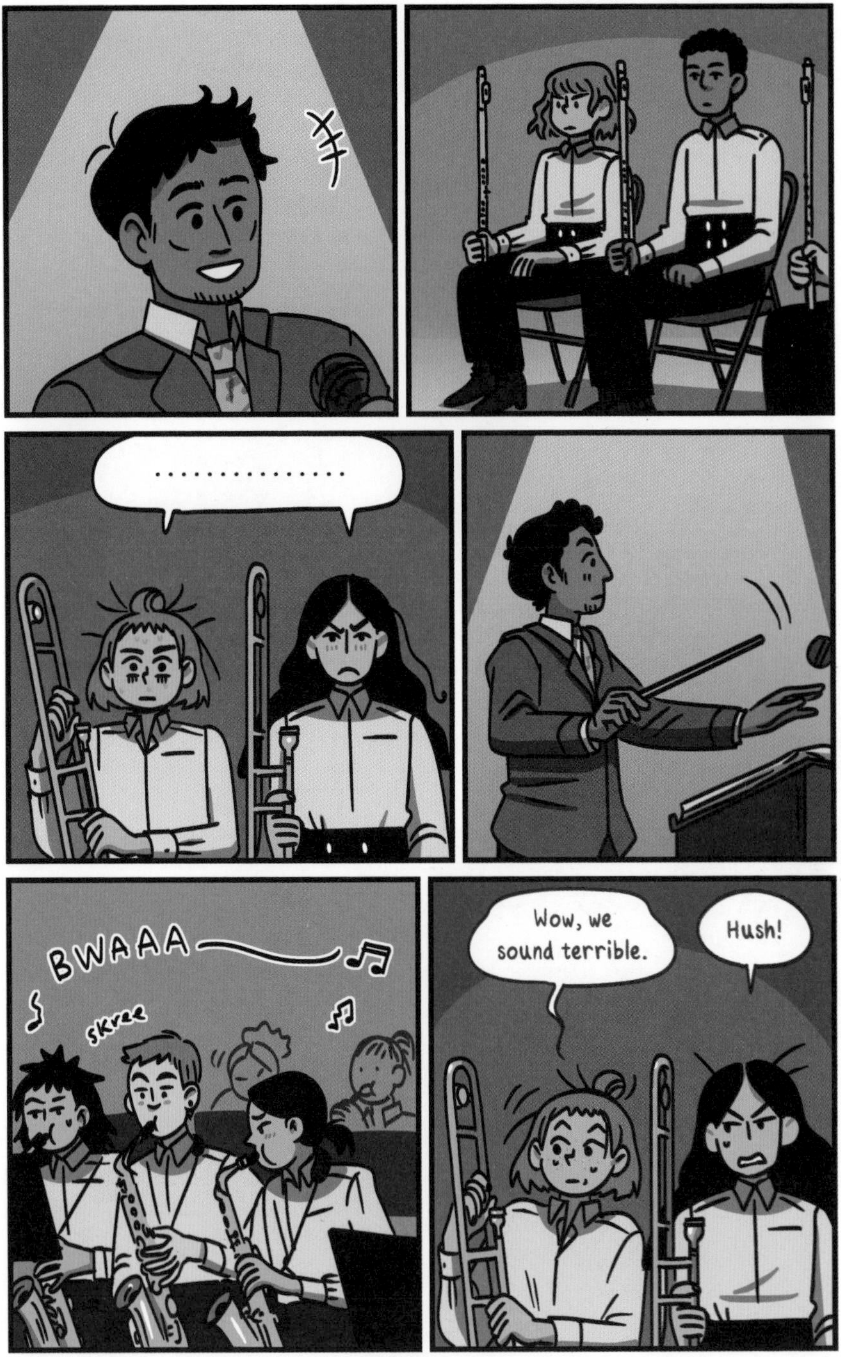

....
BWAAA
skree
Wow, we sound terrible.
Hush!

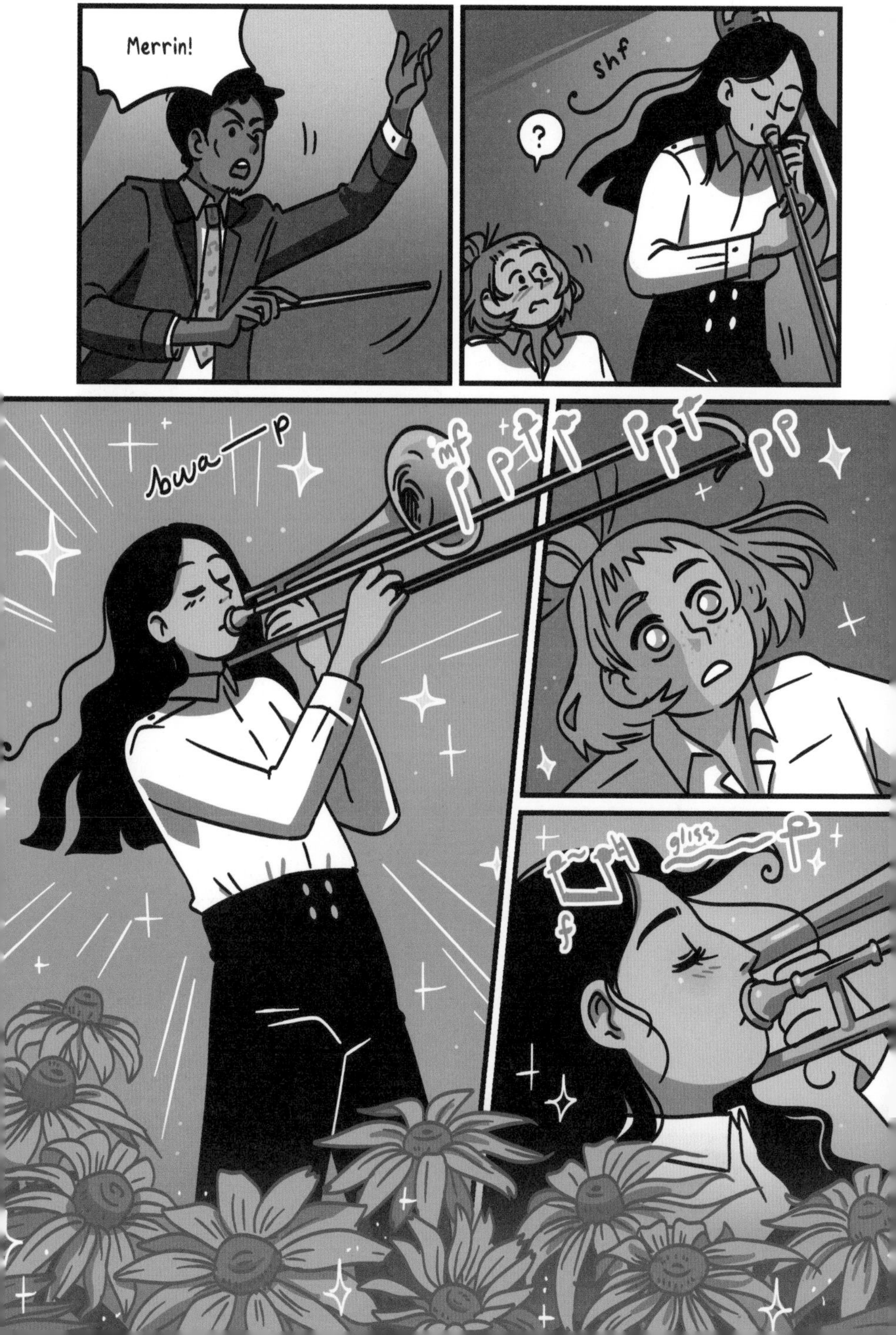
Merrin!
shf
?
bwa—p
mf
gliss
f

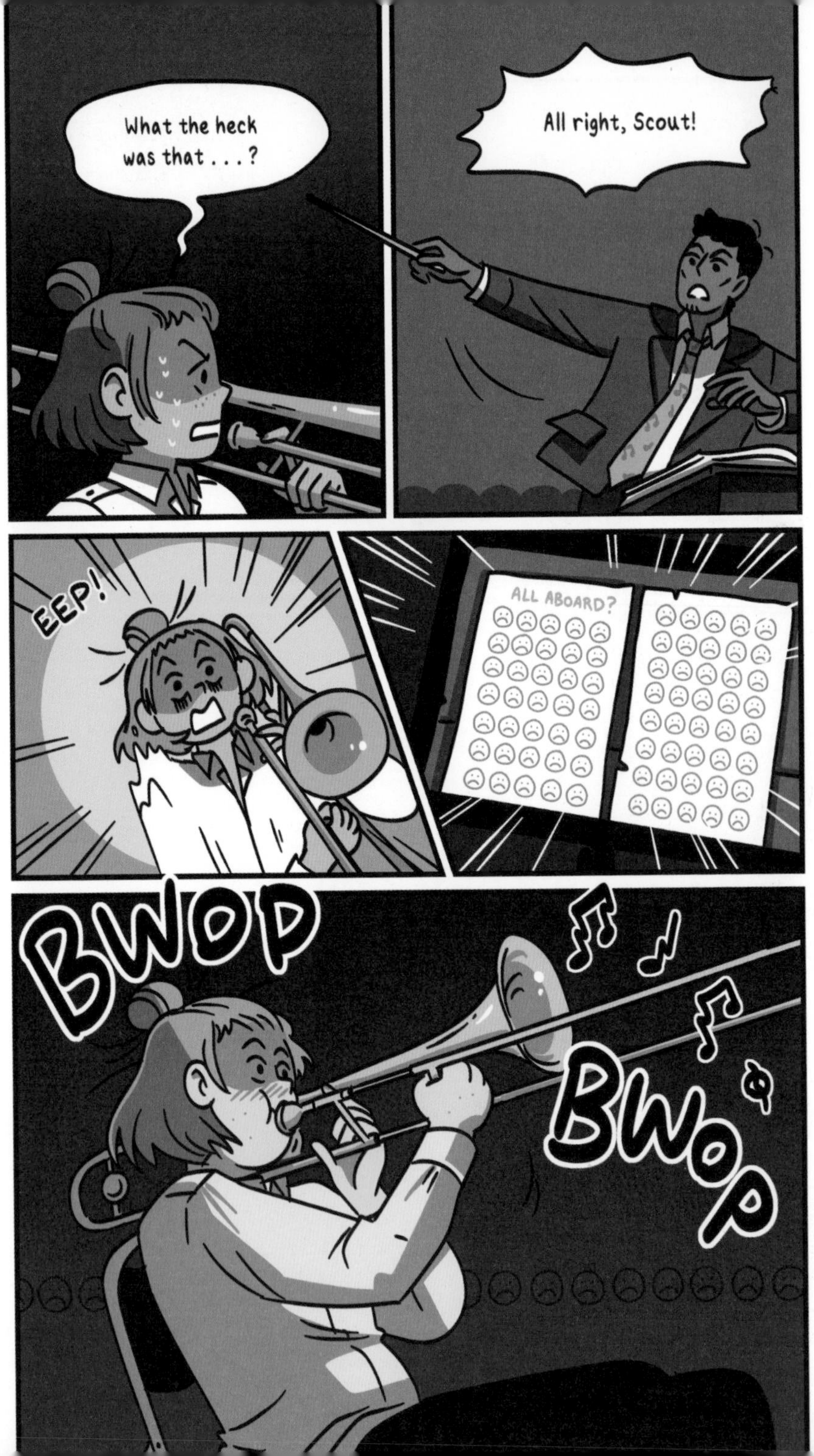
What the heck was that . . . ?
All right, Scout!
EEP!
ALL ABOARD?
BWOP
BWOP

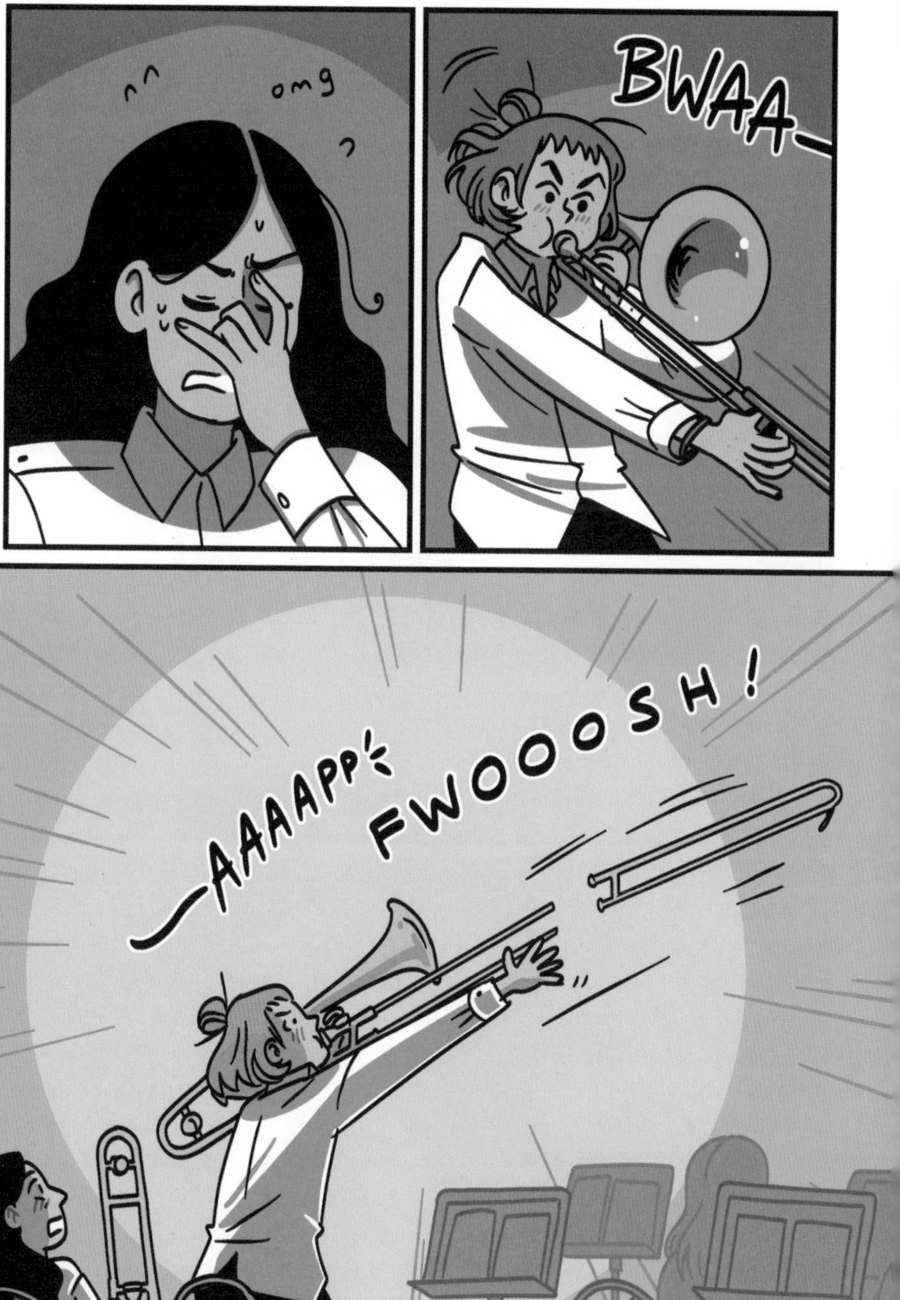
omg
BWAA—
—AAAAPP!
FWOOOOSH!

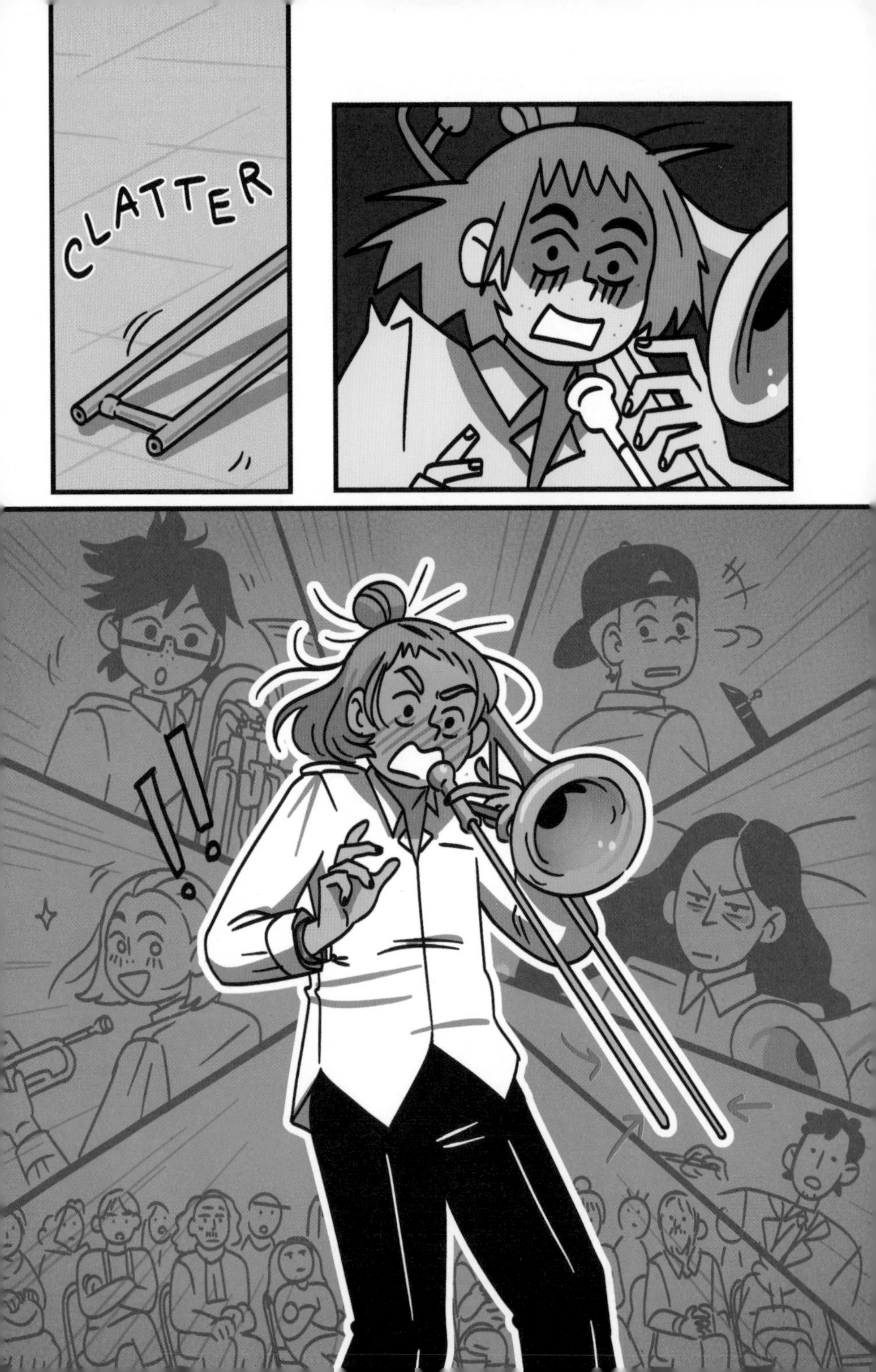
CLATTER
!!

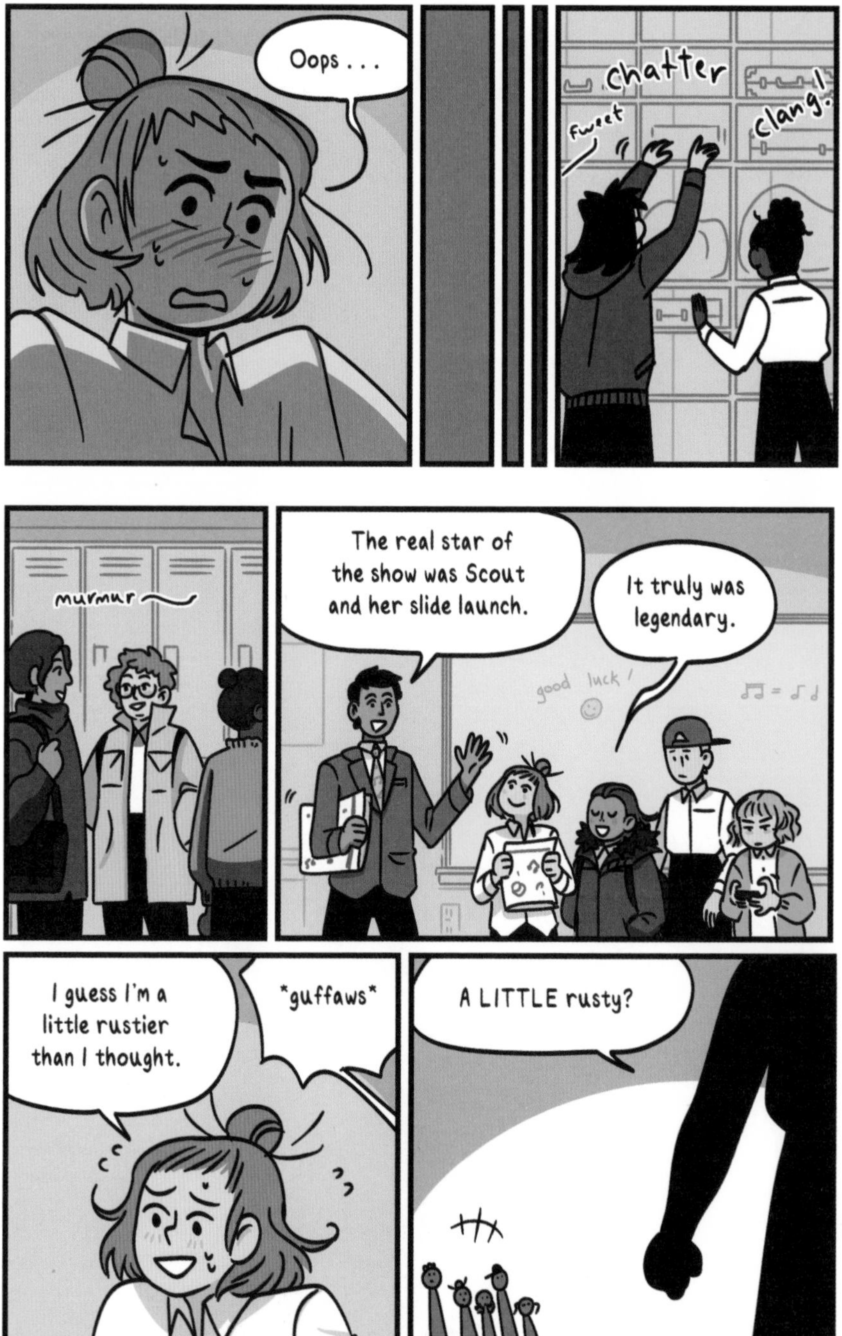
Oops . . .
chatter
fweet
clang!
murmur
The real star of the show was Scout and her slide launch.
It truly was legendary.
good luck!
I guess I'm a little rustier than I thought.
guffaws
A LITTLE rusty?

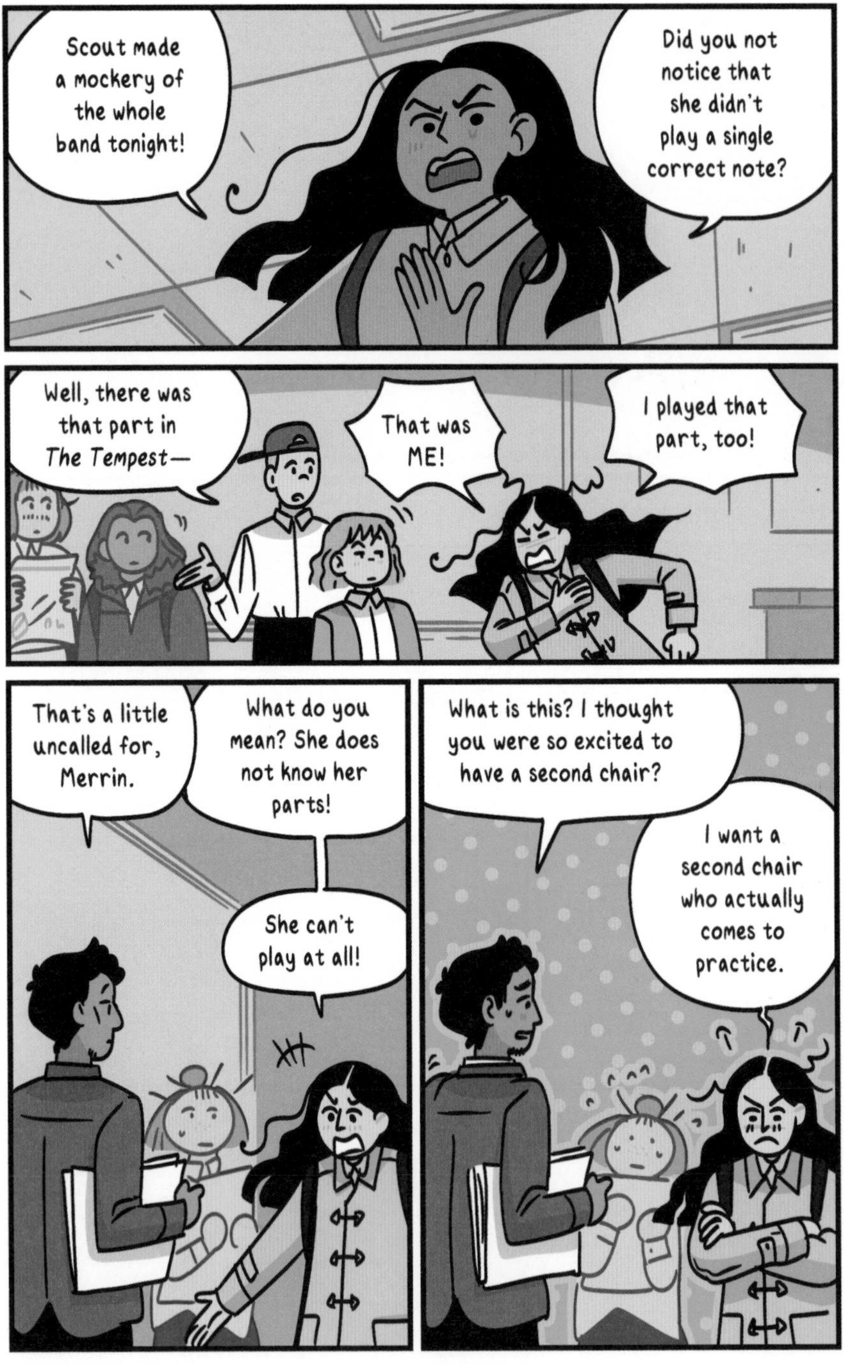
Scout made a mockery of the whole band tonight!
Did you not notice that she didn't play a single correct note?
Well, there was that part in *The Tempest*—
That was ME!
I played that part, too!
That's a little uncalled for, Merrin.
What do you mean? She does not know her parts!
She can't play at all!
What is this? I thought you were so excited to have a second chair?
I want a second chair who actually comes to practice.

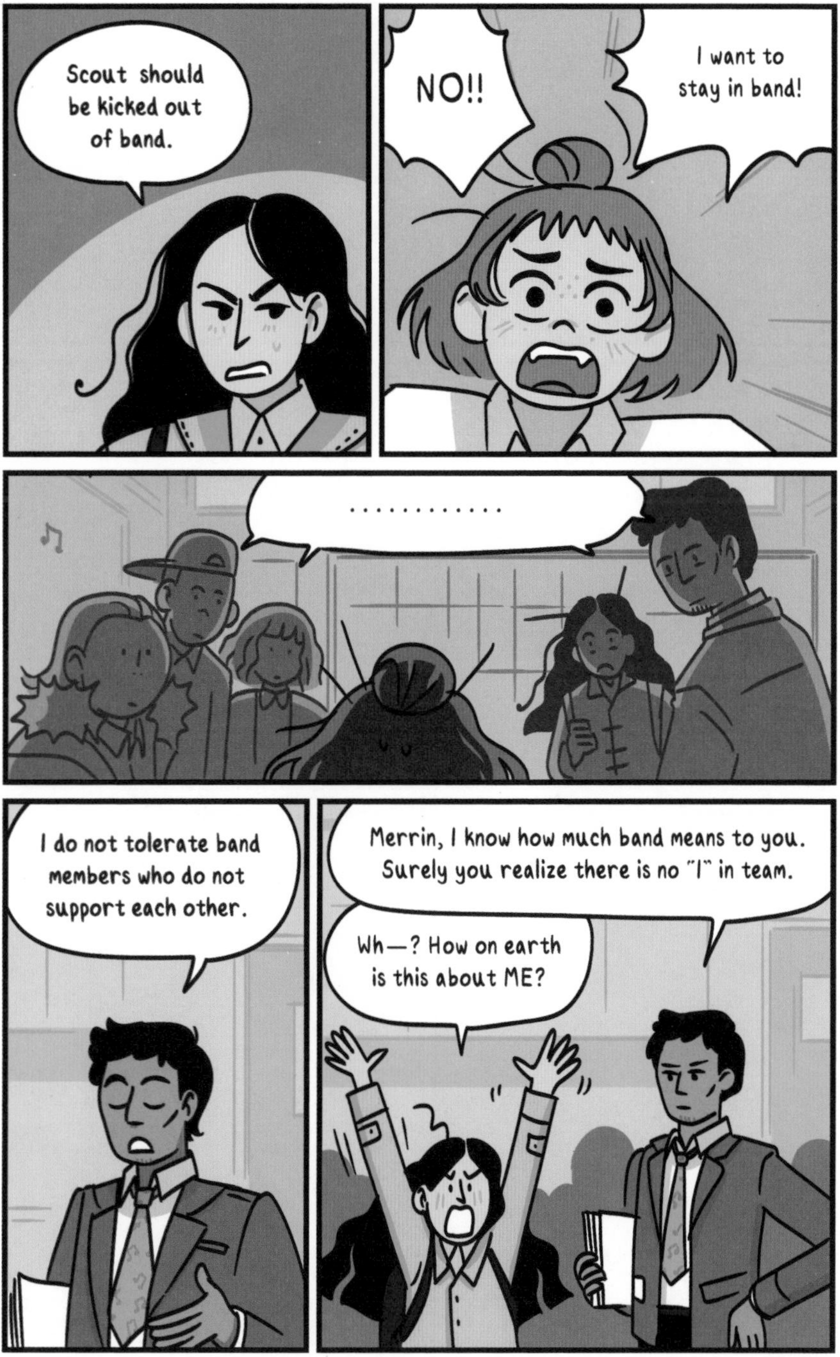
Scout should be kicked out of band.
NO!!
I want to stay in band!
....
I do not tolerate band members who do not support each other.
Merrin, I know how much band means to you. Surely you realize there is no "I" in team.
Wh—? How on earth is this about ME?

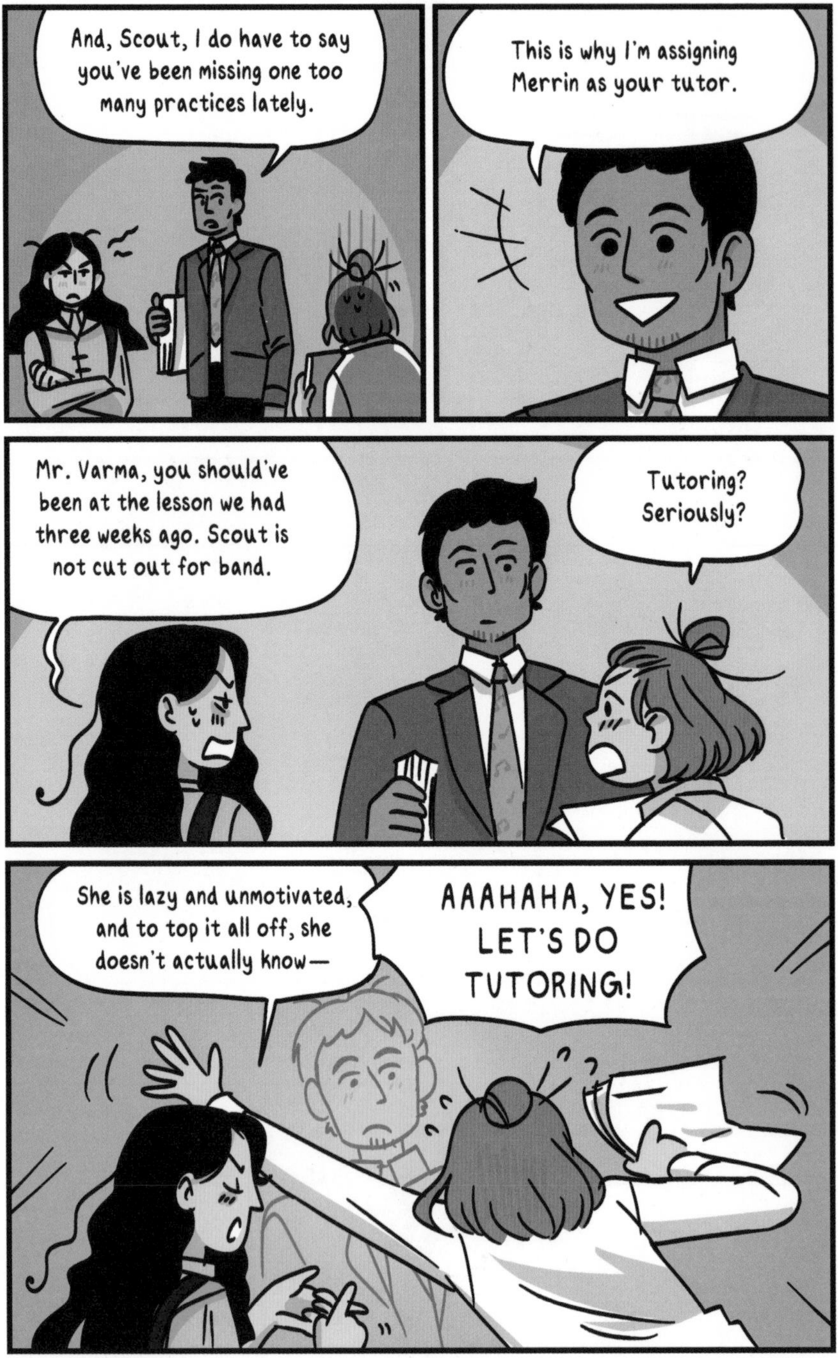
And, Scout, I do have to say you've been missing one too many practices lately.
This is why I'm assigning Merrin as your tutor.
Mr. Varma, you should've been at the lesson we had three weeks ago. Scout is not cut out for band.
Tutoring? Seriously?
She is lazy and unmotivated, and to top it all off, she doesn't actually know—
AAAHAHA, YES! LET'S DO TUTORING!

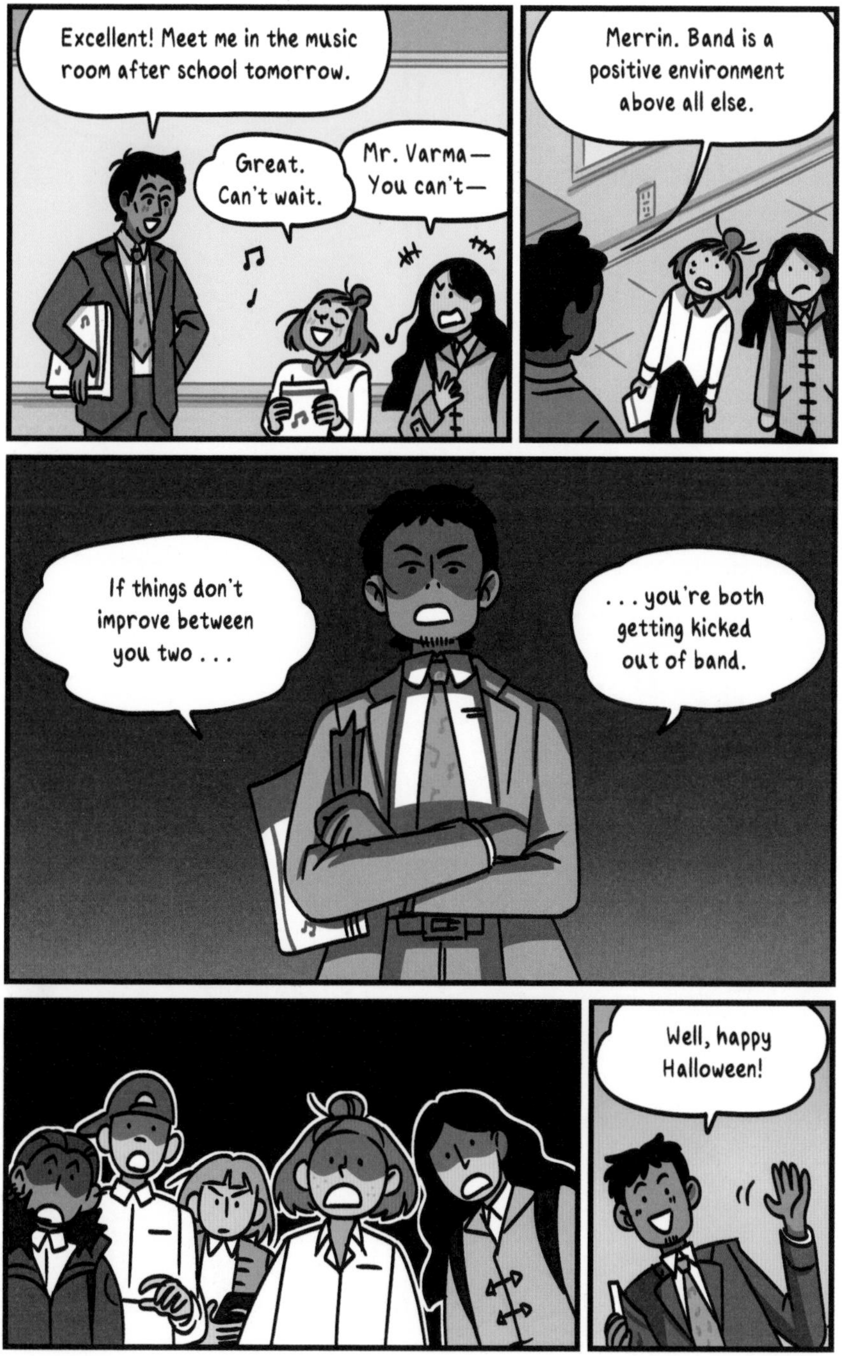
Excellent! Meet me in the music room after school tomorrow.
Great. Can't wait.
Mr. Varma— You can't—
Merrin. Band is a positive environment above all else.
If things don't improve between you two . . .
. . . you're both getting kicked out of band.
Well, happy Halloween!

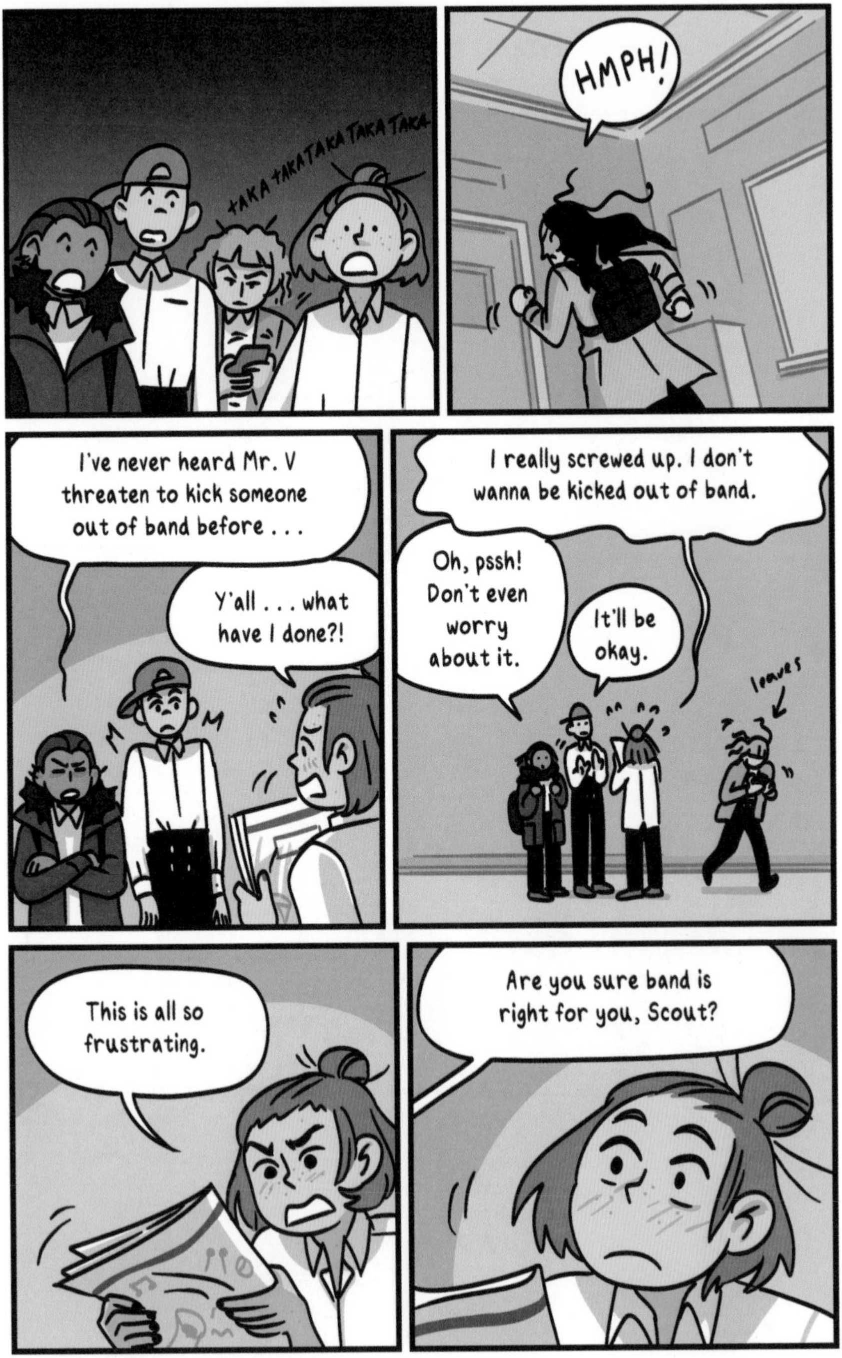
TAKA TAKA TAKA TAKA TAKA TAKA
HMPH!
I've never heard Mr. V threaten to kick someone out of band before . . .
Y'all . . . what have I done?!
I really screwed up. I don't wanna be kicked out of band.
Oh, pssh! Don't even worry about it.
It'll be okay.
leaves
This is all so frustrating.
Are you sure band is right for you, Scout?

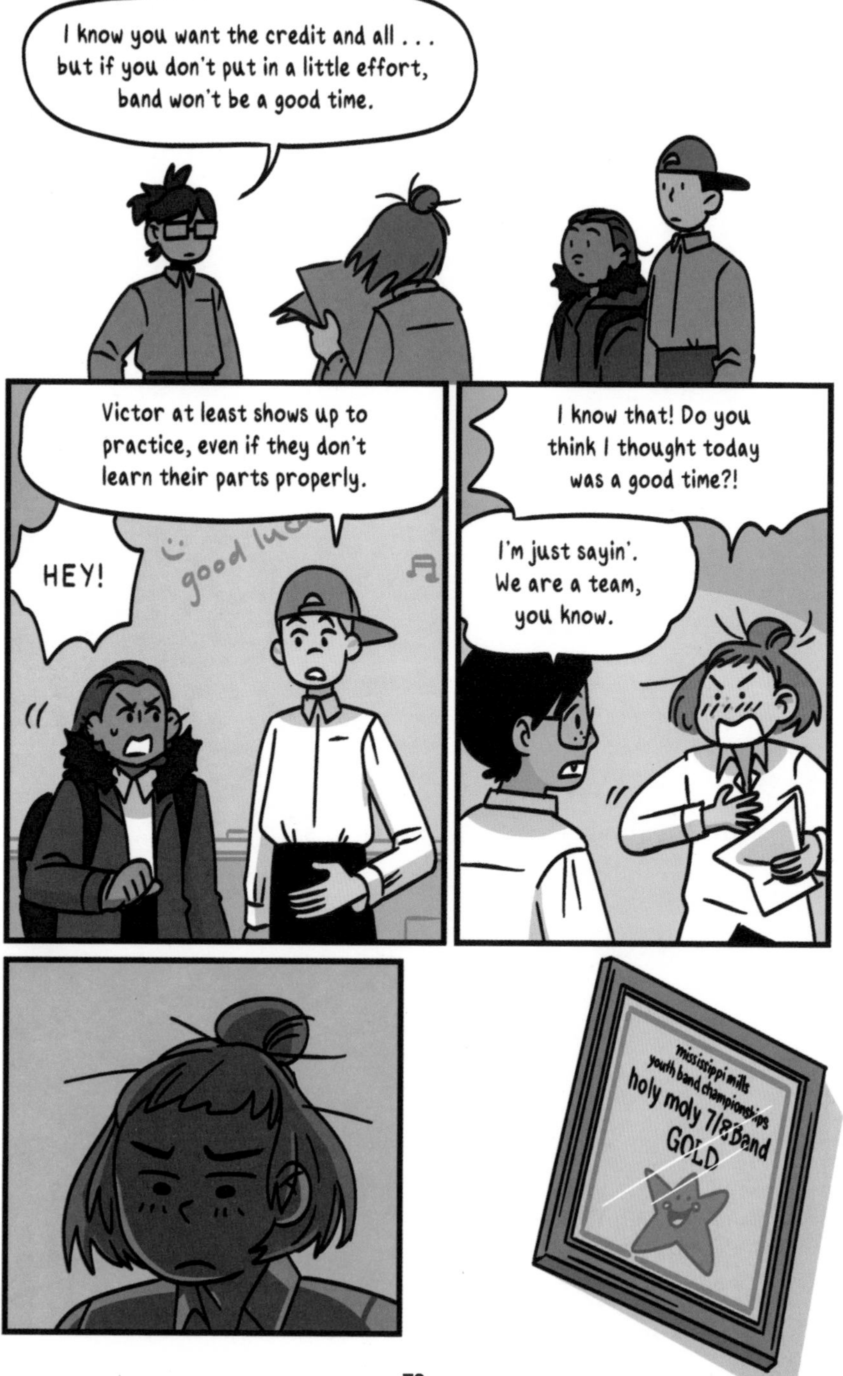
I know you want the credit and all . . . but if you don't put in a little effort, band won't be a good time.
Victor at least shows up to practice, even if they don't learn their parts properly.
HEY!
I know that! Do you think I thought today was a good time?!
I'm just sayin'. We are a team, you know.
mississippi mills
youth band championships
holy moly 7/8 Band
GOLD

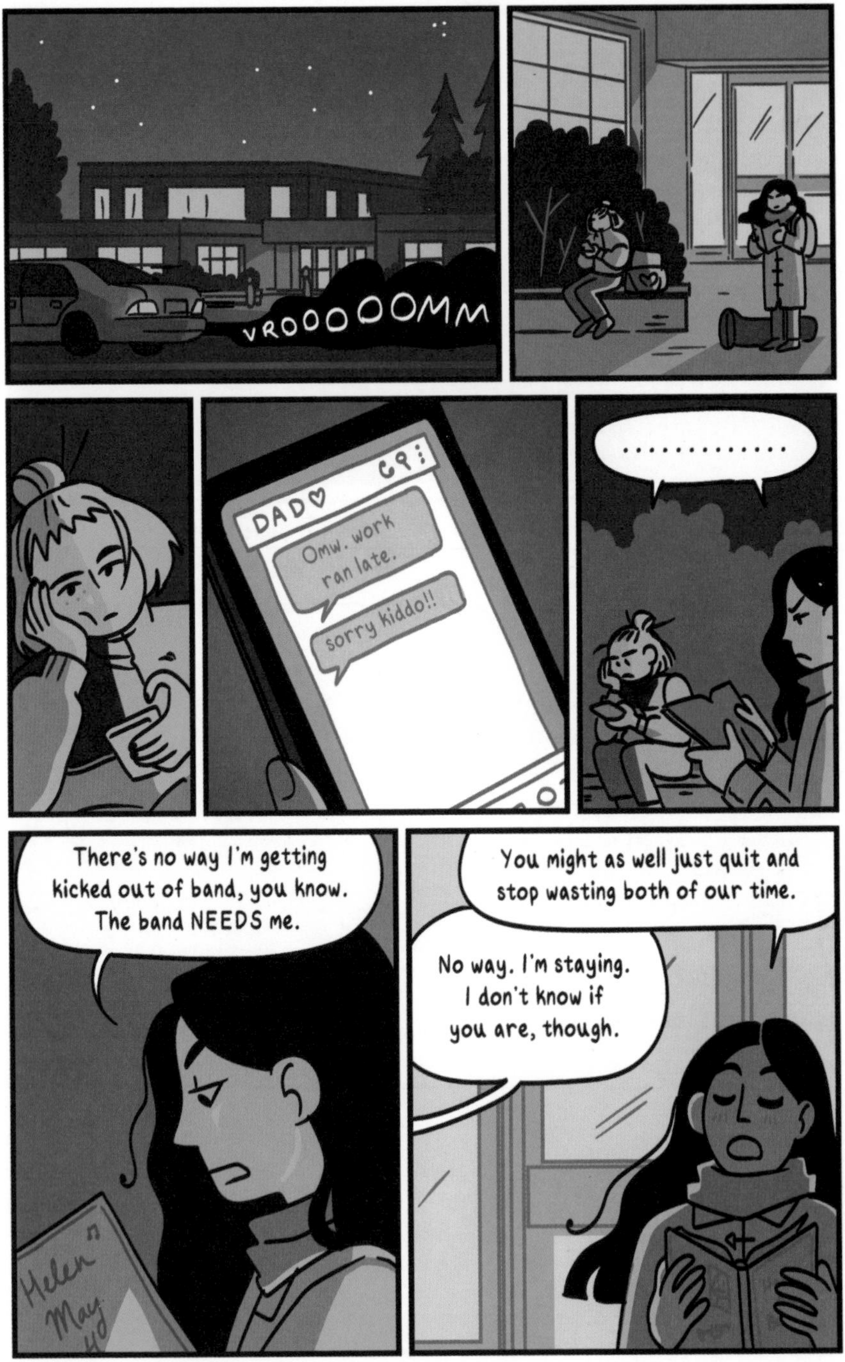
VROOOOOMM
DAD♡
Omw. work ran late.
sorry kiddo!!
....
There's no way I'm getting kicked out of band, you know. The band NEEDS me.
Helen May
You might as well just quit and stop wasting both of our time.
No way. I'm staying. I don't know if you are, though.

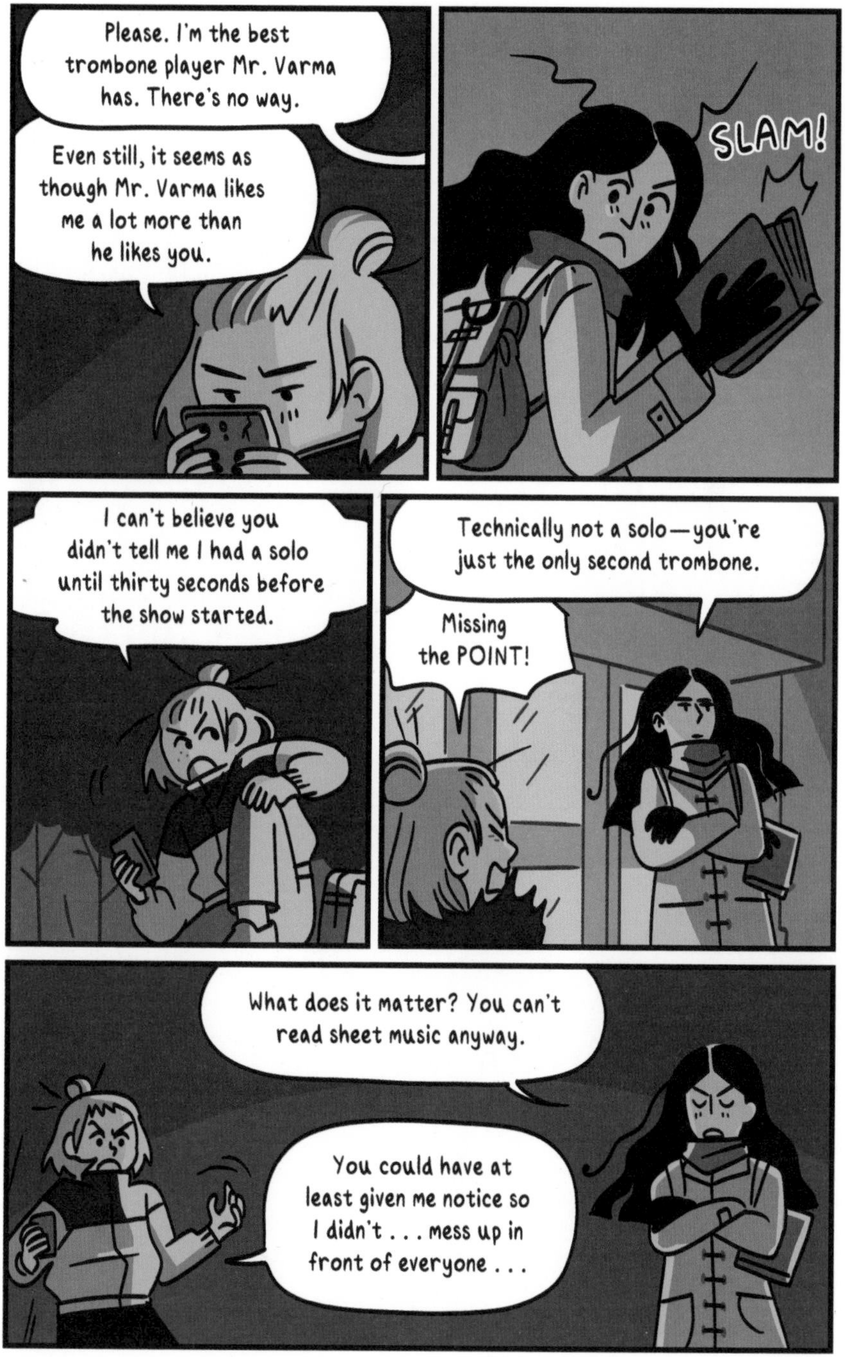

Please. I'm the best trombone player Mr. Varma has. There's no way.
Even still, it seems as though Mr. Varma likes me a lot more than he likes you.
SLAM!
I can't believe you didn't tell me I had a solo until thirty seconds before the show started.
Technically not a solo—you're just the only second trombone.
Missing the POINT!
What does it matter? You can't read sheet music anyway.
You could have at least given me notice so I didn't . . . mess up in front of everyone . . .

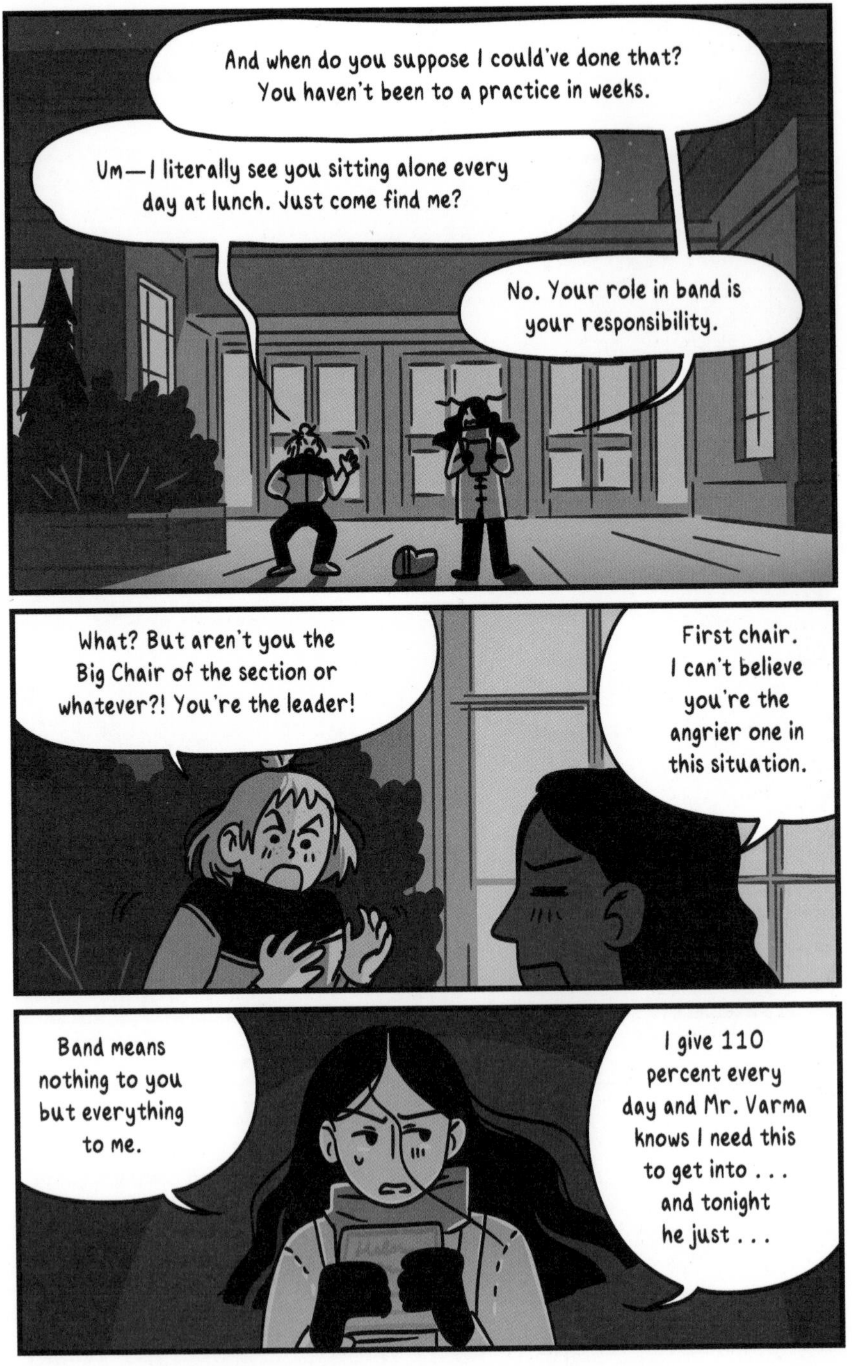
And when do you suppose I could've done that? You haven't been to a practice in weeks.
Um—I literally see you sitting alone every day at lunch. Just come find me?
No. Your role in band is your responsibility.
What? But aren't you the Big Chair of the section or whatever?! You're the leader!
First chair. I can't believe you're the angrier one in this situation.
Band means nothing to you but everything to me.
I give 110 percent every day and Mr. Varma knows I need this to get into . . . and tonight he just . . .

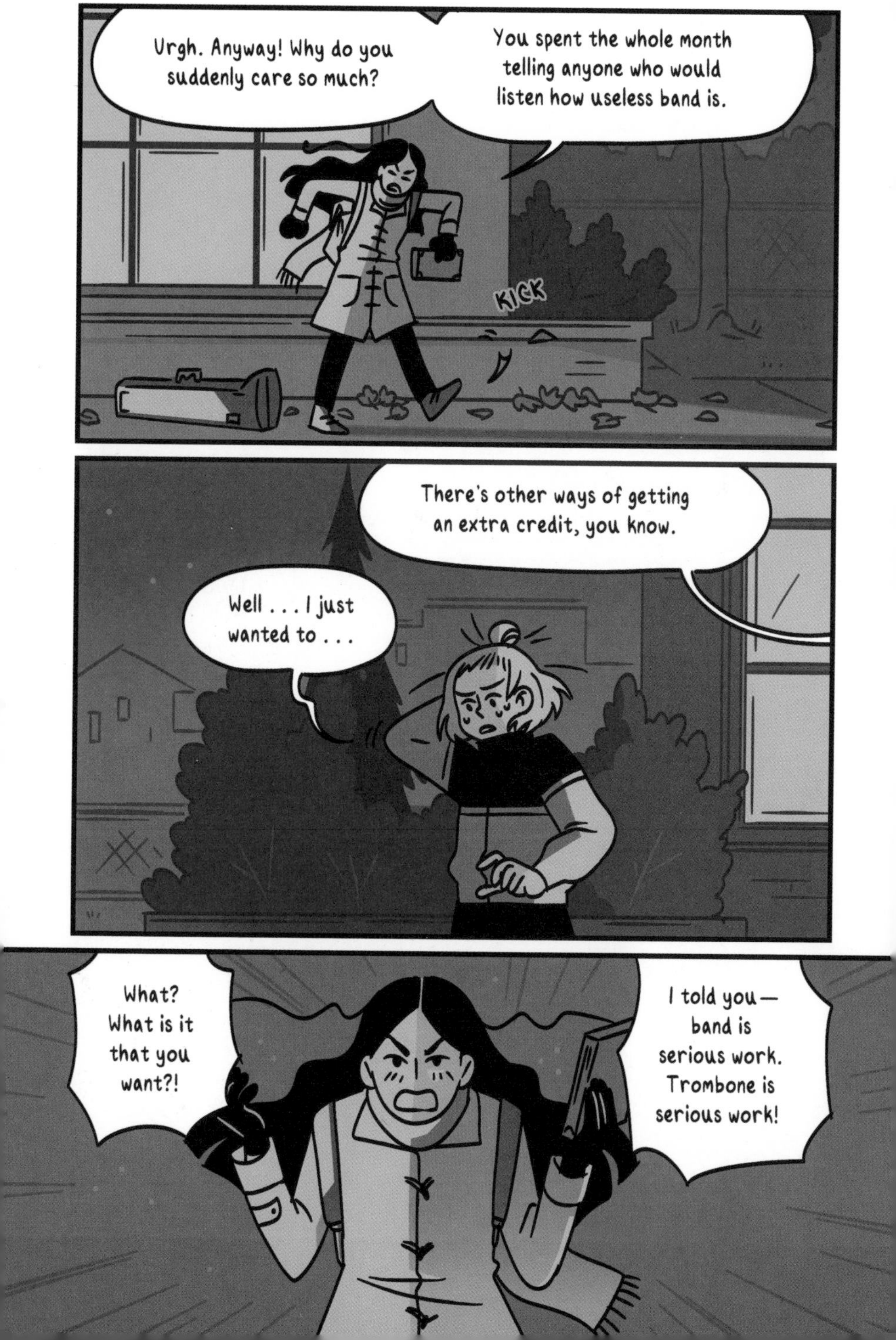
Urgh. Anyway! Why do you suddenly care so much?
You spent the whole month telling anyone who would listen how useless band is.
KICK
There's other ways of getting an extra credit, you know.
Well . . . I just wanted to . . .
What? What is it that you want?!
I told you— band is serious work. Trombone is serious work!

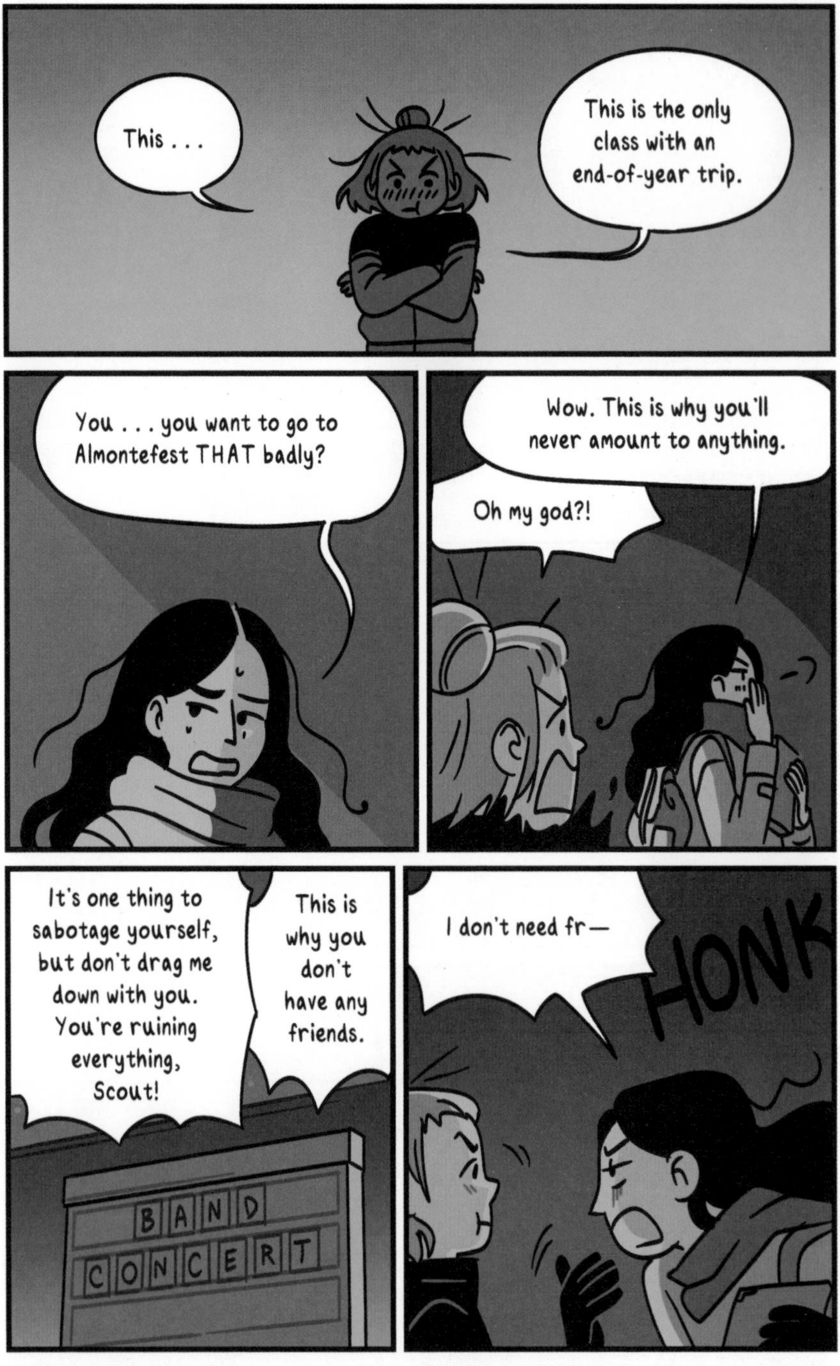
This . . .
This is the only class with an end-of-year trip.
You . . . you want to go to Almontefest THAT badly?
Wow. This is why you'll never amount to anything.
Oh my god?!
It's one thing to sabotage yourself, but don't drag me down with you. You're ruining everything, Scout!
This is why you don't have any friends.
BAND CONCERT
I don't need fr—
HONK

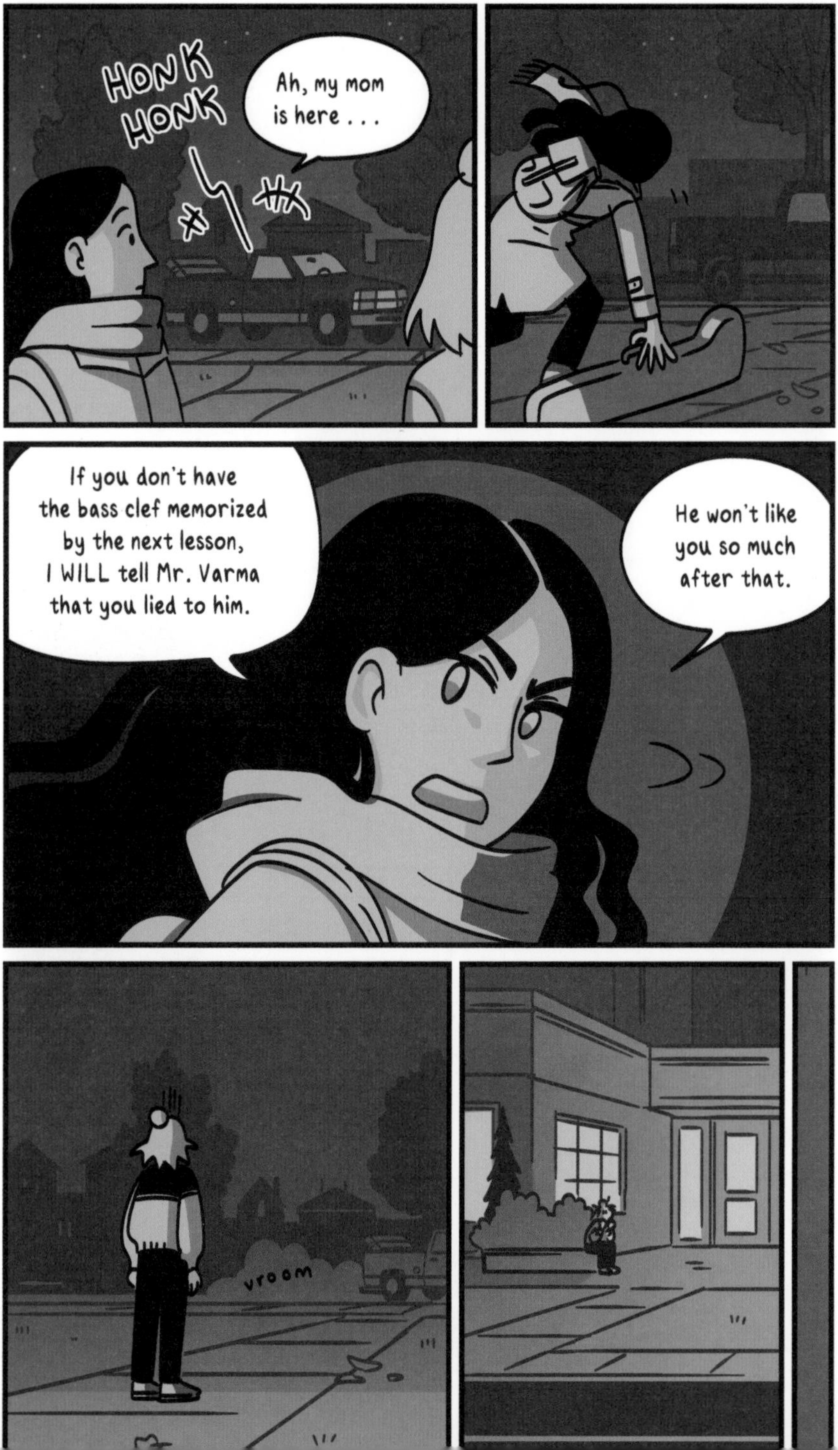
HONK HONK
Ah, my mom is here . . .
If you don't have the bass clef memorized by the next lesson, I WILL tell Mr. Varma that you lied to him.
He won't like you so much after that.
vroom

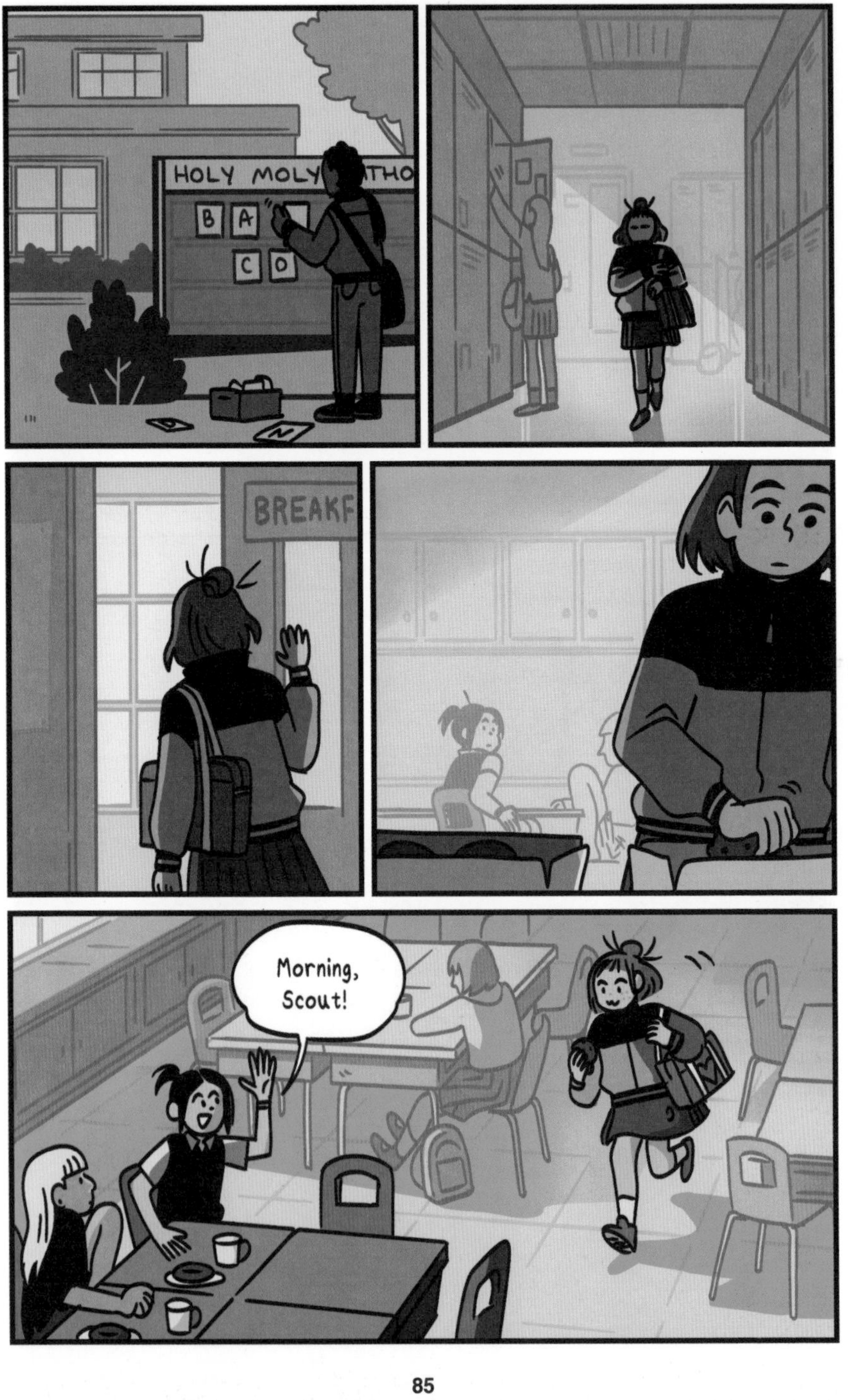
HOLY MOLY ATHO
B A
C O
N
BREAKF
Morning, Scout!

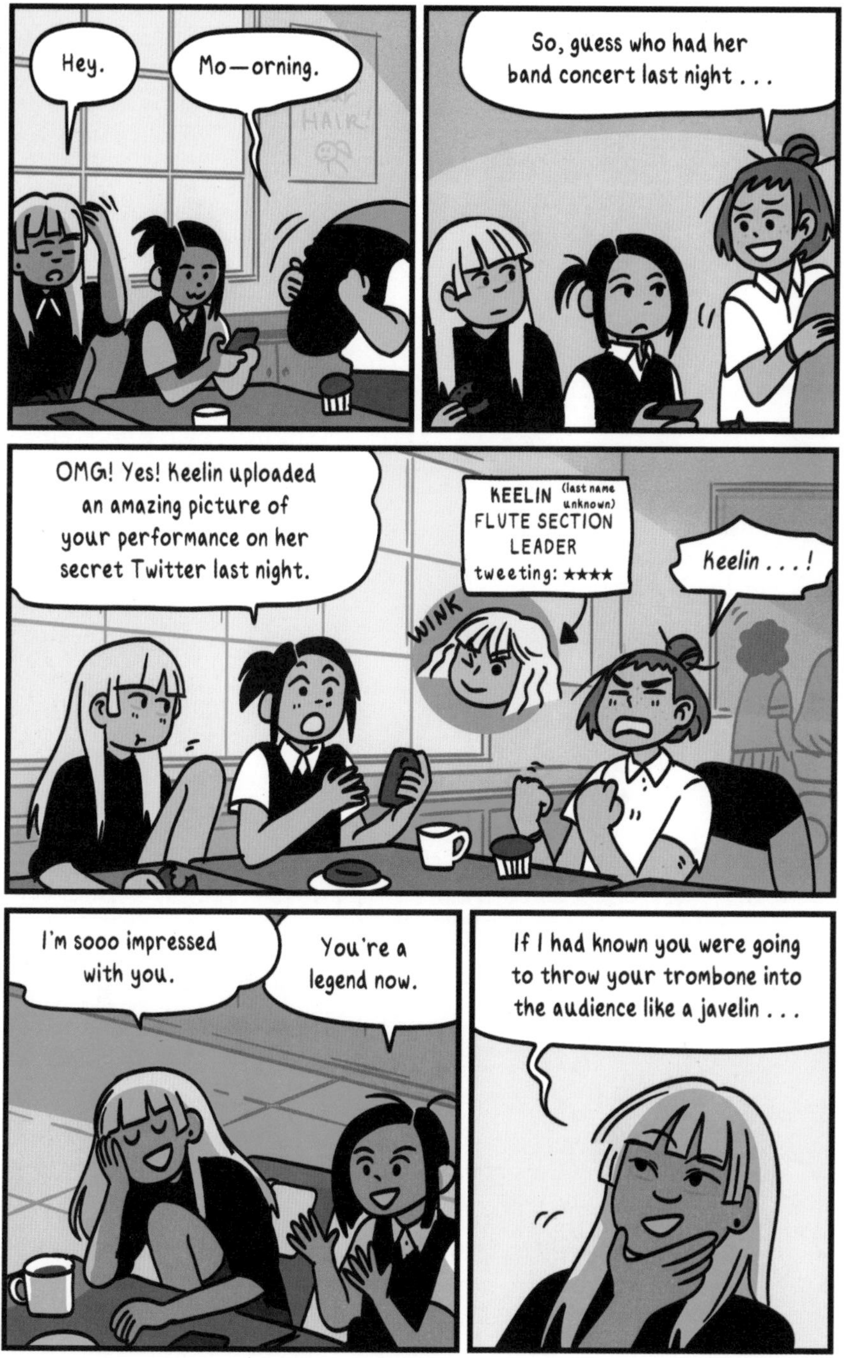
Hey.
Mo—orning.
So, guess who had her band concert last night . . .
OMG! Yes! Keelin uploaded an amazing picture of your performance on her secret Twitter last night.
KEELIN (last name unknown) FLUTE SECTION LEADER tweeting: ★★★★
WINK
Keelin . . . !
I'm sooo impressed with you.
You're a legend now.
If I had known you were going to throw your trombone into the audience like a javelin . . .

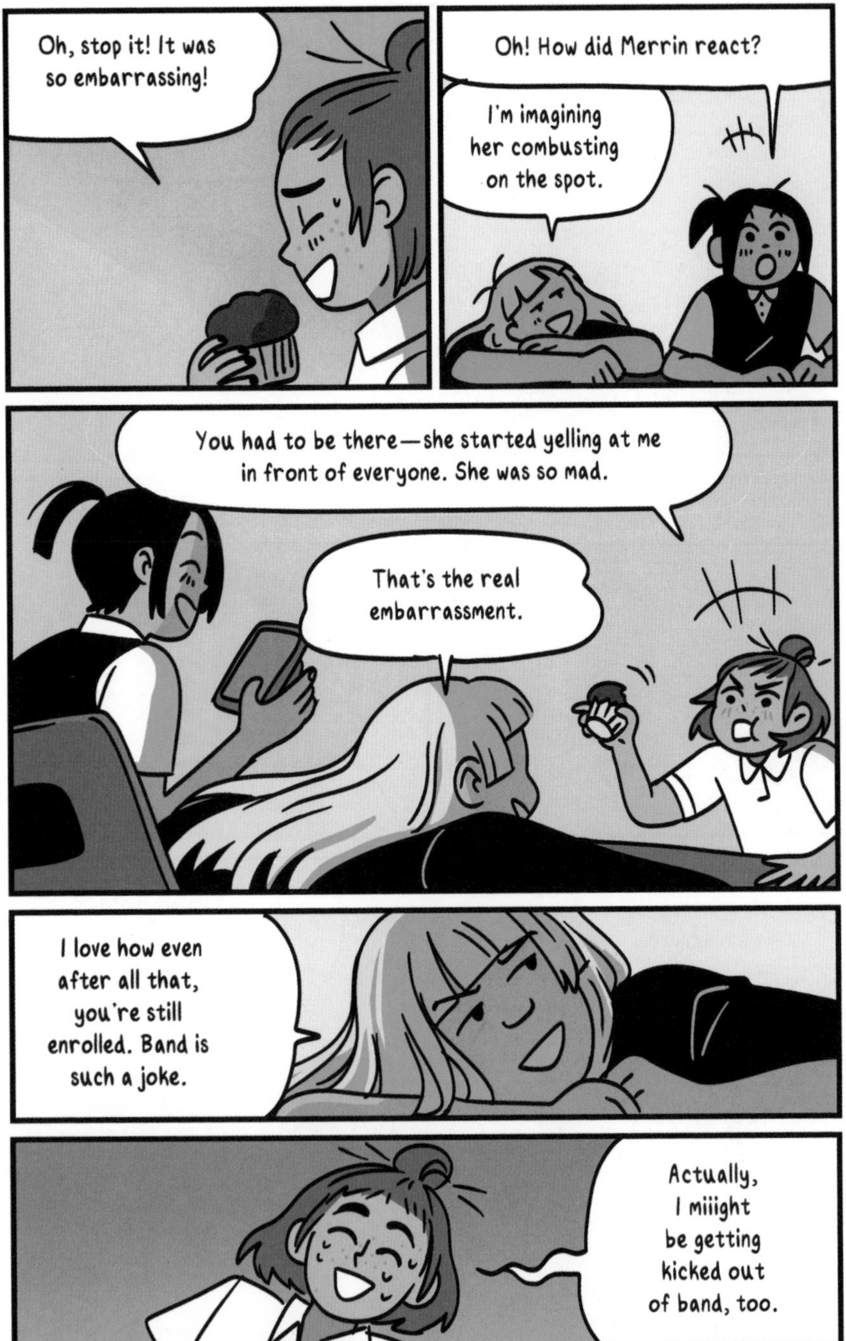
Oh, stop it! It was so embarrassing!
Oh! How did Merrin react?
I'm imagining her combusting on the spot.
You had to be there—she started yelling at me in front of everyone. She was so mad.
That's the real embarrassment.
I love how even after all that, you're still enrolled. Band is such a joke.
Actually, I miiight be getting kicked out of band, too.

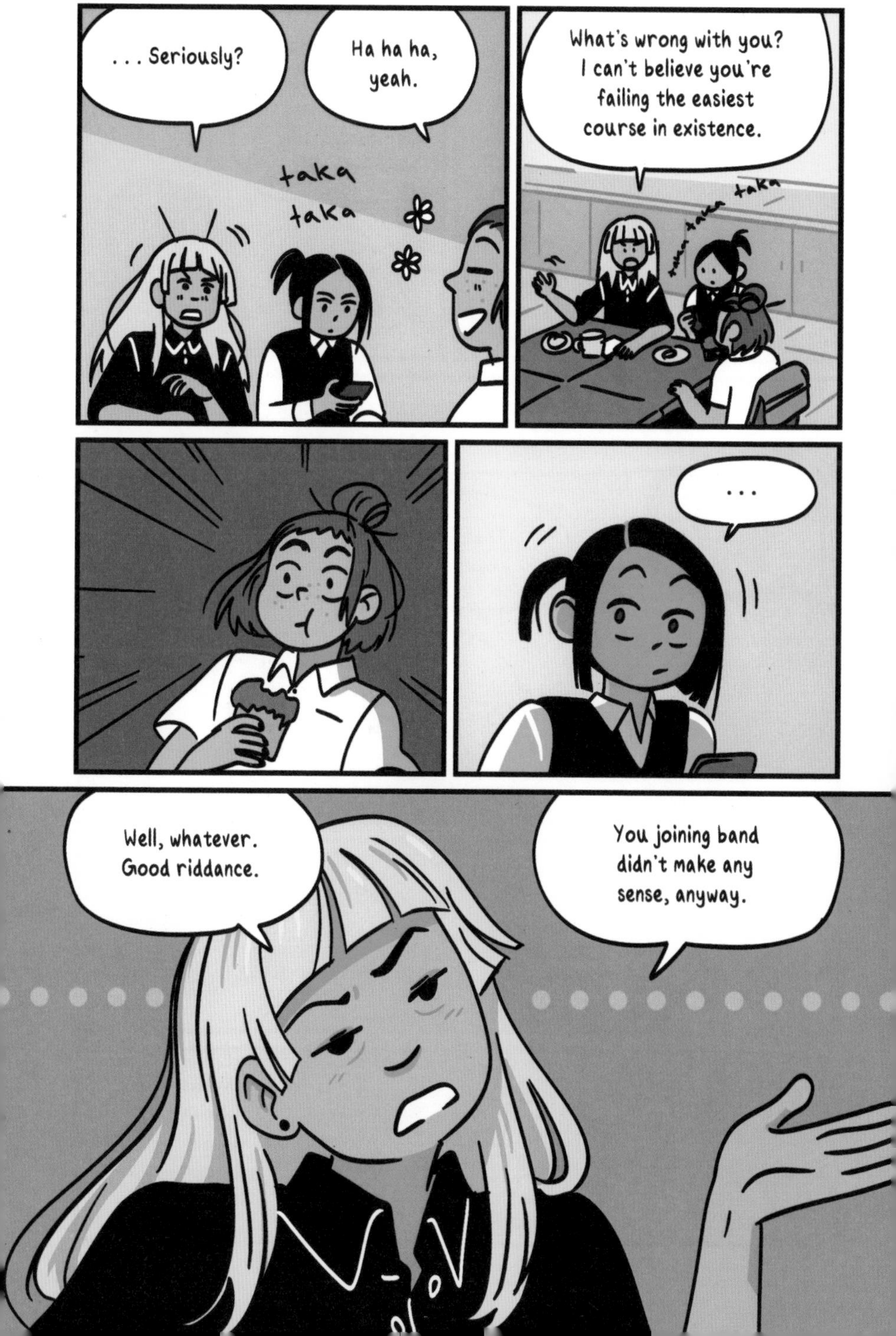
. . . Seriously?
Ha ha ha, yeah.
taka
taka
What's wrong with you? I can't believe you're failing the easiest course in existence.
taka taka taka
. . .
Well, whatever. Good riddance.
You joining band didn't make any sense, anyway.

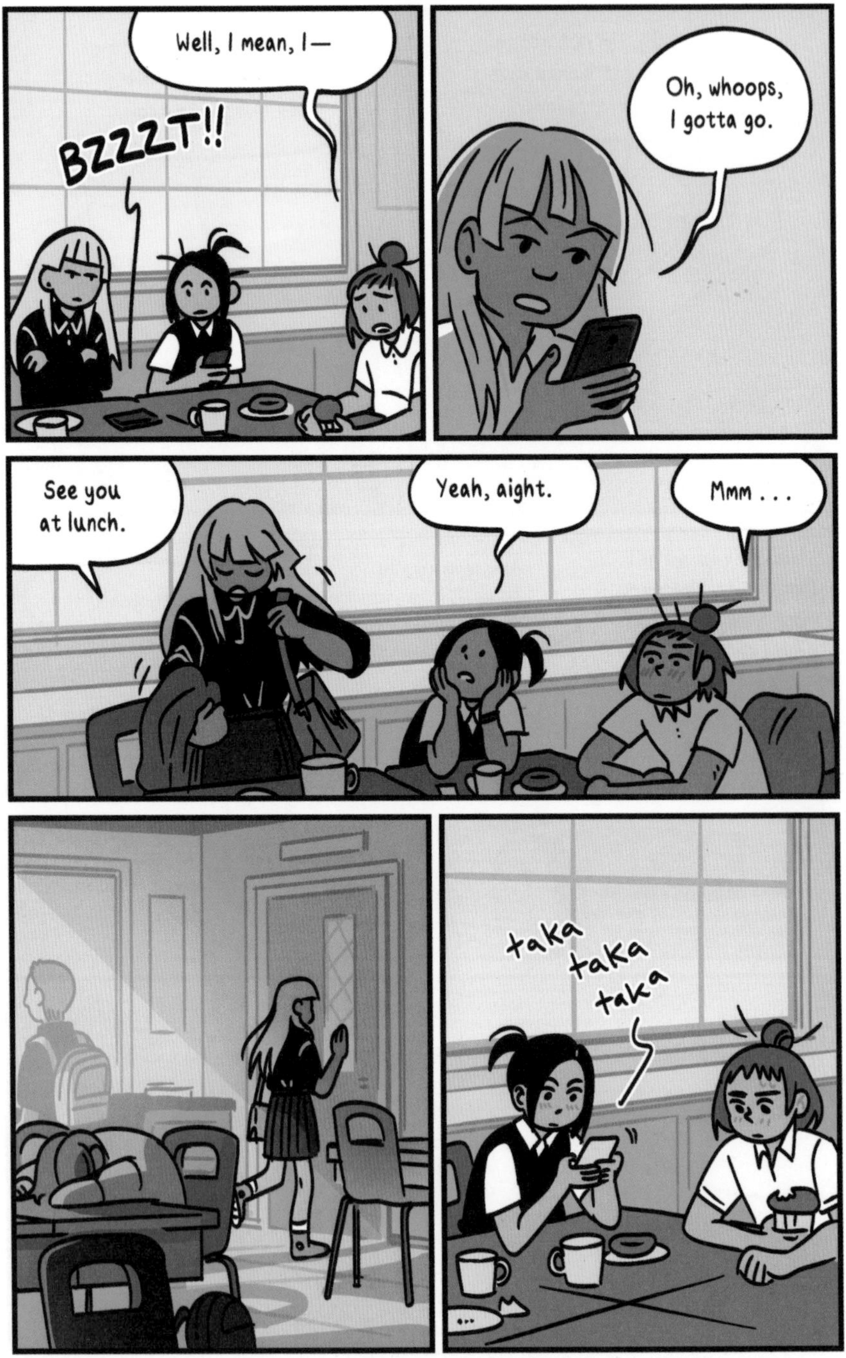
Well, I mean, I—
BZZZT!!
Oh, whoops, I gotta go.
See you at lunch.
Yeah, aight.
Mmm . . .
taka taka taka

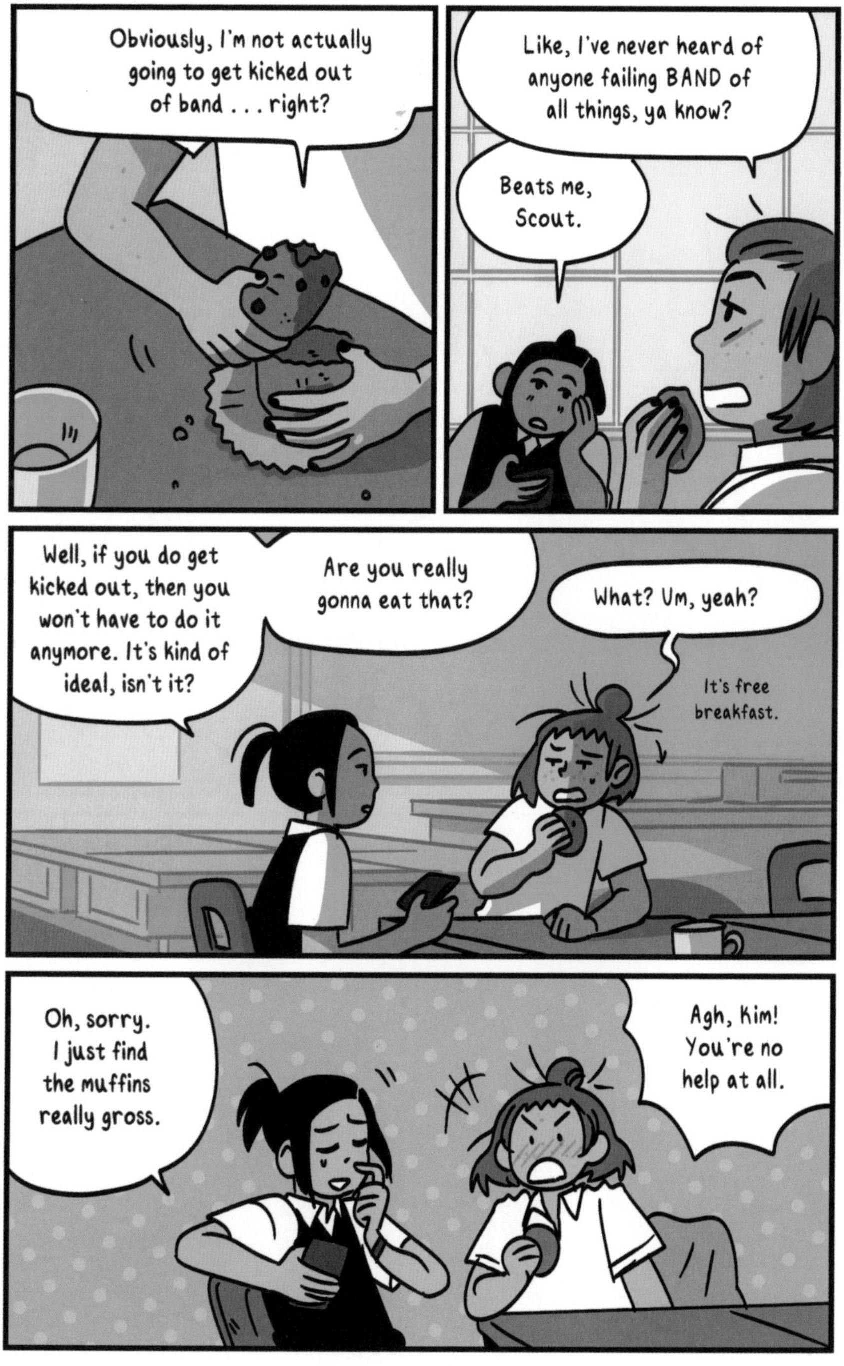
Obviously, I'm not actually going to get kicked out of band . . . right?
Like, I've never heard of anyone failing BAND of all things, ya know?
Beats me, Scout.
Well, if you do get kicked out, then you won't have to do it anymore. It's kind of ideal, isn't it?
Are you really gonna eat that?
What? Um, yeah?
It's free breakfast.
Oh, sorry. I just find the muffins really gross.
Agh, Kim! You're no help at all.

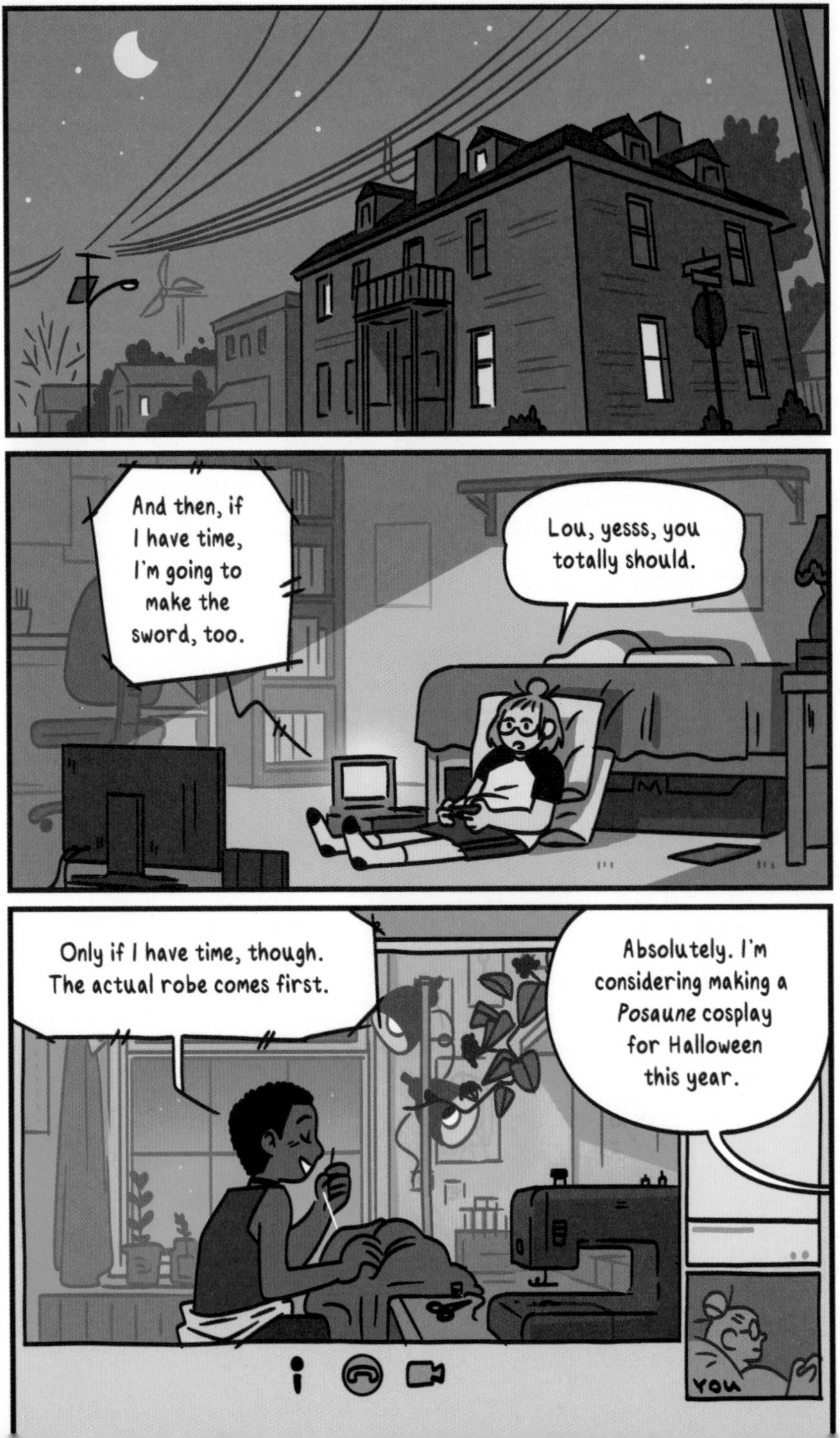
And then, if I have time, I'm going to make the sword, too.
Lou, yesss, you totally should.
Only if I have time, though. The actual robe comes first.
Absolutely. I'm considering making a *Posaune* cosplay for Halloween this year.
YOU

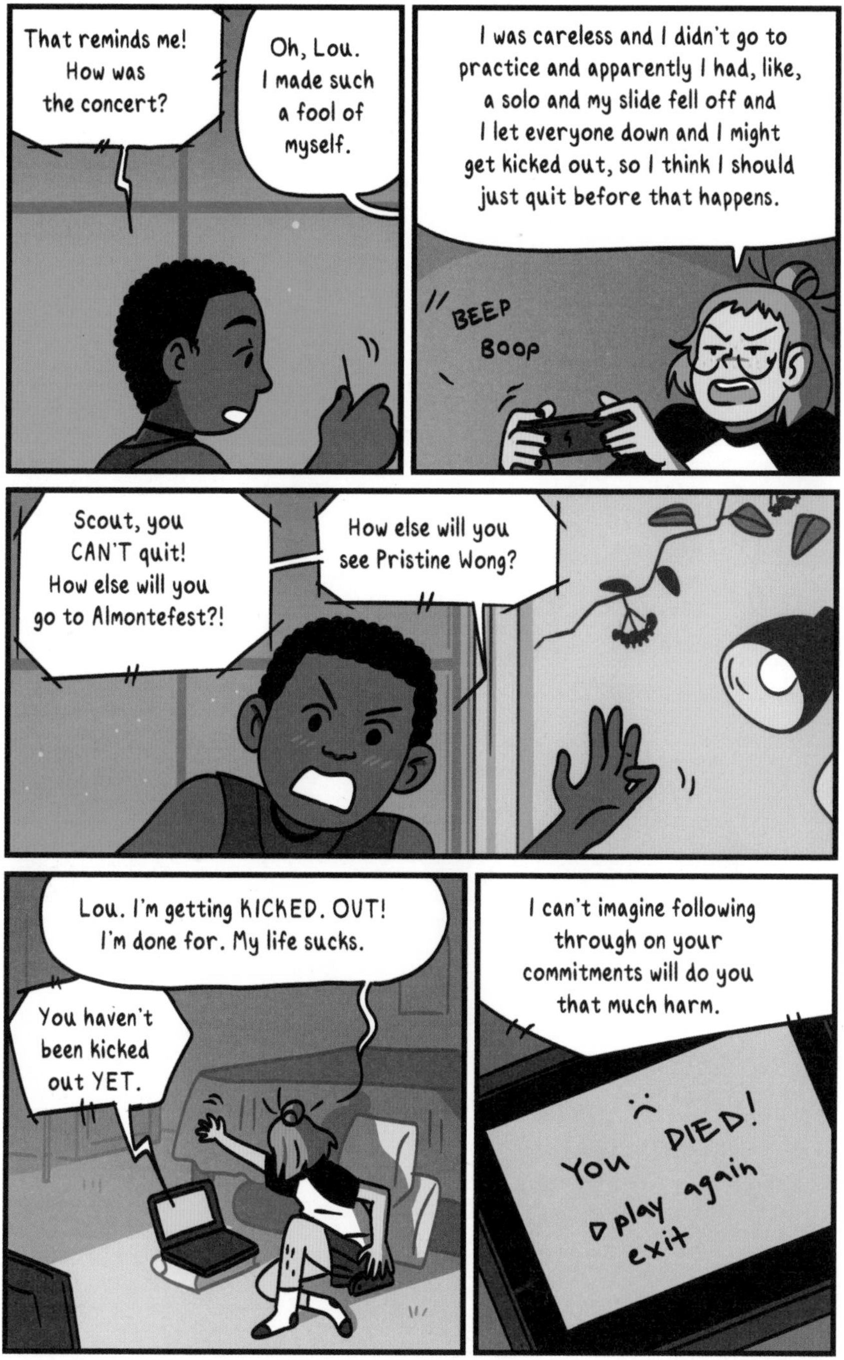
That reminds me! How was the concert?
Oh, Lou. I made such a fool of myself.
I was careless and I didn't go to practice and apparently I had, like, a solo and my slide fell off and I let everyone down and I might get kicked out, so I think I should just quit before that happens.
BEEP BOOP
Scout, you CAN'T quit! How else will you go to Almontefest?!
How else will you see Pristine Wong?
Lou. I'm getting KICKED. OUT! I'm done for. My life sucks.
You haven't been kicked out YET.
I can't imagine following through on your commitments will do you that much harm.
You DIED!
play again
exit

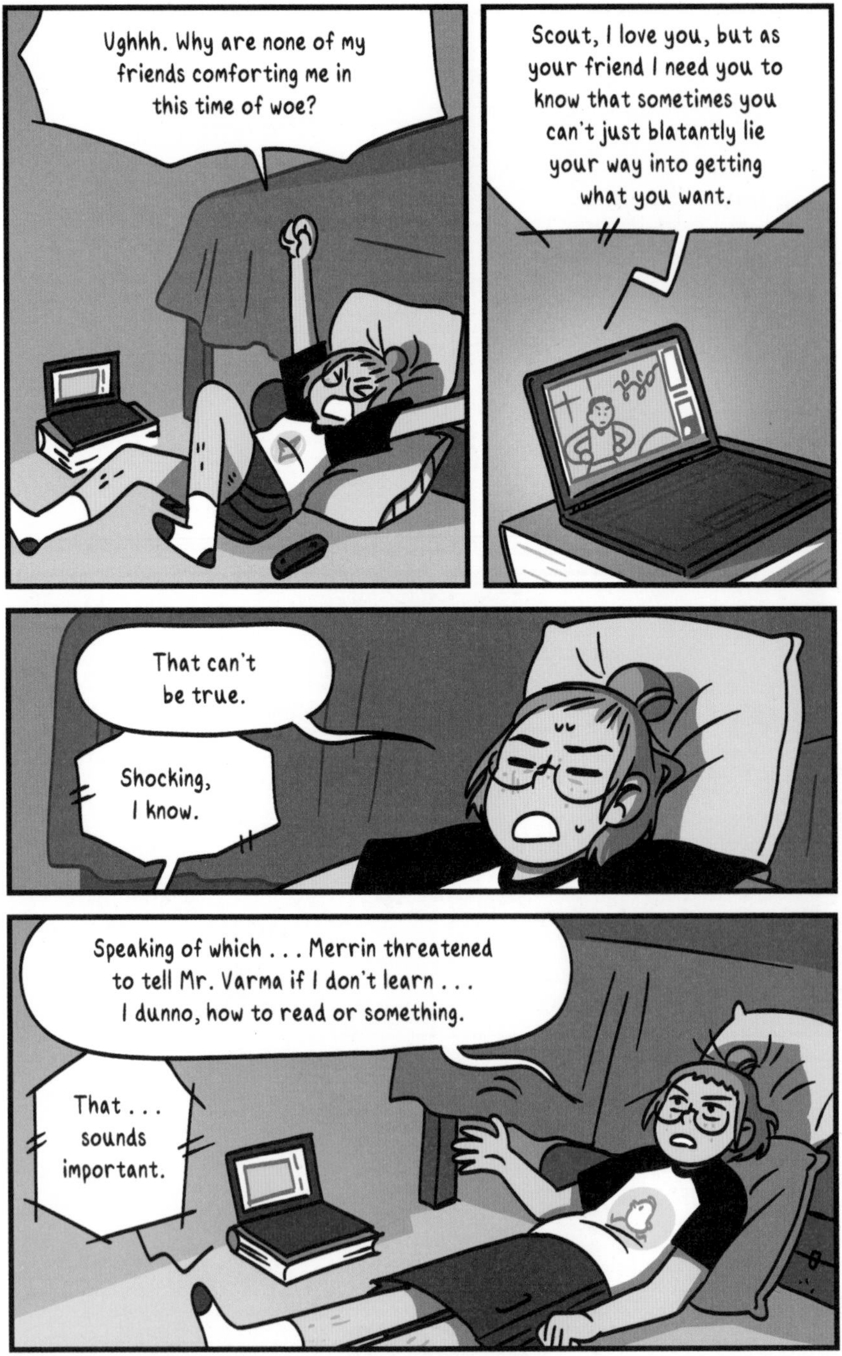
Ughhh. Why are none of my friends comforting me in this time of woe?
Scout, I love you, but as your friend I need you to know that sometimes you can't just blatantly lie your way into getting what you want.
That can't be true.
Shocking, I know.
Speaking of which . . . Merrin threatened to tell Mr. Varma if I don't learn . . . I dunno, how to read or something.
That . . . sounds important.

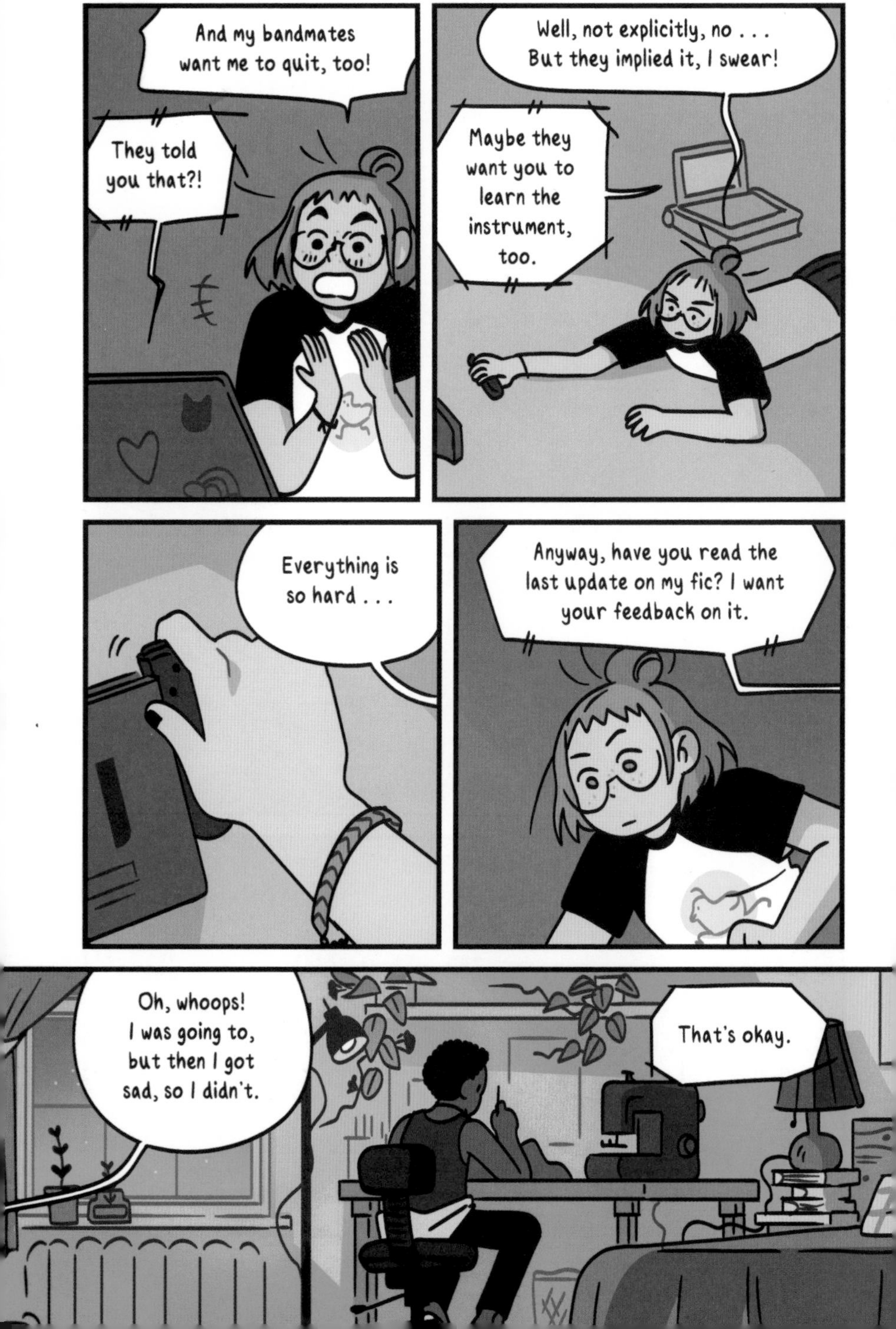
And my bandmates want me to quit, too!
They told you that?!
Well, not explicitly, no . . . But they implied it, I swear!
Maybe they want you to learn the instrument, too.
Everything is so hard . . .
Anyway, have you read the last update on my fic? I want your feedback on it.
Oh, whoops! I was going to, but then I got sad, so I didn't.
That's okay.

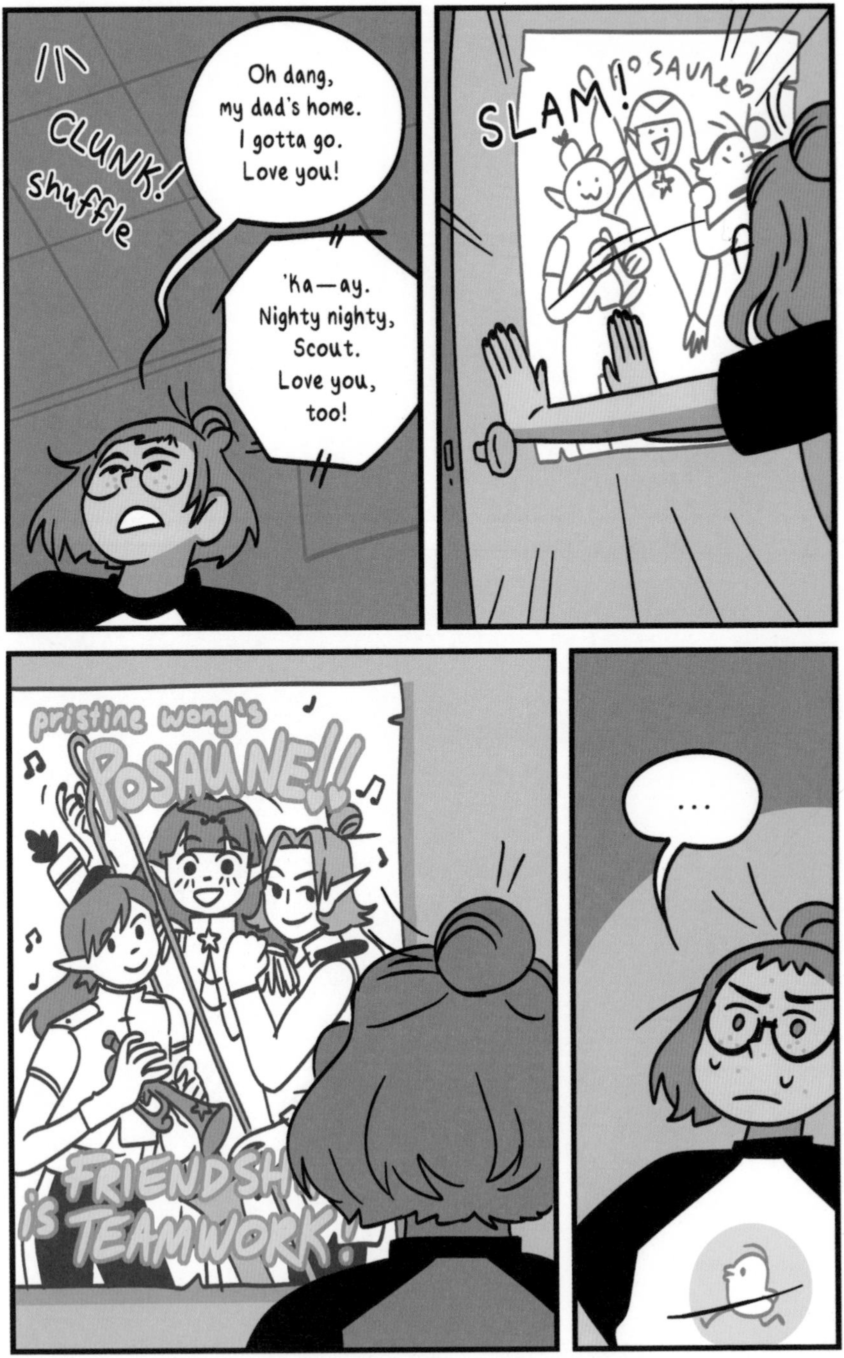
CLUNK!
shuffle
Oh dang, my dad's home. I gotta go. Love you!
'Ka—ay. Nighty nighty, Scout. Love you, too!
SLAM!
POSAUNE
pristine wong's
POSAUNE!!
FRIENDSH
is TEAMWORK!
. . .

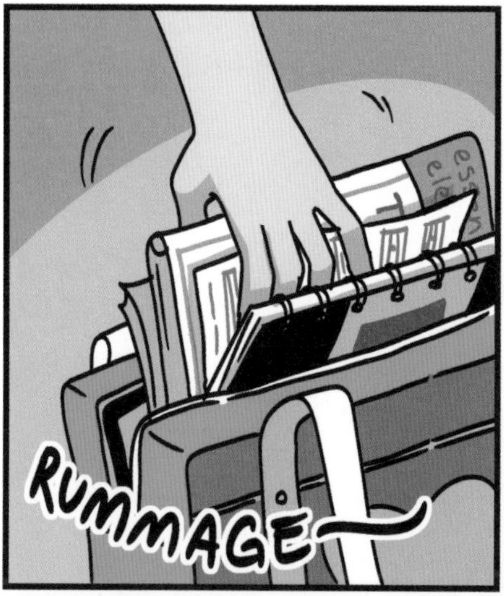
RUMMAGE—

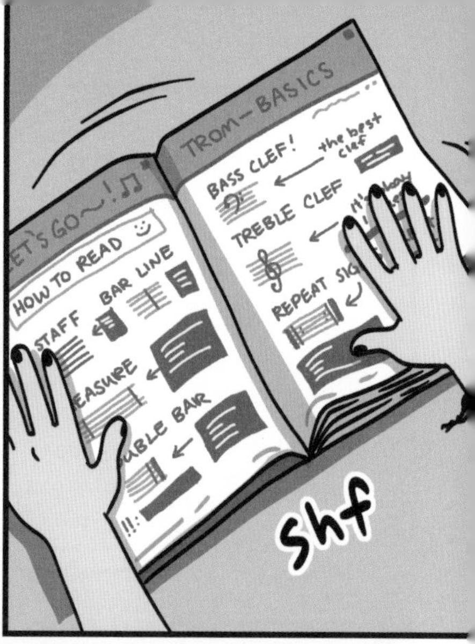
HOW TO READ
STAFF
BAR LINE
TROM-BASICS
BASS CLEF!
the best clef
TREBLE CLEF
Shf

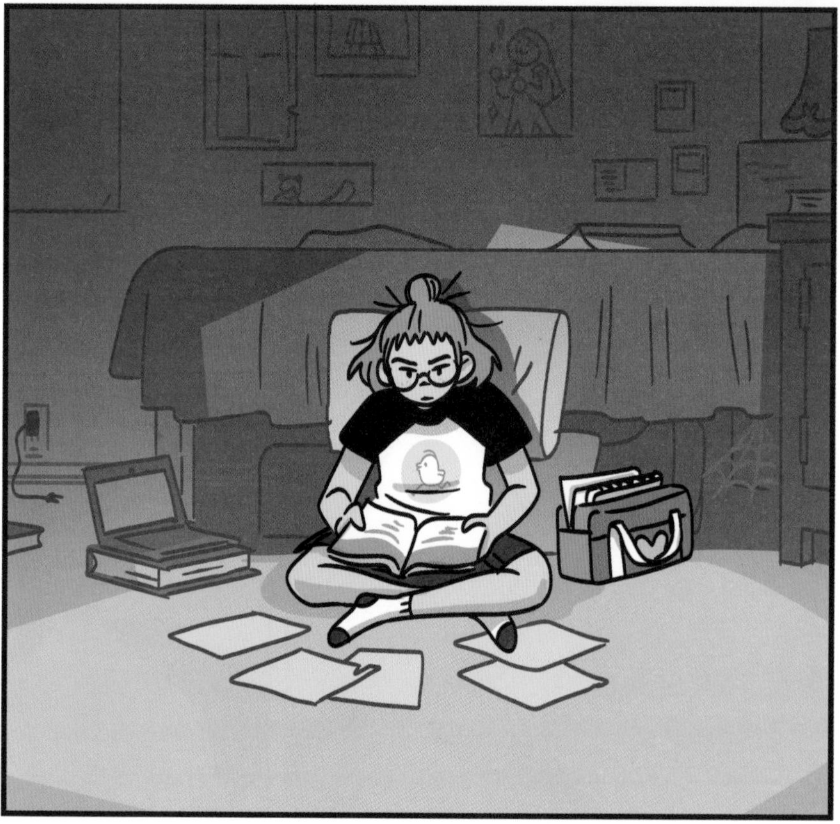

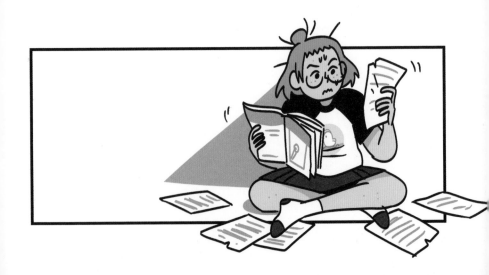

Chapter 3

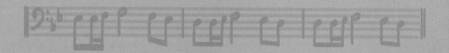

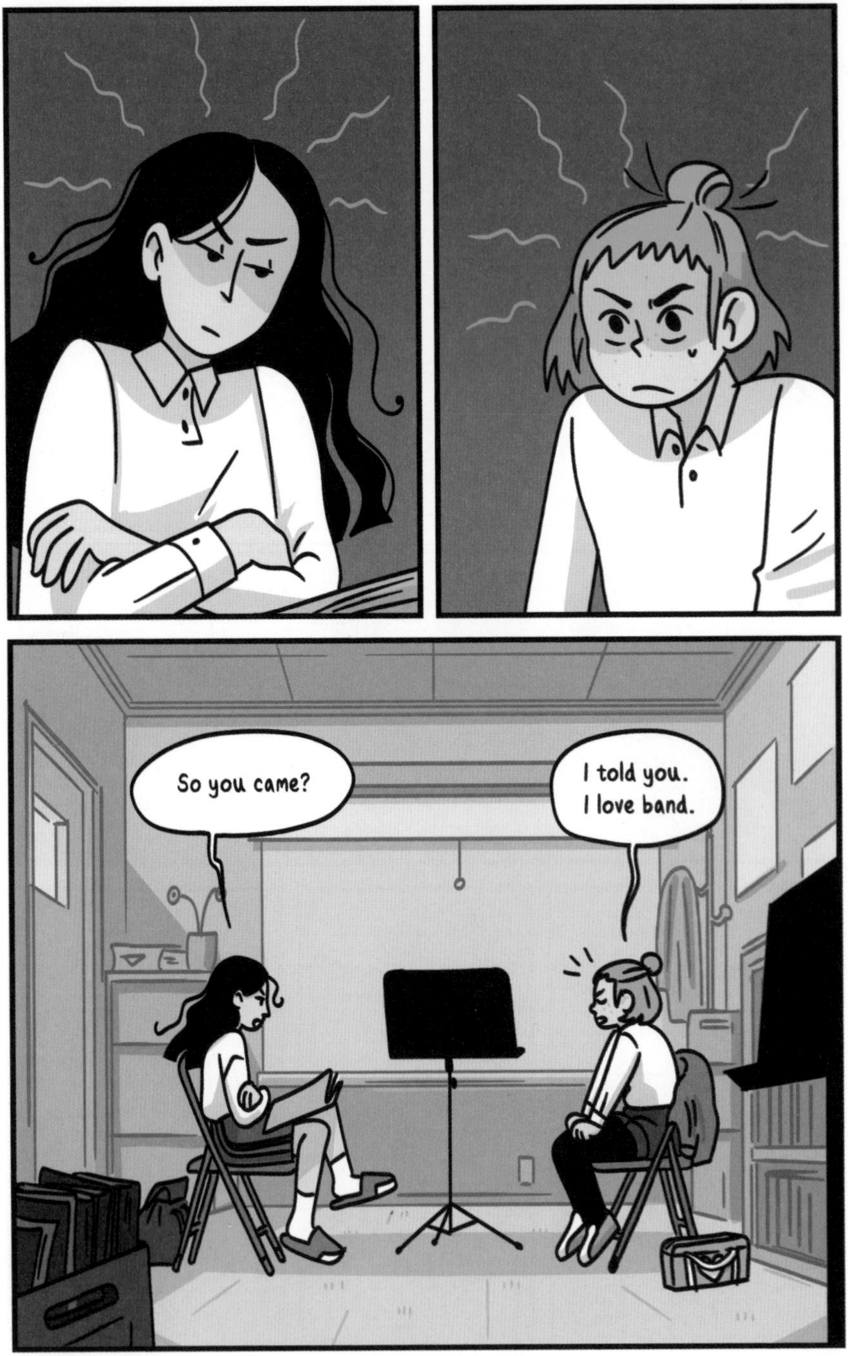
So you came?
I told you. I love band.

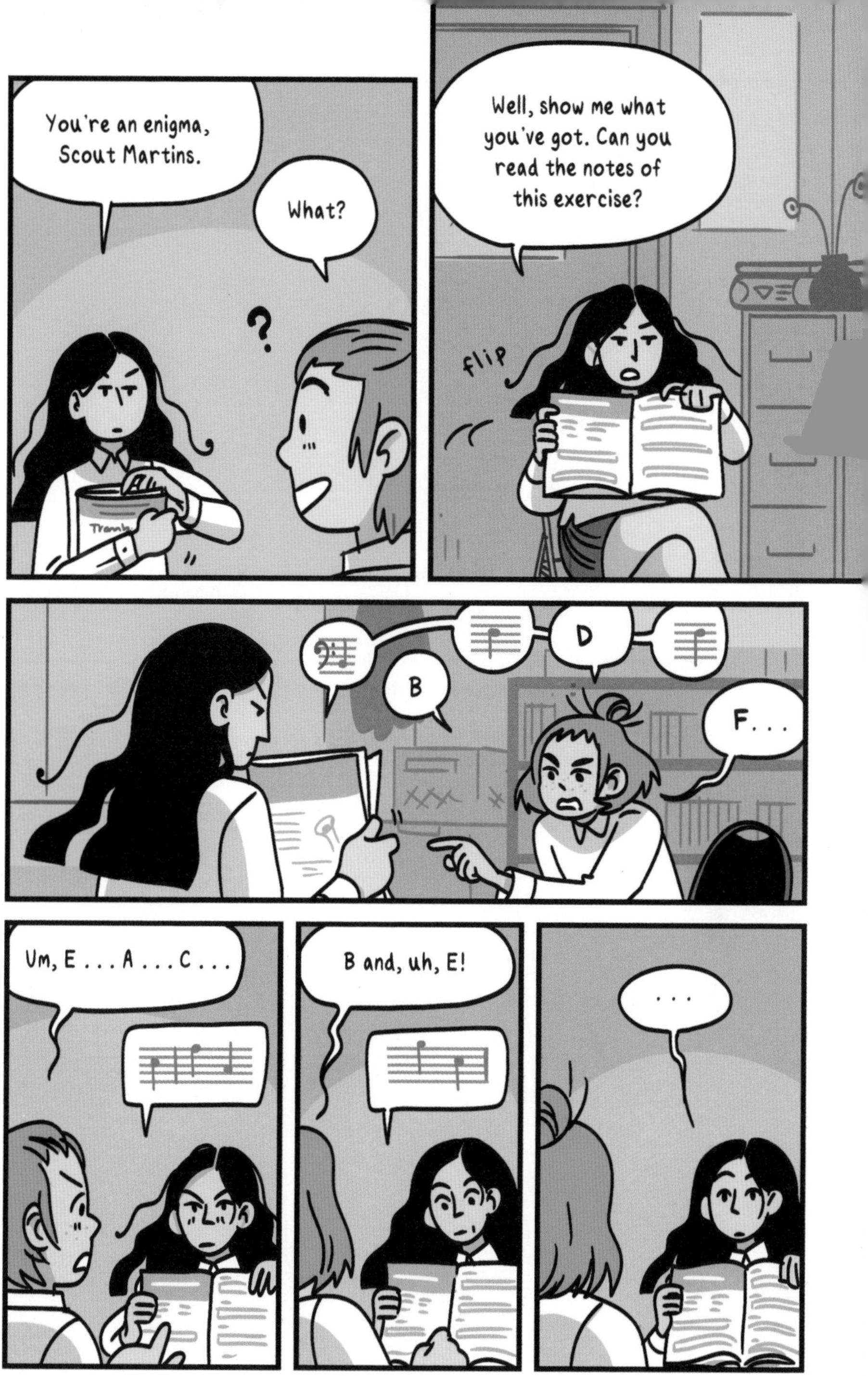
You're an enigma, Scout Martins.
What?
?
Well, show me what you've got. Can you read the notes of this exercise?
flip
B
D
F...
Um, E...A...C...
B and, uh, E!
...

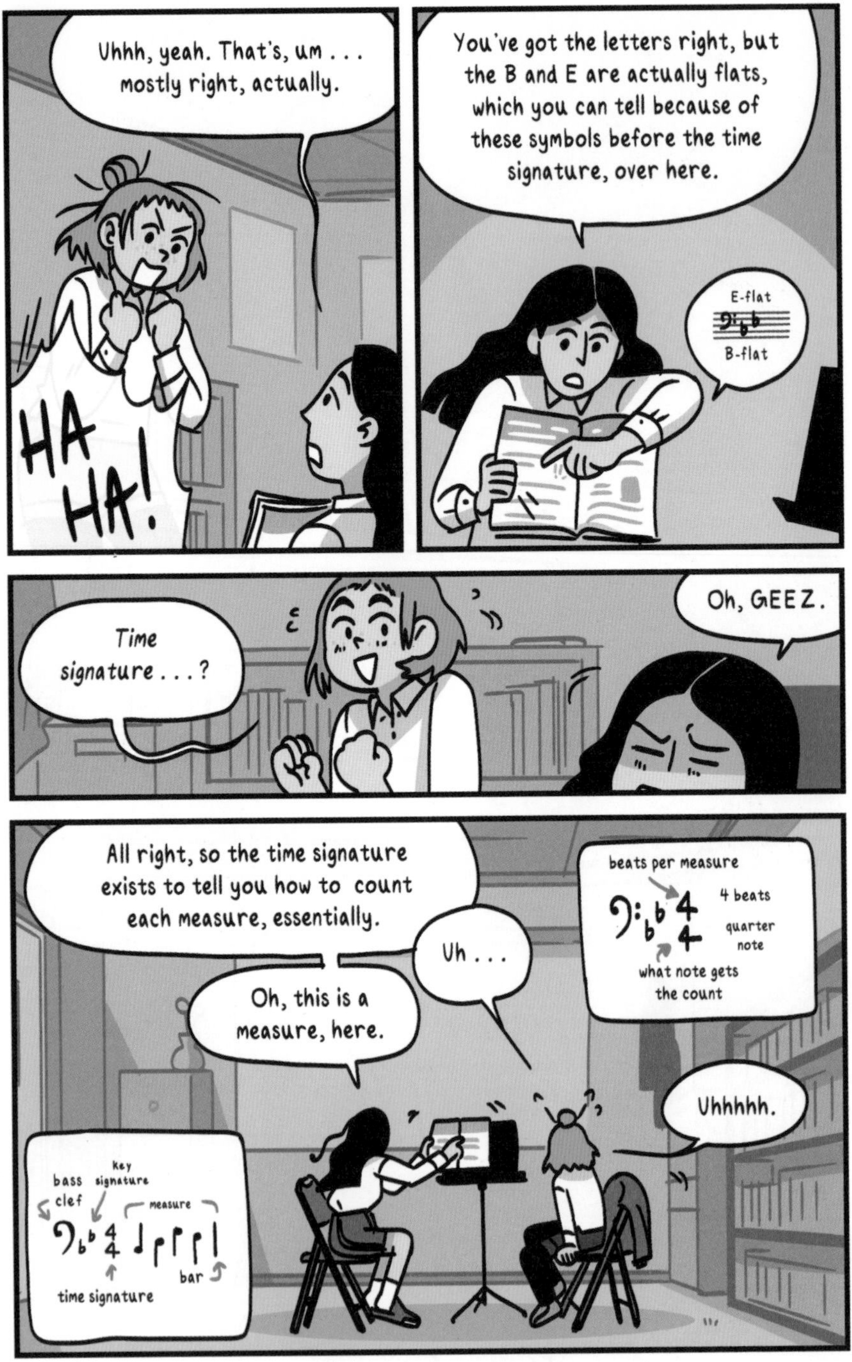

Uhhh, yeah. That's, um . . . mostly right, actually.
HA HA!
You've got the letters right, but the B and E are actually flats, which you can tell because of these symbols before the time signature, over here.
E-flat
B-flat
Time signature . . .?
Oh, GEEZ.
All right, so the time signature exists to tell you how to count each measure, essentially.
Uh . . .
Oh, this is a measure, here.
beats per measure
4 beats
quarter note
what note gets the count
Uhhhhh.
bass clef
key signature
measure
bar
time signature

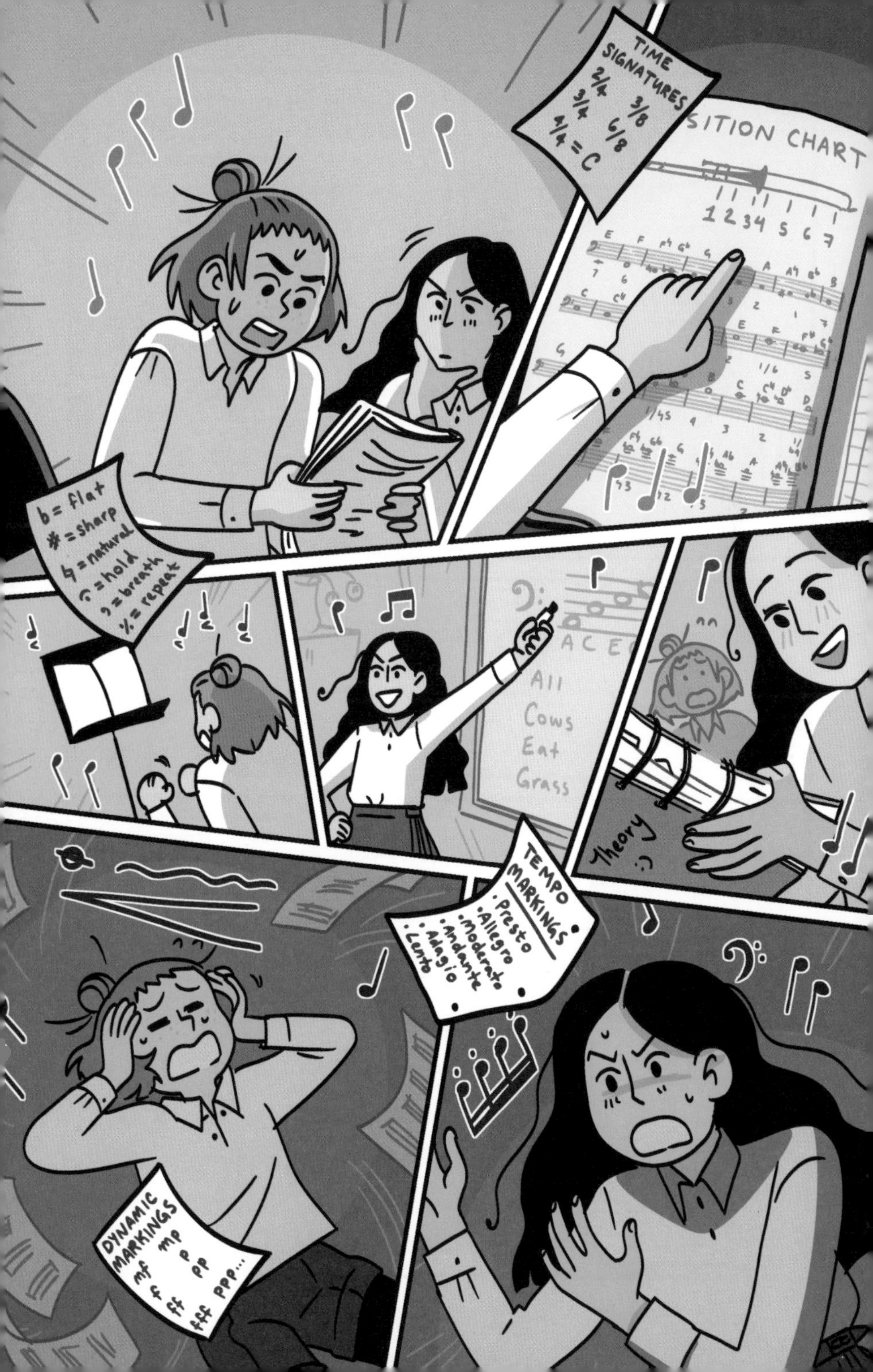
TIME SIGNATURES
2/4 3/8
3/4 6/8
4/4 = C
SITION CHART
1 2 3 4 5 6 7
b = flat
# = sharp
♮ = natural
𝄐 = hold
9 = breath
% = repeat
ACE
All
Cows
Eat
Grass
Theory
TEMPO MARKINGS
.Presto
.Allegro
.Moderato
.Andante
.Adagio
.Lento
DYNAMIC MARKINGS
mf mp
f p
ff pp
fff ppp...

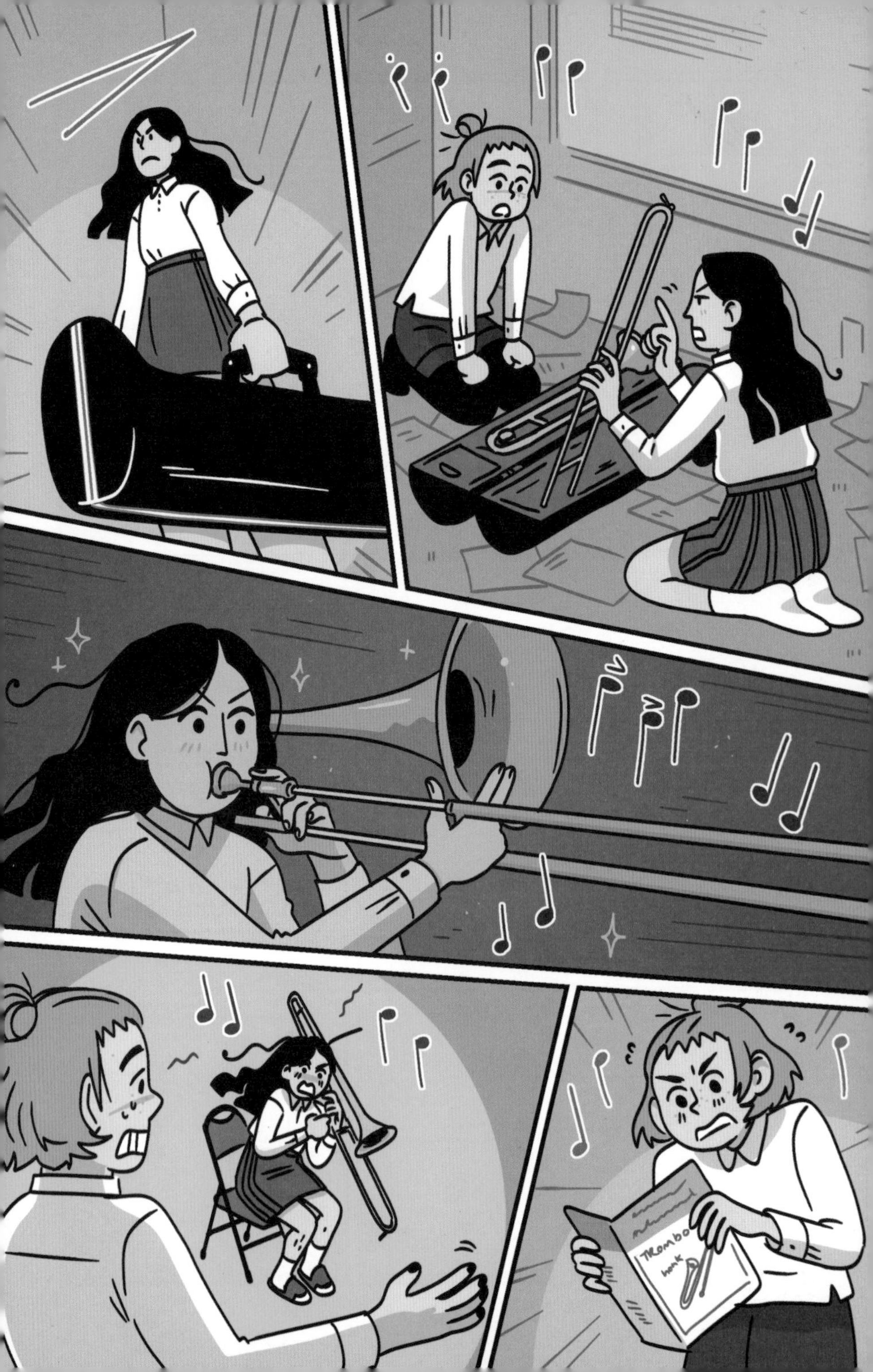
TROMBO
honk

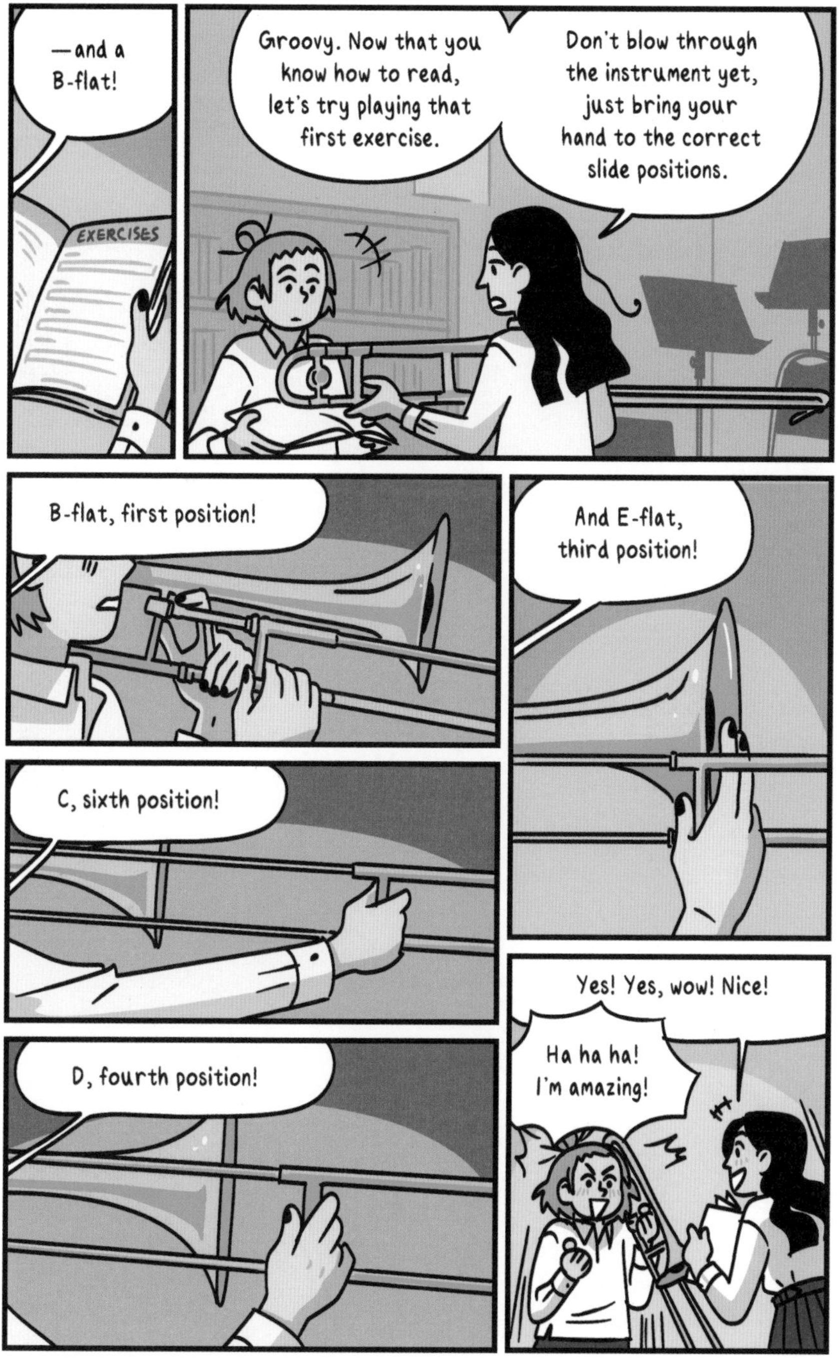
—and a B-flat!
Groovy. Now that you know how to read, let's try playing that first exercise.
Don't blow through the instrument yet, just bring your hand to the correct slide positions.
EXERCISES
B-flat, first position!
And E-flat, third position!
C, sixth position!
D, fourth position!
Yes! Yes, wow! Nice!
Ha ha ha! I'm amazing!

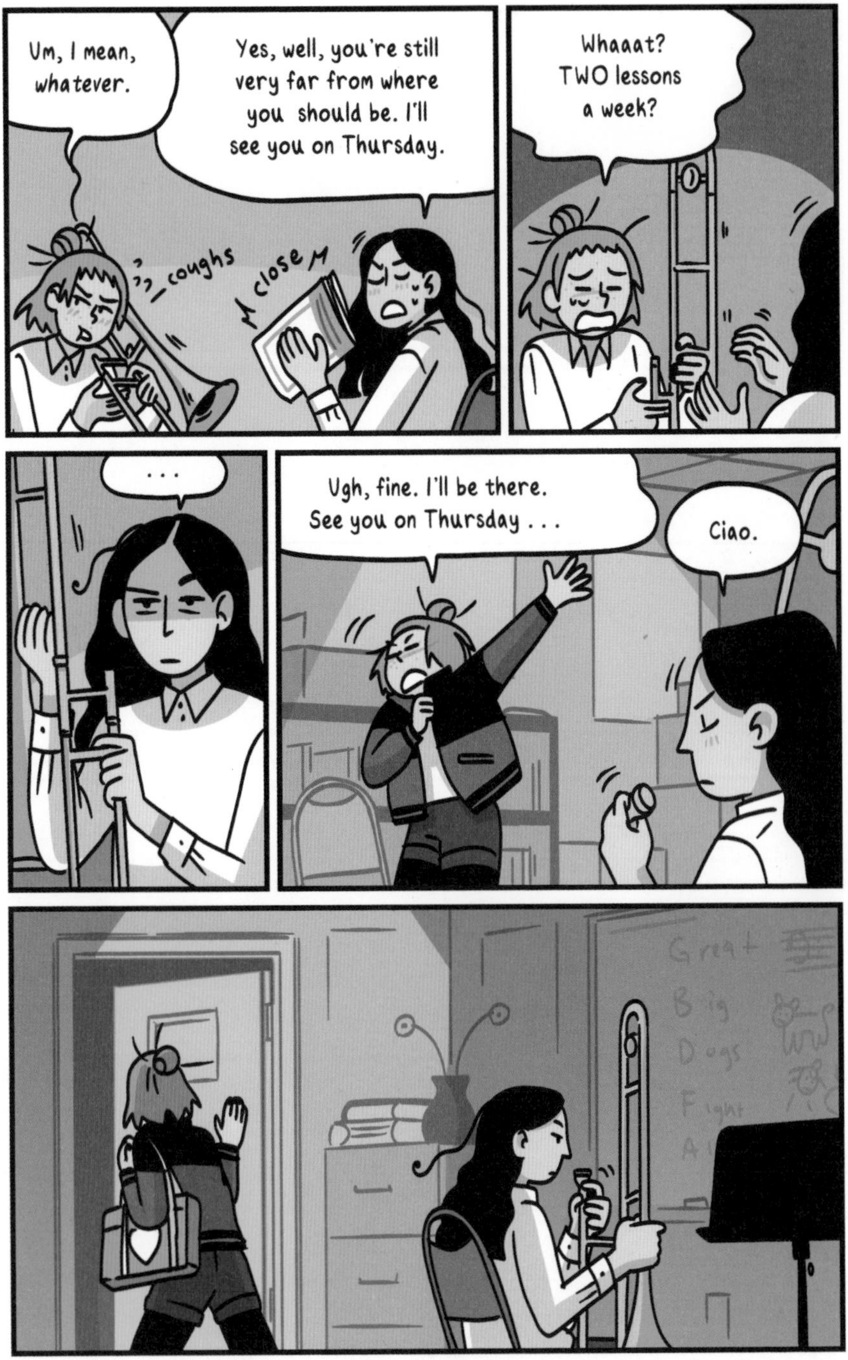
Um, I mean, whatever.
Yes, well, you're still very far from where you should be. I'll see you on Thursday.
coughs
close
Whaaat? TWO lessons a week?
. . .
Ugh, fine. I'll be there. See you on Thursday . . .
Ciao.

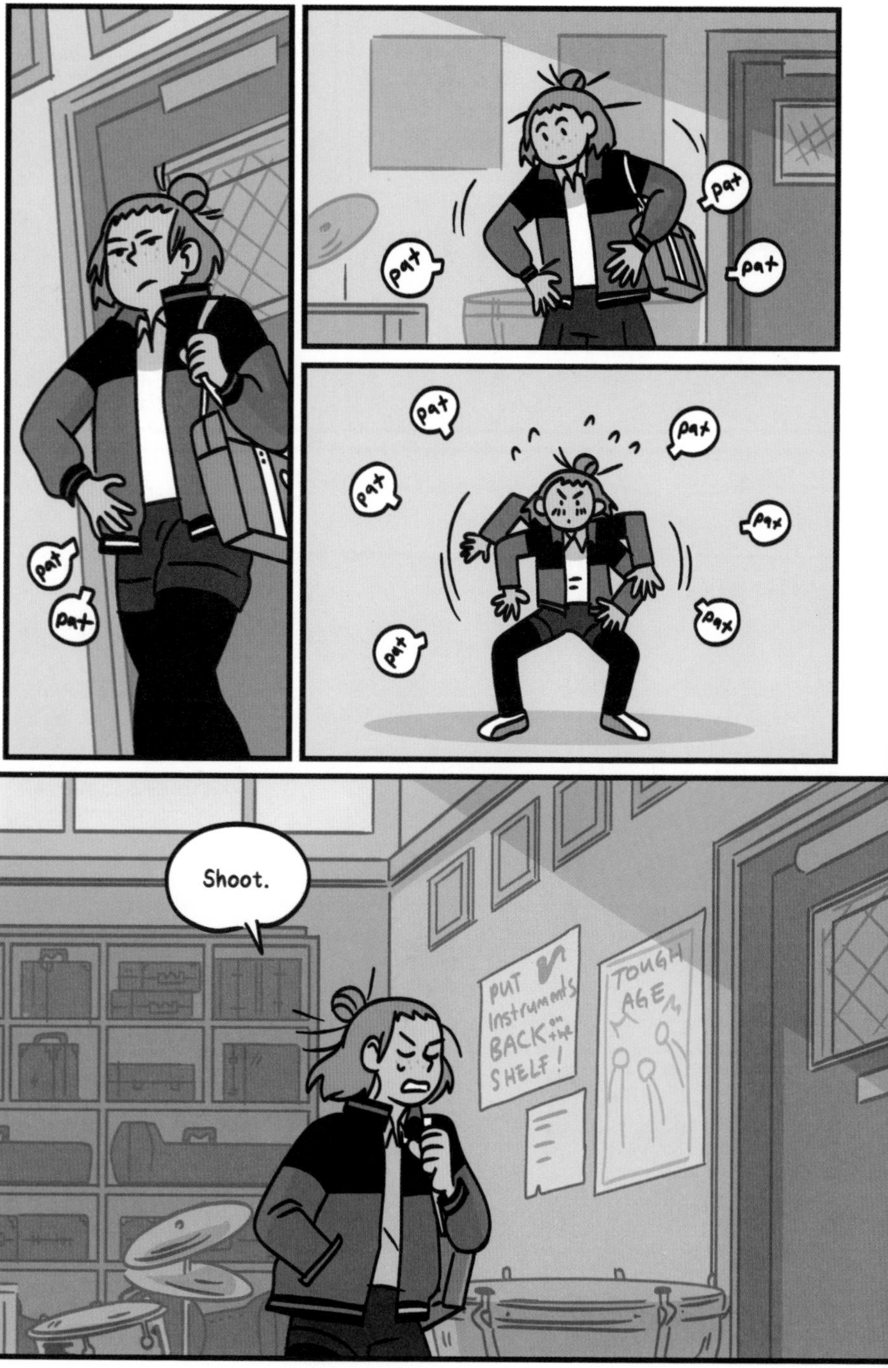
pat
pat
pat
pat
pat
pat
pat
pat
pat
pat
pat
pat
Shoot.
PUT Instruments BACK on the SHELF!
TOUGH AGE

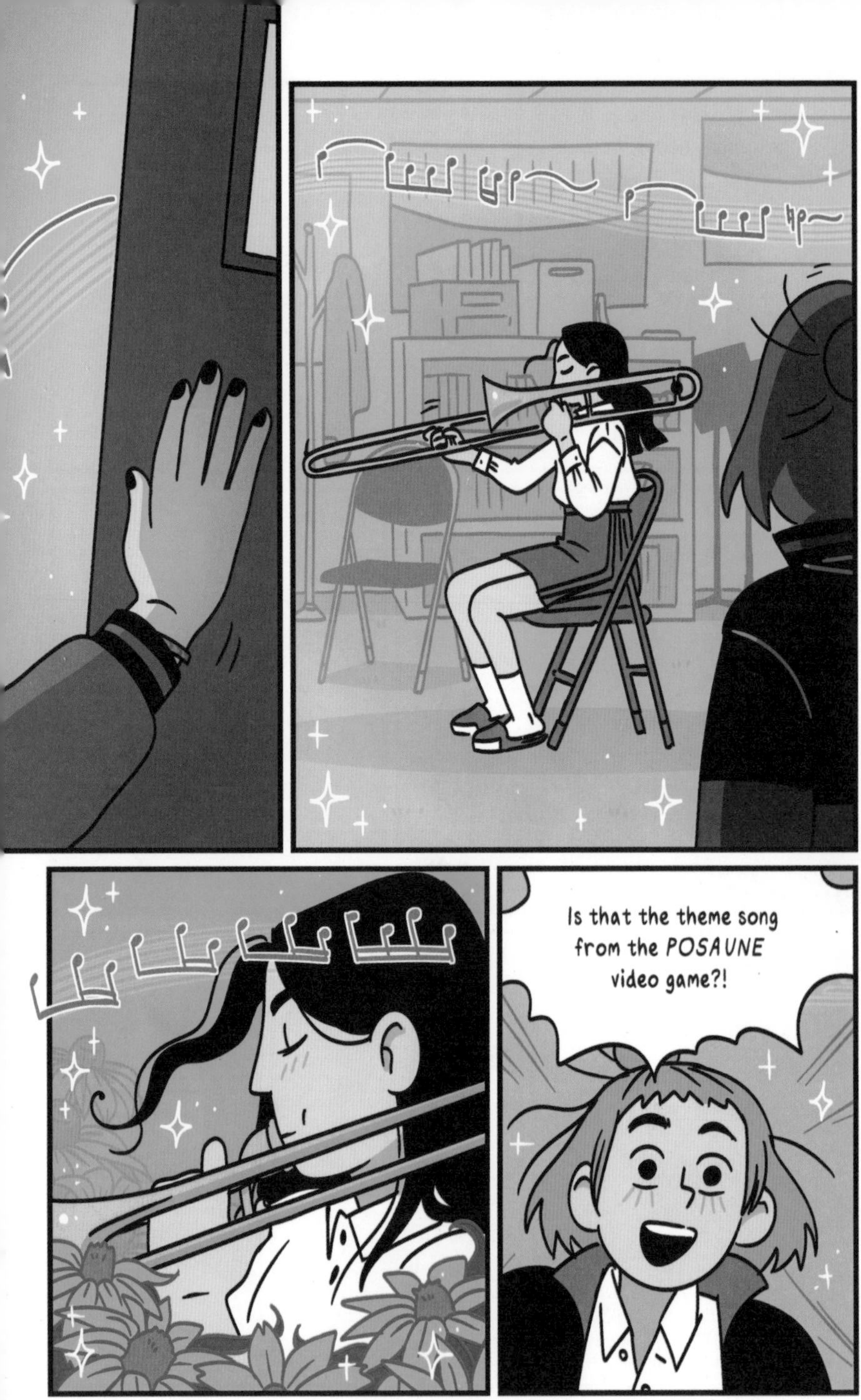
Is that the theme song from the *POSAUNE* video game?!

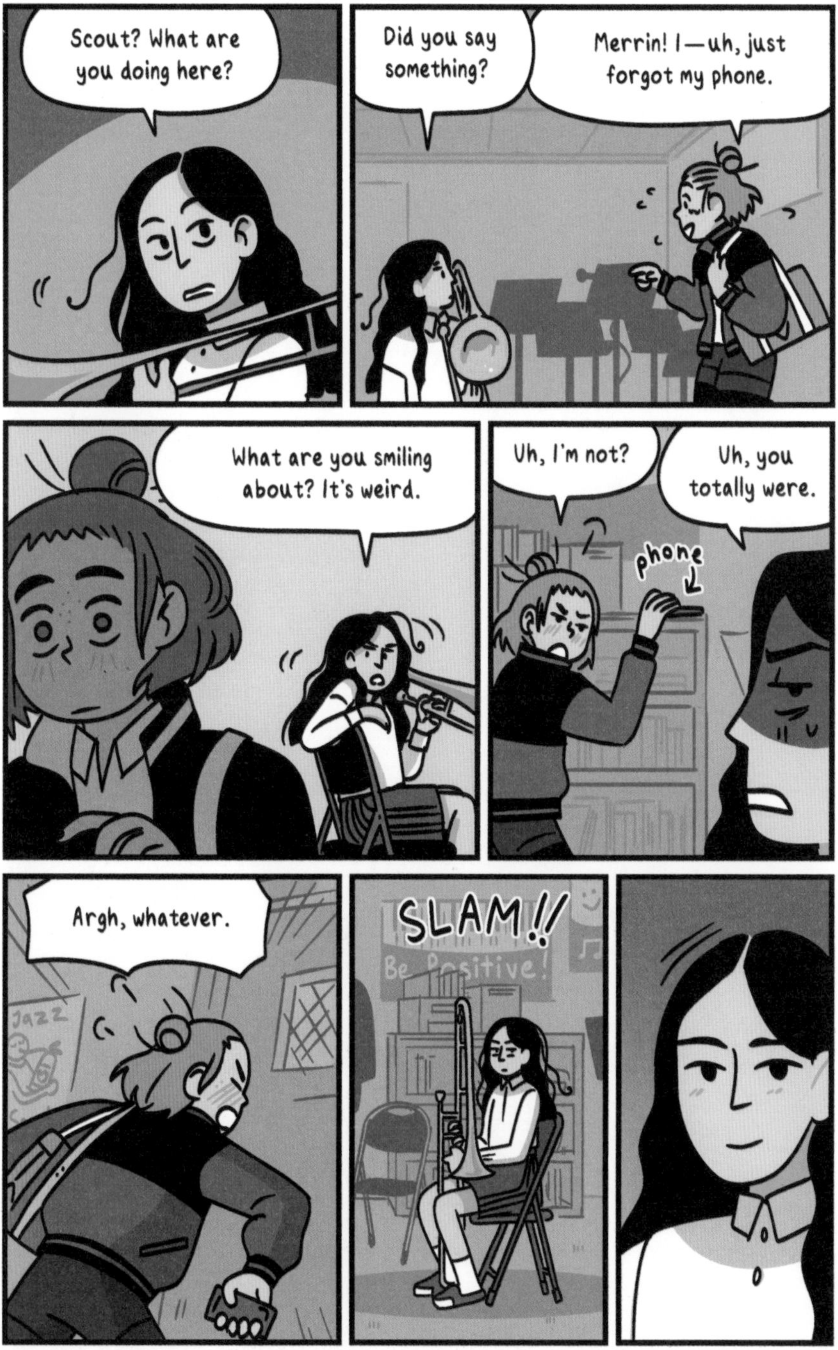
Scout? What are you doing here?
Did you say something?
Merrin! I—uh, just forgot my phone.
What are you smiling about? It's weird.
Uh, I'm not?
phone
Uh, you totally were.
Argh, whatever.
Jazz
SLAM!!

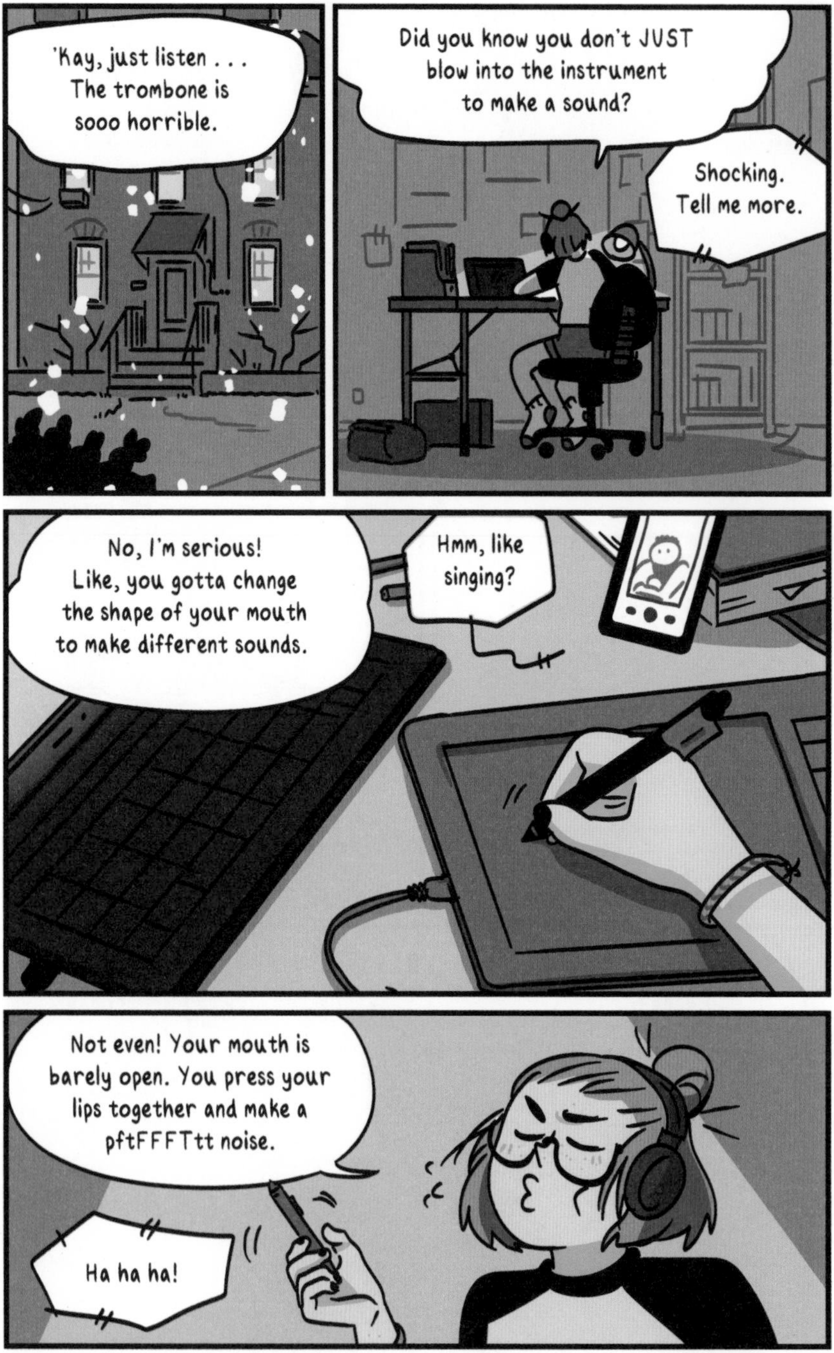
'Kay, just listen . . . The trombone is sooo horrible.
Did you know you don't JUST blow into the instrument to make a sound?
Shocking. Tell me more.
No, I'm serious! Like, you gotta change the shape of your mouth to make different sounds.
Hmm, like singing?
Not even! Your mouth is barely open. You press your lips together and make a pftFFFTtt noise.
Ha ha ha!

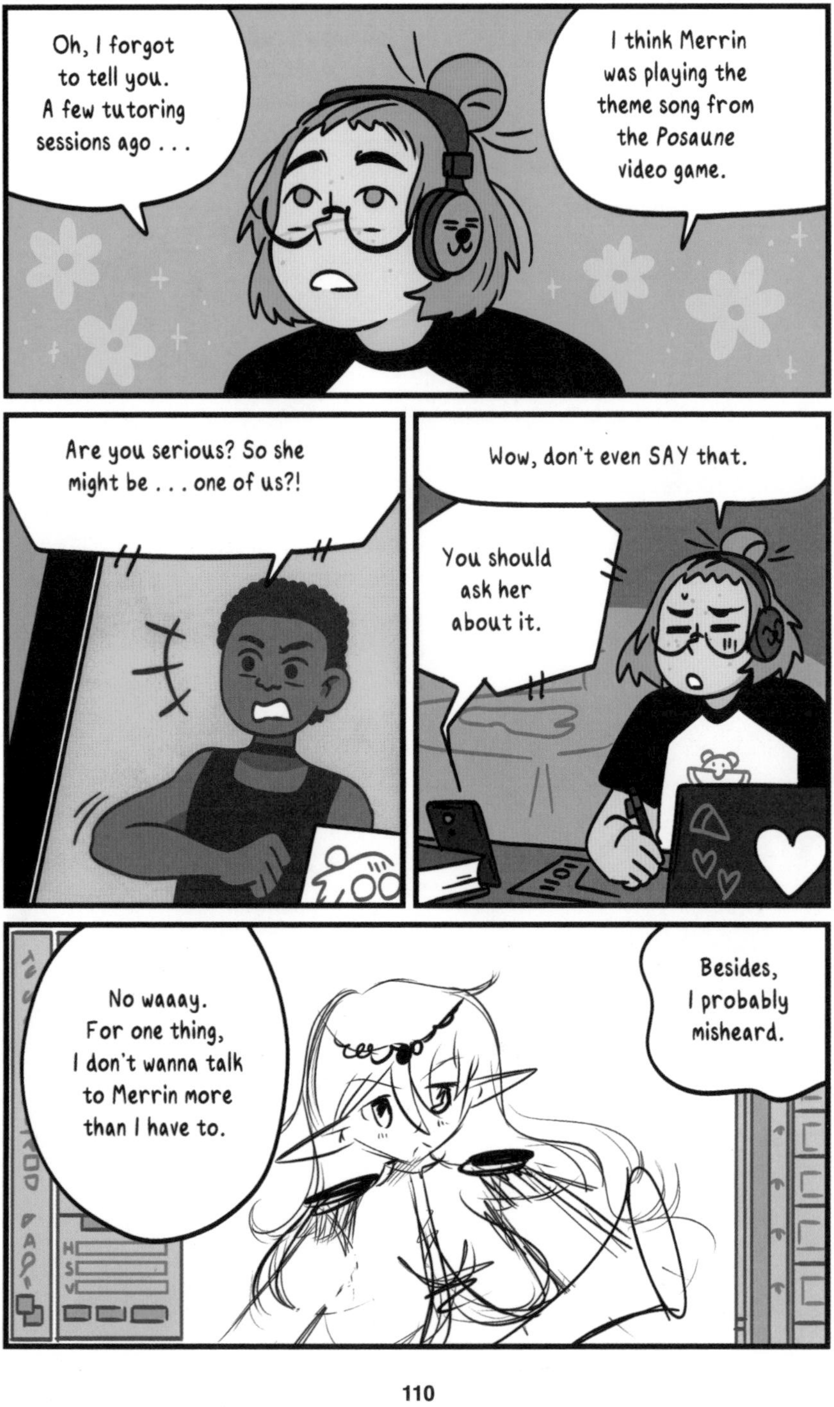
Oh, I forgot to tell you. A few tutoring sessions ago . . .
I think Merrin was playing the theme song from the *Posaune* video game.
Are you serious? So she might be . . . one of us?!
Wow, don't even SAY that.
You should ask her about it.
No waaay. For one thing, I don't wanna talk to Merrin more than I have to.
Besides, I probably misheard.

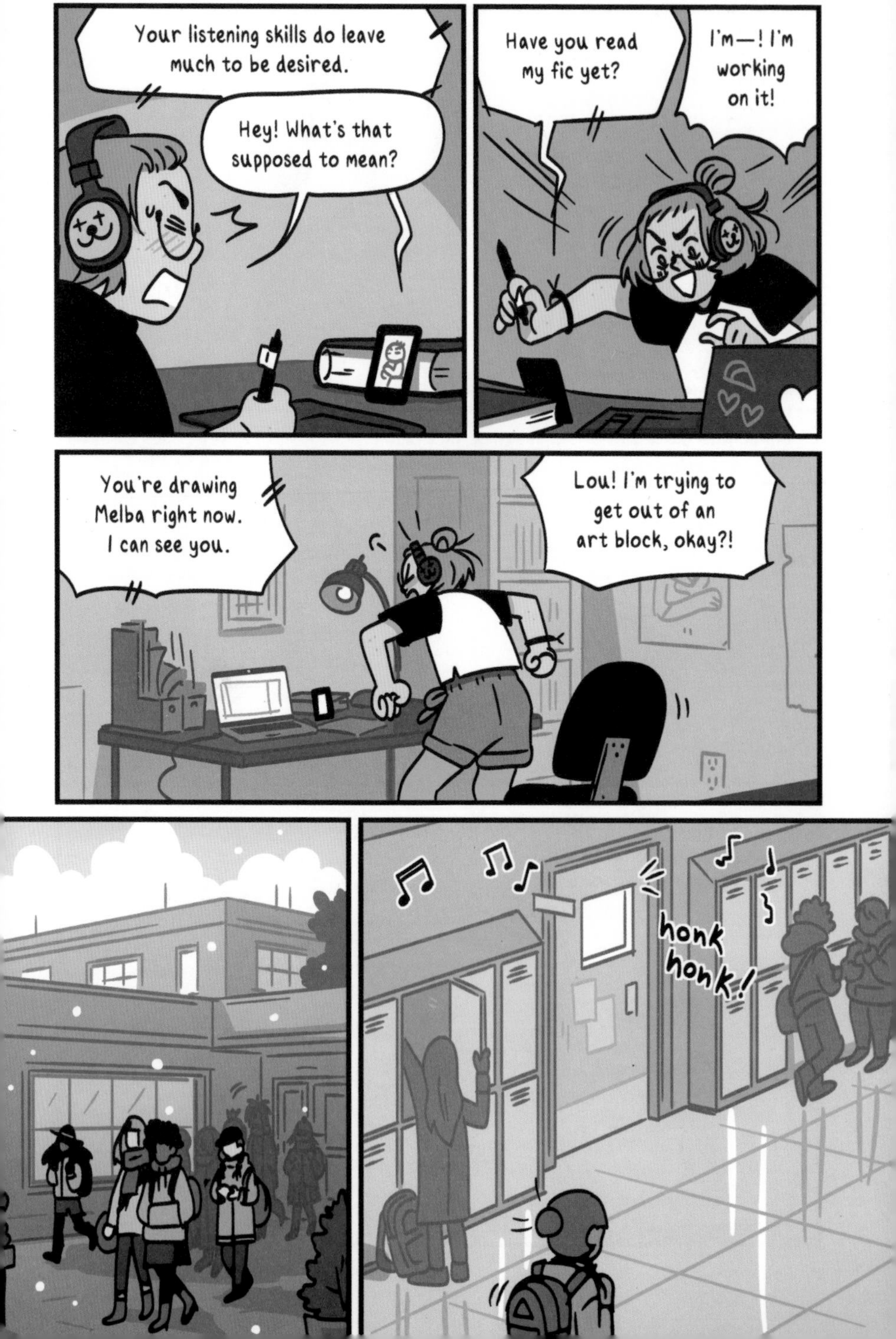
Your listening skills do leave much to be desired.
Hey! What's that supposed to mean?
Have you read my fic yet?
I'm—! I'm working on it!
You're drawing Melba right now. I can see you.
Lou! I'm trying to get out of an art block, okay?!
honk honk!

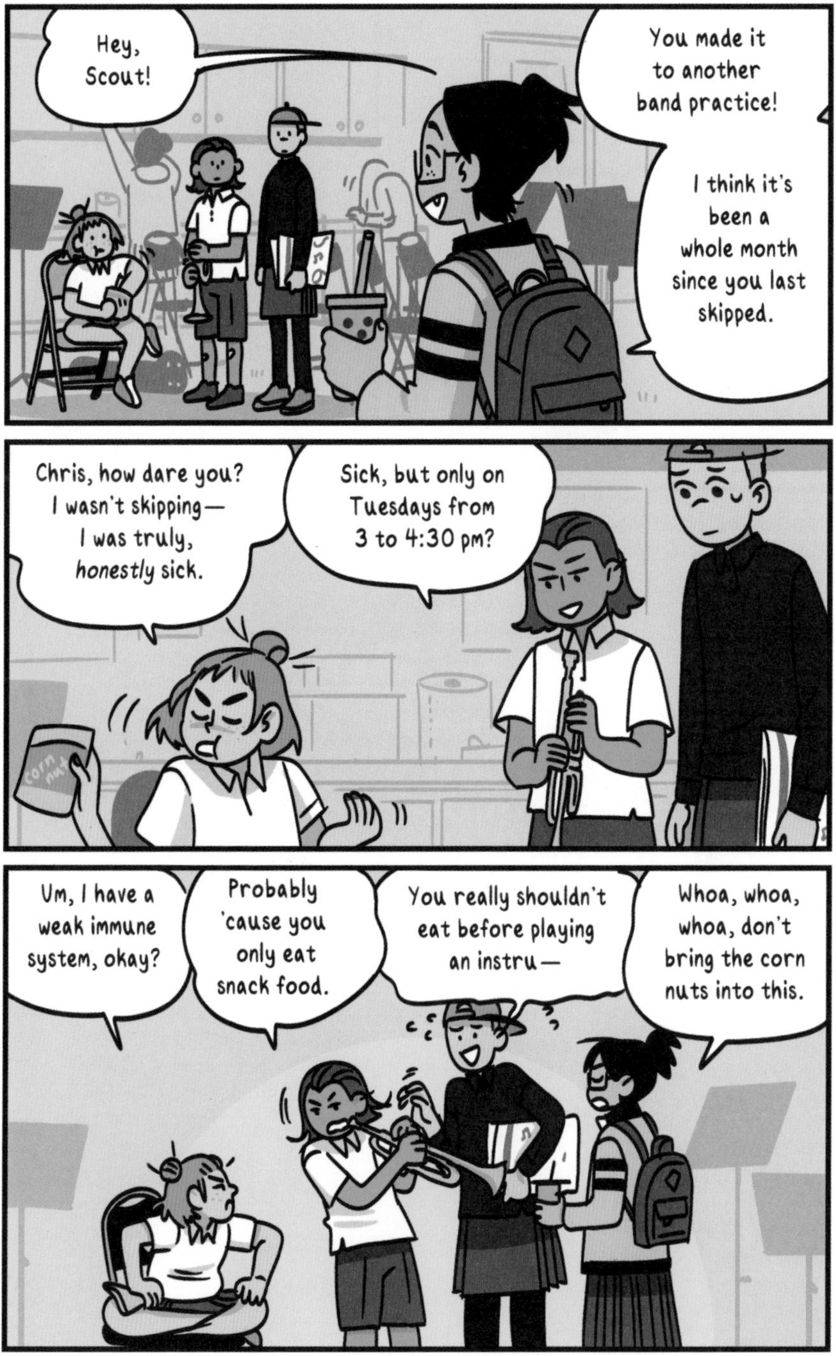
Hey, Scout!
You made it to another band practice!
I think it's been a whole month since you last skipped.
Chris, how dare you? I wasn't skipping— I was truly, *honestly* sick.
Sick, but only on Tuesdays from 3 to 4:30 pm?
corn nuts
Um, I have a weak immune system, okay?
Probably 'cause you only eat snack food.
You really shouldn't eat before playing an instru—
Whoa, whoa, whoa, don't bring the corn nuts into this.

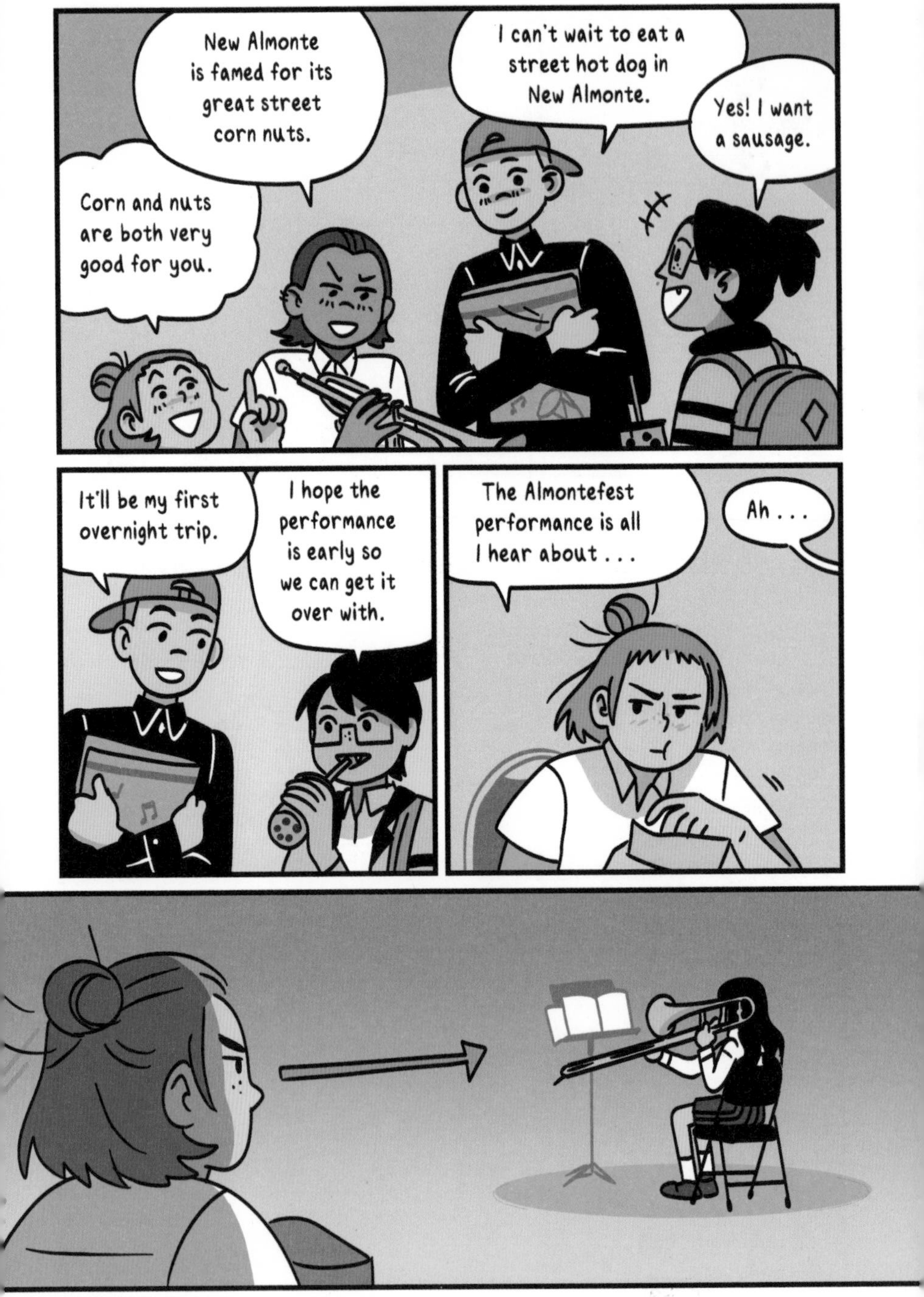

New Almonte is famed for its great street corn nuts.
Corn and nuts are both very good for you.
I can't wait to eat a street hot dog in New Almonte.
Yes! I want a sausage.
It'll be my first overnight trip.
I hope the performance is early so we can get it over with.
The Almontefest performance is all I hear about . . .
Ah . . .

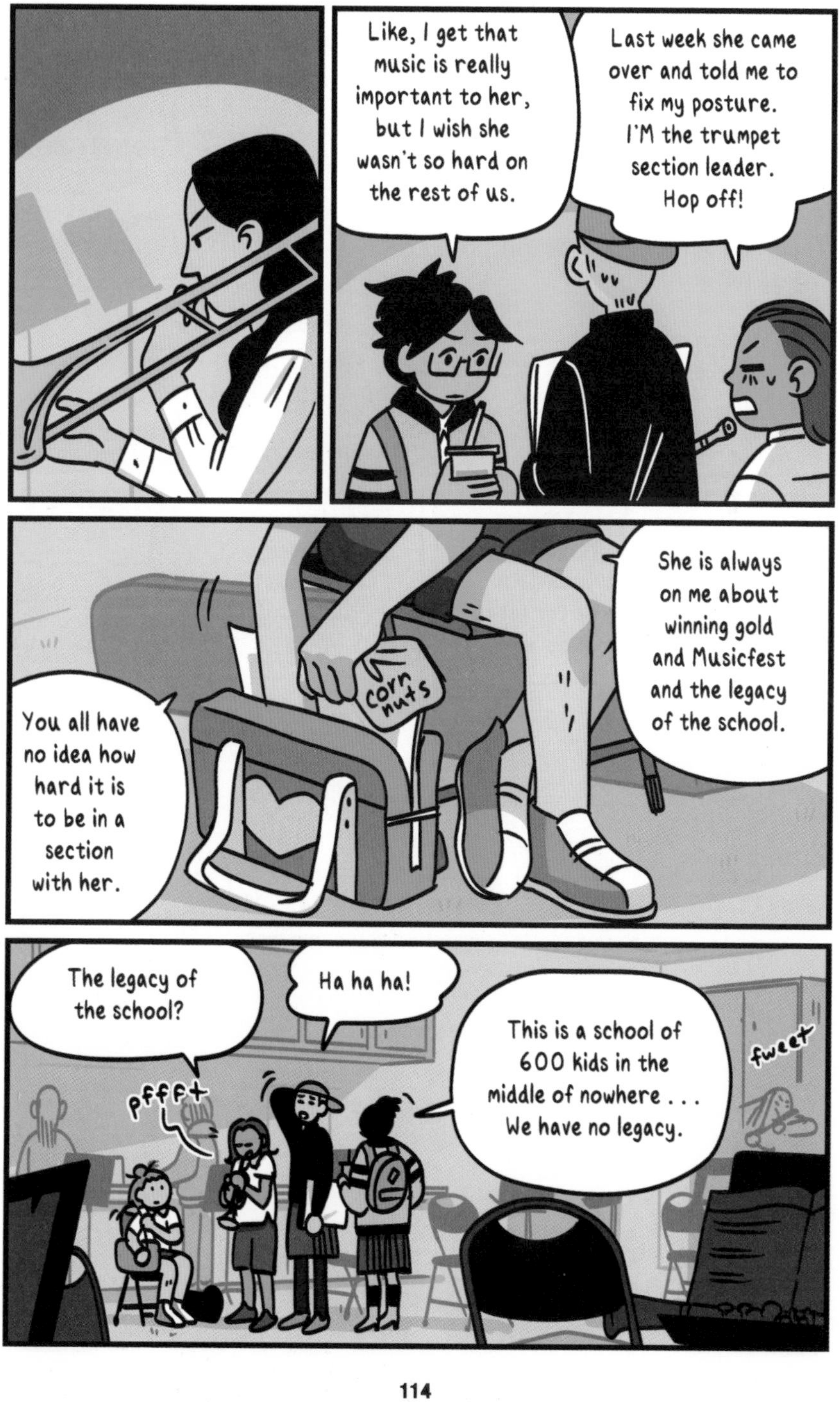
Like, I get that music is really important to her, but I wish she wasn't so hard on the rest of us.
Last week she came over and told me to fix my posture. I'M the trumpet section leader. Hop off!
corn nuts
She is always on me about winning gold and Musicfest and the legacy of the school.
You all have no idea how hard it is to be in a section with her.
The legacy of the school?
Ha ha ha!
pffft
This is a school of 600 kids in the middle of nowhere . . . We have no legacy.
fweet

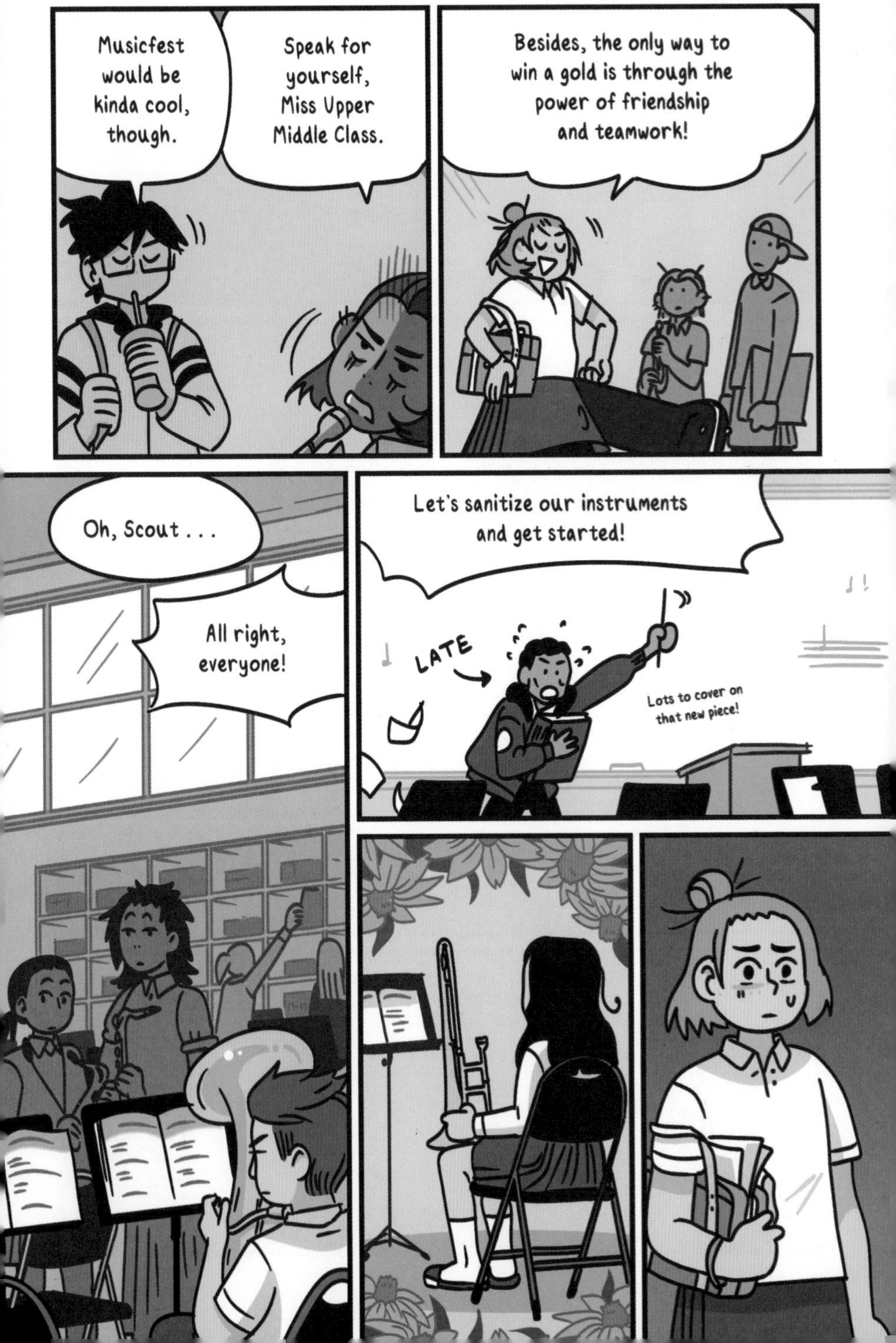
Musicfest would be kinda cool, though.
Speak for yourself, Miss Upper Middle Class.
Besides, the only way to win a gold is through the power of friendship and teamwork!
Oh, Scout . . .
All right, everyone!
Let's sanitize our instruments and get started!
LATE
Lots to cover on that new piece!

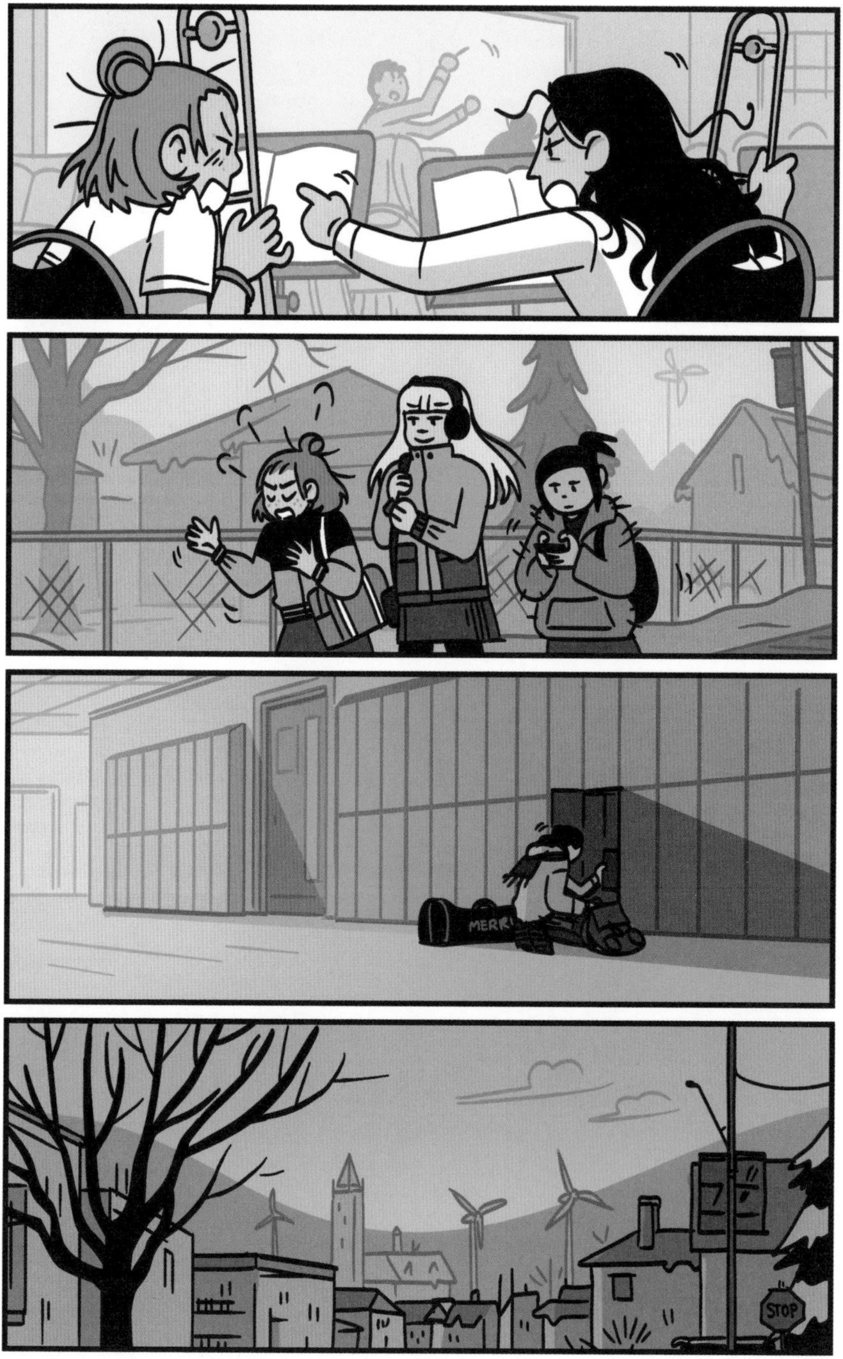
STOP

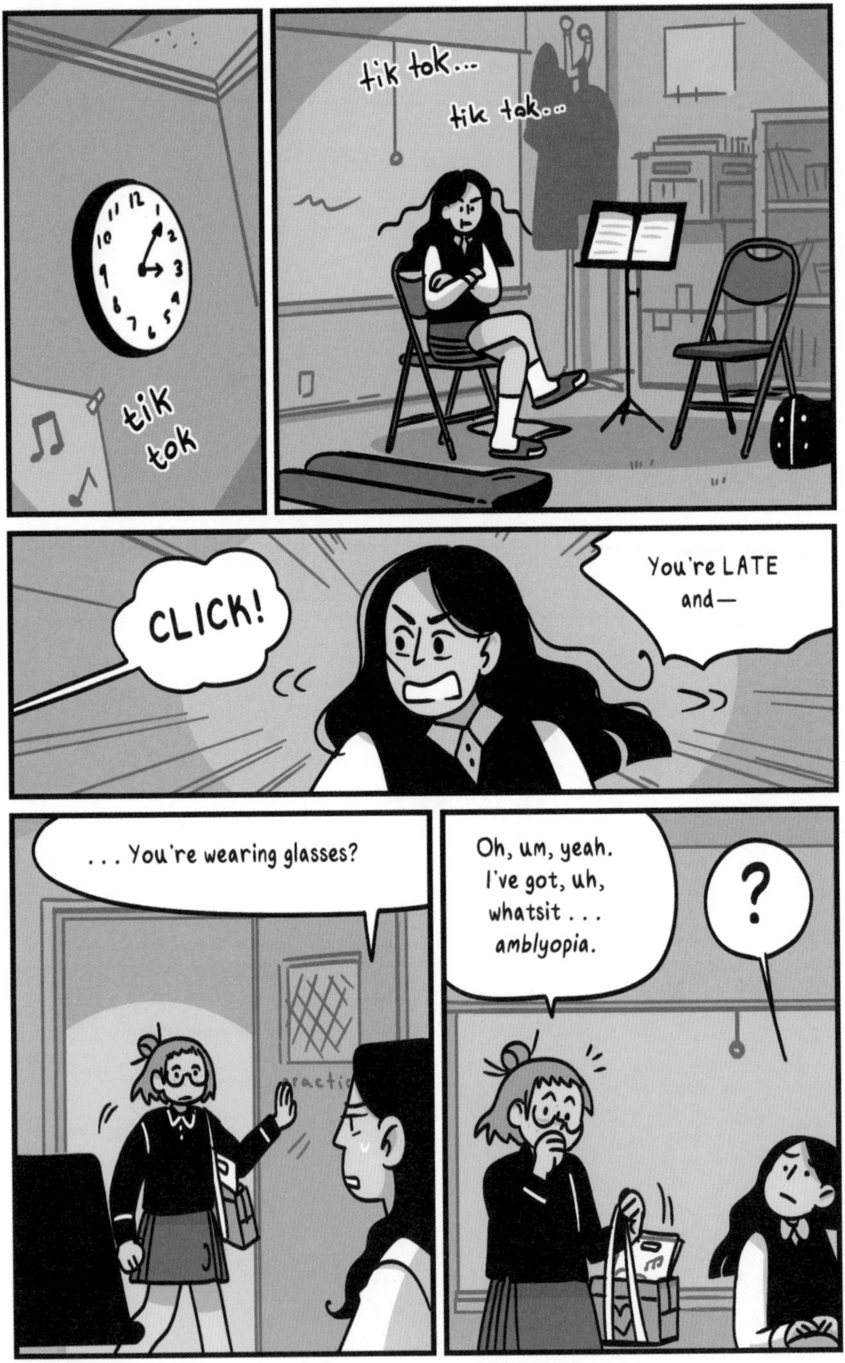
tik tok
tik tok...
tik tok...
CLICK!
You're LATE and—
. . . You're wearing glasses?
Oh, um, yeah. I've got, uh, whatsit . . . amblyopia.
?

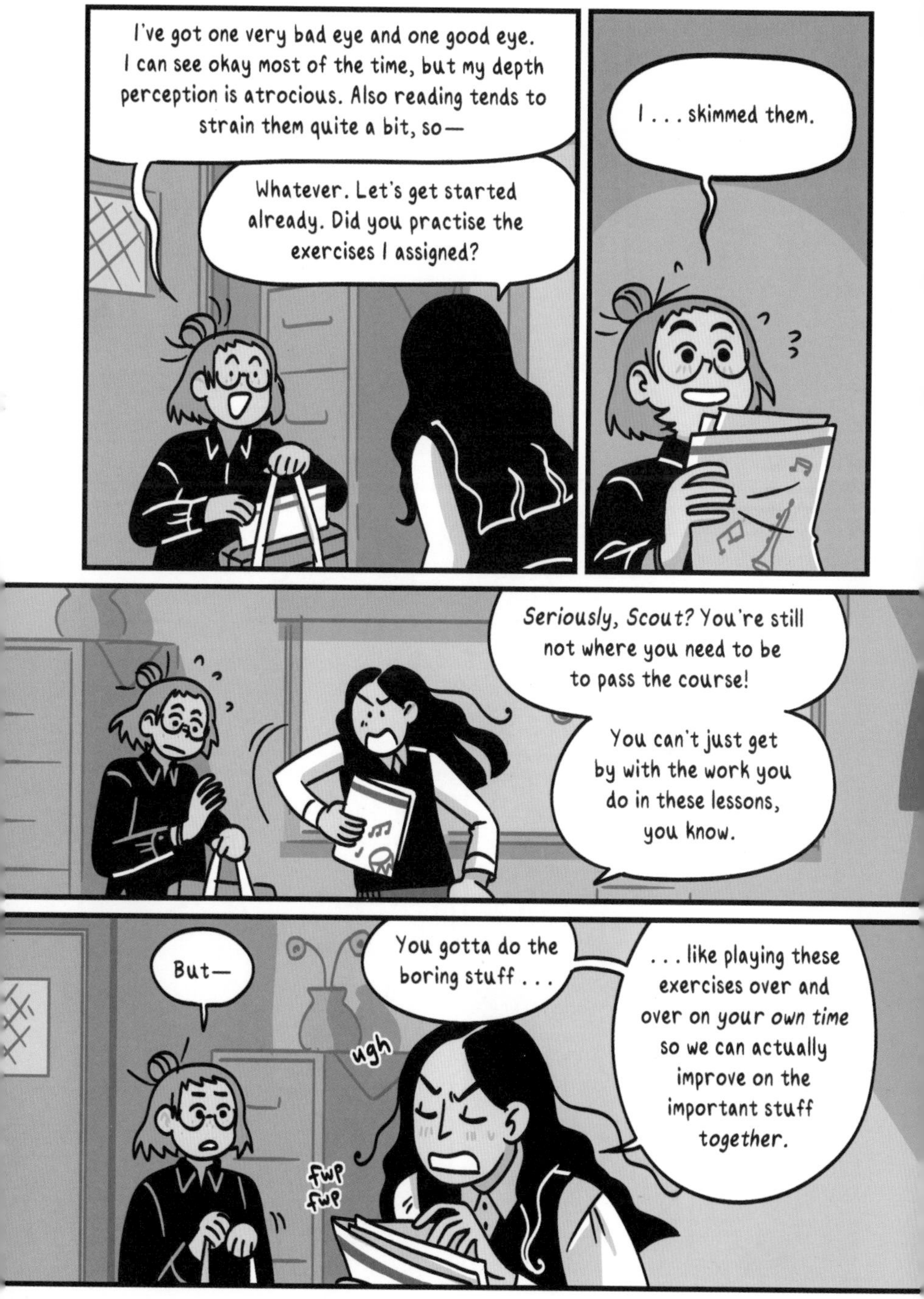

I've got one very bad eye and one good eye. I can see okay most of the time, but my depth perception is atrocious. Also reading tends to strain them quite a bit, so—
Whatever. Let's get started already. Did you practise the exercises I assigned?
I . . . skimmed them.
Seriously, Scout? You're still not where you need to be to pass the course!
You can't just get by with the work you do in these lessons, you know.
But—
You gotta do the boring stuff . . .
. . . like playing these exercises over and over on *your own time* so we can actually improve on the important stuff *together*.
ugh
fwp fwp

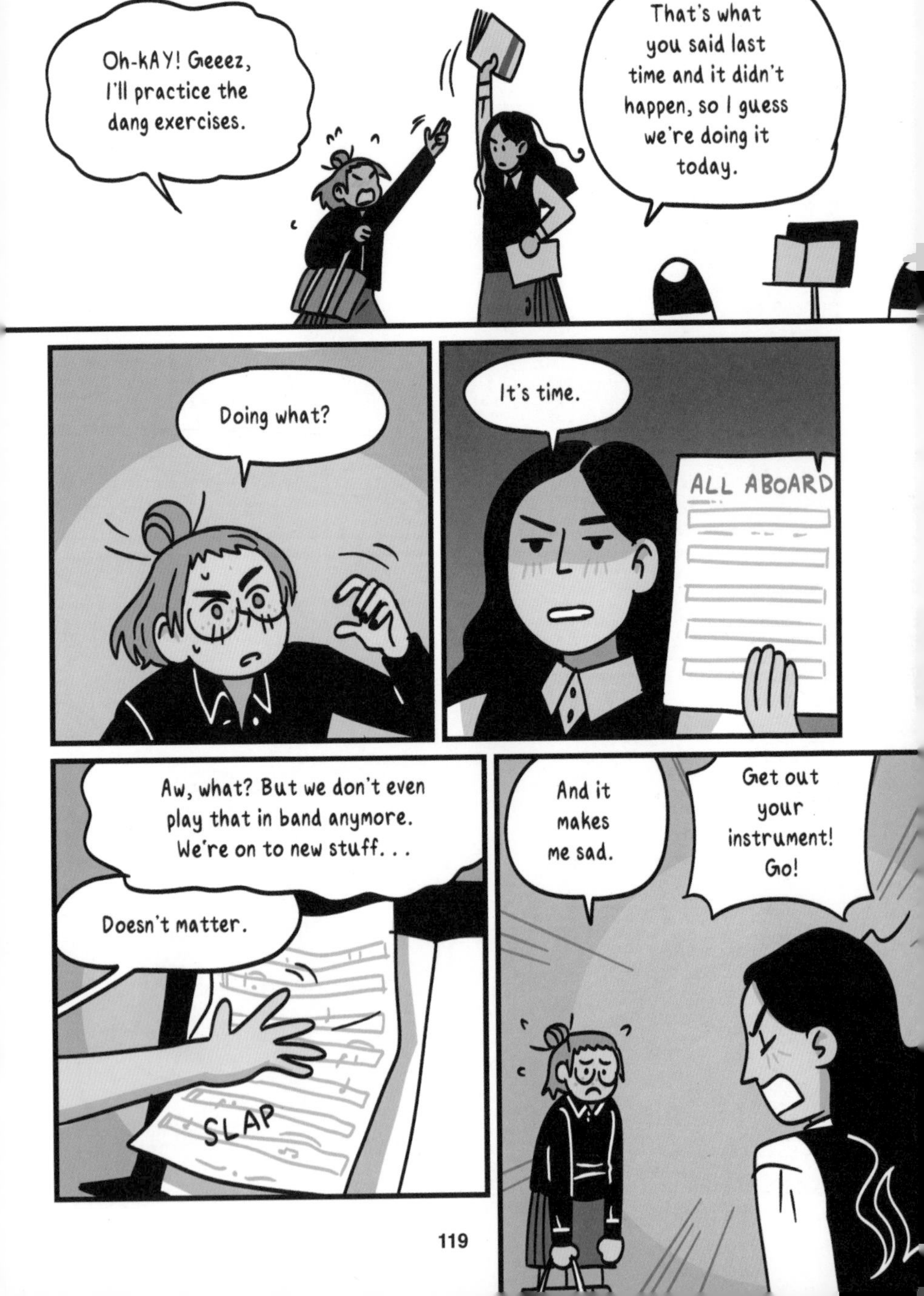
Oh-kAY! Geeez, I'll practice the dang exercises.
That's what you said last time and it didn't happen, so I guess we're doing it today.
Doing what?
It's time.
ALL ABOARD
Aw, what? But we don't even play that in band anymore. We're on to new stuff. . .
Doesn't matter.
SLAP
And it makes me sad.
Get out your instrument! Go!

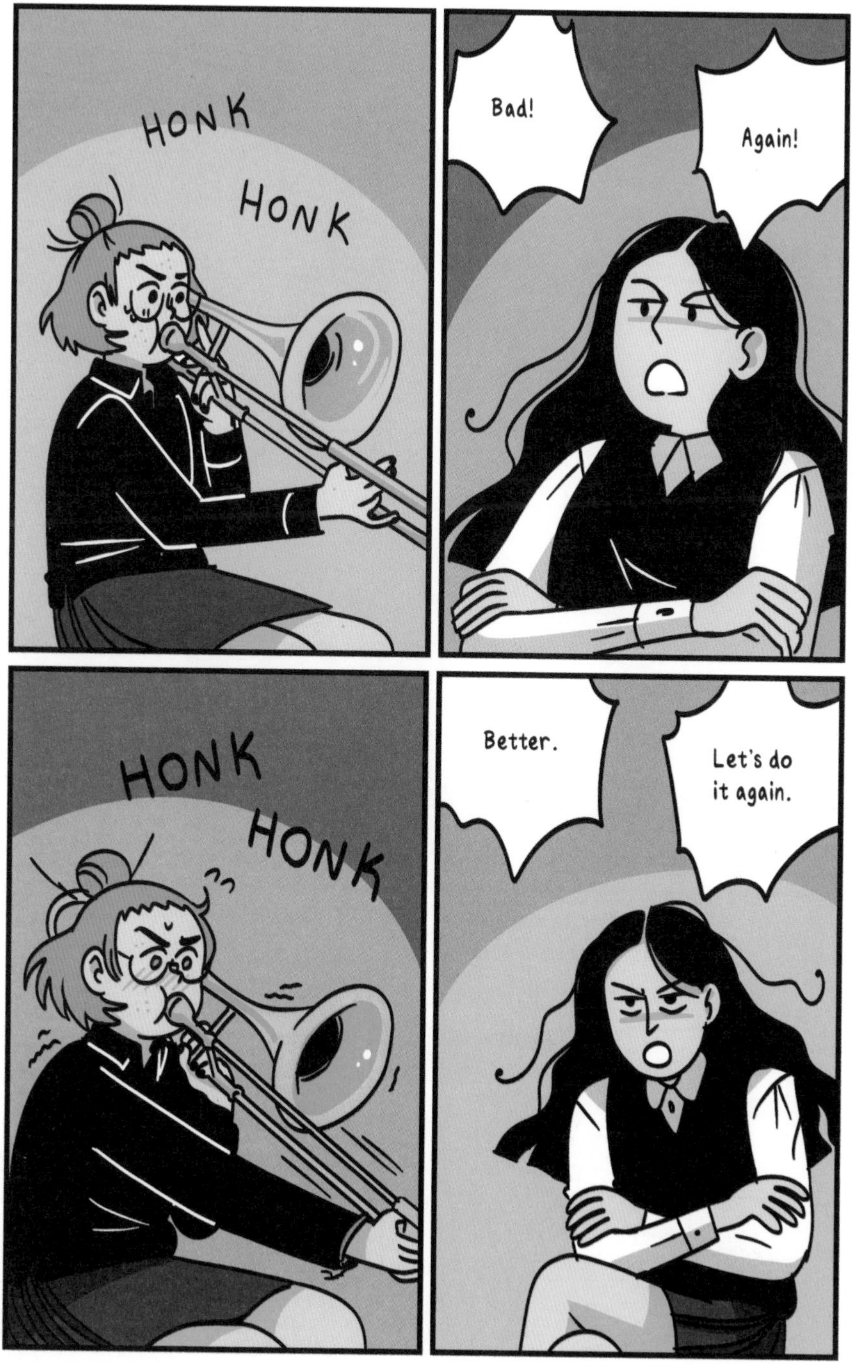
HONK
HONK
Bad!
Again!
HONK
HONK
Better.
Let's do it again.

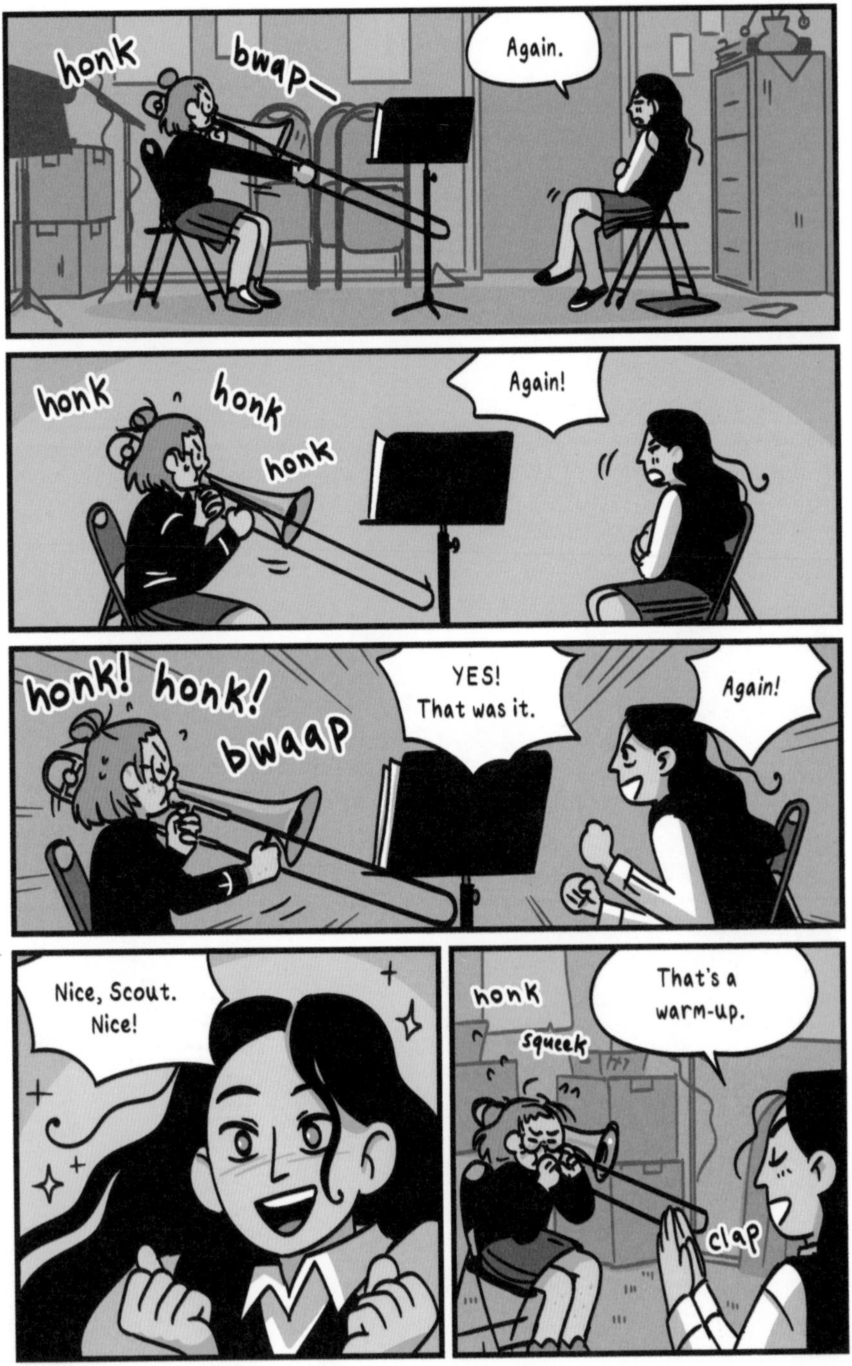
honk
bwap—
Again.
honk
honk
honk
Again!
honk! honk!
bwaap
YES! That was it.
Again!
Nice, Scout. Nice!
honk
squeek
That's a warm-up.
clap

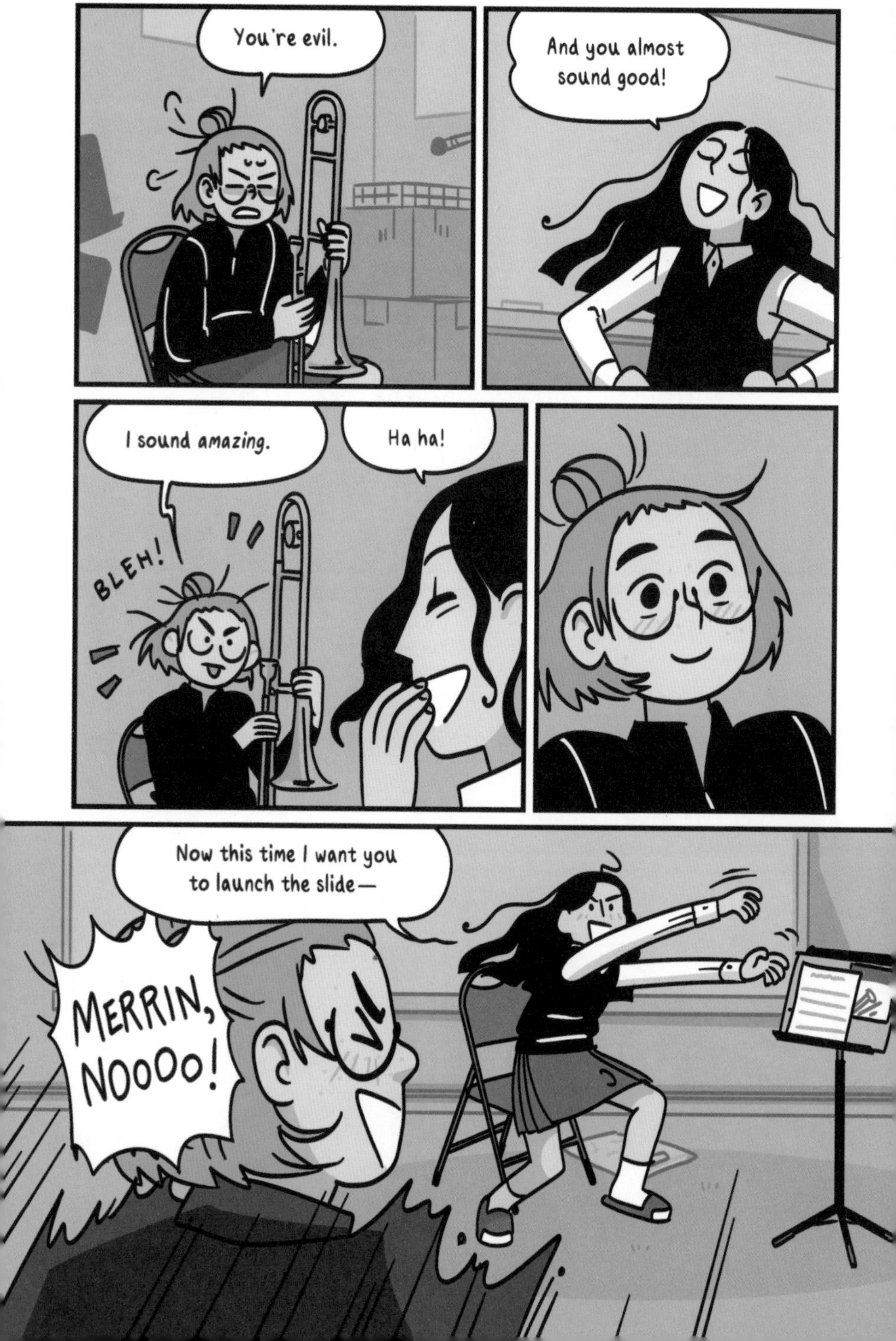

You're evil.
And you almost sound good!
I sound amazing.
BLEH!
Ha ha!
Now this time I want you to launch the slide—
MERRIN, NOOOo!

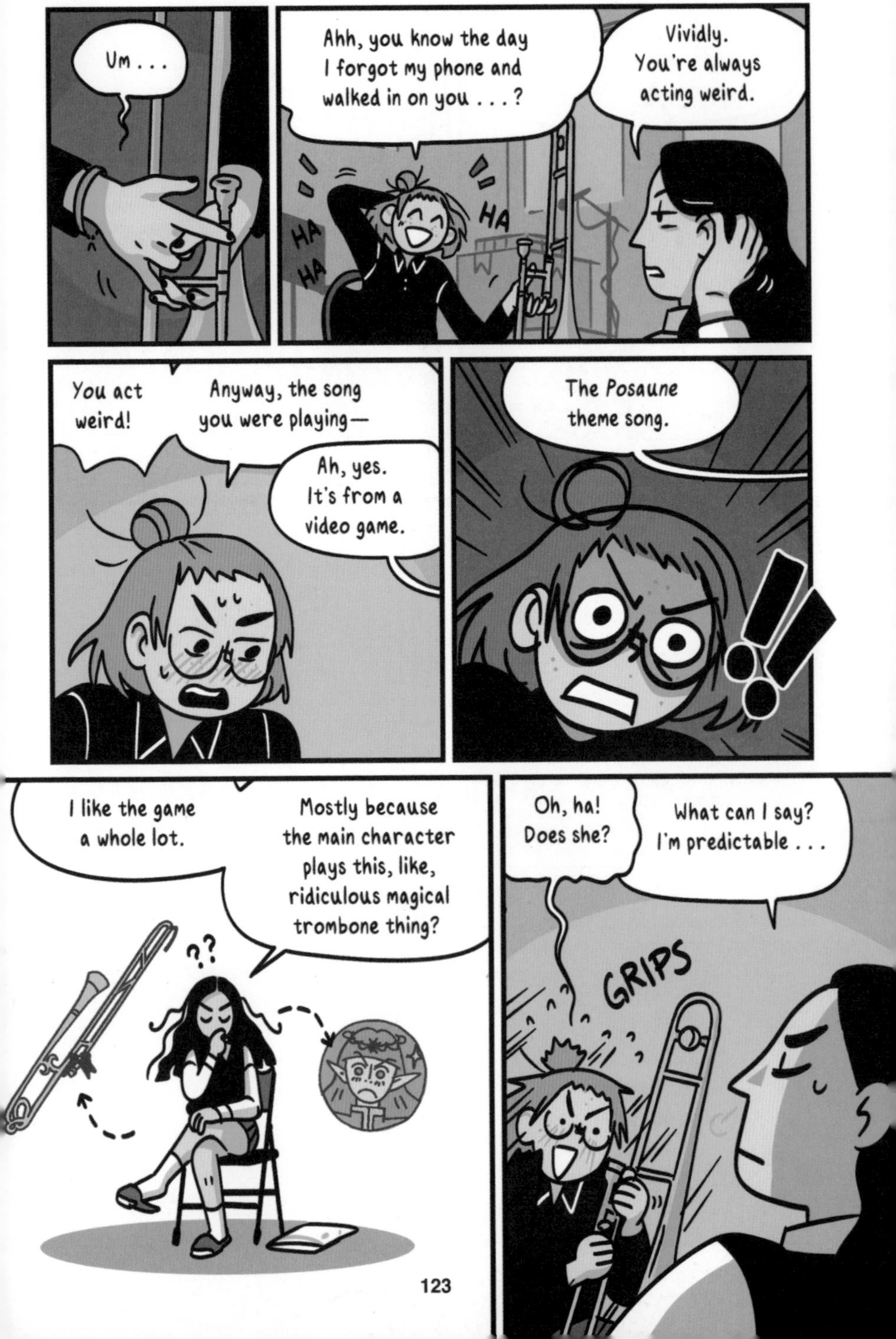

Um . . .
Ahh, you know the day I forgot my phone and walked in on you . . . ?
HA HA HA
Vividly. You're always acting weird.
You act weird!
Anyway, the song you were playing—
Ah, yes. It's from a video game.
The *Posaune* theme song.
I like the game a whole lot.
Mostly because the main character plays this, like, ridiculous magical trombone thing?
??
Oh, ha! Does she?
What can I say? I'm predictable . . .
GRIPS

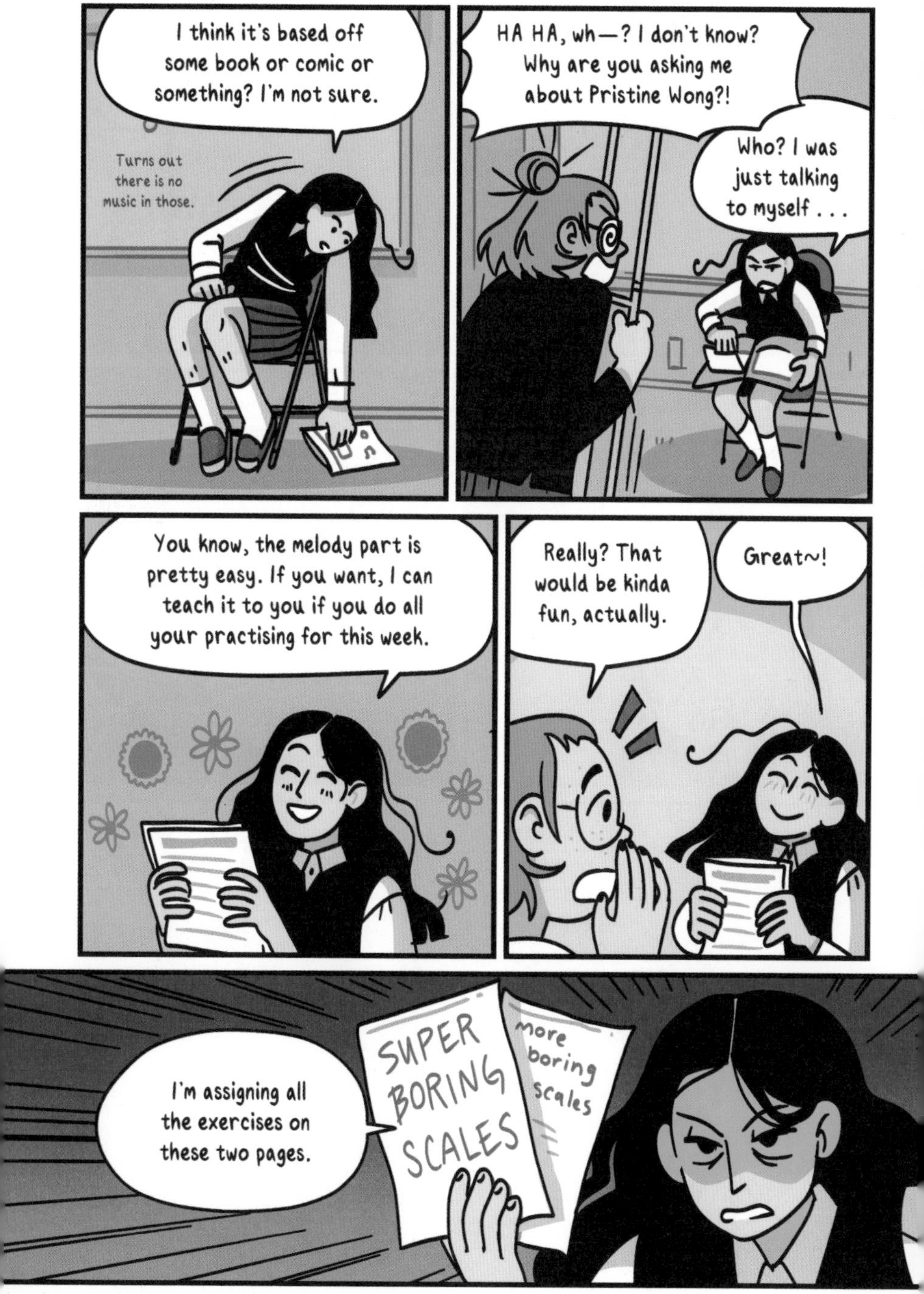

I think it's based off some book or comic or something? I'm not sure.
Turns out there is no music in those.
HA HA, wh—? I don't know? Why are you asking me about Pristine Wong?!
Who? I was just talking to myself . . .
You know, the melody part is pretty easy. If you want, I can teach it to you if you do all your practising for this week.
Really? That would be kinda fun, actually.
Great~!
I'm assigning all the exercises on these two pages.
SUPER BORING SCALES
more boring scales

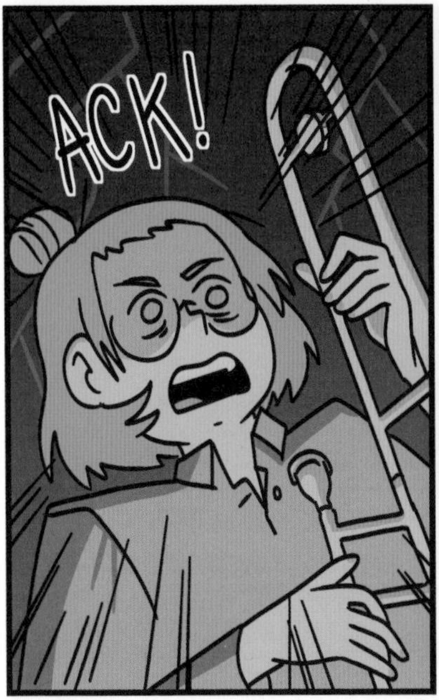
ACK!

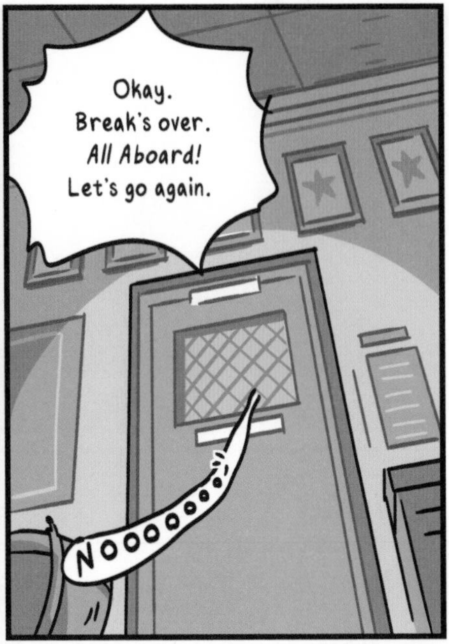
Okay.
Break's over.
All Aboard!
Let's go again.
NOOOOOOO!

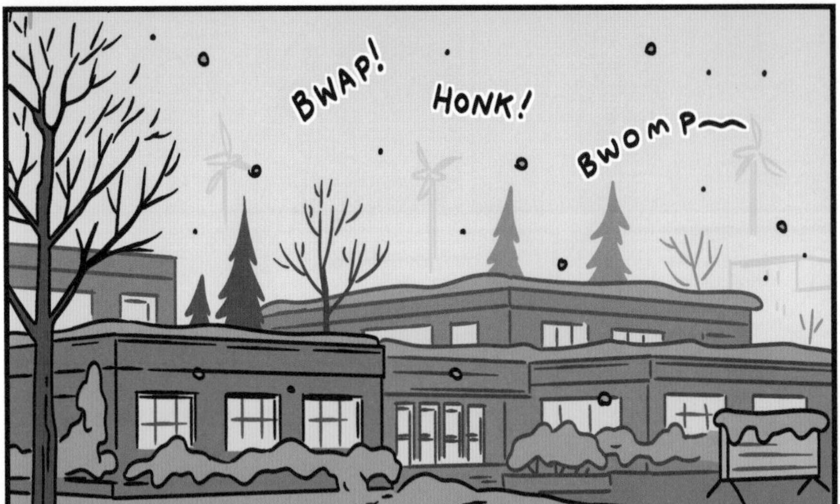
BWAP!
HONK!
BWOMP~~

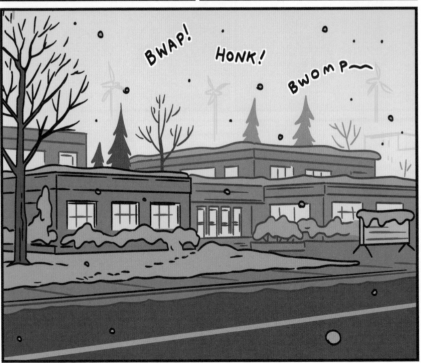

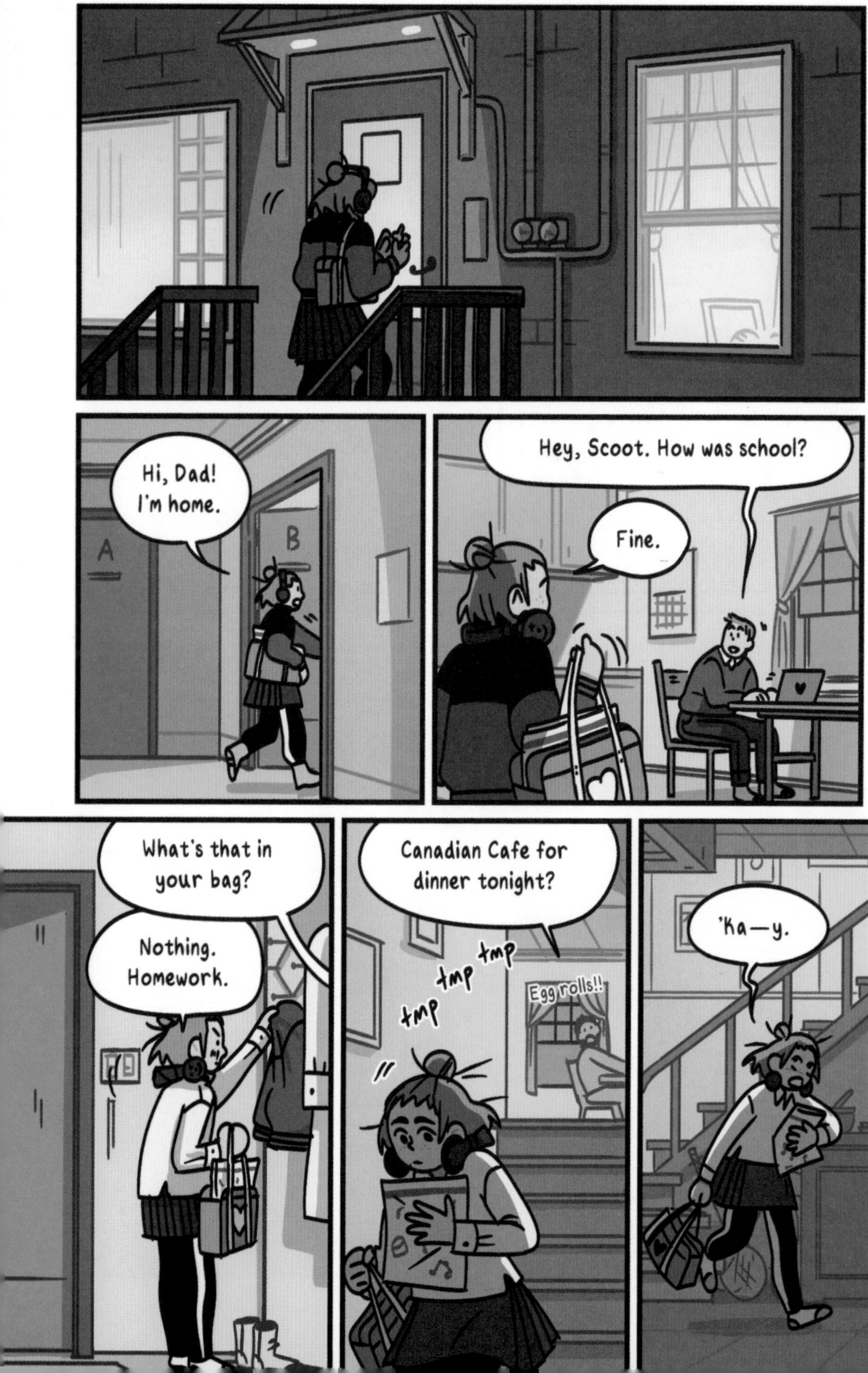

Hi, Dad! I'm home.
A
B
Hey, Scoot. How was school?
Fine.
What's that in your bag?
Nothing. Homework.
Canadian Cafe for dinner tonight?
tmp tmp tmp
Egg rolls!!
'Ka—y.

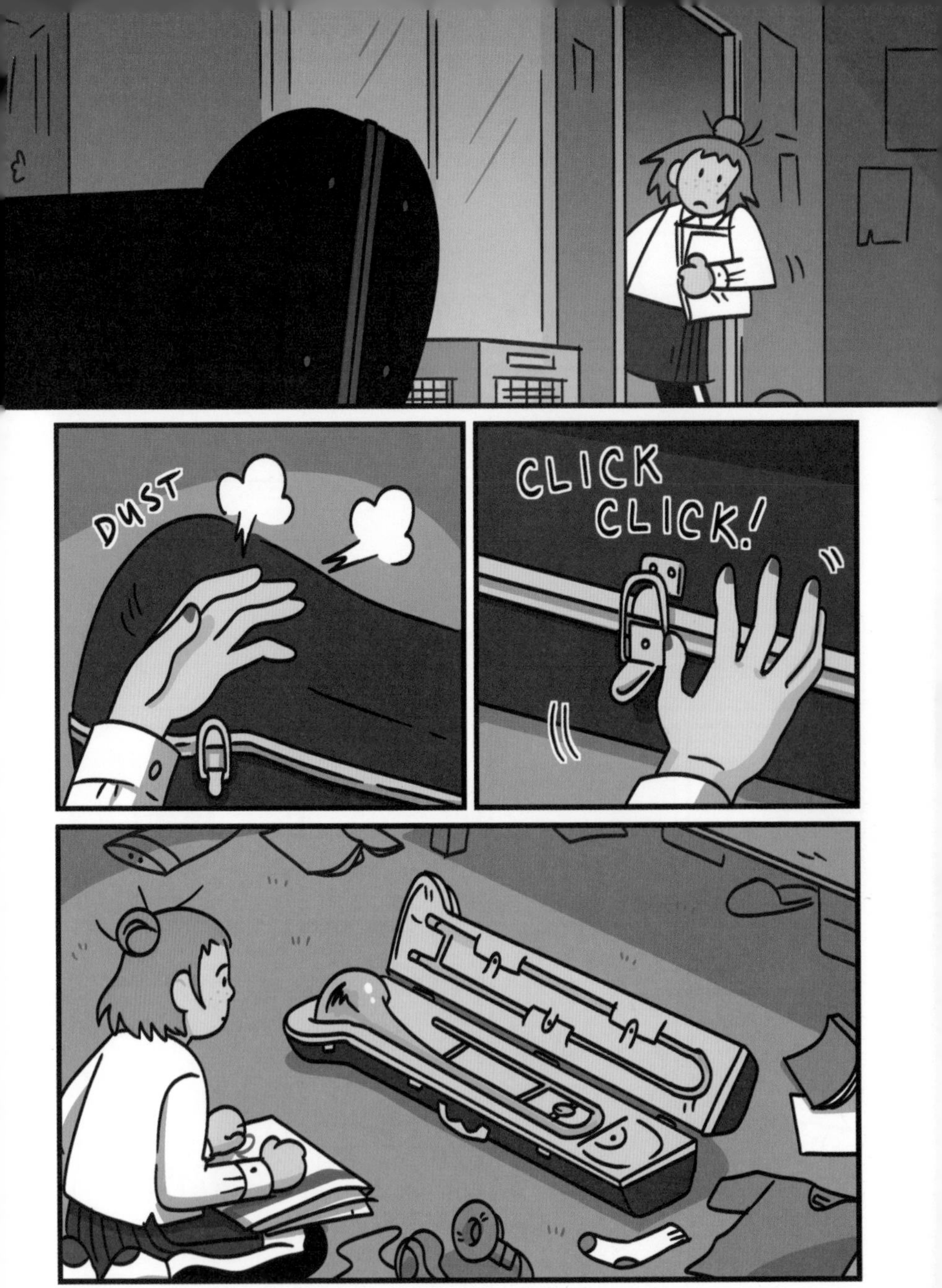
DUST
CLICK
CLICK!

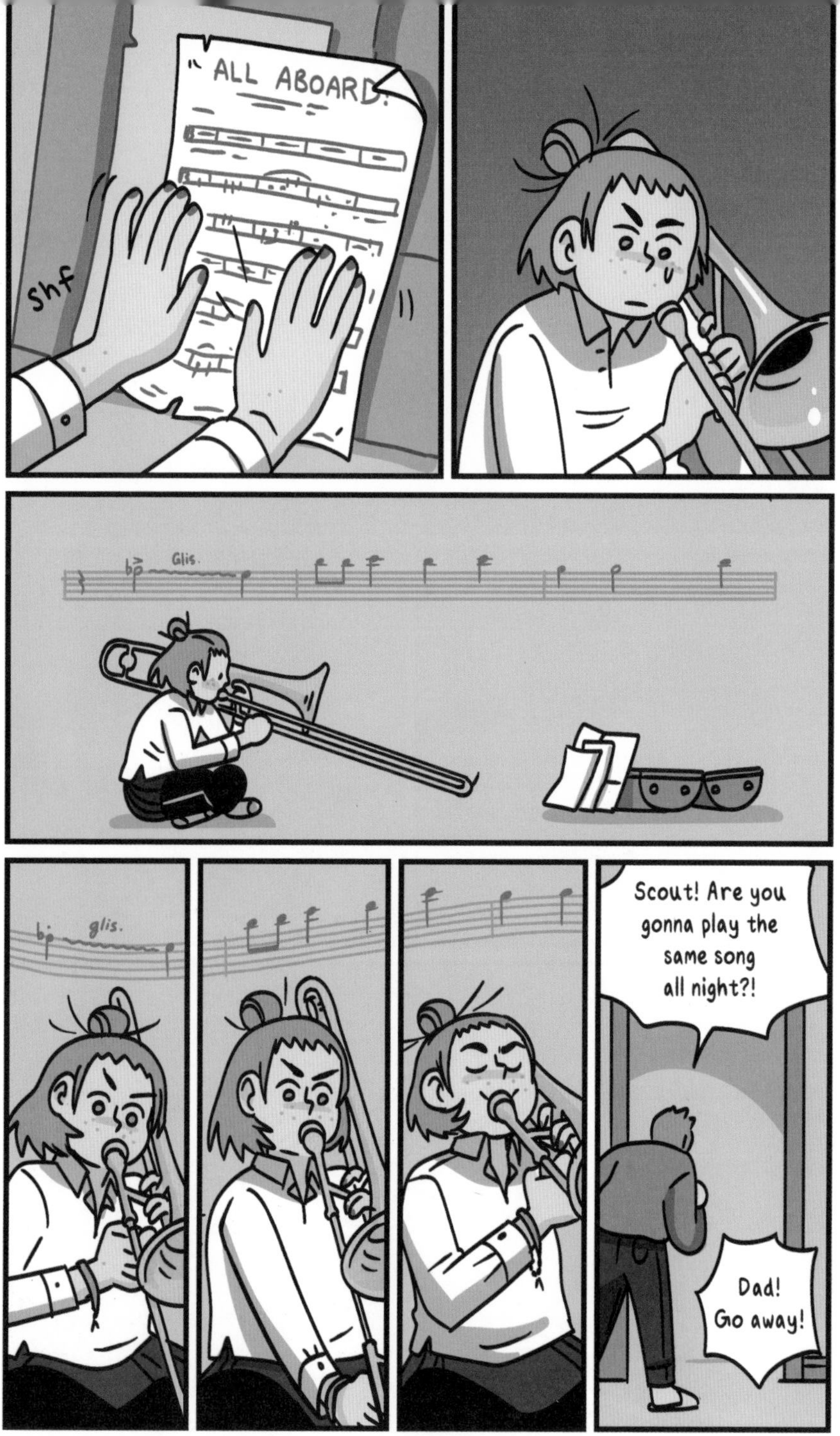
"ALL ABOARD"
Shf
Glis.
glis.
Scout! Are you gonna play the same song all night?!
Dad! Go away!

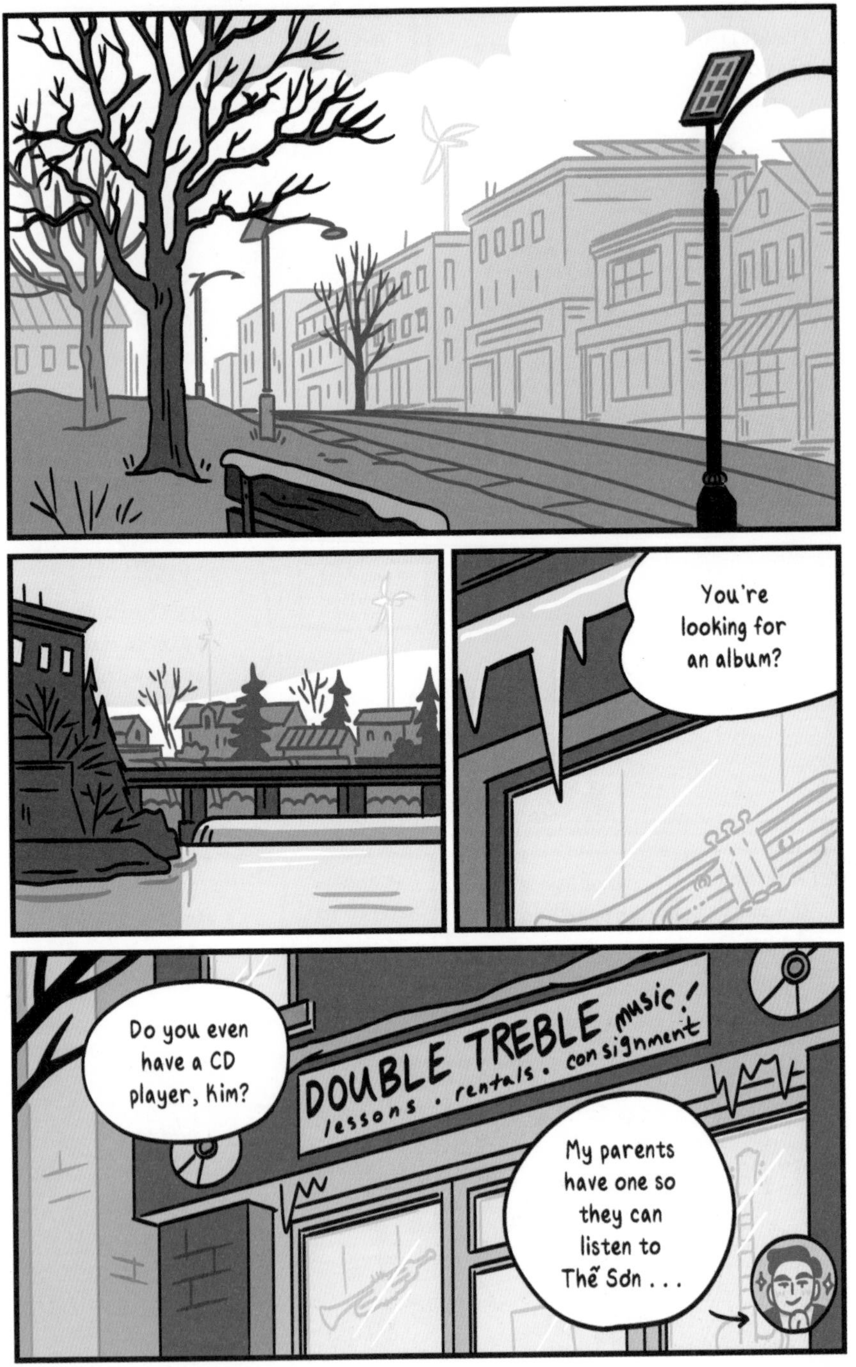
You're looking for an album?
Do you even have a CD player, Kim?
DOUBLE TREBLE music!
lessons . rentals . consignment
My parents have one so they can listen to Thế Sơn . . .

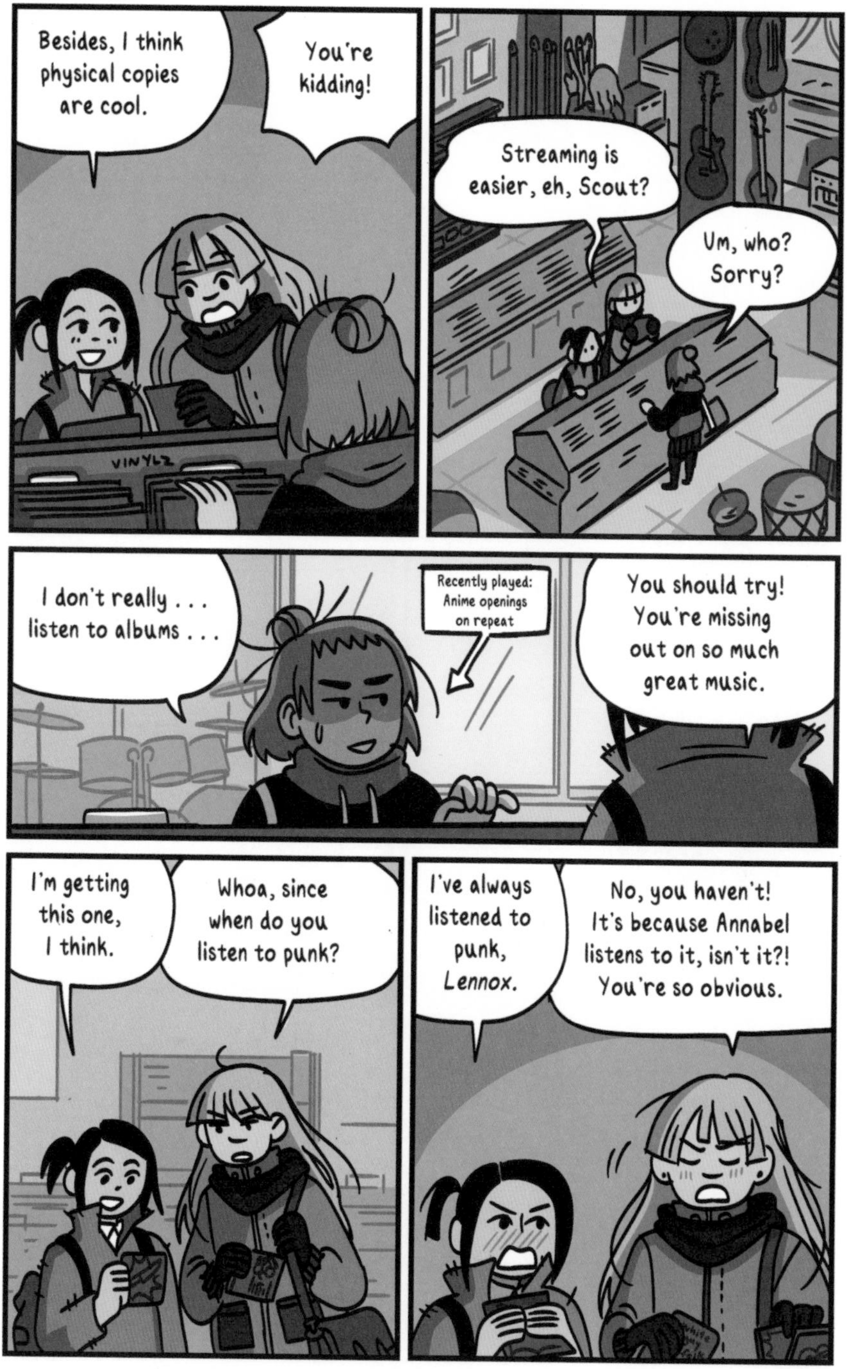
Besides, I think physical copies are cool.
You're kidding!
VINYLZ
Streaming is easier, eh, Scout?
Um, who? Sorry?
I don't really . . . listen to albums . . .
Recently played: Anime openings on repeat
You should try! You're missing out on so much great music.
I'm getting this one, I think.
Whoa, since when do you listen to punk?
I've always listened to punk, *Lennox.*
No, you haven't! It's because Annabel listens to it, isn't it?! You're so obvious.

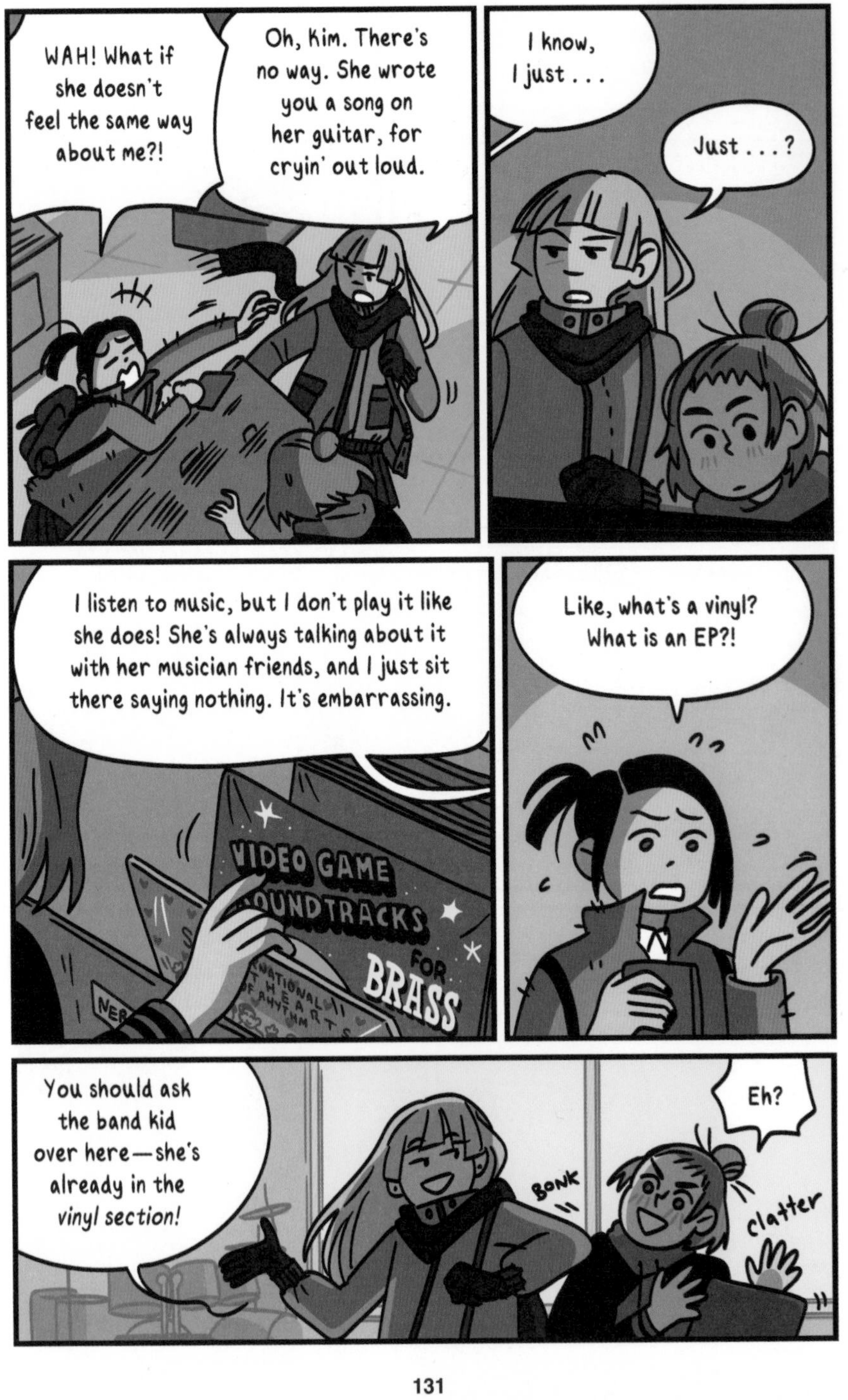
WAH! What if she doesn't feel the same way about me?!
Oh, Kim. There's no way. She wrote you a song on her guitar, for cryin' out loud.
I know, I just . . .
Just . . . ?
I listen to music, but I don't play it like she does! She's always talking about it with her musician friends, and I just sit there saying nothing. It's embarrassing.
VIDEO GAME
FOR BRASS
Like, what's a vinyl? What is an EP?!
You should ask the band kid over here—she's already in the *vinyl section!*
Eh?
BONK
clatter

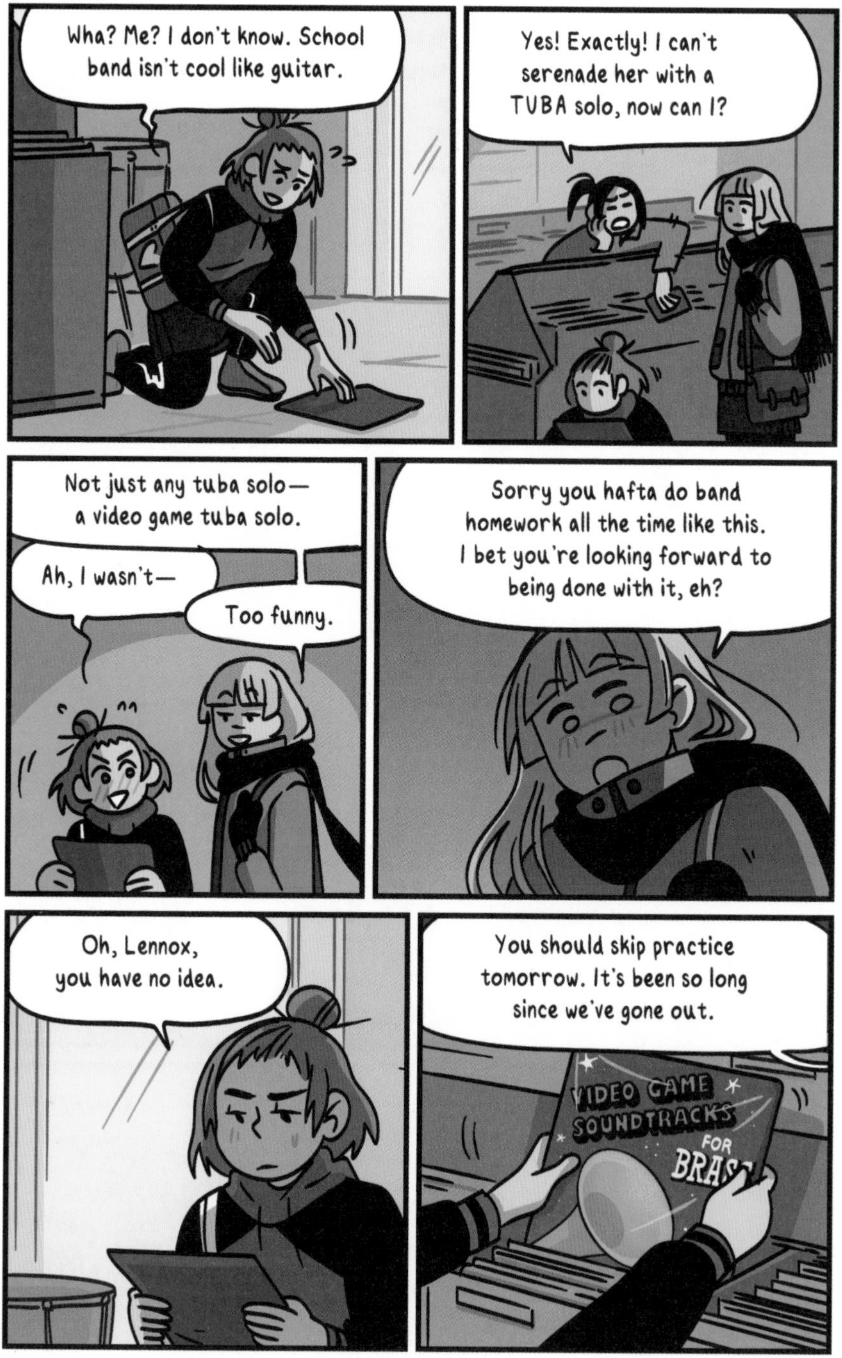
Wha? Me? I don't know. School band isn't cool like guitar.
Yes! Exactly! I can't serenade her with a TUBA solo, now can I?
Not just any tuba solo— a video game tuba solo.
Ah, I wasn't—
Too funny.
Sorry you hafta do band homework all the time like this. I bet you're looking forward to being done with it, eh?
Oh, Lennox, you have no idea.
You should skip practice tomorrow. It's been so long since we've gone out.
VIDEO GAME SOUNDTRACKS FOR

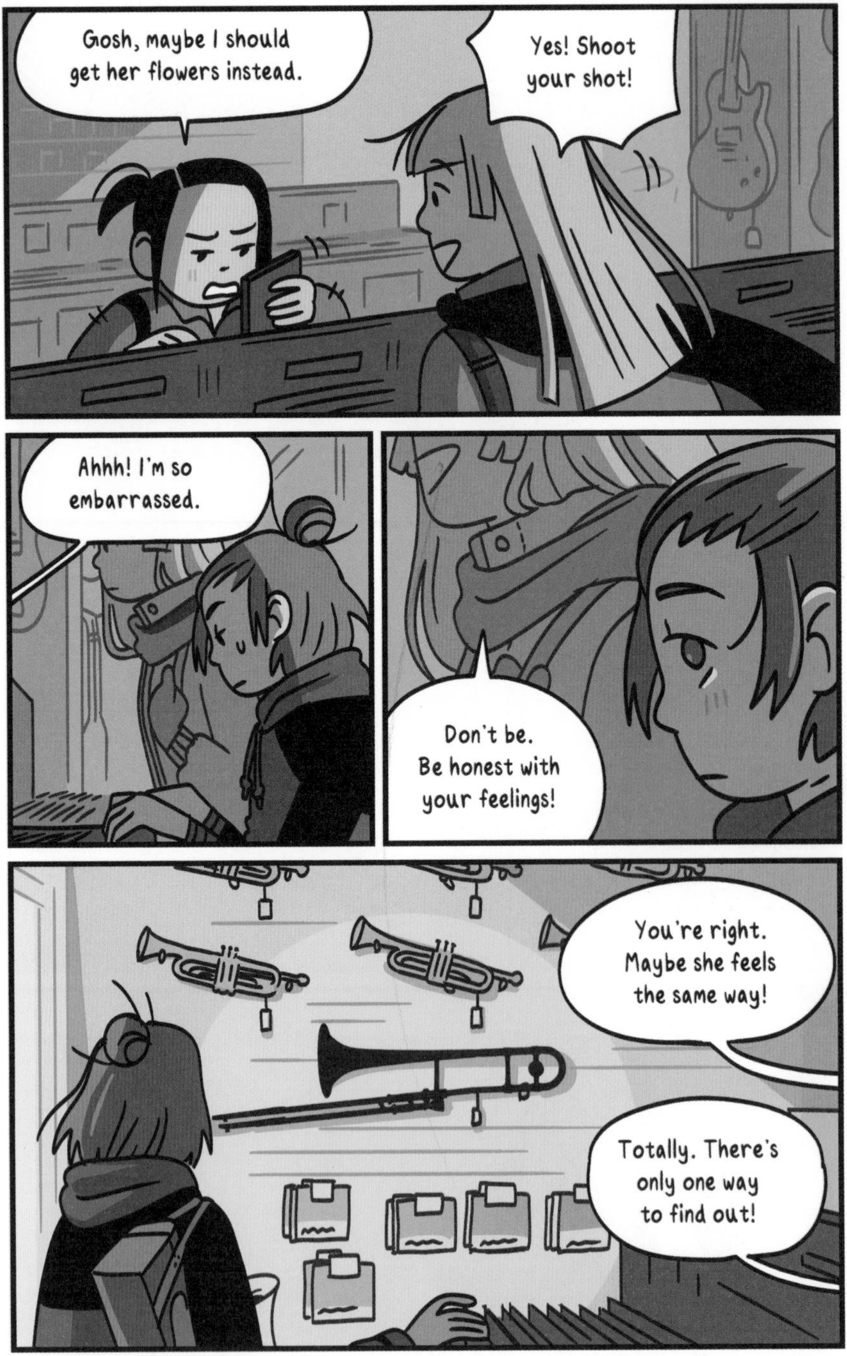
Gosh, maybe I should get her flowers instead.
Yes! Shoot your shot!
Ahhh! I'm so embarrassed.
Don't be. Be honest with your feelings!
You're right. Maybe she feels the same way!
Totally. There's only one way to find out!

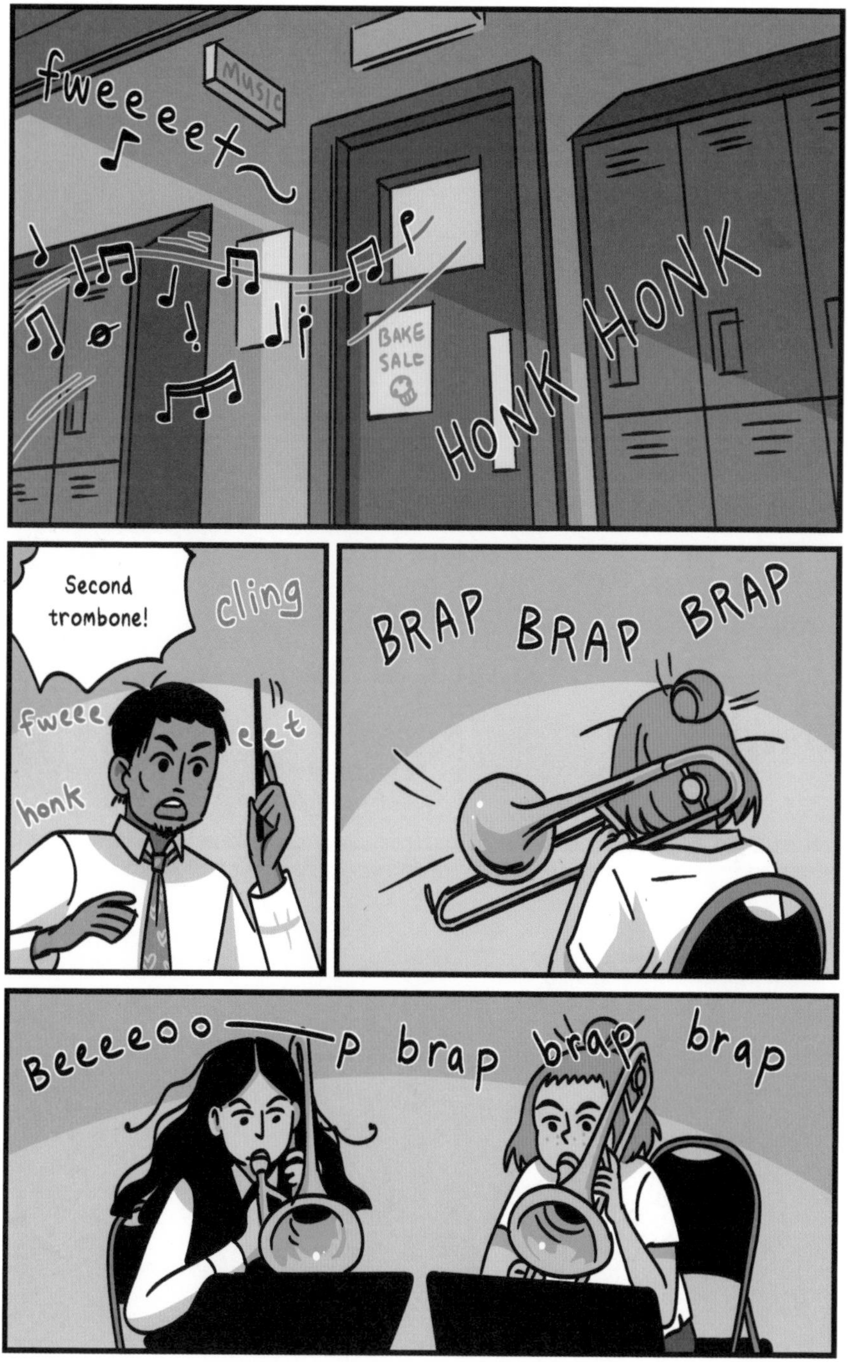
fweeeet~
MUSIC
HONK HONK
BAKE SALE
Second trombone!
cling
fweee
eet
honk
BRAP BRAP BRAP
Beeeeoo—p brap brap brap

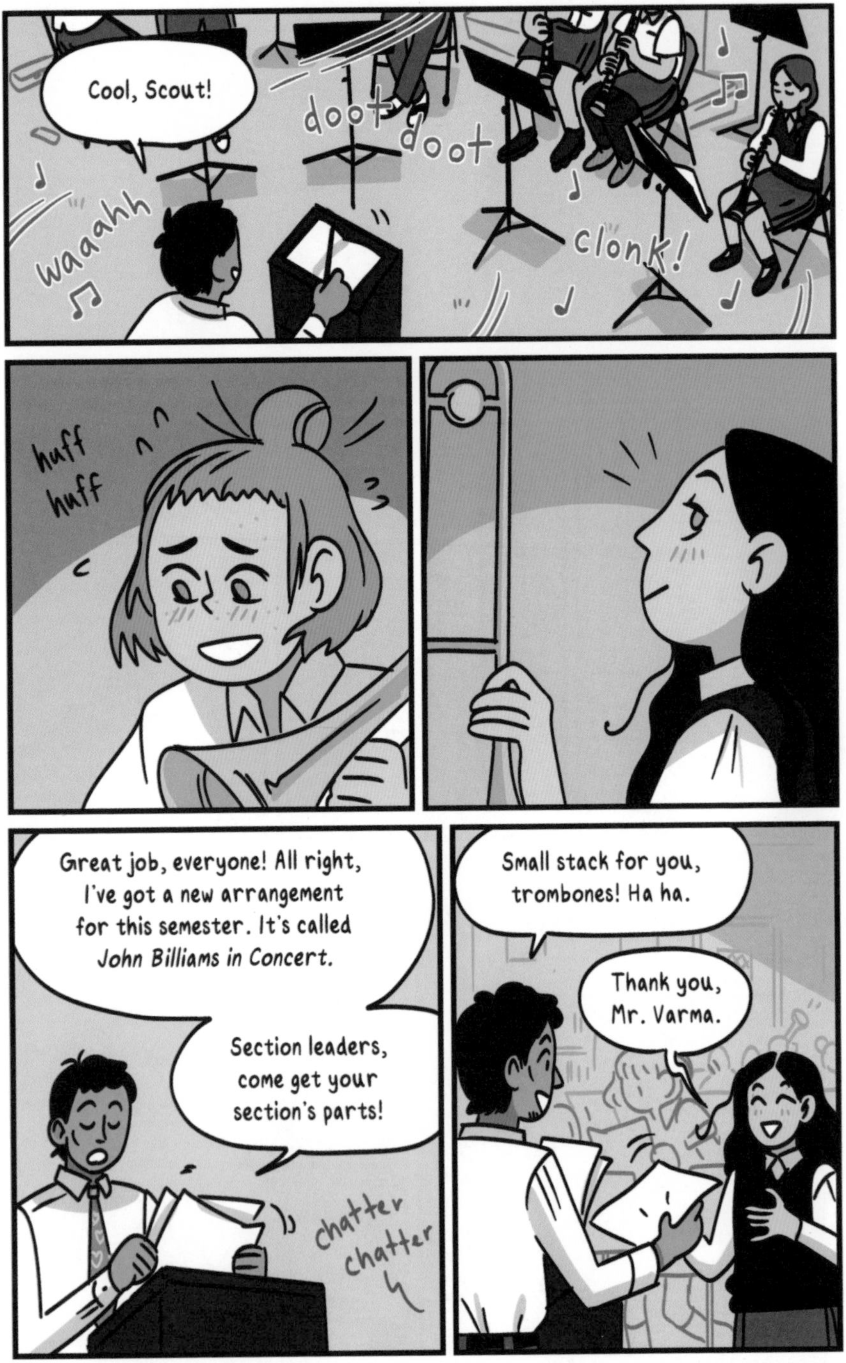
Cool, Scout!
doot doot
waaahh
clonk!
huff huff
Great job, everyone! All right, I've got a new arrangement for this semester. It's called *John Billiams in Concert*.
Section leaders, come get your section's parts!
chatter chatter
Small stack for you, trombones! Ha ha.
Thank you, Mr. Varma.

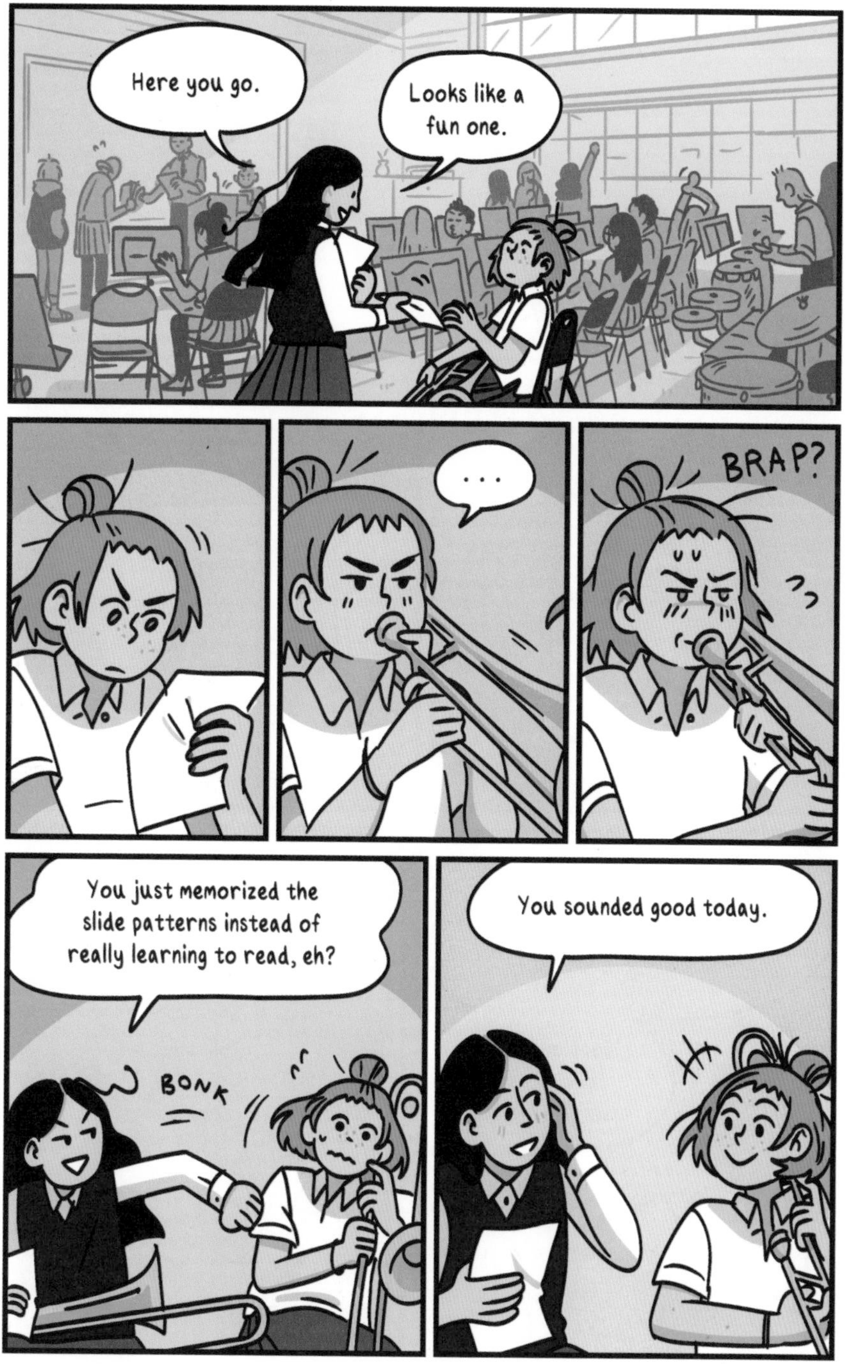
Here you go.
Looks like a fun one.
. . .
BRAP?
You just memorized the slide patterns instead of really learning to read, eh?
BONK
You sounded good today.

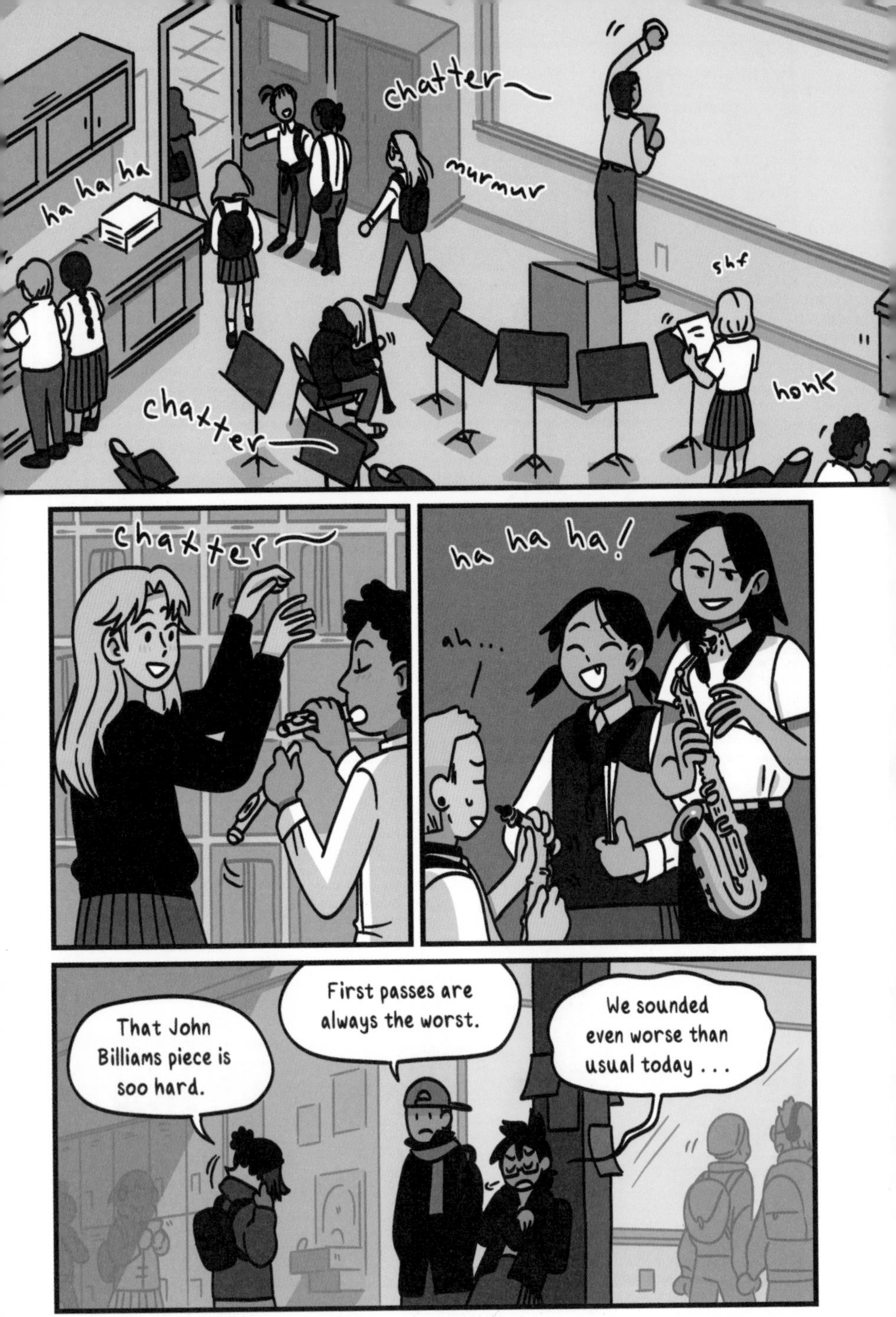
chatter~
ha ha ha
murmur
shf
honk
chatter—
chatter—
ha ha ha!
ah...
That John Billiams piece is soo hard.
First passes are always the worst.
We sounded even worse than usual today . . .

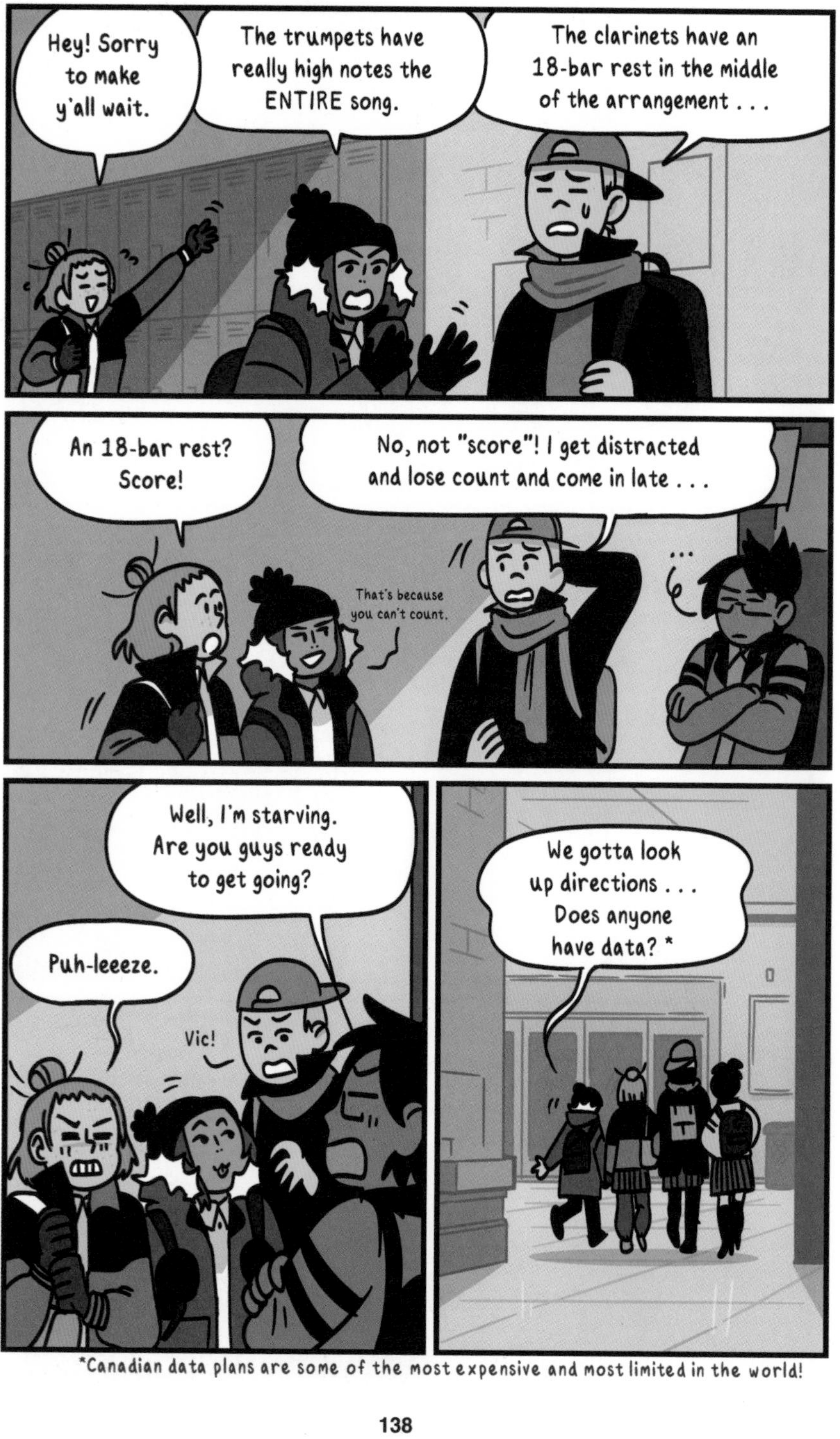
Hey! Sorry to make y'all wait.
The trumpets have really high notes the ENTIRE song.
The clarinets have an 18-bar rest in the middle of the arrangement . . .
An 18-bar rest? Score!
That's because you can't count.
No, not "score"! I get distracted and lose count and come in late . . .
. . .
Puh-leeeze.
Well, I'm starving. Are you guys ready to get going?
Vic!
We gotta look up directions . . . Does anyone have data? *

*Canadian data plans are some of the most expensive and most limited in the world!

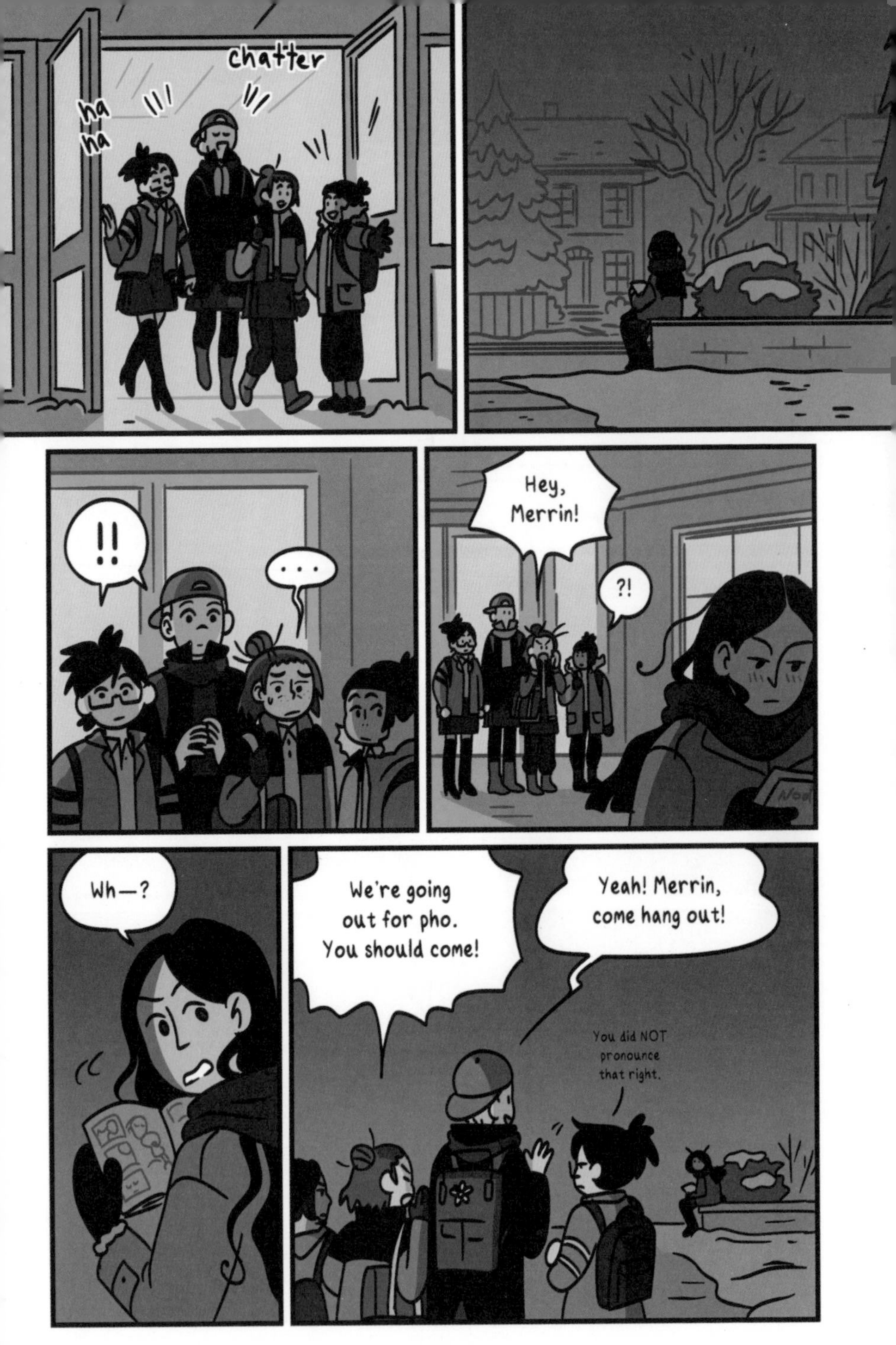
ha ha
chatter
!!
. . .
Hey, Merrin!
?!
Wh—?
We're going out for pho. You should come!
Yeah! Merrin, come hang out!
You did NOT pronounce that right.

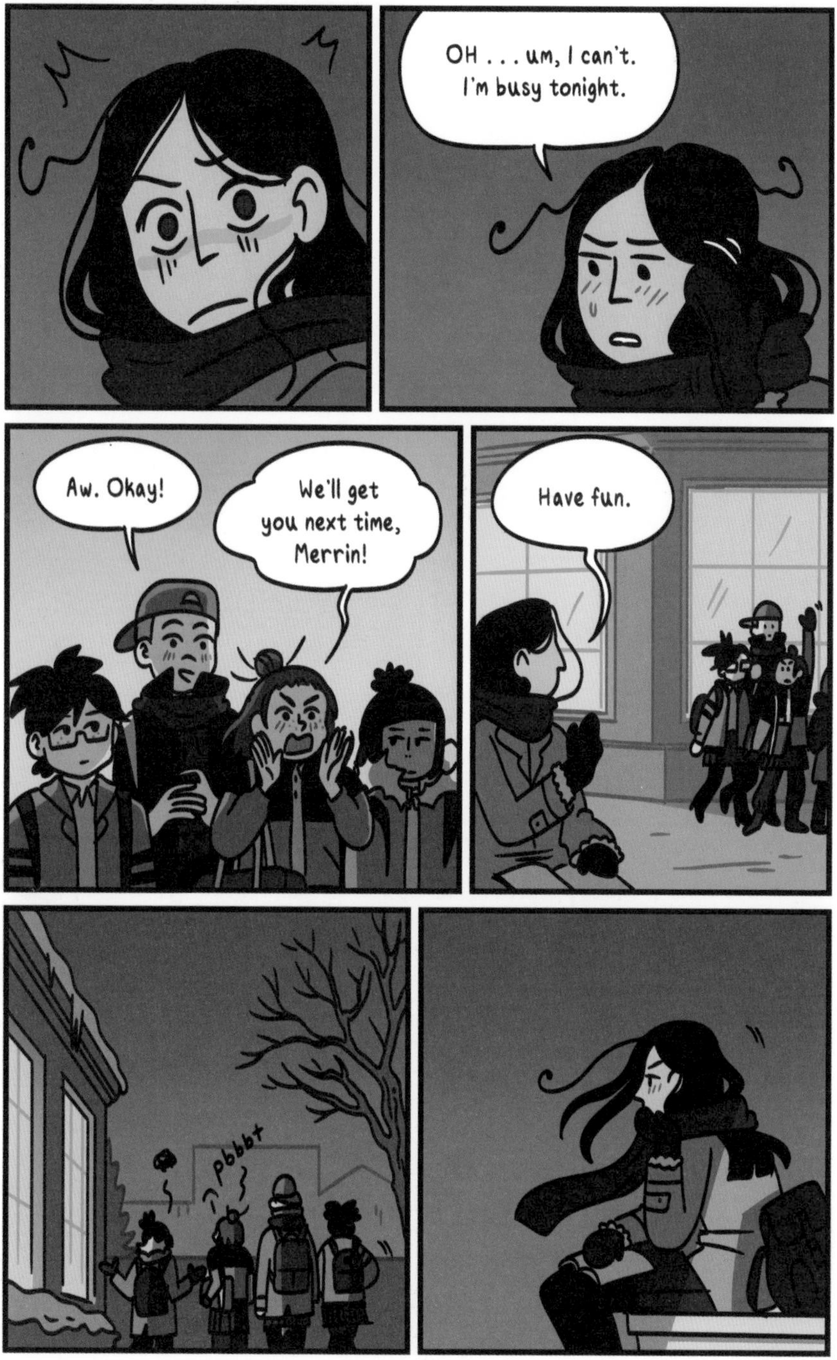
OH . . . um, I can't. I'm busy tonight.
Aw. Okay!
We'll get you next time, Merrin!
Have fun.
pbbbt

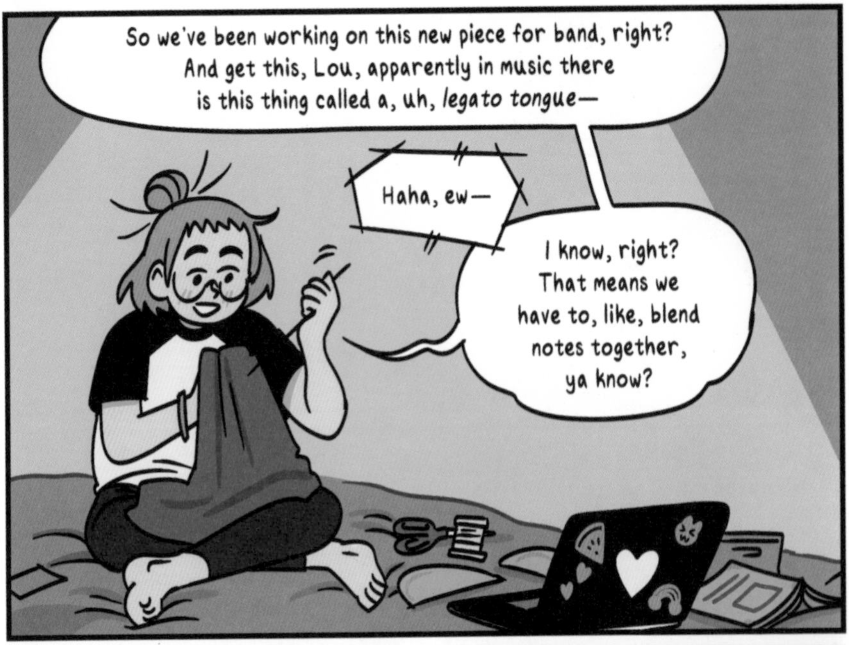
So we've been working on this new piece for band, right? And get this, Lou, apparently in music there is this thing called a, uh, *legato tongue*—
Haha, ew—
I know, right? That means we have to, like, blend notes together, ya know?
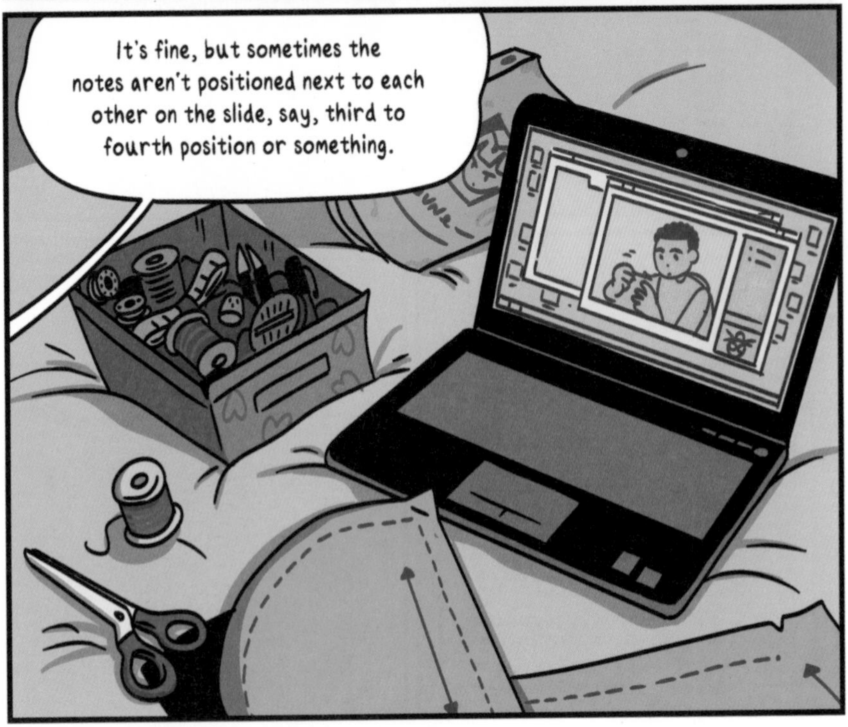
It's fine, but sometimes the notes aren't positioned next to each other on the slide, say, third to fourth position or something.

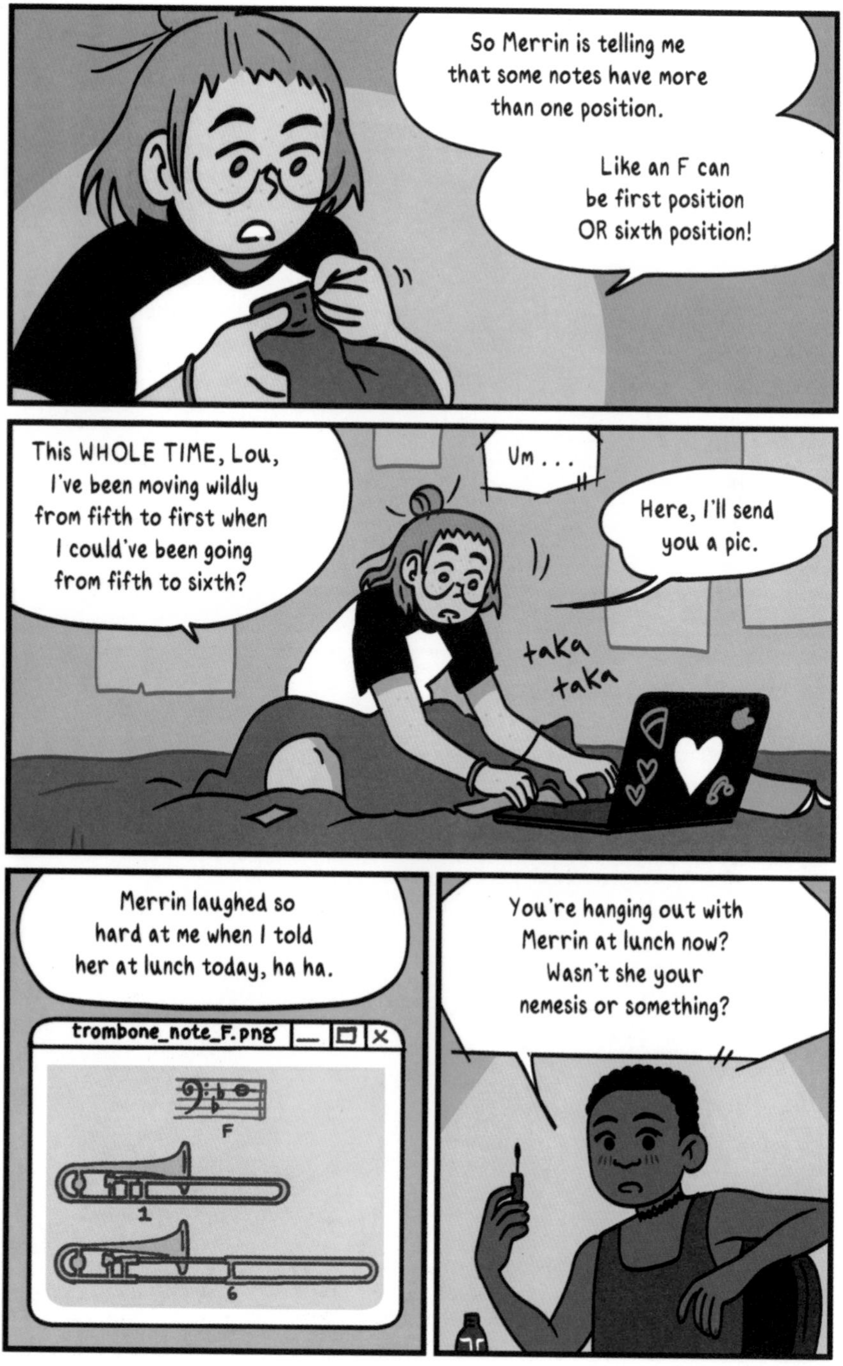
So Merrin is telling me that some notes have more than one position.
Like an F can be first position OR sixth position!
This WHOLE TIME, Lou, I've been moving wildly from fifth to first when I could've been going from fifth to sixth?
Um . . .
Here, I'll send you a pic.
taka taka
Merrin laughed so hard at me when I told her at lunch today, ha ha.
trombone_note_F.png
F
1
6
You're hanging out with Merrin at lunch now? Wasn't she your nemesis or something?

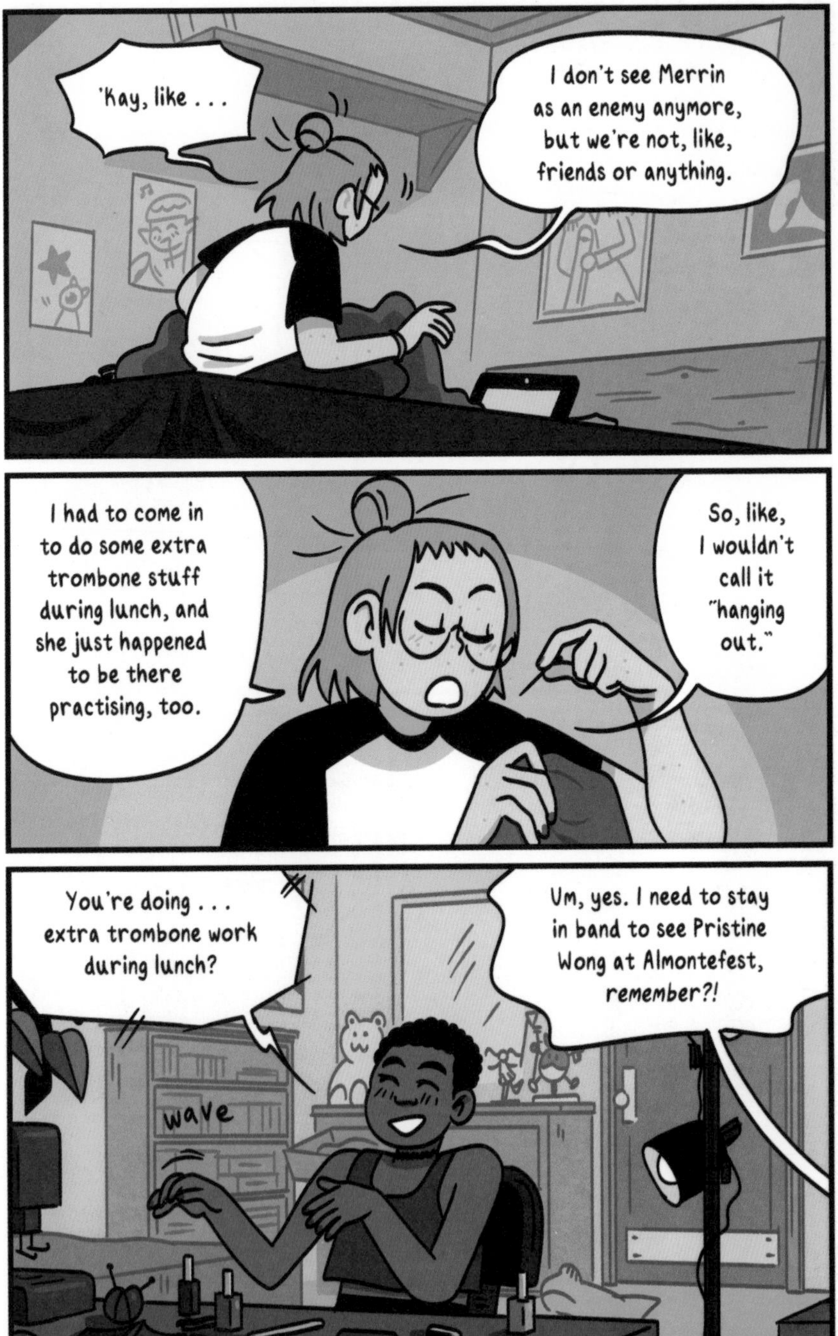
'Kay, like . . .
I don't see Merrin as an enemy anymore, but we're not, like, friends or anything.
I had to come in to do some extra trombone stuff during lunch, and she just happened to be there practising, too.
So, like, I wouldn't call it "hanging out."
You're doing . . . extra trombone work during lunch?
Um, yes. I need to stay in band to see Pristine Wong at Almontefest, remember?!
wave

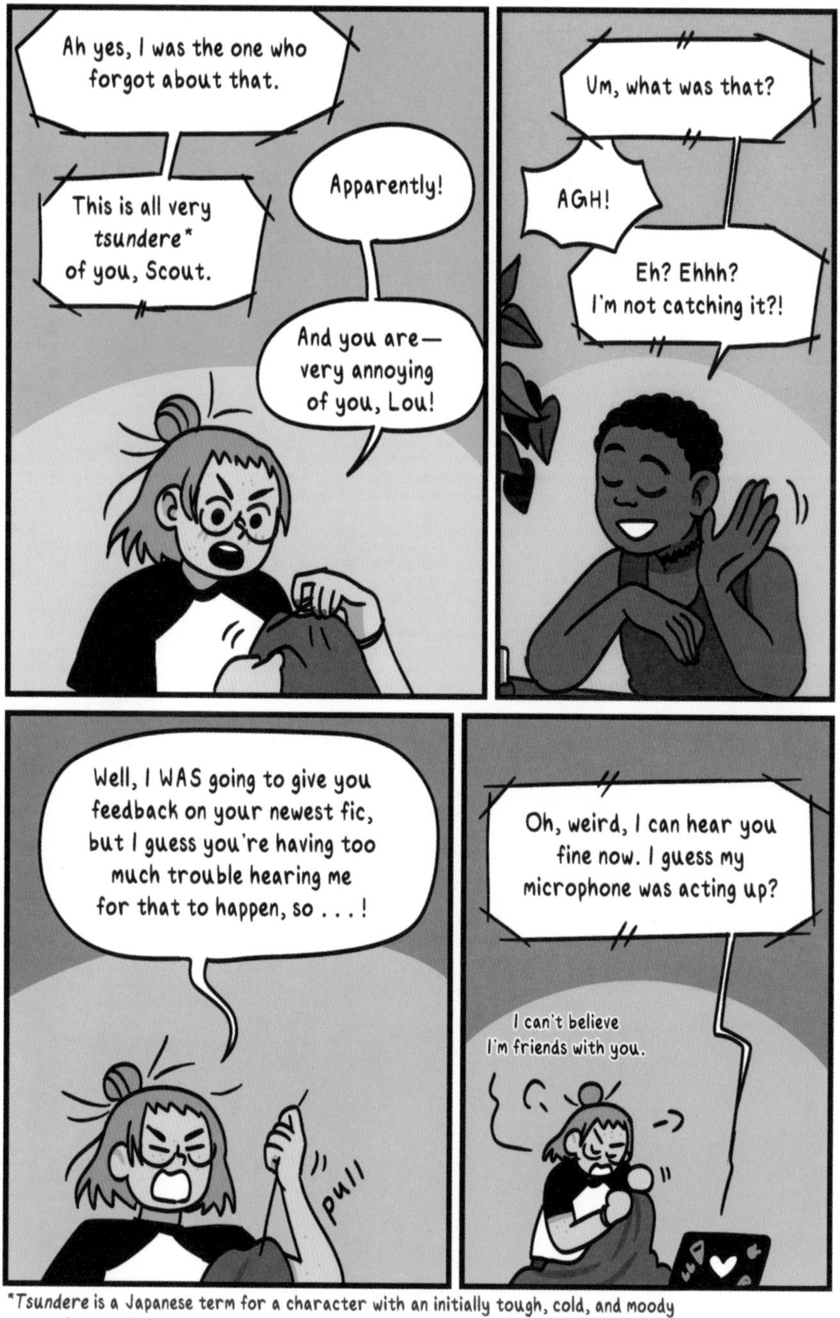
Ah yes, I was the one who forgot about that.
This is all very *tsundere** of you, Scout.
Apparently!
And you are— very annoying of you, Lou!
Um, what was that?
AGH!
Eh? Ehhh? I'm not catching it?!
Well, I WAS going to give you feedback on your newest fic, but I guess you're having too much trouble hearing me for that to happen, so . . . !
pull
Oh, weird, I can hear you fine now. I guess my microphone was acting up?
I can't believe I'm friends with you.

**Tsundere* is a Japanese term for a character with an initially tough, cold, and moody personality who later changes over time to become someone warm and friendly.

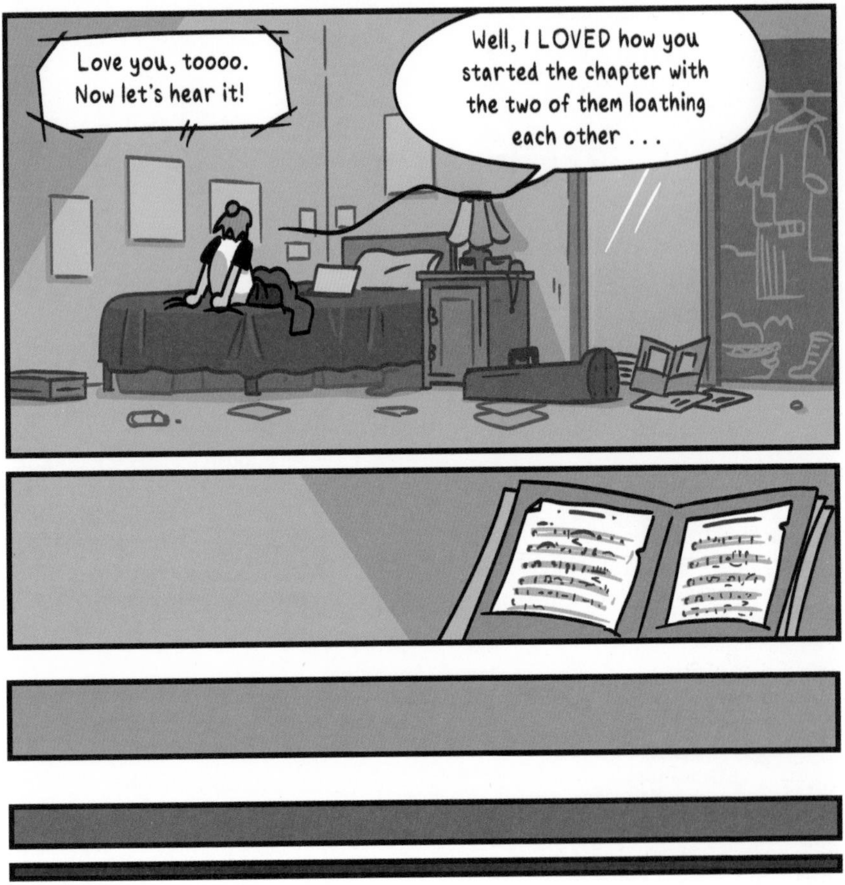
Love you, toooo. Now let's hear it!
Well, I LOVED how you started the chapter with the two of them loathing each other . . .

Chapter 4

mf
ff

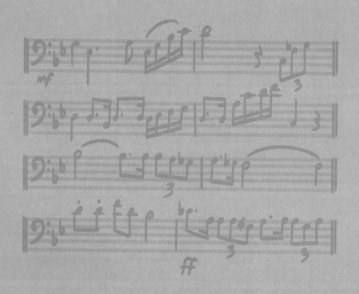

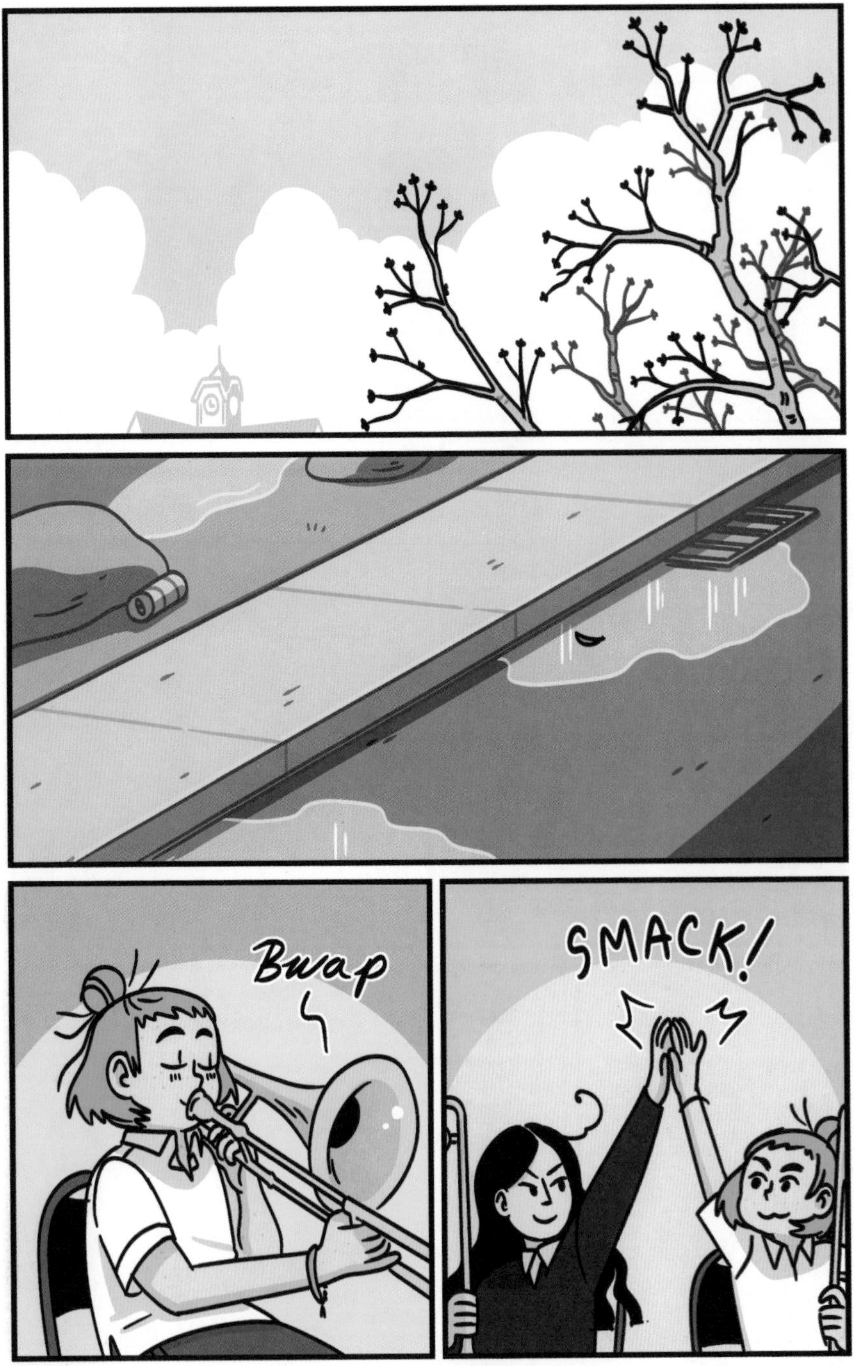
Bwap
SMACK!

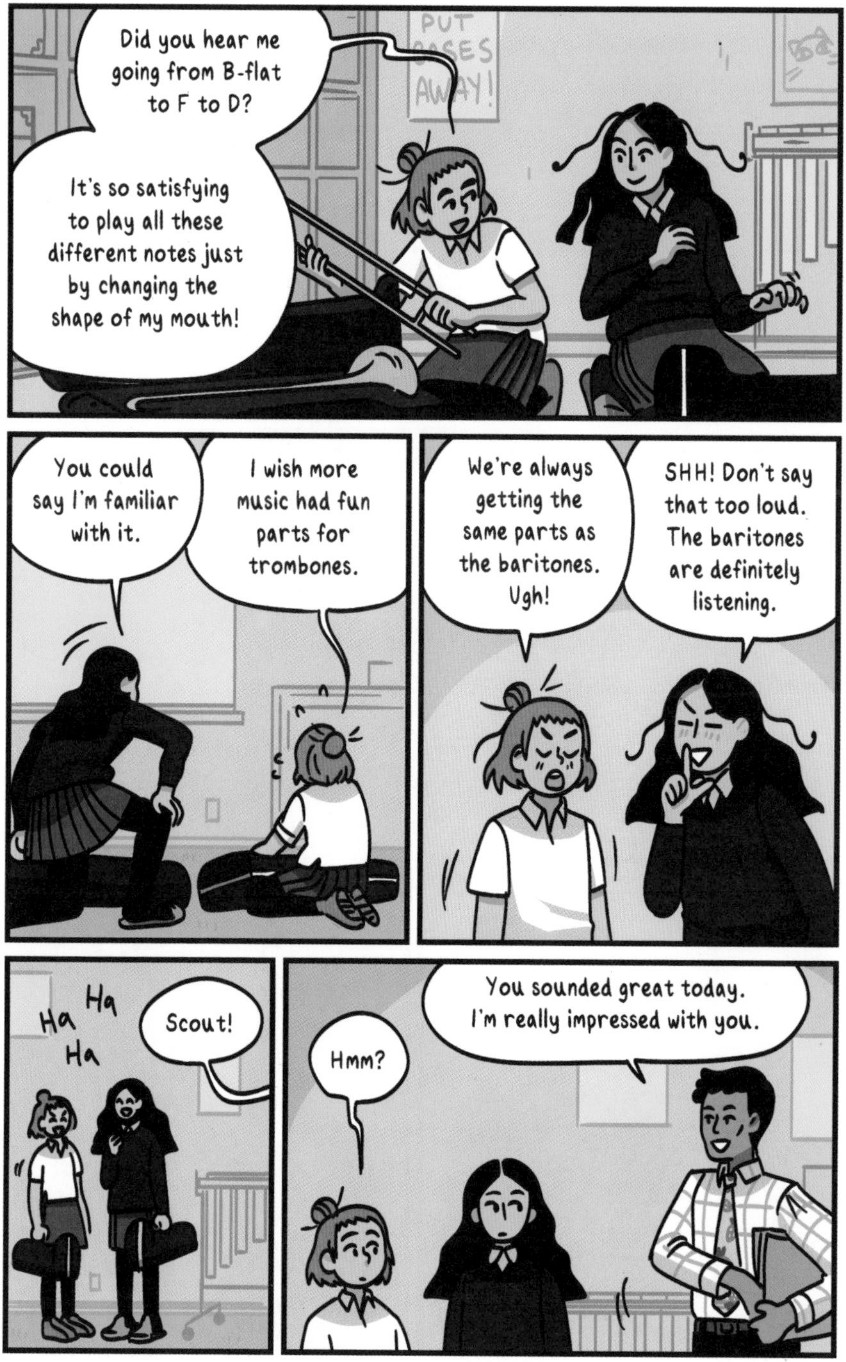
PUT CASES AWAY!
Did you hear me going from B-flat to F to D?
It's so satisfying to play all these different notes just by changing the shape of my mouth!
You could say I'm familiar with it.
I wish more music had fun parts for trombones.
We're always getting the same parts as the baritones. Ugh!
SHH! Don't say that too loud. The baritones are definitely listening.
Ha Ha Ha
Scout!
Hmm?
You sounded great today. I'm really impressed with you.

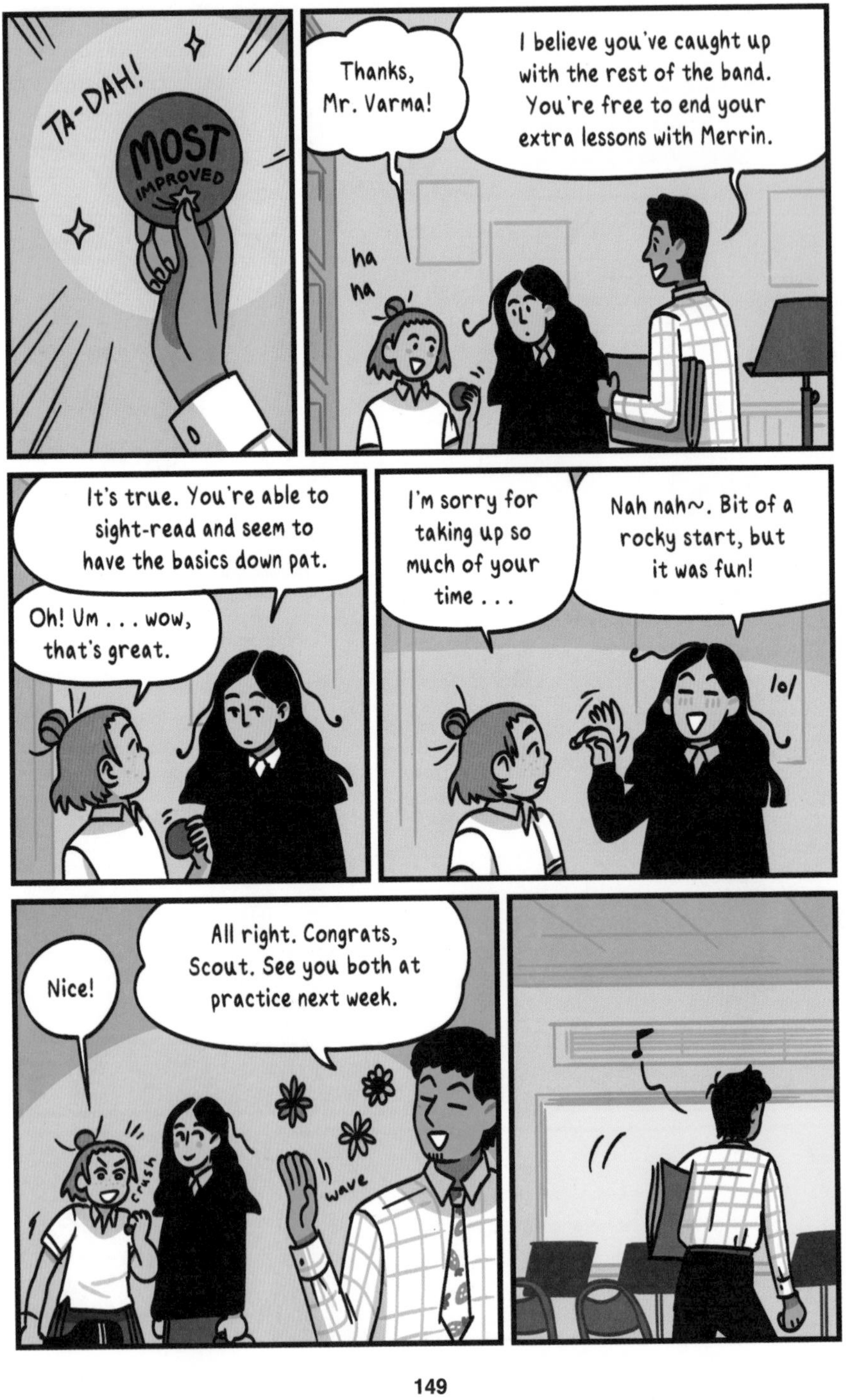
TA-DAH!
MOST IMPROVED
Thanks, Mr. Varma!
I believe you've caught up with the rest of the band. You're free to end your extra lessons with Merrin.
ha ha
It's true. You're able to sight-read and seem to have the basics down pat.
Oh! Um . . . wow, that's great.
I'm sorry for taking up so much of your time . . .
Nah nah~. Bit of a rocky start, but it was fun!
lol
Nice!
All right. Congrats, Scout. See you both at practice next week.
crush
wave

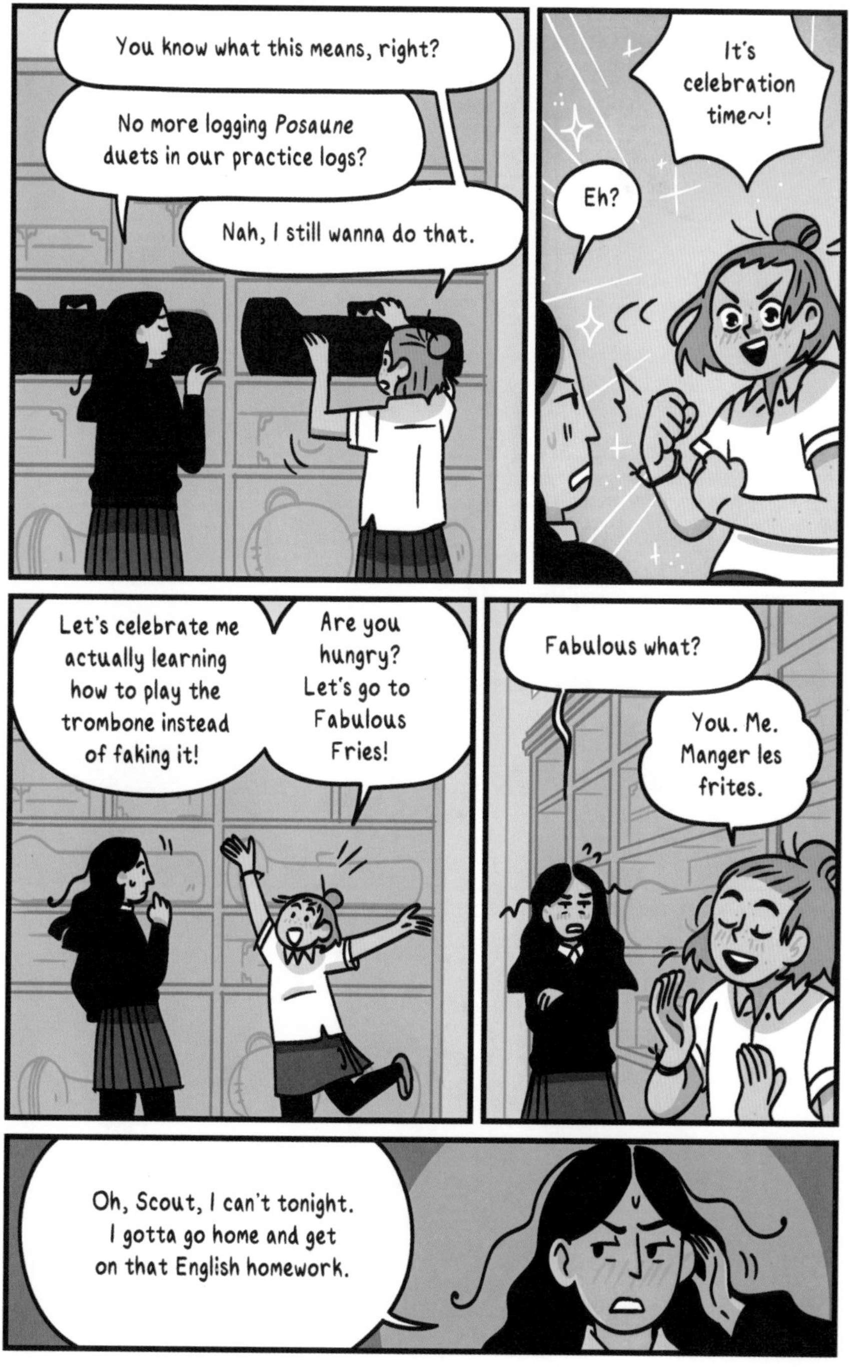
You know what this means, right?
No more logging *Posaune* duets in our practice logs?
Nah, I still wanna do that.
It's celebration time~!
Eh?
Let's celebrate me actually learning how to play the trombone instead of faking it!
Are you hungry? Let's go to Fabulous Fries!
Fabulous what?
You. Me. Manger les frites.
Oh, Scout, I can't tonight. I gotta go home and get on that English homework.

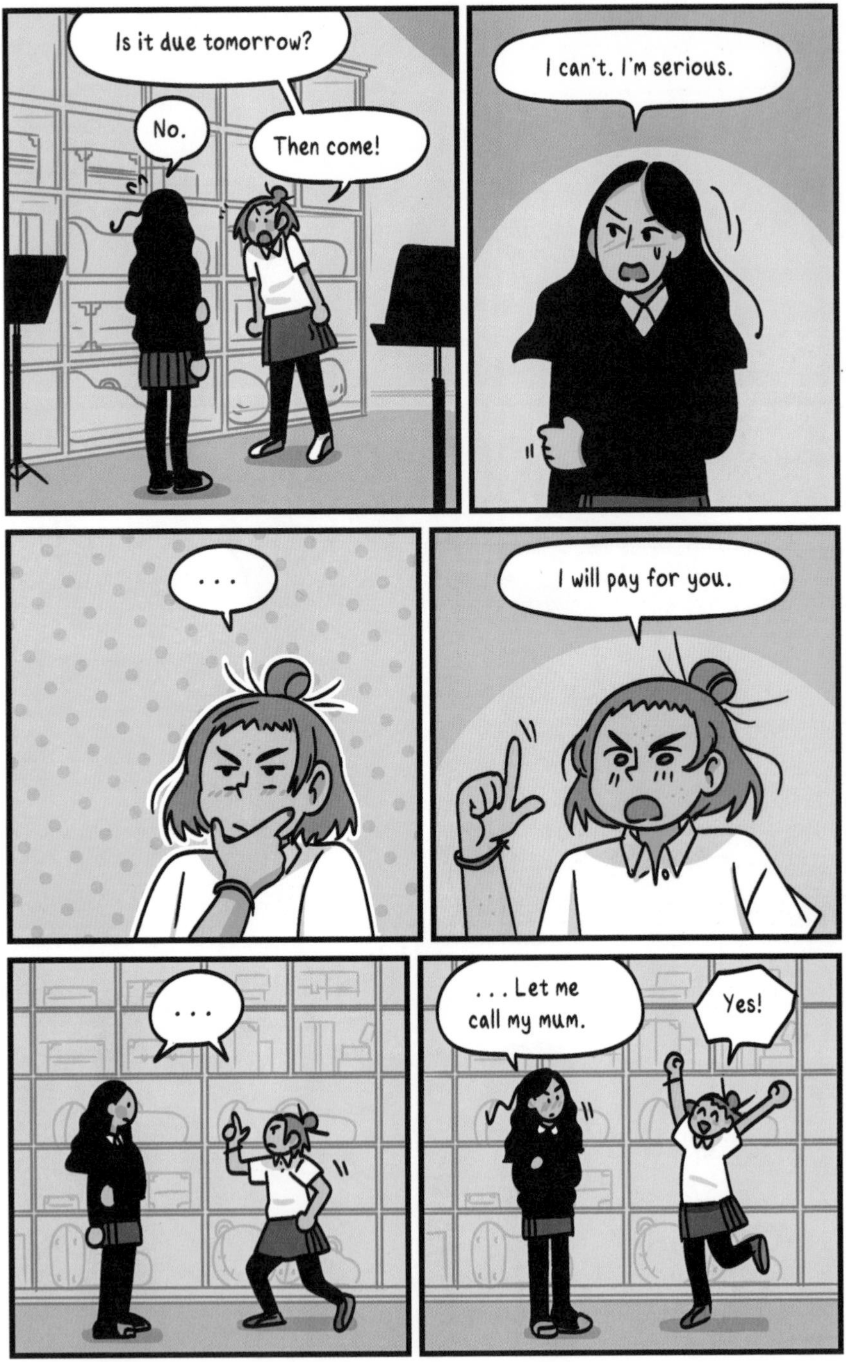
Is it due tomorrow?
No.
Then come!
I can't. I'm serious.
. . .
I will pay for you.
. . .
. . . Let me call my mum.
Yes!

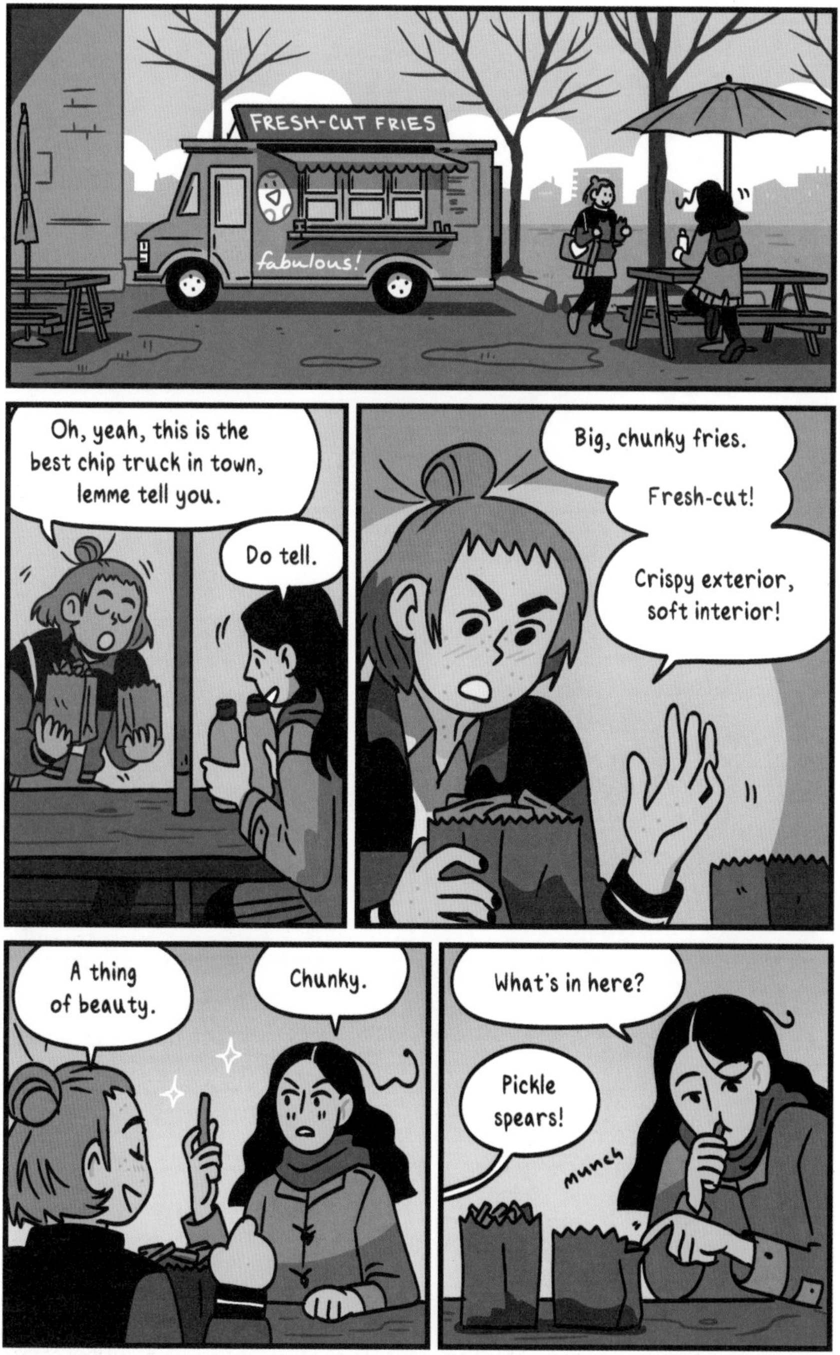
FRESH-CUT FRIES
fabulous!
Oh, yeah, this is the best chip truck in town, lemme tell you.
Do tell.
Big, chunky fries.
Fresh-cut!
Crispy exterior, soft interior!
A thing of beauty.
Chunky.
What's in here?
Pickle spears!
munch

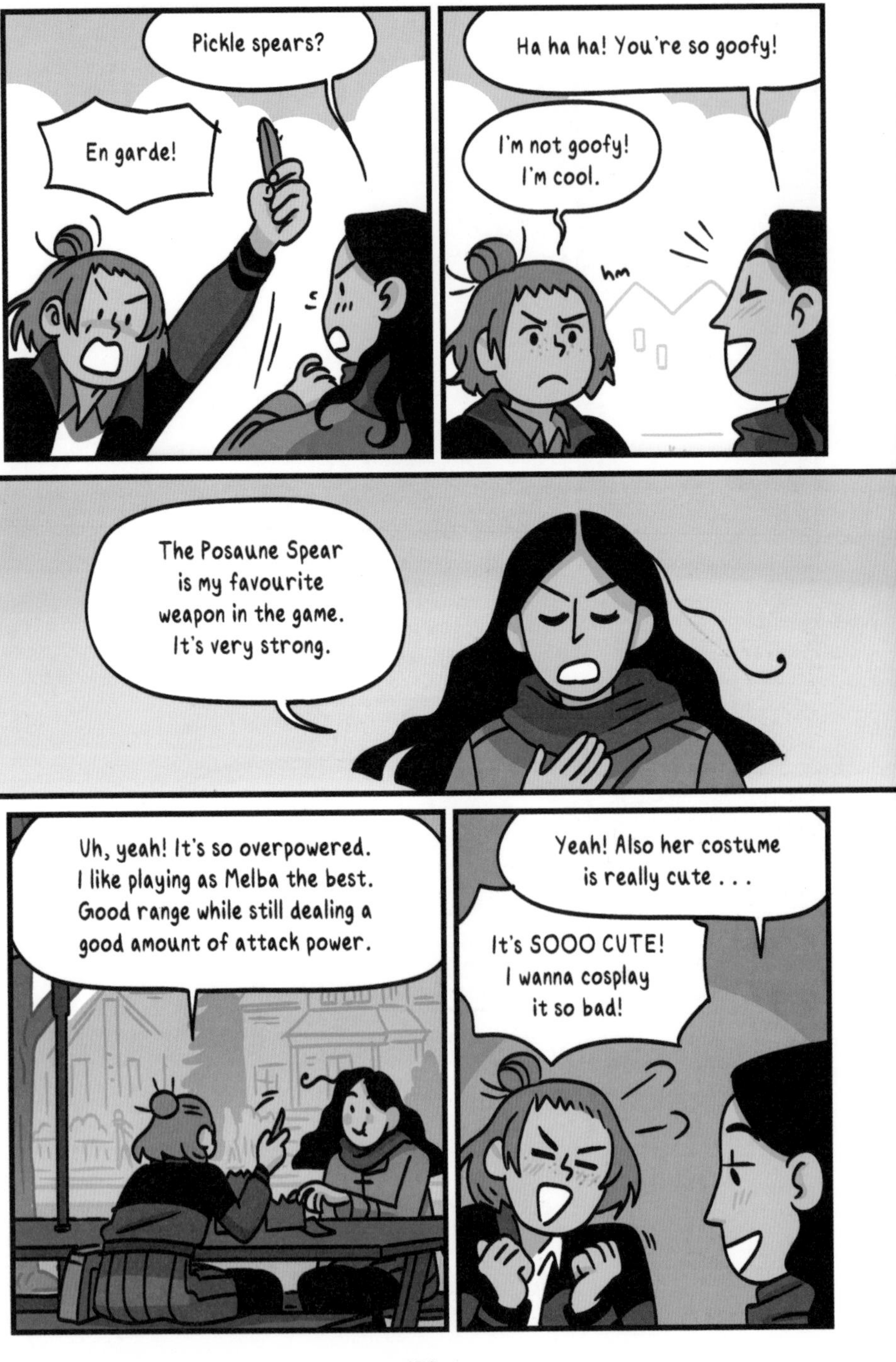

Pickle spears?
En garde!
Ha ha ha! You're so goofy!
I'm not goofy! I'm cool.
hm
The Posaune Spear is my favourite weapon in the game. It's very strong.
Uh, yeah! It's so overpowered. I like playing as Melba the best. Good range while still dealing a good amount of attack power.
Yeah! Also her costume is really cute . . .
It's SOOO CUTE! I wanna cosplay it so bad!

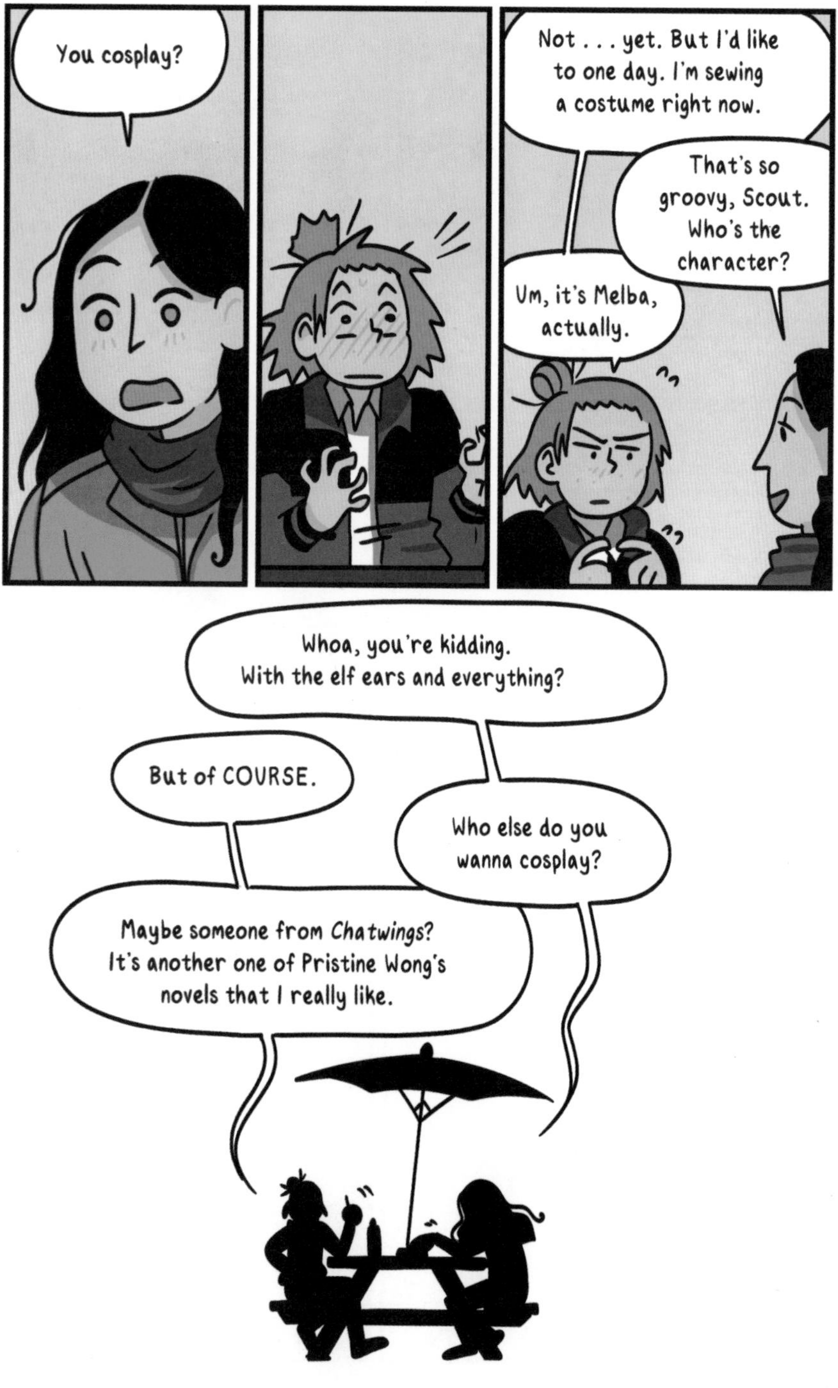
You cosplay?
Not . . . yet. But I'd like to one day. I'm sewing a costume right now.
That's so groovy, Scout. Who's the character?
Um, it's Melba, actually.
Whoa, you're kidding. With the elf ears and everything?
But of COURSE.
Who else do you wanna cosplay?
Maybe someone from *Chatwings*? It's another one of Pristine Wong's novels that I really like.

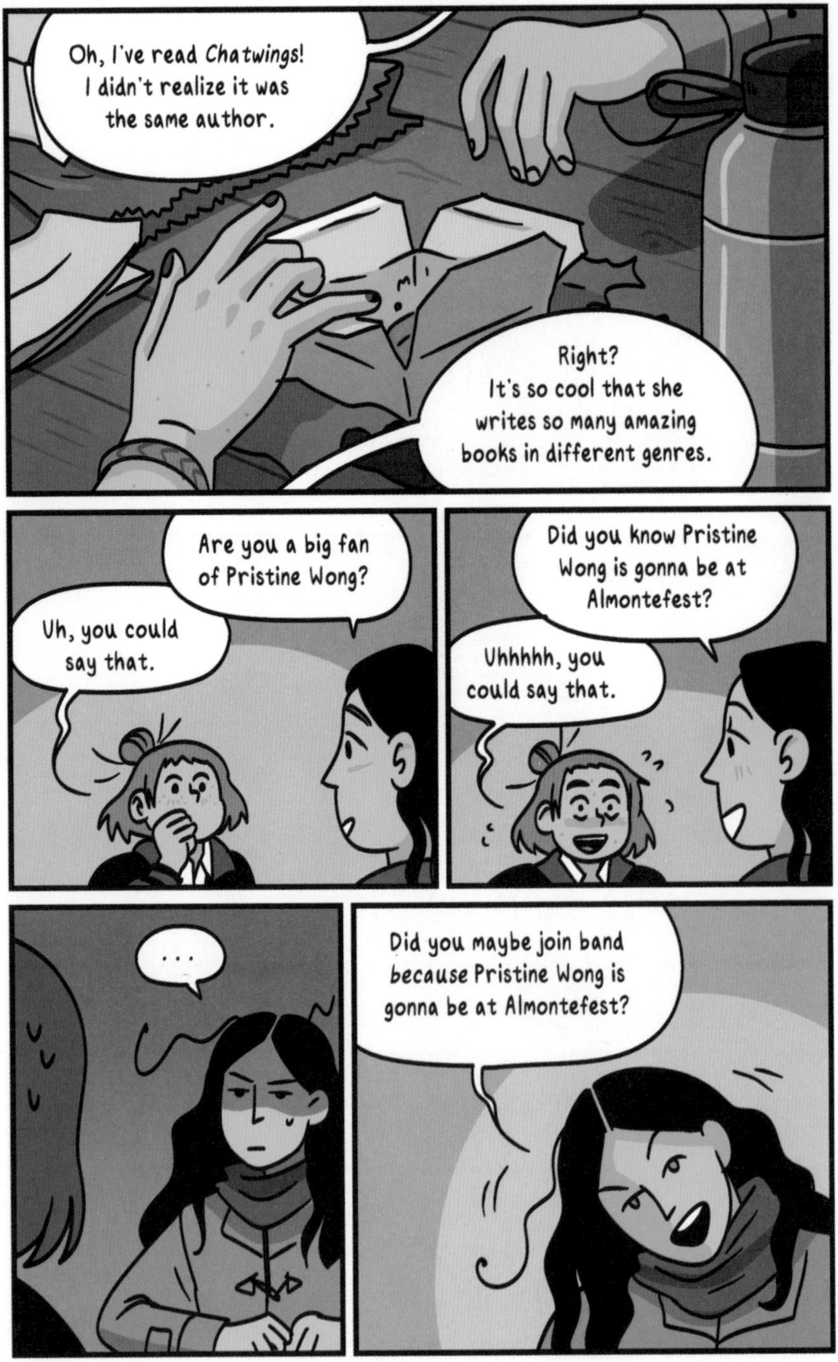
Oh, I've read *Chatwings*! I didn't realize it was the same author.
Right? It's so cool that she writes so many amazing books in different genres.
Are you a big fan of Pristine Wong?
Uh, you could say that.
Did you know Pristine Wong is gonna be at Almontefest?
Uhhhhh, you could say that.
. . .
Did you maybe join band *because* Pristine Wong is gonna be at Almontefest?

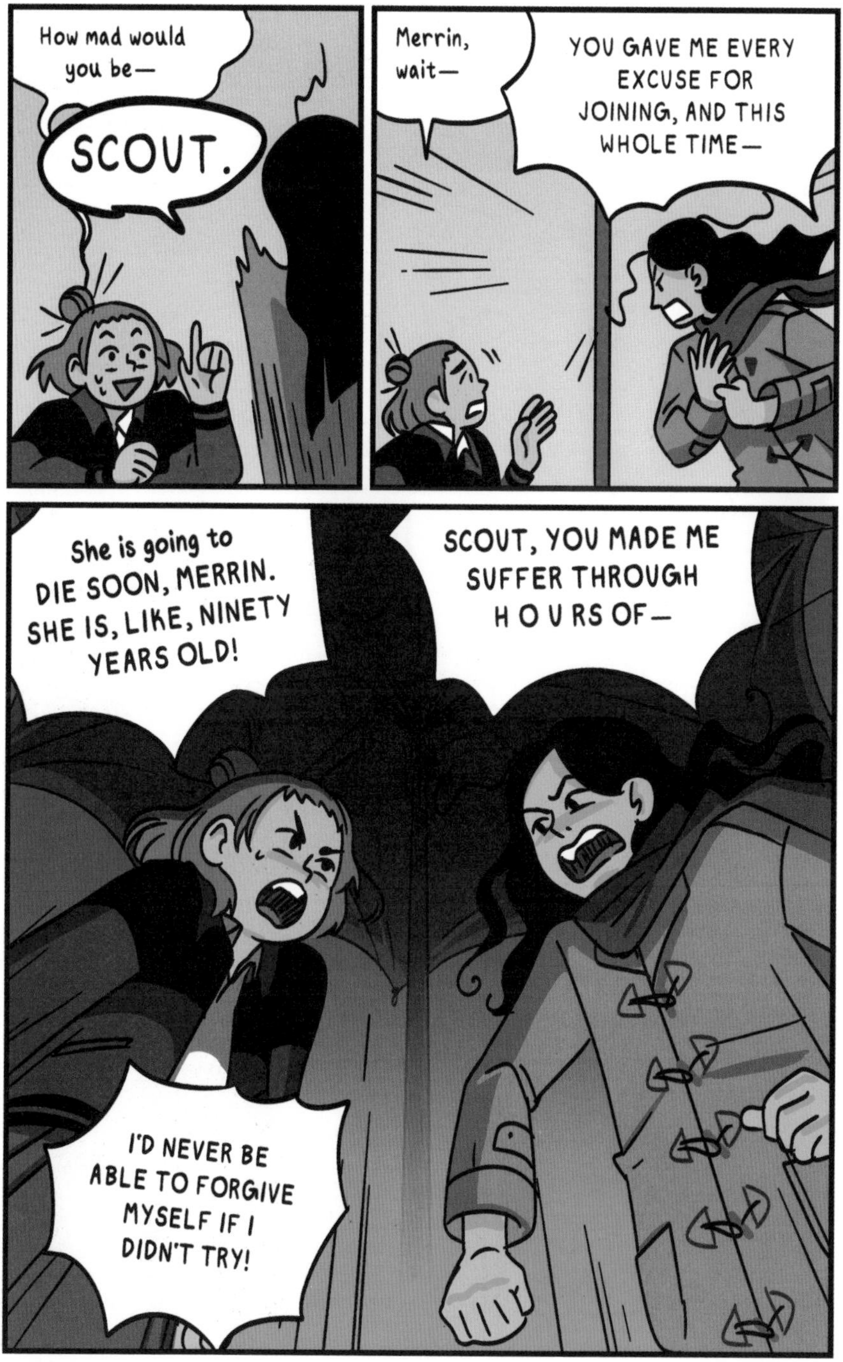
How mad would you be—
SCOUT.
Merrin, wait—
YOU GAVE ME EVERY EXCUSE FOR JOINING, AND THIS WHOLE TIME—
She is going to DIE SOON, MERRIN. SHE IS, LIKE, NINETY YEARS OLD!
SCOUT, YOU MADE ME SUFFER THROUGH H O U RS OF—
I'D NEVER BE ABLE TO FORGIVE MYSELF IF I DIDN'T TRY!

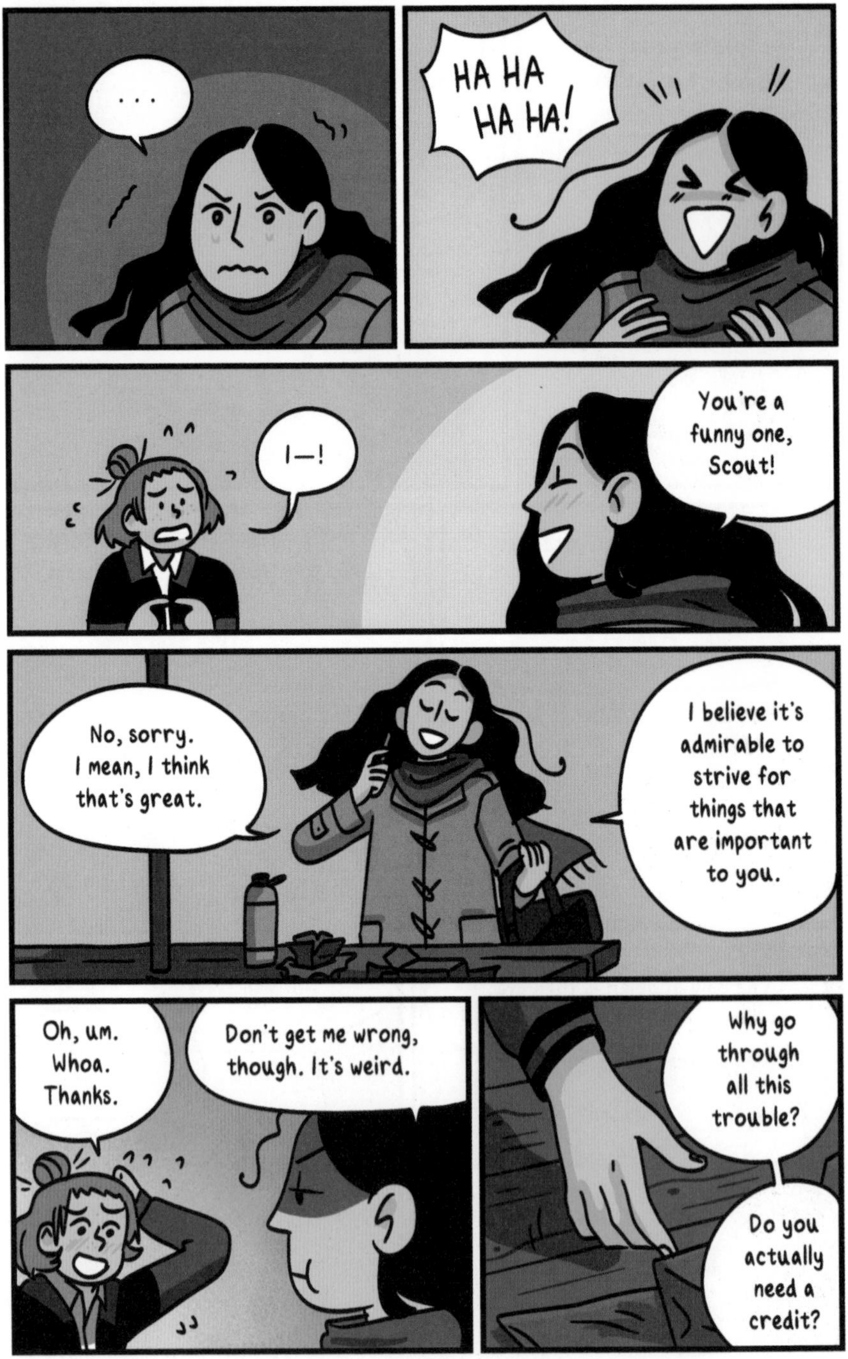
...
HA HA HA HA!
I—!
You're a funny one, Scout!
No, sorry. I mean, I think that's great.
I believe it's admirable to strive for things that are important to you.
Oh, um. Whoa. Thanks.
Don't get me wrong, though. It's weird.
Why go through all this trouble?
Do you actually need a credit?

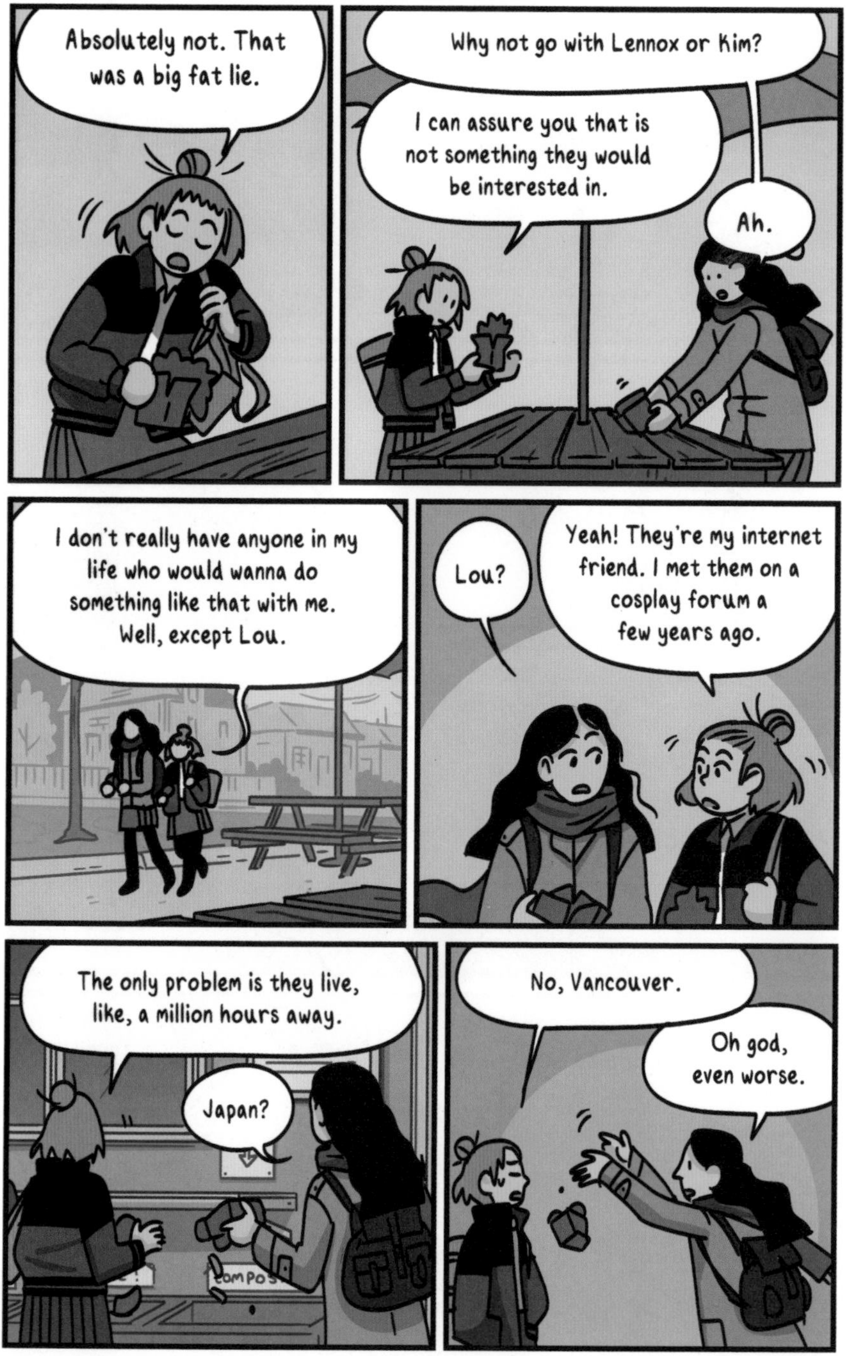
Absolutely not. That was a big fat lie.
Why not go with Lennox or Kim?
I can assure you that is not something they would be interested in.
Ah.
I don't really have anyone in my life who would wanna do something like that with me. Well, except Lou.
Lou?
Yeah! They're my internet friend. I met them on a cosplay forum a few years ago.
The only problem is they live, like, a million hours away.
Japan?
No, Vancouver.
Oh god, even worse.

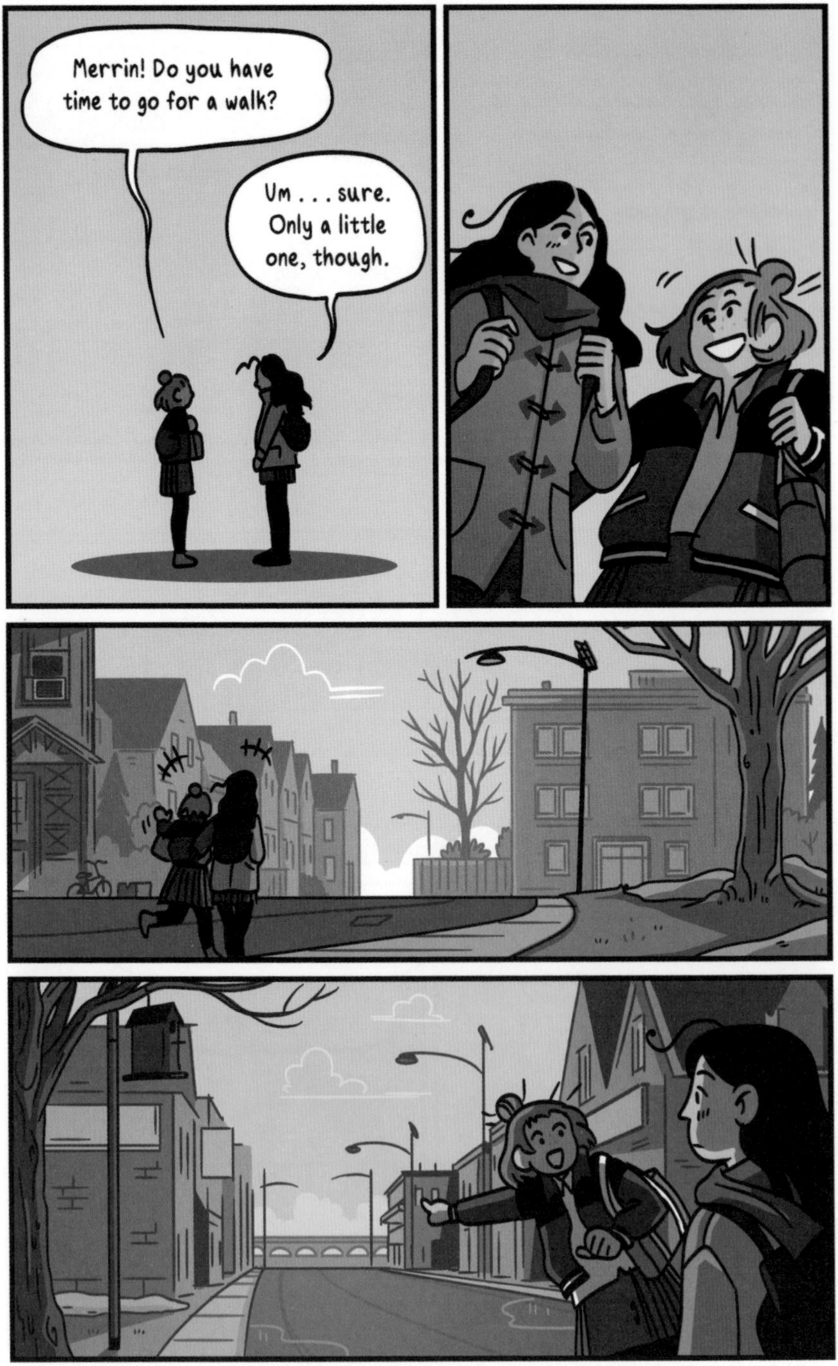
Merrin! Do you have time to go for a walk?
Um . . . sure. Only a little one, though.

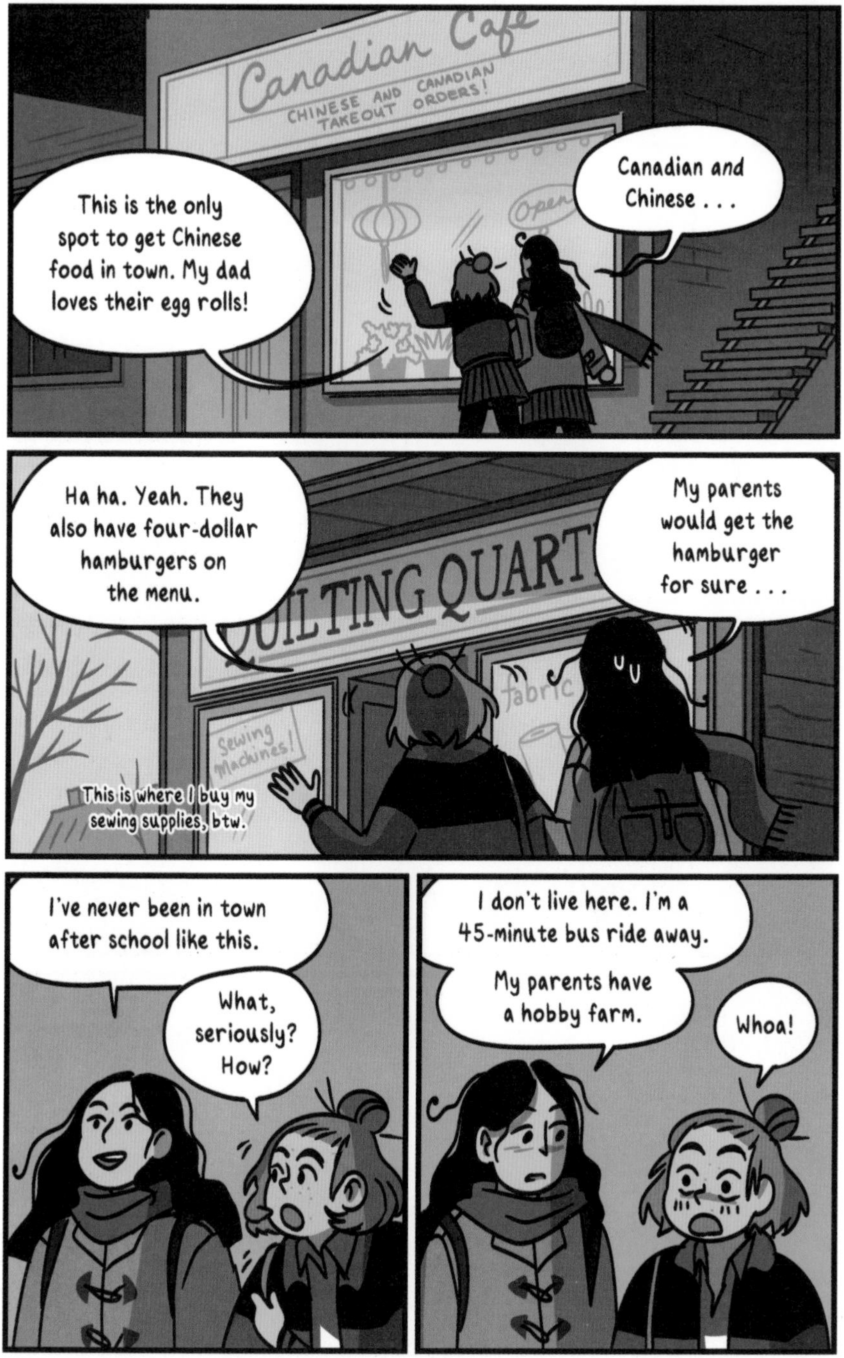
Canadian Cafe
CHINESE AND CANADIAN TAKEOUT ORDERS!
This is the only spot to get Chinese food in town. My dad loves their egg rolls!
Open
Canadian and Chinese . . .
Ha ha. Yeah. They also have four-dollar hamburgers on the menu.
QUILTING QUART
My parents would get the hamburger for sure . . .
Sewing Machines!
fabric
This is where I buy my sewing supplies, btw.
I've never been in town after school like this.
What, seriously? How?
I don't live here. I'm a 45-minute bus ride away.
My parents have a hobby farm.
Whoa!

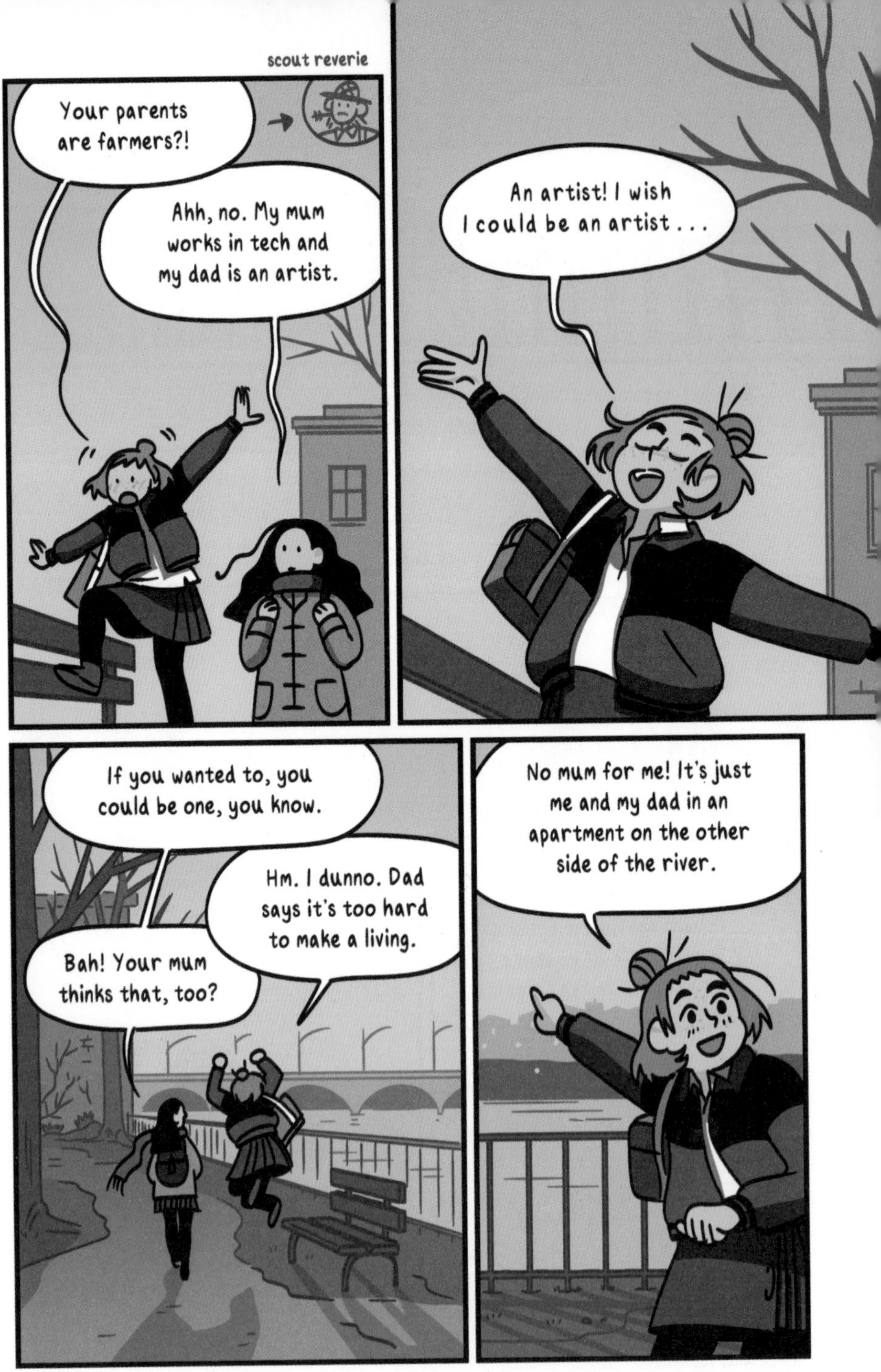
Your parents are farmers?!
Ahh, no. My mum works in tech and my dad is an artist.
An artist! I wish I could be an artist . . .
If you wanted to, you could be one, you know.
Hm. I dunno. Dad says it's too hard to make a living.
Bah! Your mum thinks that, too?
No mum for me! It's just me and my dad in an apartment on the other side of the river.

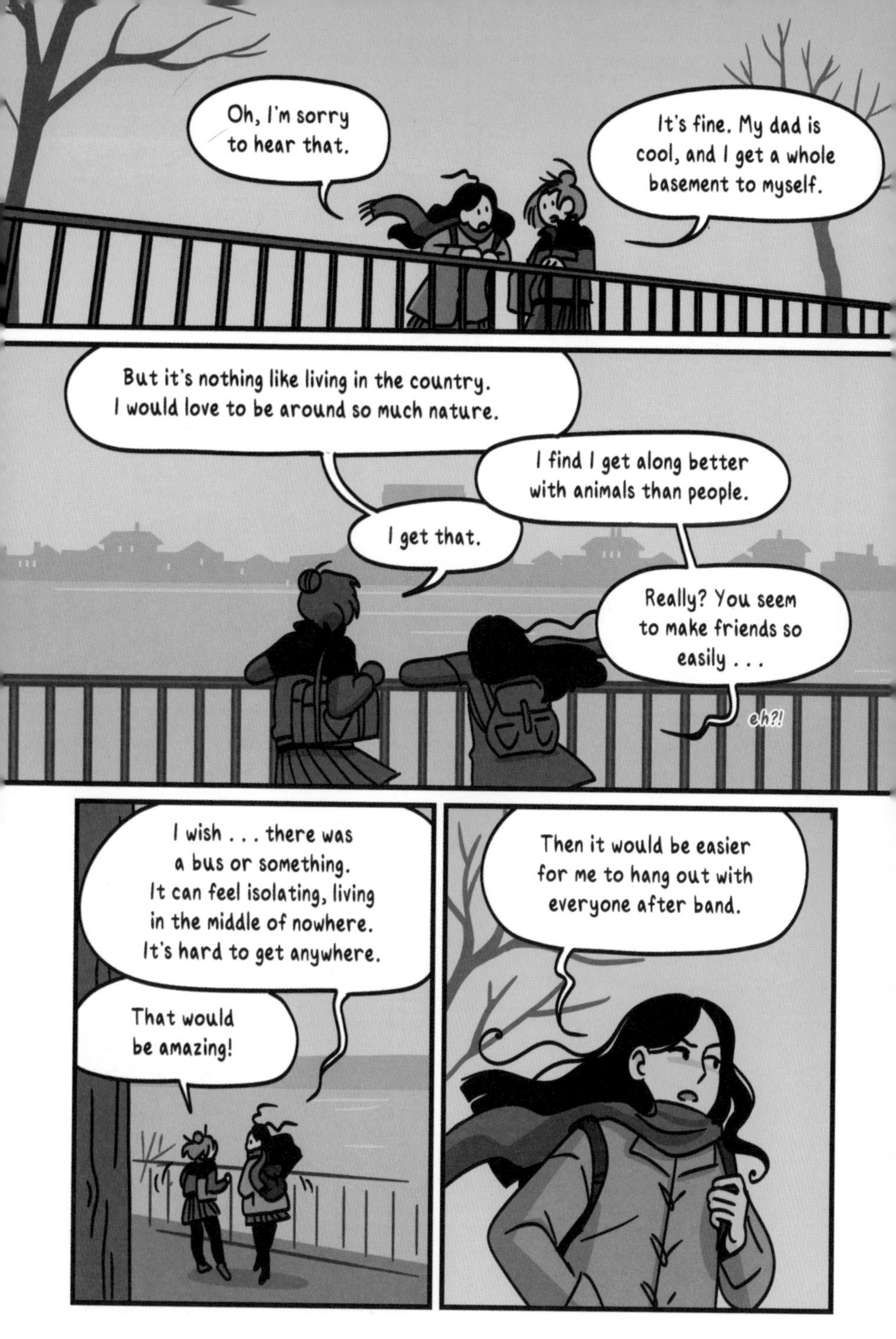
Oh, I'm sorry to hear that.
It's fine. My dad is cool, and I get a whole basement to myself.
But it's nothing like living in the country. I would love to be around so much nature.
I find I get along better with animals than people.
I get that.
Really? You seem to make friends so easily . . .
eh?!
I wish . . . there was a bus or something. It can feel isolating, living in the middle of nowhere. It's hard to get anywhere.
That would be amazing!
Then it would be easier for me to hang out with everyone after band.

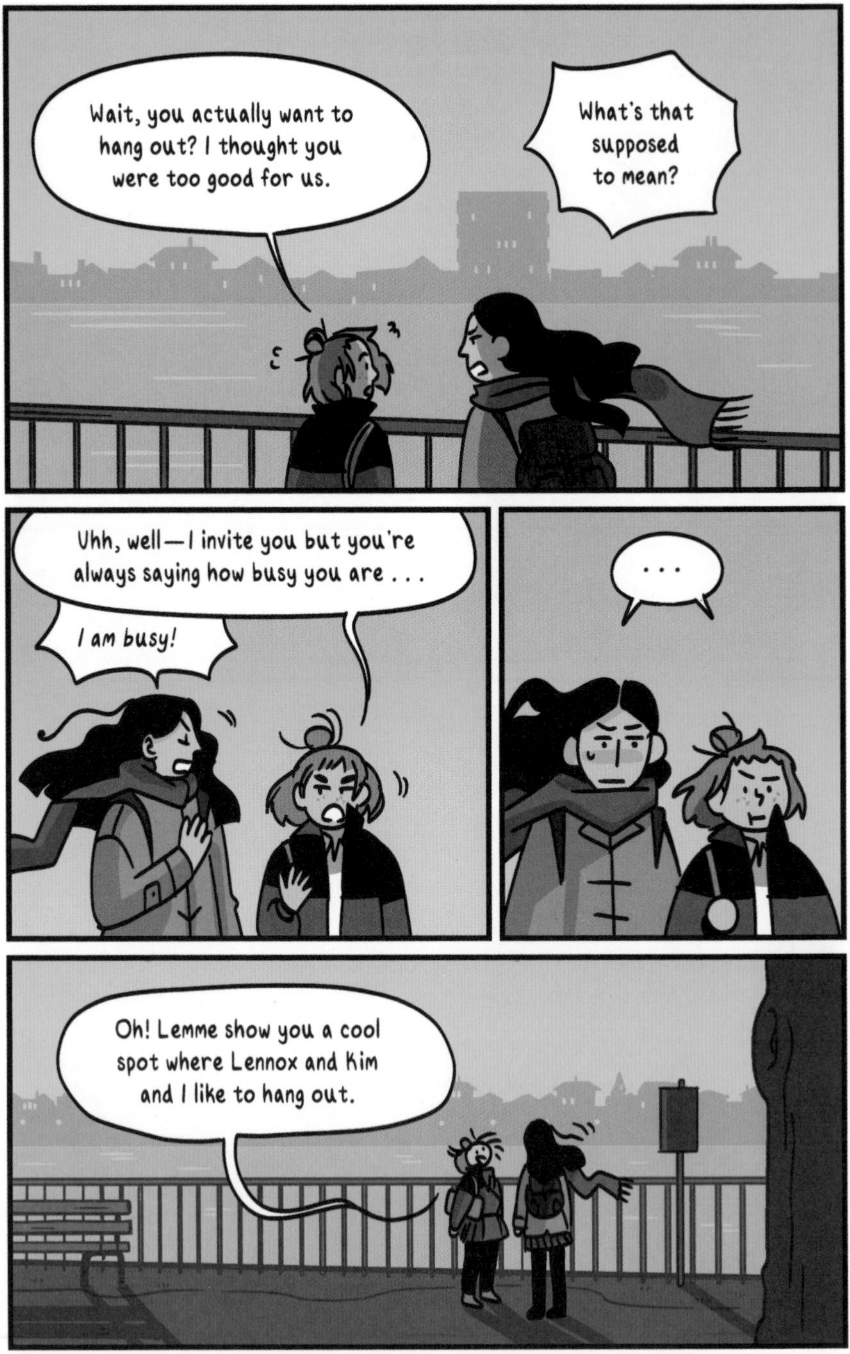
Wait, you actually want to hang out? I thought you were too good for us.
What's that supposed to mean?
Uhh, well—I invite you but you're always saying how busy you are . . .
I am busy!
. . .
Oh! Lemme show you a cool spot where Lennox and Kim and I like to hang out.

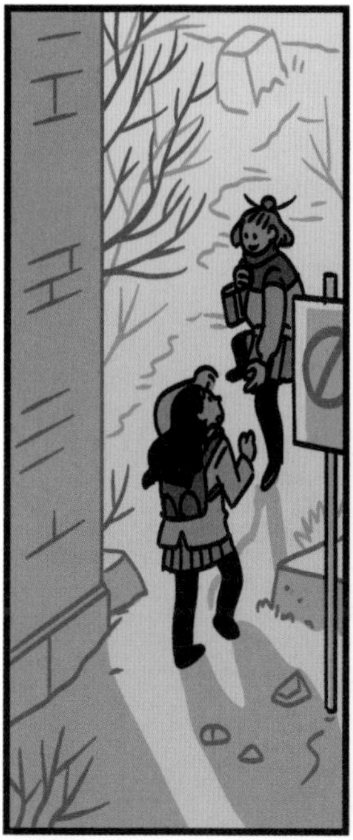
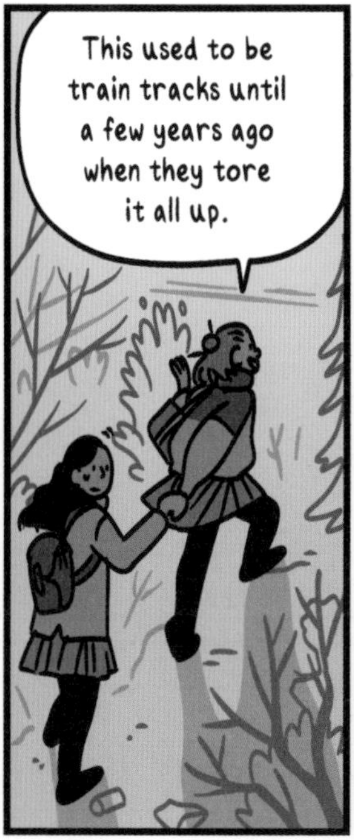
This used to be train tracks until a few years ago when they tore it all up.
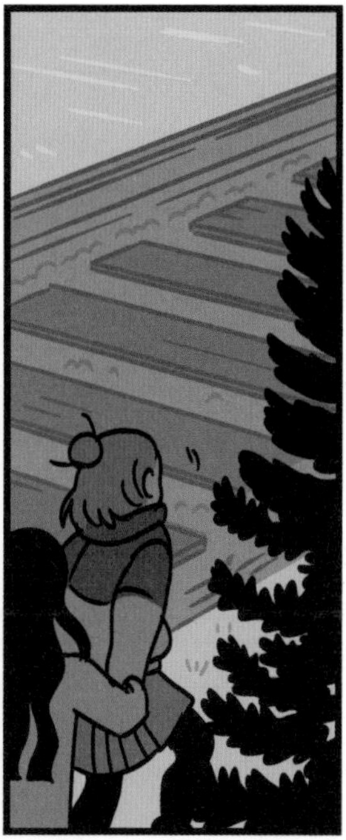
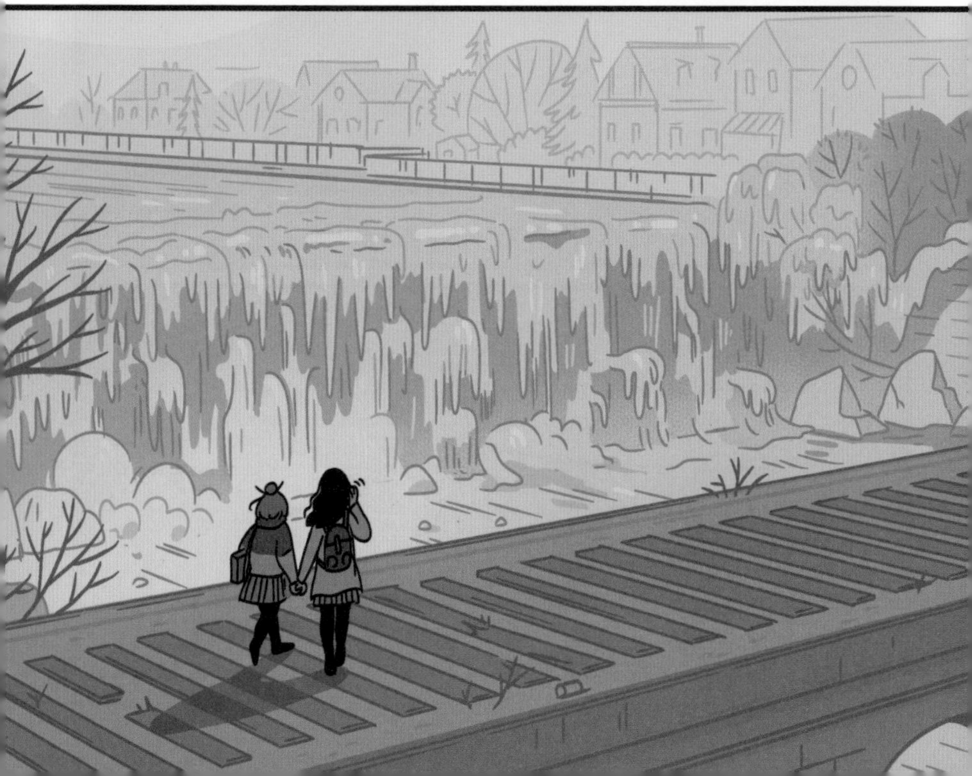

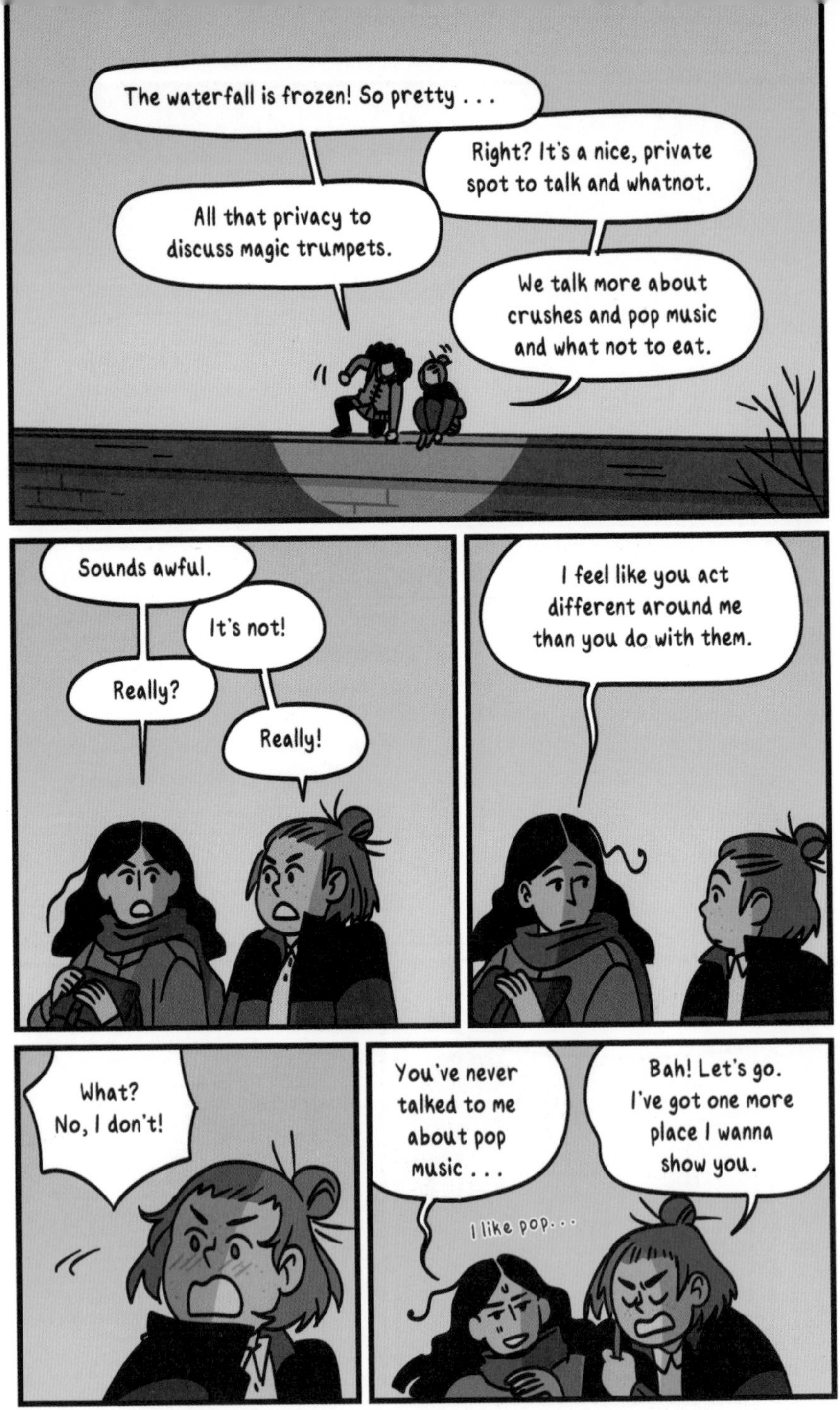
The waterfall is frozen! So pretty . . .
Right? It's a nice, private spot to talk and whatnot.
All that privacy to discuss magic trumpets.
We talk more about crushes and pop music and what not to eat.
Sounds awful.
It's not!
Really?
Really!
I feel like you act different around me than you do with them.
What? No, I don't!
You've never talked to me about pop music . . .
I like pop . . .
Bah! Let's go. I've got one more place I wanna show you.

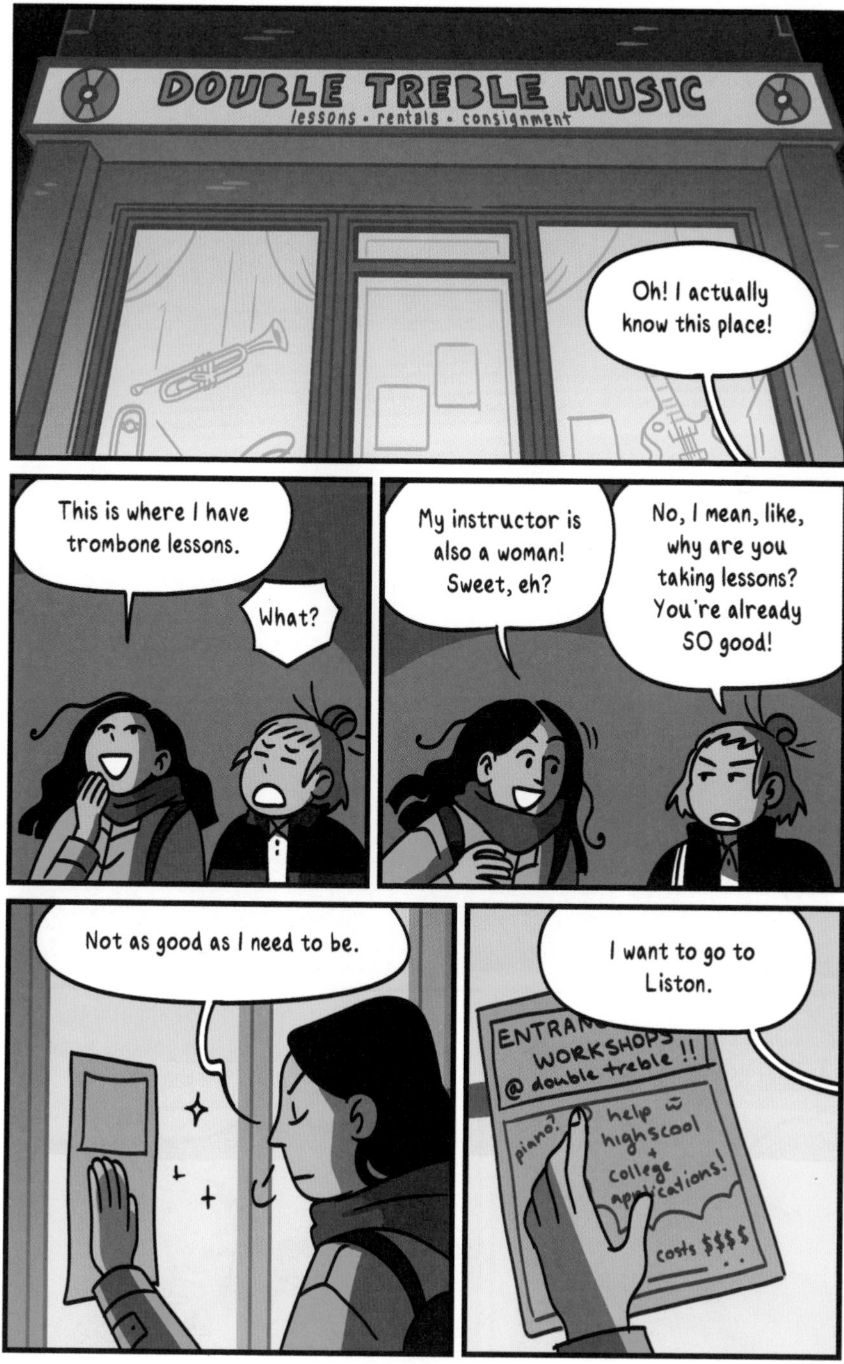
DOUBLE TREBLE MUSIC
lessons • rentals • consignment
Oh! I actually know this place!
This is where I have trombone lessons.
What?
My instructor is also a woman! Sweet, eh?
No, I mean, like, why are you taking lessons? You're already SO good!
Not as good as I need to be.
I want to go to Liston.
WORKSHOPS
@ double treble !!
help w highscool + college applications!
costs $$$$

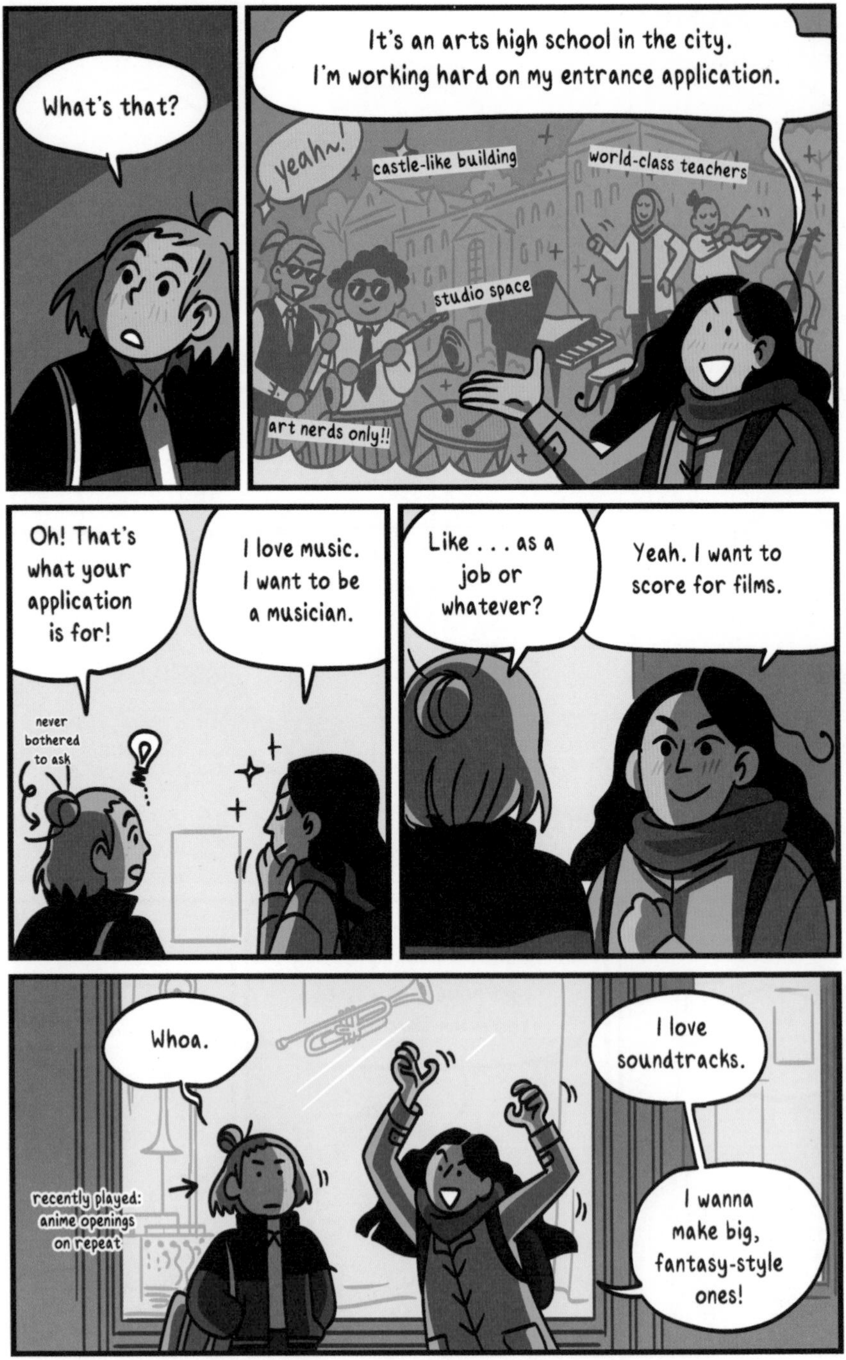
What's that?
It's an arts high school in the city. I'm working hard on my entrance application.
yeah~!
castle-like building
world-class teachers
studio space
art nerds only!!
Oh! That's what your application is for!
I love music. I want to be a musician.
never bothered to ask
Like . . . as a job or whatever?
Yeah. I want to score for films.
Whoa.
I love soundtracks.
recently played: anime openings on repeat
I wanna make big, fantasy-style ones!

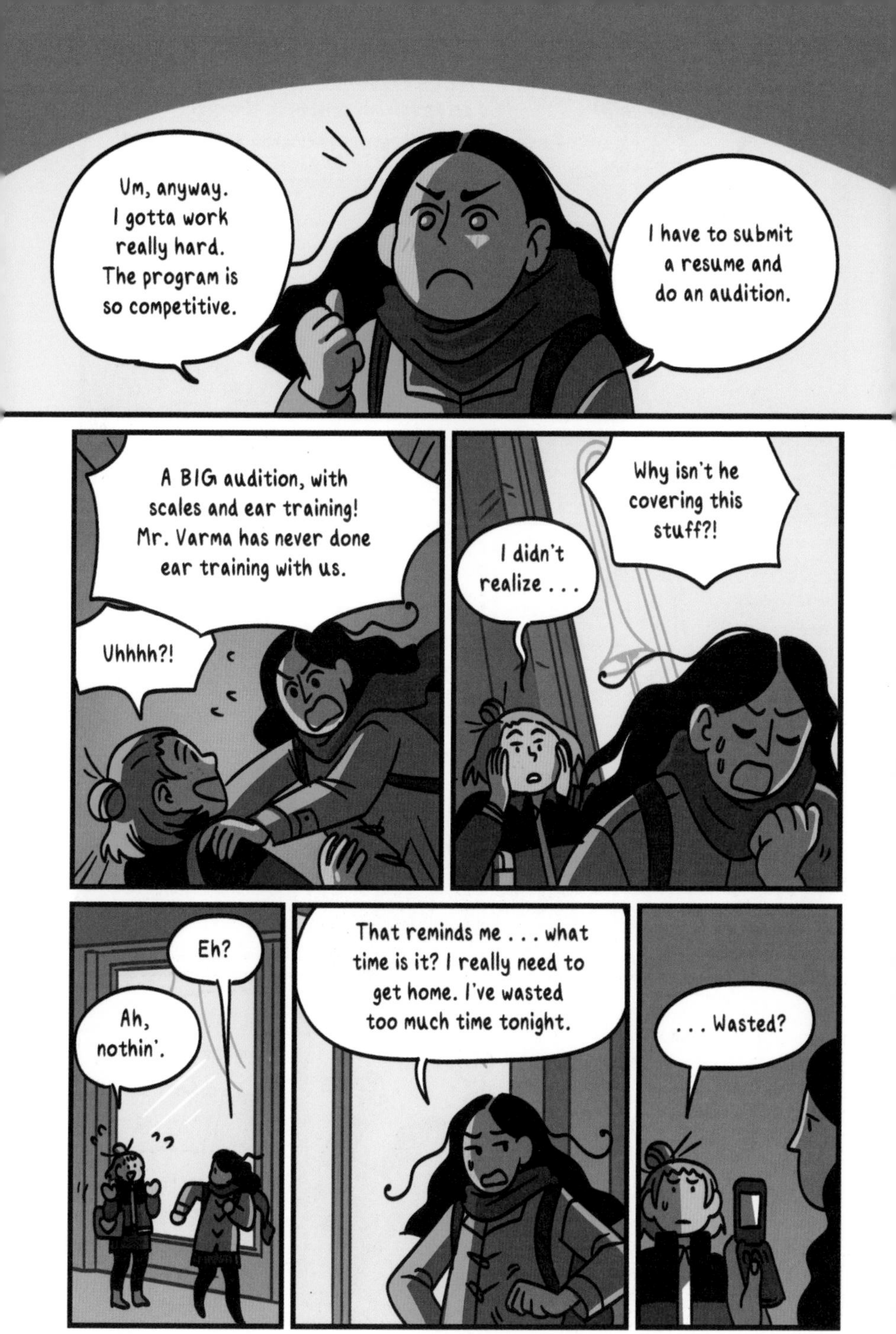
Um, anyway. I gotta work really hard. The program is so competitive.
I have to submit a resume and do an audition.
A BIG audition, with scales and ear training! Mr. Varma has never done ear training with us.
Uhhhh?!
Why isn't he covering this stuff?!
I didn't realize . . .
Eh?
Ah, nothin'.
That reminds me . . . what time is it? I really need to get home. I've wasted too much time tonight.
. . . Wasted?

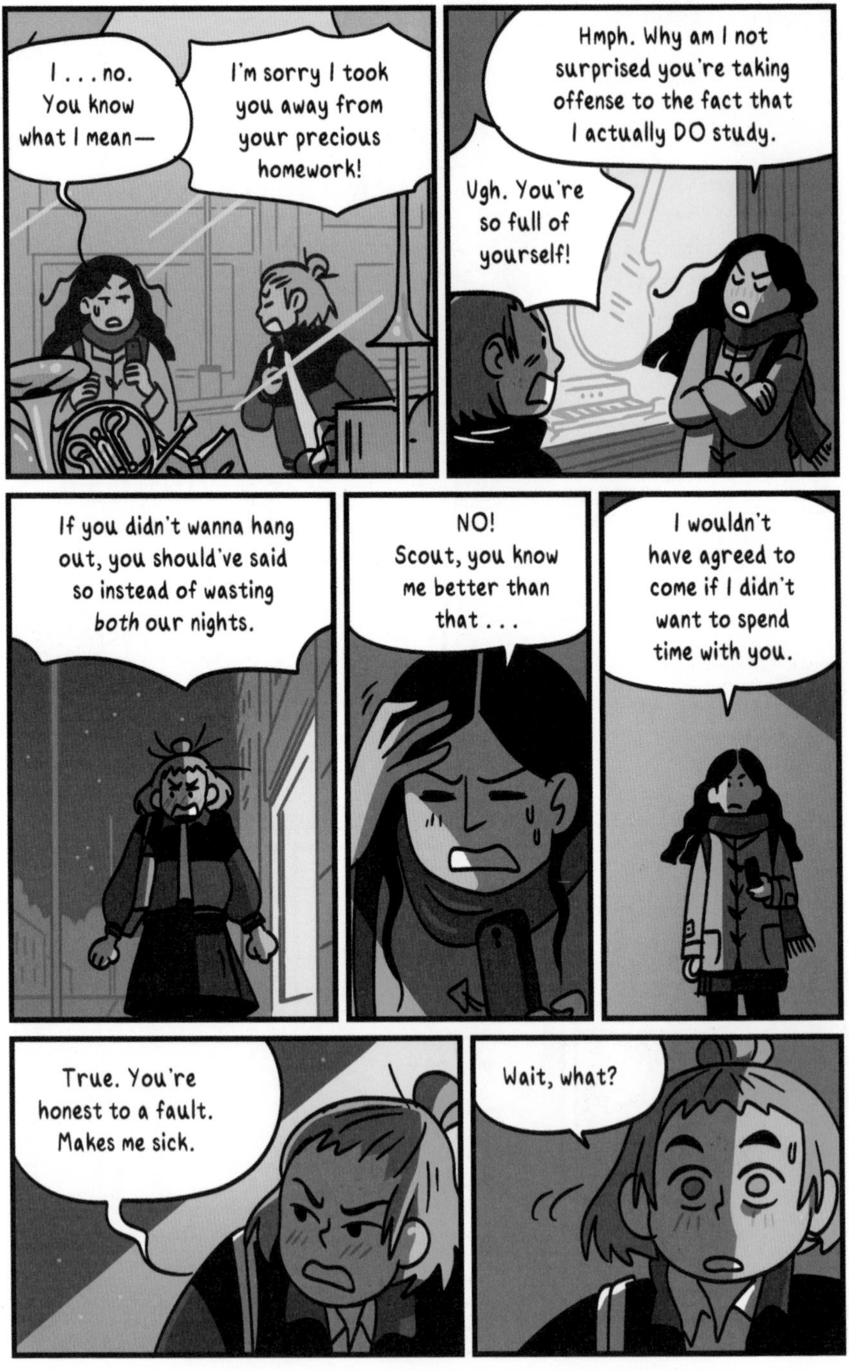
I . . . no. You know what I mean—
I'm sorry I took you away from your precious homework!
Hmph. Why am I not surprised you're taking offense to the fact that I actually DO study.
Ugh. You're so full of yourself!
If you didn't wanna hang out, you should've said so instead of wasting *both* our nights.
NO! Scout, you know me better than that . . .
I wouldn't have agreed to come if I didn't want to spend time with you.
True. You're honest to a fault. Makes me sick.
Wait, what?

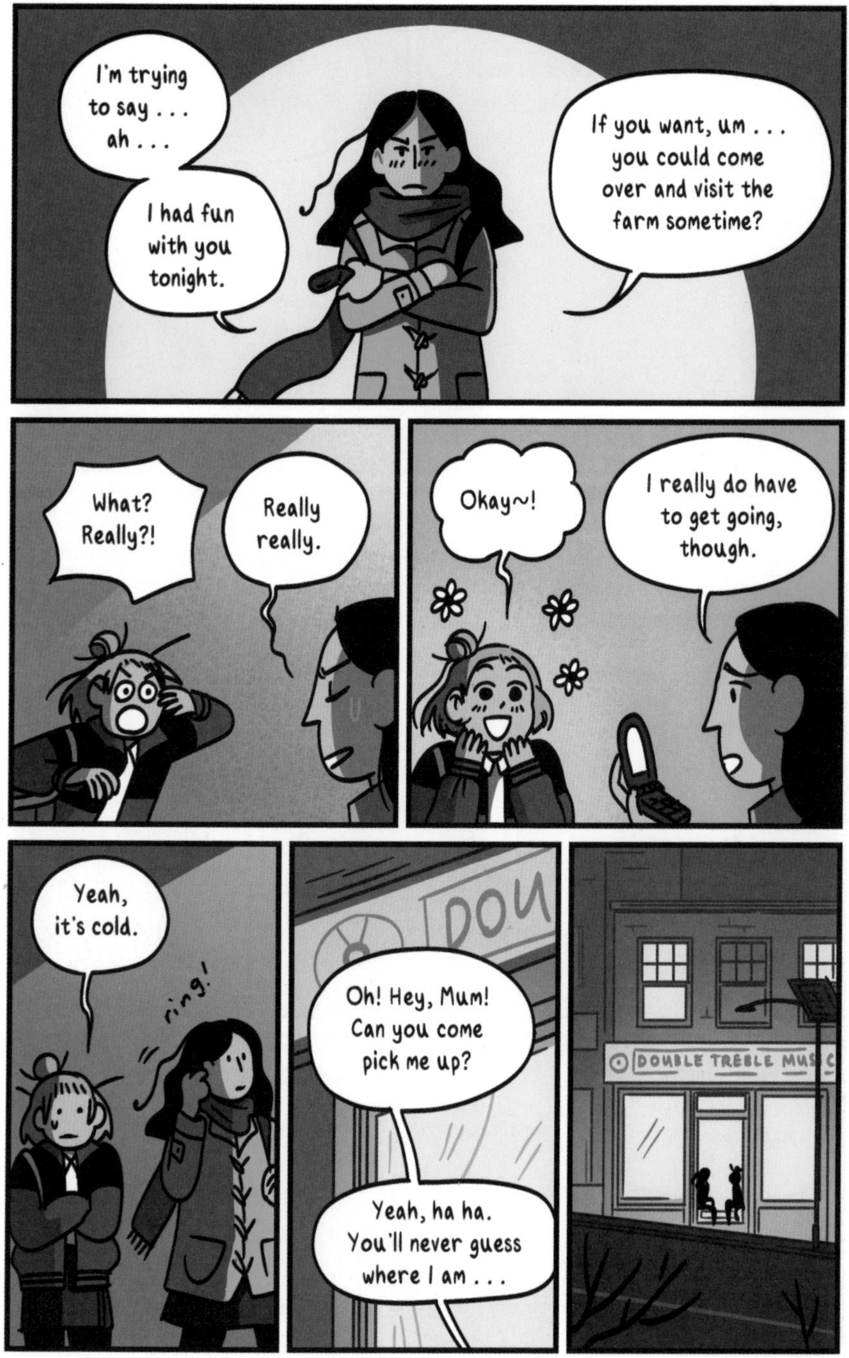
I'm trying to say . . . ah . . .
I had fun with you tonight.
If you want, um . . . you could come over and visit the farm sometime?
What? Really?!
Really really.
Okay~!
I really do have to get going, though.
Yeah, it's cold.
ring!
DOU
Oh! Hey, Mum! Can you come pick me up?
Yeah, ha ha. You'll never guess where I am . . .
DOUBLE TREBLE MUS C

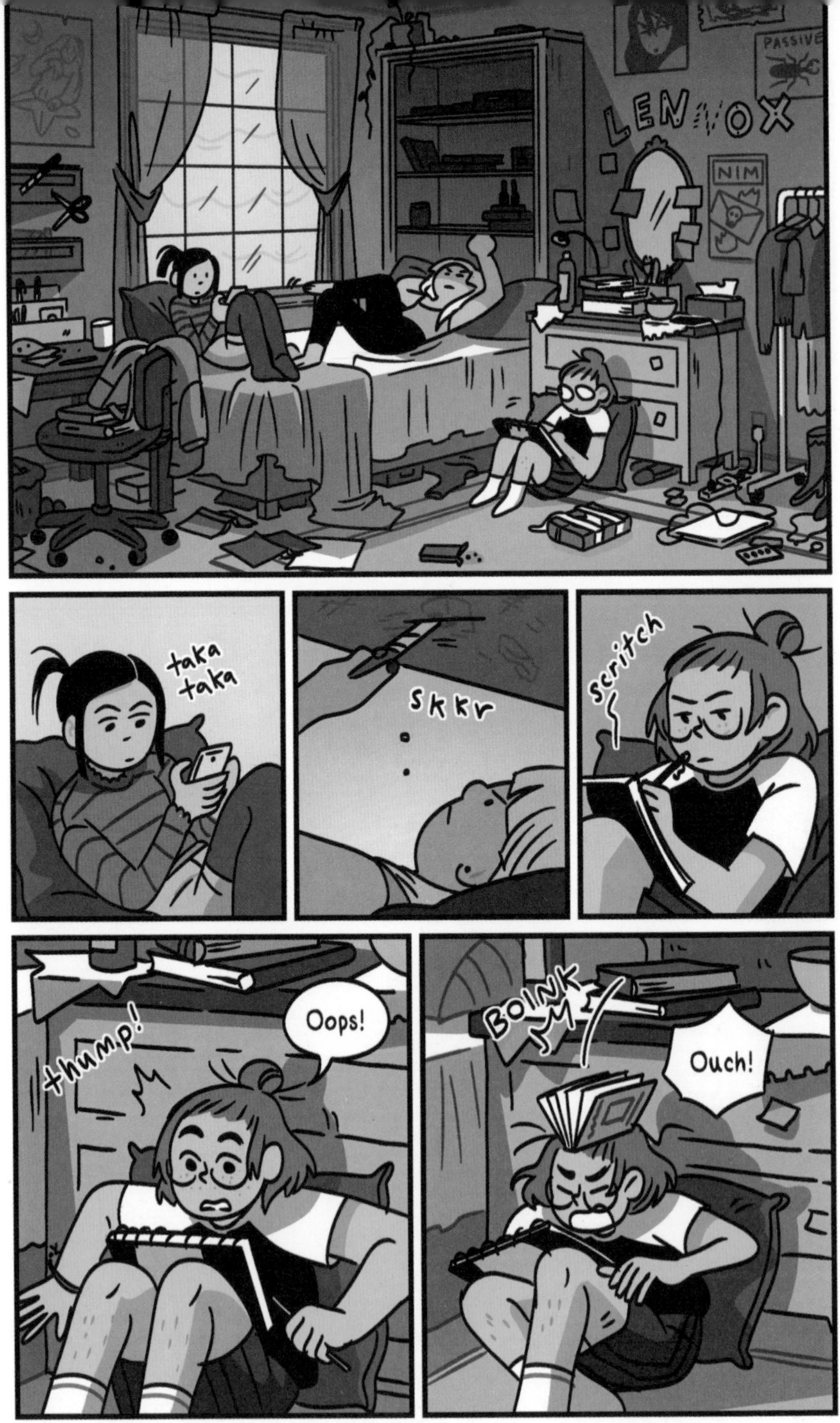
PASSIVE
LENNOX
NIM
taka taka
SKKR
scritch
thump!
Oops!
BOINK
Ouch!

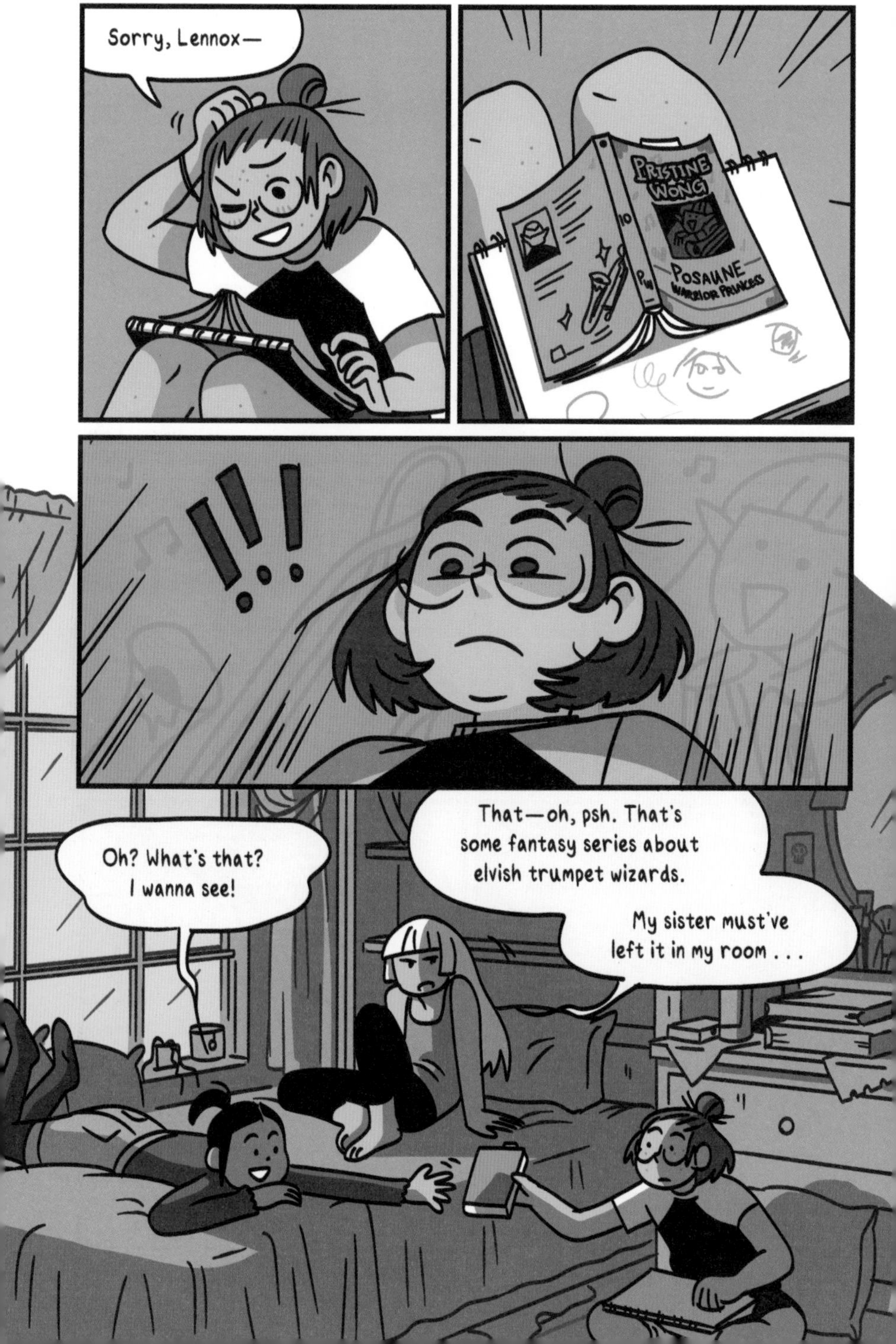

Sorry, Lennox—
PRISTINE WONG
POSAUNE WARRIOR PRINCESS
!!!
Oh? What's that? I wanna see!
That—oh, psh. That's some fantasy series about elvish trumpet wizards.
My sister must've left it in my room . . .

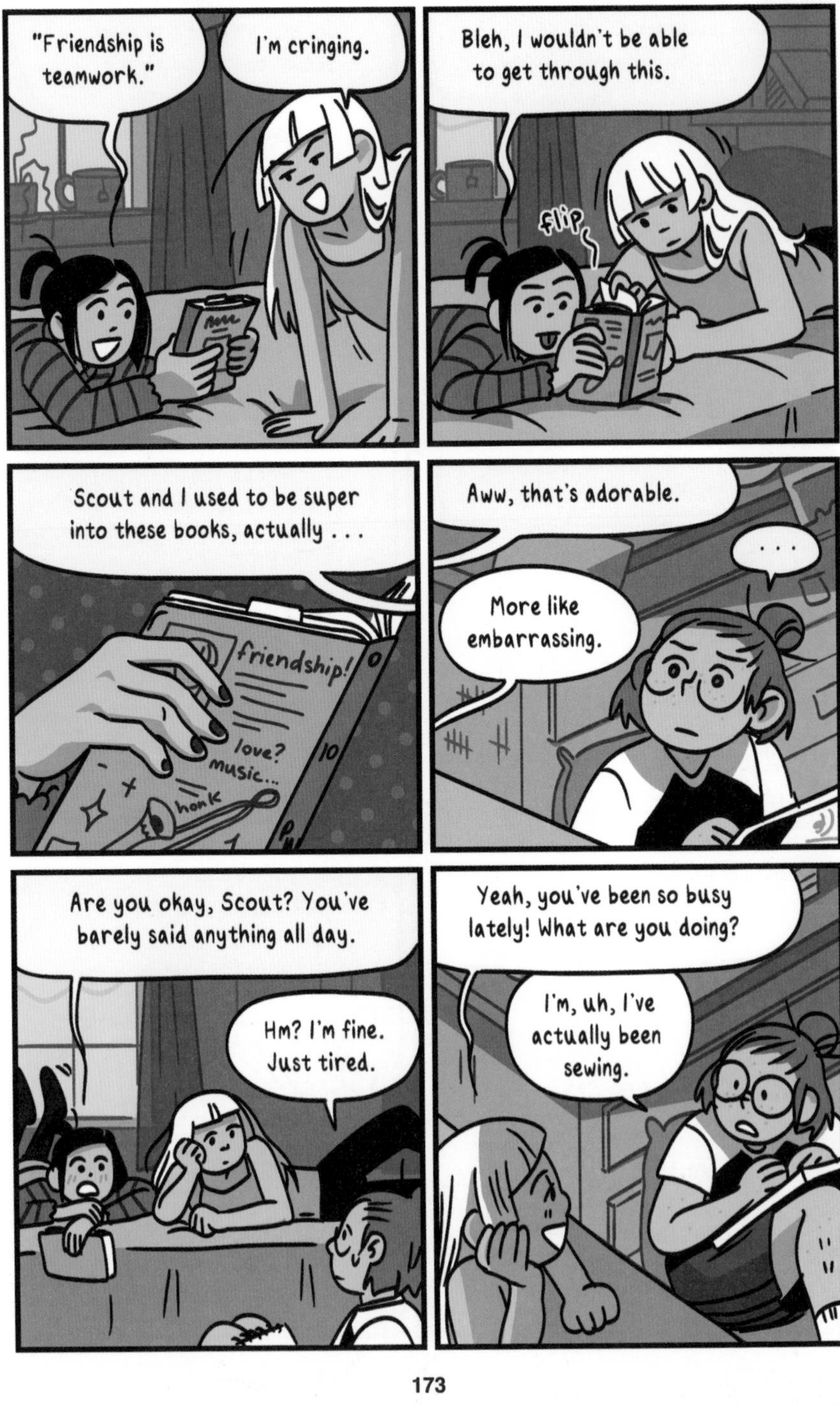
"Friendship is teamwork."
I'm cringing.
Bleh, I wouldn't be able to get through this.
flip
Scout and I used to be super into these books, actually . . .
friendship!
love?
music...
honk
10
Aww, that's adorable.
More like embarrassing.
. . .
Are you okay, Scout? You've barely said anything all day.
Hm? I'm fine. Just tired.
Yeah, you've been so busy lately! What are you doing?
I'm, uh, I've actually been sewing.

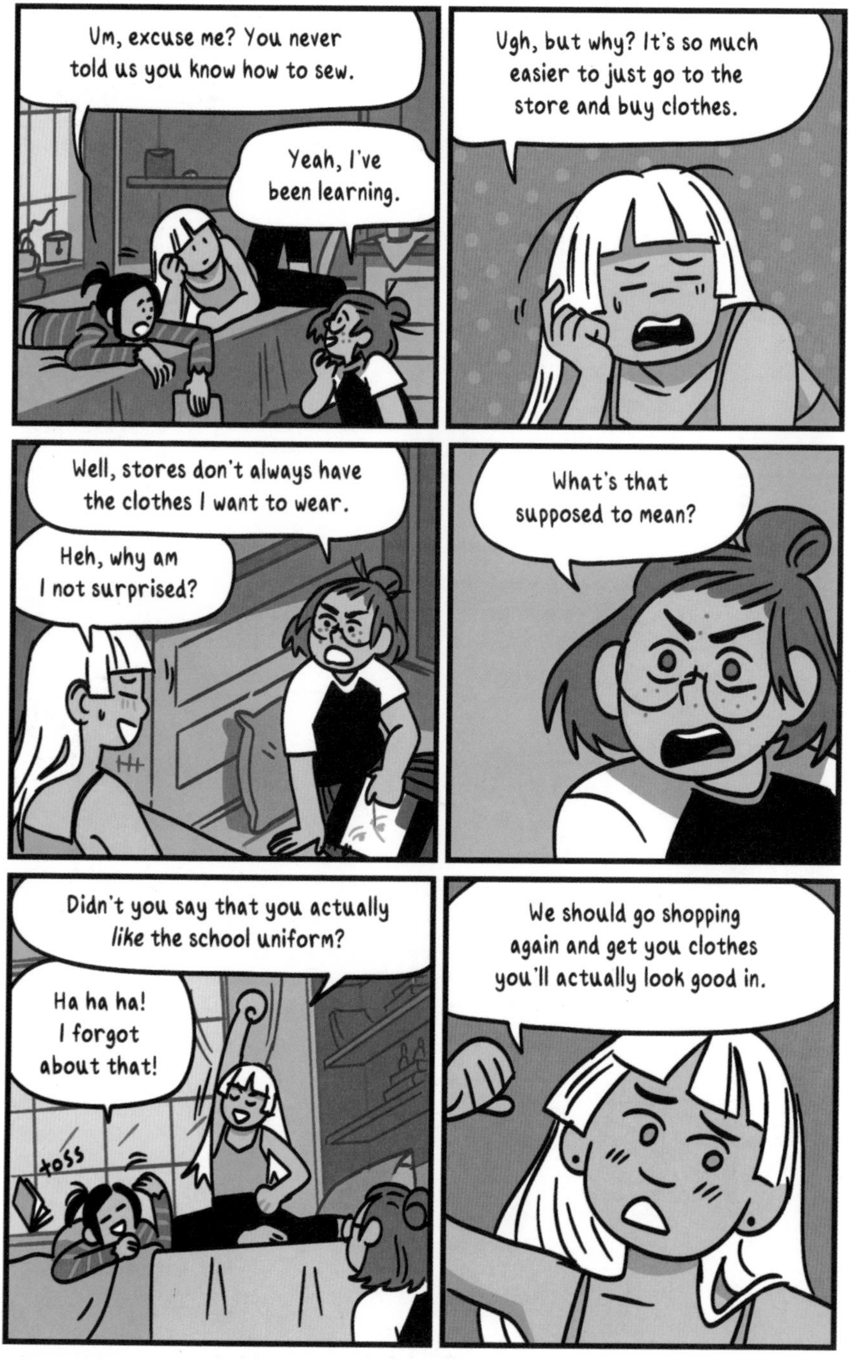
Um, excuse me? You never told us you know how to sew.
Yeah, I've been learning.
Ugh, but why? It's so much easier to just go to the store and buy clothes.
Well, stores don't always have the clothes I want to wear.
Heh, why am I not surprised?
What's that supposed to mean?
Didn't you say that you actually *like* the school uniform?
Ha ha ha! I forgot about that!
toss
We should go shopping again and get you clothes you'll actually look good in.

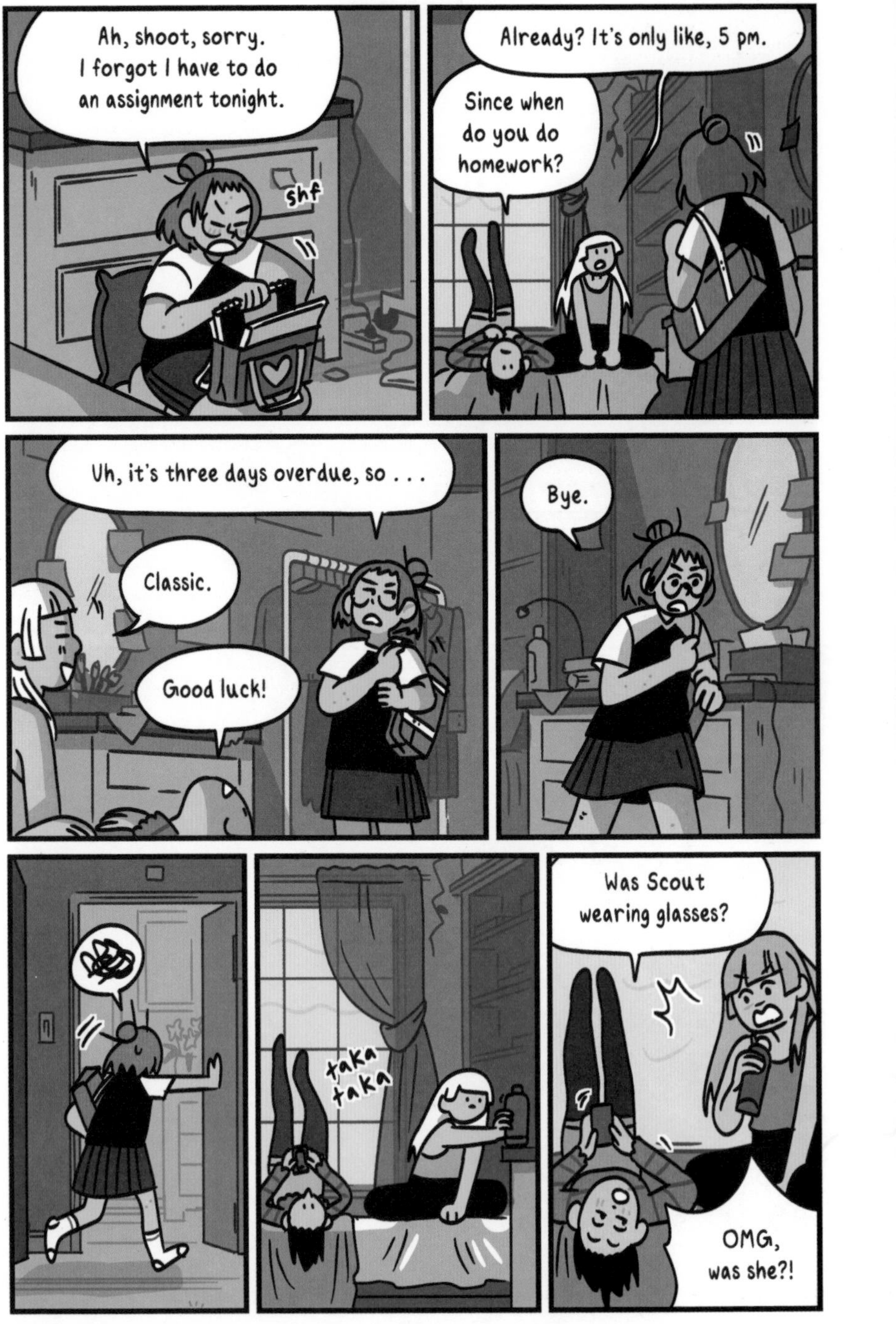
Ah, shoot, sorry.
I forgot I have to do
an assignment tonight.
shf
Already? It's only like, 5 pm.
Since when
do you do
homework?
Uh, it's three days overdue, so . . .
Classic.
Good luck!
Bye.
taka
taka
Was Scout
wearing glasses?
OMG,
was she?!

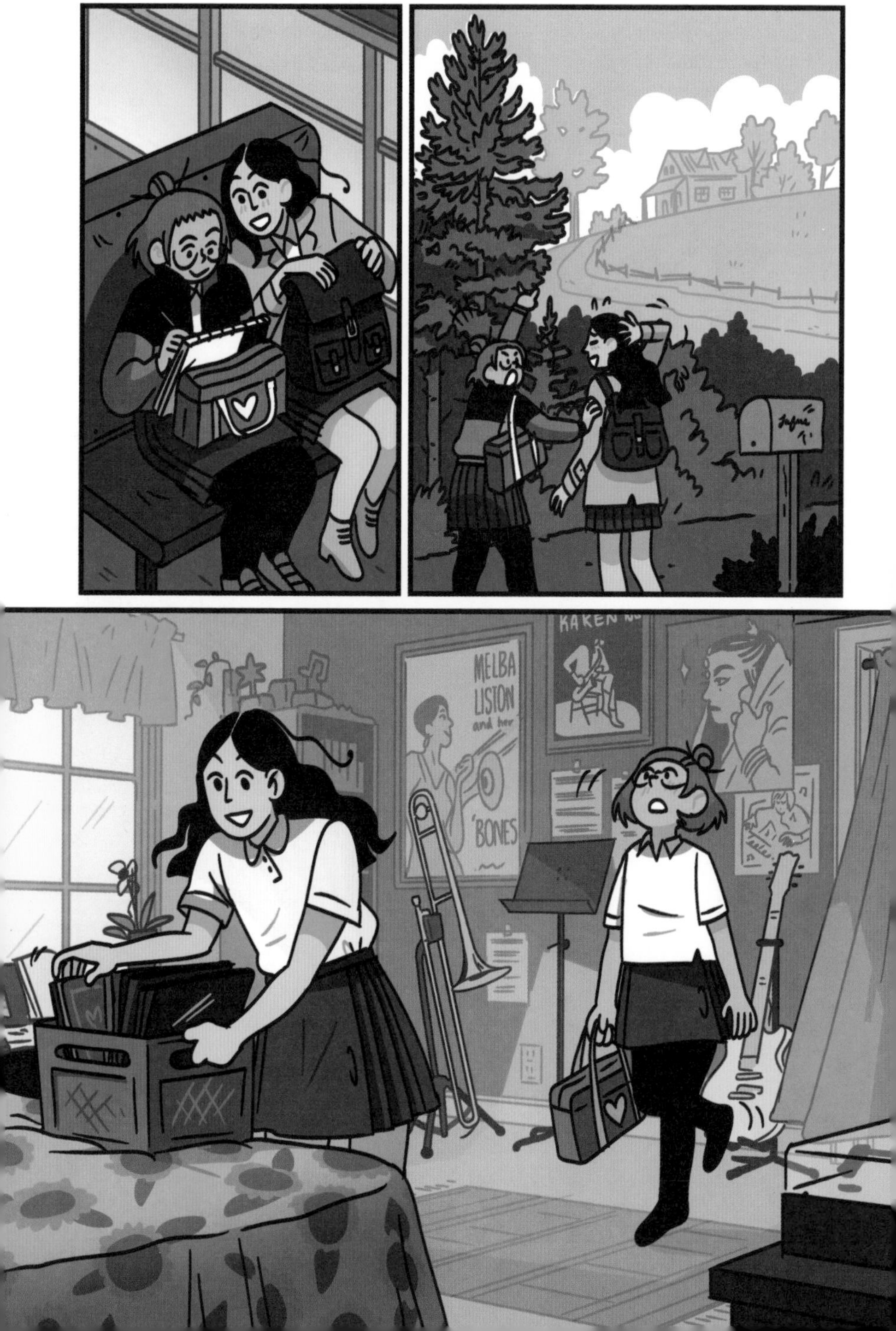

KAKEN
MELBA LISTON and her 'BONES

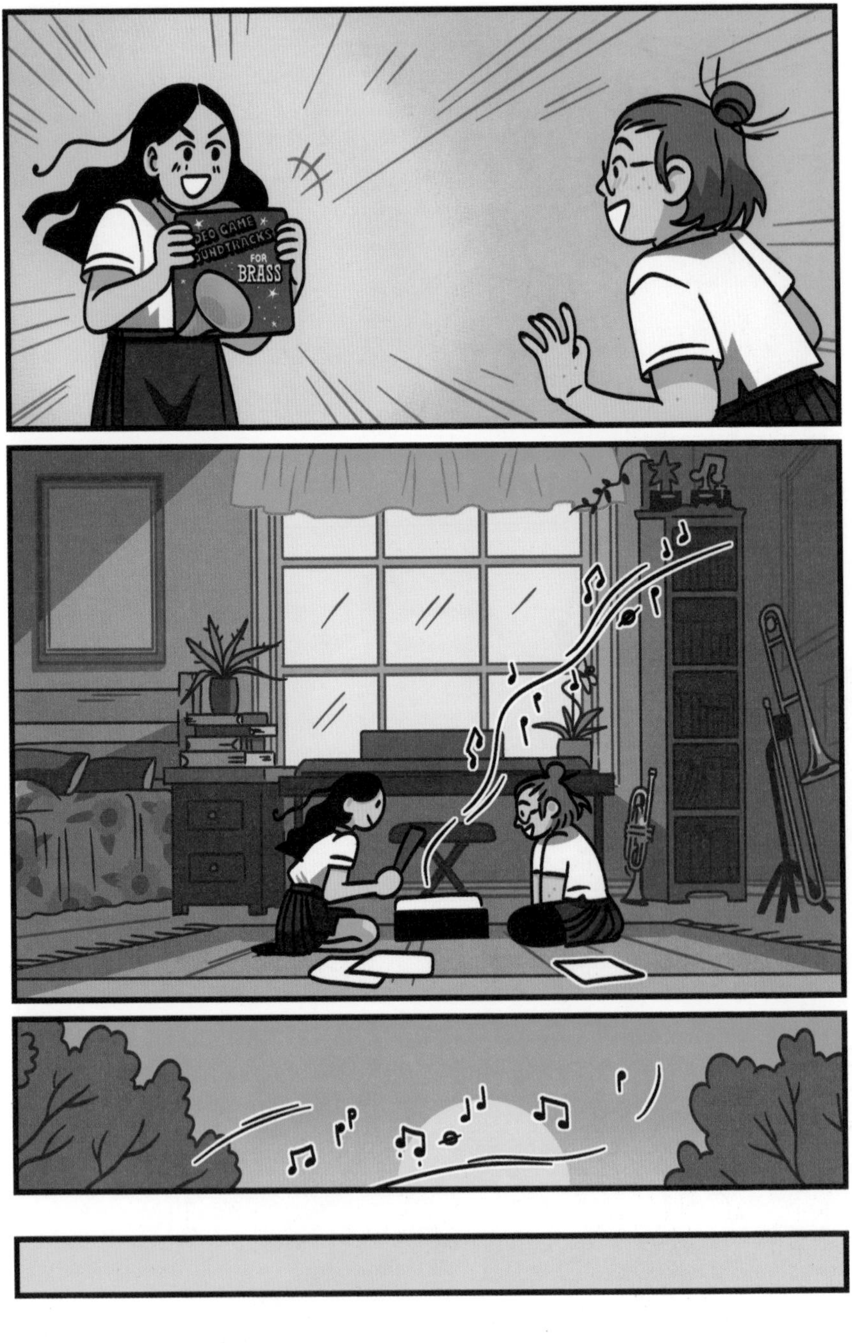
FOR BRASS

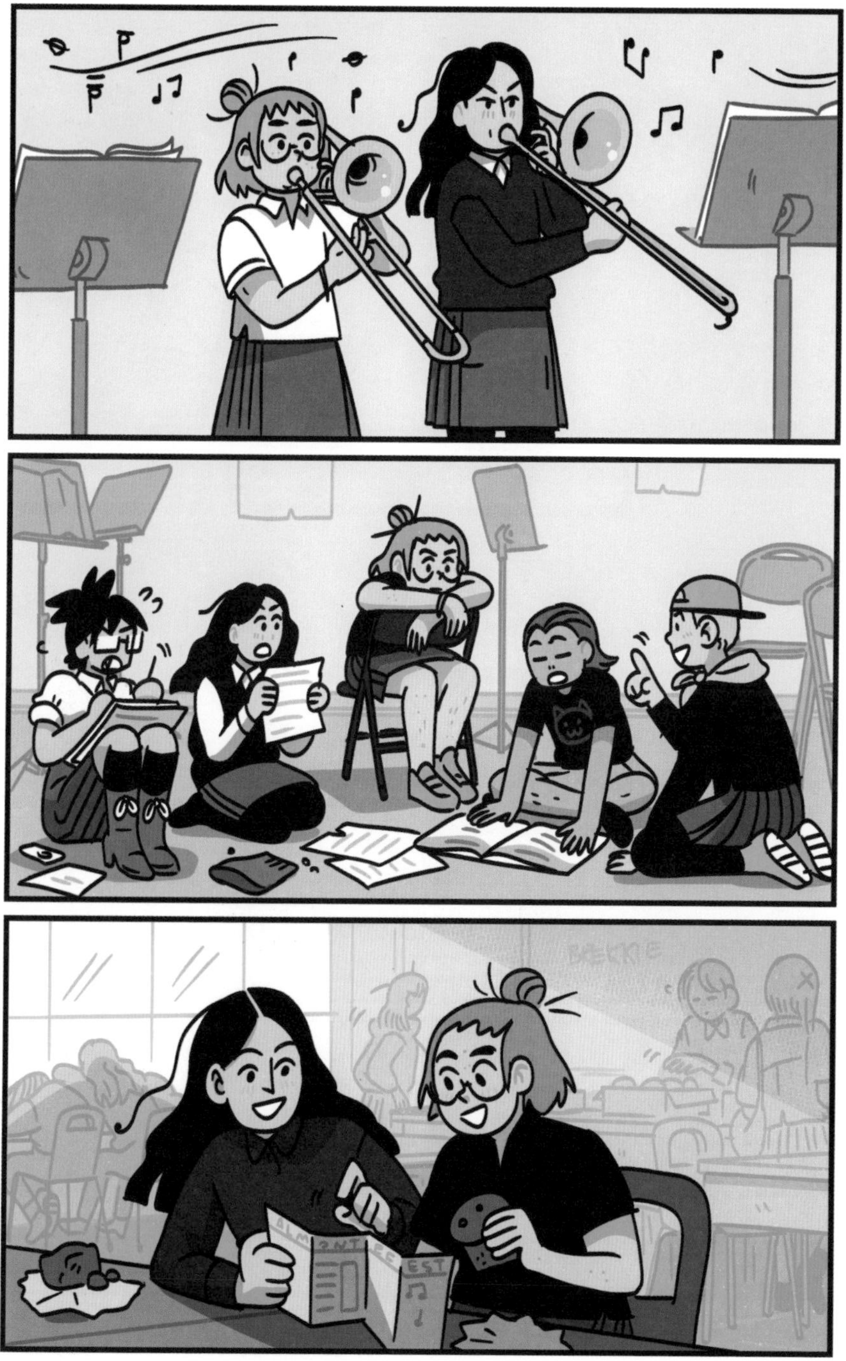
BREKKIE

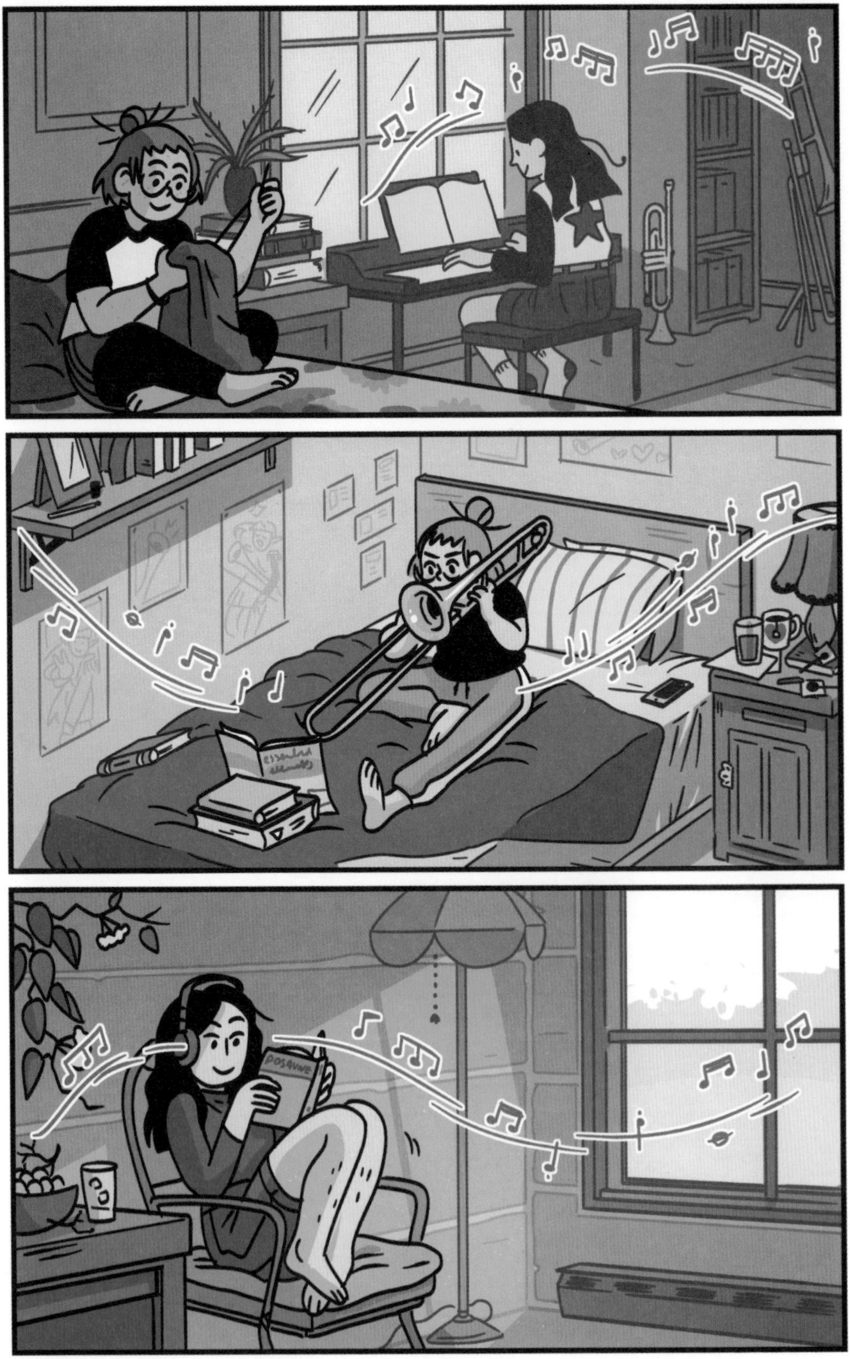
POSAUNE

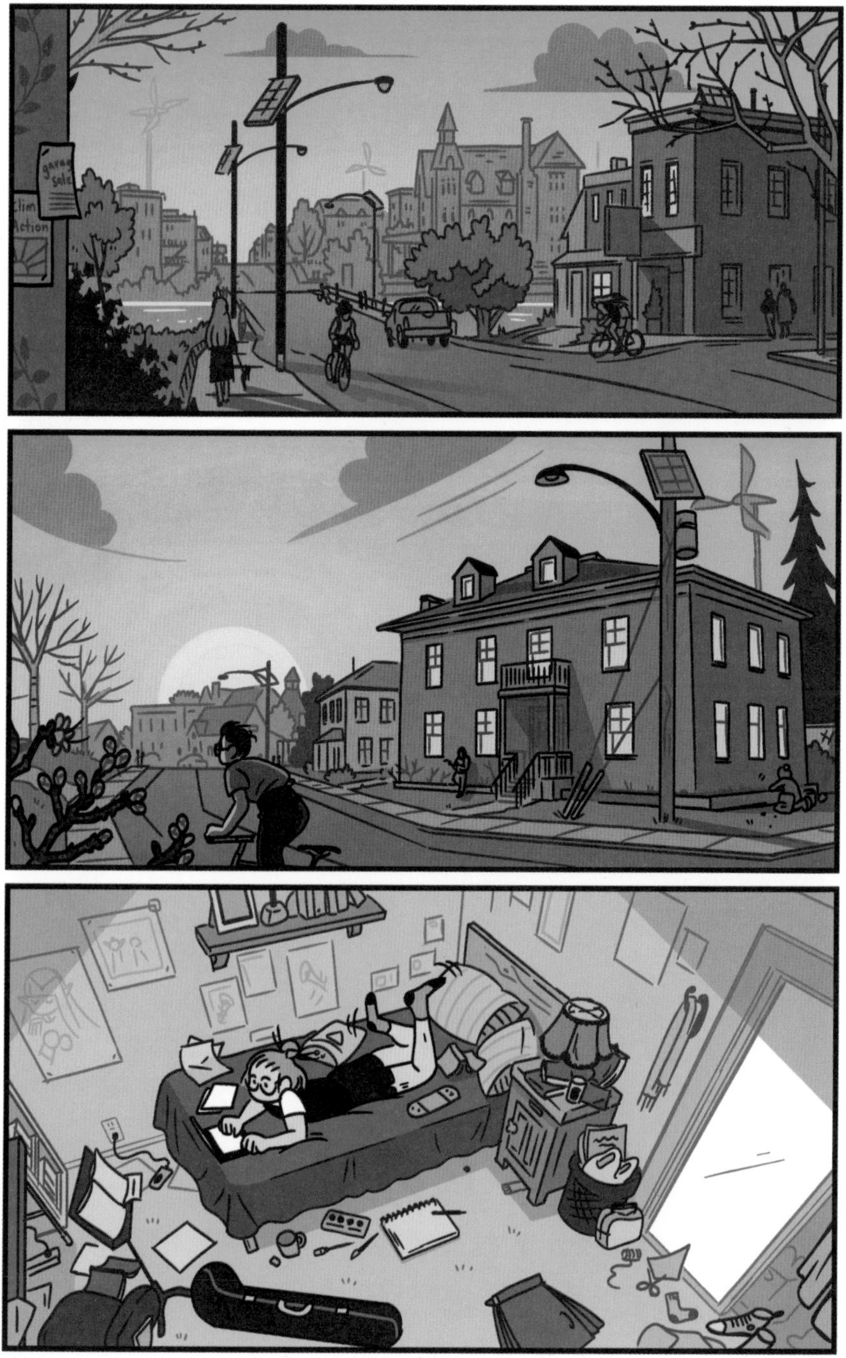

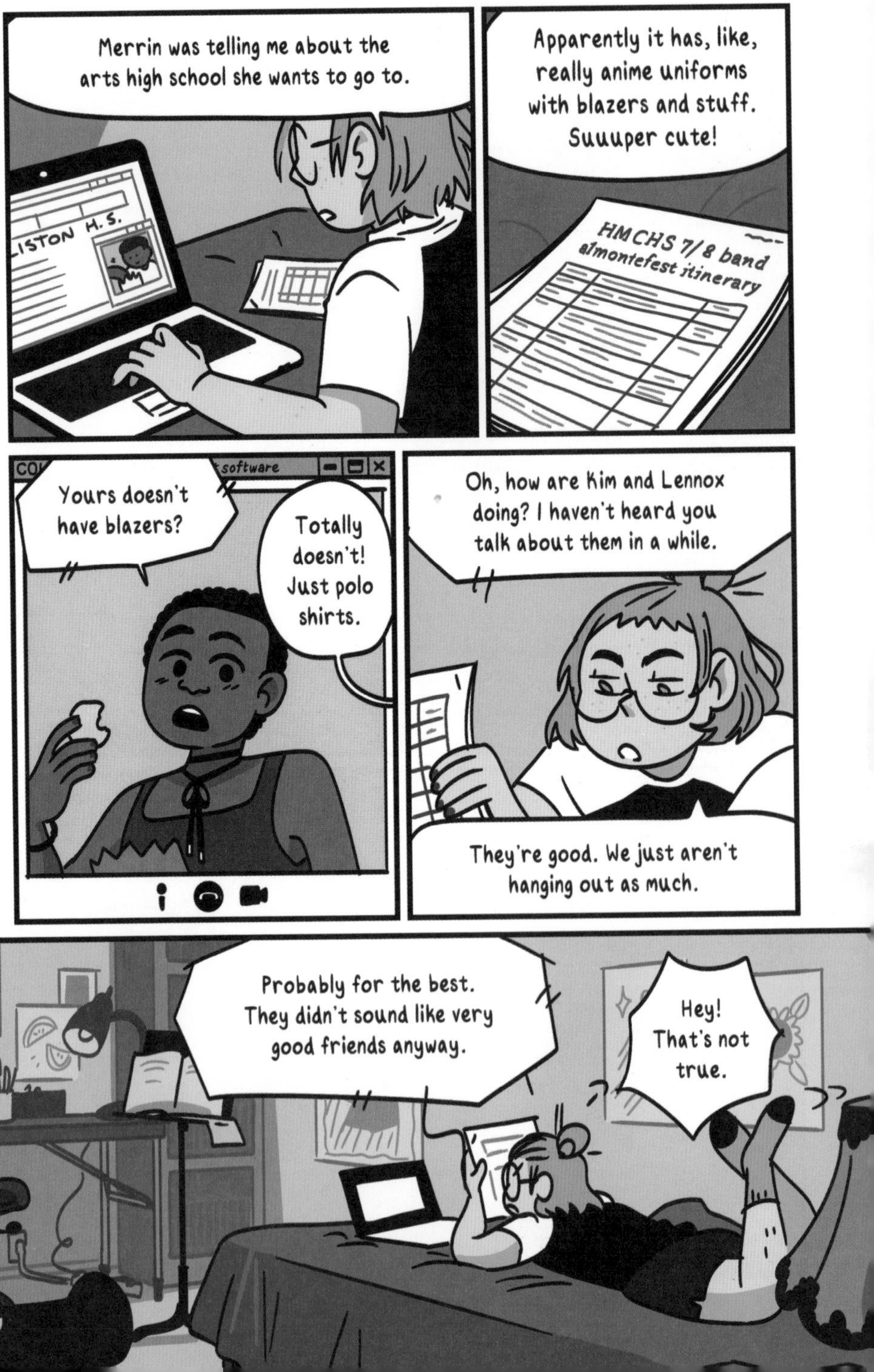
Merrin was telling me about the arts high school she wants to go to.
LISTON H. S.
Apparently it has, like, really anime uniforms with blazers and stuff. Suuuper cute!
HMCHS 7/8 band
almontefest itinerary
software
Yours doesn't have blazers?
Totally doesn't! Just polo shirts.
Oh, how are Kim and Lennox doing? I haven't heard you talk about them in a while.
They're good. We just aren't hanging out as much.
Probably for the best. They didn't sound like very good friends anyway.
Hey! That's not true.

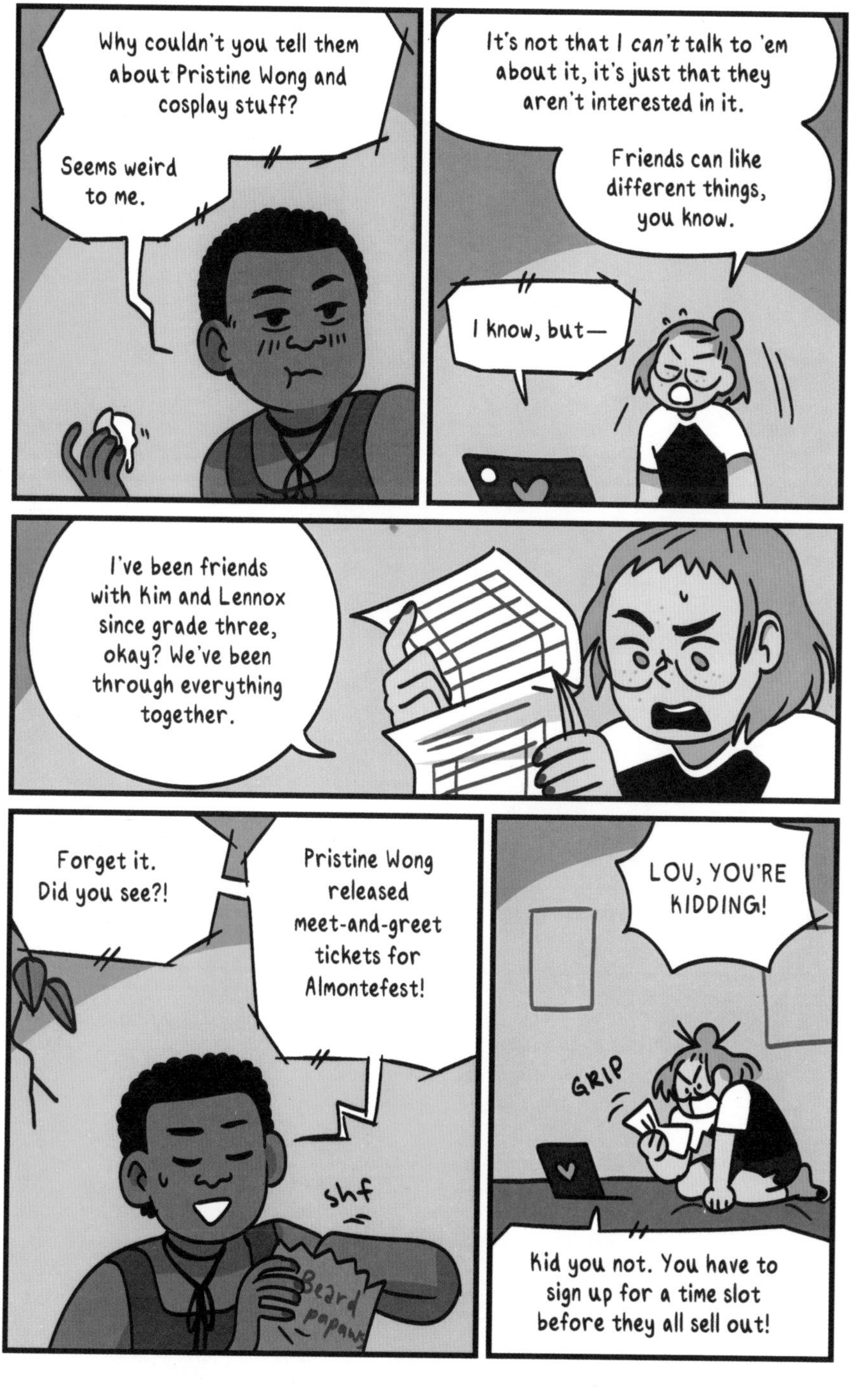
Why couldn't you tell them about Pristine Wong and cosplay stuff?
Seems weird to me.
It's not that I *can't* talk to 'em about it, it's just that they aren't interested in it.
Friends can like different things, you know.
I know, but—
I've been friends with Kim and Lennox since grade three, okay? We've been through everything together.
Forget it. Did you see?!
Pristine Wong released meet-and-greet tickets for Almontefest!
shf
Beard papa's
LOU, YOU'RE KIDDING!
GRIP
Kid you not. You have to sign up for a time slot before they all sell out!

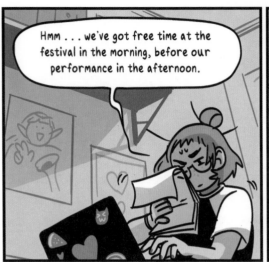

Hmm . . . we've got free time at the festival in the morning, before our performance in the afternoon.

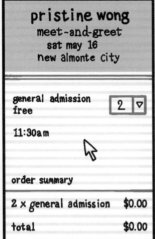

pristine wong
meet-and-greet
sat may 16
new almonte city

general admission
free   2 ▽

11:30am

order summary

2 × general admission $0.00

total $0.00

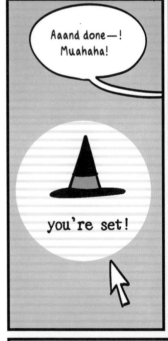

Aaand done—!
Muahaha!

you're set!

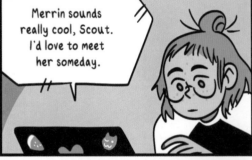

Merrin sounds really cool, Scout. I'd love to meet her someday.

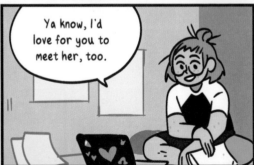

Ya know, I'd love for you to meet her, too.

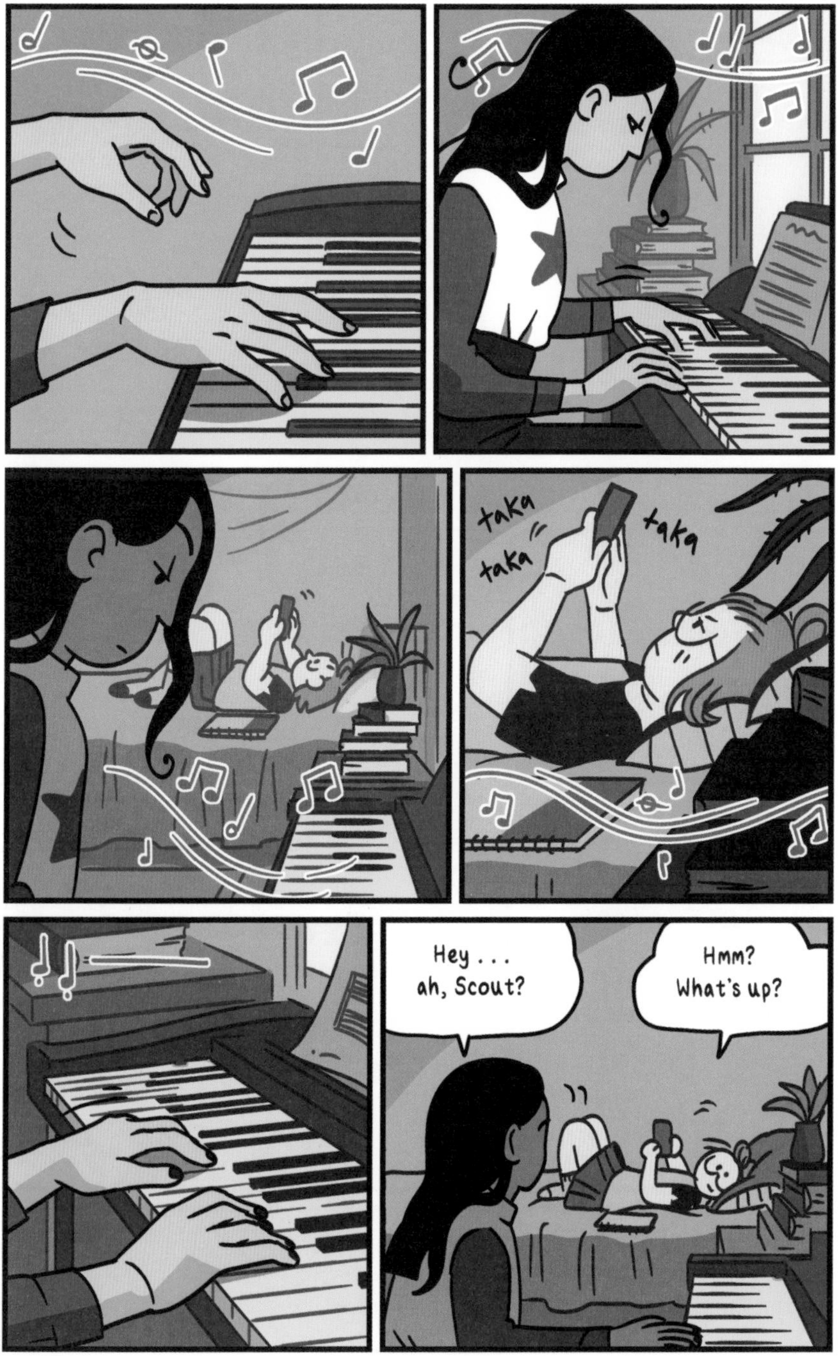
taka
taka
taka
Hey . . . ah, Scout?
Hmm? What's up?

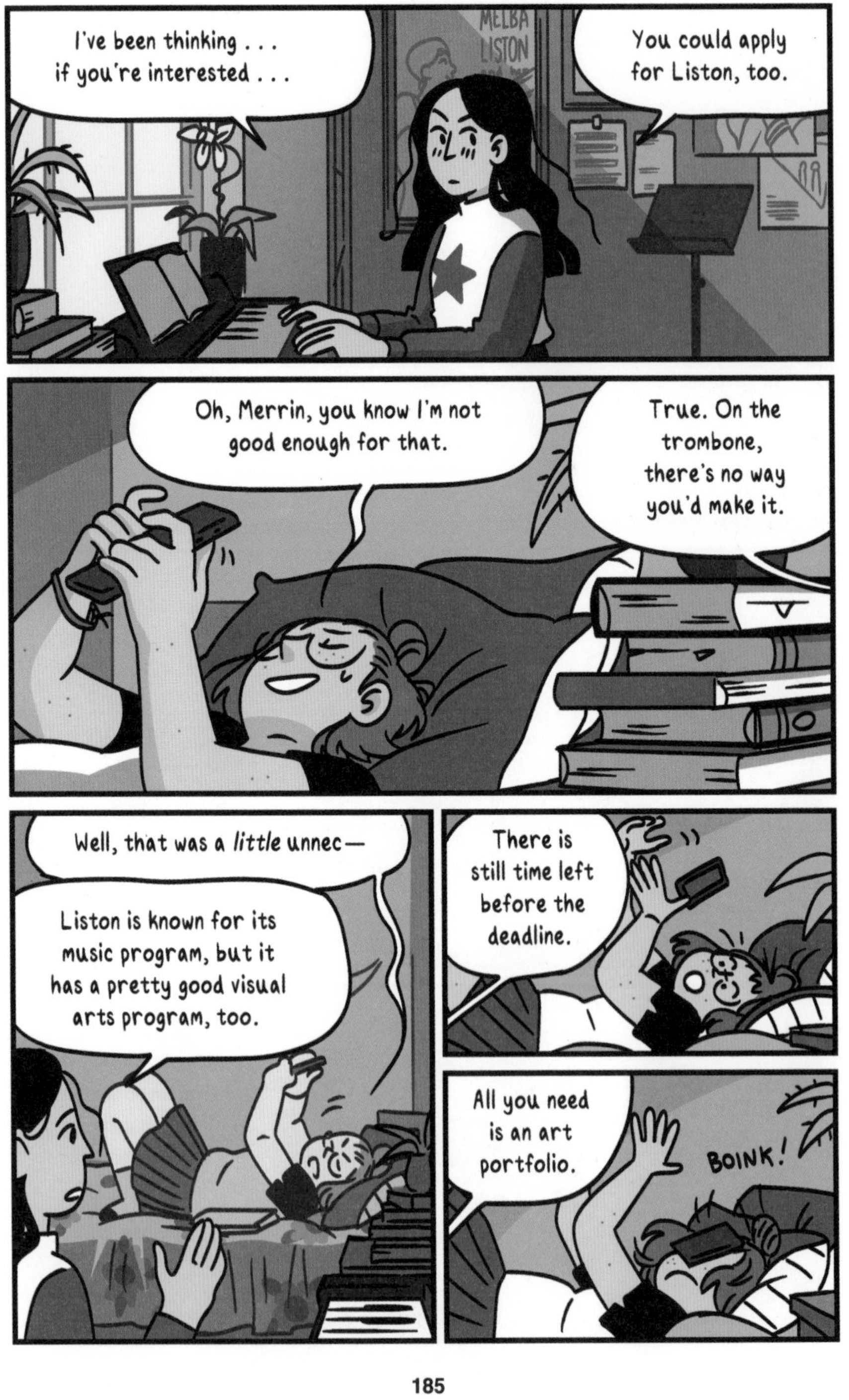
I've been thinking . . .
if you're interested . . .
MELBA
LISTON
You could apply for Liston, too.
Oh, Merrin, you know I'm not good enough for that.
True. On the trombone, there's no way you'd make it.
Well, that was a *little* unnec—
Liston is known for its music program, but it has a pretty good visual arts program, too.
There is still time left before the deadline.
All you need is an art portfolio.
BOINK!

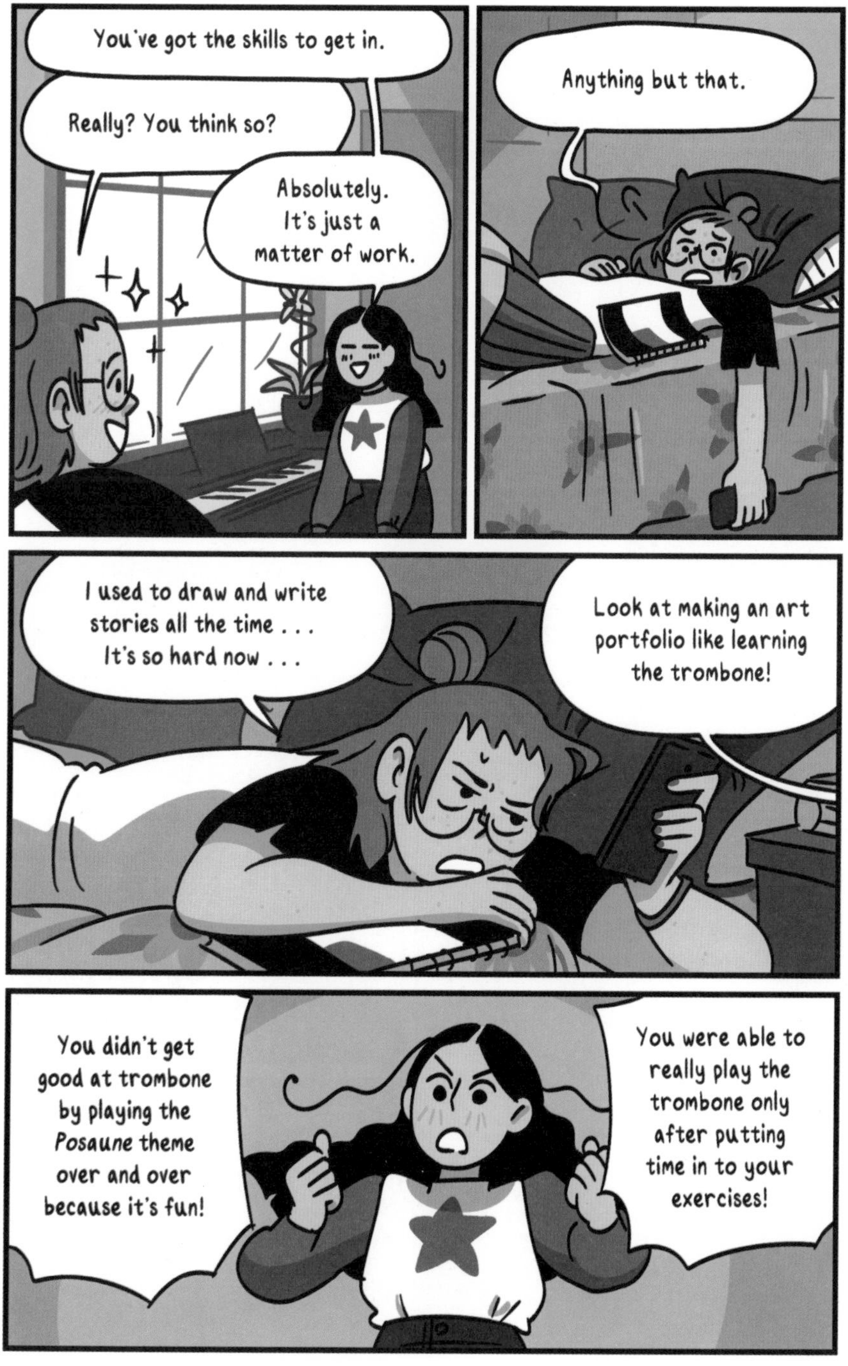
You've got the skills to get in.
Really? You think so?
Absolutely. It's just a matter of work.
Anything but that.
I used to draw and write stories all the time . . . It's so hard now . . .
Look at making an art portfolio like learning the trombone!
You didn't get good at trombone by playing the *Posaune* theme over and over because it's fun!
You were able to really play the trombone only after putting time in to your exercises!

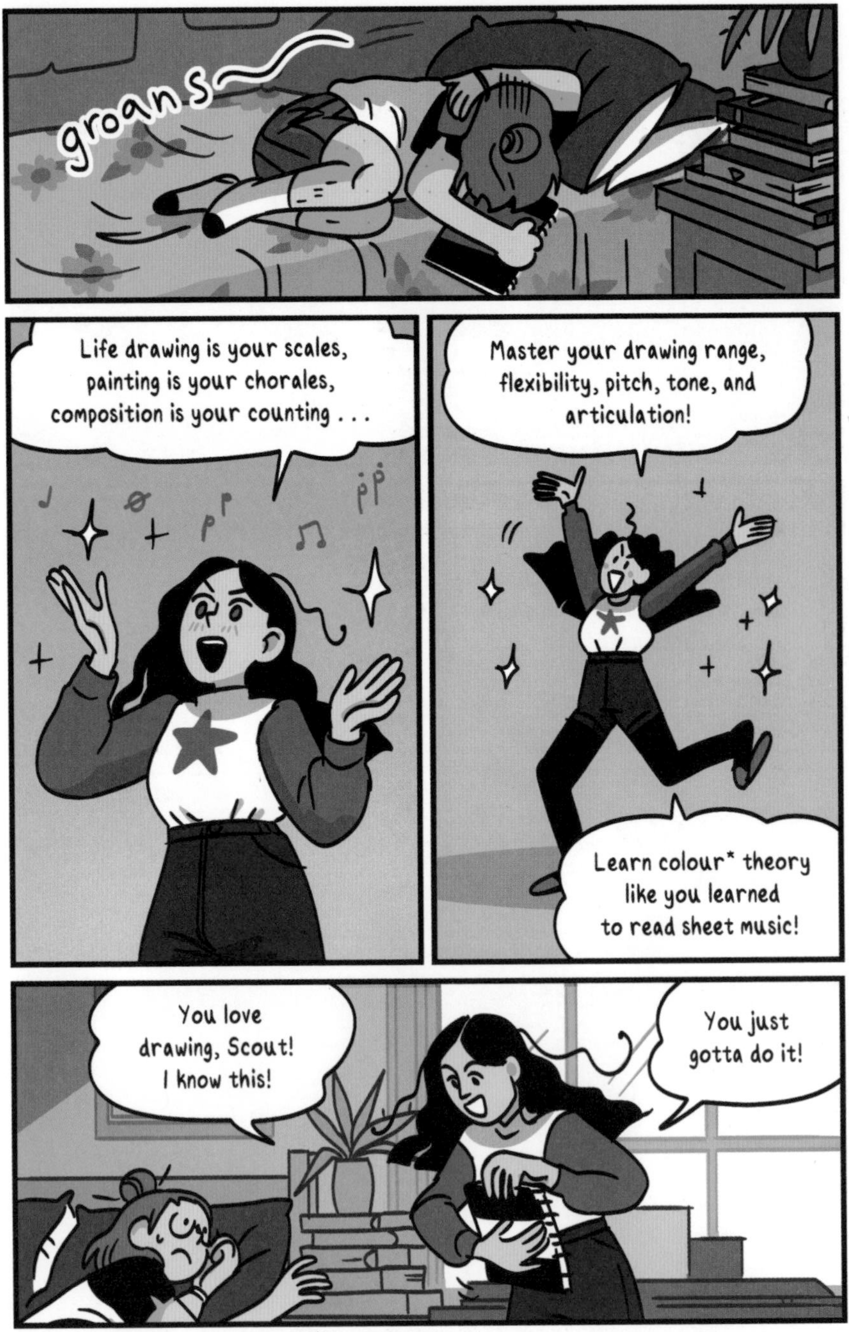
groans
Life drawing is your scales, painting is your chorales, composition is your counting . . .
Master your drawing range, flexibility, pitch, tone, and articulation!
Learn colour* theory like you learned to read sheet music!
You love drawing, Scout! I know this!
You just gotta do it!

*Color is spelt colour in Canadian English.

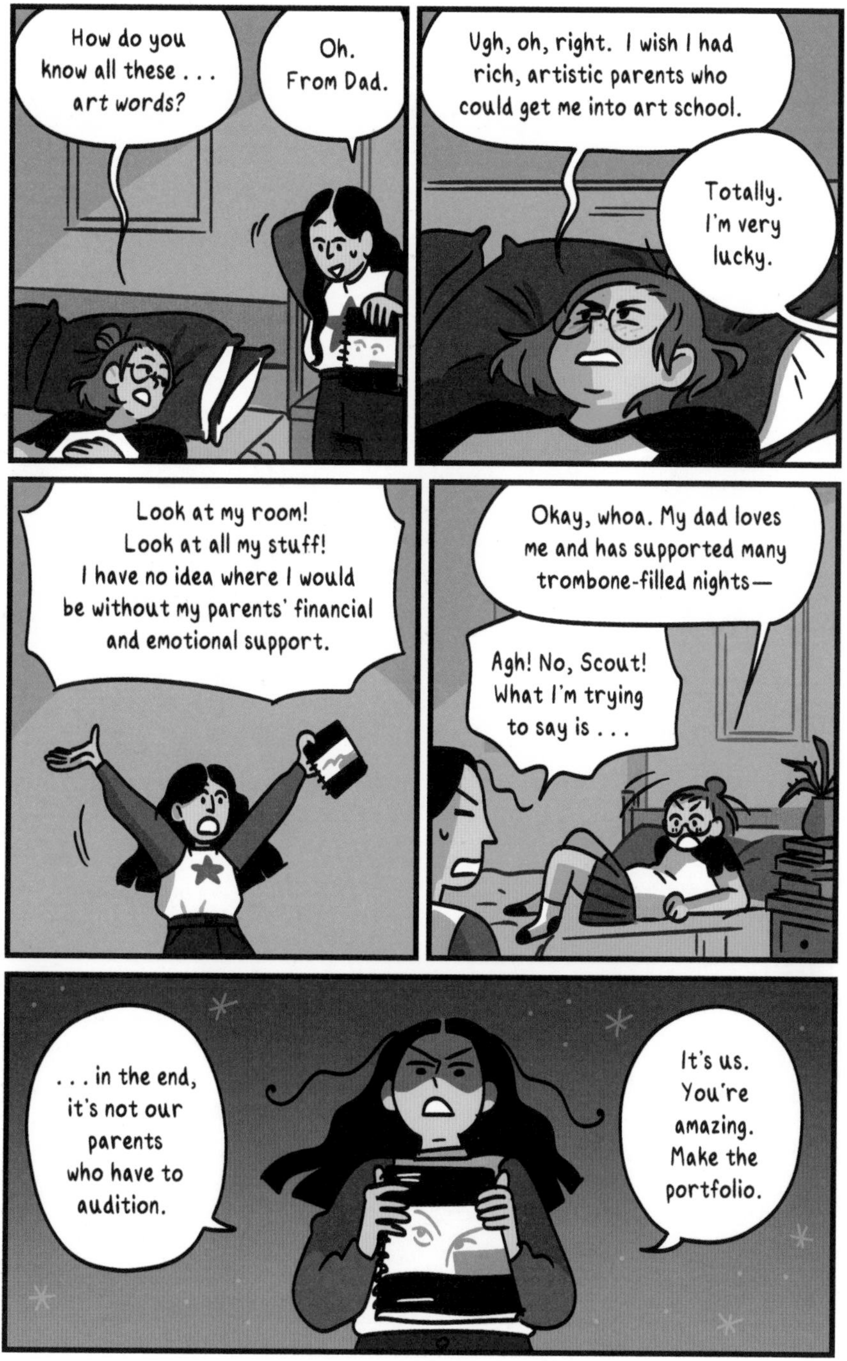
How do you know all these . . . art words?
Oh. From Dad.
Ugh, oh, right. I wish I had rich, artistic parents who could get me into art school.
Totally. I'm very lucky.
Look at my room! Look at all my stuff! I have no idea where I would be without my parents' financial and emotional support.
Okay, whoa. My dad loves me and has supported many trombone-filled nights—
Agh! No, Scout! What I'm trying to say is . . .
. . . in the end, it's not our parents who have to audition.
It's us. You're amazing. Make the portfolio.

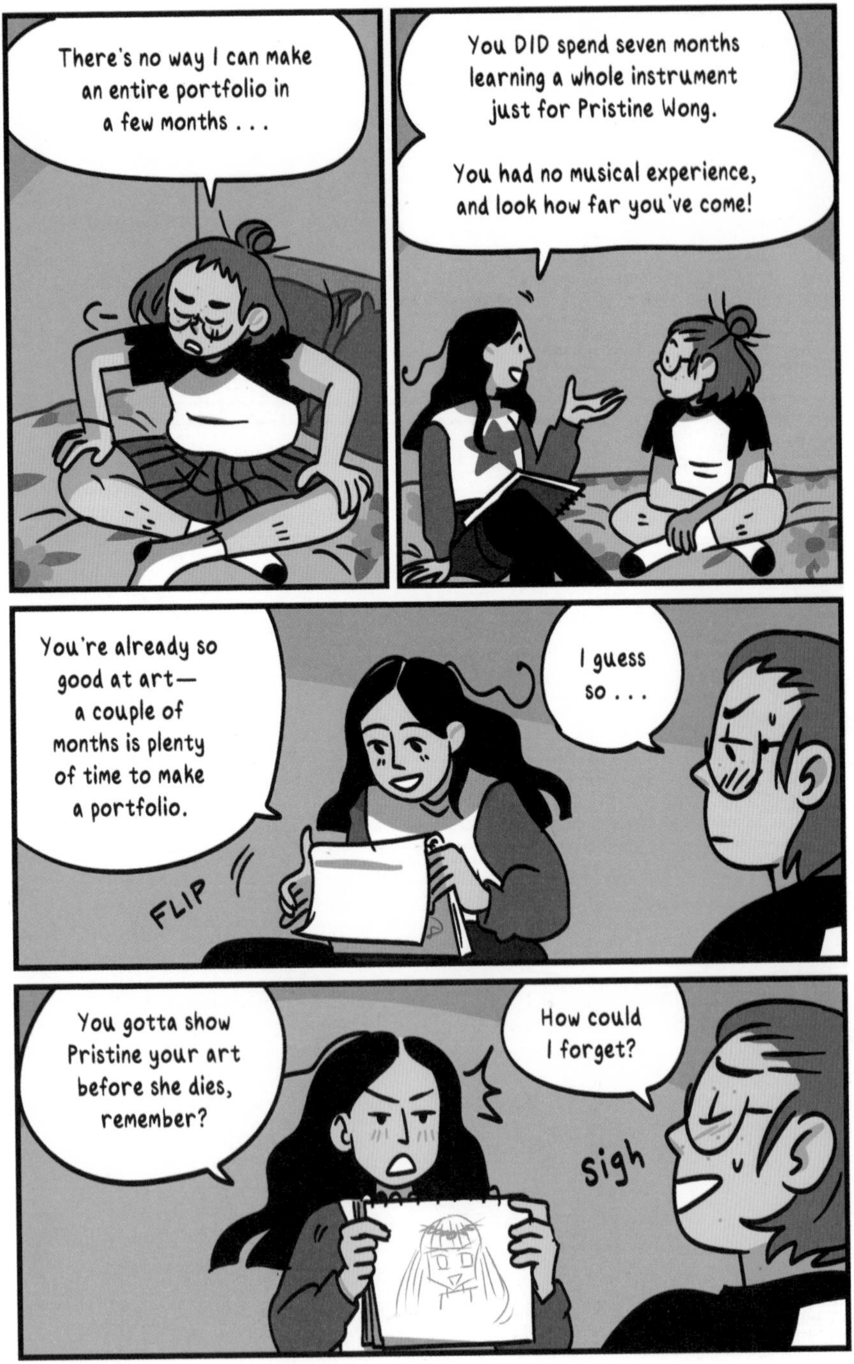
There's no way I can make an entire portfolio in a few months . . .
You DID spend seven months learning a whole instrument just for Pristine Wong.
You had no musical experience, and look how far you've come!
You're already so good at art— a couple of months is plenty of time to make a portfolio.
FLIP
I guess so . . .
You gotta show Pristine your art before she dies, remember?
How could I forget?
Sigh

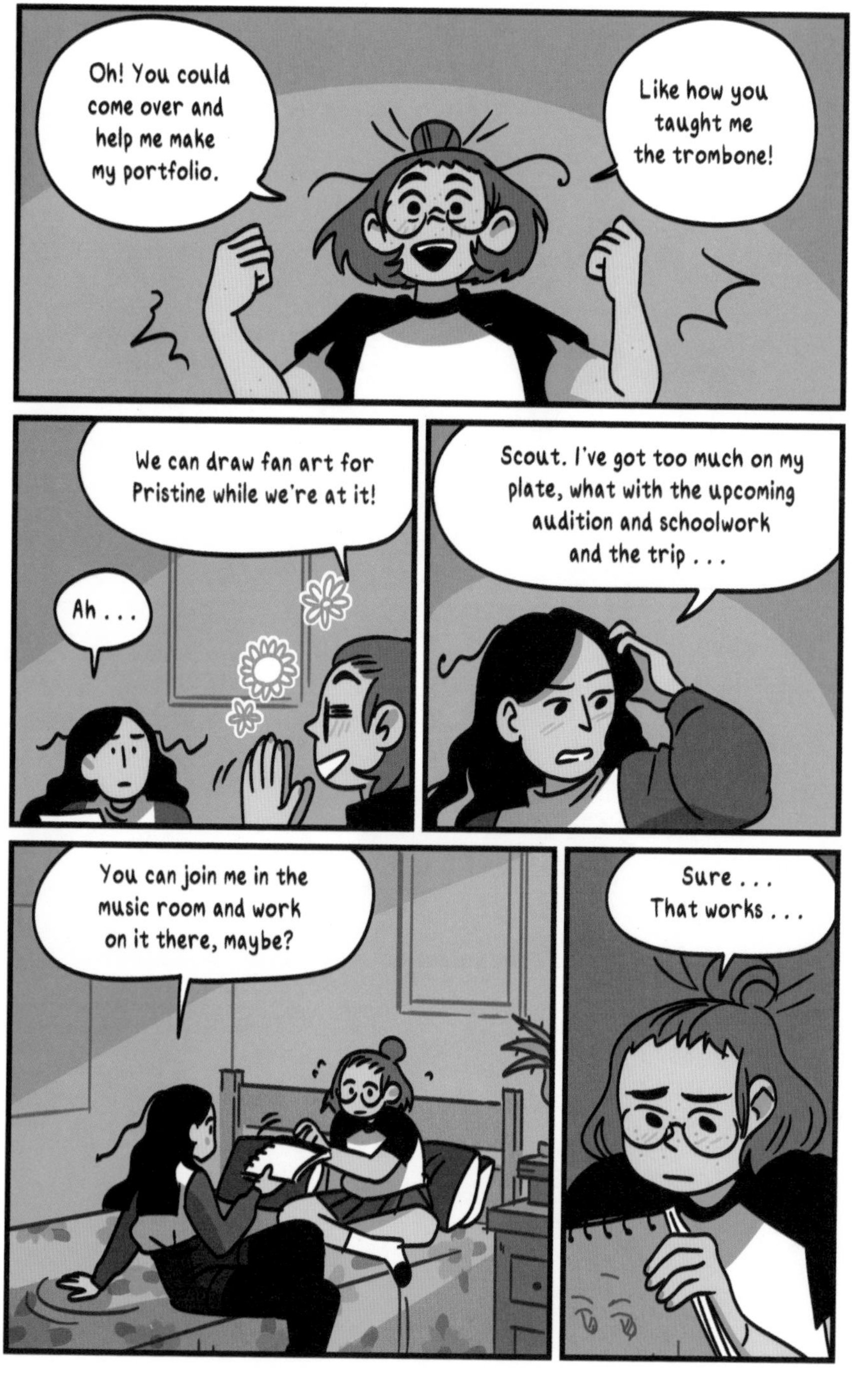
Oh! You could come over and help me make my portfolio.
Like how you taught me the trombone!
We can draw fan art for Pristine while we're at it!
Ah . . .
Scout. I've got too much on my plate, what with the upcoming audition and schoolwork and the trip . . .
You can join me in the music room and work on it there, maybe?
Sure . . . That works . . .

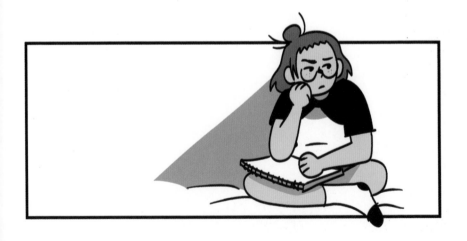

Chapter 5

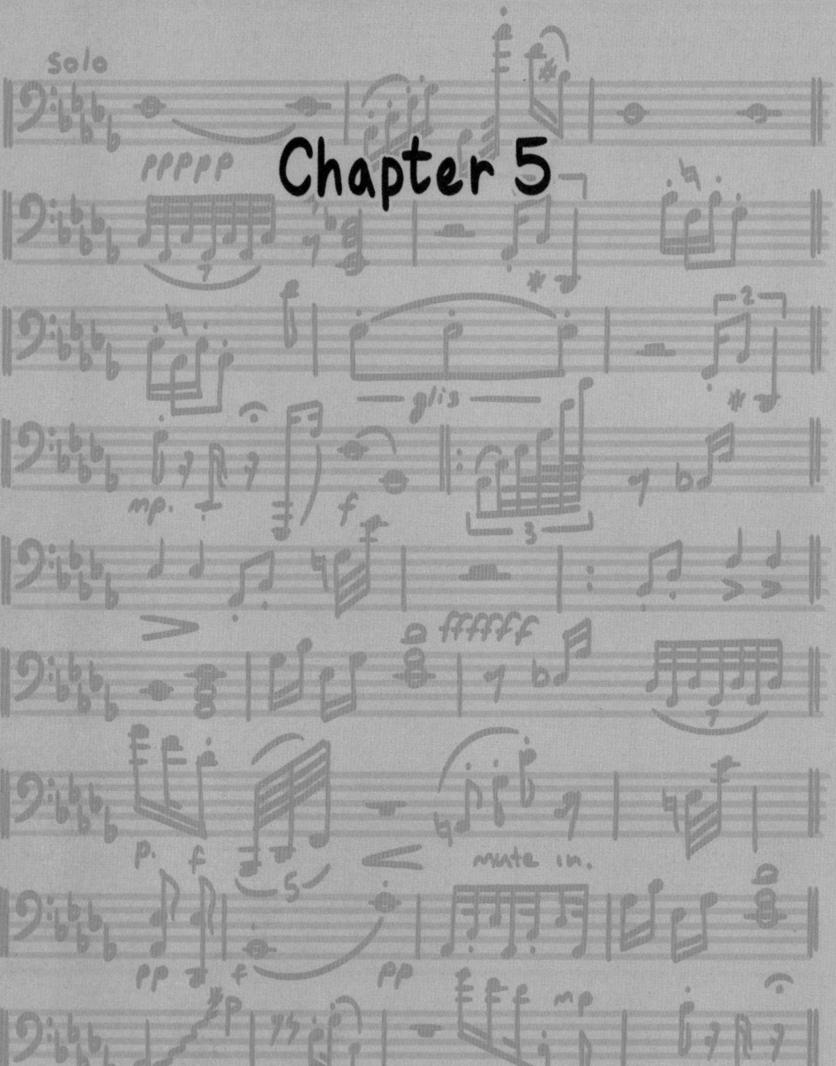
Solo
glis
mute in.

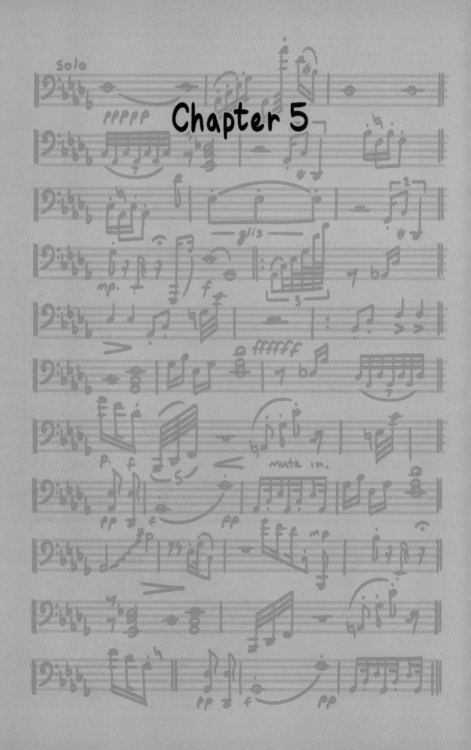

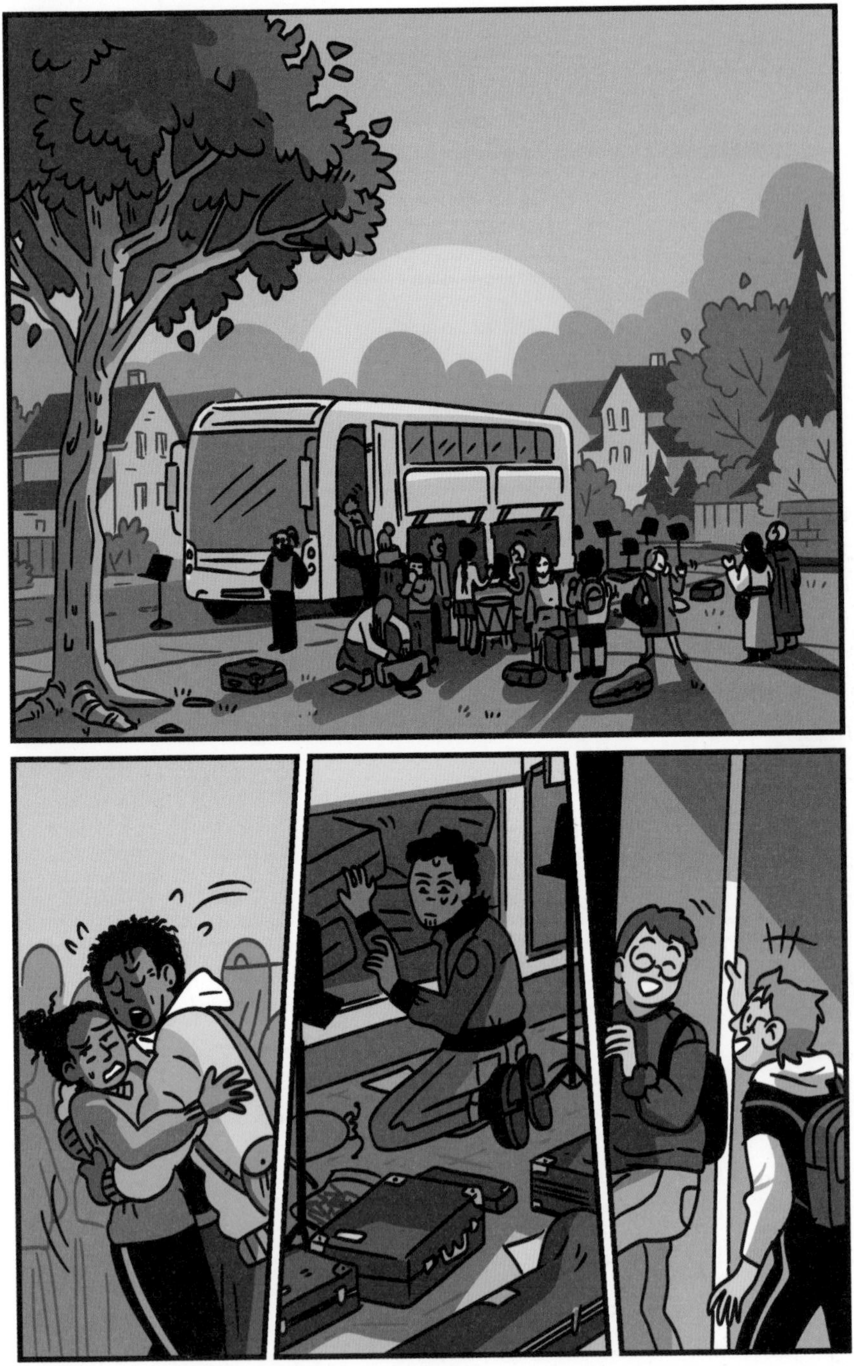

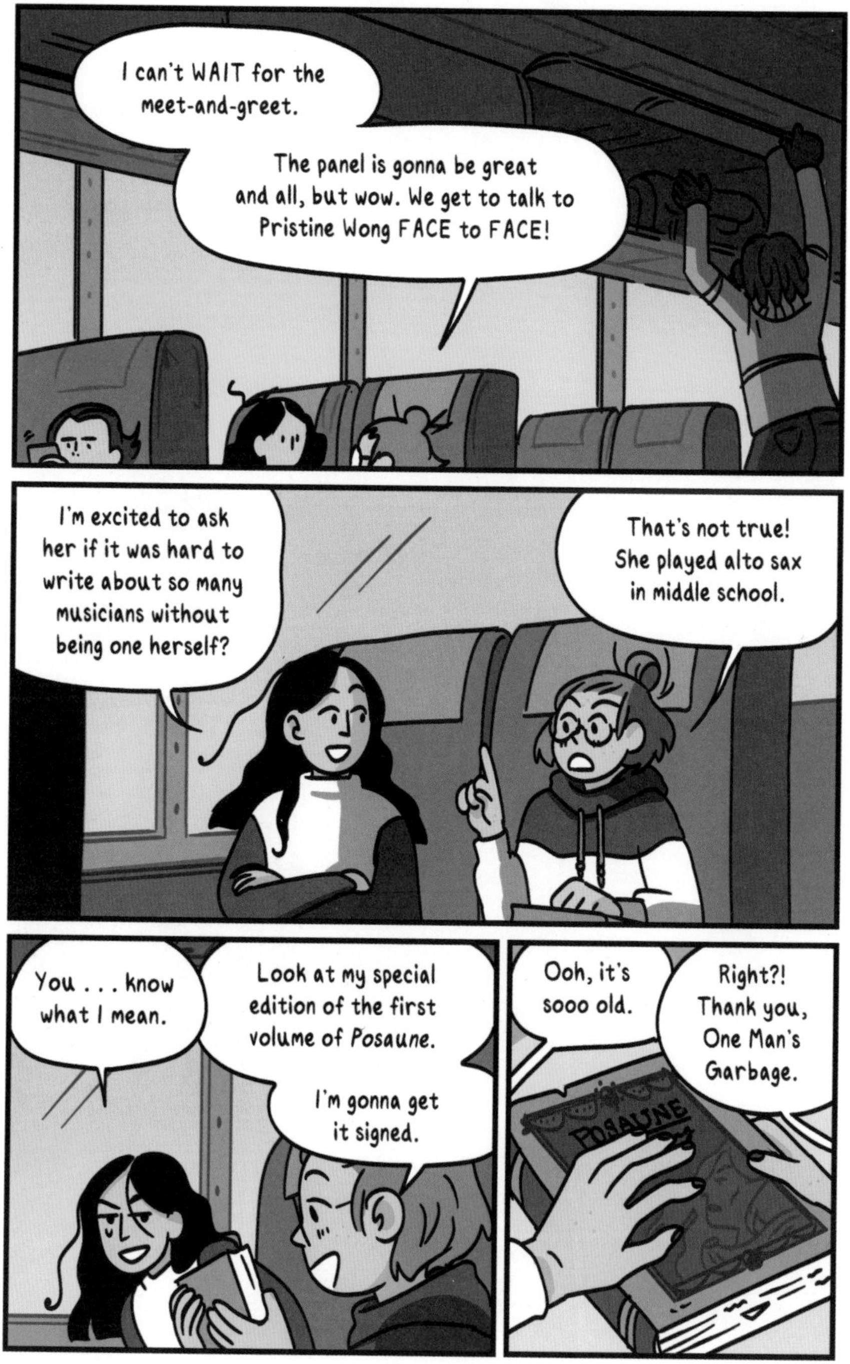
I can't WAIT for the meet-and-greet.
The panel is gonna be great and all, but wow. We get to talk to Pristine Wong FACE to FACE!
I'm excited to ask her if it was hard to write about so many musicians without being one herself?
That's not true! She played alto sax in middle school.
You . . . know what I mean.
Look at my special edition of the first volume of *Posaune*.
I'm gonna get it signed.
Ooh, it's sooo old.
Right?! Thank you, One Man's Garbage.
POSAUNE

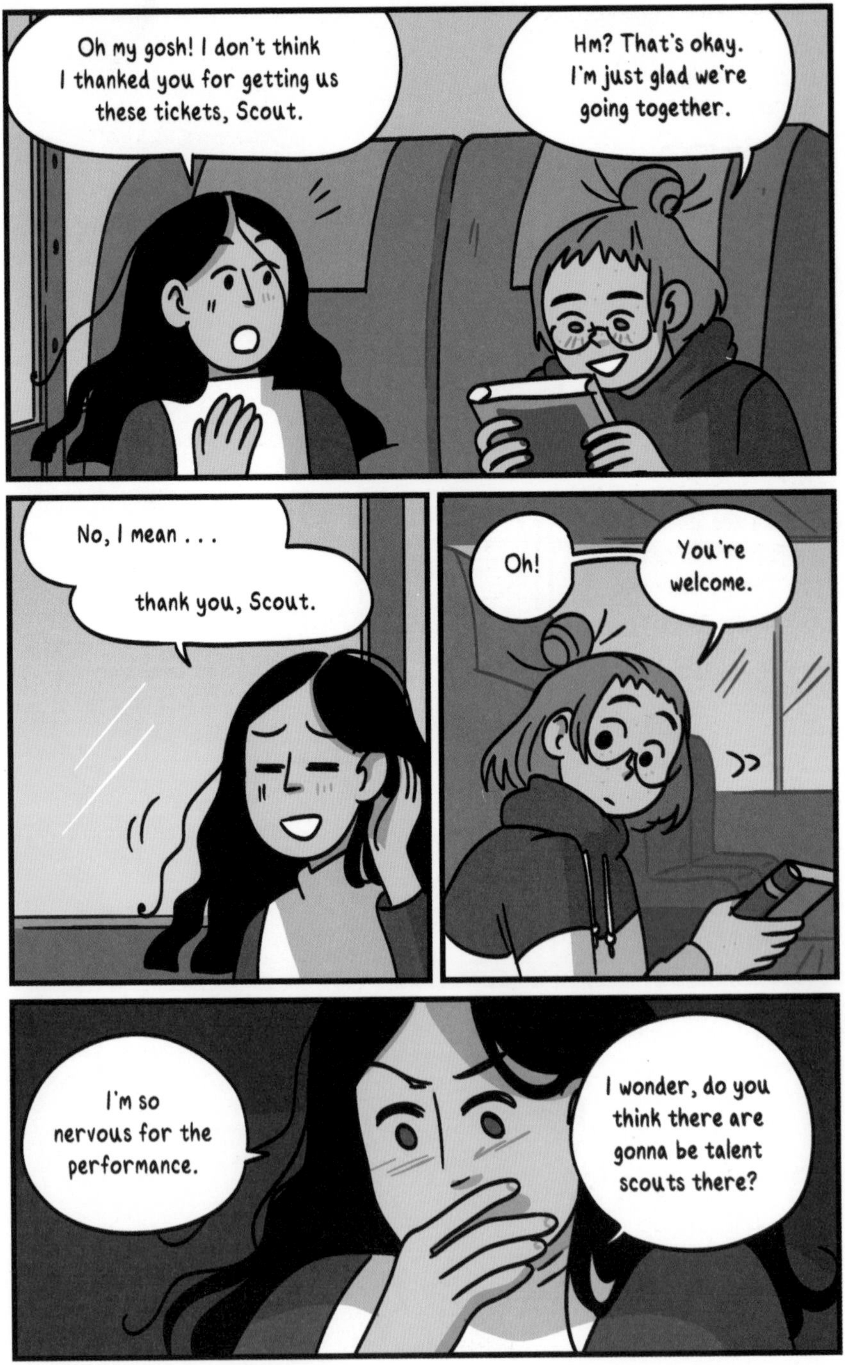

Oh my gosh! I don't think I thanked you for getting us these tickets, Scout.
Hm? That's okay. I'm just glad we're going together.
No, I mean . . .
thank you, Scout.
Oh!
You're welcome.
I'm so nervous for the performance.
I wonder, do you think there are gonna be talent scouts there?

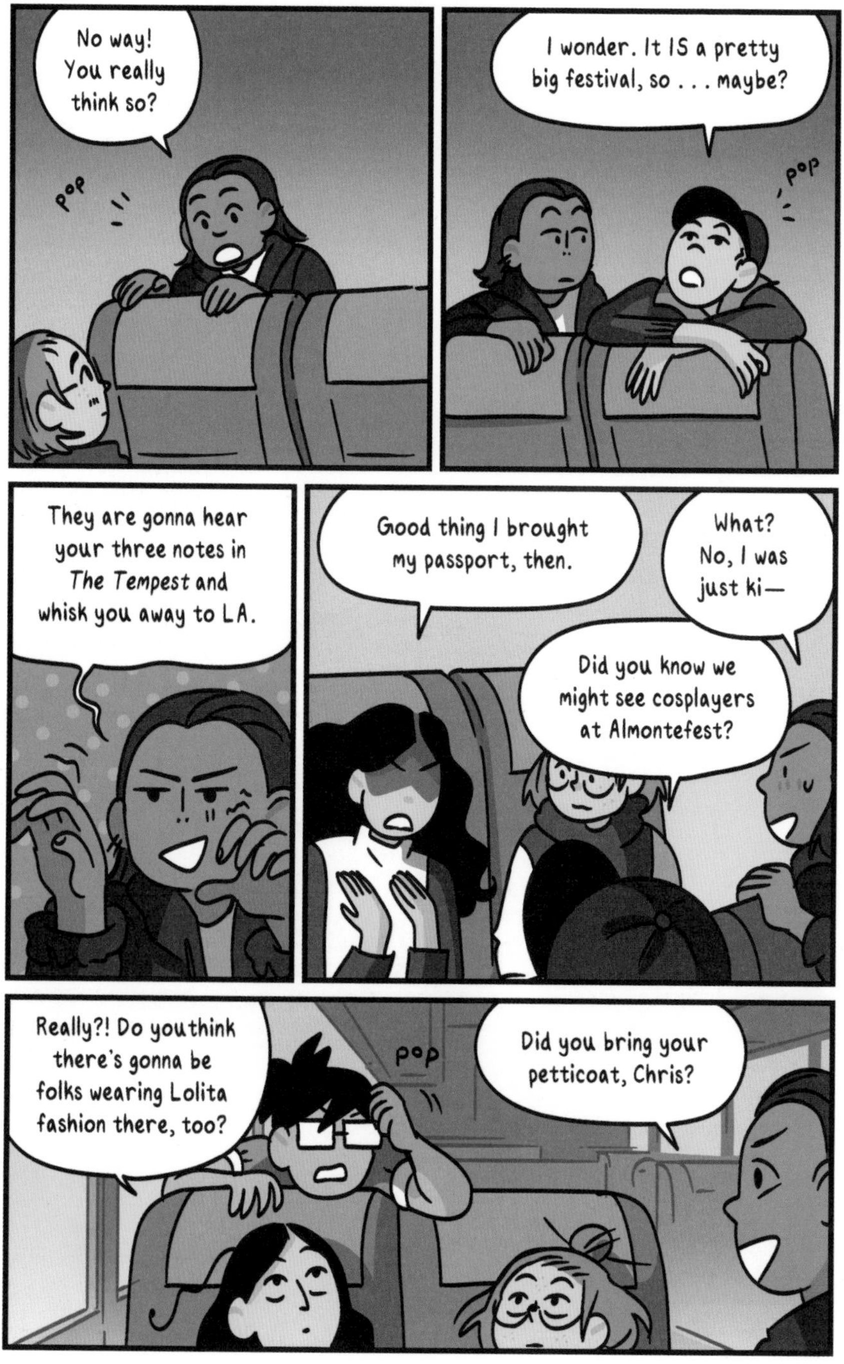
No way! You really think so?
pop
I wonder. It IS a pretty big festival, so . . . maybe?
pop
They are gonna hear your three notes in *The Tempest* and whisk you away to LA.
Good thing I brought my passport, then.
What? No, I was just ki—
Did you know we might see cosplayers at Almontefest?
Really?! Do you think there's gonna be folks wearing Lolita fashion there, too?
pop
Did you bring your petticoat, Chris?

*Overalls or pinafore, often worn as a part of Lolita fashion.

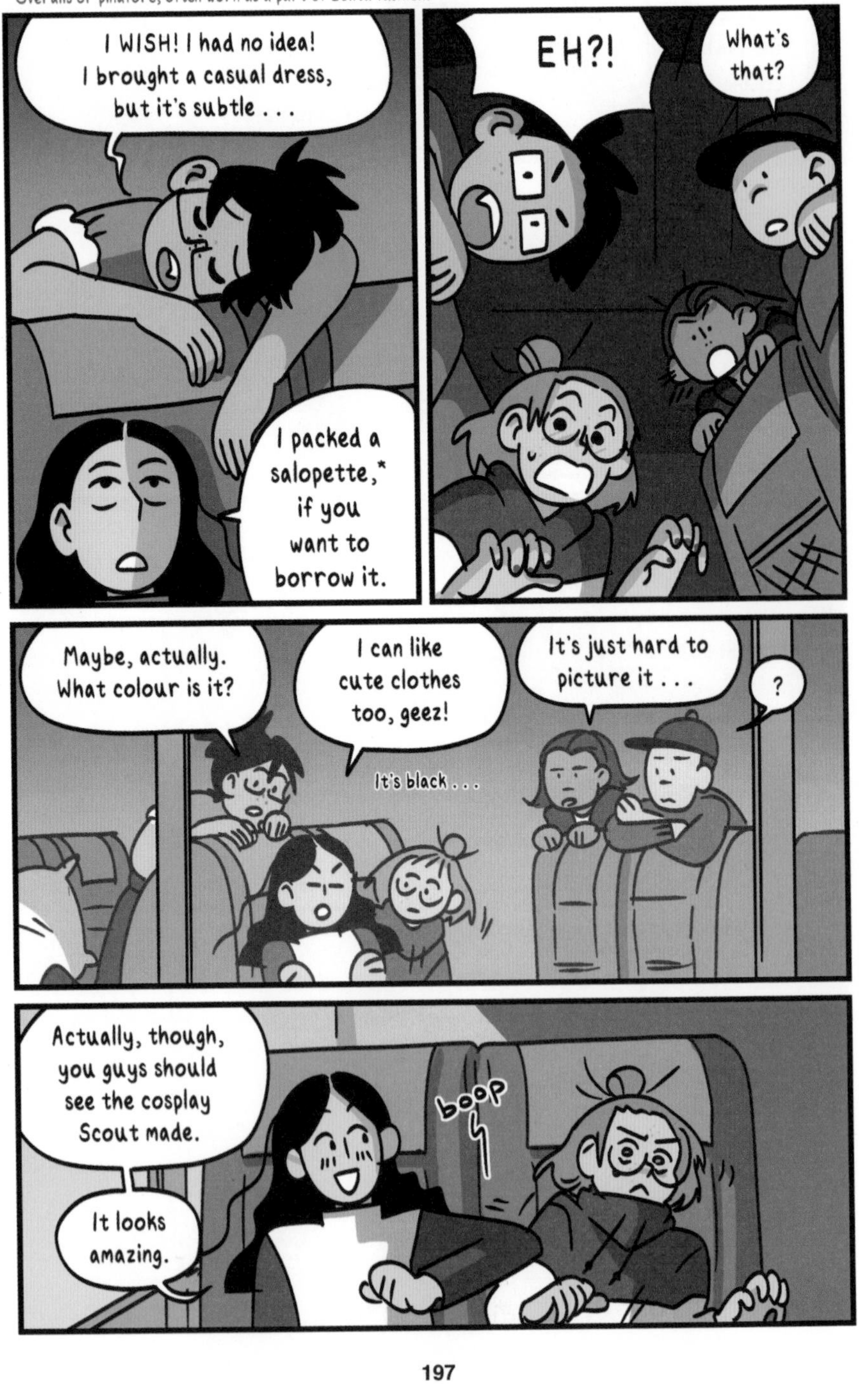

I WISH! I had no idea! I brought a casual dress, but it's subtle . . .
I packed a salopette,* if you want to borrow it.
EH?!
What's that?
Maybe, actually. What colour is it?
I can like cute clothes too, geez!
It's black . . .
It's just hard to picture it . . .
?
Actually, though, you guys should see the cosplay Scout made.
boop
It looks amazing.

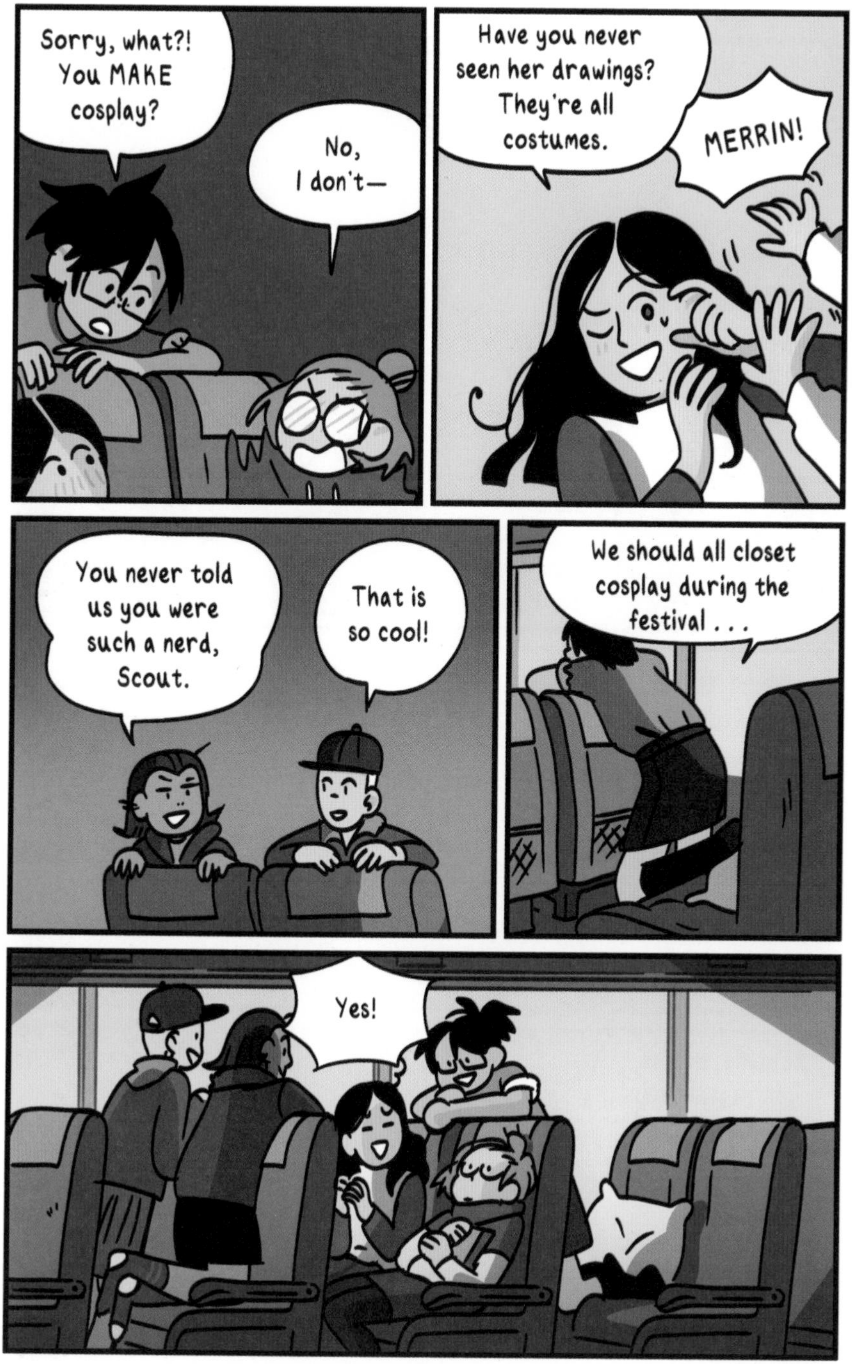
Sorry, what?! You MAKE cosplay?
No, I don't—
Have you never seen her drawings? They're all costumes.
MERRIN!
You never told us you were such a nerd, Scout.
That is so cool!
We should all closet cosplay during the festival . . .
Yes!

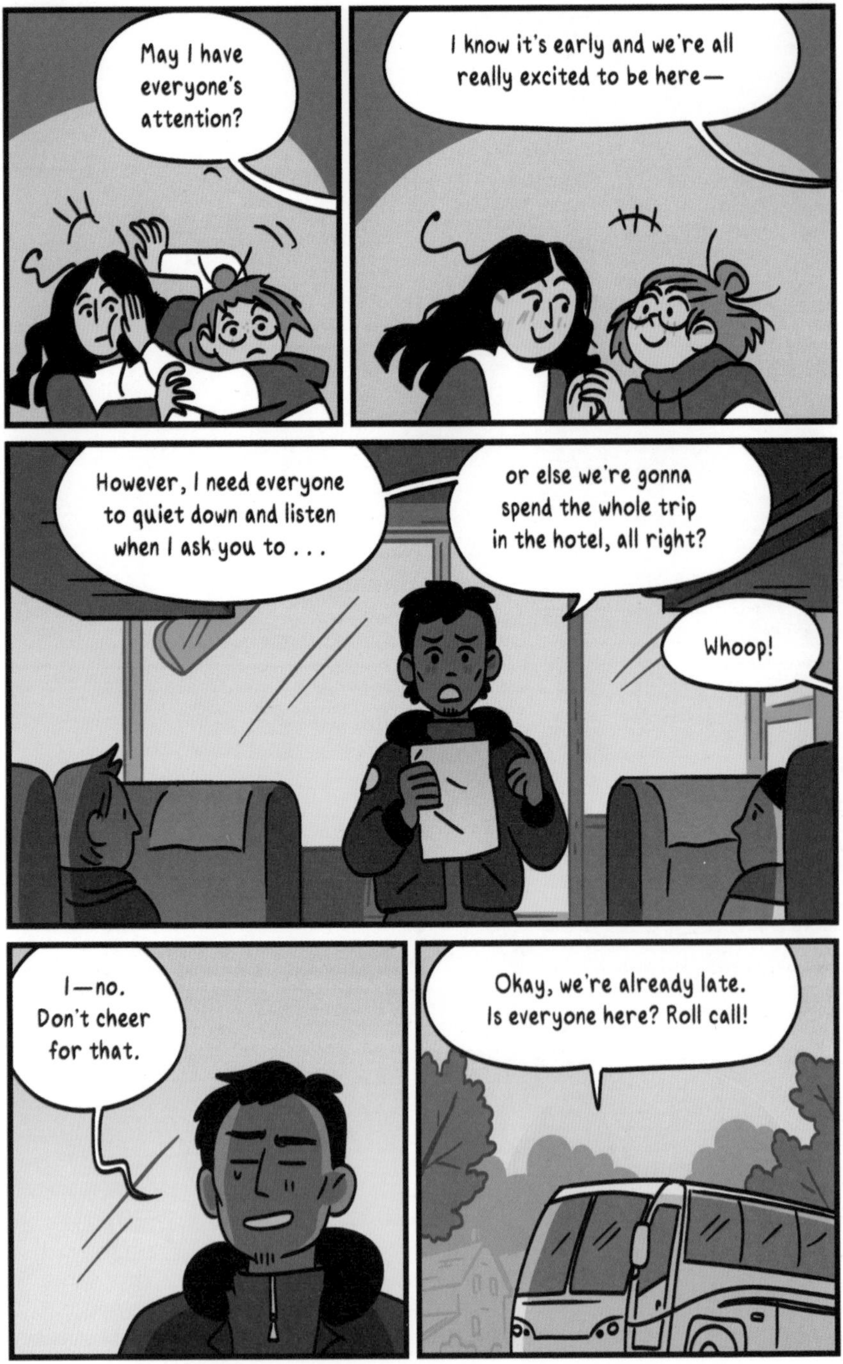
May I have everyone's attention?
I know it's early and we're all really excited to be here—
However, I need everyone to quiet down and listen when I ask you to . . .
or else we're gonna spend the whole trip in the hotel, all right?
Whoop!
I—no. Don't cheer for that.
Okay, we're already late. Is everyone here? Roll call!

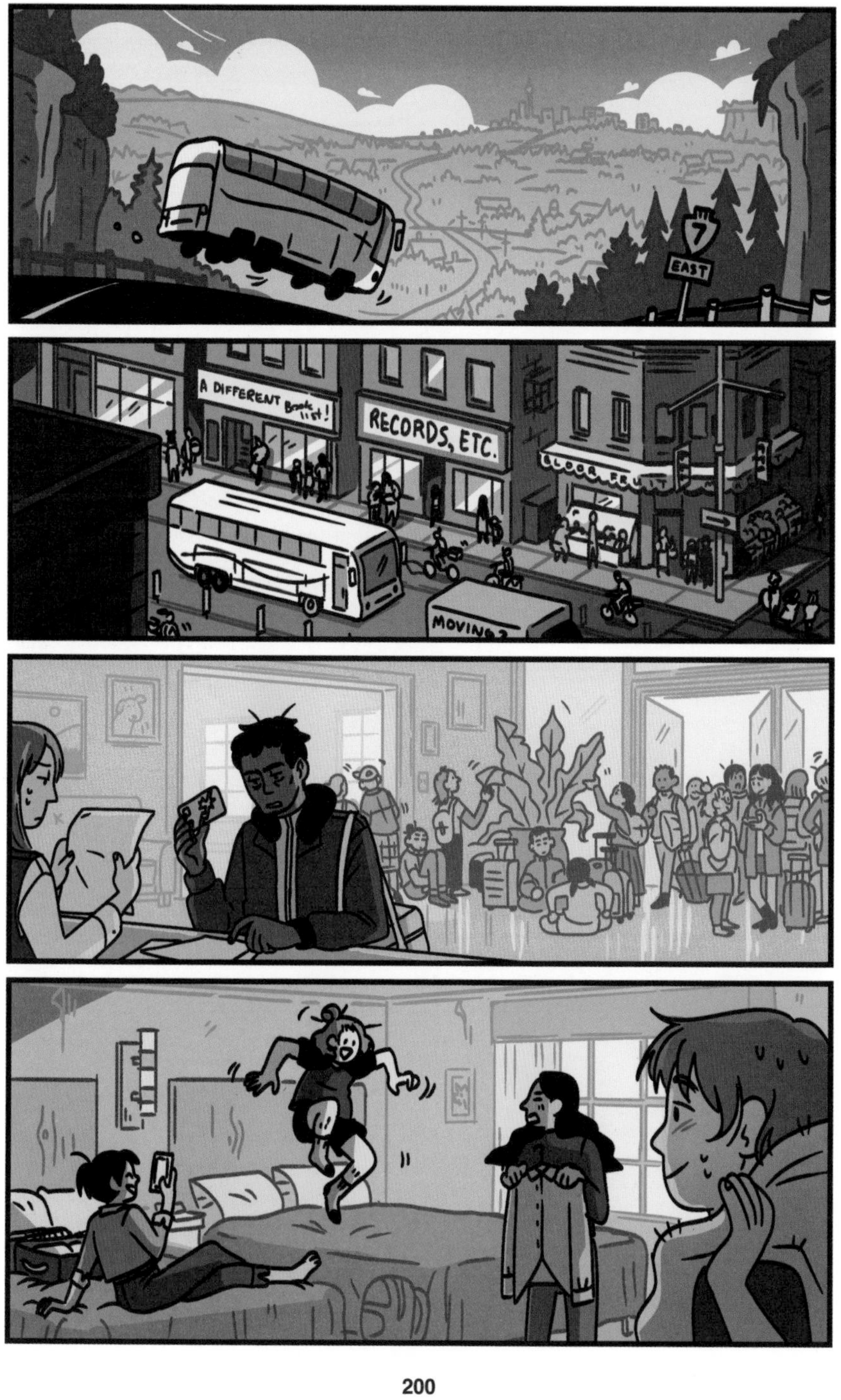
7
EAST
A DIFFERENT Book list!
RECORDS, ETC.
BLOOR FRUIT
MOVING?

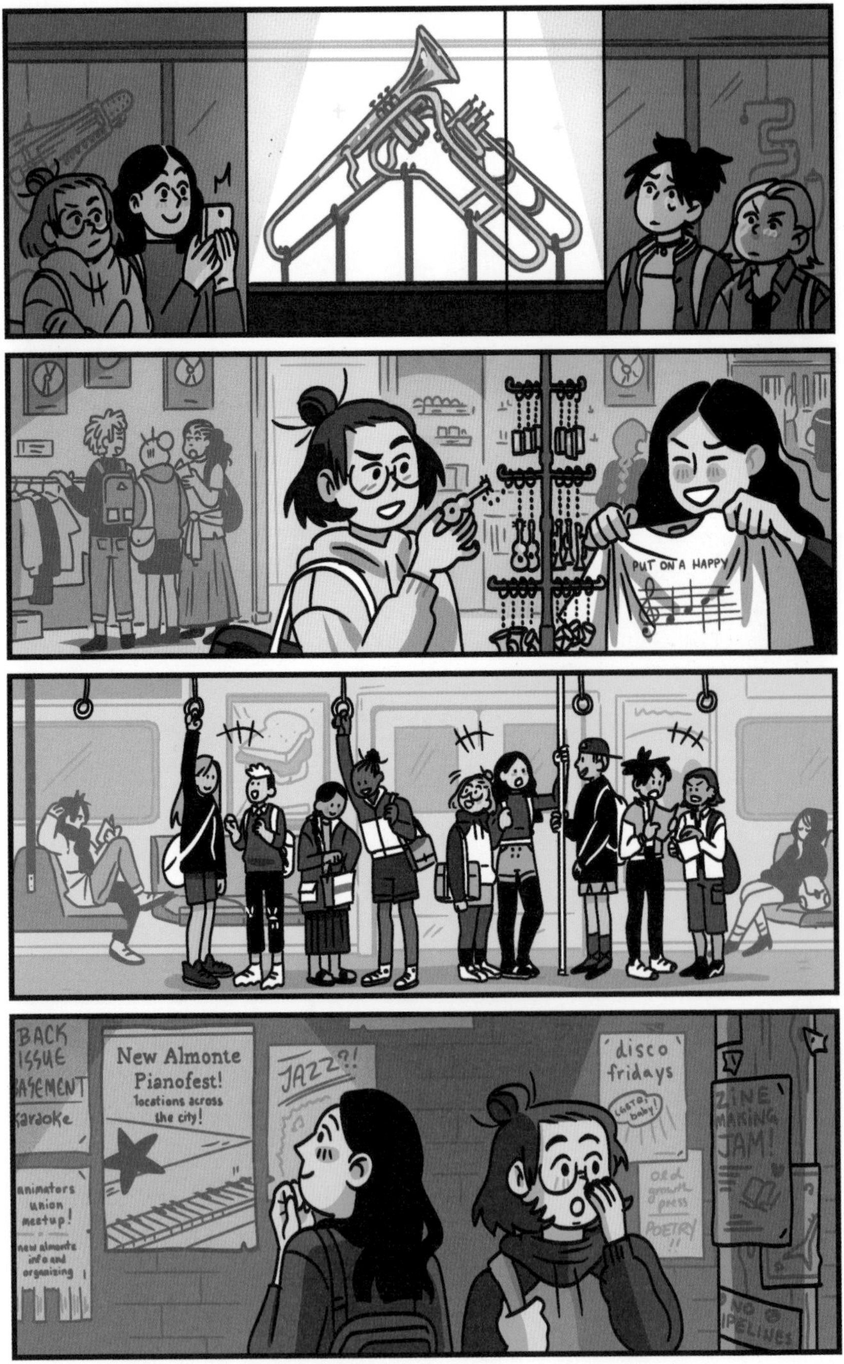
PUT ON A HAPPY
BACK ISSUE ASEMENT
aradoke
New Almonte Pianofest!
locations across the city!
JAZZ?!
animators union meetup!
new almonte info and organizing
disco fridays
LGBTQ, baby!
old growth press
POETRY!!
ZINE MAKING JAM!
NO
IPELINES

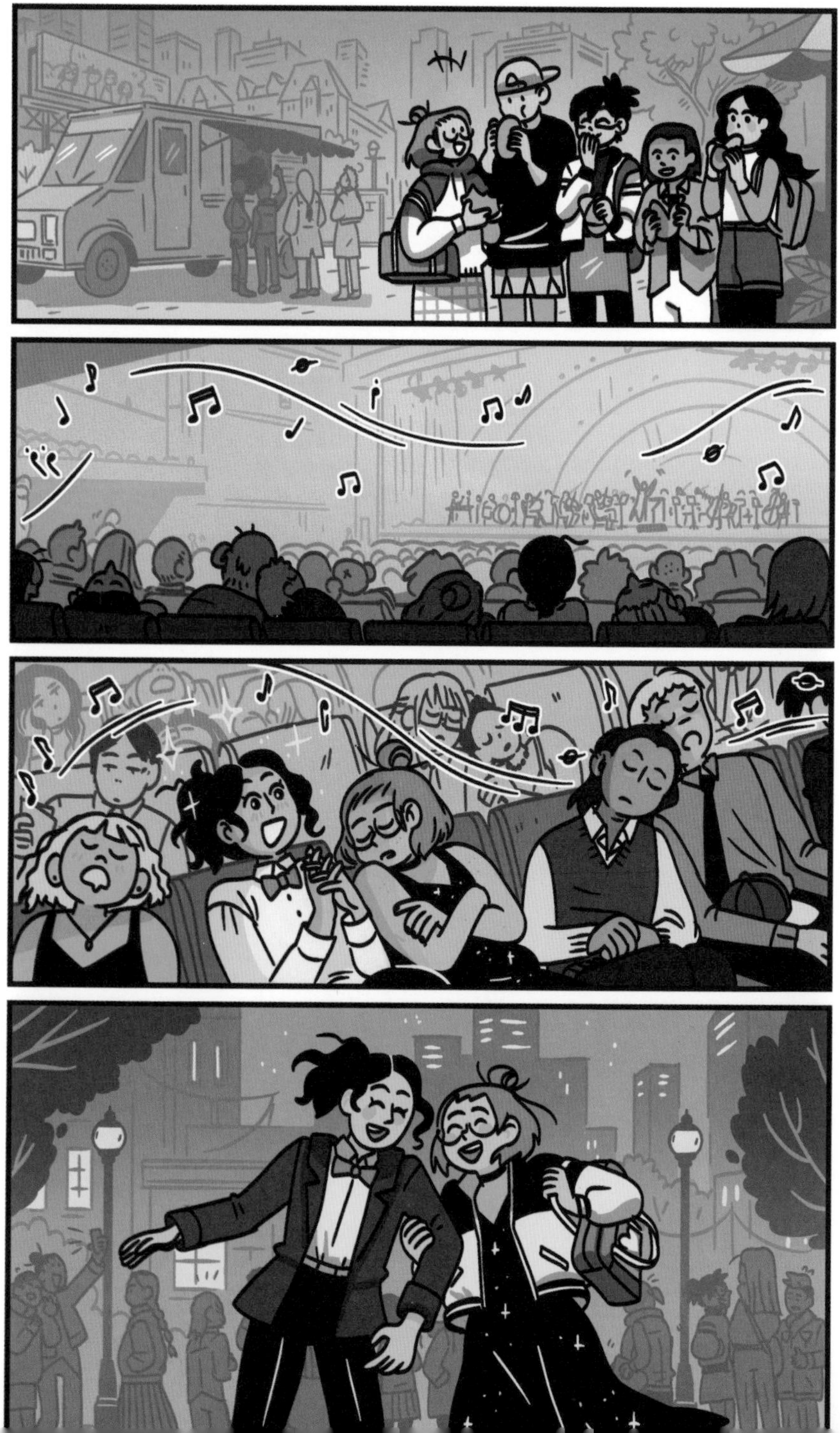

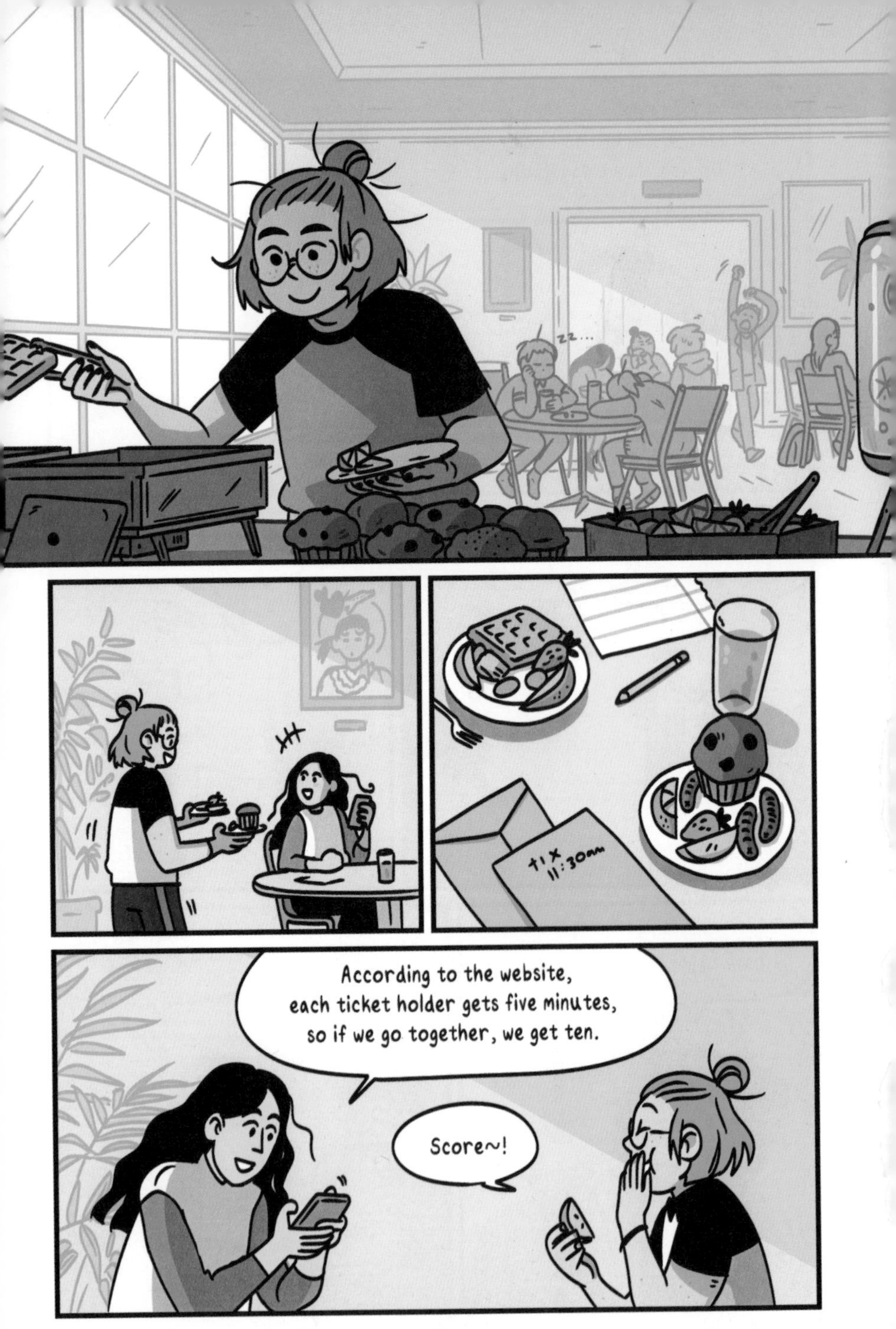
ZZ...
TIX
11:30AM
According to the website, each ticket holder gets five minutes, so if we go together, we get ten.
Score~!

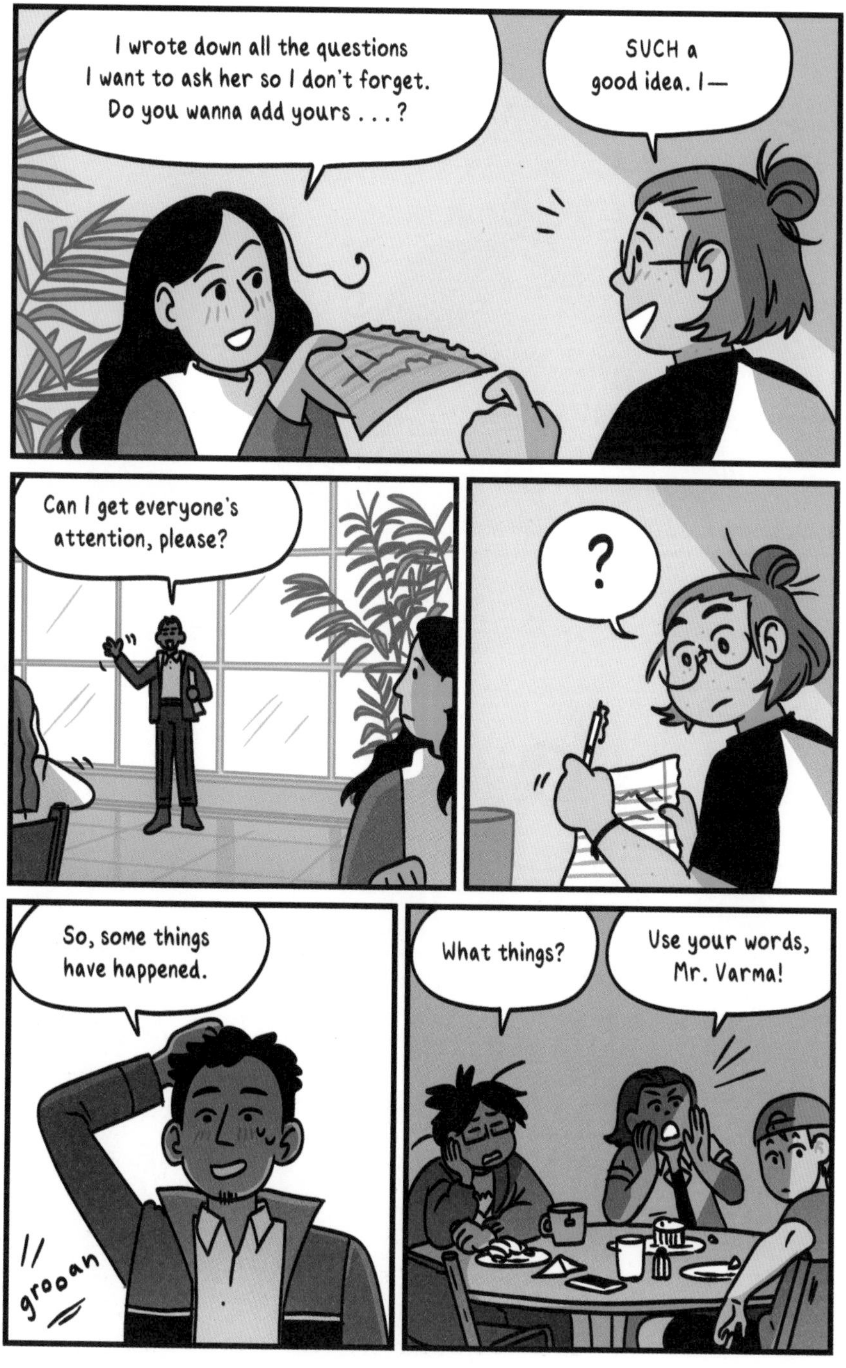
I wrote down all the questions I want to ask her so I don't forget. Do you wanna add yours . . . ?
SUCH a good idea. I—
Can I get everyone's attention, please?
?
So, some things have happened.
groan
What things?
Use your words, Mr. Varma!

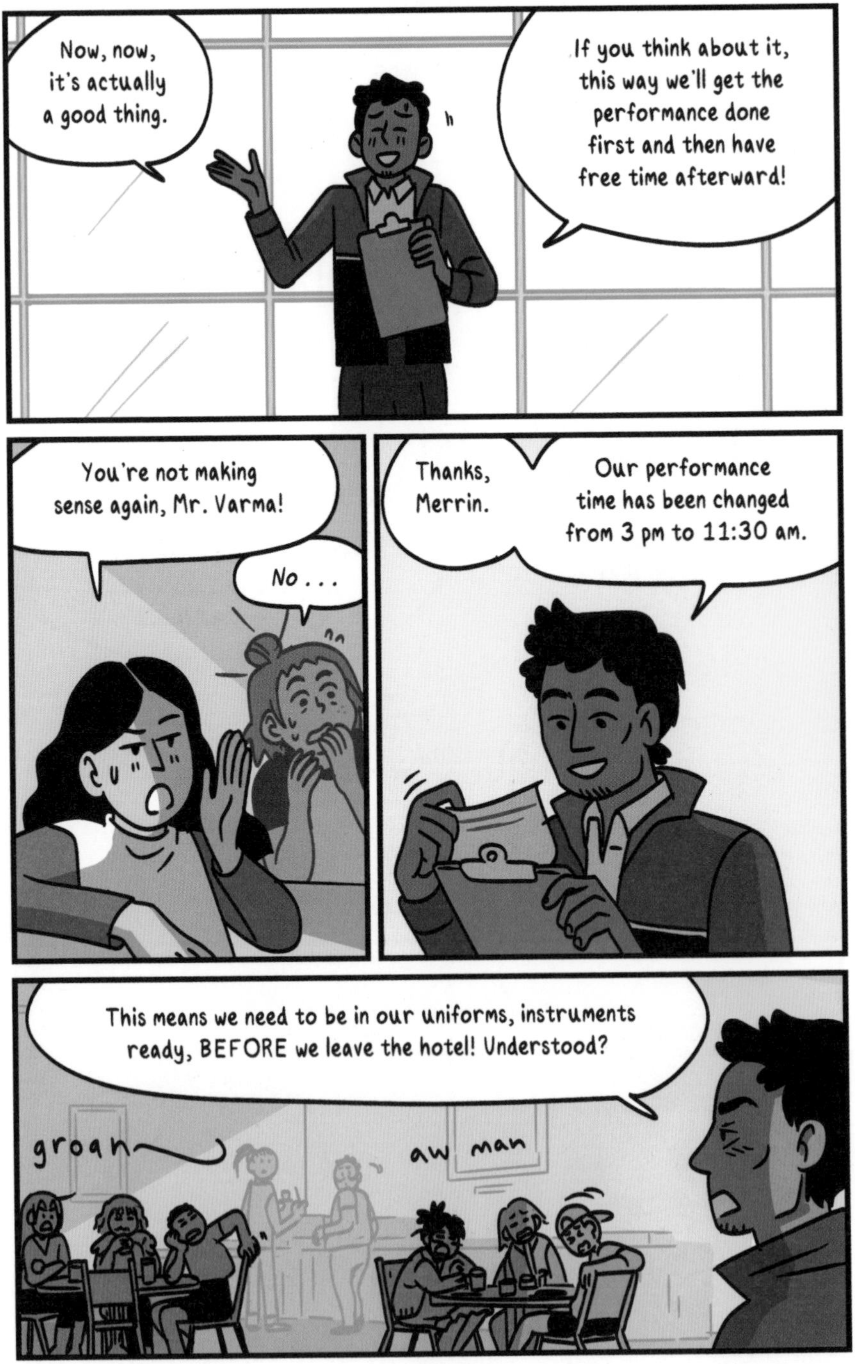

Now, now, it's actually a good thing.
If you think about it, this way we'll get the performance done first and then have free time afterward!
You're not making sense again, Mr. Varma!
No . . .
Thanks, Merrin.
Our performance time has been changed from 3 pm to 11:30 am.
This means we need to be in our uniforms, instruments ready, BEFORE we leave the hotel! Understood?
groan
aw man

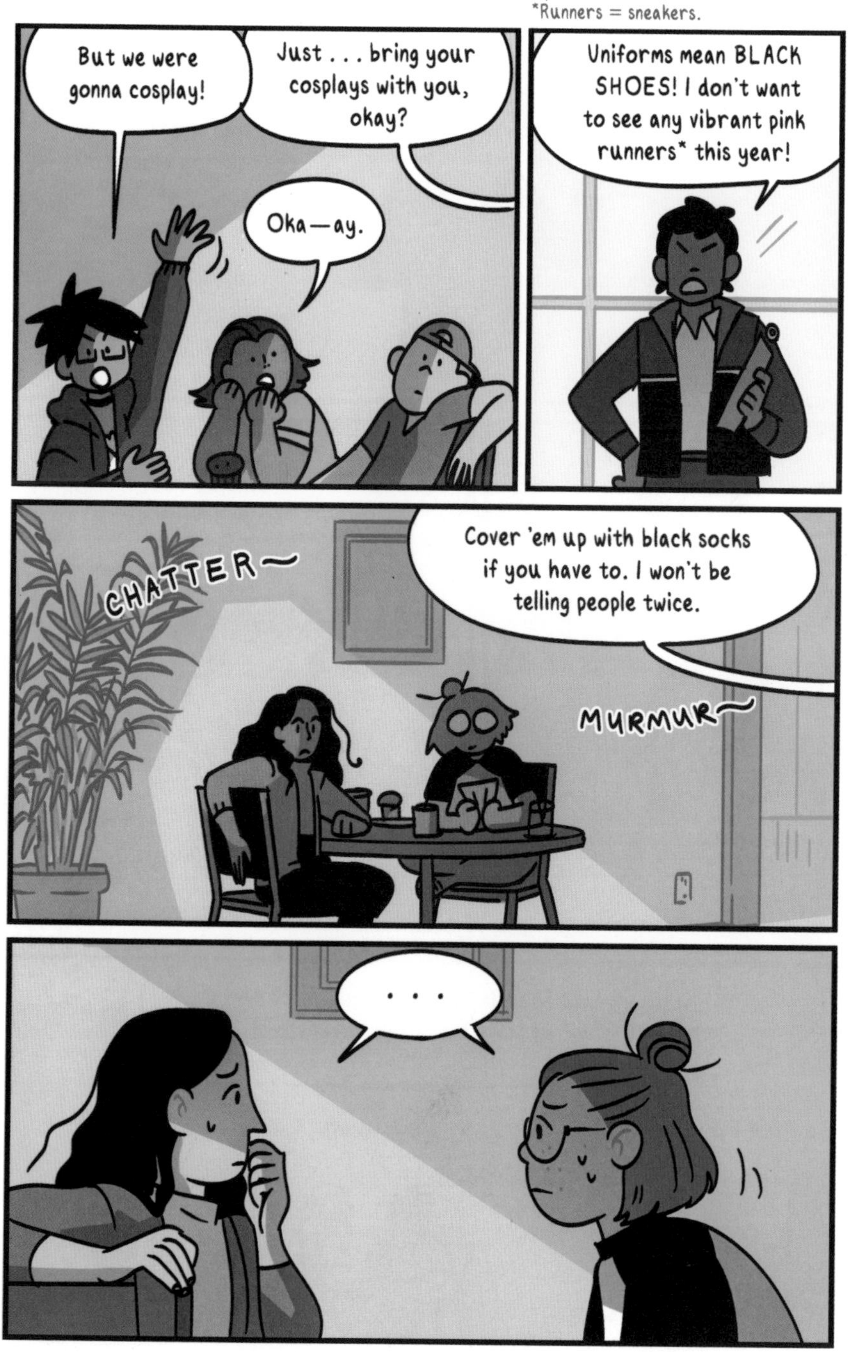
*Runners = sneakers.
But we were gonna cosplay!
Just . . . bring your cosplays with you, okay?
Oka—ay.
Uniforms mean BLACK SHOES! I don't want to see any vibrant pink runners* this year!
CHATTER~
Cover 'em up with black socks if you have to. I won't be telling people twice.
MURMUR~
. . .

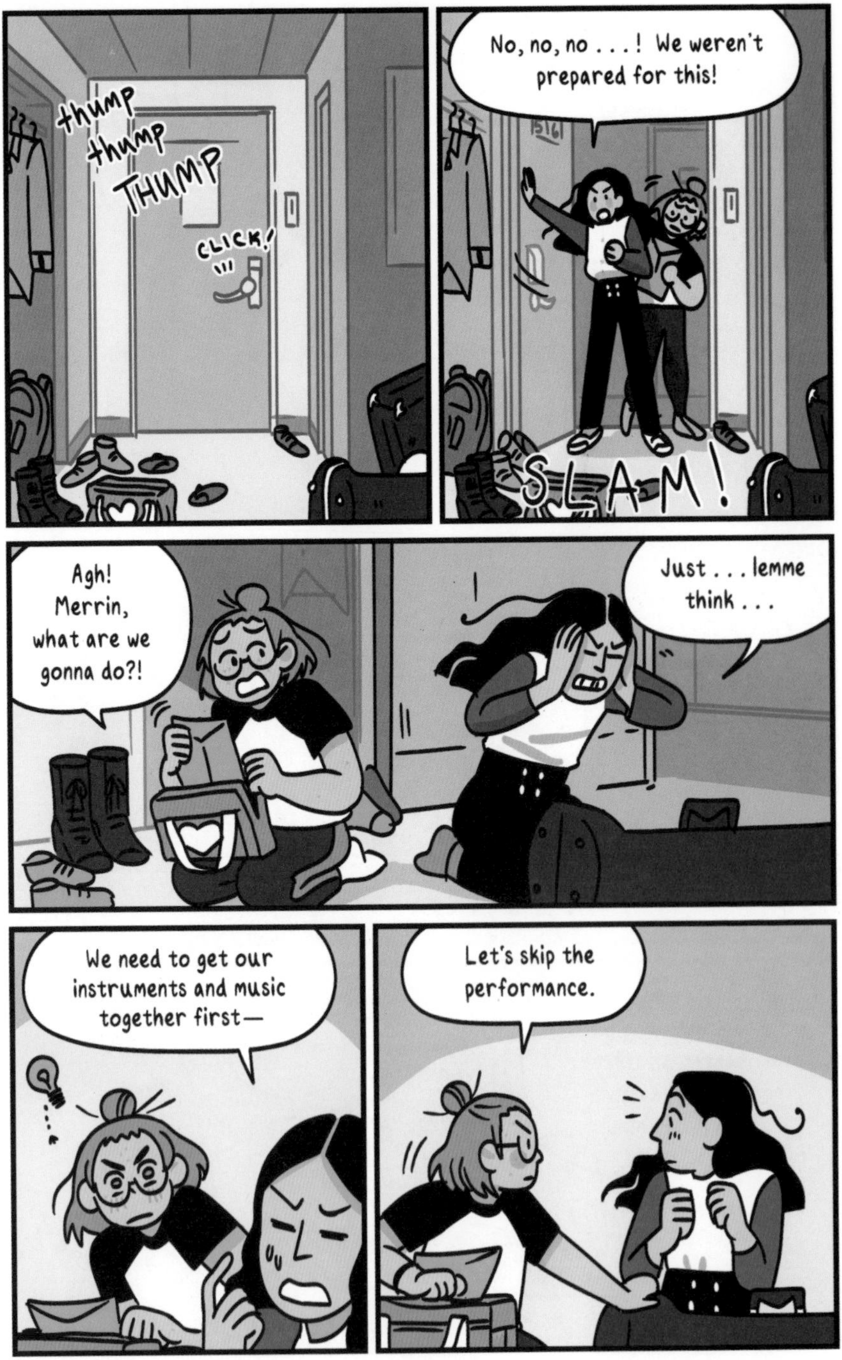
thump
thump
THUMP
CLICK!
No, no, no . . . ! We weren't prepared for this!
SLAM!
Agh! Merrin, what are we gonna do?!
Just . . . lemme think . . .
We need to get our instruments and music together first—
Let's skip the performance.

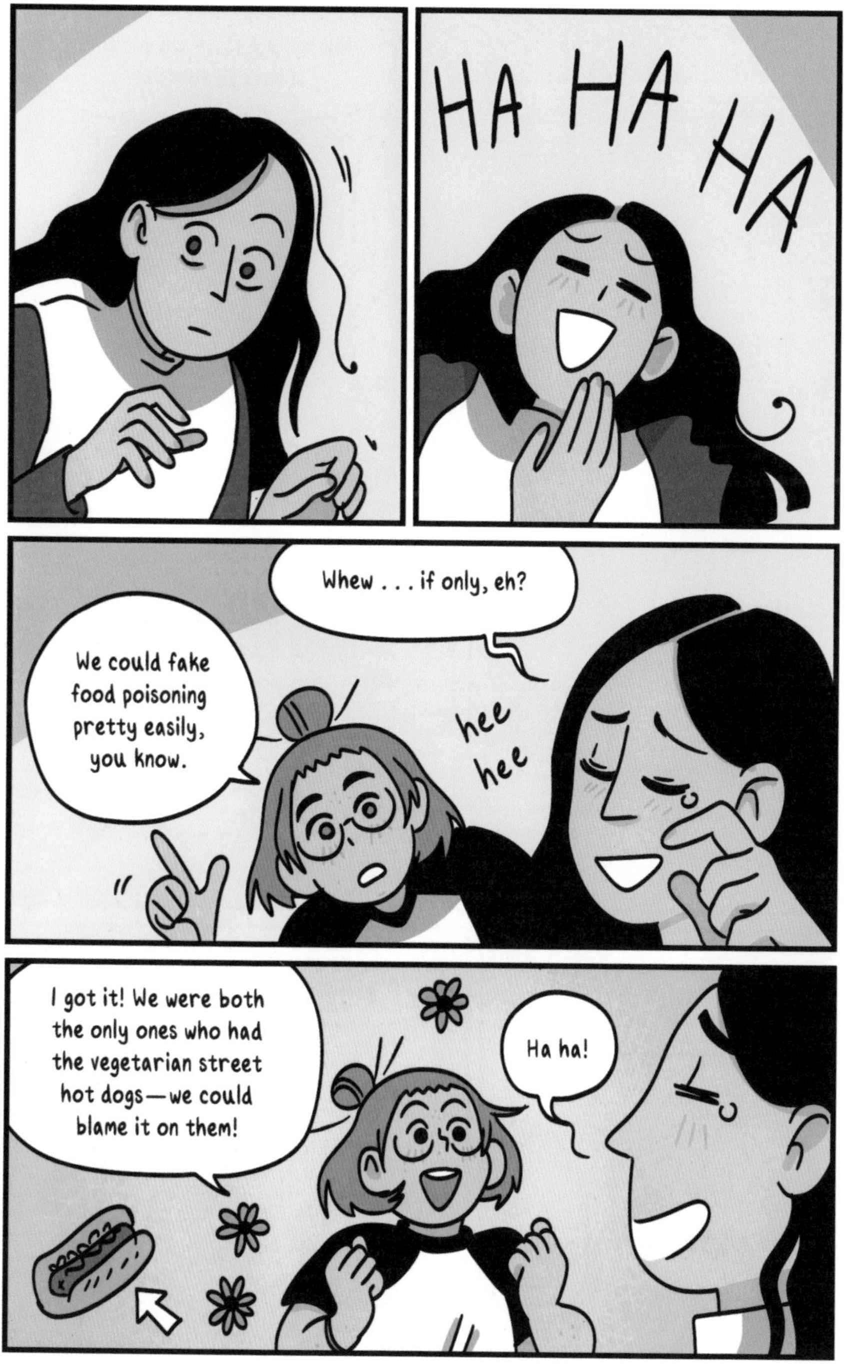
HA HA HA
Whew . . . if only, eh?
We could fake food poisoning pretty easily, you know.
hee hee
I got it! We were both the only ones who had the vegetarian street hot dogs—we could blame it on them!
Ha ha!

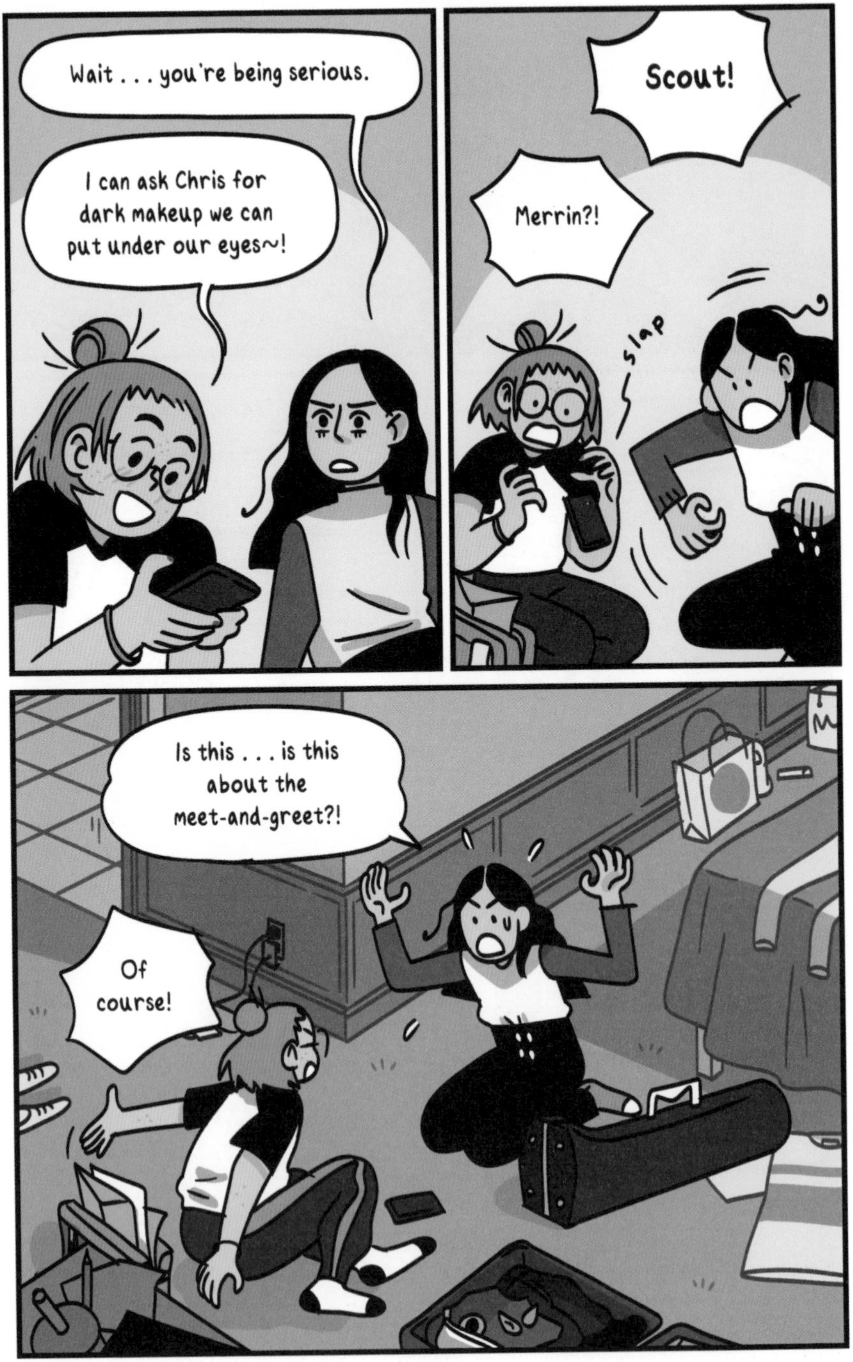
Wait . . . you're being serious.
I can ask Chris for dark makeup we can put under our eyes~!
Scout!
Merrin?!
slap
Is this . . . is this about the meet-and-greet?!
Of course!

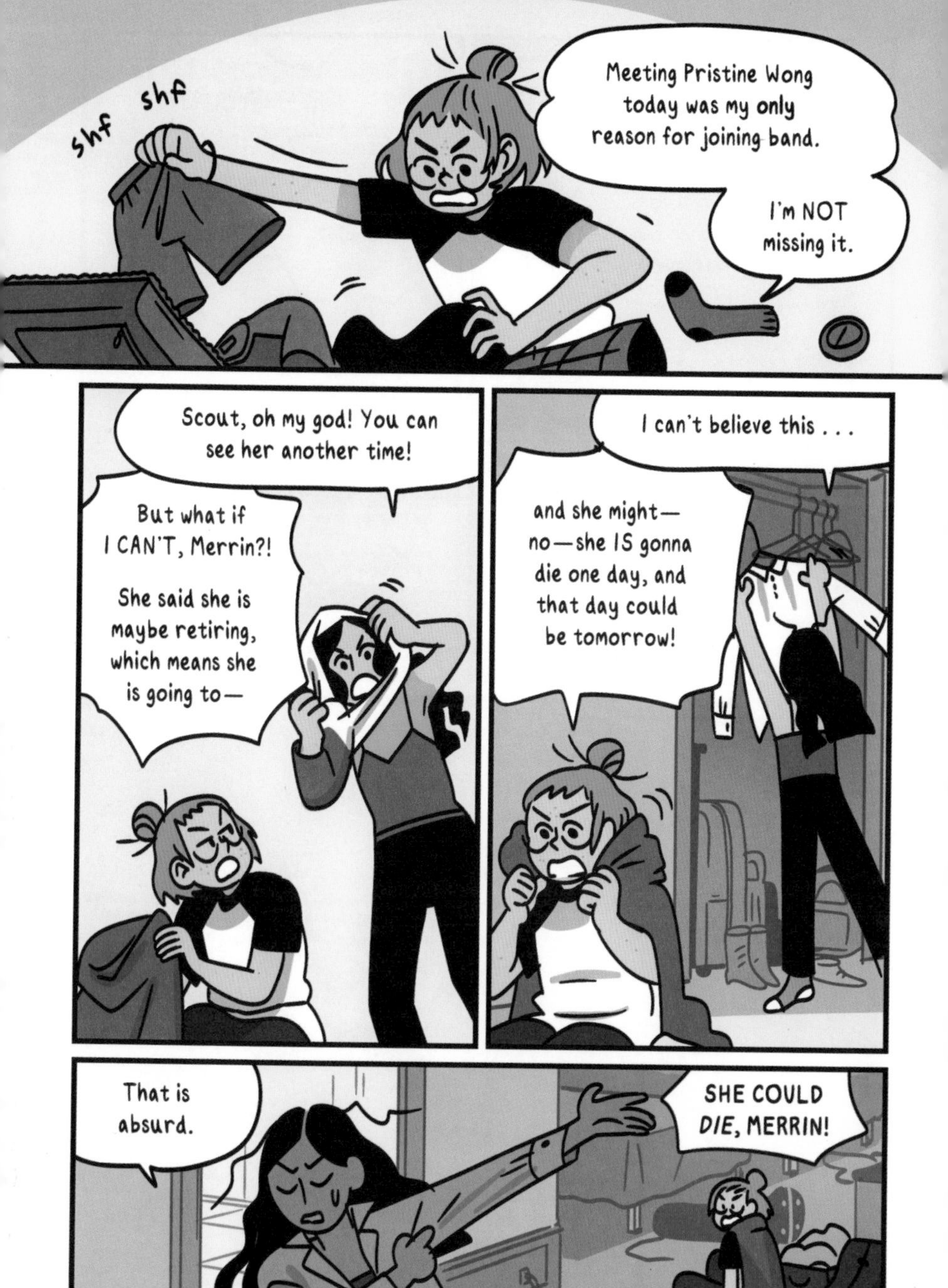
shf shf
Meeting Pristine Wong today was my only reason for joining band.
I'm NOT missing it.
Scout, oh my god! You can see her another time!
But what if I CAN'T, Merrin?!
She said she is maybe retiring, which means she is going to—
I can't believe this . . .
and she might—no—she IS gonna die one day, and that day could be tomorrow!
That is absurd.
SHE COULD *DIE*, MERRIN!

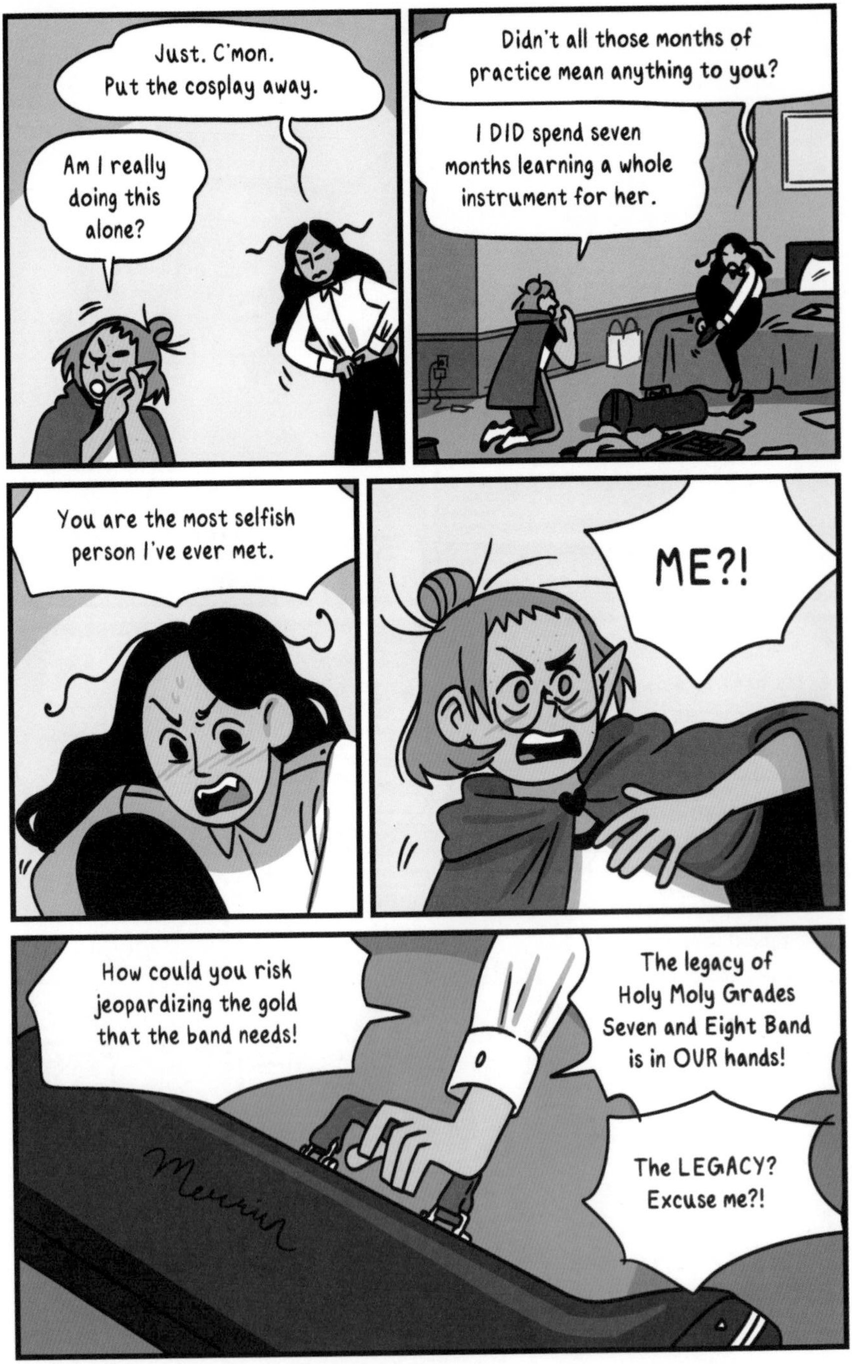
Just. C'mon.
Put the cosplay away.
Am I really doing this alone?
Didn't all those months of practice mean anything to you?
I DID spend seven months learning a whole instrument for her.
You are the most selfish person I've ever met.
ME?!
How could you risk jeopardizing the gold that the band needs!
The legacy of Holy Moly Grades Seven and Eight Band is in OUR hands!
The LEGACY? Excuse me?!

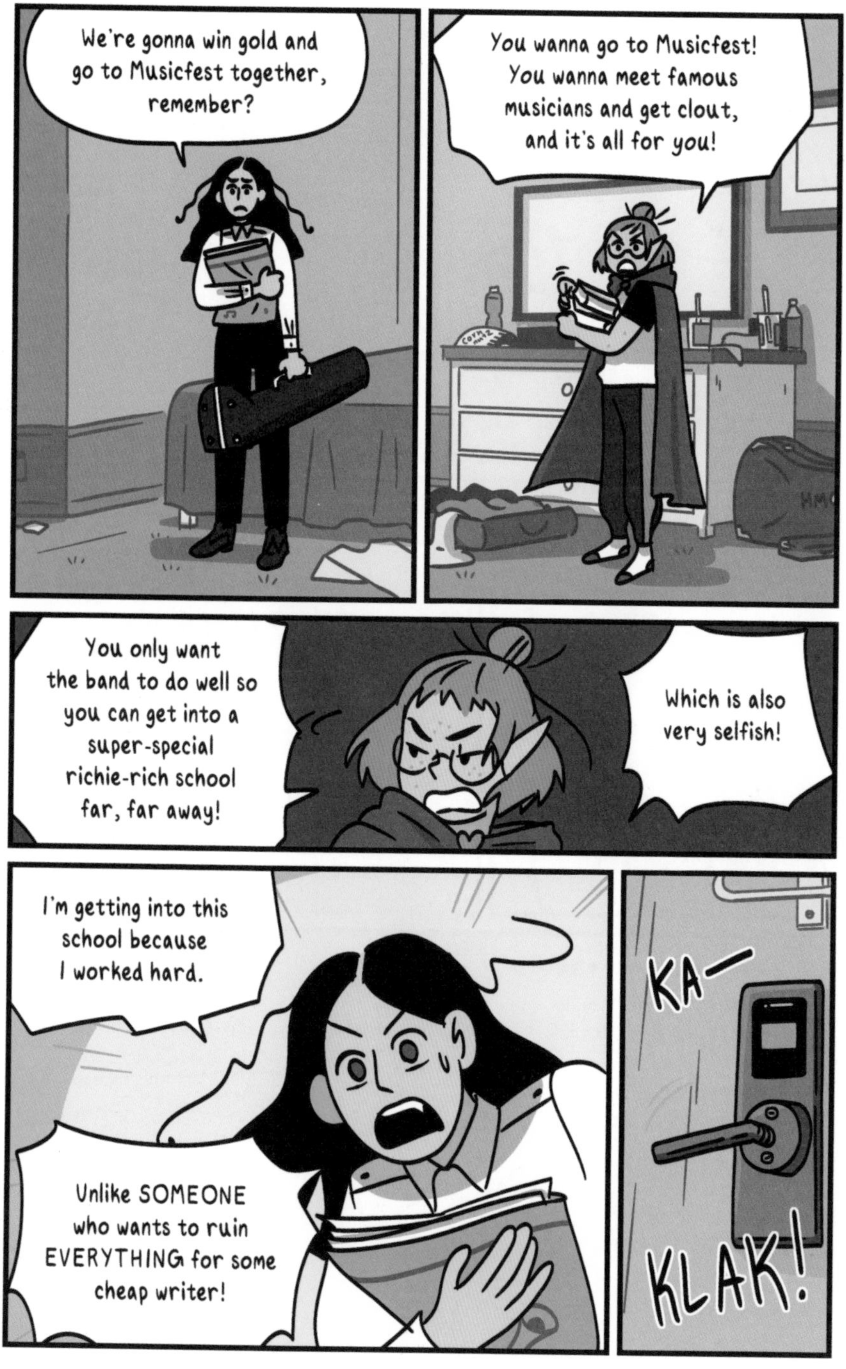
We're gonna win gold and go to Musicfest together, remember?
You wanna go to Musicfest! You wanna meet famous musicians and get clout, and it's all for you!
You only want the band to do well so you can get into a super-special richie-rich school far, far away!
Which is also very selfish!
I'm getting into this school because I worked hard.
Unlike SOMEONE who wants to ruin EVERYTHING for some cheap writer!
KA—
KLAK!

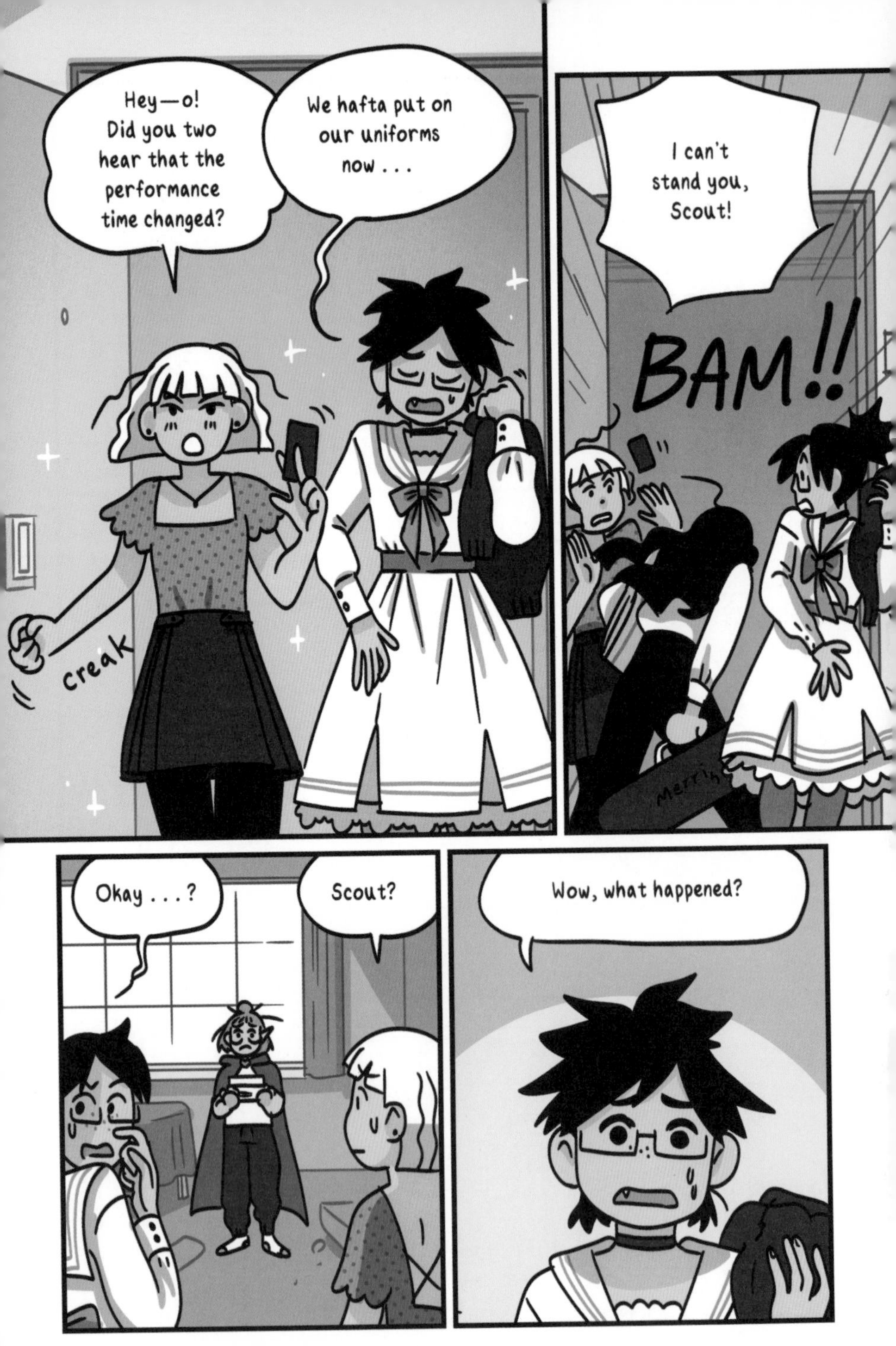
Hey—o!
Did you two hear that the performance time changed?
We hafta put on our uniforms now . . .
creak
I can't stand you, Scout!
BAM!!
Okay . . . ?
Scout?
Wow, what happened?

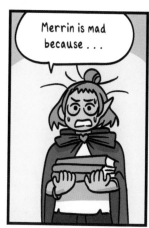

Merrin is mad because . . .

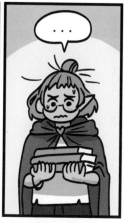

. . .

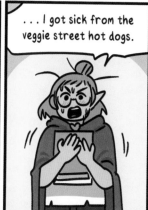

. . . I got sick from the veggie street hot dogs.

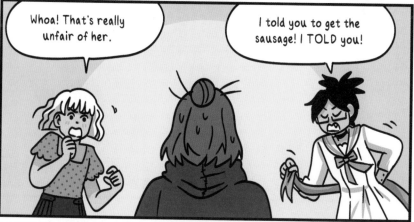

Whoa! That's really unfair of her.

I told you to get the sausage! I TOLD you!

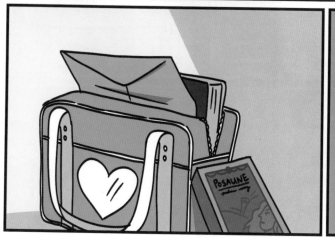
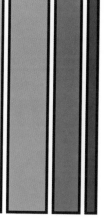

POSAUNE

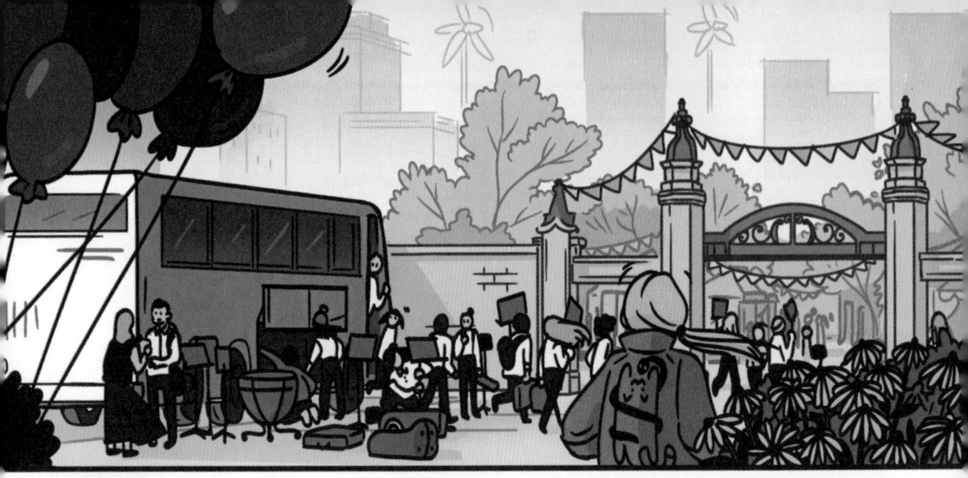

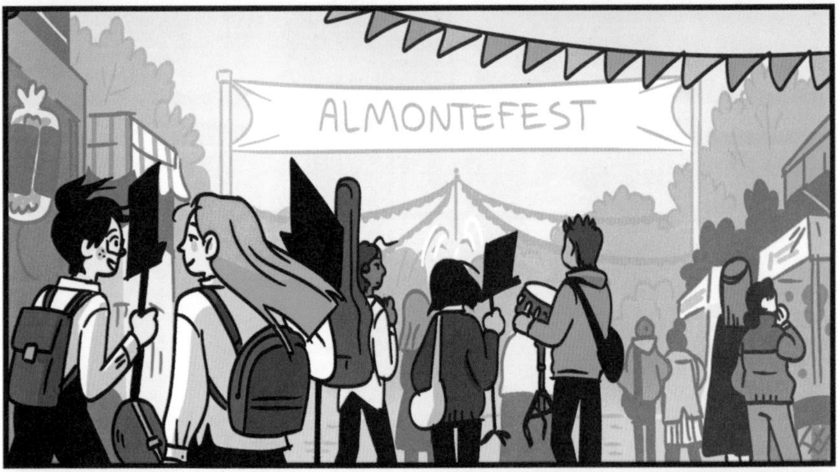
ALMONTEFEST

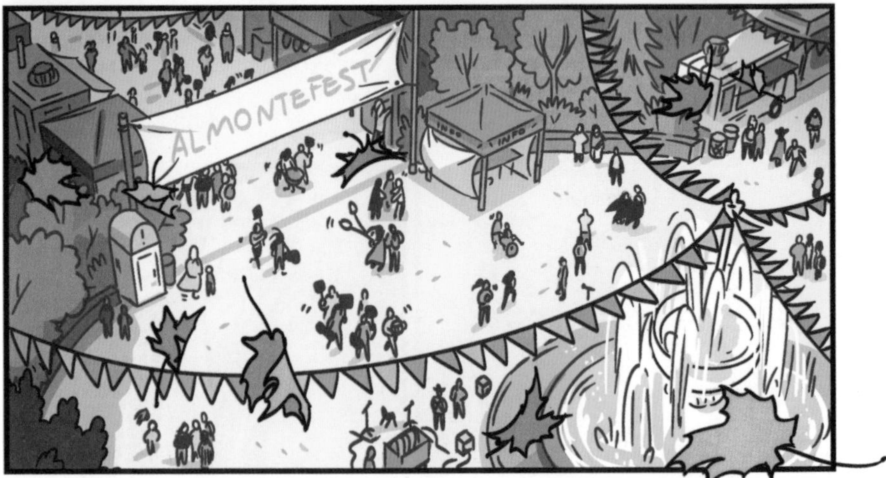
ALMONTEFEST
INFO
INFO

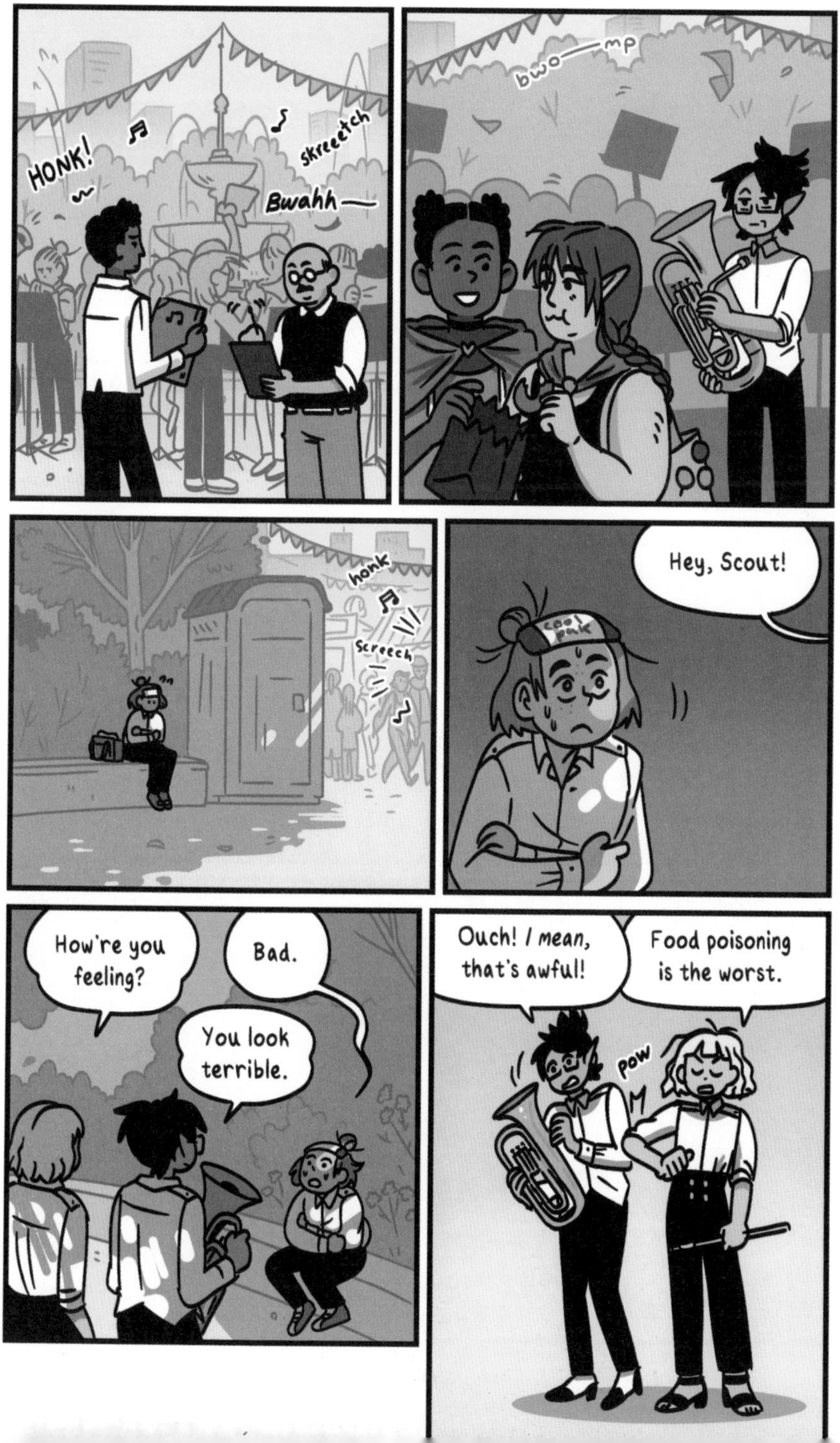
HONK!
skreeetch
Bwahh—
bwo—mp
honk
Screech
Hey, Scout!
cool pak
How're you feeling?
Bad.
You look terrible.
Ouch! *I mean,* that's awful!
Food poisoning is the worst.
pow

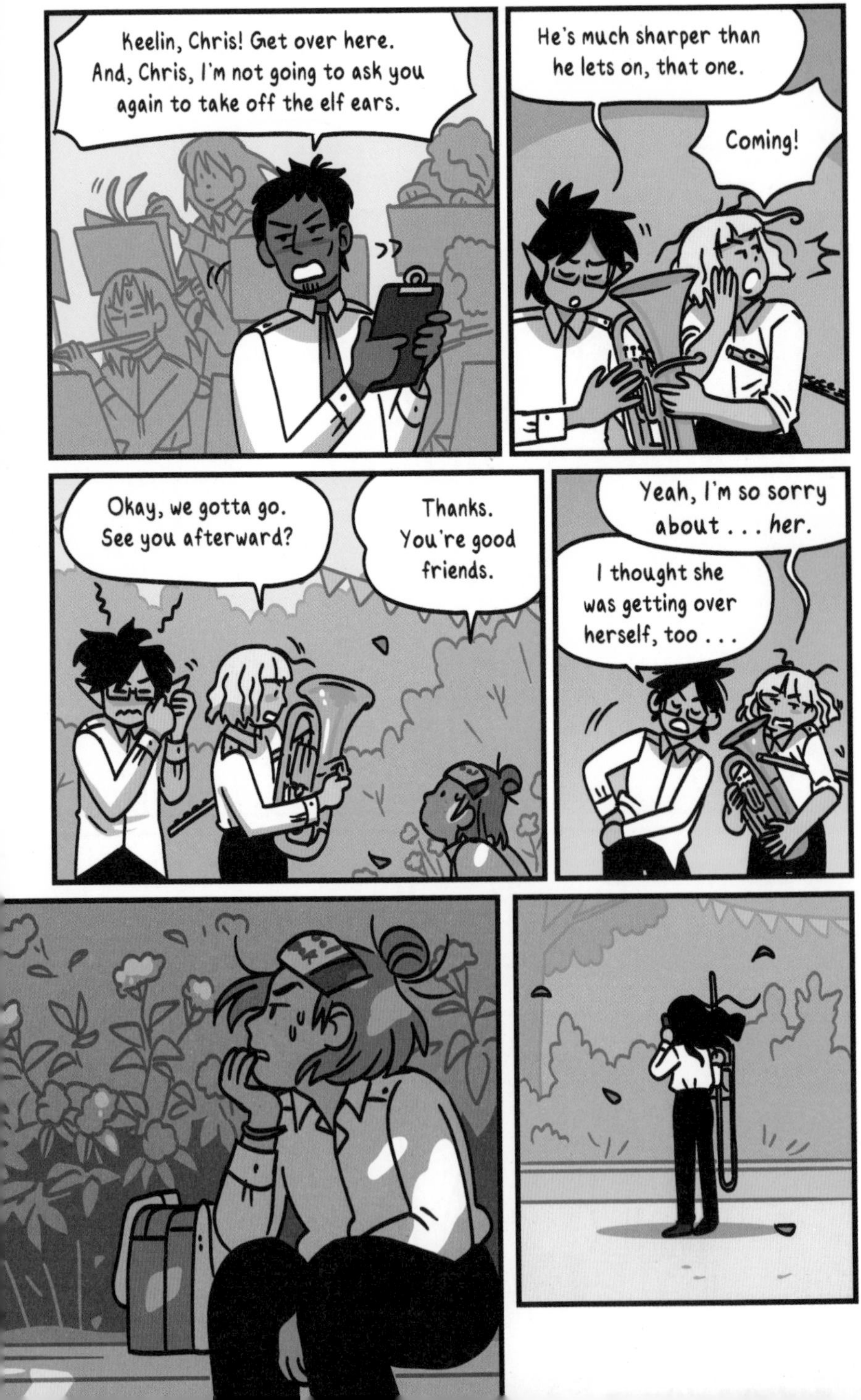
Keelin, Chris! Get over here. And, Chris, I'm not going to ask you again to take off the elf ears.
He's much sharper than he lets on, that one.
Coming!
Okay, we gotta go. See you afterward?
Thanks. You're good friends.
Yeah, I'm so sorry about . . . her.
I thought she was getting over herself, too . . .

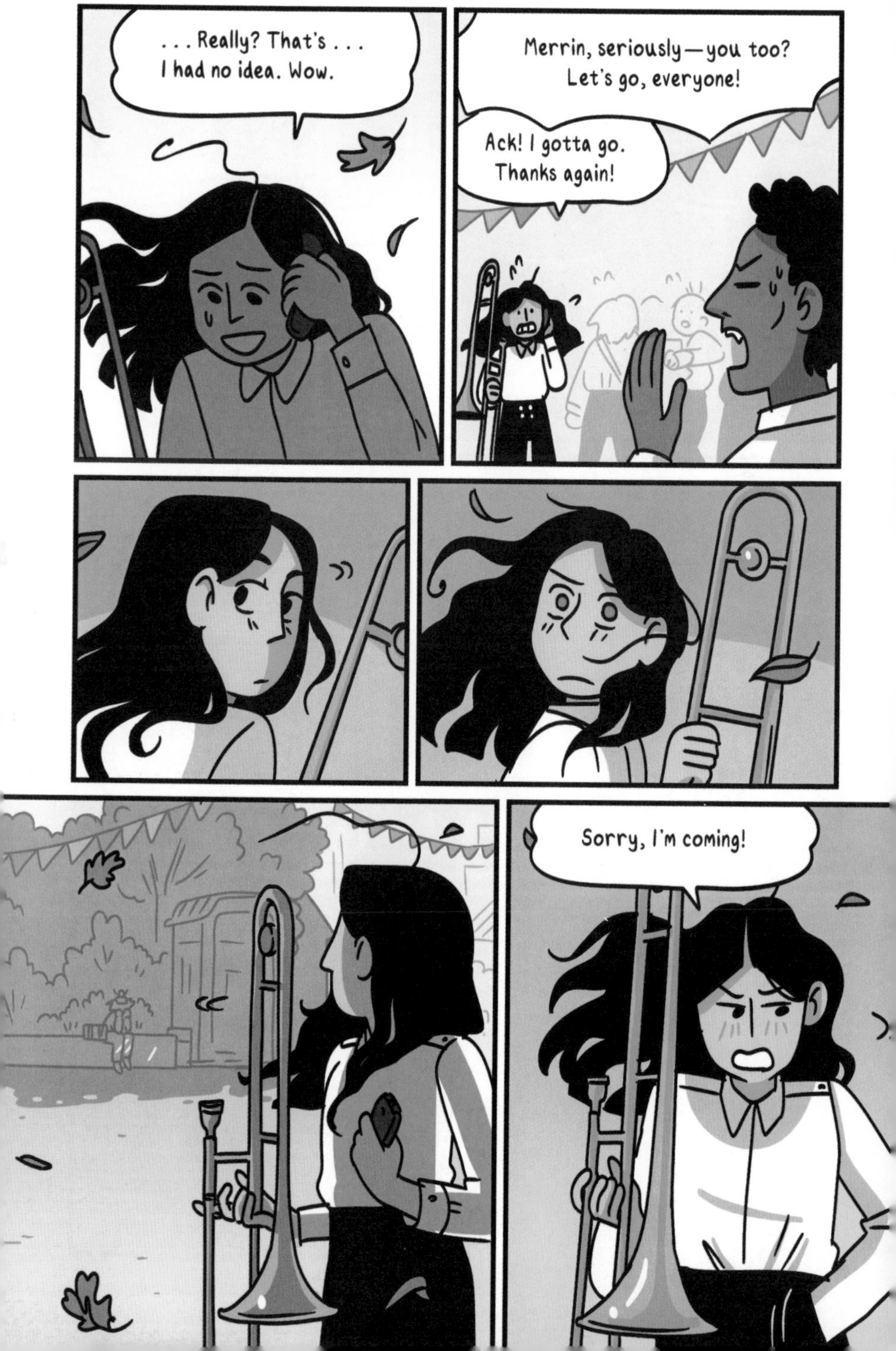
. . . Really? That's . . .
I had no idea. Wow.
Merrin, seriously—you too?
Let's go, everyone!
Ack! I gotta go.
Thanks again!
Sorry, I'm coming!

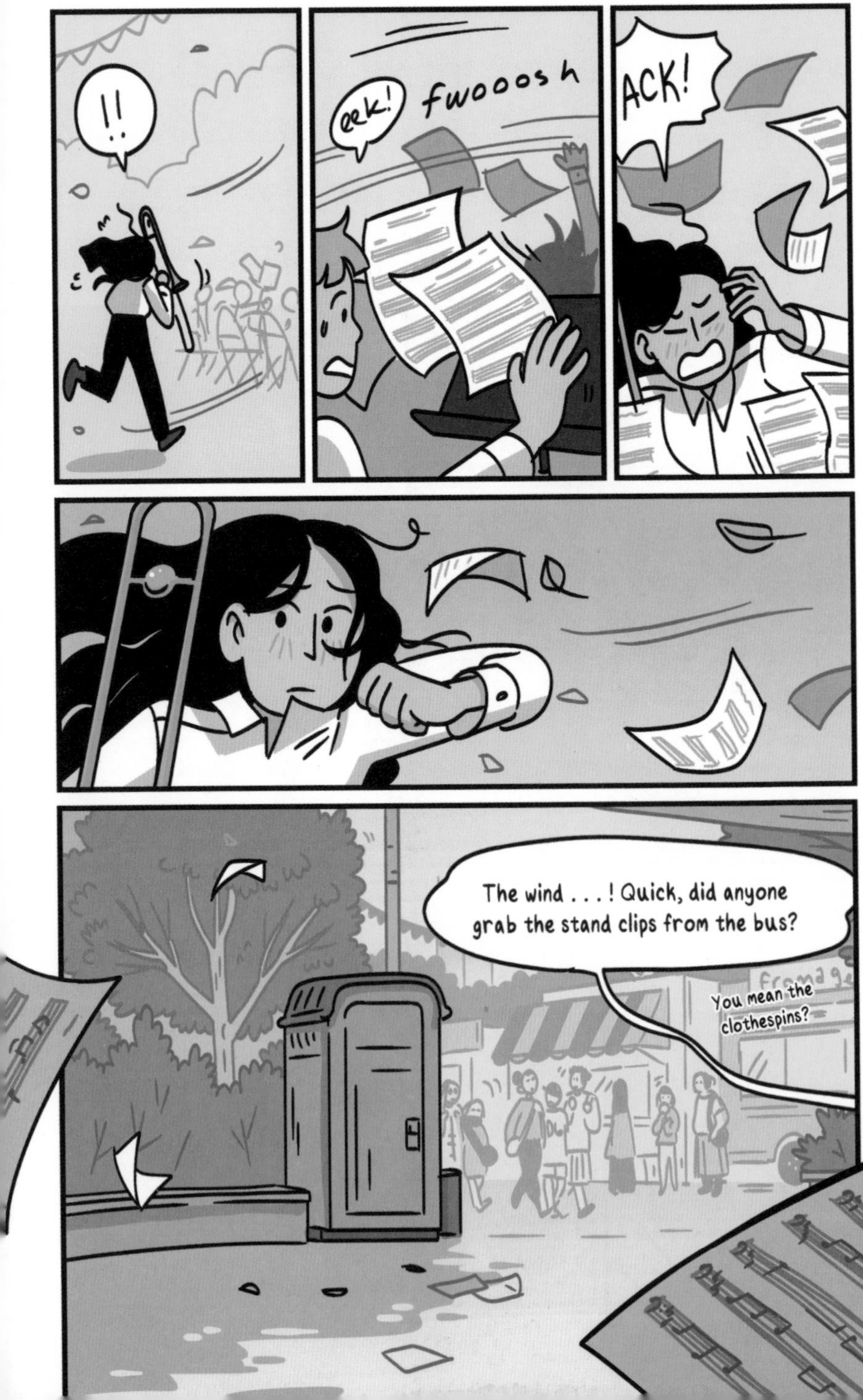
!!
eek!
fwooosh
ACK!
The wind . . . ! Quick, did anyone grab the stand clips from the bus?
You mean the clothespins?
fromage

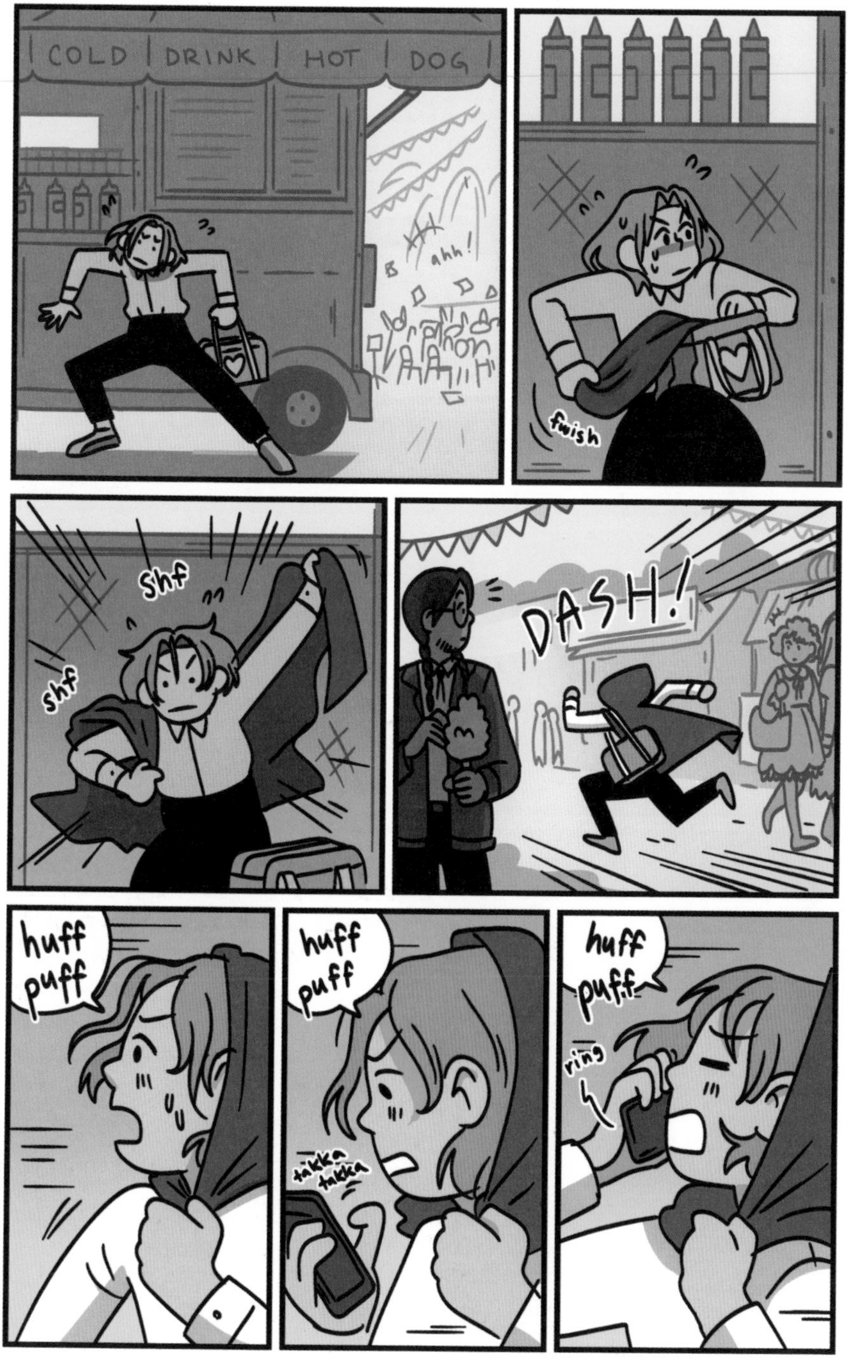
COLD DRINK HOT DOG
ahh!
fwish
shf
shf
DASH!
huff puff
huff puff
takka takka
huff puff
ring

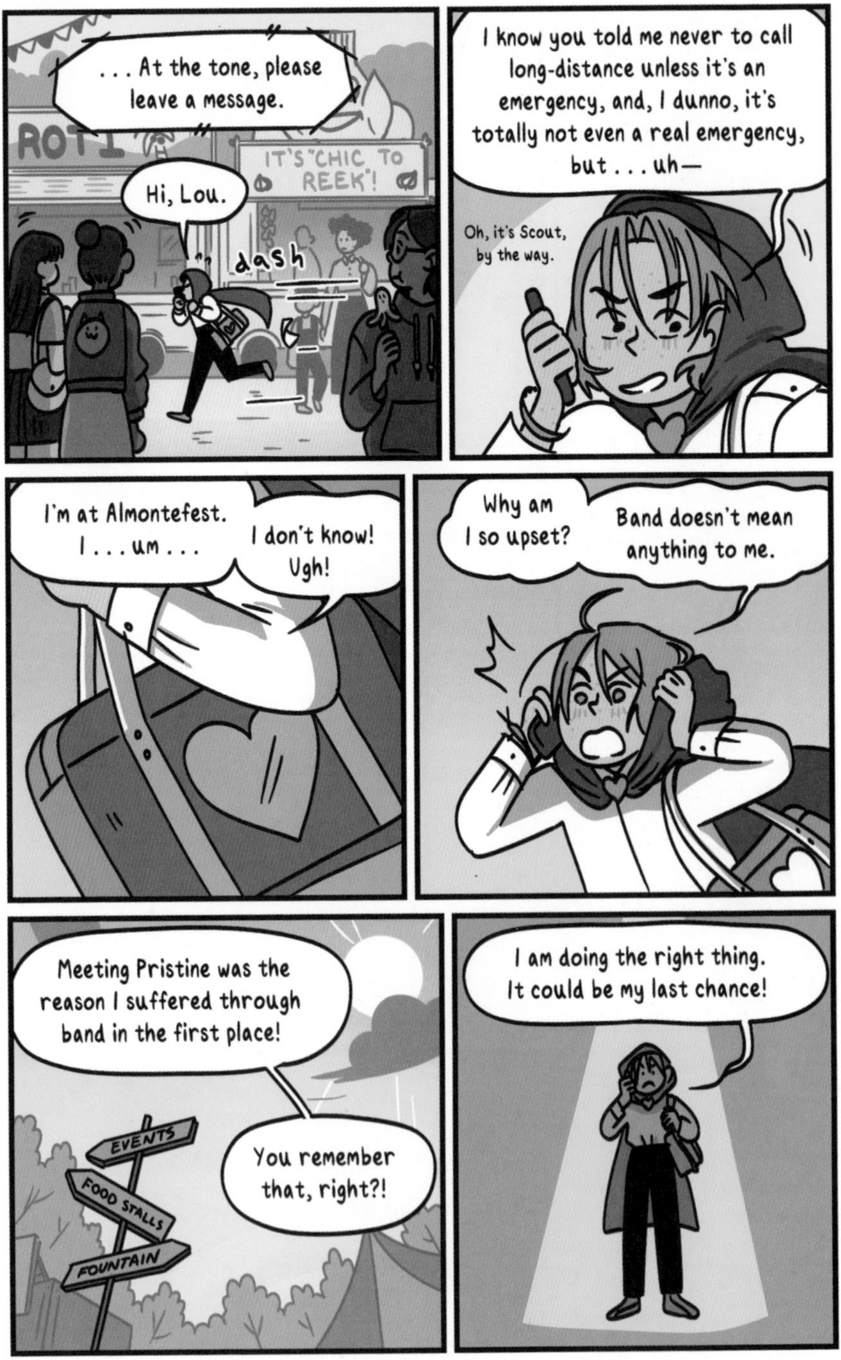

. . . At the tone, please leave a message.
ROTI
IT'S "CHIC TO REEK"!
Hi, Lou.
dash
I know you told me never to call long-distance unless it's an emergency, and, I dunno, it's totally not even a real emergency, but . . . uh—
Oh, it's Scout, by the way.
I'm at Almontefest. I . . . um . . .
I don't know! Ugh!
Why am I so upset?
Band doesn't mean anything to me.
Meeting Pristine was the reason I suffered through band in the first place!
You remember that, right?!
EVENTS
FOOD STALLS
FOUNTAIN
I am doing the right thing. It could be my last chance!

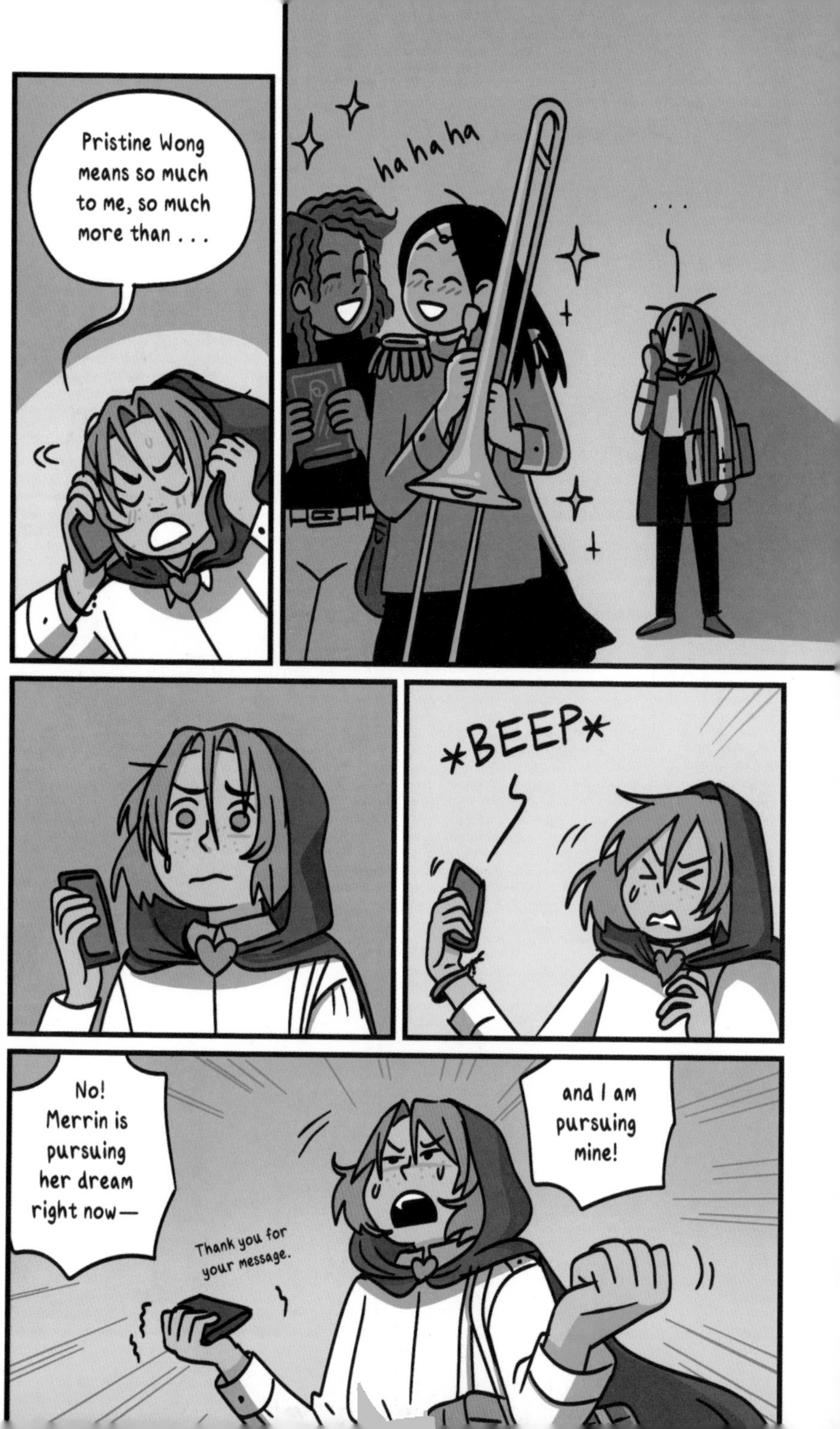
Pristine Wong means so much to me, so much more than . . .
ha ha ha
. . .
BEEP
No! Merrin is pursuing her dream right now—
Thank you for your message.
and I am pursuing mine!

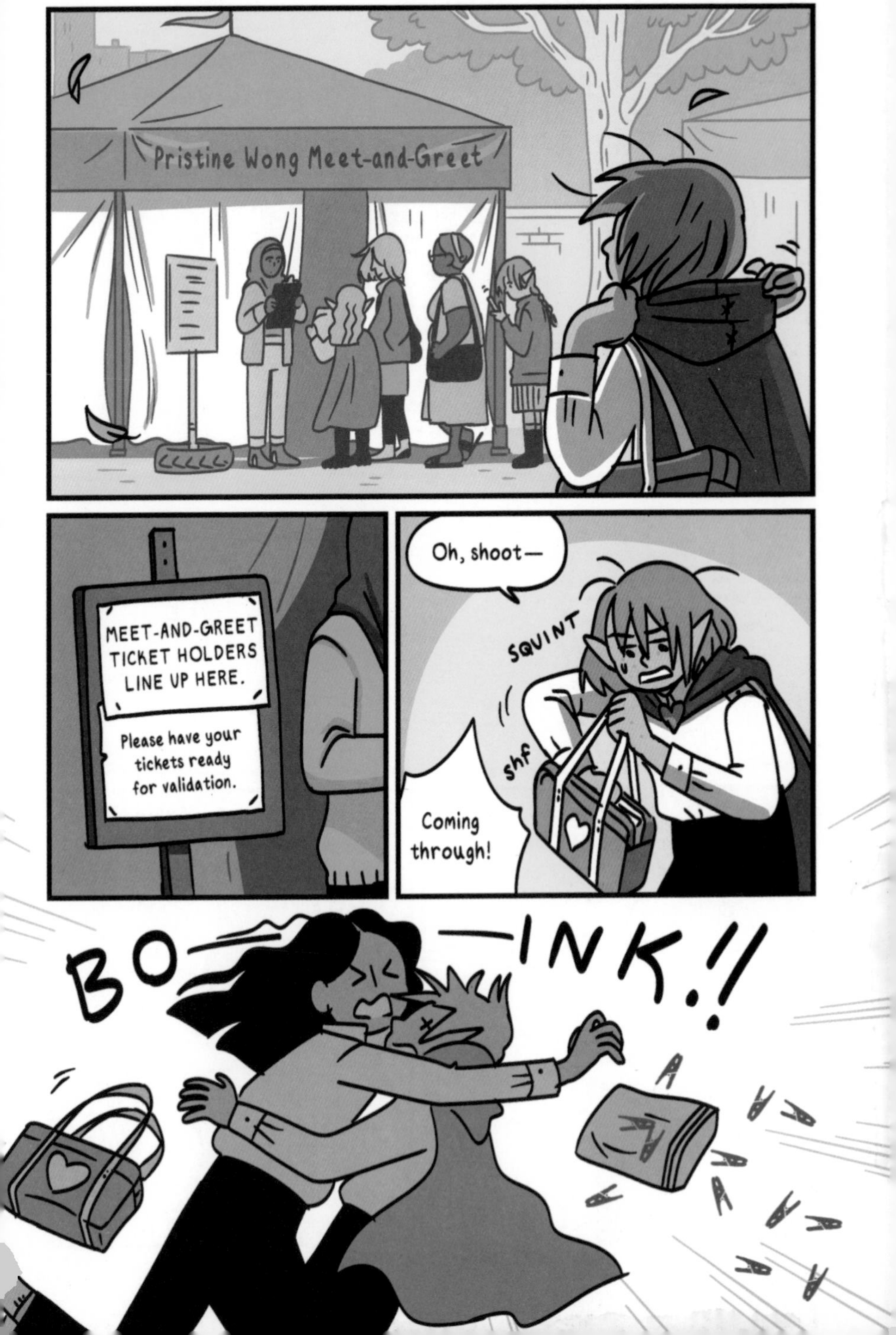
Pristine Wong Meet-and-Greet
MEET-AND-GREET TICKET HOLDERS LINE UP HERE.
Please have your tickets ready for validation.
Oh, shoot—
SQUINT
shf
Coming through!
BO—
—INK!!

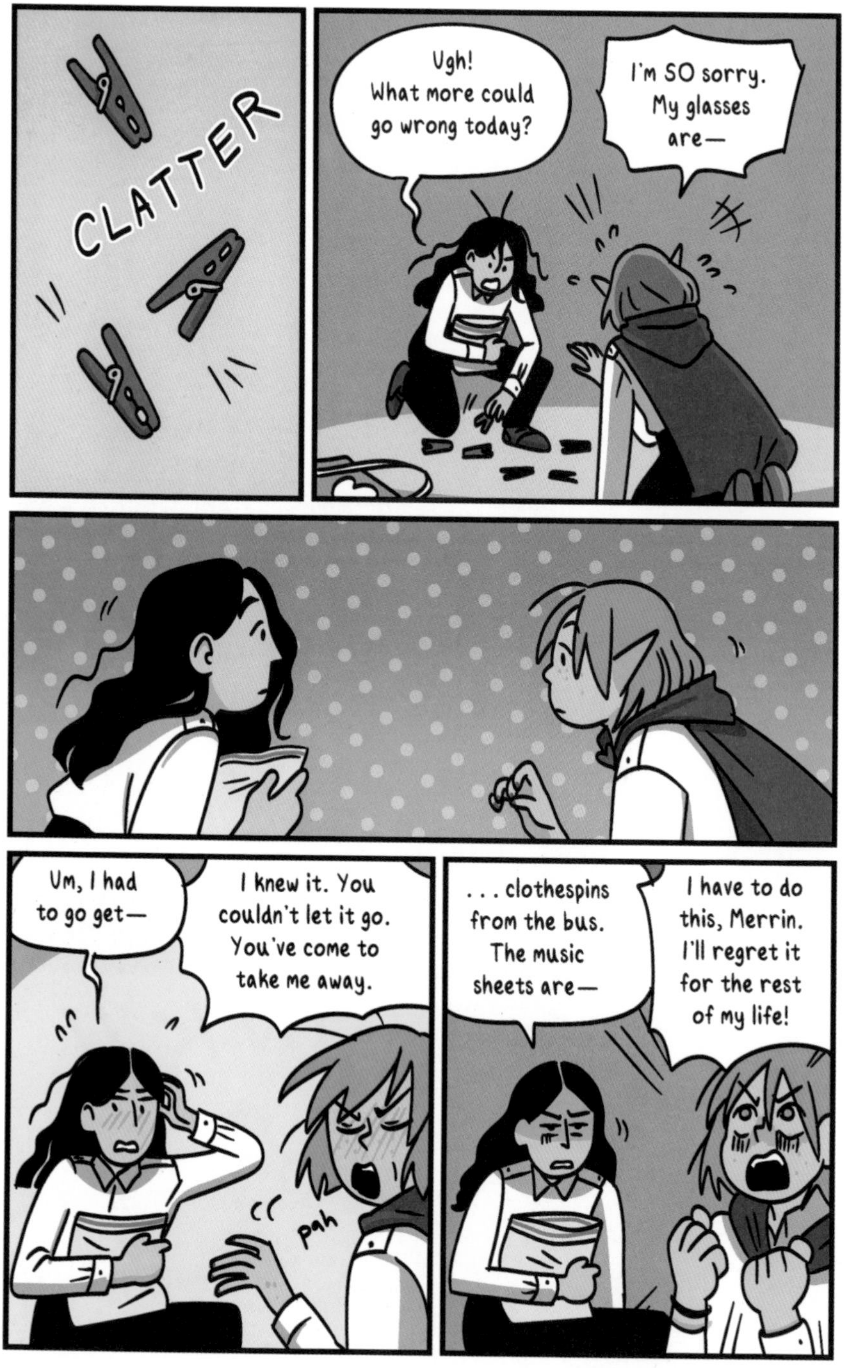
CLATTER
Ugh! What more could go wrong today?
I'm SO sorry. My glasses are—
Um, I had to go get—
I knew it. You couldn't let it go. You've come to take me away.
pah
. . . clothespins from the bus. The music sheets are—
I have to do this, Merrin. I'll regret it for the rest of my life!

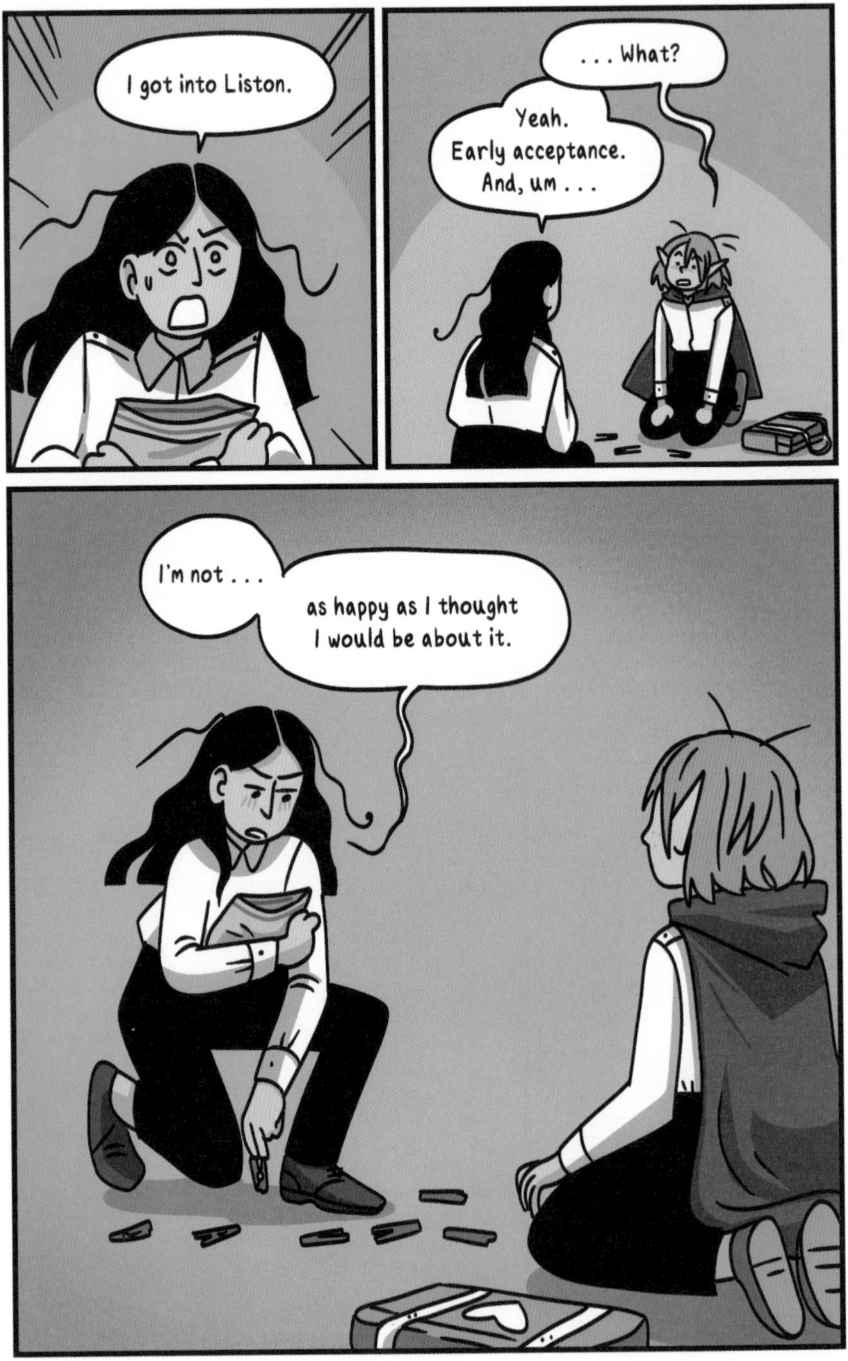

I got into Liston.
. . . What?
Yeah.
Early acceptance.
And, um . . .
I'm not . . .
as happy as I thought
I would be about it.

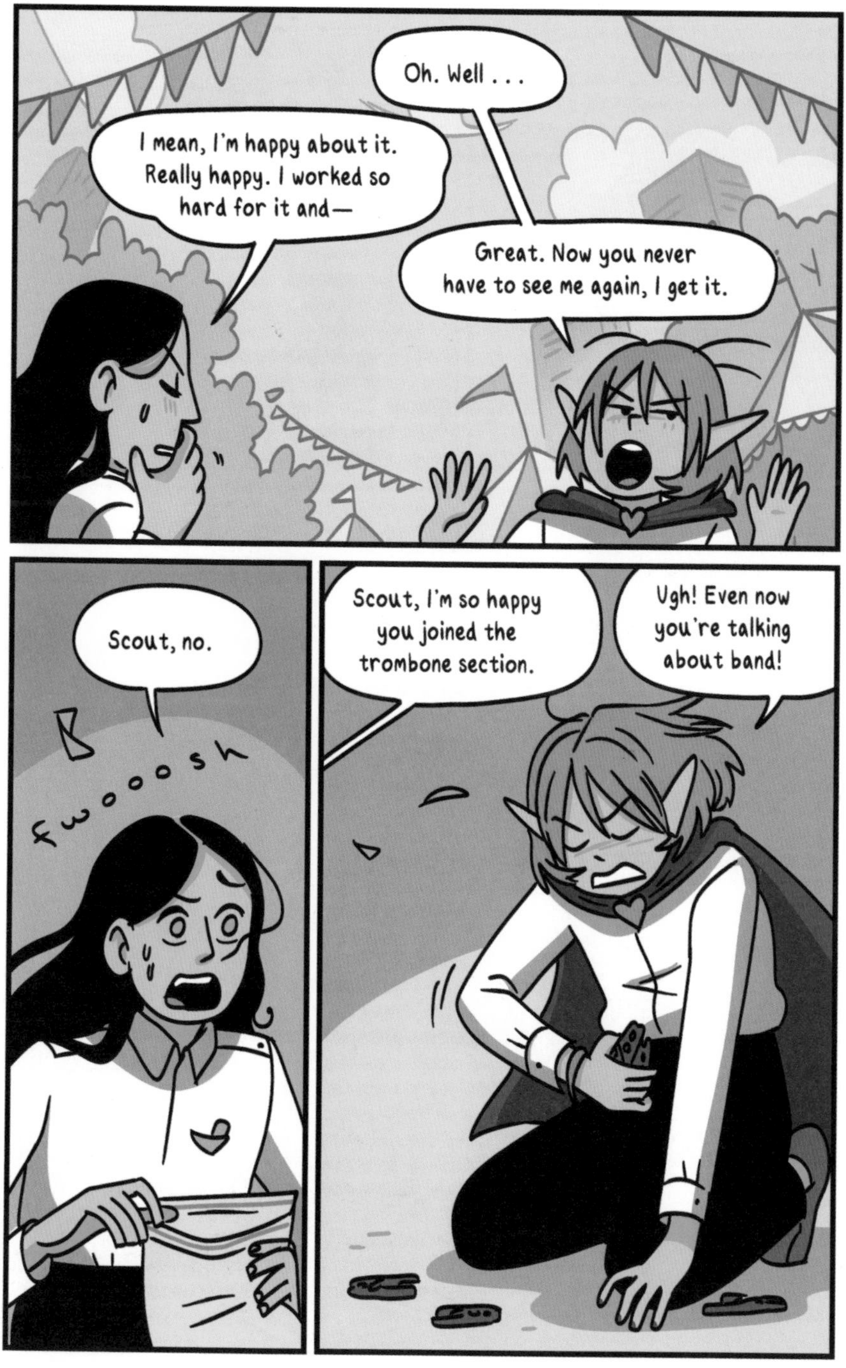
I mean, I'm happy about it. Really happy. I worked so hard for it and—
Oh. Well . . .
Great. Now you never have to see me again, I get it.
Scout, no.
fwooosh
Scout, I'm so happy you joined the trombone section.
Ugh! Even now you're talking about band!

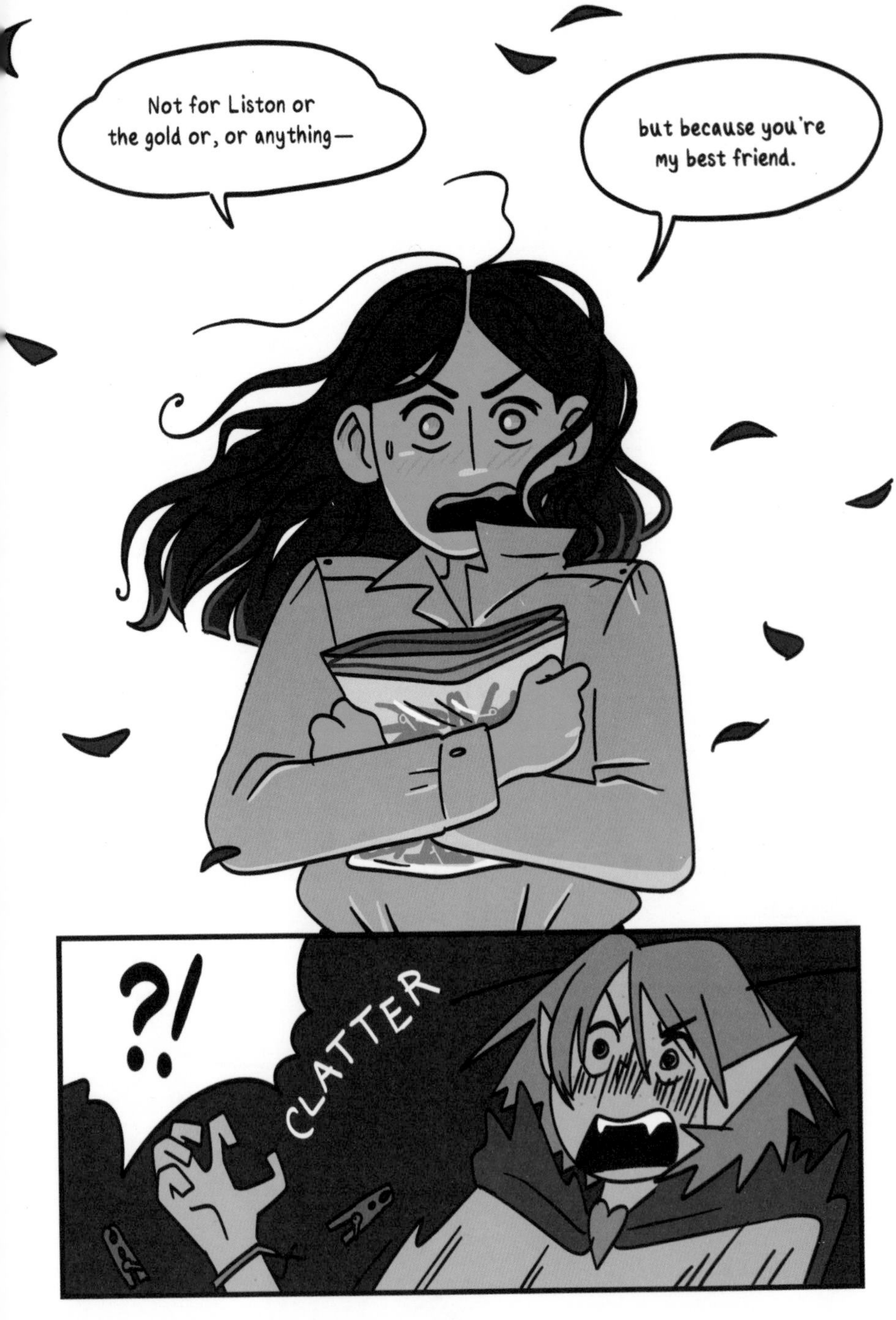
Not for Liston or the gold or, or anything—
but because you're my best friend.
?!
CLATTER

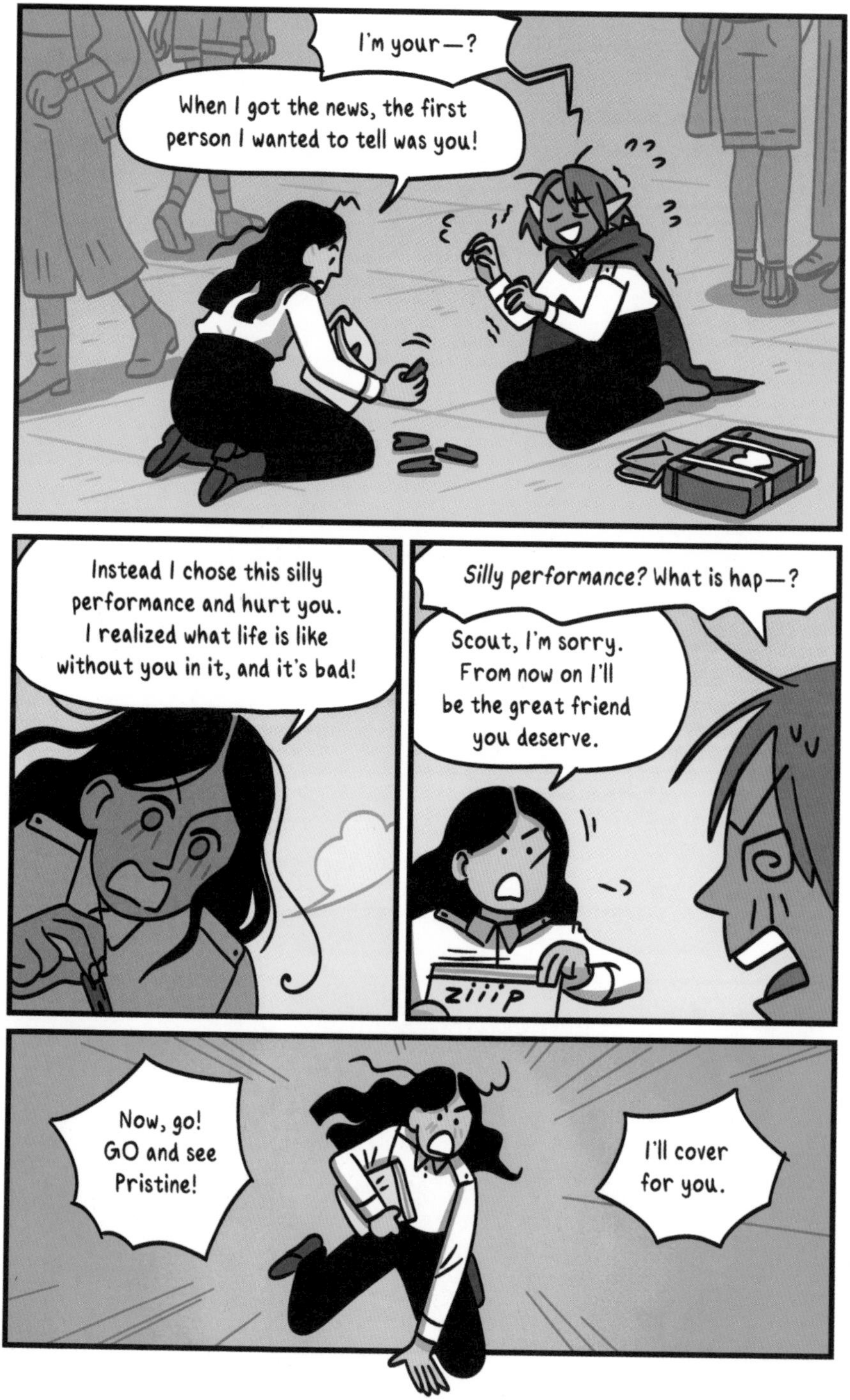
I'm your—?
When I got the news, the first person I wanted to tell was you!
Instead I chose this silly performance and hurt you. I realized what life is like without you in it, and it's bad!
Silly performance? What is hap—?
Scout, I'm sorry. From now on I'll be the great friend you deserve.
ziiip
Now, go! GO and see Pristine!
I'll cover for you.

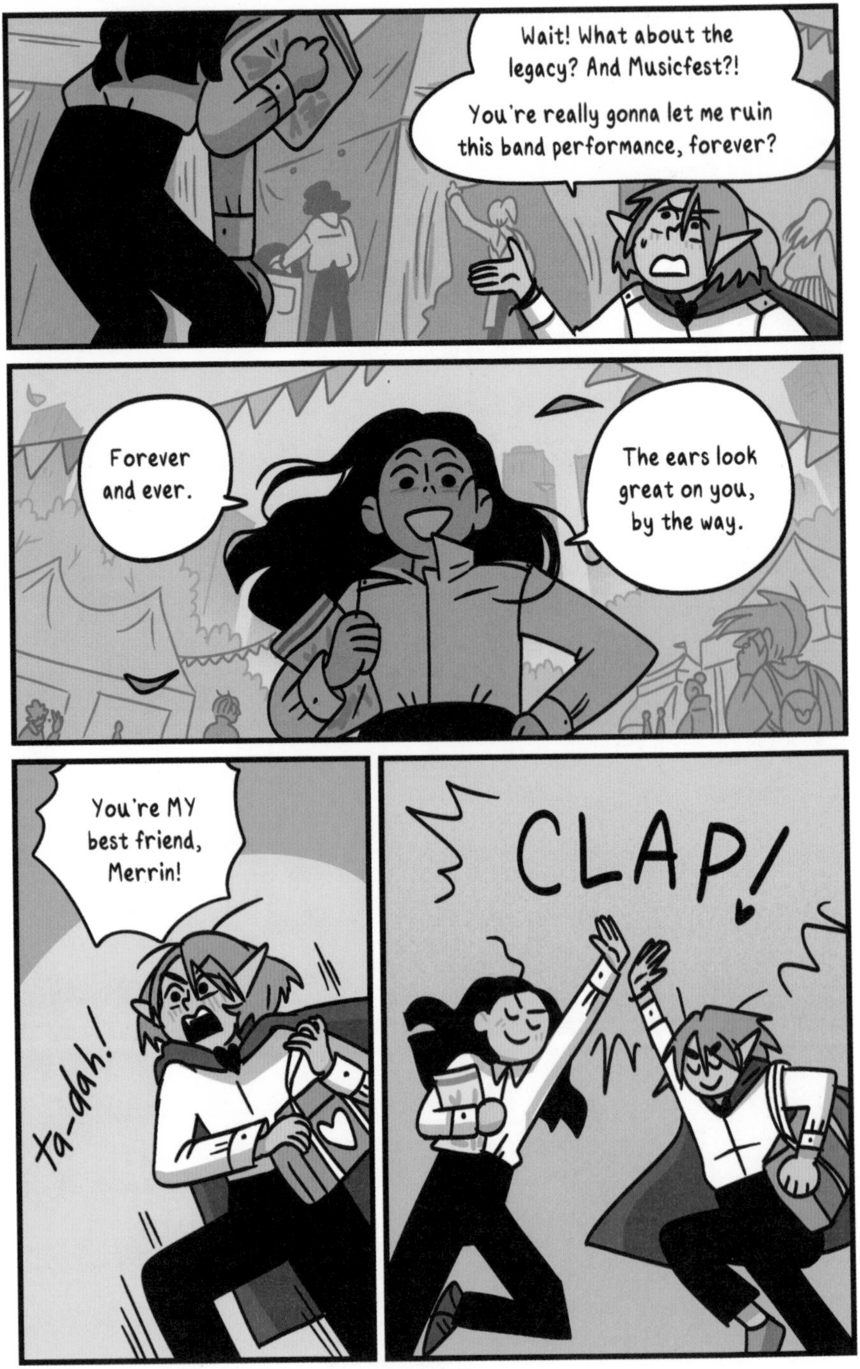
Wait! What about the legacy? And Musicfest?!
You're really gonna let me ruin this band performance, forever?
Forever and ever.
The ears look great on you, by the way.
You're MY best friend, Merrin!
ta-dah!
CLAP!

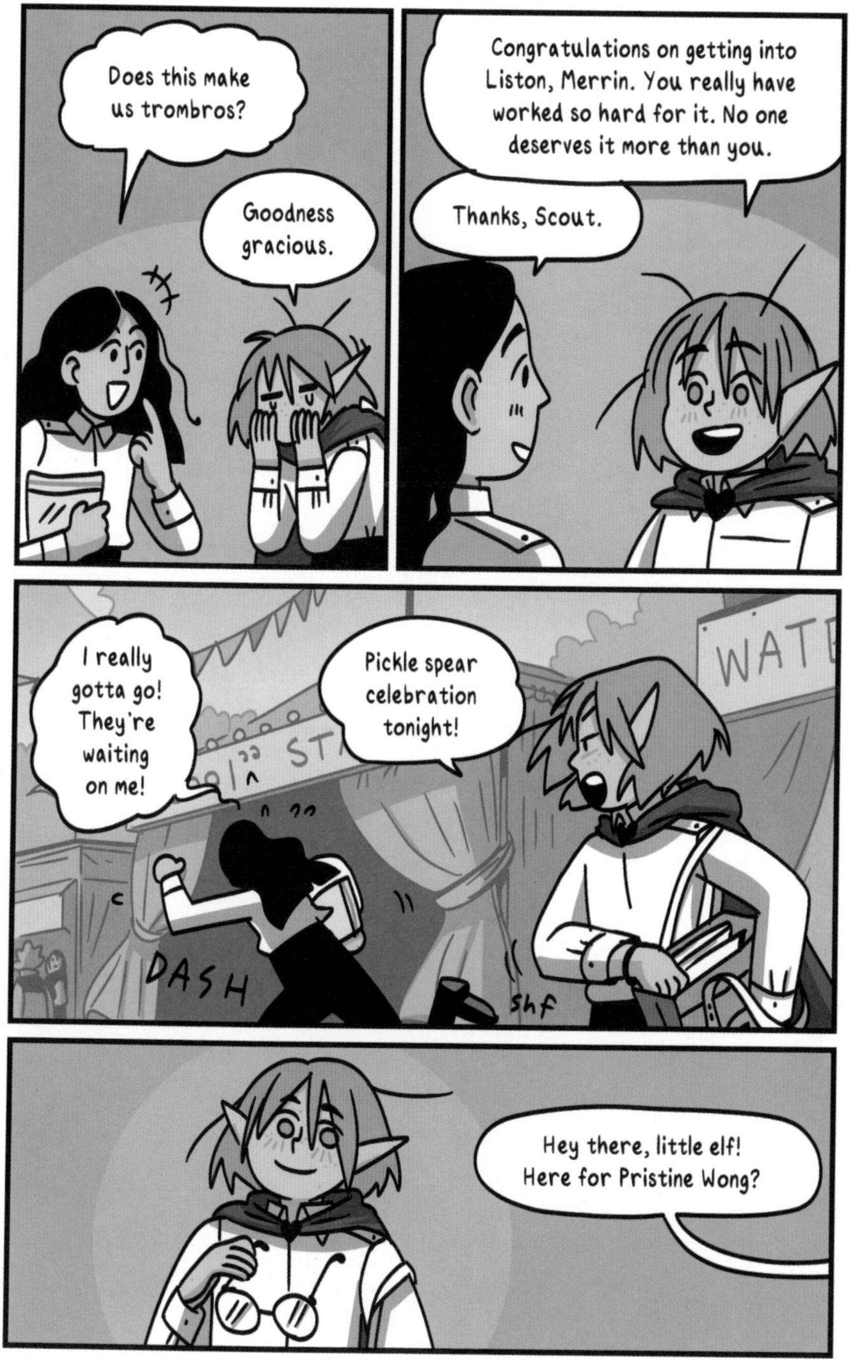
Does this make us trombros?
Goodness gracious.
Congratulations on getting into Liston, Merrin. You really have worked so hard for it. No one deserves it more than you.
Thanks, Scout.
WATE
I really gotta go! They're waiting on me!
Pickle spear celebration tonight!
DASH
shf
Hey there, little elf! Here for Pristine Wong?

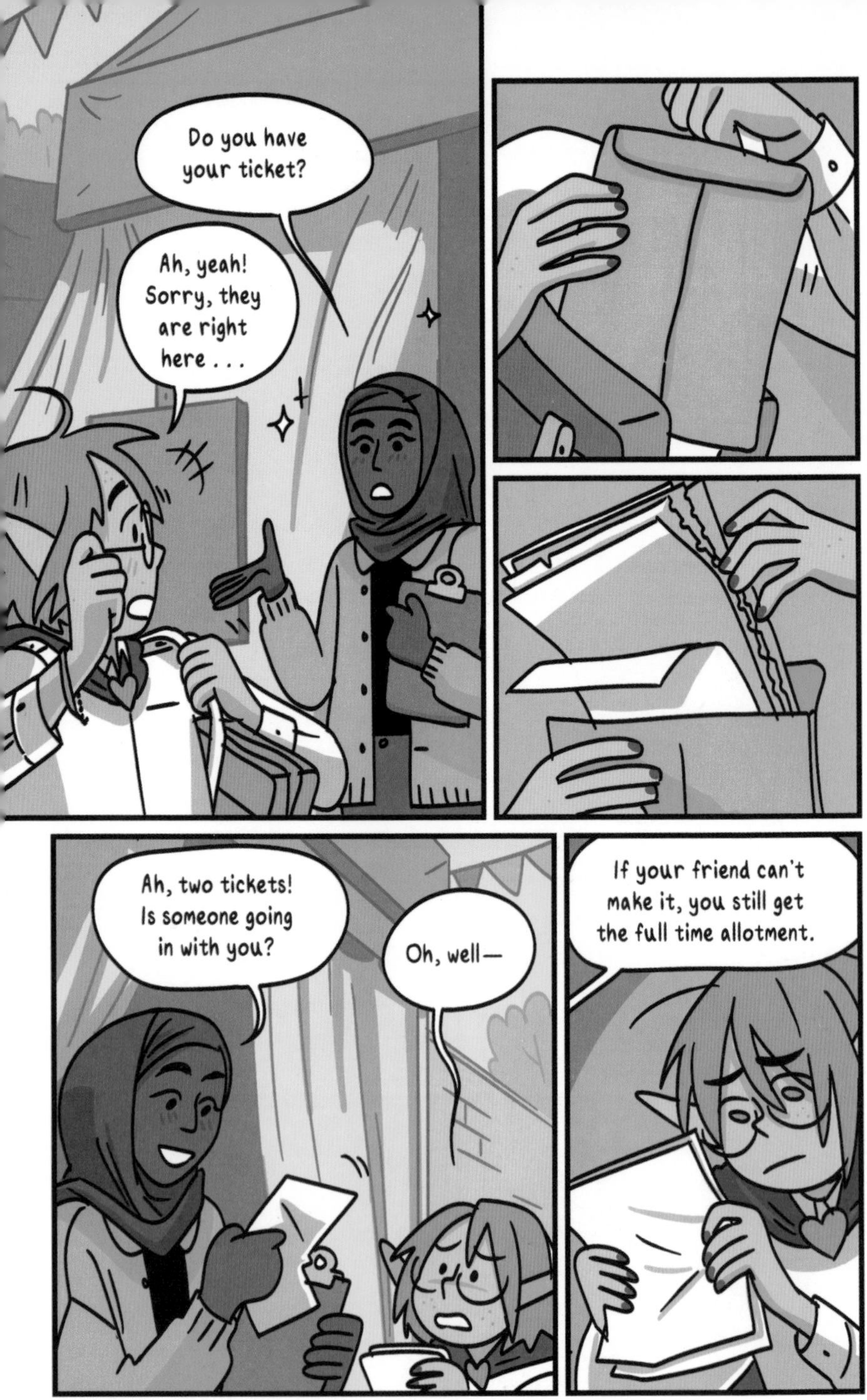
Do you have your ticket?
Ah, yeah! Sorry, they are right here . . .
Ah, two tickets! Is someone going in with you?
Oh, well—
If your friend can't make it, you still get the full time allotment.

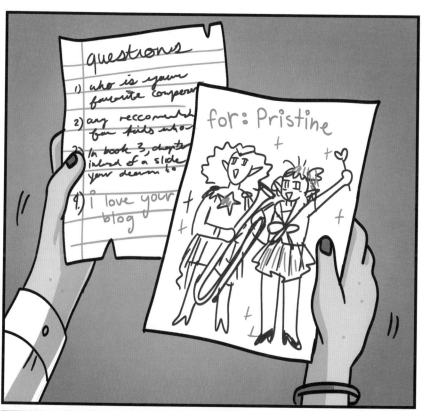

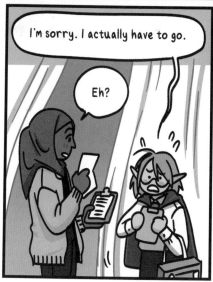

questions
1) who is your
2) any
3) In book 3,
4.) I love your blog
for: Pristine
I'm sorry. I actually have to go.
Eh?
I—I got food poisoning from a street hot dog!
Bathrooms are by the pavilion!

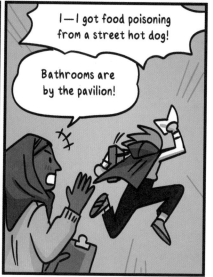

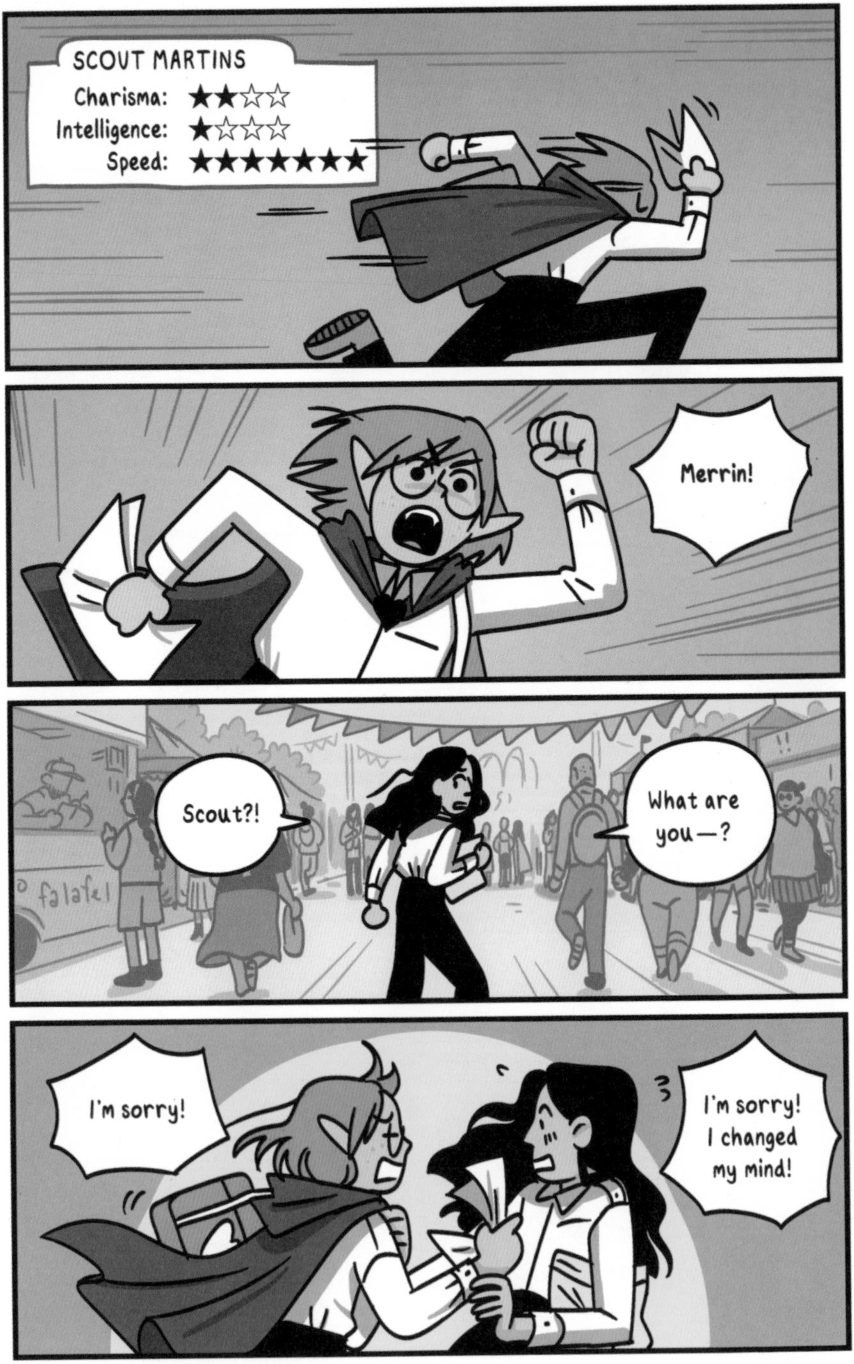
SCOUT MARTINS
Charisma: ★★☆☆
Intelligence: ★☆☆☆
Speed: ★★★★★★★
Merrin!
Scout?!
What are you—?
falafel
I'm sorry!
I'm sorry! I changed my mind!

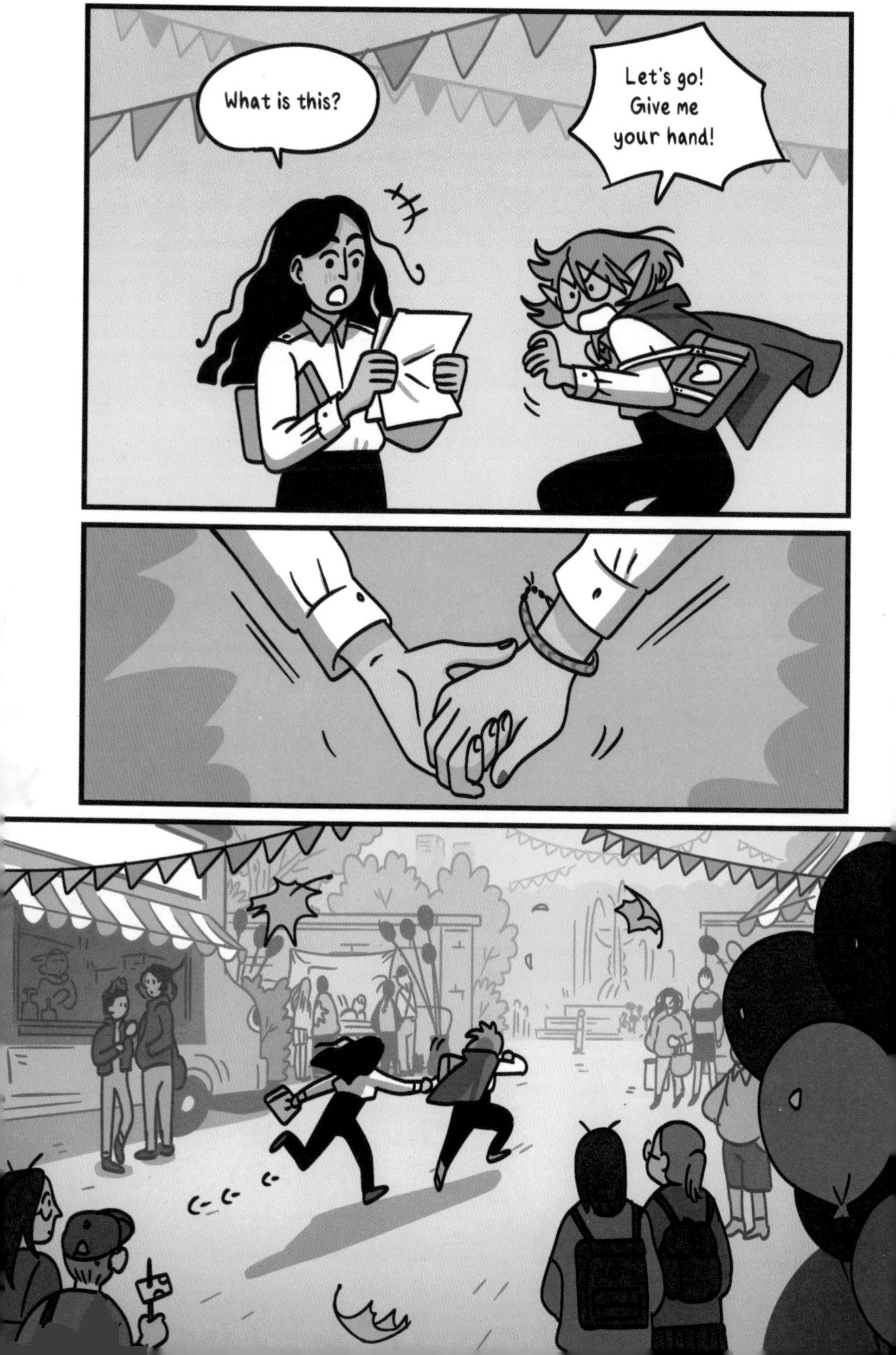
What is this?
Let's go! Give me your hand!

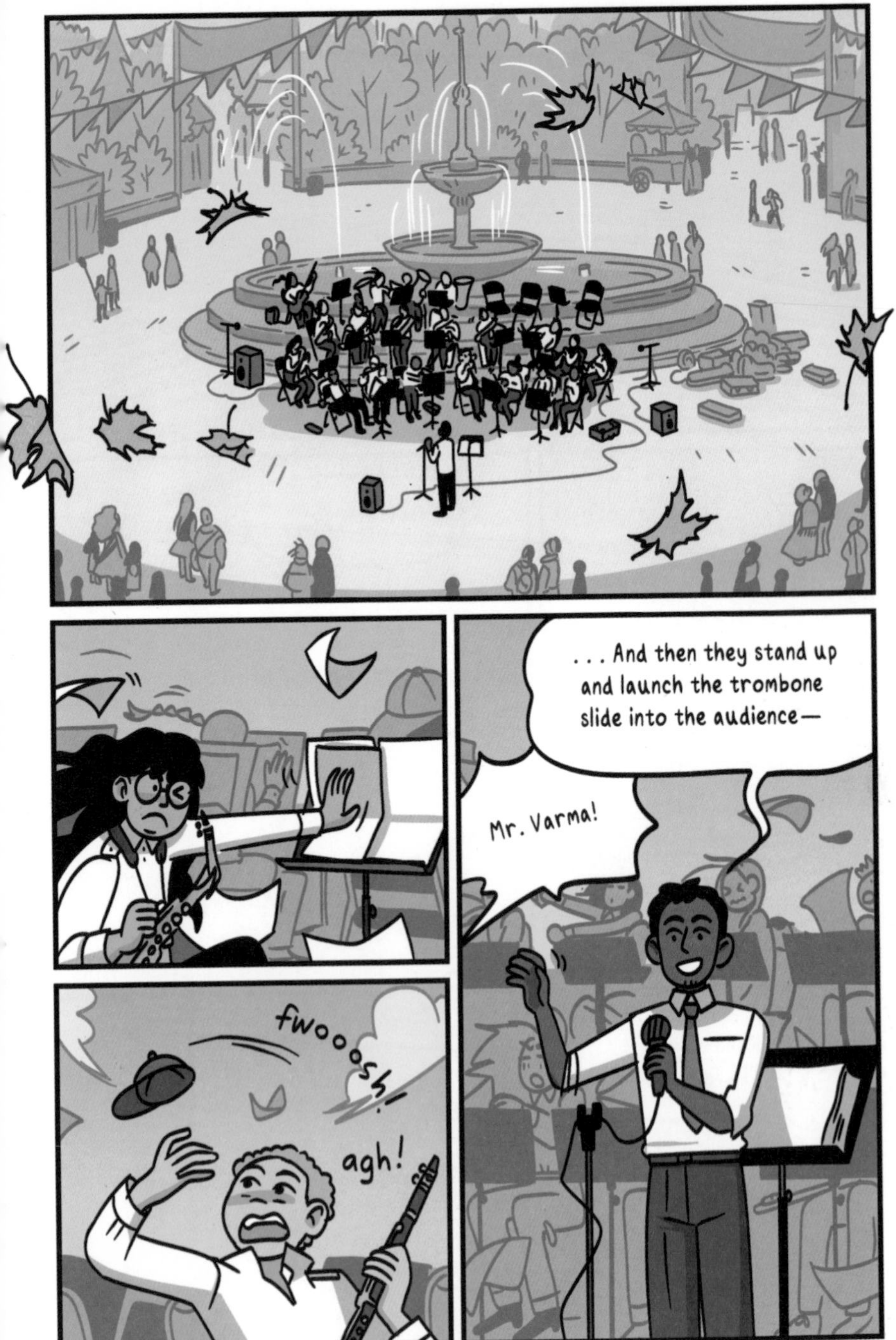
. . . And then they stand up and launch the trombone slide into the audience—
Mr. Varma!
fwoooosh!
agh!

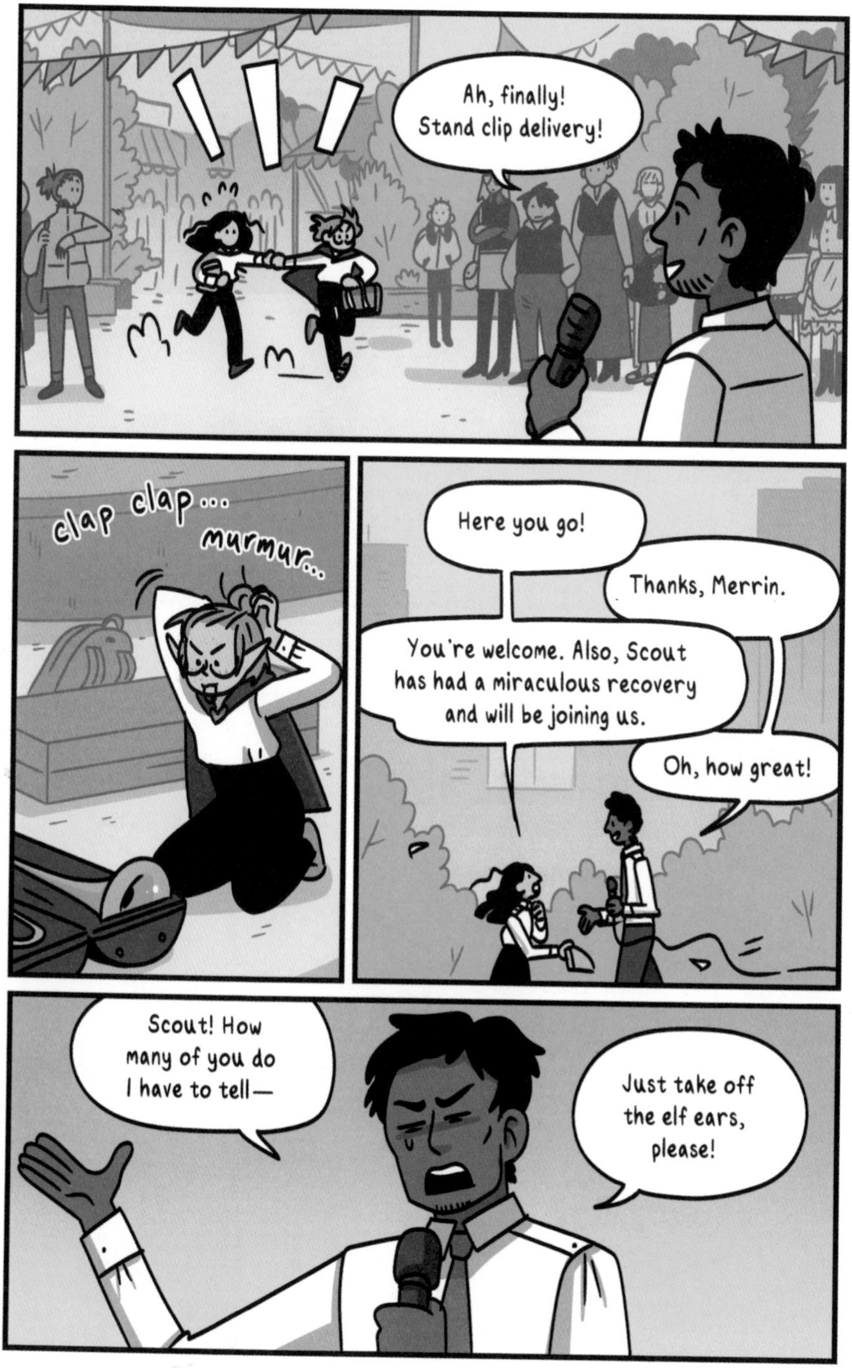
Ah, finally! Stand clip delivery!
clap clap...
murmur...
Here you go!
Thanks, Merrin.
You're welcome. Also, Scout has had a miraculous recovery and will be joining us.
Oh, how great!
Scout! How many of you do I have to tell—
Just take off the elf ears, please!

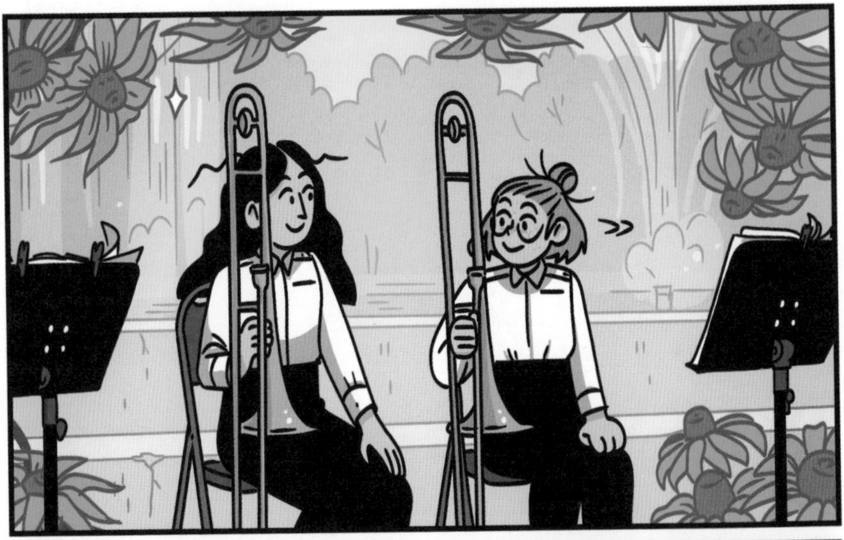

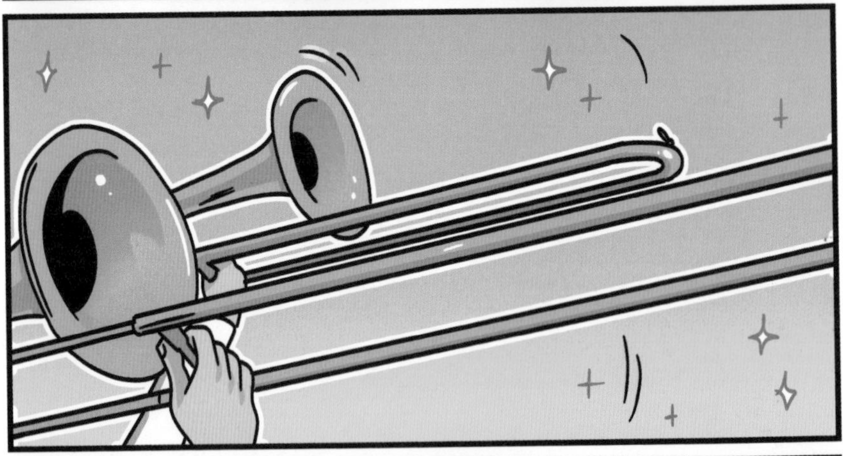

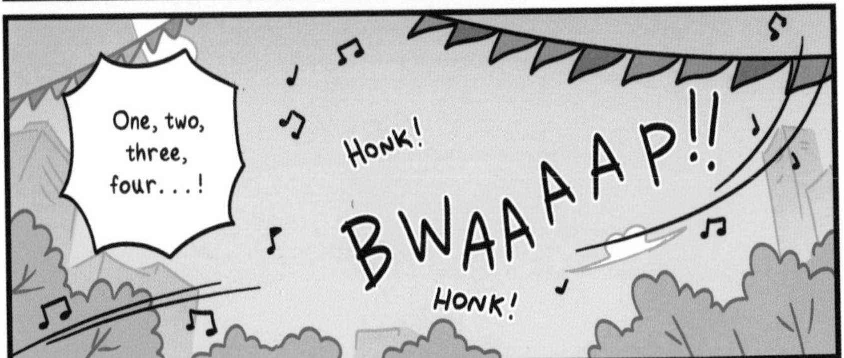
One, two, three, four...!
HONK!
BWAAAAP!!
HONK!

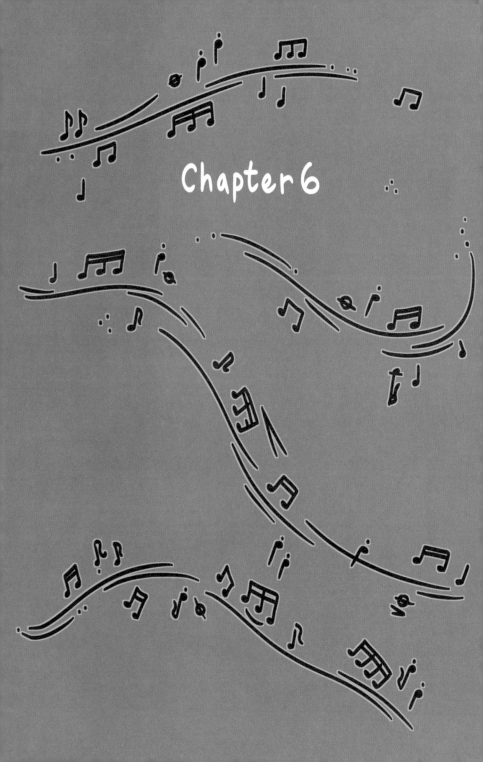

Chapter 6

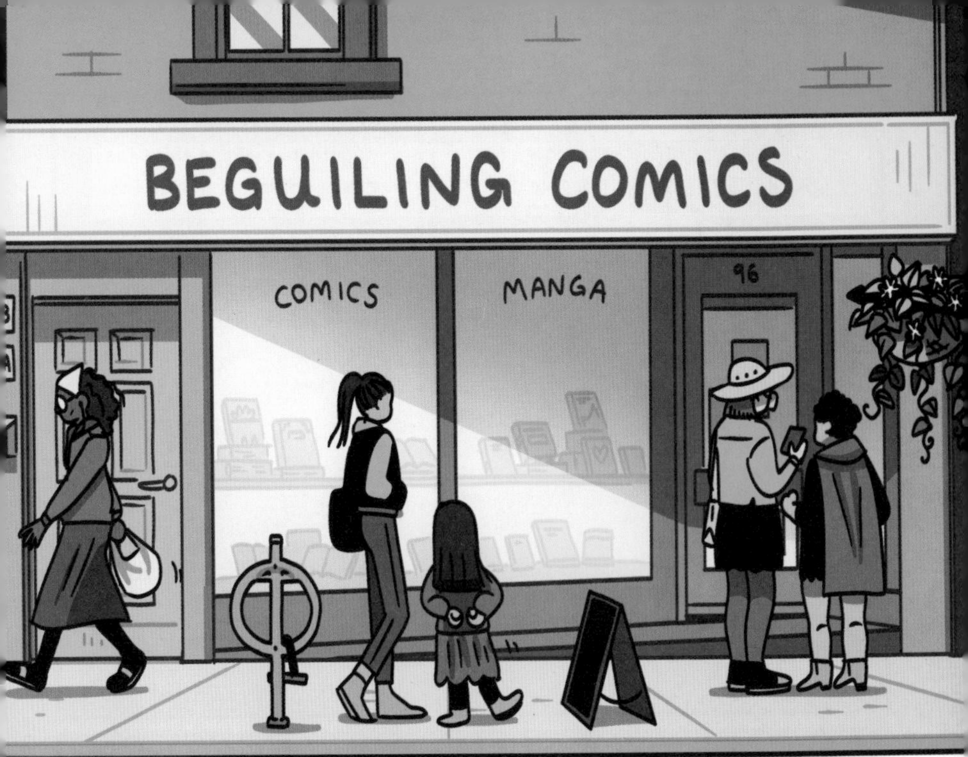
BEGUILING COMICS
COMICS
MANGA
96

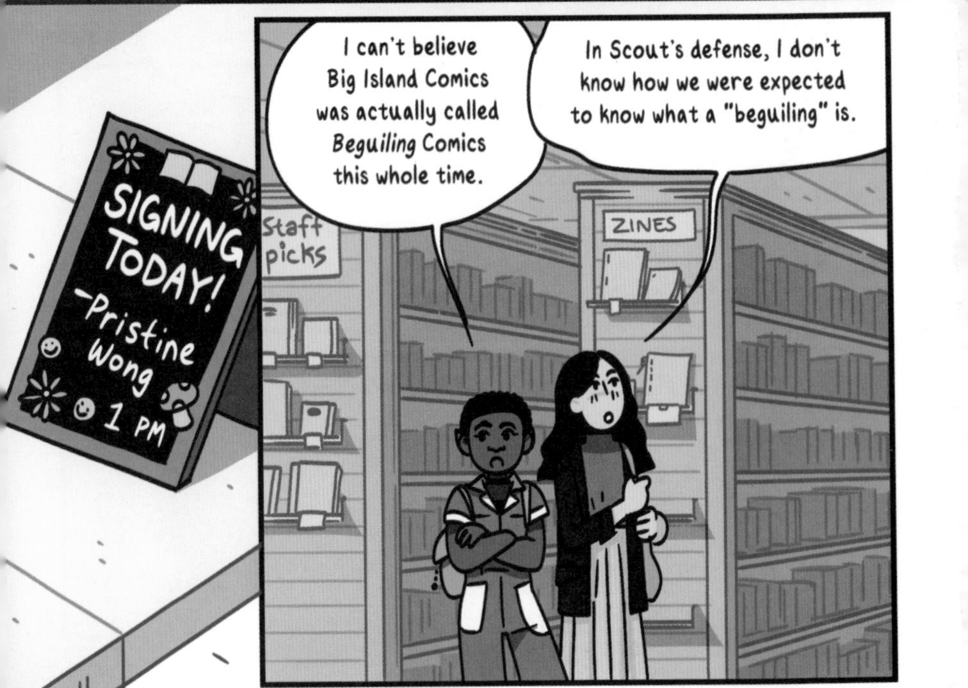
SIGNING TODAY! -Pristine Wong 1 PM
Staff picks
I can't believe Big Island Comics was actually called *Beguiling* Comics this whole time.
In Scout's defense, I don't know how we were expected to know what a "beguiling" is.
ZINES

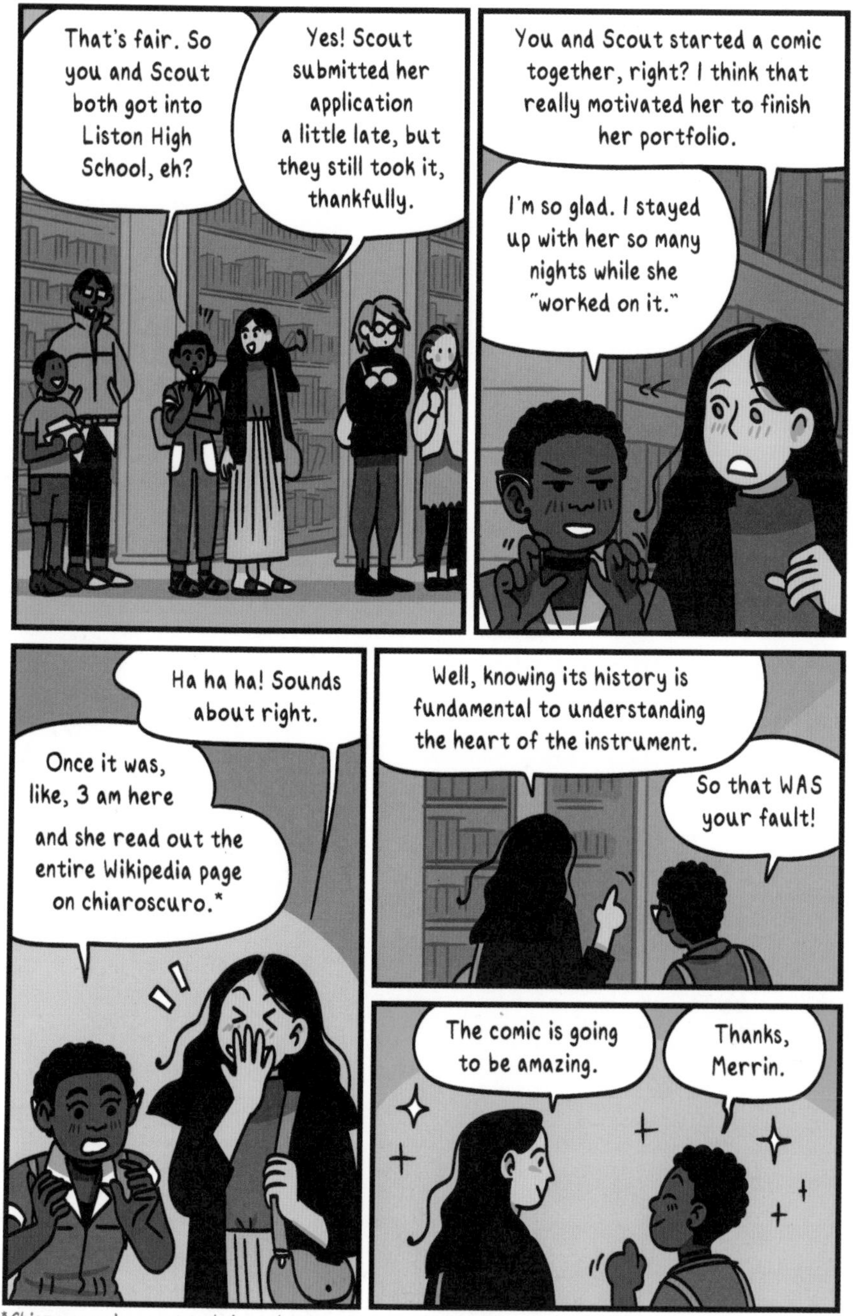
That's fair. So you and Scout both got into Liston High School, eh?
Yes! Scout submitted her application a little late, but they still took it, thankfully.
You and Scout started a comic together, right? I think that really motivated her to finish her portfolio.
I'm so glad. I stayed up with her so many nights while she "worked on it."
Ha ha ha! Sounds about right.
Once it was, like, 3 am here
and she read out the entire Wikipedia page on chiaroscuro.*
Well, knowing its history is fundamental to understanding the heart of the instrument.
So that WAS your fault!
The comic is going to be amazing.
Thanks, Merrin.

**Chiaroscuro* is an art technique that uses strong contrasts between light and dark.

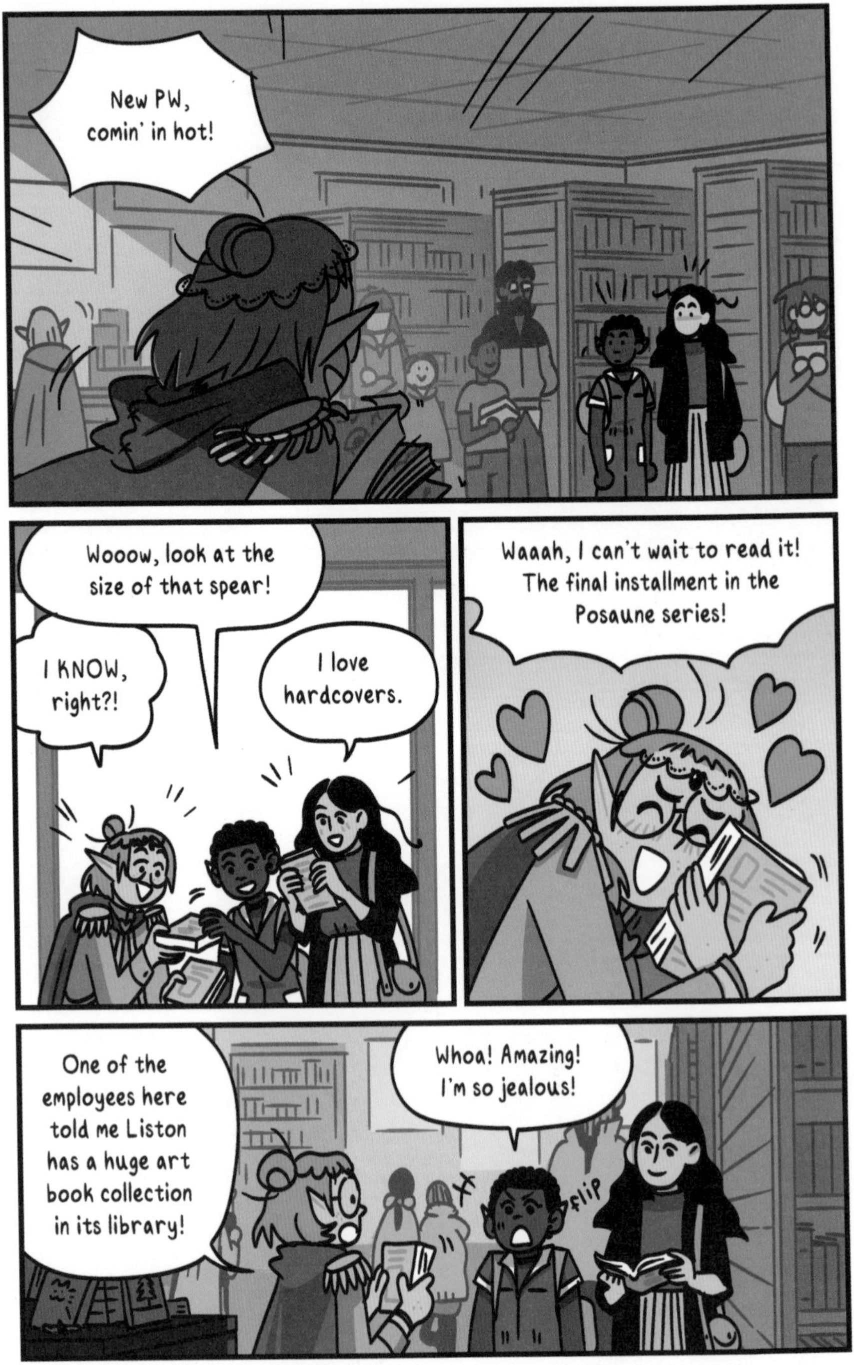

New PW, comin' in hot!
Wooow, look at the size of that spear!
I KNOW, right?!
I love hardcovers.
Waaah, I can't wait to read it! The final installment in the Posaune series!
One of the employees here told me Liston has a huge art book collection in its library!
Whoa! Amazing! I'm so jealous!
flip

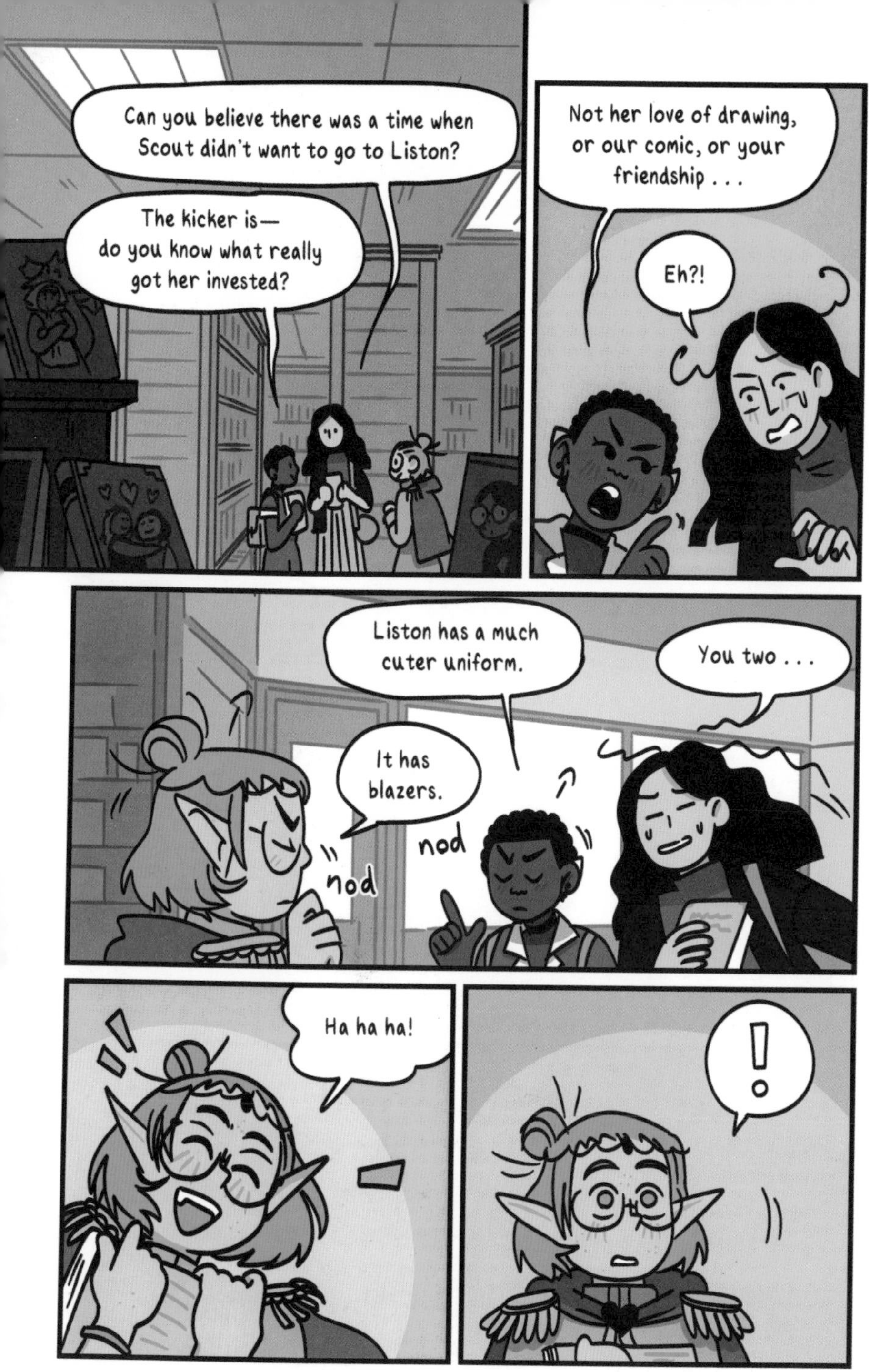
Can you believe there was a time when Scout didn't want to go to Liston?
The kicker is—do you know what really got her invested?
Not her love of drawing, or our comic, or your friendship . . .
Eh?!
Liston has a much cuter uniform.
You two . . .
It has blazers.
nod
nod
Ha ha ha!
!

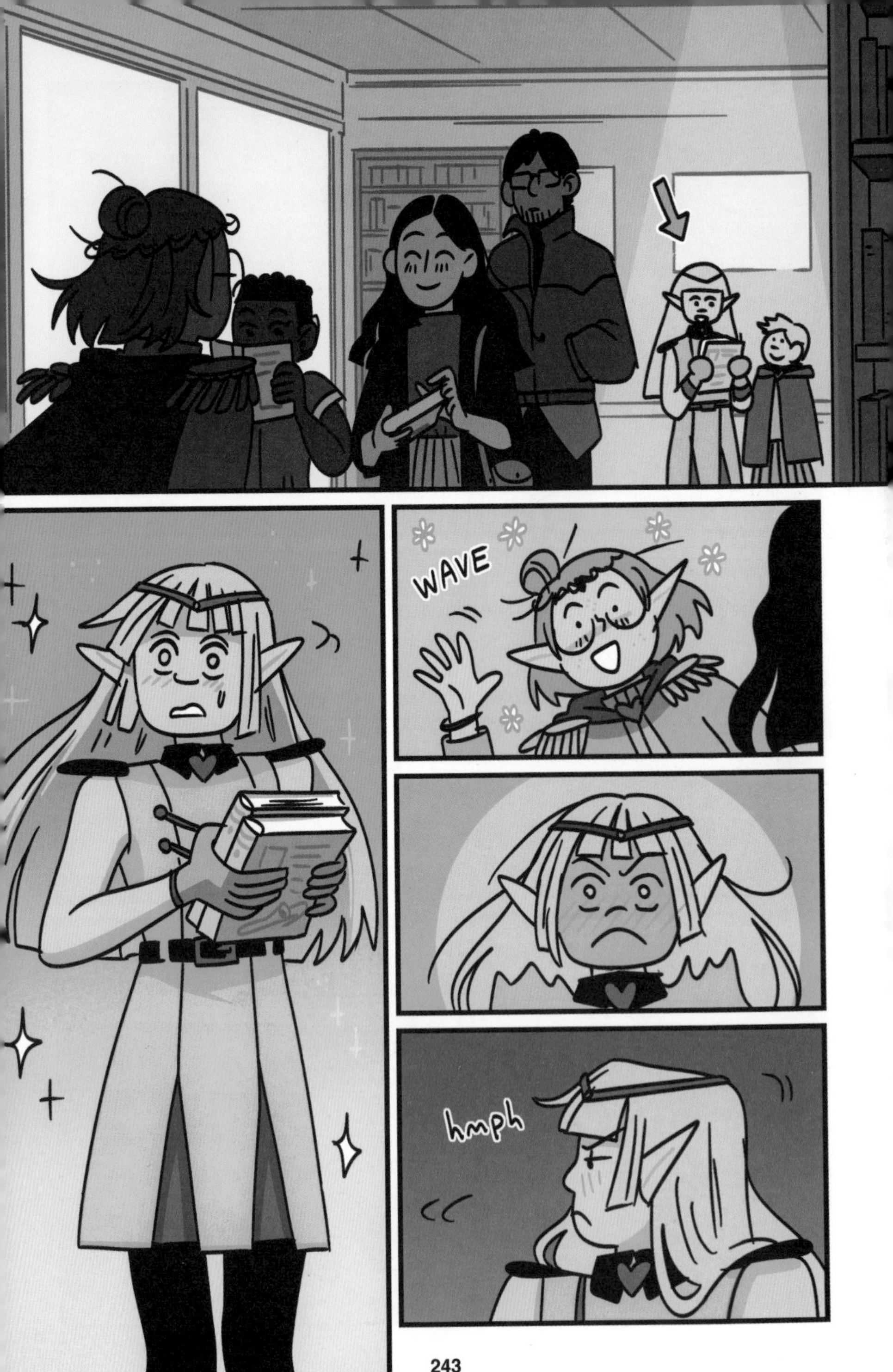
WAVE
hmph

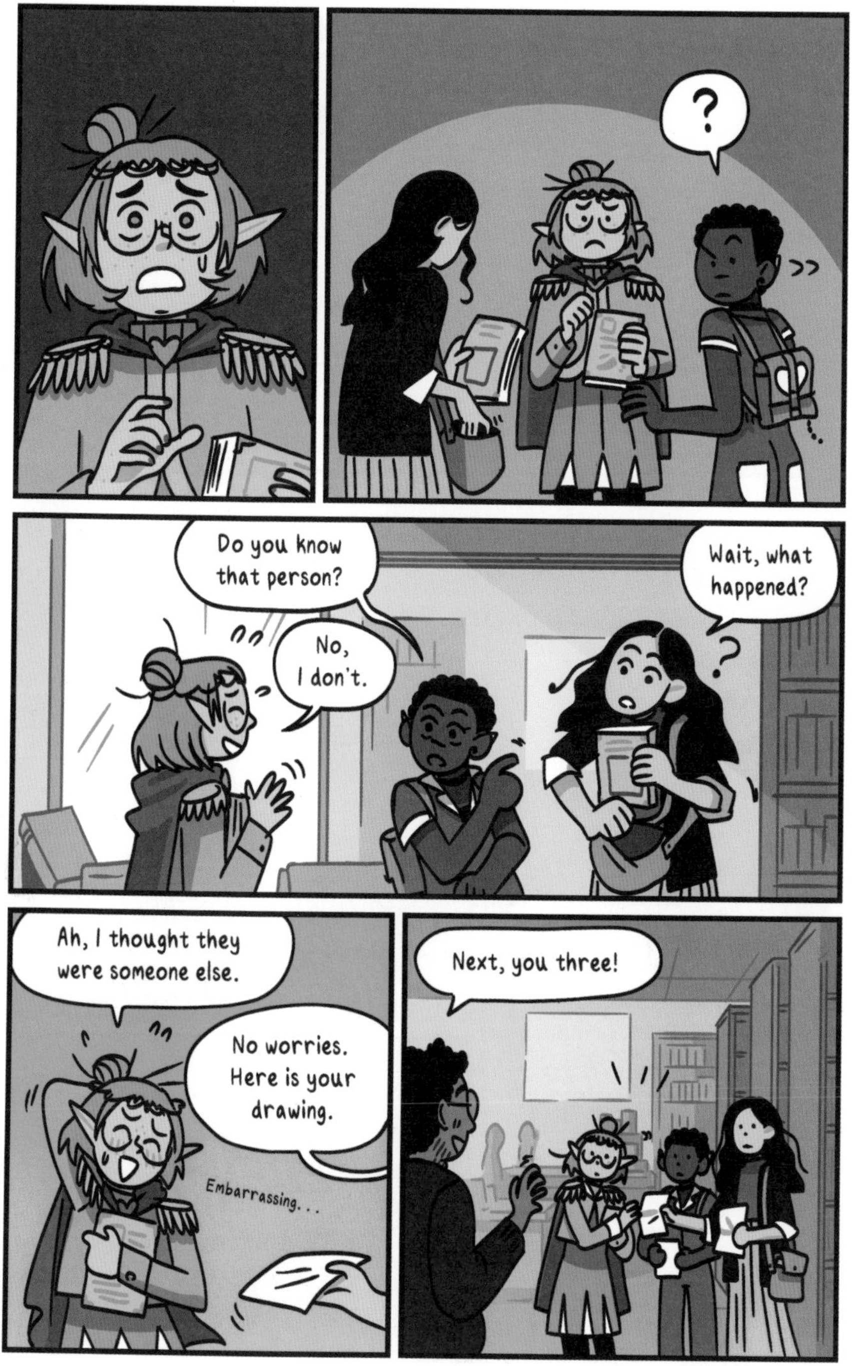
?
Do you know that person?
No, I don't.
Wait, what happened?
?
Ah, I thought they were someone else.
No worries. Here is your drawing.
Embarrassing...
Next, you three!

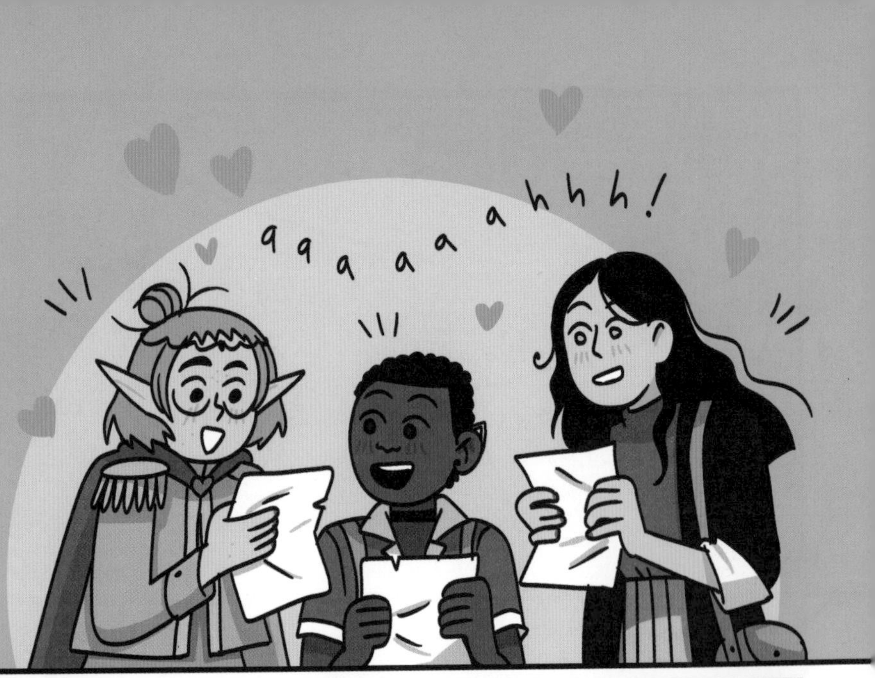
aaaaaaahhhh!
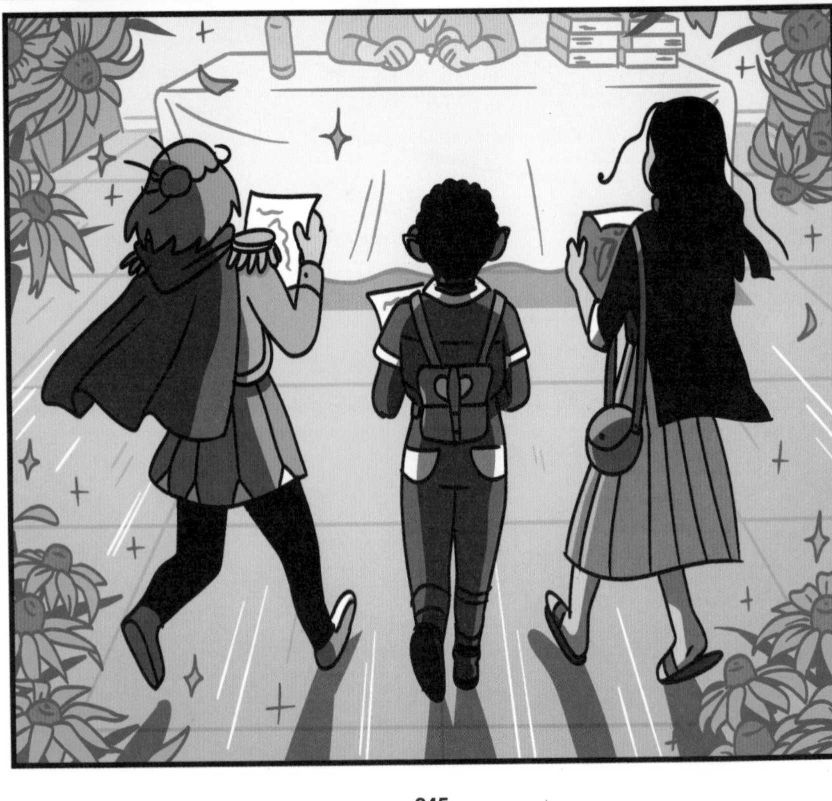

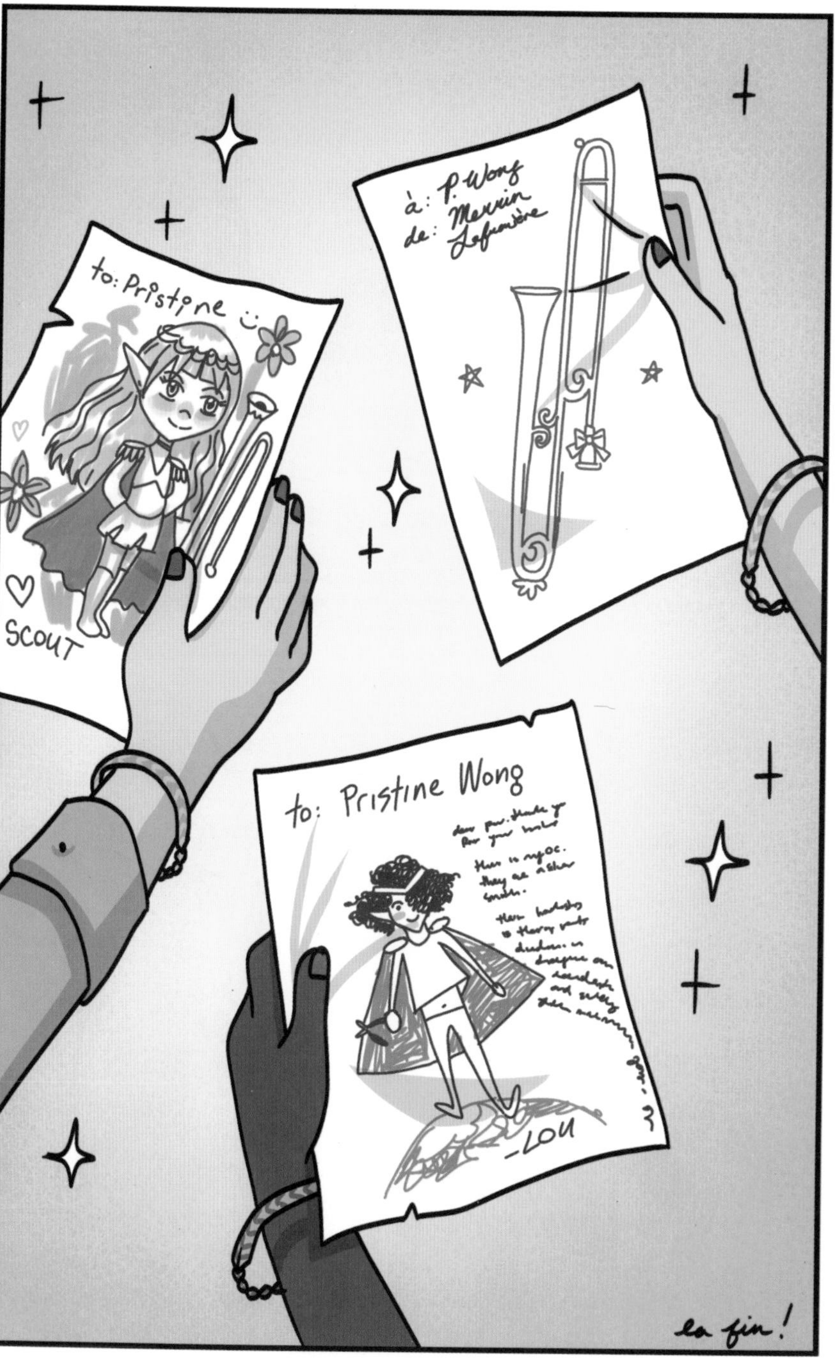
to: Pristine :)
♡
SCOUT
à: P. Wong
de: Merrin Lefumière
to: Pristine Wong
-LOU
la fin!

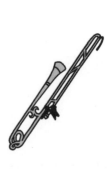

Scout!

these are some of the designs
i would reference when drawing
scout in this book.

i love her so much, but i struggled
a lot with drawing her in a way
i was happy with! as i was penciling,
i kept telling myself, "i'll figure it
out eventually!" but i don't think
i ever did (lol).

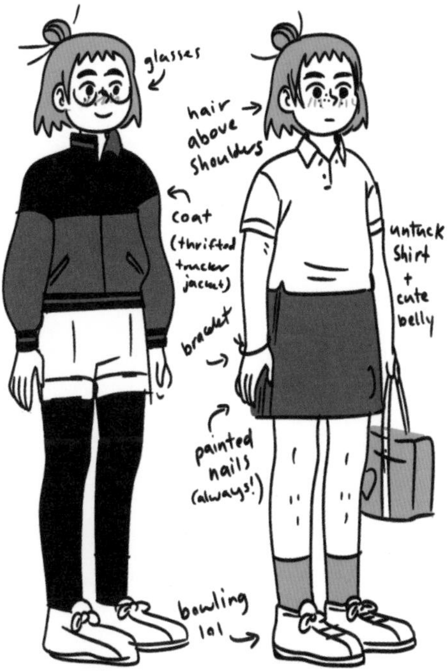
glasses
hair above shoulders
coat (thrifted tracker jacket)
untuck shirt + cute belly
bracelet
painted nails (always!)
bowling lol

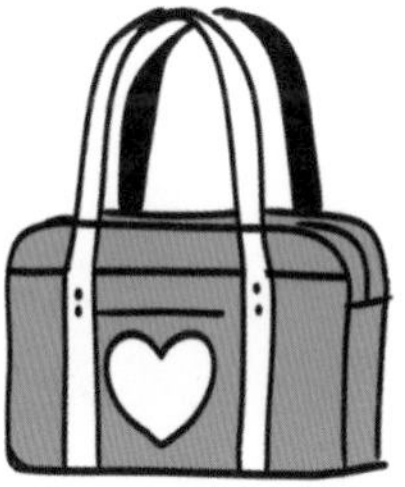

bag

scout's bag.
i almost gave up
on this design
because it was
so hard for
me to draw.

scout's laptop

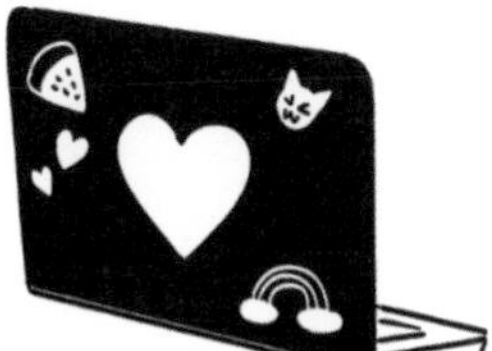

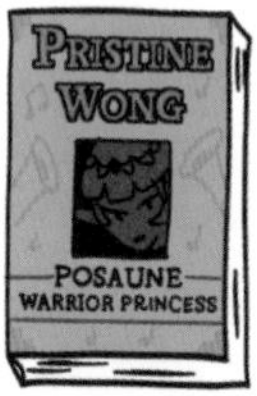
PRISTINE WONG
POSAUNE
WARRIOR PRINCESS

i drew these prop designs
after inking 75 percent
of the book and had to
go back and change what
i drew originally.

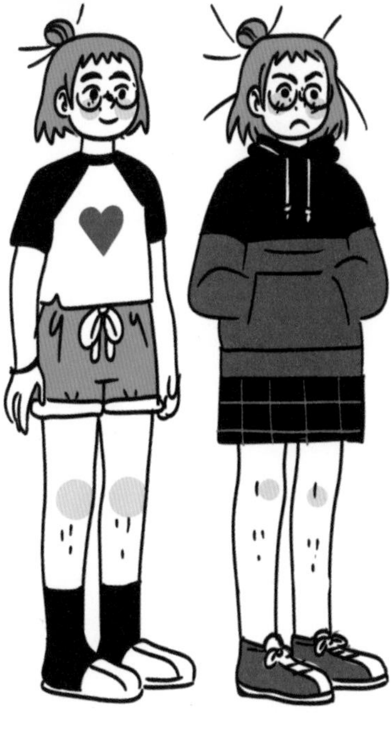

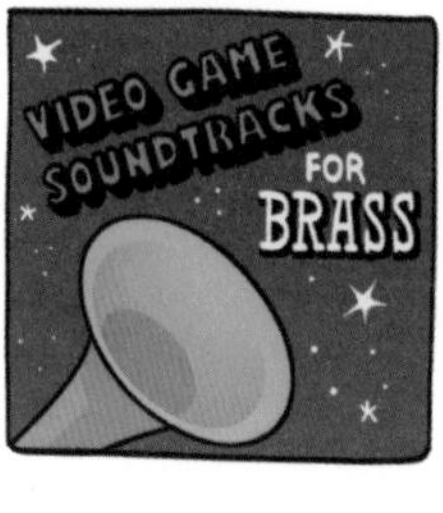
VIDEO GAME SOUNDTRACKS FOR BRASS

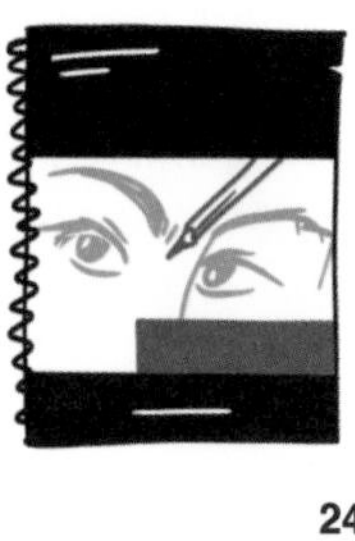

Merrin

merrin was easier for me to draw from the beginning. i think her hair length changes all throughout the book, but maybe we can pretend it grows really fast and she cuts it a lot?

the straight cut at the bottom makes me think she chops it off herself. her hair is very thick. when she braids it, the braid is so heavy it hurts her scalp! she absolutely can't put it up in a ponytail for too long for the same reason . . .

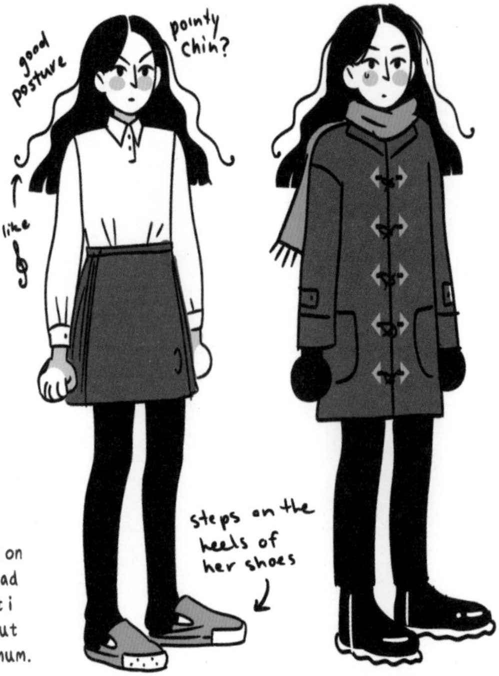
good posture
pointy chin?
like
steps on the heels of her shoes

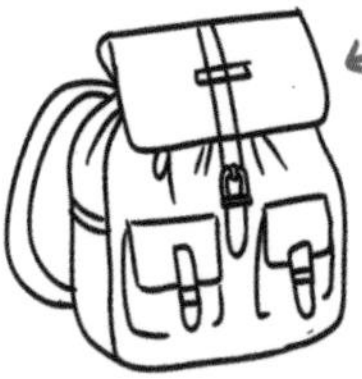

merrin's bag. based on the leather bag i had in high school that i "borrowed" without permission from my mum. (sorry ,mum.)

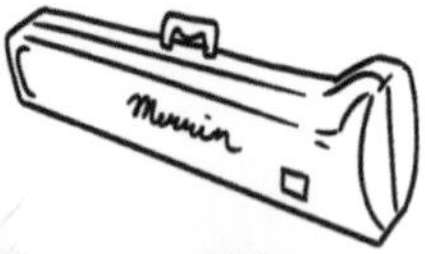
Merrin

merrin definitely has her own trombone. i bet she had one of those colourful novelty trombones at one point but then thought it wasn't "mature." (incorrect opinion. sorry, merrin.)

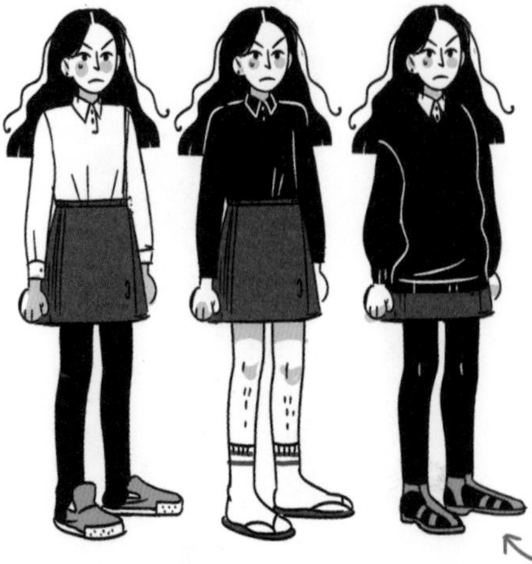

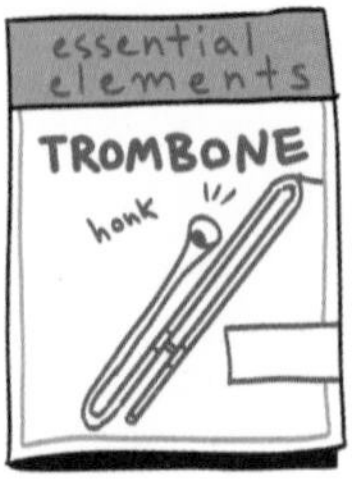
essential elements
TROMBONE
honk

music book

music folder

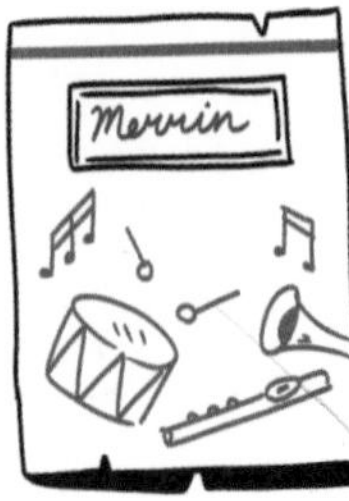
Merrin

did she ever even wear these shoes . . . ?

Lennox and Kim

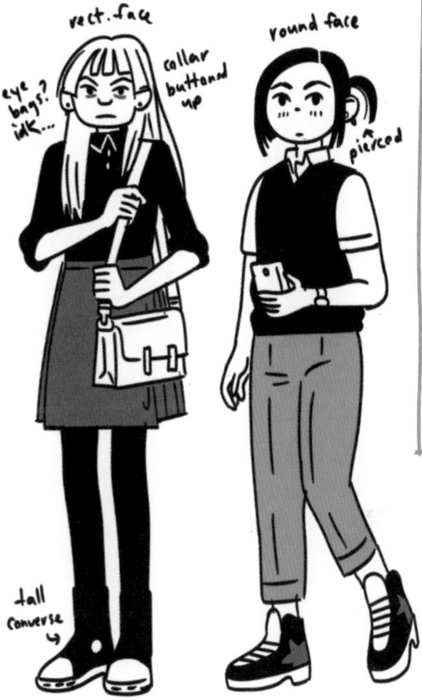
rect. face
eye bangs? idk...
collar buttoned up
round face
pierced
tall converse

lennox was my favourite girl to draw. while all the characters in the book are "very me," i feel like lennox is the most me. whenever lennox showed up in this book, i was like, "ah! here i am!" it's probably the bangs.

i loved writing kim a lot. i really wanted to bring the feeling of young crushes and how distracting and horrible they can be. kim is a girl with her head constantly in the clouds.

don't think i drew these shoes on her once.

Lou

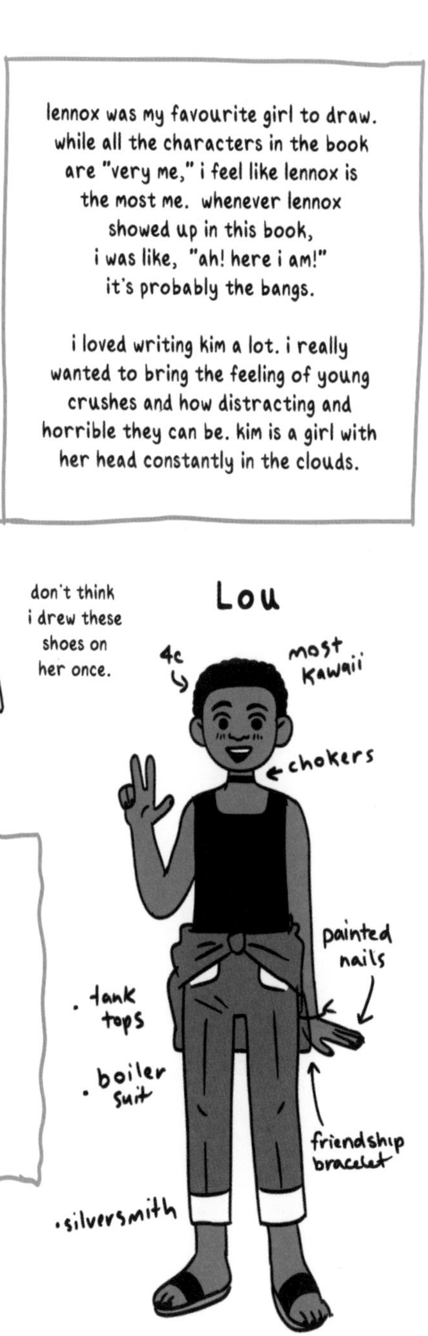
4c
most kawaii
chokers
painted nails
friendship bracelet
• tank tops
• boiler suit
• silversmith

lou was named after mary lou williams, but apparently lou williams is also a professional basketball player?! that is kind of cool, too! i don't follow sports that much, obviously.

i had a few internet friends growing up who i still talk to and cherish to this day. one of which was my first non-cis friend, so i really wanted someone similar in the book!

Chris, Vic, and PB

chris basically had the same design since day one, although putting together these pages i noticed i gave her a long kilt in the concept art? why did i change that? it's so cool.

vic originally had a buzz cut hairstyle but i got bored of drawing it after pencils so i changed it to mid-length hair.

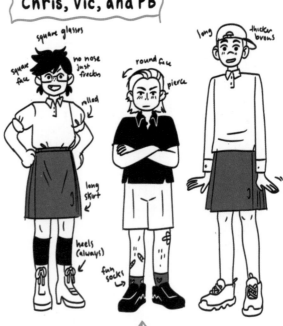

square glasses
square face
no nose just freckles
rolled
long skirt
heels (always)
round face
pierce
fun socks
long
thicker brows

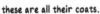

these are all their coats.

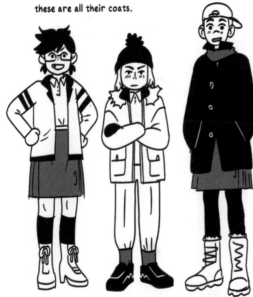

i changed PB's name, like, probably six times in the course of writing this book. i'm very bad at naming characters.

i settled on PB because my deadline was coming up and I liked to think it was short for "peanut butter," which is very cute and funny.

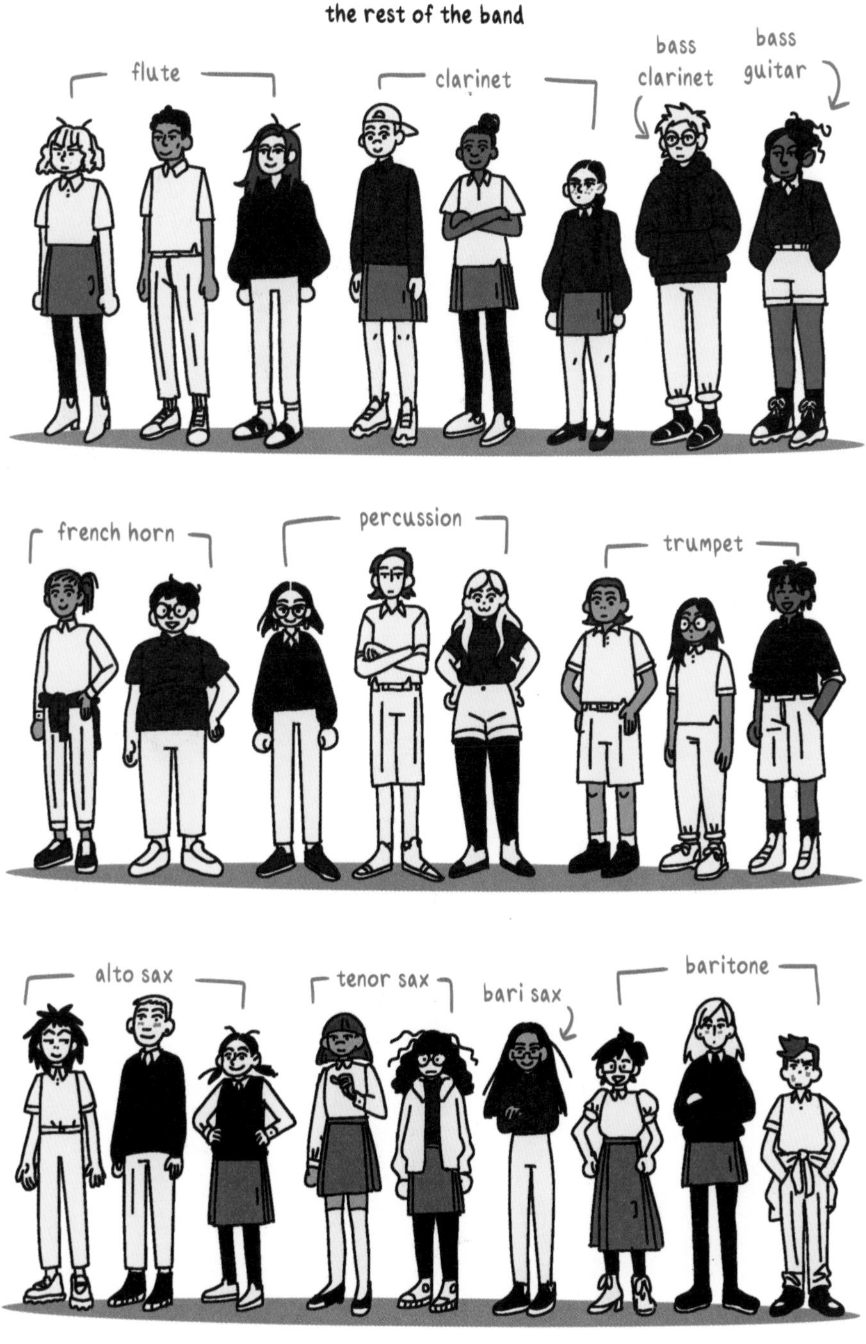
the rest of the band
flute
clarinet
bass clarinet
bass guitar
french horn
percussion
trumpet
alto sax
tenor sax
bari sax
baritone

band uniform concepts

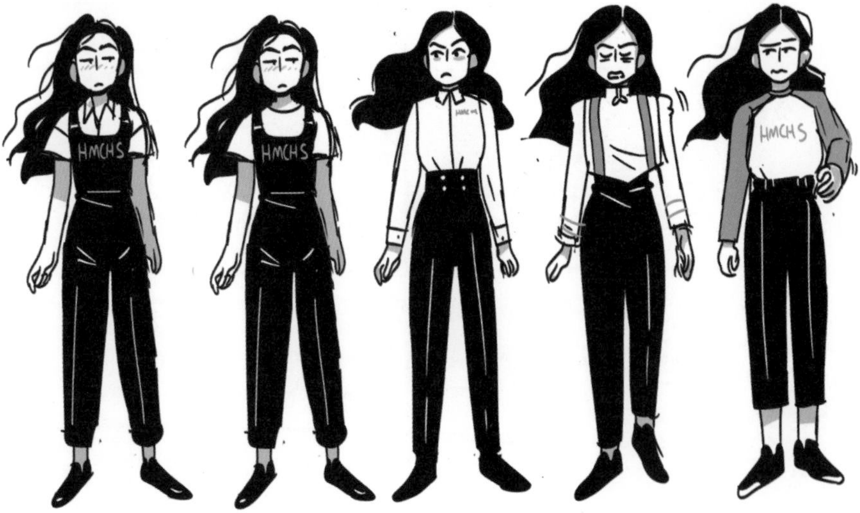
HMCHS
HMCHS
HMCHS

old *posaune* designs

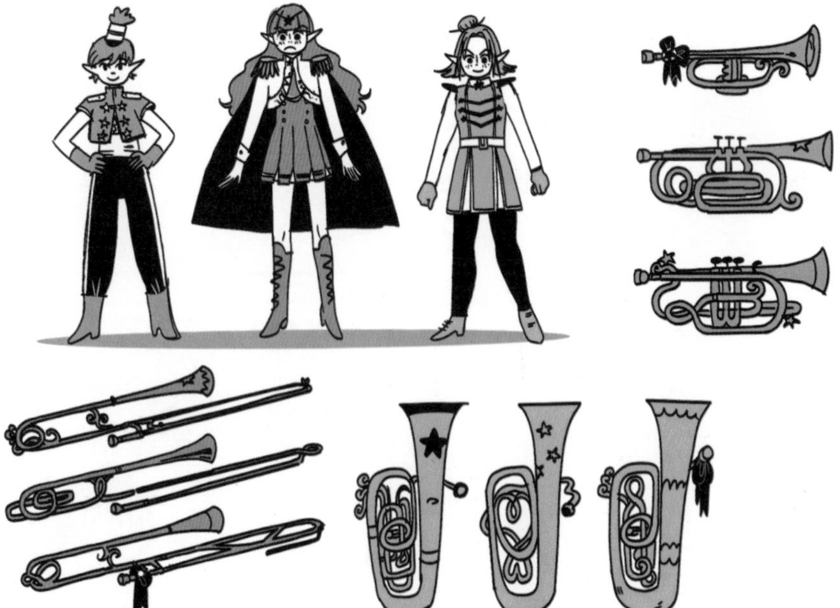

spotlight on: mr. varma!!

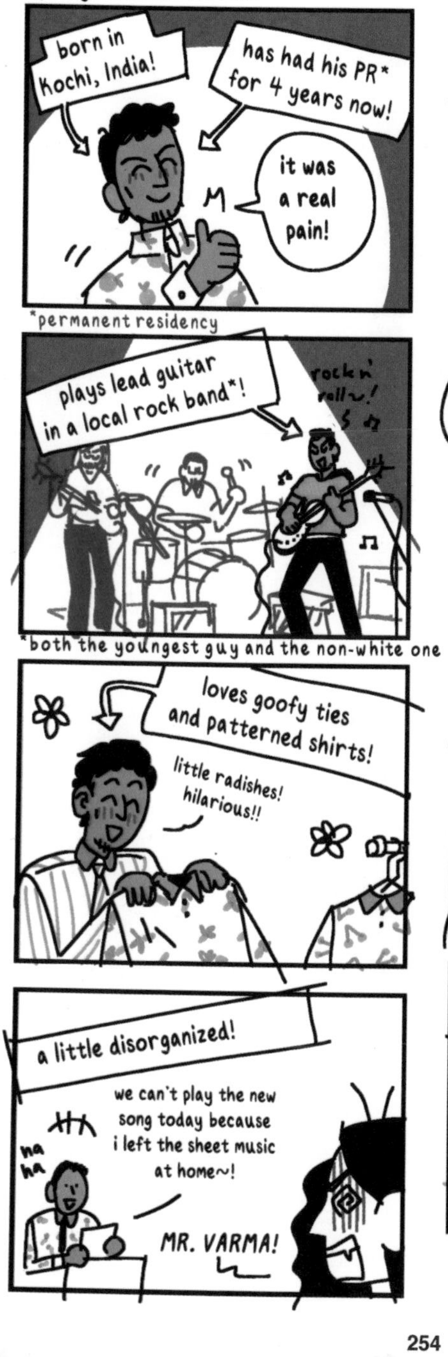
born in Kochi, India!
has had his PR* for 4 years now!
it was a real pain!
*permanent residency
plays lead guitar in a local rock band*!
rock n' roll~!
*both the youngest guy and the non-white one
loves goofy ties and patterned shirts!
little radishes! hilarious!!
a little disorganized!
ha ha
we can't play the new song today because i left the sheet music at home~!
MR. VARMA!

band 4 credit

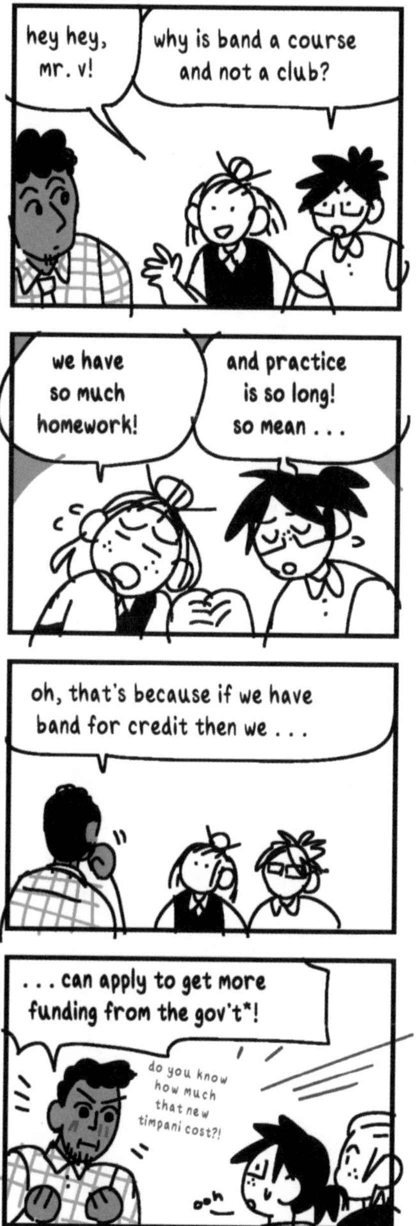
hey hey, mr. v!
why is band a course and not a club?
we have so much homework!
and practice is so long! so mean . . .
oh, that's because if we have band for credit then we . . .
. . . can apply to get more funding from the gov't*!
do you know how much that new timpani cost?!
ooh
*the ontario gov't supports catholic schools with tax money, but no other religious group, which is unfair and discriminatory!

spit rug

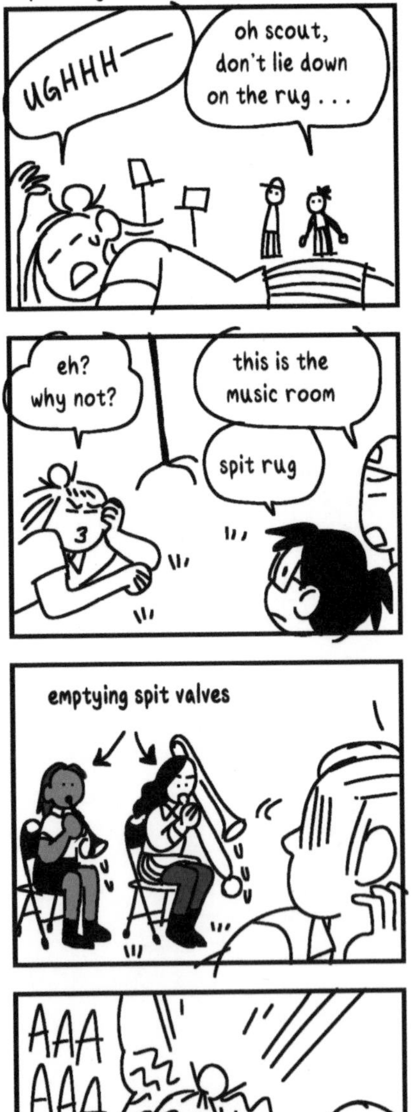
UGHHH—
oh scout, don't lie down on the rug . . .
eh? why not?
this is the music room
spit rug
emptying spit valves
AAA AAA
yark

spit cannon

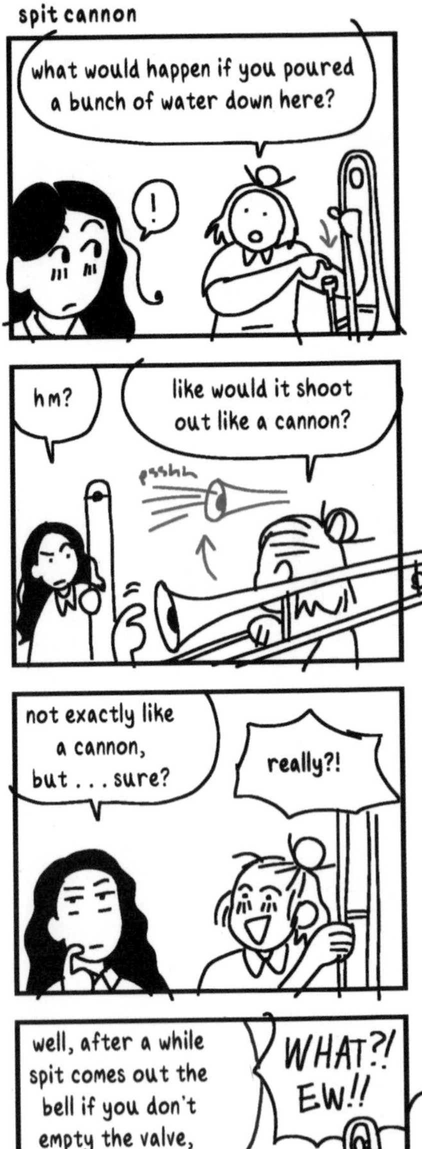
what would happen if you poured a bunch of water down here?
!
hm?
like would it shoot out like a cannon?
psshh
not exactly like a cannon, but . . . sure?
really?!
well, after a while spit comes out the bell if you don't empty the valve, so . . .
WHAT?! EW!!
drip

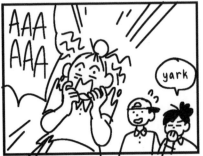

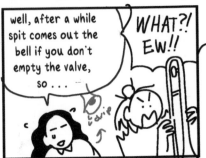

band folders exist for a reason

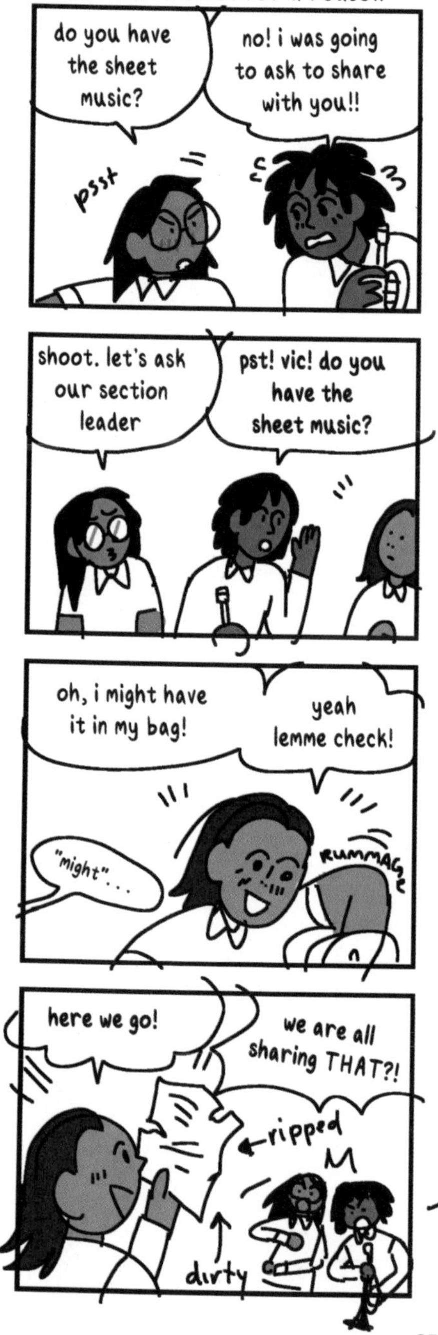
do you have the sheet music?
psst
no! i was going to ask to share with you!!
shoot. let's ask our section leader
pst! vic! do you have the sheet music?
oh, i might have it in my bag!
yeah lemme check!
"might"...
RUMMAGE
here we go!
we are all sharing THAT?!
ripped
dirty

recording

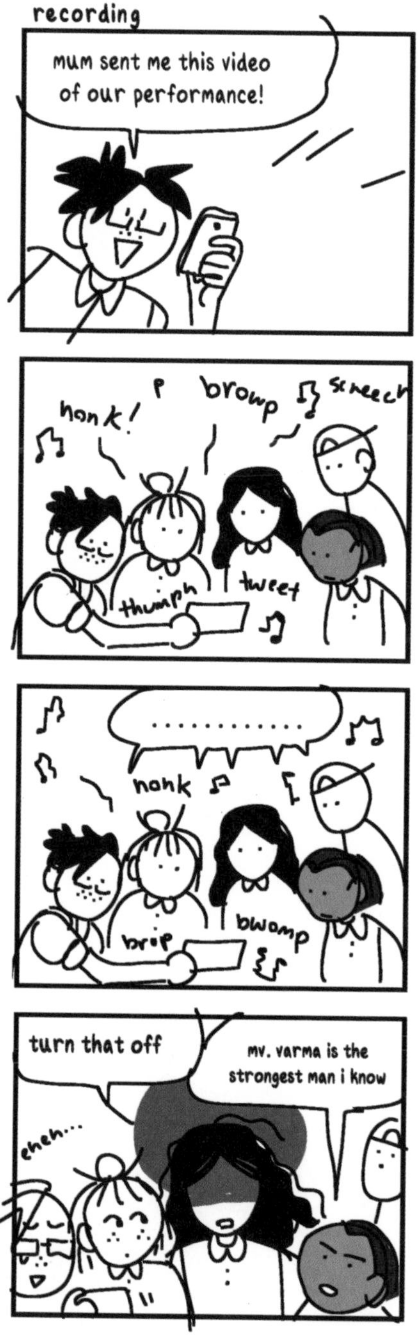
mum sent me this video of our performance!
honk!
p
browp
screech
thumph
tweet
....
honk
brip
bwomp
turn that off
mr. varma is the strongest man i know
eheh...

agnostic

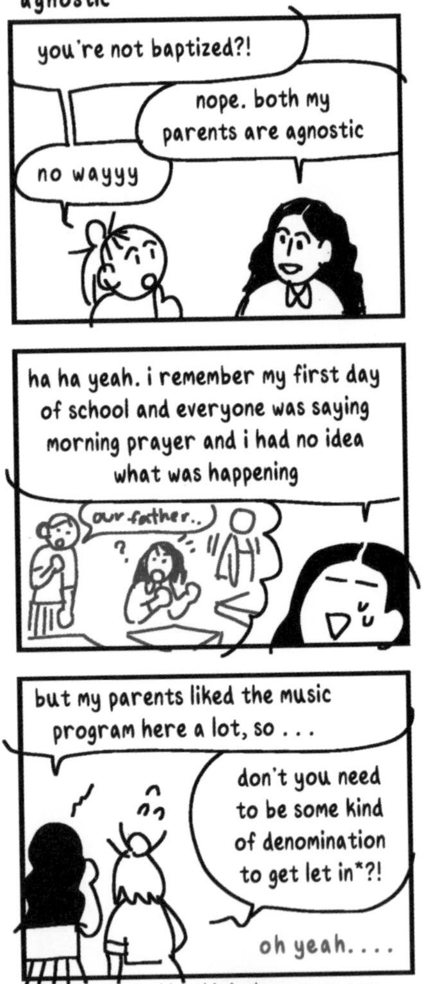
you're not baptized?!
nope. both my parents are agnostic
no wayyy
ha ha yeah. i remember my first day of school and everyone was saying morning prayer and i had no idea what was happening
our father..
but my parents liked the music program here a lot, so . . .
don't you need to be some kind of denomination to get let in*?!
oh yeah. . . .

*2021: i don't think this is the case anymore

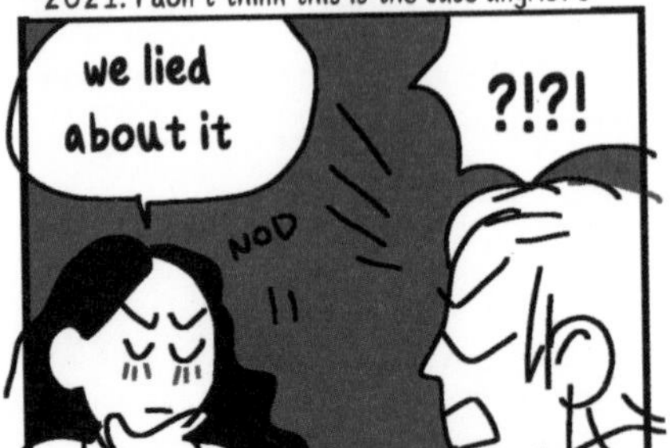
we lied about it
?!?!
NOD

off to mass

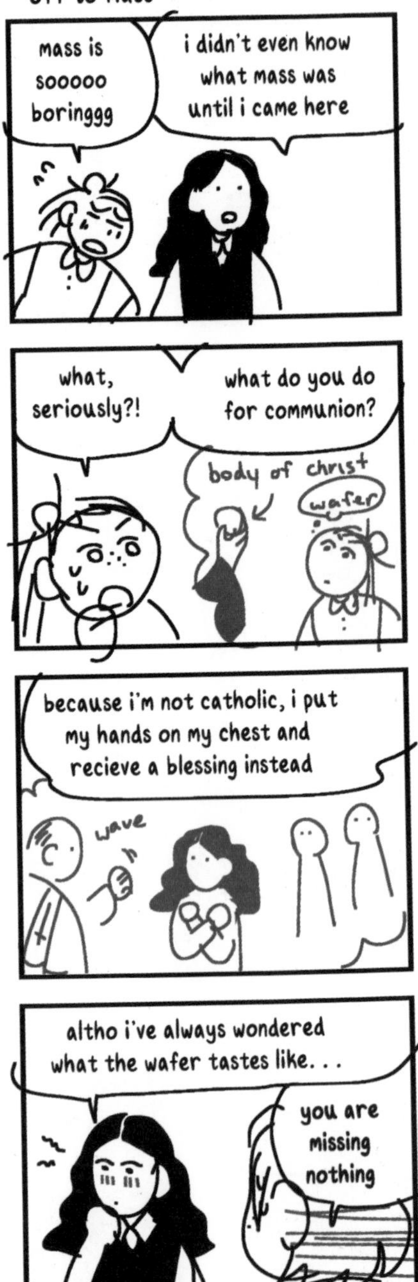
mass is sooooo boringgg
i didn't even know what mass was until i came here
what, seriously?!
what do you do for communion?
body of christ
wafer
because i'm not catholic, i put my hands on my chest and recieve a blessing instead
wave
altho i've always wondered what the wafer tastes like. . .
you are missing nothing

lost

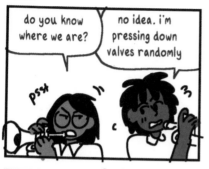

do you know where we are?

no idea. i'm pressing down valves randomly

pst

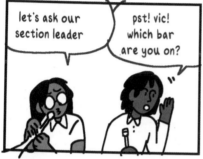

let's ask our section leader

pst! vic! which bar are you on?

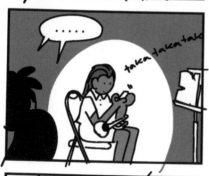

. . . . .

taka takatak

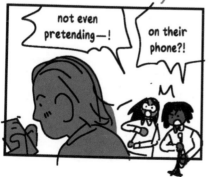

not even pretending—!

on their phone?!

inviting lou

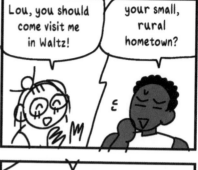

Lou, you should come visit me in Waltz!

your small, rural hometown?

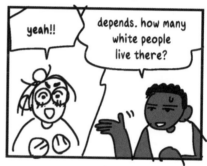

yeah!!

depends. how many white people live there?

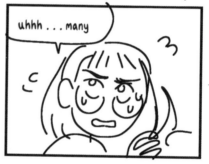

uhhh . . . many

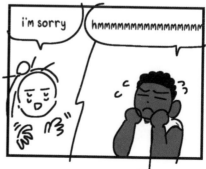

i'm sorry

hmmmmmmmmmmmmmmmm

cellular data

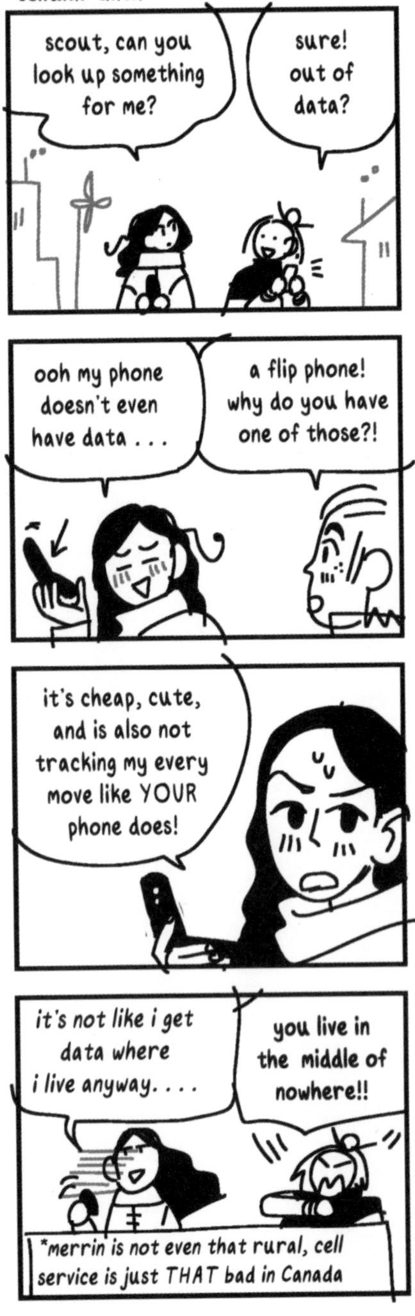
scout, can you look up something for me?
sure! out of data?
ooh my phone doesn't even have data . . .
a flip phone! why do you have one of those?!
it's cheap, cute, and is also not tracking my every move like YOUR phone does!
it's not like i get data where i live anyway. . . .
you live in the middle of nowhere!!
*merrin is not even that rural, cell service is just THAT bad in Canada

crush

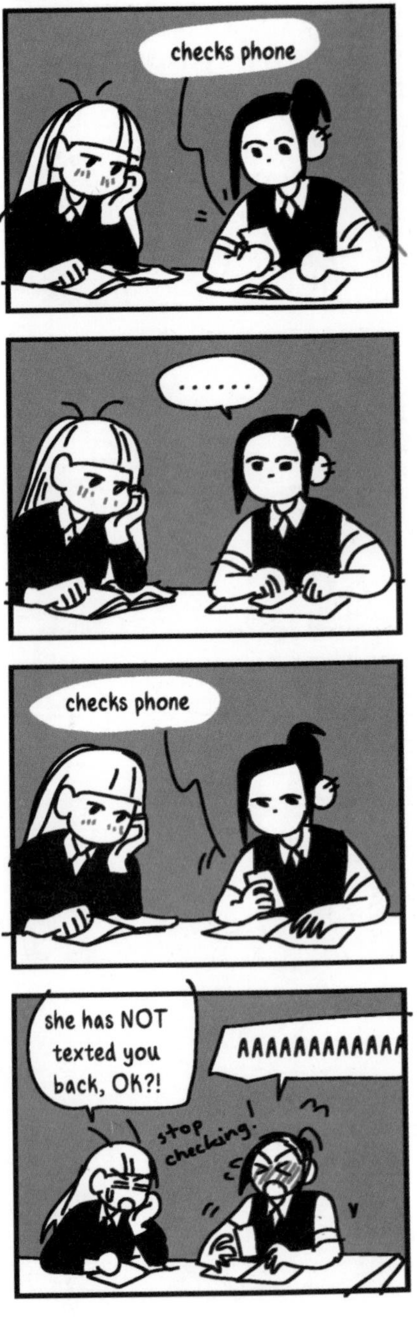
checks phone
. . . . . .
checks phone
she has NOT texted you back, OK?!
AAAAAAAAAAA
stop checking!

pew-pew

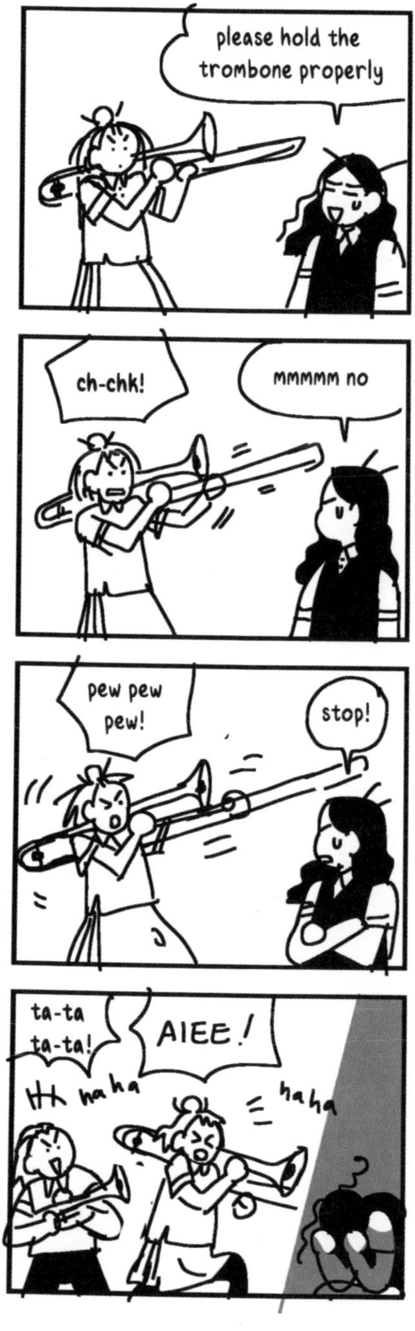

please hold the trombone properly
ch-chk!
mmmmm no
pew pew pew!
stop!
ta-ta ta-ta!
AIEE!
ha ha
haha

"sheet music online free"

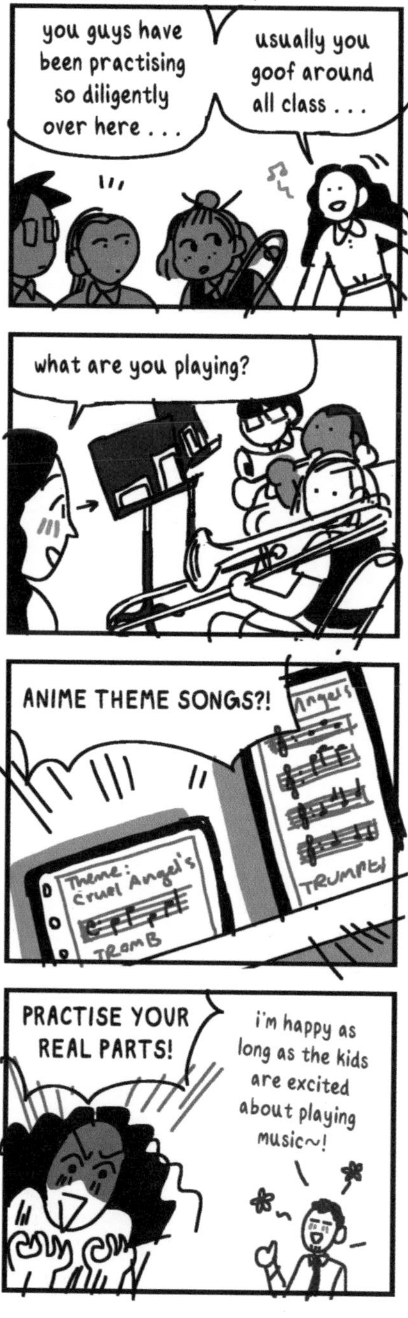

you guys have been practising so diligently over here . . .
usually you goof around all class . . .
what are you playing?
ANIME THEME SONGS?!
Angel's
TRUMPET
Theme: Cruel Angel's
TROMB
PRACTISE YOUR REAL PARTS!
i'm happy as long as the kids are excited about playing music~!

mum means well

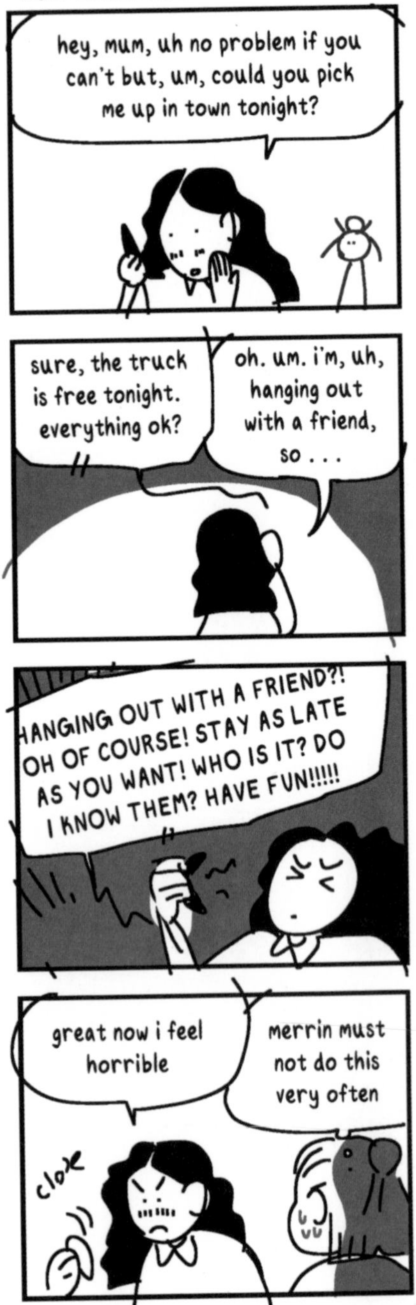
hey, mum, uh no problem if you can't but, um, could you pick me up in town tonight?
sure, the truck is free tonight. everything ok?
oh. um. i'm, uh, hanging out with a friend, so . . .
HANGING OUT WITH A FRIEND?! OH OF COURSE! STAY AS LATE AS YOU WANT! WHO IS IT? DO I KNOW THEM? HAVE FUN!!!!!
great now i feel horrible
merrin must not do this very often

cat person

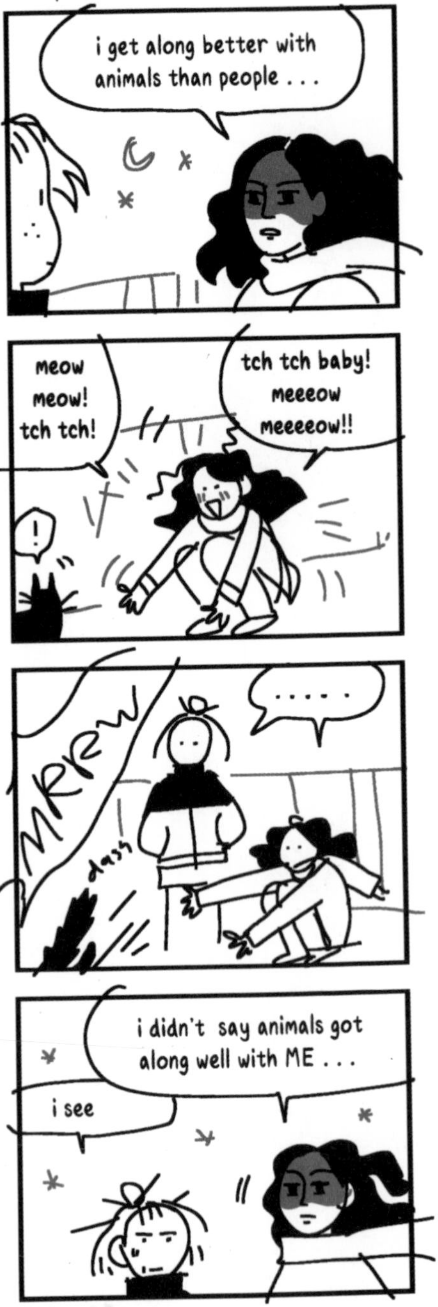
i get along better with animals than people . . .
meow meow! tch tch!
tch tch baby! meeeow meeeeow!!
!
MRRRW
. . . . .
i didn't say animals got along well with ME . . .
i see

freetalk

hello, everyone. 2021-05-14

thanks for coming to my freetalk. it's 11 am on a friday. i want a steamed pork bun and a soda and i am going to have a nice lil picnic in the park.

when i was 11 i switched from the local public school to a catholic school in the next town over, even though i knew nothing about religion nor knew anyone at the school. i did it because i wanted to wear a school uniform with a pleated skirt so badly.

my best friend and i met when i opened my locker and had my anime fanart taped up on the inside and she asked if i had a deviantart. we have been best friends ever since and talk to each other every day :)

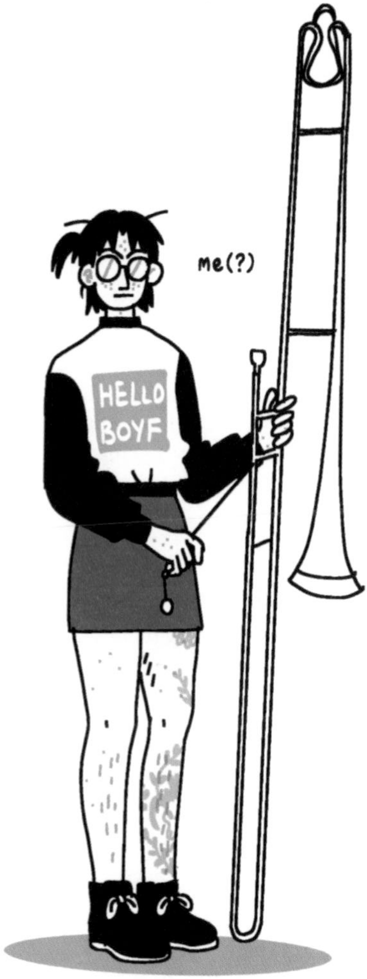
me(?)
HELLO
BOYF

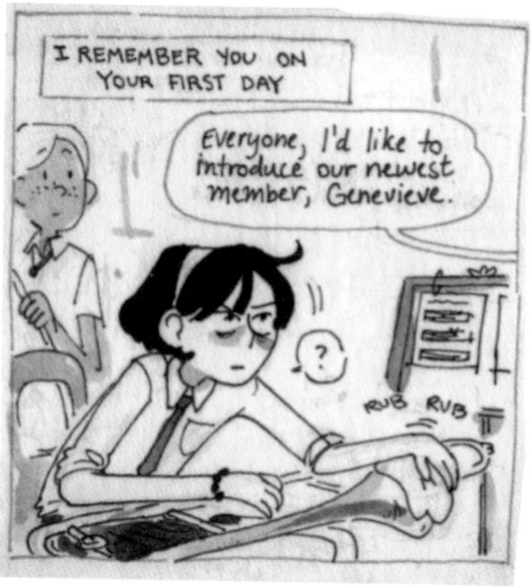
I REMEMBER YOU ON YOUR FIRST DAY
Everyone, I'd like to introduce our newest member, Genevieve.
?
RUB RUB

this book was inspired by a short comic i drew in 2018. it was about a trombone player who murders another trombone player for making fun of band (and being too pretty). i quickly realized i couldn't write a full-length book about murder so it eventually became this!

thank you from the bottom of my heart for reading.

love, jade

Special Thanks

Deep gratitude and appreciation to my family for their unwavering support and love. Thank you, Mom, Dad, Keely, and Selena. Thank you to Annabel Scott for being the best friend anyone could ever ask for. Thank you to my dearest friends and fellow collective members Victor Martins, Keelin Gorlewski, and Christine Wong, whose incredible comic work inspires me to no end and whose friendship I cherish. Special thanks to Rabeea S, D. Chouk, Jarrett S, Emma H, Kim + Serge, Beena M, Kristina L, the Luu Nguyen family, Sara C, Lis S, Anna K, Andrew T, my middle school music teacher Mr. Stuart, everyone in Friendo Art Share Jamboree, Gundam consultant Dan, colour consultant Killian Ng, longtime internet pals Alex and Lina, my agent Seth, designer extraordinaire P. Crotty, and my editor Whitney for taking a chance on me so long ago. Shout-out to Diskette Press and Koyama Press for their inspiring and wide support of the arts, and to Olivia at Pindot Press for printing all our zines so beautifully even when we don't format them correctly. Thanks to The Beguiling for letting me and HBF use their basement to work on comics and definitely not goof off. Shout-out to the broader support from the arts communities of Toronto, Montréal, and Almonte, and any person who has ever picked up a zine from me. Thank you so much!

Special thanks to my flatters Natalie Mark and Kristen Cooper for all their hard work and attention to detail, and for working with line art that had so many broken lines.

I would like to acknowledge the support of the Ontario Arts Council, an agency of the Government of Ontario, in the creation of this book.

I moved five times creating this graphic novel! Never doing that again. As such, I would like to acknowledge that this book was written on the unceded traditional territories of many nations including the Mississaugas of the Credit, the Anishinaabeg, the Ojibwa, the Haudenosaunee, the Mohawk, and the Wendat peoples. This book was written on and based upon unceded traditional Omàmìwininì (Algonquin) territory.

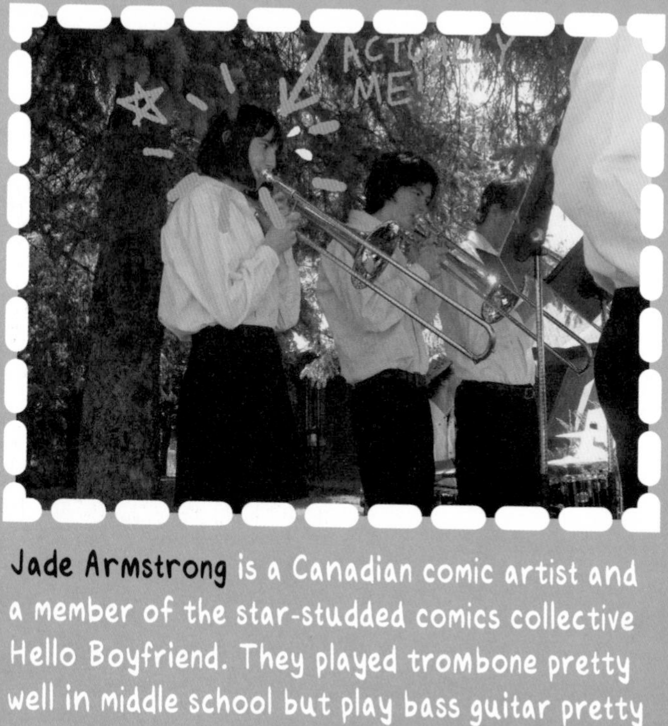
ACTUALLY ME!

Jade Armstrong is a Canadian comic artist and a member of the star-studded comics collective Hello Boyfriend. They played trombone pretty well in middle school but play bass guitar pretty badly now. *Scout Is Not a Band Kid* is their first graphic novel.

This book was brought to life with the help of a very heavy Cintiq that I bought off of Kijiji, Clip Studio Paint, Adobe Illustrator, and a 200-page 1-subject ruled notebook (blue cover).

This is a work of fiction. Names, characters, places, and incidents either are the product of the author's imagination or are used fictitiously. Any resemblance to actual persons, living or dead, events, or locales is entirely coincidental.

Text, cover art, and interior illustrations copyright © 2022 by Jade Armstrong

All rights reserved. Published in the United States by RH Graphic, an imprint of Random House Children's Books, a division of Penguin Random House LLC, New York.

RH Graphic with the book design is a trademark of Penguin Random House LLC.

Visit us on the web! RHKidsGraphic.com • @RHKidsGraphic

Educators and librarians, for a variety of teaching tools, visit us at RHTeachersLibrarians.com

Library of Congress Cataloging-in-Publication Data is available upon request.
ISBN 978-0-593-17623-8 (hardcover) — ISBN 978-0-593-17622-1 (paperback)
ISBN 978-0-593-17625-2 (ebook) — ISBN 978-0-593-17624-5 (lib. bdg.)

Paper-over-board cover illustration by Christine Wong
Flats by Natalie Mark and Kristen Cooper
Designed by Patrick Crotty

MANUFACTURED IN CHINA
10 9 8 7 6 5 4 3 2 1
First Edition

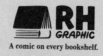

A comic on every bookshelf.

PO!

SCOUT IS NOT A BAND KID